CURSED WORLD

BOOKS 1-3

STEPHANIE FOXE

STEEL FOX MEDIA LLC

Cursed World
Misfit Pack
Misfit Angel
Misfit Fortune
All rights reserved.

First edition, May 2020
ISBN 978-1-950310-12-8

The Foxey Betas

A big thank you to my ART (Advanced Reader Team). Their advice polished up the book and helped me to be more confident launching a new series.

Misfit Pack ~

Amber Searcy, Janice Day, Jen Plumstead, Laura Rogers, Natasha O'Brien, Stephanie Johnson, Tami Cowles, Thomas Ryan

To my proofreader Ranting Raven, you provided me with a clean draft to send to the ART team. Thanks for the hard work!

To Alida with Word Essential, thank you for your help with the outline. The story *did* need more tension and danger, and that bit of advice helped me take the book to the next level.

Lastly, I want to thank Sarah Burton at An Avid Reader Editing. Writing in third person, especially with multiple points of view, was new to me. Your advice made a huge difference in the finished product. Thank you so much for sharing your knowledge!

Misfit Angel ~

David Ravita, Jen Plumstead, Larry Diaz Tushman, Laura Cadger Rogers, Stephanie Johnson, Tami Cowles, Thomas Ryan

To Sarah, thank you so much for your feedback on the story. I will always have something to learn and your edits are always so insightful.

And to Carol, thank you for a speedy and thorough proofread to catch all those pesky typos!

Misfit Fortune ~

Terri Adkisson, Tami Cowles, Morgan Davis, Janice Day, Stephanie Johnson, Denise King, Jessica Mack, Jen Maggio Plumstead, David Ravita, Laura Cadger Rogers, Samantha Rooney, Thomas Ryan, Amber L Searcy, Larry Diaz Tushman

CONTENTS

MISFIT PACK

MISFIT ANGEL

MISFIT FORTUNE

MISFIT PACK

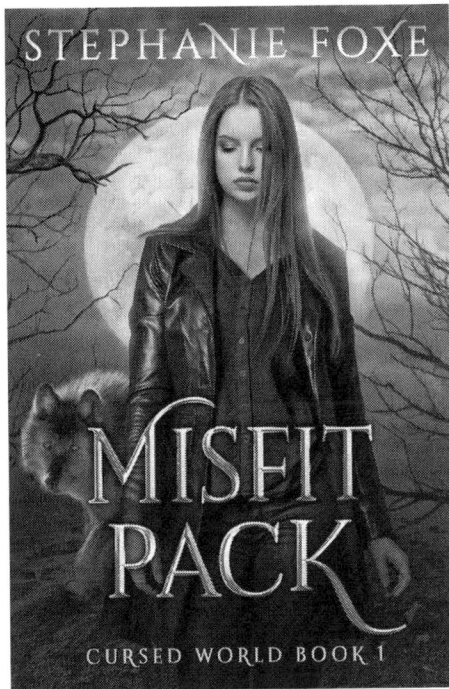

what is stronger
than the human heart
which shatters over and over
and still lives
- rupi kaur

The Sun and Her Flowers

To the strong-willed, the resilient, and the misfits. To the families we choose. To the ones who love
us unconditionally.

CHAPTER 1

AMBER

"There are reports that yet another area has been discovered where magic simply does not work. Jan Compton is on the ground with the most recent update. Over to you, Jan," the reporter said, her face a serious picture of concern.

Amber tied off her braid and snorted. "Unable to use magic? What a tragedy," she muttered as she snatched up the remote and shut off the television.

Witches and Elves and all the rest of them were so dependent on magic. As a human, she had no problem getting by without it. She didn't hate it or anything, but the panic over three little spots where magic didn't work had gotten old real fast. They had probably always been there, and it just so happened that someone had finally stumbled across them.

She grabbed her leather jacket and pulled it on, running her fingers over the material that was soft from regular use. When the weather was cool enough, she wore it every day. And in Portland, it was almost always cool enough in the evenings to want a light jacket.

Amber patted her pockets. Keys. Wallet. Mace. With a nod, she slipped out of her studio apartment and locked the door behind her.

Her neighbor, Mrs. Huntington, was just coming in. She narrowed her eyes at Amber, then hurried into her own apartment. That woman was nosy as hell and a pain in the ass. Last week she had reported Amber for "coming back too late" and "slamming her door." The woman had *As the Witch Burns* blaring out of her television twenty-four seven. There's no way she heard anyone doing anything.

Amber was tempted to kick her door as she walked past, but she shook off the pettiness. Tonight wasn't about crappy neighbors. It was supposed to be fun...whatever that was.

There was a free concert in the park with some new local bands, and a few older ones whose popularity had fizzled as their fan base had grown up. The Troll Bangs was going to be on stage around eleven that night. Since that was the only band she was interested in seeing, she had skipped the first few hours of the concert.

Her twin, Dylan, had loved The Troll Bangs to an almost embarrassing extent. He had dragged her to three of their concerts in high school one summer. Amber hadn't hated them, but Dylan had taken his fanboying to a whole new level. She pulled out her keys to unlock the ugly, old red truck she drove, shaking her head at the memory. Watching the band without him would be bittersweet.

The truck didn't have keyless entry or elf-spelled air conditioning like a new model would. She had rebuilt it with her dad as a graduation gift, one of the few things she ever did with him one-on-one. It still ran, but only thanks to her constant maintenance. Maybe in a year or two she'd be able to afford something new.

In order to avoid the traffic of downtown Portland, she took the long way to the concert. The Market had appeared there a couple of weeks ago, and for the next two weeks it was going to remain a pain in her ass to get to work.

Despite her annoyance with the traffic, she was glad The Market had popped up nearby. She hadn't been in years, not since it showed up in Texas a few months before she moved away. The Market was old and made up of so much magic that no one knew how it worked anymore. It disappeared and reappeared every new moon, always in a different location, and always completely unpredictable. The only things that were sure about The Market were that it liked populated areas and that it somehow always made room for itself no matter where it landed.

The merchants who traveled with it had to sign an unbreakable contract that lasted for at least one year. Openings were hard to come by, though; merchants who got a spot never seemed to want to leave.

The narrow streets that led to the concert were lined with vehicles. She parked her truck at the first open spot. There was no point in driving around for thirty minutes, hoping for something closer, when she didn't mind the walk.

A group of elves clambered out of a car that had parked a few spaces ahead of her. They wore flower crowns that shimmered with magic. Fluorescent butterflies fluttered around their heads every few seconds. They must have been to The Market before coming there.

A pixie flew out of the bushes and chased one of the butterflies around an elven girl's head, trying to eat the magical illusion. She shrieked and batted it away, knocking her crown askew. The pixie jabbered its displeasure, then landed on a car and watched them walk away sullenly. Pixies were odd, gray little creatures with wide mouths like a frog and wings like a bat. They'd eat almost anything, but preferred metal and bugs. Amber's dad had always been chasing them out of the garage when they got into the screws.

Her phone vibrated in her pocket, and the custom ringtone, an engine revving, rumbled loudly. She hesitated, then pulled out her phone. Her oldest brother, Derek, would just call over and over until she picked up. He was persistent like that.

"Hey, big brother. Grandma Kelly didn't kick the bucket, did she?"

Derek chuckled. "You're so morbid. And no. She does have a date tomorrow, though."

She grimaced. "I didn't need to know that."

"Neither did I," Derek said. She could hear the shudder of horror through the phone. "Anyhow, that's not why I called."

"Well, I'm waiting," she said when he didn't immediately continue.

Derek sighed. "Dad got in a wreck this afternoon."

"What?" She stopped in her tracks. "And you're just now calling me?"

"He's fine. No one got hurt," Derek said quickly. "The only reason I called is because Mom—because I just thought you should know. It's a problem with his eyesight. We've been trying to get him to go to the doctor for months, but it took this to get him to make a damn appointment."

Amber sighed. She got her stubbornness from him. They all did. But he was in a category all by himself.

"Thanks for letting me know. It's probably going to take another wreck to get him to actually do what the doctors tell him, though," she grumbled, kicking at a rock as she started walking again.

"Tell me about it. He was still trying to argue he was fine in the ambulance."

"Hard-headed idiot," she said, shaking her head. She hesitated before she asked her next question. She wanted to know…and she didn't. "How is Mom doing?"

Derek stayed silent for a beat. "You have her number, Amber. Just call her."

"She has mine, too, and you don't see her calling me. She doesn't want to talk to me, Derek."

"You don't know that—"

"Yeah, actually I do." She was tired of this old argument. Derek refused to believe her. "I know that because she told me when she kicked me out of the house."

"That was almost six years ago," Derek argued.

"We'll talk again when she invites me back," she said, her tone making it clear she was done talking about it. She took a deep breath to ease the knot of guilt in her chest. "Thanks for calling, okay? I appreciate it."

"Yeah, of course," Derek replied, his words clipped. "I'll keep you updated."

"Thanks, bro. Talk to you again soon."

"Sure. Bye," Derek said, ending the call.

She lowered the phone from her ear and shoved it in her pocket. It was never good news when family called. She used to be close with all her brothers, but so long away from home and the relationships had just…fizzled.

The sound of familiar music drifted toward her. A sense of nostalgia warmed her, and she picked up the pace. The main parking lot was packed. She wove through the cars, passing a few people that were leaving the concert already.

A growl cut through the sounds of the concert and chatter.

She frowned. That was odd. Shifters didn't normally run around shifted in public. One of them was probably messing with a friend.

She scanned the area as she walked toward the pavilion. She didn't see any wolves or bears roaming around trying to startle people, but she couldn't quite shake the unsettled feeling the growl had given her.

She stepped out from between two cars. A loud scream rattled her eardrums, and a girl with pink hair crashed into her. A growl made all the hair on her arms stand on end. It was a lot closer this time.

Amber shoved the girl behind her and faced the source of the growling. Bright yellow eyes locked onto hers, and a huge black wolf bared its teeth. Saliva dripped from fangs as long as her hand. The wolf took a step forward, and Amber reached for the mace in her pocket.

She was too slow.

～

GENEVIEVE

The woman that Genevieve ran into had an arm stretched out in front of her. Like that could stop the werewolf. Genevieve took a step back, trying to decide if she could run fast enough to get away from the crazy-ass wolf. There was something in its eyes that made it seem wild. It looked insane.

Her heel slipped on a large chunk of gravel. She gasped and tipped backward, her hand flying out to grab the woman's leather jacket, but her fingers slipped.

The wolf lunged at them with a snarl, and the woman's body slammed into Genevieve, driving them both to the ground.

Sharp claws cut into her side, and gravel dug into her bare arms. She screamed, trying to cover her head with her arms, but she couldn't move with the weight of the woman and the wolf pressing down on her. The woman was fighting back and shouting, but her words were lost among the growls. Genevieve couldn't tell if it was aimed at her or the beast.

Teeth clamped around her thigh. She screamed and slapped at whatever had her. The dull pain grew sharp as her leg was wrenched from side to side with vicious shakes. Her hands hit fur and teeth. The pain kept her from taking a full breath.

The woman had her arm wrapped around the wolf's throat as though she were trying to strangle it, but she couldn't pull it away. Genevieve lifted her other foot and drove her heel into the wolf's face in a frantic stomping motion.

A rock bounced off the side of the wolf's head, and the creature turned toward whoever had thrown it with an enraged growl. In an instant, the weight was gone, and so was the woman. Genevieve forced herself upright, frantically looking around for somewhere safe to run to.

A teenager with a shocked look on his face stood right in the path of the charging creature. He threw another rock, hitting it right in the face, but it would take a whole hell of a lot more than that to stop two-hundred pounds of muscles and rage.

The wolf barreled into him, latching onto his shoulder, and he went down with a yell. The red-headed woman that had tried to help Genevieve jumped on the back of the wolf with a crazed shout. It turned, locked its jaws around her arm, and shook her like a rag doll. The woman slammed into the ground, still trying to fight back.

Before she had time to regret it, Genevieve jumped to her feet. Her leg almost gave out on her, and pain shot all the way up to her hip, but she gritted her teeth against it. Her foot hit the same stupid rock she had tripped over. If she could distract the creature for just a moment...maybe they could get away.

She picked the rock up and flung it at the wolf.

It hit the wolf's neck. The creature paused in its attack, dropping the woman's arm, and turned its freaky, yellow gaze on her. The red-headed woman grabbed something from her pocket with her uninjured arm, and a stream of liquid hit the wolf in the eyes.

It yelped and flinched back, shaking its head back and forth, pawing at its face. The woman jumped up and kicked it square in the chin. The wolf turned and ran, snaking the through the cars until it disappeared.

Genevieve looked down. Her dress was ripped, and blood dripped from a deep bite on her thigh.

"Well, fuck."

~

TOMMY

No. No no no.

Tommy lay in the dirt with his hand clutched to the ragged bite on his shoulder. He choked back tears of pain and struggled to sit up. He should have just run. He shouldn't have gotten involved.

A woman in a leather jacket stood over him with a can of mace in her hand, panting. Everyone else that had been in the parking lot had fled. He doubted anyone had even bothered to call the police.

"Shit, kid, are you okay?" she asked, extending her uninjured arm to help him up. Her other arm was smeared with blood that dripped down from the bite.

He took it and let her pull him to his feet. "I just—shit. I've been bit." The implications of what had happened sunk in.

"I've been bit," he repeated uselessly. This couldn't be happening. He took a step back and looked up to the sky. It was a full moon.

The woman followed his gaze. "Yeah, this is not great," she said.

The girl with the pink hair she had been protecting walked up behind her. Blood was streaming down her leg. "Did we all get bit?" she asked, her voice shaking.

"Unfortunately," the woman said, looking back at her. "What's your name?"

"Genevieve," she replied.

"I'm Amber," the woman in the leather jacket replied with a nod. Amber turned back to him. "What's your name, kid?"

"Don't call me that," Tommy snapped. His whole body shook, but not just with adrenaline. He could already feel some freaky magic shit starting inside of him. This couldn't be happening. His life was already hell. He couldn't deal with this on top of it.

He took a step away from the women. Amber watched him, worried. She held out a hand like she might try to grab him.

"Look, calm down, okay?" she said, stepping closer.

"I just got bit by a werewolf on the *full moon* and you want me to calm down?" he shouted at her, taking another step back. "Are you kidding me?"

She grit her teeth. "I get it. I'm freaking out too. Just don't—"

Tommy turned and fled. He had to get away. He couldn't stay around people and let someone trap him. He had to *run*.

CHAPTER 2

AMBER

"Shit," Amber said as the nameless kid took off at a run. He could hurt somebody. Hell, so could she.

"Are we going to change?" Genevieve asked.

She turned to face her. "Yeah. Assuming we don't die."

Her hands shook and her insides churned with guilt and fear as memories she desperately wanted to forget rose to the surface. Dylan screaming. His body twisted in pain as his bones broke, but couldn't reform. His eyes as the magic tortured him and stole his life.

A thump of something *other* beat inside Amber's chest. "We need to get to the woods," she said, her voice edged with a growl.

She grabbed Genevieve's arm and dragged her toward the dark line of trees. It looked like safety. She had to get Genevieve there, and she had to find the boy. The drive to do so overwhelmed the fear and guilt.

Genevieve struggled against her grip. "What are you doing?"

Amber stopped in her tracks. "Can't you feel it?" she asked, looking straight at Genevieve. "Do you want to be standing next to some stranger when the change happens?"

Genevieve shook her head and she dropped her arm.

"Just follow me. Please."

Genevieve nodded, biting her lip uncertainly, and Amber turned back to the tree line. She would follow or she wouldn't.

Footsteps crunched in the gravel behind her, and Amber breathed a sigh of relief.

"How long do we have?" Genevieve asked, jogging a little to catch up and walk beside her.

"I don't know exactly," she said. "It varies from person to person. Not long, though."

Genevieve was silent for a moment, then asked, "How bad is it going to hurt?"

"It won't hurt if your body can take the magic," she said, closing her eyes against the memory of the alternative.

"And if it doesn't?" Genevieve pressed.

Amber stopped and whipped around to face her. "Then you die a painful and bloody death."

Genevieve stared at her with wide eyes. "Shit."

"That about sums it up," she agreed, continuing into the forest. Something inside her relaxed as they passed under the cover of the trees.

"Do you know a shifter or something?" Genevieve asked.

"No," she said tersely. "I knew someone that didn't survive the change."

"Oh," Genevieve replied, her voice much quieter.

A strange warmth curled through her limbs. She stopped and looked up at the sky, her breaths coming a little faster. Something woke up inside of her, opening its eyes for the first time. They stared up through the leaves as her muscles twitched.

The shift rippled along Amber's skin. She watched as claws extended from her fingertips and fur prickled down her arm. Grief warred with the foreign elation inside of her. Why? Dylan had been the one they chose. Why did this kill him and not her? Why did she have to be the one to survive?

~

TOMMY

Tommy fell to the ground as a panic attack stole his breath and blurred his vision. His muscles trembled, and he wheezed as claws pushed painlessly from his fingertips, digging into the soft dirt. It didn't hurt. He thought it would.

Barely able to process what was happening, he forced himself upright and pulled off his shirt. It felt like it was suffocating him. He tried to pull off his jeans, but they got hung up on his shoes.

He fell backward and blinked up at the sky. The moon peeked through the trees, and he couldn't tear his eyes away from its bright face. It was brighter than he had ever seen before. It sang to him, and something inside of him sang back.

With a sickening snap, his bones began to shift. Fur rolled over his skin and his feet fell out of his shoes as they narrowed into paws. His face lengthened into a snout, and his teeth morphed into sharp fangs. Light his human eyes couldn't process now illuminated the dark forest. He could see every branch and every leaf perfectly.

He lifted his hand toward the moon, but a paw attached to a long leg was what moved instead. With a yelp, he twisted and tried to stand. Four wobbly legs scrambled against the dirt underneath him. He stood, panting and shaking.

Tommy was afraid, but there was something else in his mind, and it was not scared at all. It was exultant. The wolf yipped in excitement, turning in a circle and sniffing at the clothes that lay in a pile where he had changed. He picked them up gently and stuck them

12

by a tree, nosing leaves over the top of them. They were poorly hidden, but the wolf seemed pleased.

With an approving huff, the wolf turned and sprinted deeper into the forest. Human feelings warred with the wolf's instincts, but Tommy's worry couldn't overcome the joy of the wolf. It was a full moon. It was a night for running and hunting, not thinking. The wolf lifted its head and howled as it ran.

The forest was silent for a moment, then an answering howl echoed through the trees. He slid to a halt. Another howl joined it.

Pack. Family. Home. He turned and ran toward the other wolves.

~

GENEVIEVE

Genevieve stared at the ruddy wolf across from her. She shifted on her paws, muscles tensed and ready to flee. The wolf watched her with yellow eyes that glinted in the bright moonlight, then took a step forward.

Genevieve hunched down. Something about this other wolf made her want to show her belly. She didn't like the feeling. It was unnatural. To her at least. The wolf inside of her was practically purring; it *wanted* to submit.

Amber made a rumbling noise in the back of her throat, then turned away. She looked back over her shoulder as though she was asking her to follow.

Genevieve took a careful step forward, and Amber took off at a run. A thrill ran through her and she raced after the larger wolf.

Her new body sang with emotions she didn't recognize. Curiosity at every scent. Delight at her speed. A fierce desire to win the race. Genevieve hated competition of any kind, but the new presence inside of her loved it. She dug in and pushed her strange new legs to go faster. Though she was smaller than the reddish wolf, she was gaining on her.

A howl cut through the night. Amber stopped short and Genevieve slid in the leaves, bouncing off the other wolf's flank. She shook her head to clear it and waited, tense, to make sure she hadn't pissed Amber off.

Amber was looking through the trees, ears standing straight up. She tilted her head back and howled in return. The sound did something to Genevieve. To the wolf inside of her. It coursed through her with a mixture of longing and a desire to prove herself.

She lifted her snout toward the moon and joined her howl with Amber's. After a moment, Amber stopped and waited for a response, but the forest was silent. She took off in the direction it had originally come from.

Genevieve raced after her, determined to beat her this time. She had to show the other wolf she was fast and strong. The creature inside of her knew she wasn't just some submissive puppy. Her muscles strained against their limits, and slowly, Genevieve gained on Amber. She willed her legs to go faster and she began to pass the larger wolf.

A bitter scent distracted her. The wolf inside of her growled in anger. Human. Intruders. This was her pack's territory now.

Trespasser.

She snarled in anger and veered away from Amber, racing toward the smell of unwashed human. Fury coursed through Genevieve's body. It wasn't her emotion, it was pouring out of the creature that now shared her mind. She couldn't think. Instinct took over, driving her forward. Protect. *Kill.*

Genevieve could see the human now. He was laying under a tree in an old sleeping bag. She lunged toward him, but teeth closed around her leg and jerked her to the ground. She yelped and turned on whatever stopped her, teeth snapping as she growled her displeasure.

The ruddy wolf growled right back and leaped toward her, wrapping her jaws around the back of Genevieve's neck. Amber's teeth didn't break the skin, but Genevieve knew they could. Her body went limp. She twisted, showing her vulnerable belly to her alpha.

Alpha. The word felt right to her and the wolf inside of her.

But Amber wasn't letting go. Her teeth tightened on Genevieve's neck, and a growl vibrated in her mouth. Genevieve twisted farther and whimpered. Her alpha was rejecting her.

A branch cracked behind them, and Amber whipped around, dragging Genevieve with her. A gray wolf stood a few feet away, watching them anxiously. He shifted from paw to paw, then lowered down to his belly.

He slunk forward, staying low to the ground, his eyes never leaving Amber. He slid up beside Genevieve and lay his snout over her neck. Tommy looked up into Amber's eyes and whined, the sound pleading.

Amber huffed around her mouthful of skin and fur. Something changed. Amber's teeth broke through her skin but it didn't hurt. A new magic flooded through Genevieve. Warm. Bright. Comforting.

Amber dropped her and gently wrapped her jaws around the back of Tommy's neck. Genevieve felt the moment Tommy accepted Amber as alpha.

For a brief moment, golden threads shimmered between them, connecting them all. Amber's eyes flared bright red. The golden threads disappeared, but the new bond did not. They were a pack.

CHAPTER 3

AMBER

What the hell had she done? Amber stared at her now-human hands. The pack bond was a steady presence at the back of her mind, along with the wolf. It was curious and intelligent.

Her hands shook. She was a werewolf. A shifter. Amber felt strange new instincts she didn't completely understand. She wanted to claim the forest around her, protect it and her pack.

Amber put her face in her hands. God help her, she had a pack.

"Amber?" Genevieve asked tentatively.

She curled her fingers into a fist and took a deep breath to calm herself down before looking over her shoulder at the other woman. "Yeah?"

"I don't suppose you remember where we left our clothes, do you?" Genevieve asked, standing with one arm crossed over her chest, and the other hand hiding her crotch. The pink hair that had perched on top of her head in matching buns last night was a mess of tangles around her face.

They had slept in a pile after running through the forest most of the night. Unfortunately, they had woken up this morning human and very nude.

"Vaguely." Amber shrugged. She looked at the boy and sighed. "You don't want me to call you kid, right?" she prompted.

The boy looked back at her, then covered his eyes and turned his head away again. "My name is Tommy," he said, a blush creeping up his neck.

"Alright, Tommy," Amber said with a nod. "Nice to meet you. Genevieve and me are going to go retrieve our clothes. Hopefully. Did you manage to get yours off before you changed?"

"Um, yeah, I think so," he said.

"Well, why don't you go get yours too, and we can meet back up in the parking lot?" Amber asked.

"Sounds great," Tommy said as he scrambled to his feet. He hurried into the trees without a backward glance.

Genevieve covered her mouth to stifle a laugh. "I thought he was going to die of embarrassment," she whispered.

Amber grinned. "He's probably never seen a boob before in real life."

Genevieve snorted, losing her battle to keep from laughing. "He was blushing so bad."

"Better that than gawking at us," Amber said, feeling fond of Tommy already.

"Agreed," Genevieve said with a smile.

Amber turned in a circle and sniffed the air. Then felt stupid for trying to sniff her way back to their clothes. The wolf was peering out of her eyes, and its instincts were getting mixed up with her own.

"This way, I think," Amber pointed in the opposite direction from where Tommy had headed.

Genevieve nodded and fell into step beside Amber. They walked silently. Genevieve stared at the ground, and Amber looked straight ahead. Being naked was awkward even though they were both girls. No one wants to go hiking in the nude. Especially with a stranger.

"Thanks for…you know," Genevieve said, making a biting motion with her hand. "The homeless guy."

Amber nodded. "No problem. I'm just glad neither of us were alone. I think it made it easier."

"You can feel the thing, right? The bond or whatever?" Genevieve asked.

"Yes." Amber rubbed her hand against her sternum. She could feel how far away Tommy was and had a vague sense of both of her new pack member's emotions. She thought she might be able to tell more if she focused on it, but it seemed intrusive. She certainly hoped they couldn't feel hers.

After a few more minutes, they found their clothes strewn in the small area where they had shifted the night before. Amber pulled on her underwear and jeans first, then picked up her jacket. The sleeve had a jagged hole where she had been bitten. She stared at it and tried to decide if she would be able to patch it or stitch it back up.

"That thing has seen better days," Genevieve said with a laugh.

"I'm going to fix it, "Amber snarled at her before she could stop her overreaction.

Genevieve lifted her hands in apology. "Sorry," she said. "I didn't realize it was important to you."

Her shoulders slumped and she turned away. "It was my brother's."

She wanted to tell Genevieve it was okay, but her emotions were all over the place. She didn't want to be a werewolf. Not after what had happened to her brother. Her family would never accept it, not that they wanted her around now anyhow.

Genevieve didn't ask any more questions after that. Amber pulled on her shirt and draped the ruined jacket over her arm.

They headed back towards the parking lot. She could feel the tension in Genevieve and had an urge to try to mend it. Her wolf was frustrated and irritated with her for hurting Genevieve. It was protective of its pack members. Amber was irritated with it for existing, much less having an opinion.

CHAPTER 4

AMBER

The first thing Amber heard was a snarl, then she felt Tommy's fear. She broke into a run, and Genevieve followed her.

Some big, bald guy had Tommy backed up against a car. His hands were fisted in the collar of Tommy's shirt. Fury ripped through Amber. Neither she, nor the wolf inside her, would stand for someone threatening her pack.

With a speed not her own, she sprinted toward them, hitting the other werewolf from the side. Tommy's shirt ripped as the guy's claws were torn out of the fabric.

"Don't touch him," Amber growled, shoving the other wolf back again. She made sure she was between him and Tommy.

The werewolf snarled, but didn't move toward her. The scent of other shifters drifted toward them. Amber looked up and saw three bulky men headed their way through the mostly empty parking lot.

The man in front wore a blazer over a plain shirt. He walked a few steps ahead of the other two, and Amber immediately identified him as the leader of this little group. Whether he was the alpha of the pack or just the highest-ranking werewolf present, he was definitely in charge.

Amber put herself between him and her pack.

He stopped next to the man that had been threatening Tommy and looked her up and down. "I guess we just discovered what that omega got up to last night," the man said. "Did you idiots kill anyone?"

"Touch my pack again and I might," Amber said. The wolf inside her wanted to charge this man and tear him down in front of the others. The desire to challenge him was almost overwhelming, but Amber resisted. No matter what instincts she had now, she wasn't going to be stupid. They were outnumbered, and challenging him would put the two wolves she was responsible for in danger.

The man gave a disbelieving snort. "I'm sorry, your what?"

Amber bit the inside of her cheek, uncertain. She had intended to keep the whole alpha thing under wraps before she had blurted out that Tommy was hers. She wasn't sure what it meant to be an alpha, or if she even wanted the responsibility.

"You heard me," Amber said. Now that it was out there, she'd be damned if she'd let this douchebag laugh at her for it.

The guy shook his head. "Bitten wolves can't be alphas," he said, looking at her like she was stupid. "You don't have what it takes."

Amber straightened. This guy was a bully and a bigot. Something in his tone told her he wasn't an alpha himself. She curled her lip in disdain. The wolf peered out of her eyes, and red tinted her vision as she felt alpha power rise in her. The wolf's instincts told her that the other werewolf had to back down, or challenge her.

An angry blush crept up his neck and he took a step back, lowering his eyes. "How the fuck did you do that?"

"How about you tell me why a werewolf that you seem to know was running around a concert last night attacking people?" She took another step toward the other werewolves and was satisfied to see the wolves move back again to keep distance between them.

"That would be because Samuel didn't do his job," a deep voice said from Amber's left.

Amber turned, startled. She hadn't heard the guy coming at all.

The man walked toward them; he was different from the others. There was a weight to him that was unnatural. This was their alpha.

The werewolf that had been taunting her stared hard at the ground. If he had a tail, it would be tucked tightly between his legs. She was surprised Samuel didn't drop to his stomach in human form.

"We're close to finding Peter—" Samuel began.

The alpha looked at Samuel, who snapped his mouth shut. Turning back to Amber, he put on a more pleasant face. "My name is Donovan Lockhart. I'm sorry for the way my *gamma* embarrassed himself today, Samuel is correct that it is unusual to see a bitten wolf take up the mantle of alpha. It is, of course, also not legally permitted. However, I can help you with that if you would like to join my pack."

Amber racked her brain for where gammas fit into the pack. It had been a long time since she had studied the pack hierarchy. All she could remember was that they were below the beta, but somewhere above a regular pack member.

Even more confusing, this had taken a turn in a direction she had not seen coming. "Join your pack? There's normally an application process that takes a year," Amber said, skeptical of the offer. The way this alpha was speaking to her was all wrong; and her wolf hated him. "I don't want to be in a pack with a douchebag like Samuel either," she said, pointing at the idiot who was still staring at the ground.

Donovan bristled slightly, but kept his expression calm. "You would be of a higher rank than Samuel. I'm sure you could cope."

"Why would you want us?" she asked, gesturing to Tommy and Genevieve behind her. More than anything, she was suspicious of his offer. It was too good to be true. "You don't know anything about the three of us."

"Us? The offer is for you, and you alone. There is a limit to how many wolves I can add to my pack each year. Going over the quota would force me to pay some very hefty fines. Besides," he said, eyeing Tommy and Genevieve distastefully, "I'm not interested in weak wolves."

"Then what would happen to us without an alpha?" Tommy blurted out. He immediately shrunk back when all eyes turned to him.

"The other two would be put into the system," Donovan said, speaking directly to Amber and ignoring Tommy. "They would find a pack, eventually."

Tommy's panic ripped through Amber like an alarm. Her heart beat like a drum in her chest and the wolf in her head snarled angrily. She had to protect him, but what could she do? She wouldn't be able to stay his alpha if it was illegal. Hell, she didn't even *want* to be a werewolf. Being an alpha came with responsibilities she knew nothing about.

"This is your fault," Amber snapped, stepping forward. "Whether Samuel was supposed to be watching that omega or not, this is still on you, *Alpha*."

Donovan's expression grew dark, and his eyes flashed red. "You are in no position to chastise me, little girl," he said, his voice edging toward a growl. "I offered you a chance. Take it or leave it. If you want to go in the system with the others, who am I to stop you?"

"I am not leaving them behind," Amber insisted. "And how many more people did Peter attack last night? How can you be so callous?"

~

GENEVIEVE

Genevieve watched the exchange grow more heated by the moment. Amber was refusing his offer, which was insane. The *system*, as the other alpha put it, was terrible. Bitten werewolves went in for a year, but they never came out with a pack. After their stay was up, they'd be dumped back in a city and told not to make trouble. Most ended up homeless.

Tommy edged closer to her. He was trembling. Putting a comforting hand on his shoulder, she shut her eyes and took a deep breath. She didn't get involved with shit like this normally. There was a reason that she hadn't used her degree, despite having passed the bar exam almost two years ago. She didn't want anyone depending on her; she always ended up letting them down.

Amber yelled at the other alpha again and Genevieve stepped up to her side, putting a hand on her elbow.

"This whole conversation is stupid." Her voice came out quieter than she had intended. Clearing her throat self-consciously, she continued, "Amber can remain our alpha. She doesn't have to join anyone's pack," she said, louder this time.

Donovan turned his creepy red gaze on her. "You have no idea what you're talking about," he said, dismissing her.

"Actually, I do," she said, stepping past Amber. "A bitten werewolf may become an alpha the same way a born wolf can. The Alpha Trials are open to anyone that can find a sponsor."

Donovan curled his hand into a fist and glared at her, losing the final remnants of his friendly pretense. "And who would sponsor her?" he asked, spreading his arms wide as if he expected her to have someone volunteer right then. "No pack around here would do something that stupid."

"It doesn't have to be a werewolf," she said, jutting out her chin stubbornly. Her heart was racing in her chest and she thought she might vomit, but there was no backing down now. "It can be any paranormal that can fund the pledge. Amber has until the next full moon to prepare."

The alpha snorted. "She will never pass the Trials."

"Yes, I will," Amber said, stepping up next to Genevieve. Her expression was one hundred percent determined.

She had no idea how Amber could be so fearless, but it bolstered her own confidence. "She has the right to try. You can't stop her."

"We'll see about that," the other alpha said. He turned away, snapping his fingers at the other three werewolves. They followed him to an SUV on the other side of the parking lot and climbed inside.

Genevieve couldn't see them through the darkly tinted windows, but as they sped off, gravel flying from under their tires, she got the impression she was being flicked off. She slumped in relief. She never did that kind of thing. Part of her wanted to take it all back and just let whatever happened...happen.

"A sponsor?" Amber asked quietly, glancing at her.

"Yeah," she said, feeling awkward for volunteering Amber for something she barely understood. Finding a sponsor wasn't going to be easy either. "We'll have to find one soon. At least a week before the Trials."

"What exactly are the Alpha Trials? I've never heard of them," Amber said.

"Um, that's because they're kind of shrouded in secrecy." She twisted her fingers in the hem of her shirt, feeling like an idiot. She had volunteered Amber for something crazy and Amber had just backed her up without question, giving up her chance at getting a pack. "I actually don't know much about them, other than that they exist, and any wolf is eligible to take them with a sponsor."

Amber stared at her blank-faced for a moment before speaking again. "What is the sponsor for?"

"From what I remember, they have to cover any fines should the alpha or pack do something stupid," Genevieve explained, trying to remember the details she learned in her magical law classes. "The month between the time the werewolf claims alpha status and the Alpha Trials are a test of sorts. If they can't keep control of their pack during that first month, there's no point in them completing the Trials. The sponsor is also somehow responsible for whatever the pack does. I don't remember the details, though."

"I'm surprised it doesn't have to be a werewolf." Amber running her fingers through her tangled hair.

Genevieve shrugged. "A technical loophole. A werewolf sponsor is expected, but not legally required."

Amber looked back at Tommy, who, now that Genevieve thought about it, was being weirdly quiet. Tommy stood with his arms wrapped around himself, staring at his bare feet.

"Tommy," Amber said, "I'm not going to let them put you in the system."

He looked up and laughed once, a despairing sound. "You're going to *try*, but you don't know anything about being a werewolf. None of us do."

"Hey," Amber said, marching up to him and grabbing his shoulders. "If I became an alpha, there has to be a reason. I'll jump through these assholes' legal hoops, and then we'll all be fine."

"Well, technically the only reason you became alpha is because you happen to be naturally more dominant than either of us. It doesn't really mean..." Genevieve trailed off at the irritation on Amber's face. Oh. She was trying to calm him down. "But you seem to be a natural, so I'm sure it'll all be fine," she said, plastering a fake smile on her face.

Tommy jerked out of Amber's grip and scuffed his bare toes on the pavement. "I couldn't find my shoes," he muttered.

"I can take you back home to get some more," Amber said gently.

Tommy scowled at her. "I don't have a home," he snapped.

Looking at him more closely, it was obvious. His clothes were dirty and threadbare like he wore them every day. His shaggy hair hung almost to his shoulders and was knotted pretty badly. He couldn't have been more than sixteen.

"Then you can come and stay with me," Amber responded without hesitation. "I'll get you shoes and some clothes too. And a haircut if you want one."

Genevieve thought about going back to her friend's apartment, but the wolf inside of her really didn't like that idea.

"Can...I come too?" Genevieve asked, feeling like an idiot.

"Of course," Amber said with a frown, rubbing her hand against her stomach. "The idea of being separated makes me feel all wrong inside."

Amber fished her keys out of her pocket. "Come on," she said, waving at them to follow. "Food, shoes, and then sleep. In that order."

Tommy looked at Genevieve, waiting for her to follow Amber before he did as well. They walked silently behind her, each of them lost in their own thoughts.

CHAPTER 5

AMBER

Early morning sunlight streamed into the small apartment, muted by smoke drifting past the window. Amber hurriedly flipped the bacon out of the pan. Half of it landed on the floor, the rest on the counter. The bitter smell of burned food filled the kitchen.

"I think I have some ramen in the pantry," Amber said, eyeing the bacon with distaste. She could rebuild an engine, and stick an IV, but cooking just wasn't her thing. They had gone through everything easy to make in the refrigerator the evening before, which, to be fair, wasn't much for three people.

Tommy's stomach growled loudly behind her. She threw down the spatula and turned to face him and Genevieve, hands on her hips. "You know what, let's just go to The Market. They have food stalls. My treat."

"The Market?" Tommy asked tearing his eyes away from the ruined food and perking up. His face cracked into the first smile Amber had seen. "I've never been."

"If you've never been, then we have to go. It'd be stupid to miss it while it's in town," Amber said. The wolf inside her watched eagerly as excitement shivered through the pack bond. Providing for them felt right.

"Anything to get food," Genevieve agreed. "I've never been this hungry in my life."

"Is that a werewolf thing?" Tommy asked as he carefully pulled on his new shoes. He treated them like they were made of glass. Amber was surprised he was willing to walk in them.

Amber wiped sweat from her brow and nodded. "We haven't had a proper meal since we shifted. It takes a lot of energy and makes you super hungry. We need protein more than anything else right now."

Before she could sweep it all into the trashcan, Genevieve swiped the least burnt piece of bacon from the counter. Amber raised a brow.

"I'm really hungry," Genevieve said, shoving the blackened pork into her mouth. She grimaced, but swallowed resolutely.

"How do you know so much about werewolves?" Tommy asked, his voice was carefully neutral, casual almost, but Amber could feel his suspicion like an alarm bell through the pack bond.

She swept the last of the bacon that had fallen on the floor into the dustpan before answering. "I applied to join a pack when I turned eighteen," she explained carefully. The last thing she wanted was to get into the details of what had actually happened. "Didn't get accepted, but I spent close to a year learning about basic werewolf stuff. Unfortunately, nothing about being an alpha, since I didn't think it mattered."

"You'd have had a hard time finding any information on it anyhow," Genevieve piped up. "The werewolves don't like all their rules being public knowledge."

"Speaking of," Amber said, eager to turn the attention away from her history. "How do *you* know all this stuff that isn't supposed to be public knowledge?"

Genevieve shrugged and looked at the floor. "I studied magical law in college."

Amber narrowed her eyes. Genevieve didn't look old enough to have gotten through college, but she decided not to push it. She didn't want to talk about her past, either.

She grabbed her keys and reached for her jacket, then remembered it was shredded.

"Do you want me to try to patch it?" Tommy asked hesitantly.

Amber looked at him. "You could do that?" She knew she had said it too harshly as soon as the words came out of her mouth. Her desperation to have it fixed had come off like she was angry, which was far from the truth.

Tommy shrank back. "Yeah, it wouldn't be perfect or anything, but it would hold together."

Amber forced herself to relax and stop freaking Tommy out. "Anything you could do would be great. Thank you," she said softly. "We'll get whatever you need to patch it while we're out, if that's okay?"

Tommy straightened a little and nodded. "Yeah, that's fine."

"Let's go," Genevieve said, waiting by the door impatiently.

They headed downstairs and piled in the truck. Genevieve sat in the middle of the bench seat while Tommy scooted as close to the door as he could get.

"How old is this thing?" Genevieve asked, eyeing the dials on the dash skeptically.

"Old on the outside, but the engine was replaced six years ago," Amber said, patting the steering wheel. "She's built like a tank."

She cranked the engine and it sputtered ominously. Genevieve raised a brow and turned to say something, but Amber raised a hand in warning.

"Speak ill of her and you'll be walking to The Market," she threatened.

Genevieve snapped her mouth shut and turned back to the front. On the second try the engine turned over and rumbled to life. Amber threw it into gear and glared at her passengers one last time before pulling out of her parking spot.

~

TOMMY

They'd had to park almost a mile away from the Market. Tommy's stomach growled impatiently. A few food trucks were parked along the street, and the smell of cooking food made him ravenous. His new shoes pinched at the sides of his feet, but Tommy was relieved to have something without holes to wear. Something *clean*. He hadn't appreciated how nice it was to be able to wash his clothes regularly until he couldn't anymore.

"There it is," Amber said, pointing in the opposite direction he had been looking.

The Market was…magical. He stopped in his tracks as people surged around him and stared at the archway that led inside. It had planted itself between two one-hundred story office buildings in the center of downtown. The sight hurt his eyes; it shouldn't have fit, but there it was.

The archway itself shone like a beacon even in the bright sunlight. The word MARKET hovered overhead, spelled out in green fire that twisted in on itself, making each letter appear to writhe. The concrete sidewalk gave way to opalescent cobblestone that shimmered every time a step landed on it. With so many people walking on it, the path seemed to wobble.

"Come on," Genevieve said with a grin, grabbing his sleeve. "It gets better."

Even Amber was smiling softly. She was less intimidating when she wasn't scowling at everything that moved. Tommy followed Genevieve. She'd put her hair up in those buns again; they made her look like she was eighteen or nineteen, but he got the impression she was actually in her mid-twenties. She slipped sometimes, shifting from teenager to adult when she wasn't thinking about it.

Amber never slipped. She was wary, and angry. They were all upset about being turned, but he knew there was something worse going on with Amber. He just had no clue what it was. She'd practically bitten his head off this morning when he'd mentioned he could patch her jacket, but she hadn't been angry. She was just desperate, which was even weirder.

They passed under the archway, and all thoughts of why Amber was acting weird fled from Tommy's mind. Music and chatter pounded against his newly sensitive hearing, but he didn't care. This place was *magic*. Not just magical. Every part of it seemed to be created from pure magic itself.

The first stall was formed out of a flowering tree. The workers stood inside the trunk, leaning over a counter created by a low hanging branch that curved at a ninety-degree angle. Purple and pink blooms unfurled as people approached, releasing a sweet scent. A pretty elvish girl harvested a few flowers and wove them into a hairband that was then sold to the next customer.

Ahead of them a man dressed in colorful silk was juggling fire. Actual fire, not flaming batons or chainsaws, but large balls of fire. Every few rounds he tossed one high in the air and it exploded with a shower of blue sparks, then snapped back into shape before he caught it again.

A weird scraping noise overhead caused Tommy to look up, and where the sky should have been, there was water. Strange shapes flitted through the darkness. A face appeared, and Tommy startled. Webbed hands pressed against the surface of the water, and the slitted, green eyes of a mermaid stared down at him. Her tail swished behind her. It was a brilliant rainbow of colors, but the fins were lined with serrated spikes. She smiled, her teeth razor sharp, then disappeared from view.

"Don't worry, they can't get you," Amber whispered with a grin right next to his shoulder.

"I'm not—it's just cool. I've never met a mermaid before," Tommy stuttered out.

Amber grinned. "You can trade with them farther down, I think."

"I don't have anything to trade." Tommy shrugged.

"You might be surprised," Amber said cryptically before walking further down the path.

He moved to follow, but a familiar scent stopped him short. Curious, he turned back toward the entrance, but couldn't see anything. He wasn't sure what he was smelling, anyhow.

A bony hand wrapped around his arm, and claw-like fingers bit into his flesh. He spun around and found an old woman draped in shawls leaning out of her stall. Her arm was stretched taut between them. If he took another step forward, he'd drag her right out of the opening. Her foggy eyes looked past him, unfocused.

"Care to hear your fortune?" she asked, her voice strangely distant. It beckoned him…it…

"No thanks," Amber said.

Her voice cut through the haze in Tommy's mind. He shook his head to clear it and jerked out of the crone's grip.

"She's not even a real fortune teller," Amber muttered, dragging Tommy further down the road.

"Aww, you should have let her read him. I bet he would have freaked out when she predicted death and dismemberment," Genevieve said, licking a glittery ice cream cone.

"Death and dismemberment?" Tommy asked, looking back at the old woman. She flipped them off, then disappeared in a puff of green smoke.

"She's a witch," Amber explained. "They use spells to put on a convincing show, but they have no way of telling the future. And they always predict you're going to die for some reason."

"I mean, they're not wrong," Genevieve said with a shrug. "We all die eventually."

Amber rolled her eyes. "Come on, I smell barbecue."

They wove through the crowd following the smell of meat. The stalls got larger as they went. In the distance, a tower loomed. It was at least fifteen stories high and wrapped in glittering balconies. The golden exterior shone in the sun.

The smell of perfectly cooked steak pulled Tommy's attention away from the tower. The source of the scent was a massive barbecue pit, with *Devil May Grill* emblazoned on the side. It was manned by the biggest troll he had ever seen. The pyrotechnic pit erupted with fire, and the flames morphed into a horned demon that cackled loudly.

Genevieve took off for the outdoor restaurant at a jog, followed closely by him and Amber. They got in line, and Tommy's stomach growled loudly. Even though they were at least ten people back, the line moved quickly.

They reached the front of the line and the troll loomed over them, his bulging muscles glistening with a sheen of sweat from the heat of the grill. His tusks jutted sharply up toward his upper lip. The ivory bones were pierced three times on each side. He had no idea how they managed to pierce something like that.

Most trolls were nerds. Buff nerds, but they liked to read and collect knowledge way more than they liked to fight. This troll looked like he ate nerds for breakfast.

"What'll you have?" the troll asked in a deep, rough voice. His purple eyes scanned their faces expectantly.

"I'll take the Fresh Kill Special and whatever they want," Amber said, gesturing at him and Genevieve.

"Same, that looks amazing," Genevieve said, standing on her toes to look at the piles of meat to the troll's right.

"I'll take the Roadkill Roast," Tommy said, mouth watering as he eyed the hunk of meat.

"Aye, and you'll all take it rare, won't you?" the troll asked with a laugh.

Amber grinned, all teeth. "Aye," she mocked.

The troll winked and slapped their meat down on the grill. It sizzled, the juices igniting the flames beneath it. Everything cooked in fast motion, sped along by magic. The troll tossed their orders on plates the size of platters, then waved them down the counter to pay.

Amber handed over the money and they hurried to a table. Tommy picked his slab of beef up with his hands and took the biggest bite he could. Juices dripped down his chin as he closed his eyes in pleasure. There was nothing like a good, hot meal when you were starving. He hadn't had that in longer than he could remember.

They didn't speak as they ate; their mouths were too busy being stuffed with amazing barbecue. He could feel his body relaxing as the hunger was finally sated.

That scent drifted toward him again and he looked up sharply. The wolf, previously sated by the food, awoke in his mind. Shit, he knew who that scent was. It was the werewolf that slammed him up against the car the day before.

He hunched over his plate and took another bite, scanning the crowds carefully. The wind shifted and the scent grew stronger. A bald head glinted in the sunlight. Tommy looked away, keeping track of the werewolf in his peripheral vision. He was watching them.

"What's wrong?" Amber asked, plastic fork clenched in her hand like a weapon. Her eyes flicked between him and the people around them.

"One of the werewolves from yesterday is here." Anger boiled in his gut. He was used to being scared when he was threatened, not angry. He had an urge to confront the guy, which he shoved down. "He's looking at us right now. I thought I smelled him when we first came in, too."

"It's possible one of them is just at The Market today," Genevieve suggested.

Amber shook her head. "I don't like coincidences," she said, anger clear in her voice as she stared at the remnants of food on her plate. She wasn't going to let this go. He almost regretted saying something, but the idea that they were being followed filled him with dread.

Amber wiped her face off and threw down her napkin. "Let's keep walking around. If they're following us, I want to catch them in the act."

"And then do what, exactly?" Genevieve asked, raising an eyebrow. "Are you going to pick a fight in the middle of The Market? It'll chew you up and spit you out."

"I know that," Amber retorted. "That's why this is the perfect place. If they try to attack, The Market will kick their asses for us. It's our best chance."

Tommy hadn't been here before, but everyone knew The Market was a neutral zone. It would dump whoever threw the first punch outside and never let them back in. A few idiots still started fights, but they were over in the blink of an eye.

"We should probably split up if we want to catch them following us," he said. "If I go off on my own, they'll probably follow me since I'm alone. The two of you can get behind them, then we can corner them."

Amber cocked her head to the side and gave him an odd look. "That's...a great idea. Do you get stalked often?"

Tommy shrugged and looked down at his feet. "No, it just seems logical."

The real answer was that he had been obsessed with *Werespy* when he'd still had access to a TV. It was a ridiculous show, with loads of action and hot women. The main character had used this technique before. That didn't make the plan stupid, but he still wasn't going to admit any of that.

"Alright, let's walk around for a little bit together. When you smell him again, break off from the group. I'll give you a few minutes to lead them away, then we'll corner them under the tower," Amber said.

He nodded in agreement. Genevieve shook her head and tossed her napkin down on the table, but didn't object further.

This area of The Market was mostly food stalls and small cafes. It was three solid minutes of walking before they made it to more shopping. The closer they got to the center, the larger and more ornate everything became. Instead of stalls there were buildings, some a couple of stories high. The luminescent cobblestone gave way to large, inky black stones. The smells changed too; everything here was old.

Tommy paused in front of a building, turning just far enough to see that Baldy and some douchebag werewolf in a fedora were still following them. Amber glanced back, and he nodded at her. She looked hesitant for a moment, but kept walking.

Slowing his pace, he fell behind the others, then took a right down one of the narrow paths that led away from the main street. A vendor shoved a sample in his face that smelled like old fish. He dodged the foul snack and hurried through the crush of people. When he glanced back, the werewolves were gone. They hadn't followed him.

He froze for a moment, then decided it didn't matter. The plan would still work, just in reverse. He jogged ahead, then cut across another side street, and came back out onto the main street, catching glimpse of Baldy as he turned a corner. Genevieve's bright pink hair was easy to spot in the crowds. Amber was still with her. The werewolves were keeping a decent distance between them.

He slipped back onto the main street and stalked after them, barely seeing anything around him; he was completely focused on the threat to his pack. Slowly, the distance closed between him and the werewolves. The thrill of the chase pounded in his chest.

The wind shifted again, blowing past Tommy toward the wolves. Baldy stopped and turned his head to the right, his nose twitching. Tommy ducked down and pretended to look in the window to his left. They started walking again, but faster.

Unease filled him as he trailed behind them. They had probably made him. What if there were more of them? He glanced over his shoulder, but he couldn't make out a threat in the crowd. His muscles tensed with the urge to shift.

The wolf urgently drew his attention back to the men following his pack. Baldy had split off from Fedora and was disappearing down a side street. With only a split second to make a decision, he let the wolf's instincts guide him. He followed Baldy.

This street was much narrower, and less crowded. The scents were sharper and the shadows seemed longer, like this was a place you went if you needed to hide what you were doing. The wolf urged him forward; it wanted to corner its prey. It wanted a fight.

He had to step around a small group of witches whispering about a hard to find ingredient when he noticed that the other werewolf had followed him. And he was closing in.

Resisting the urge to panic, he tried to think logically. If they were following him, then he just needed to get to the tower. He picked up his pace, but realized he had lost sight of Baldy completely.

A large, burly man with a beard down to his chest bumped his shoulder and scowled down at him. "Watch where yer goin', *puppy*," he grumbled.

Curling his hands into fists, he hurried around the man, or whatever he was. He smelled like magic and blood, which wasn't exactly a friendly combination. He had to get out of here. The wolf wanted to stay, to fight, but that wasn't what he did.

With a quick glance behind him, he took off at a run, darting down an alley, then behind a stall and down another street. Every turn he took the tower grew closer. He just needed to get back to Amber. If the werewolves were following him, then they could confront them that way. He wasn't going to risk getting trapped alone with them.

After two more turns, he paused to catch his breath. He couldn't see either of them, and this place was eerie. The fake sky dipped down in pillars of greenish water, casting an unearthly glow over the whole area. This must have been the place Amber was talking about where you could trade with the mermaids.

He pressed his back against what he thought was a glass tank, but cold water seeped through his shirt and trickled down his back, and a hand pressed against his shoulder. Jerking away, he bit down on a yelp.

A mermaid hovered directly behind him. Her vibrant, luminescent hair waved around her head in the gentle currents. She wasn't beautiful exactly, at least not by human standards, but Tommy couldn't tear his eyes away. She swam closer and pushed her face out of the water. Her green skin was dull in the direct sunlight.

"I'll offer you a trade," she whispered. Her silky voice echoed around Tommy, and he wasn't exactly sure if she was speaking out loud or in his mind.

"I don't have anything to trade," he said, taking a step back.

She grinned. "I want what's in your pocket."

"My pocket? Look, I'm sorry, but I'm in a rush," he said, catching sight of Baldy headed toward the tower, he was scanning the crowds looking for either him or Amber. Tommy took another step back.

"I'll tell you what they've been whispering if you trade," the mermaid said, stretching her webbed fingers toward him eagerly.

Tommy stopped and looked back at her, surprised. How could she hear them? They were getting farther and farther away, but if she knew what they wanted, he had to try to find out.

He pulled out the contents of his pocket. A paperclip, a two inch bit of copper wire he had stripped from a power cord, and a dime. The mermaid wiggled her fingers, eager and demanding. He dropped the items in her hand, confused how she knew he had them, much less why she wanted any of it. She closed her fingers around it and held the payment tightly to her chest.

"Please, I have to hurry," Tommy begged. The wolf inside of him wanted to chase after the men following his pack.

"They whisper about the red one. She's the only one they care about," the mermaid said before she sunk back into the brackish water and vanished.

Tommy ran in the direction Baldy had been heading, but skidded to a halt when the werewolf stepped out from between two stalls, blocking his path.

"You seem like you're in a hurry," Baldy commented, stalking forward with even steps.

He didn't have to turn around to know that the other werewolf was right behind him. "Not really, just stretching my legs."

Fedora huffed behind him. "I can smell your fear."

Tommy looked over his shoulder. "Stop sniffing me, weirdo," he said, narrowing his eyes. Splitting up with Amber had been a bad idea. He made a vow to never volunteer to be bait again. "Why are you following us, anyhow?" he asked, deciding he might as well be blunt.

Baldy chuckled. "Just making sure the dangerous new werewolves don't cause any trouble. It's a public service, really."

He snorted. "I don't have to be a werewolf to know that's a lie."

"You're not kidding," Genevieve said, walking up from his left. He had been focusing on the other two wolves so hard that he hadn't noticed her approach at all.

Amber stalked up behind Baldy, her expression furious. She stopped right behind him and leaned in to whisper in his ear. Baldy stiffened and jerked around to the side so that she wasn't standing at his back.

Fedora stepped around Tommy and walked toward Amber, a growl rumbling in his chest. Genevieve jumped in front of their alpha and bared her teeth at him. Her eyes glinted yellow as her fingers curled into claws.

"Gen," Tommy said carefully, "it's not worth it."

"Don't worry, it's not like she could land a blow on me anyhow," Fedora taunted.

"Why did Donovan put you up to this?" Amber demanded, walking toward Genevieve, whom she was eyeing warily. Tommy was too. Genevieve was way too close to shifting and losing control.

"Genevieve," he whispered, trying to draw her attention away from their stalkers. His wolf was restless. It wanted to protect his packmate, it wanted to attack, but he knew that would be a huge mistake.

"Donovan is responsible for the safety of everyone in this city. If a werewolf were to embarrass us by losing control, it would reflect poorly on him," Baldy said in a conde-scending tone. "This is for your safety and the safety of everyone around you."

"Everyone knows bitten bitches can't be trusted," Fedora taunted, leaning in close to Genevieve.

Genevieve's low growl turned into a roar and she took a step toward the asshole werewolf.

"Genevieve, don't!" Amber shouted as she lunged toward her. Tommy managed to grab her arm, but it was too late. She swung at the werewolf with a growl. A moment before her hand connected with his face, she disappeared in a flash of light.

Tommy stumbled forward, his hand abruptly empty. Amber caught him and shoved him behind her.

Fedora burst into laughter. "The way she lost it was almost poetic," he taunted, a self-satisfied grin plastered on his face.

"When I find you outside of this place, I'm going to make you pay for that," Amber said. The power in her voice made Tommy want to drop to his belly.

Even Fedora flinched, though he jutted out his chin like it hadn't affected him.

"Let's go." She pushed Tommy forward and took a few steps backward before turning and walking beside him.

He looked over his shoulder at them. The other werewolves watched them walk away with a hungry expression on their faces. They wanted to chase after them.

"Is Gen okay?" he asked quietly.

"Getting cast out doesn't hurt anything but your pride. I don't think she completely lost control, but she's probably not happy," Amber replied, her brows pinched tightly together like she was listening for something really far away.

He was almost sure at this point that she could feel them somehow, but didn't want to ask about it. "It's weird," he said, a sense of foreboding settling in his chest. "They haven't reported us to the police, but they're still following us. Why does Donovan want you so badly?"

Amber looked at him, confused. "You think he wants me?"

"Even when I split off from the group, they kept following you at first," he said. "And you were the one he made the offer to. Even then, it just seemed like..." he let the thought trail off, uncomfortable with speaking so plainly.

"Seemed like what?" Amber asked, nudging him with her elbow.

"It seemed like he was lying. About letting you in the pack. He was almost desperate for it, which doesn't make any sense. I don't know, it's stupid."

"No, it's not." She shook her head firmly. "The way he showed up the next morning and wasn't surprised to see people had been bitten is odd. Werewolves, bitten or not, don't lose control every day. Donovan wanted us to be changed, and he knew we would be. They found us, but they acted like they had no idea where or who the omega that attacked was."

"There's easier ways to get new pack members," he said.

"Yeah, but I wonder how many ways there are for someone to become an alpha?" Amber asked, her face tight with anger as she looked over her shoulder to make sure the two werewolves weren't still sniffing around for them.

"One of the mermaids overheard them talking," he said, shoving his hands in his pockets. "She said they only cared about you."

"A mermaid? How'd you manage to get that out of one of them?" Amber asked, raising both eyebrows in surprise.

"I made a trade, just like you suggested," he said with a sly grin. It was nice to be the one with a secret for once.

Amber snorted in amusement and smiled at him. "You're resourceful, I'll give you that."

He was almost embarrassed by the way he swelled with pride, but it was the first time in a long time that he'd been given a compliment like that.

CHAPTER 6

AMBER

Amber went through the motions of brushing her teeth while staring into the mirror with a blank expression. Her eyes used to be hazel; now they leaned more toward brown with a hint of red. She leaned over and spit in the sink then rinsed her mouth with water.

Dylan would have loved it. He would have wanted to catalogue every change and post pictures on social media. Her fingers clenched tightly on the edge of the sink. Claws crept out of the tips. The porcelain cracked under her hands and her breath came in short pants. Angry that she was in this situation and having to relive these memories all over again pushed her eyes all the way to red.

A hesitant knock on the door startled Amber. She stepped away and the claws slipped back into her fingers. With a deep breath, her eyes returned to normal.

"Are you…okay?" Tommy asked hesitantly. "I thought I heard something break?"

Through the pack bond, she was flooded with concern, and a little fear. It was brave of Tommy to approach her when he thought she was freaking out. She had to get it together. They deserved better than an unstable alpha who might bite their heads off.

She plastered a smile on her face and opened the bathroom door. "I'm fine, just had a…" she sighed, then finished lamely. "I dropped something in the sink. Did you find the extra blankets?"

It was apparent from Tommy's expression that he knew she was lying, but he didn't call her on it; he just nodded and walked back to the living room. Amber followed. She didn't want to be by herself right now. All that did was give her time to think about things she didn't want to think about.

Tommy seemed to want to intrude in her apartment as little as possible, but Genevieve did not have that problem. She was sprawled on the couch with a bag of chips and a beer from the fridge.

"Why is your reception so crappy?" Genevieve asked as she flipped to another grainy channel on the television. She had been grumpy and embarrassed the entire drive back to the apartment, but once she had settled on the couch with more food, she had calmed down. Any attempts to talk about what had happened had been met with stubborn silence, so Amber had given up for now and decided they'd had enough arguments for one day.

"I don't pay for the enchanted signal," Amber shrugged. "I don't really have time to watch TV."

Genevieve looked at her like she was an alien, then flinched away from the window. "There's someone—"

A knock at the door interrupted her warning.

Amber waved Tommy behind her and approached the door as quietly as she could. She was nervous, and the wolf prowled inside of her, ready to face any threat to her territory. The peephole showed Donovan standing in front of the door, a pleasant expression on his face.

Donovan, she mouthed to the other two, motioning for them to stay back. She unlocked the door, but left the chain, and cracked the door open.

Donovan raised a brow. "Amber," he greeted with a nod. "I'd like to talk."

"How do you know where I live?" she asked.

Something flickered across Donovan's face. "I simply asked arou—"

"So you didn't have two of your pack members following us all day?" She was fed up with the bullshitting.

Donovan took a deep breath like he was trying to remain patient. "May I come in? I wanted this to be a friendly conversation."

She yanked the chain out of the latch and opened the door wide. It wouldn't have stopped him if he'd really wanted to get in anyhow; keeping it closed was just petty.

He walked in, eyeing the other two before taking a seat at the small table. Tommy crossed his arms and stood in the middle of the living room while Genevieve stayed on the couch and shoved a chip into her mouth. Her chewing was the only sound for a moment before he cleared his throat and turned his attention to Amber.

"I have been thinking over the offer I gave you yesterday morning, and have decided it was unfair to not extend the invitation to all three of you," he said, looking around the room at the pack. "Your new instincts won't allow you to split your pack up like that, and honestly, if you had accepted, it wouldn't have reflected well on either of us."

Amber crossed her arms and looked at him closely. This reeked of desperation. "If we were to even consider this offer, I'm going to need some honesty first. How did the wolf that attacked us lose control? What happened to him?"

"Loss of control is an issue for bitten wolves," Donovan said, leaning back in his chair in a display of nonchalance. He traced his thumb along a groove in the table. "And he has been punished appropriately for his actions, but the nature of that punishment isn't something I can share with you."

"Why not?" Genevieve asked, licking chip dust from her fingers.

Donovan's jaw clenched. "Despite your education, there are still some things you don't know about werewolf laws. Things you will not know until you are part of a *proper* pack."

"It's amazing to me that even while you're here practically begging us to join your pack, you still talk down to us, like we're less than you because we've been bitten," Amber snapped.

Donovan bristled immediately and rose to his feet. He seemed to grow in size as his eyes bled red. "I am offering you something no other pack would ever consider, but if you are going to throw my generosity back in my face with insults, then you can consider my offer withdrawn," he bit out.

Genevieve dropped the bag of chips and stood, advancing on Donovan. "You can't call it generosity when you told your wolf to turn us."

"Careful what you accuse me of, little girl," Donovan growled.

Amber dropped her arms, claws pricking at her fingertips. "Get out of my apartment, and don't come back."

Tommy and Genevieve stepped closer, and she was relieved to feel their determination through the pack bond. Donovan didn't intimidate them.

The last of the facade fell away and he snarled at them. "I will make you regret this," he threatened before turning and yanking the door open. He slammed it shut behind him, and Mrs. Huntington banged on the wall they shared, shouting demands for quiet.

Amber walked over to the wall and banged right back. "Kiss my ass, Mrs. Huntington."

The woman huffed and shuffled away. Amber let her head drop against the sheetrock. She was drained, and while she knew turning Donovan away had been the only option, that didn't mean she was confident everything would be okay.

"He needs you for some reason," Tommy said, echoing his comments at The Market.

"It's because she's an alpha," Genevieve said, crossing her arms. "I'm just not sure how that helps him."

"We keep coming up with more questions and no answers," Amber said, laughing humorlessly. She ran a hand down her face and squared her shoulders. "We'll figure it out tomorrow. We have a little time."

CHAPTER 7

AMBER

The smells of the hospital were almost overwhelming. Amber tried breathing through her mouth, then grimaced. That made it worse. She had gotten used to the smell of antiseptic when she first started working as a nurse, but now, she could easily smell the rot of infection and the feces from someone a nurse hadn't gotten to help yet.

Pressing her hand over her mouth and nose, she grabbed a file to distract herself. She'd get used to this, too. Eventually.

Burning through her time off wasn't an option, especially with the money she had spent getting Tommy a new wardrobe. Since he needed a place to stay, she was already thinking about seeing if she could upgrade to a two bedroom apartment without breaking her lease. She'd be able to afford it; she just wouldn't be able to put money in savings like she had intended.

It had been cramped with all three of them in the studio apartment, but she was glad they both agreed to stay with her for now. Having to come to work today made her uneasy. The wolf inside her was practically pacing, constantly tugging at the pack bond to make sure it was still there.

"Amber, can I speak with you?" her boss Cory asked.

They got along fairly well, though Cory did have a reputation for playing favorites. But now, the elf's voice was off. The tips of her pointed ears were pink, and she was staring at the floor intently.

"Sure," Amber said, setting the patient's chart down on the nurse's station. An ominous feeling crept up her spine. She thought of every patient she had worked with for the past month. She hadn't screwed anything up, at least nothing too bad. Everyone made mistakes. If she had really messed up, surely she would remember what she'd done.

Cory led her away from the ICU and into a little office. A man from HR, the one that none of the nurses liked, was waiting for them.

"What's going on?" Amber demanded, stopping just inside the doorway.

Cory had a hand on the door, but couldn't shut it without hitting her.

"Please stay calm, ma'am," the HR representative said, lifting his hands and moving them in an overly deliberate manner. "Neither of us will attempt to harm you. You are safe here. You are not trapped in this room."

Amber looked at him like he was crazy, then at her boss. "Cory, is there something wrong with him?" she asked.

Cory shifted on her feet. "Look, it was reported this morning that you are an unregistered, bitten werewolf. It's against hospital policy. No one would insure us if we let someone who had been a werewolf for less than a year work here. I'm sorry."

The HR representative pushed some paperwork toward Amber. "This is your final write up for nondisclosure of a condition that makes you ineligible to work here. Please sign it, and we can give you your final paycheck," the HR representative said, tapping an envelope next to the paperwork.

A series of thoughts tore through her mind. Who reported it? It had to have been Donovan. He had found out where she lived, and apparently where she worked.

She bit her tongue to keep from shouting at the two people tensely watching her. They expected her to attack them. That was the stereotype after all. Bitten werewolves were out of control when they were new, while born wolves were zen masters of control. It was all bullshit.

Still, the rage she felt was amplified by the rage of the wolf inside her. She wanted to find the other alpha and rip him apart.

Forcing her arm to move, she grabbed the pen and scratched her signature onto the paper.

"This isn't right," she said, looking up into the eyes of the HR representative. "And you know it."

"Legally, the hospital is obligated to—"

She grabbed her final paycheck and walked away. Her claws dug into her palm as the howling in her head drowned out everything else.

CHAPTER 8

AMBER

Amber sat in her truck staring at the contact list on her phone. She could call her dad; he would give her whatever she needed. Tightening her grip on the phone she dropped her hands in her lap. No. She refused to slink back home a failure. She had lost her nursing job, but she could do something else. Fix cars maybe, or work as a waitress.

She flung her phone into the passenger seat and started her truck. It grumbled and clanked, then turned on. Genevieve and Tommy weren't expecting her back at the apartment until tonight. She was supposed to be working a twelve hour shift. That gave her almost eleven hours to try to find something else. Anything.

With her tires screeching against the pavement, she sped out of the parking lot, leaving the hospital in the rearview mirror. She cranked up the radio and tried to drown out the whirlwind of negative thoughts racing through her mind.

The wolf was restless, and angry. It was ready to fight, but there was no one to fight. She couldn't growl at the insurance company or at a policy that wasn't even written by the asshole who fired her.

She gripped the steering wheel tightly. Donovan was responsible for all of this. For the attack and for taking away the job she had studied four years to get.

The light turned red just before she was able to get through. She slammed on the brakes and skidded to a stop halfway onto the crosswalk. A guy walked past and smacked the hood of her truck then gestured rudely.

She snarled and had the door halfway open, intending to beat his ass, before she realized what she was doing. Yanking the door shut, she counted down from ten with deep breaths. This wasn't what she wanted, at all, but she wasn't going to let it ruin her life. Somehow, she was going to make it through the Trials and become an alpha. She was going to prove everyone wrong.

Amber parked in front of a small cafe with a woodsy theme and a "Help Wanted" sign in the window. The restaurant was built into a massive tree that was obviously grown by elven magic. No tree grew that wide naturally.

The outside seating was covered by a canopy of heavy, flowery branches. As she walked up the pathway cool air skated across her skin. They had likely charmed the area to be a perfect seventy degrees year-round.

Pixies were fighting with birds over dropped food, trying to grab little morsels and hide under the bushes that fenced in the property. She ducked under one that flew straight across the path in front of her.

The door opened ahead of her as a couple walked out of the cafe. The scent of coffee and fried food drifted toward her, making her stomach growl. She hadn't even thought about lunch after she'd been fired, but her new appetite was more than happy to remind her.

She stepped inside and looked for the hostess, but the post was empty. The place was nice but not too fancy. Elves tended to go for the *be one with nature* vibe. She'd always liked it, and their food was great. Nobody could grow a vegetable quite as well as an elf.

She was startled by a loud squeal and then a shout. "No, you can't have him!"

The angry shout brought the wolf to the surface as Amber whipped around to see what was going on. A witch with curly, blonde hair floating around her head like she just stuck her finger in a light socket had grabbed a pixie around the middle. Another witch with black hair had the small creature by the wings.

"It's a stupid, little pest," the dark-haired witch snapped. "I can take it if I want. You don't own it!"

"I won't let you—"

The other witch yanked back and the pixie's wings were ripped from its body. It let out a piercing squeal of pain.

"You bitch!" the blonde witch yelled, lifting her hand to cast a spell.

The other witch's friend moved faster and Blondie was thrown back, the pixie flopping out of her hands onto the floor. The witch that ripped off its wings jumped forward, foot poised to crush the pixie.

Amber stepped in her path and shoved her from the side just in time for her foot to come down on the tile floor instead.

"What the hell is wrong with you?" she shouted, forcing herself between the witch and the pixie. "Leave it alone." Nobody really liked pixies, but that was just cruel. There was no reason to torture the damn thing.

The witch lifted her hand, turning her hateful gaze on Amber. Amber grabbed it, squeezing the witch's wrist tightly.

"Try it and see what happens," she growled, her eyes flashing red. She had just ruined her chance to get a job here, but she'd be damned if she just stood by and watch those witches pick on a defenseless little animal. She couldn't fix everything that had gone wrong today, but she could stop this.

The witch smirked and a flash of green hit Amber in the face. She doubled over and vomited, lumpy slime pouring from her mouth. She shoved the witch with a growl, then vomited again.

Light flashed through the cafe, blinding her and everyone else. A hand wrapped around her arm and someone dragged her toward the back.

"We need to run," the blonde girl whispered.

At least she hoped it was her. She smelled right. The cool air of the patio swept over them as she let the woman drag her outside. She stopped and vomited, the putrid slime making her gag all over again.

"Come on," the blonde said impatiently. "Vomit and run."

Amber tried to glare at her, but she still couldn't see right. Spots danced in her vision, and everything was blurry.

"What did you do to me?" she asked the woman leading her farther away from the restaurant.

"Just a blinding light spell," the witch said. "Sorry, I couldn't warn you without tipping them off, and we really needed to get out of there."

They slipped behind a building and her vision finally cleared. The witch clutched the bleeding pixie to her chest, but it looked like it was dead.

"I'm Ceri, by the way," the witch said, smiling at her. "Thanks for trying to help back there. Most people don't give a crap about pixies."

"It's messed up to hurt them like that," she said, shaking her head. "And I'm Amber."

Another wave of nausea hit and she doubled over, vomit splattering on her shoes.

"Witch on a stick, she really hit you hard with that spell," Ceri exclaimed. "If you come back to my house I can make you something to counteract that. It'll last for hours if I don't."

Amber burped loudly, and unpleasantly. "Please. This is fucking awful."

Ceri peered around the corner, to make sure it was safe. "Come on, my car is parked down the street."

CHAPTER 9

CERI

Ceri ran two tires up on the curb in her haste to get the car parked. Amber flung her door open and hit her knees in the grass, vomiting for a third time on their drive here.

The witch grimaced and jumped out of the car. The sooner she got a remedy down this girl's throat the better. The pixie, still in her hand, was worrying as well.

"Just come inside when you can," she shouted back over her shoulder while unlocking the door. She left it open behind her and jogged toward the family spell room. Even though she wasn't part of her family's coven, she still used the spell room when she needed to. Well…she did when her mother wasn't pissed at her.

Carefully, she laid the pixie on a small towel on the table. Its gray body was limp. There was a little stub of a wing left on one side, but on the other side the wing was broken off at the joint and a strip of skin had been torn away.

She grabbed a wound-mending elixir off the shelf and doused the pixie's back. It was a lot of magic for such a little thing, but she had to try. It would take at least twenty minutes for it to work, so she turned her focus to the other urgent issue.

Her mind whirled through the possibilities for a remedy. The slime-vomiting hex was a childish spell mostly used by bullies in school. It was obvious the witch that used it on Amber intended it as an insult, *you're as threatening as a child*. She felt a little guilty for thinking it, but the way Amber had tried to help had been a little…stupid. You didn't just grab a witch. Every werewolf knew that; especially an alpha.

She grabbed a lighter and a half-burned bundle of sage, then stuck it in its holder. Smoke curled from the tightly bound herbs as soon as the flames of the lighter touched it. She blew lightly across the top to encourage it, and the sharp, cool scent cleared the stench of the slime from her nose.

"Ceri?" Amber said from the front of the house.

"Back here!" she shouted back. "Just follow your nose!"

Amber muttered something but appeared in the doorway a few moments later. She closed her eyes in relief as she stepped into the room. "That smells so much better."

Ceri grinned. "Just vomit in the trashcan if you get nauseous again," she said, pointing at it in the corner.

Amber nodded, but she was distracted, looking around the room.

"Never been in a spell room before?" she asked as she picked the ingredients she needed off the shelves.

"No," Amber said. "I've known a few witches, but they never let anyone but coven inside."

"My mother probably wouldn't be thrilled if she knew," she admitted. That was closer to a lie than an understatement. Her mother would be furious, but she didn't have to know. "I've always thought that was kind of silly if your clan wasn't in the running for a position with the conclave or something. No one is trying to steal our family magic."

"Y'all have one of those family covens?" Amber asked.

Ceri looked up with a laugh. "Y'aaall," she said, exaggerating the drawl. "Are you from Texas or something? I didn't think anyone actually said that."

Amber gave her an unimpressed look. "Yes, I'm from Texas."

"Sorry," she held up her hands in apology, "I wasn't trying to mock you. Anyhow, my family does have a coven, but I'm not part of it." her smile faltered, eyes straying to the pixie. She'd have to get the pixie out of here, or her mother would chop it up for parts.

"Sorry," Amber said quietly. "Didn't mean to bring up…" She let her thought trail off and waved her hand at Ceri's expression.

"Perfectly normal assumption," she said, forcing a smile back on her face. Flipping open her old spellbook, she scanned through the list of remedies, then flipped to the recipe. She froze when she saw the ingredients, pressing her lips into a thin, white line. So, the insult wasn't directed toward Amber after all. It was meant for her. The remedy required pixie wings.

She slammed the spellbook shut. She'd just have to come up with something else. Really, what the magic wanted was a sacrifice. Ritual, ingredients, and the spoken phrase were all part of the trade. She could come up with her own remedy.

The reason most witches wouldn't let anyone into their spell room was to make sure their coven's spells weren't stolen. There were standardized spells, but every coven, and every witch, had their own. Ceri had always enjoyed inventing new spells, but as she grew older, it had changed from passion to necessity.

She took a deep breath to steady herself and immediately regretted it as Amber vomited into the trashcan.

"I'm going to kill that witch," Amber croaked from the corner of the room.

"I'll help," she said, forcing herself to reopen the spellbook. If she wanted to modify the remedy, she needed to understand it first.

Poring over the smudgy text, she studied each step. It had three parts. The potion, the purge, and the spell. The potion pulled the spell from the body into itself, the purge expelled them both, and the spell restored. She straightened as a thought raced through her mind. The potion was there to make the purge easier, but it wasn't absolutely necessary if she knew another way to pull the spell from the body. Luckily for Amber, she did.

"Alright," she announced, turning to face her unhappy patient. "I know how to fix this, but it's going to be a little uncomfortable."

"I don't care as long as it stops," Amber groaned, and she immediately vomited again.

Ceri cringed. It was getting worse. She grabbed and lit another bundle of sage, then dragged Amber and the trashcan to the center of the room.

"The remedy involves more vomiting," she explained. "But then it'll all be over."

Amber looked unhappy about the news, but nodded resolutely and braced her hands on the rim of the trashcan.

All spells, especially hexes, were limited and temporary. Even this one would wear off on its own eventually. Ceri's grandmother had always told her that if she was lousy enough to get hit with a hex, she should at least know how to get back on her feet quickly. Grandma Gallagher had then proceeded to hex her. She had then made Ceri learn the counter-hex she had invented while she was under the painful effects of the nasty spell.

She could still hear Grandma Gallagher's gruff voice in her head. *"If yer stupid enough ta get hexed, then ya ought ta pay the price, lassie."* Ceri grabbed the boning knife from the counter and jabbed her finger, then grabbed Amber's and repeated the process.

"What the hell—"

Ceri slapped her hand against Amber's chest and chanted the counter-hex under her breath. Amber's face turned green and she bent over the trashcan as the slime and the magic were purged from her body violently.

She grabbed the sage and continued with the rest of the remedy. Hands together, clockwise twice, the Chant of the Sun for restoration, then finally, the cast. She spread her hands an inch apart, then turned her palms outward. The magic flowed from her hands into Amber in a bright stream of light.

Amber straightened slowly. The color returned to her cheeks as the magic poured into her body. Her eyes bled red and her hands shook at her side.

Ceri completed the spell and opened her mouth to ask Amber how she felt, but she was shaking. "Uhh, Amber, are you okay?" she asked, trying not to freak out.

Amber shut her eyes and clenched her hands tightly. "The magic made me feel weird and...like I needed to shift."

"Of course, it's restorative. Pretty much any helpful spell will do that to you, especially as an alpha. How do you not know that?" she asked, trying not to sound too critical. She wanted to like Amber, but first she had grabbed a witch, and now this?

"Because I was bit two days ago," Amber said, clenching her jaw tightly.

Ceri took a step back. "Two days ago? There's no way you can be an alpha!"

"So I've heard," Amber snapped. "But here I am. I didn't ask to get bitten. Some crazed werewolf just ran through a parking lot and attacked me and my...pack."

"You were changed against your will?" she asked, horrified.

Amber nodded. "Three of us were, and since I was the most dominant of the three, I ended up the alpha." She crossed her arms, practically daring Ceri to challenge her on it again.

"That explains a lot," she said instead.

"I should go," Amber sighed, turning toward the door. "I need to find a job and somehow get a sponsor so I can go through some kind of alpha trial."

"You're going through the Alpha Trials?" Ceri asked, eyes going wide. Amber had been human, and she obviously didn't know what she was getting into. "Do you have any idea how dangerous they are?"

Amber paused at the door. "No, I don't. I know the basics of pack life, but it's not like information on werewolves is freely available to the general public. So I don't know what I'm getting myself into, but I have no choice. I can't let my pack end up in the system. They'll be omegas for the rest of their lives," Amber said, getting angrier and angrier as she spoke.

Ceri crossed her arms. She had an idea that may or may not work. Part of her didn't want to use the favor that creepy, old elf owed her like this, but she knew it was a selfish thought. Amber had jumped in to help her with nothing to gain. Helping her in return was the right thing to do, but more importantly, she just wanted to. Goddess knew she had little enough chance to actually make a difference in the world. "I might be able to help you get a sponsor."

"What?" Amber asked, the anger switching to hope.

"There's someone that owes me a favor, and he's more than capable of sponsoring someone," she explained.

"Why would you help me like that?"

"You jumped in to help me save a pixie. It was kind of crazy, and kind of dumb, but you did it anyway because you thought it was the right thing to do," Ceri said, squaring her shoulders. "I'm helping you for the same reason. I know what happens to shifters who get put in the system. Besides, you saved my ass, and now I can save yours."

Amber looked like she might reject the offer for a moment, then nodded and held out her hand. "It's a deal."

Ceri took her hand and shook it. A subtle twist of magic shivered between them, but Amber didn't seem to notice. Ceri flexed her fingers. She'd have to figure out what that was later.

CHAPTER 10

TOMMY

Tommy jerked awake, swiping at the dark figure leaning over him with a growl. They jumped back with a curse.

"Tommy! It's me!" Genevieve shouted.

His heart raced in his chest, and the urge to shift and fight pounded along his skin. He blinked up at Genevieve, his eyes adjusting to the light streaming in the apartment window. Her hair was tied back in a neat bun, and she was wearing a pant suit. She looked like a completely different person.

"Sorry," he said quietly. "I'm not used to being woken up by anyone friendly."

"Right," Genevieve said awkwardly. "I didn't think about that, sorry."

"You can just throw something at me next time." He didn't want her to feel bad. It wasn't her fault. He'd been living on the streets for the past year, and after being jumped while asleep, he'd learned to wake up swinging.

She smirked at that. "I have to go to work. Just didn't want you to wake up to an empty apartment. Amber left super early and said she'd be back around six this evening."

"Alright, thanks." He could barely believe his good fortune. He'd have the whole apartment to himself all day.

Genevieve waved goodbye and hurried out the front door. He listened intently as her footsteps led away from the apartment, then started down the stairs. He lost her after that, but it was good enough, she was definitely gone.

He leapt off the air mattress. The clock on the microwave said it was just past noon. He couldn't believe he had slept so late, but the apartment did feel safe. He couldn't remember the last time he had felt safe in the place he was sleeping. Not even before he got kicked out.

He put his new clothes in a pile first, then started looking around the apartment for anything valuable. Guilt gnawed in his gut, but he had to make a run for it before things got any worse. Amber meant well, but she had no clue what she was doing. There was no way she was going to pass some weird trial to become an alpha. Especially not with another alpha having it out for her.

The wolf in his mind fought his every step. It hated what he was doing, but he ignored the feeling. He was good at ignoring things. Hunger. Fear. Exhaustion. None of it mattered more than just surviving.

There was no cash in the apartment other than a small jar full of coins. He grabbed it. There was probably twenty or thirty bucks in there. There was no medicine in the cabinet in the bathroom. He yanked open the drawers and found a small box. Inside was some jewelry. Most of it was fake, but there was one necklace with a diamond that might be real. It looked old, like some kind of family heirloom.

He picked it up, but froze. His hand shook a little. He looked at the open drawers, the pile of things on the bed, and he wanted to throw up. He hadn't meant to become like *her*.

The memories overwhelmed him, and for a moment he was standing in that little two bedroom house that reeked of cigarettes and old beer.

"Where is it?" Tommy demanded, shoving the empty ring box in his stepmother's face. "What did you do?"

She slapped his hand away and surged up off the couch. "Show a little fucking respect to your mother," she snapped, her voice slurred from the alcohol and who knew what else.

"You're not my mother!" he shouted.

She snorted. "Your mother is dead, kid. I'm all you got, and it's not like she needed it anymore."

Rage and anguish rushed through him at her callous words. He barely realized he was moving before he shoved her back as hard as he could. "What the fuck did you do with it?"

She slapped him across the face, her nails scratching his skin. He stumbled back. Tears stung at his eyes, but he refused to let them fall. He wouldn't ever let her see him cry.

She yanked a crumpled dollar bill from her pocket and threw it at his face. "Here's what's left," she sneered.

He grabbed the money, staring at it in horror. "You sold it?"

"The pawn shop gave me like two-fifty," she said, swaying unsteadily.

He lunged at her with a shout. Pain lanced through his fist as it connected with her bony face.

Tommy dropped the necklace and slammed the box shut. He'd only gotten one hit in before his dad had dragged him off her. He had managed to escape before his dad could beat the hell out of him, but he had never dared to go back.

He wanted to throw up. He couldn't do this. He *wouldn't* do this. He'd survived this long without stealing from people that didn't deserve it, and he could keep going. He'd take the clothes, because she had given them to him, but that was it. He put everything back exactly as it had been in the bathroom, then hurried out to fix the rest of the apartment.

CHAPTER 11

AMBER

They had intended to go straight to the elf's house, but Amber had felt Tommy practically panicking through the pack bond. She had decided to go back and see if he'd come with them. Her wolf would feel better being able to keep an eye on him.

Ceri followed her up to the apartment, looking around curiously. She'd poked at all the truck dials on the way here too. She reminded her a little of a pixie, especially with her wide blue eyes.

She unlocked the door and walked into the apartment. Tommy was sitting on the couch looking particularly guilty, which wasn't what Amber had expected, but the expression was replaced with surprise when Ceri followed her inside.

"Tommy, this is Ceri. Ceri, Tommy." He kept glancing at Ceri like she was a threat, so she added, "She's a new friend, and she thinks she can help us get a sponsor."

"I thought you were at work until really late." He shuffled slightly to move in front of his bag on the ground. It was packed.

Self consciously, she smoothed her hair back. She didn't want to tell him what had happened, especially if he had already been trying to run away, but she had a feeling he'd know if she lied. "I got fired this morning. They don't allow newly bitten werewolves to work as nurses, apparently."

"Oh," Tommy said quietly. He tugged his beanie down on his head and crossed his arms. "Sorry, that sucks."

For an awkward moment they were all silent. Ceri's face lit up with a grin and she beamed at Tommy, who, in return, looked alarmed.

"Do you have a job?" she asked out of nowhere.

"Me?" he asked, pinching his brows together. When Ceri nodded he replied, "No, I mostly just fix computers for people when I can. Resell stuff."

"The shop I work at needs a temporary, part-time stocker. It'd be about twenty hours a week, and you could start tomorrow. If you're interested."

Amber felt a tangle of emotions run through the pack bond. Surprise, hope, frustration, worry, and more guilt. This kid was more of a mess than she was.

"Ok, I guess I could try, but I've never had a job like that," Tommy said.

"It's just putting stuff on shelves," Ceri said.

The box in her hand let out a squeak and Tommy flinched at the noise. "What…is that?"

Ceri cracked the lid open then pulled a small vial out of her pocket. She poured a little liquid in the box and closed it again. "A pixie," she explained, putting the vial back in her pocket. "Some witches ripped his wings off earlier. That's actually how I met Amber. She came to our rescue."

Tommy snorted. "She does that a lot."

Ceri grinned, then turned to Amber. "Mind if I leave the pixie here? He's gonna be out cold for a while."

"That's fine," she said, ready to get this sponsor thing over with. "Tommy, want to come with us to meet this potential sponsor?" She really needed him to say yes. She had a feeling that if he didn't come with them, he might not be here when they got back.

Tommy hesitated for a moment, glancing at Ceri before seeming to make a decision. "Sure, I guess."

CHAPTER 12

AMBER

The potential sponsor's estate was outside of Portland, away from the bustle of the city and past the sprawling suburbs. The property was wedged between the Multnomah Channel, just north of where it split off the Willamette River, and one of the small lakes that dotted the area.

Based on the location, which was prime real estate for elves and other races that were fond of the outdoors, she had expected something nice. She stopped the truck at the entrance to the property and turned to look at Ceri.

"Are you sure someone lives here?" she asked. The rusted gate was overgrown with vines, and the driveway had more ruts than gravel. Elves were usually meticulous about maintaining their yards and gardens. They were called the flower children for a reason.

"Yeah," Ceri said. "He's a little…eccentric. I'm not really sure what his deal is, but he doesn't go outside much, and the place is falling apart. Obviously."

"How do we get in?" she asked, still skeptical.

"Just pull forward," Ceri said, waving her on. "The gate will open."

Amber inched the truck forward and, sure enough, the gate creaked open. As she drove through the gate a shiver of magic rolled over her skin. Runes glowed on the stone pillars that held the gate. The vines shivered, and a few reached toward the truck like they wanted to grab it.

"The property is falling apart, but he still keeps active wards on the gate?" Amber asked, incredulous. Those kinds of spells were *expensive*, not to mention hard to get. Enchanting was a difficult branch of magic that not many practiced; most chose to study witchcraft like Ceri.

"Eccentric, like I said." Ceri shrugged.

"This place gives me the creeps," Tommy said. His discomfort crackled through the pack bond like a warning.

Amber silently agreed. The truck bounced down the driveway in the shadow of towering maple trees. It was late October and the branches were heavy with brilliantly colored leaves. It should have been beautiful, but her skin crawled with the sensation of being watched. She wanted to trust Ceri, but she was starting to wonder if the witch actually had any idea what she was getting them into.

The driveway and the lane of trees framed what must have once been a beautiful mansion. The grey stone exterior was hidden behind creeping vines, but what was visible was dirty and worn. The front of the mansion had three sharply angled sides, with towers standing guard on the front corners. The spire on the left one had broken off, and it looked like it had taken half the wooden shingles with it. A tarp covering the hole flapped in the light breeze. A balcony with a crumbling balustrade stretched between the two towers, sheltering the entryway.

Bay windows protruded from the house every few feet, but no light came from any of them. The driveway ended abruptly in front of the house. Amber parked the truck and squinted up at the windows. They were all boarded up from the inside.

"Okay," Ceri said, appearing to brace herself. "Don't let him intimidate you. He's all bark and no bite."

Amber glanced back at Tommy, already regretting bringing him. He was flighty enough when he wasn't scared.

"Let's get this over with," she sighed, pushing the truck door open. Ceri climbed out on the other side after Tommy.

To the left of the house, set back in the trees, was a cottage. It wasn't as ornate as the mansion, but it looked cozy with a chimney and a wraparound porch. It must have been the groundskeeper's house back in the day.

Grass and weeds grew over the cobblestone that was once intended as pathway up to the main house. They picked their way over it, then walked up a short flight of steps. A wide walkway covered in leaves and other debris led all the way around the house.

Ceri walked ahead of the group and approached a dark green door set back in a stone archway. A brass knocker hung askew, pulled sideways by a delicate green vine. She tugged the knocker out of its grasp and rapped firmly on the door three times.

Amber listened intently, but the old mansion remained silent. Ceri waited with hands on her hips, then knocked again, louder this time. The sound echoed through the house.

"You're sure he still lives here?" Amber asked as the silence continued.

Ceri nodded firmly. "I was here just a few weeks ago."

"What did you do for him that he owes you a favor now?" Amber asked. She hadn't wanted to pry before, but she was starting to realize she needed to have a better idea of what she was getting into.

"It's kind of complicated," Ceri deflected. She grabbed the knocker and slammed it against the door as hard as she could. "This is stupid," she muttered. "I know Thallan's just hiding out in his study being a damn hermit."

"Then let's go find him." Amber walked up to the door and tried the handle. It was unlocked. "Seems like an invitation to me," she said as she pushed the door open with a creak.

"Wait, don't—" Ceri said, reaching for Amber's arm.

She shrugged out of her grip and walked inside. The entryway was dimly lit. It would have been completely dark if it wasn't for the sunlight streaming in through the french doors tucked behind the staircase.

"This is a bad idea," Ceri muttered as she and Tommy followed her inside.

The house extended in two directions. To their left, the hallway led into darkness, and the floor itself was dusty. To their right, a single light bulb illuminated the hallway. It still looked barely used, but it was moderately clean.

"His study is this way," Ceri said, pointing to the right.

Amber started down the hallway. She desperately needed a sponsor, but everything about this elf was off. The house seemed abandoned, the grounds were falling apart, and anyone that ignored someone banging on their front door for five minutes obviously didn't want visitors. She hated needing help like this. She glanced at Tommy and grit her teeth. If it weren't for her pack, there'd be no way she would stoop to begging a stranger for a handout like this.

Ceri jogged to catch up and walk beside her. "I'm sorry this is so weird, but I really think he'll help."

"You didn't have to try to help me with this. Whether it works out or not, I really appreciate you trying at all," she said, forcing a smile onto her face.

They passed a few rooms as they walked down the gently curving hallway. The furniture inside was draped with sheets that were covered in a layer of dust. As Amber had seen from the outside, even the windows on the first floor were boarded up. Whoever had done it had simply slapped plywood over the windows without caring what they damaged. The antique wood paneling was split in places from the nails.

Ceri slowed and pointed at the room at the end of the hallway. The door to the study stood open, Amber's nose twitched as the cloying scent of cigars—or something equally smelly—drifted out of the room. Ceri squared her shoulders, took a deep breath, and marched inside.

The study was the cleanest room Amber had seen so far. A tall window overlooking an unruly garden illuminated the space. To her left were bookshelves that extended to the ceiling. A desk covered in stacks of unopened mail sat in front of the shelves.

"Has old age finally gotten to you and made you go deaf?" Ceri demanded. "I knocked for almost five minutes."

A chuckle emanated from a wingback chair set in front of the tall window. A curl of smoke drifted up from a slender hand that lay on the plush velvet armrest. Thallan tapped a long finger rhythmically against a worn spot on the velvet. "Hearing a knock at the door and caring about it are two different things, little witch," Thallan said. His voice was smooth, but he sounded strangely tired. "There's no need to sound so offended. I unlocked the door for you."

Amber looked at Ceri, wondering if that was possible. Ceri just shrugged.

"I have a couple of friends with me that I'd like to introduce to you," Ceri said, gesturing at them.

"What do you want?" Thallan asked. "Skip the pleasantries. I know you didn't come here to chat."

Amber stepped forward. "I was bitten a few nights ago, on the full moon along with two others. Since we changed together, I ended up the alpha. No pack will take us, and if I want to be able to stay an alpha, there are these trials I have to go through."

Thallan's finger stilled. "And you need a sponsor."

"Yes," she said, her fingers curling into a tight fist.

"No," Thallan said. He didn't sound angry, or even annoyed, simply uninterested.

"I'm calling in my favor," Ceri interjected. "You owe me."

Thallan stood from the chair. White-blond hair extended halfway down his back, the sides neatly plaited. He turned to Ceri. His face must have been handsome once, but a twisted, red scar cut through his patrician features.

"The favor you ask is not equal to the favor owed," Thallan said sharply. "In fact, the favor I owe you is worth so much less than what you are asking that I find the demand insulting." The calm tone he had held at the beginning of the conversation was gone. He stubbed out his slender cigar in an ashtray and stalked toward Ceri. "Take your little band of misfits and get out of my house. As a *favor*, I'll refrain from calling the police to report you for trespassing."

Ceri's pale face went red in anger and embarrassment. "All you'd have to do is put down a bond and show up to the Trials, I don't see how that's—"

"I'm not risking that money and what's left of my reputation on a newly bitten were-wolf I don't even know," Thallan snapped. "Get out of my house."

Amber had to turn to face Tommy to keep from lunging at the elf. It had been stupid to think there was a chance he would help. Her hands shook with anger. Tommy watched her with a worried expression. He looked like he was ready to bolt.

"Let's go," she said, glancing back at Ceri. Thallan stood in front of the fireplace, disdain apparent on his scarred face. He looked at her briefly before turning back to his window.

Ceri threw one last glare at Thallan, then followed her out the door.

CHAPTER 13

GENEVIEVE

Genevieve was tired, angry, and hungry. She wasn't sure why she had bothered to come here. There was no way she'd be able to talk him into helping, but for some reason, she wanted to try.

"Steven, just open the door!" She pounded her fist against the stained dorm room door. She could hear him in there, typing away and ignoring her. Either that or the music blasting out of his headphones was drowning her out. He always listened to it way too loud. He was stupid, and thoughtless, and always so busy with his precious thesis.

Irritation turned to anger, and she took a step back from the door, then slammed her foot into it. The door flew open, splinters of wood flying from where the latch used to be. Steven, who was leaning back in his chair, flailed and toppled out of it.

"What the fuck?" he demanded, ripping his noise-canceling headphones off of his ears.

She stood in the doorway, panting, and asked herself the same question. The door was busted, and it had dented the sheetrock. She hadn't paused to think before she had kicked the door open, she had been so mad—just like in The Market.

"I—" she hesitated. "I need your help," she said finally, straightening her shoulders and trying to look reasonable.

"You broke my door down!" Steven shouted, clearly not ready for the calm part of the conversation. "How the hell did you break my door? You weigh like ninety pounds!"

"That's not important," she said, brushing a piece of door off her slacks. "The point is, I could really use your help."

He ran his hands down his face and groaned. "You are insane. Less than a month ago, you dumped me because, and this is a direct quote, 'you are too clingy, and you never have time for me,' which is a complete contradiction by the way." His voice rose into a shout. "And now you've literally kicked down my door for no reason because *you need my help?!*"

She cleared her throat uncomfortably. "I was knocking and you didn't answer." Maybe kicking down the door had been an...overreaction.

"You were..." He let the thought trail off and stared at her with wide eyes. "Oh my god, you've finally cracked. I always thought it was inevitable, but it's happened. You've lost your mind completely."

"What do you mean it was inevitable?" she demanded, anger shocking her out of her embarrassment.

"You refuse to talk about anything! You bottle everything up and...and let it fester! And now this." He threw his arms up, waving them over his head like an explosion.

"I wouldn't have come here if it wasn't important," she said through gritted teeth.

"Oh really," he said, acting like what she had just said was insulting. "Then please explain what is so important that it compelled you to come back to the one place you swore you would never return to when you dumped me."

She crossed her arms. "It's...personal."

"Get out," he pointed at the hallway behind her. "Leave now."

"Fine," she said, dropping her arms with a sigh. "If it's that big of a deal I'll explain."

"No," Steven snapped. "I don't want to hear it. You are still exactly the same, and I am *so done*. Get out."

Genevieve wanted to rake her claws across the scowl look on Steven's face. He'd be sorry then. He'd probably beg to help. He'd...

Genevieve ground her teeth together, turned on her heel, and walked away. She had to, or she knew she would kill him.

CHAPTER 14

GENEVIEVE

Genevieve hesitated in front of the door, but the smell of Chinese food compelled her to walk inside.

"Hey, sorry I'm..." she trailed off, staring at a woman with curly blonde hair sitting at the table next to Tommy. She was dressed like an elf in frilly dress, but she didn't have the pointed ears.

"This is Ceri. We met earlier today," Amber said, nodding toward the woman.

Ceri waved at Genevieve with her chopsticks. "Hey," she said with a smile. "Me and Amber got into it with some witches."

"Is that a pixie?" Genevieve asked. A little gray creature was stumbling around on a hand towel, squeaking.

"Yeah, some witches ripped its wings off," Amber said with a frown. "We saved you a little of everything. Weren't sure what you liked." She gestured at the half empty cartons that littered the table.

"Oh thank Merlin. I'm so hungry," Genevieve exclaimed, dumping her purse by the door. She grabbed a carton and began shoveling food in her mouth.

Ceri passed the pixie a piece of chicken with her chopsticks. It grabbed it, shoving the whole bite in its mouth at once. Its cheeks bulged as it chewed happily.

Genevieve's wolf growled, anxious and irritated. It didn't like intruders in the den.

She paused at the thought. Her wolf's instincts were getting out of hand, and she had no idea how to handle it. Magical law didn't get into how werewolves controlled their urges, just that they had to.

"Were you working late or something?" Amber asked. Her tone was even and calm, but Genevieve felt the distrust she implied like a punch to the gut. She shifted uncomfortably in her heels and shrugged.

"Yeah, and I might have to work late a few nights this week," she said before shoving a huge bite of shrimp in her mouth.

STEPHANIE FOXE

It was a lie, and Amber looked like she could tell somehow, but she wasn't ready to explain everything to her. She wasn't sure she would get Steven to help, and if she couldn't there was no reason to give Amber another reason to dislike her. So far, Genevieve knew she had been worse than useless. Getting kicked out of The Market still made her want to die of embarrassment.

The pixie squeaked loudly, then toppled off the table. Tommy's hand shot out, catching it before it hit the ground.

"Dude, you can't fly," Tommy said as he set it back on the hand towel. The pixie flailed its arms angrily, then fell over.

"It will probably take a while for it to understand," Ceri said, worry creasing her brows.

"What happened to its wings?" Genevieve asked, happy to turn the conversation to a different topic.

Ceri's face darkened with anger. "Some Blackwood witches ripped them off."

"Blackwood? Aren't they that huge coven that owns half of Portland?" she asked.

The pixie glanced at Tommy, then took a running start for the edge of the table. He caught it again and held onto it while it wriggled instead of setting it back down.

"Yeah, those Blackwoods," Ceri confirmed. "Pixie wings are used in a lot of spells. It's barbaric to rip their wings off, but they don't care because they're just *pests*." She spit out the word like a curse.

"It's mean to mutilate them like that, but they are just frogs with wings," Genevieve said with a shrug.

"They're not," Ceri said, leaning forward and bracing her arms on the table. "No one ever pays attention, but they talk to each other. I think they can understand us to a certain extent, they just can't speak our language."

"You think they're what...sentient?" Genevieve asked, glancing at Amber and Tommy to see if she was the only one that thought Ceri was crazy.

"Everyone looks at me like that," Ceri said, "and I don't care. I'll prove it one day."

The pixie made another frantic run for the edge of the table and Ceri grabbed him just in time.

"You're going to have to stick it in the bathtub tonight to keep it from jumping to its death," Amber said, amused.

Ceri's shoulders slumped. "I don't think it's safe to keep him at home actually," she said. "If my mother finds out, she'll chop him up for parts just to spite me."

Tommy looked up sharply. "Then you have to leave him here," Tommy demanded. "I'll take care of him." He paused and glanced back at Amber. "If that's okay?"

"Yeah, of course," Amber said without hesitation. "I don't mind it being in the apartment."

"What about tomorrow at work?" Tommy asked. "We can't leave him here alone, can we?"

"We can take him to work with us," Ceri said with a smile before exchanging a glance with Amber when Tommy wasn't looking.

Genevieve felt completely out of the loop. There was obviously something going on with Tommy that this stranger knew about and she didn't. She looked back down into her carton and picked out the last shrimp. There was no reason for her to feel so hurt, it was just the instincts again. She shoved the shrimp in her mouth and glared at the ugly, wingless pixie that had everyone's attention.

CHAPTER 15

TOMMY

Tommy looked curiously around the stockroom. It was stacked with boxes and shelves of items waiting to be placed in the store. The front of the shop was half bookstore and half supplies for witches. Aileen, Ceri's aunt, owned the shop. She'd sent them back here and told Ceri to put him to work.

He walked over to one shelf that held what looked suspiciously like pickled rabbits feet. Grimacing he turned away and poked at a dusty old jar. A weird scent tickled his nose, and he sneezed loudly.

"Blessings," Ceri said politely as she dug around through a pile of discarded boxes. She found an empty box with a lid and set the pixie, now dubbed Woggy, inside.

He squeaked in irritation, reaching his spindly arms up to her.

"Sorry, buddy." She set a small cup of water and a bowl of shredded tuna in the box next to him, which improved his mood immediately. He crouched over the tuna and stuck his face in it, chewing loudly. "Can you check on him every half hour or so and make sure he's okay?"

"Sure," Tommy said. Woggy still kept trying to fly; he would have kept an eye on him even if Ceri hadn't asked. It was stupid to get attached to Woggy since he probably wouldn't survive, but he couldn't help it. He had a soft spot for underdogs and broken things.

The door to the back room opened, and a young troll walked in.

"Deward, hi! I'd like you to come meet Tommy. He's going to be helping out for a little while," Ceri said, waving him over.

He must have been around Tommy's age, since his tusks barely extended over his lips. His bright blue mohawk lay neatly slicked back, and his biceps bulged against the sleeves of his crisp button-up shirt. Black-framed glasses were perched on his nose. He had a book tucked under one arm. Deward was a walking stereotype, unlike the troll that had served them barbecue the day before.

"Deward Tuskbreaker," the troll said, extending his moss green hand in greeting.

Tommy shook his hand, able to match the firm grip with werewolf strength. "Just Tommy."

"No last name?" Deward's thick brows drew together in confusion.

"I'm not on speaking terms with my family," he said with a shrug.

Aileen shouted for Ceri from the front of the store.

"Coming!" Ceri shouted back before turning to Deward. "Can you show him the ropes? Aileen just wanted him unloading the truck, then stocking the shelves today."

"Of course, my pleasure," Deward said politely.

"Thanks a billion," Ceri said with a grin before hurrying out of the back room.

Deward looked at Tommy nervously before clearing his throat and setting his book down next to the box. "I prefer to stay in the back and unload, so I'll show you how to stock the shelves before the store gets too busy."

"Okay," Tommy said, shoving his hands in his pockets. He was nervous about screwing up since he'd never had a real job before, but he was still excited to have this chance. He'd volunteered for various things after school, and he'd been paid for tutoring most of his junior year, but this was different. This made him want to stay.

~

Tommy sat down in the a folding chair in the stockroom and chugged half a bottle of water. He had *thought* stocking the shelves might be the easier job, but it still involved lugging around fifty pound boxes. For the first time, he was truly glad of the extra strength he'd gained. The exercise even felt good.

Taking another long drink of cold water, he leaned back in the chair. A tug at his jeans startled him. He looked down and saw Woggy climbing up his pant leg with shaky arms.

"How did you get out of your box, little guy?"

Woggy squeaked imperiously in reply.

"Ah, of course," he said as he leaned down and plucked Woggy from his jeans and set him on his shoulder. Woggy babbled excitedly and pointed around the room. He must have wanted to be up high where he could see.

"Is that some sort of pet?" Deward stood to his left holding out another stack of books for Tommy.

He hadn't heard him walk up. It was creepy how quiet he was. "Yeah, I guess," he said, standing to take the books. "Ceri rescued him, and I'm helping take care of him until he adjusts to not having wings anymore."

"The odds that the pixie will be able to be reintroduced back into its natural habitat are nonexistent," Deward said, adjusting the glasses on his nose.

He resisted the urge to knock them askew for that comment. Deward was technically right, but he hoped Ceri would find a way to beat the odds. "I figured. I don't think Ceri is going to try that, she just needs him to stop jumping off the table. He doesn't understand why he can't fly yet," he said with a shrug.

"It is incapable of rational thought," Deward said before turning and walking away.

Tommy shook his head. Trolls were odd. He adjusted the books in his arms and noticed that the top book was titled Sign Language: Magical Chants for the Deaf. He had learned Sign language in school. One of the many after-school programs he had joined to avoid going home. He'd picked it up quickly, but it had been a long time since he had signed, so he'd be rusty at best.

Woggy hopped down onto the books. Tommy adjusted to hold them with one hand and signed hello at the pixie. To his surprise, Woggy repeated the motion. Leaving the pixie perched on the books, he headed out to the store front to put up the books. Woggy signed hello over and over, though the motion was garbled after a bit, turning into more of a salute than a hello.

Ceri thought Woggy could learn to communicate, though. This might be the way he could. As soon as she had a break, he'd have to show her.

He knelt and set the books down on the floor. Woggy hopped off the books and scampered toward the end of the aisle.

"Get back here," he said trying to grab him, and missing.

The pixie crawled under a shelf and ran out the other side. Jumping to his feet, he ran around the end of the aisle just in time to see a witch viciously trying to stomp on the pixie.

"Wait!" he shouted, lunging for Woggy. He grabbed him, but the witch's heeled boot still came down on the back of his arm. Jerking his hand back, he looked up in at her in alarm. His heart pounding in his ears as adrenaline rushed through him. He hadn't even seen the woman coming, and Woggy had almost been crushed.

"Why would you do that?" he snapped, rising to his feet.

The woman standing in front of him narrowed her eyes. She had long black hair that hung down to her waist, and bright green eyes that sparked with malice. He knew that kind of look well, he'd been at the receiving end of it most of his life.

"You shouldn't let pests into stores," she said tightly. Her fingers twitched, and the sharp scent of magic filled the area. "That one looks half dead, anyhow."

Nervous, he moved the pixie behind his back. He didn't trust this witch for a second. "He's healing," he replied tersely.

The witch glanced over her shoulder, then flicked her index finger in his direction. A sharp pain stole his breath, and he stumbled, grasping his side. His vision blurred from the shock as he looked down; his hand came away bloody.

"What the hell did you do to me?" he growled.

The witch looked at him with a smirk, then screamed. She stumbled away from him and lifted her hand. Purple light flashed from her palm and fiery agony clawed at his chest. The magic shredded his shirt and the skin beneath.

"He attacked me!" the witch shrieked. "He's losing control!"

He crouched with one hand on the floor, but Woggy still safe behind his back, panting against the pain in his chest. Blood dripped steadily onto the floor. His teeth lengthened and fur grew along the edges of his face as he growled at the witch. His hands curled into claws. She had threatened Woggy, and now attacked him. He wanted to tear her apart.

He took a step forward, but Ceri jumped in front of him. "Get away from him, Selena!"

"*He* attacked *me*," Selena replied with a sneer.

He tried to shove Ceri away, but she grabbed his arms with surprising strength and forced him backward. "Tommy, you can't change here," she hissed in his ear. "They'll arrest you!" Her face was pale and fearful.

"She tried to hurt Woggy," he growled.

"I know," Ceri said, clenching her jaw tight. "But you stopped her. That's what matters."

"She's going to get away with it," he said, standing from his crouch and taking a step forward. He could see the black-haired witch just past Ceri. She was putting on her act for the store manager. She was a *liar*.

"Tommy, please," Ceri begged.

"Get that bitten piece of trash out of here! I can't believe you brought him here to work," Aileen shouted at Ceri before turning to Tommy. "You're fired if that wasn't clear," the woman bit out.

CHAPTER 16

AMBER

Amber had filled out applications at four different businesses, but she doubted any of them would call her back. Even if they did, it was unlikely the pay would cover her apartment and other bills. She slammed the truck door shut and jogged up the stairs. Maybe she could get Ceri to charm her boobs bigger so she could start stripping.

She paused at the top of the stairs. The hairs on her arms stood on end. Something wasn't right.

Slowly, she walked toward her apartment door, but a familiar scent made her pause again. A piece of paper taped to her apartment door fluttered in the breeze.

She approached it slowly. Her wolf pressed its claws into her mind, urging her to shift. She pushed down the instinct, but the hair on the back of her neck prickled. She was being watched, but she didn't know how or from where. There was no one behind her, and there was no one else on the walkway.

The lock on the apartment door was shiny and new. She grabbed the paper and skimmed it. An eviction notice. Her fingers dented the paper as rage tore through her. Getting her fired wasn't enough? Donovan was taking her apartment from her too? How was he even doing this?

The notice cited a report that there were multiple unauthorized people living in the apartments as grounds for eviction. The curtain next door moved and Amber jerked her gaze upward, catching Mrs. Huntington peering at her. The shift crept down her arms. Her muscles twitched as her fingers extended into claws and a growl erupted from her throat.

"Typical," a deep voice muttered behind her.

Amber whipped around. A man with shaggy brown hair and two days' worth of stubble was leaning against the banister watching her with a smirk. She hadn't heard him walk up.

"Who the hell are you?" she asked, her words slurred from the enlarged incisors crowding her mouth.

"Mark Jackson, beta of the Lockhart Pack," he said, giving her a mock bow.

Amber took a deep breath and pulled back the shift. Mark's eyes never strayed from her face as she struggled for control, but he didn't look worried, only mildly interested.

"Donovan sent you?" she demanded as soon as she could speak clearly again.

"No, of course not," he scoffed. "I was simply in the area and saw you about to lose control. I had to step in before you hurt your poor neighbor." He took a step forward. "Everyone knows newly bitten wolves can lose control at any moment."

She grit her teeth. "Stay away from me and my pack."

"Your pack?" Mark scoffed. He walked into her personal space, forcing her to take a step back. "You don't have a pack. Your eyes might glow red, but you aren't a real alpha, and you never will be."

He took another step forward and her back hit the wall. A power she hadn't felt before surged up inside of her. Donovan had fucked with her life. It was his fault she was bitten in the first place, then he had gotten her fired, and now evicted. Now he thought he could send his beta to intimidate her.

She laughed in his face and closed the distance between them until they were almost touching. "Why is Donovan so desperate to have me in his pack?" she asked, peering into Mark's eyes. He hesitated, just for a moment, but it was enough. "Oh, did he not tell you he's been trying to recruit me? Or that he promised me your position in the pack?"

He snorted in amusement. "Like hell he did."

She grinned, then shoved him back as hard as she could. Her shove lifted him off his feet and he hit the banister. The place where the iron connected with the concrete cracked loudly and the banister swayed out.

He pushed himself upright. A golden glow flickered in his eyes as a growl rumbled in his chest. "You're going to pay for that."

Red flashed at the edges of her vision and the wolf tensed in her mind. "I'm not the one that's going to pay," she snapped.

Mark lunged for her. She sidestepped and swung her leg into his stomach, snapping it back before he could grab it. Having grown up with five brothers, she knew how to brawl. The kick caught Mark off-guard and he wheezed, his breath knocked out of him.

The shift tugged at her bones and she stumbled. The wolf wanted out, but she couldn't afford to lose control now. Mark's fist connected with her cheek. The strike jarred painfully through her skull but she managed to stay on her feet.

"You hit like a pixie," she taunted, throwing a punch at his gut. He slipped out of reach and kicked her in the side as the momentum drug her forward. She hit the wall, rattling the windows.

Mark growled, his face contorting as he began shifting. Amber slid to the right and his fist slammed against the wall where her head had been. She punched twice, catching him under the jaw, then in the throat.

His half-shifted claws raked across her shoulder, ripping her shirt. Blood splattered on the concrete as she ducked under his follow-up attack. Ready to end this, she lunged forward. Catching him in the stomach with her uninjured shoulder, she lifted him off his feet and slammed him down against the concrete.

The air rushed from his lungs in a wheeze. She grabbed his arm and wrist, then stepped across his body, forcing him onto his stomach. He struggled against her grip so she drove her heel into his kidney. A low growl rumbled in her chest. He could fight all he wanted, but she had better leverage, and she was stronger.

Wild instincts rushed through her. It was time to send Donovan a message. Mark was born a werewolf, but to join a pack, there had to be a bite. A bite to change a human was always on the wrist, it was tradition. The bite to seal the pack bond was always on the back of the neck.

Her claws cut through Mark's flannel shirt easily. The white, raised scar from the bite contrasted sharply against his tanned skin. She set her claws over the pack mark. Magic pulsed under her fingertips, Donovan's magic. The pack bond. She dug her claws into his skin, cutting through the scar tissue. He shouted in agony, increasing his struggles against her.

Foreign magic flowed through her as the strength of her will fought against his. Dominance in werewolf packs was more than just who was bossier. Whatever magic enabled them to shift into wolves changed their will into something more tangible. Even though she was an alpha, there was still a chance that he was actually more dominant. This battle of wills was about proving that he was not. If Donovan wanted to challenge her, he'd have to do it himself instead of sending a lackey in his place.

The beta twitched, then shifted, ripping his clothes. His wolf form was twice the size of his human one, but she was still able to hold him down easily. He lay under her grip, his tail tucked between his legs.

"If I see you again, I will rip you apart," she whispered in his ear. She tore her claws free and stood up.

Mark drug himself forward on his stomach, keeping his head low.

"I never wanted any of this, but I won't let Donovan hurt my pack," she threatened.

Mark snarled at her, but turned and fled down the stairs. Mrs. Huntington cracked her door open and pressed her face up to the narrow opening.

"I'm calling the police," she announced in her shrill voice.

"Go ahead, you miserable old hag," she snapped.

Mrs. Huntington gasped and slammed her door shut. Amber turned to her own door. The locks had been changed, but that was not going to stop her. They could evict her, but they had no right to lock all her things up inside. She lifted her foot and kicked the door down.

CHAPTER 17

AMBER

Amber was stuffing a fistful of clothes into her backpack when pain and fear—Tommy's
—ripped through the pack bond. Her knees hit the floor, and the shift began to roll over
her. She wanted to run and rip apart whoever was hurting him. Her back curved sharply,
and her shirt split as the shift rushed over her. She ripped her jeans off in shreds with her
teeth.

She raced out of the apartment, letting the wolf take over. For once, they were in
complete agreement. The wolf drove her forward; her legs moving faster than she had
even thought possible.

The parking lot blurred as she wove through the cars. Since she didn't have to stick to
the road, she was halfway into town in a matter of minutes. Tommy was moving, she
thought. Still in pain. Still angry. Still afraid.

Faster, she urged the wolf. Her paws pounded against hot pavement and cool grass.
The scents of the city would have been fascinating in any other moment, but she ignored
them as she ran.

Tommy's pull led her into a subdivision she recognized, and after another minute, she
was racing up to Ceri's front door. She hit it running, but a ward flared and threw her
back, singeing her fur.

Amber growled at the display of magic and prowled forward. She tensed her muscles
to try again when the door was yanked open.

Ceri waved her inside. There was blood on her hands.

She raced inside, following her nose and the pack bonds straight to Tommy. His shirt
hung from his shoulders, bloody and shredded. She whined and walked over, sniffing at
the injuries. His chest had already healed, but she couldn't get past the scent of blood. The
wolf needed something to *do*.

"Amber," Ceri said, tentatively touching her shoulder. "Please shift back. Tommy is
going to be okay."

Amber huffed and nosed at Tommy's hand. He patted her head. "I healed, and the witch didn't hurt Woggy," Tommy said.

Ceri held out a dress. "Come and put on some clothes."

Giving in, she followed Ceri into what must be her bedroom, and shifted. The wolf wasn't happy about it, but seemed to agree that she could help Tommy better if she wasn't a wolf.

Ceri handed her the dress, keeping her eyes glued to Amber's face. Amber pulled the dress on over her head. It was flowy and girly and nothing like she normally wore. The material was soft, but she still felt naked with it on. She marched out of the room and headed back to Tommy.

Tommy was still in the same chair, though he had on a fresh shirt now.

"Who hurt you?" Amber demanded.

"It doesn't matter right now—"

"Tell me!" she shouted. Her voice echoed around the apartment.

Tommy slipped out of the chair and fell to his knees, his shoulders hunched in pain. "Blackwood...coven..." Tommy gasped as the words were forced out of him.

Amber took a step back, panting from the strain of forcing Tommy to submit like that. She hadn't realized it was even possible. That wasn't something they put in the werewolf literature.

"Which one? Was is the same witch that attacked Ceri?" she demanded, pointing back at her.

"Why does it matter? There's nothing you can do about it!" Tommy retorted.

Amber took a step back. The wolf was insulted, but she was overwhelmed with guilt. She hated this powerlessness. Enough was enough.

"Stay with Ceri," she snapped. "I'll come get you when I'm done."

"What are you going to do?" Ceri asked, alarm clear on her face.

"Nothing, apparently," Amber said, brushing past her. Tommy glared at her from the floor. He could hate her all he wanted, but she couldn't protect them if they tried to hide things from her.

She had let Donovan stomp all over her life, and then she had let that elf shut them down without even the courtesy of hearing them out. She was done taking no for an answer.

CHAPTER 18

AMBER

Amber's truck skid to a halt, the right wheel bumping up onto the first step in front of Thallan's house. She jumped out and marched toward the imposing house. He had laughed them out of the place last time, but she wouldn't allow him to do it again.

She kicked the door open and walked inside. "Thallan, where are you hiding?" Amber shouted into the dark house. Her voice echoing off the dark, wood floors was the only reply.

She turned down the hallway that led to the study. Her hand curled into a fist, the claws digging into her palm. The pain kept her focused enough to stop the shift, despite her anger. She couldn't control anything else, but she could damn well control herself. No one was going to take that from her.

The door to the study was closed, but not locked. She threw it open and walked inside. The chair Thallan had sat in last time faced the fireplace. It, and the room, were empty.

"I let you leave without considering you a trespasser once," Thallan said from behind her. "I'm not inclined to do so again."

Amber turned to face him slowly. "I came here to negotiate for you to be my sponsor."

Thallan snorted and took a drag on his long cigarette, blowing the smoke toward her. "Then you wasted your time, and mine."

"There has to be something you want," she insisted. "I need a sponsor and I'm not leaving here until you agree to be mine, or give me a damn good reason why you won't."

Thallan sneered. "I don't owe you any answers."

"Never said you did." She crossed her arms. "But I'm still not leaving until I get what I came here for."

He tapped the end of his cigarette thoughtfully. "You're desperate, and desperate people make mistakes."

"I don't care and I don't have time to worry about the consequences," Amber said. "If you've ever been desperate, then you'd understand."

Thallan laughed, a dry sound that bubbled out of his chest. He looked at her and tugged his linen shirt to the side. Over his heart lay a twisted black scar.

"I know desperation better than anyone," he said, jabbing his finger into the scar. As he pressed against the black mark, the smell of dark magic filled the room. "Do you know what this is?"

"No." She forced herself not to cringe away from Thallan, but that thing on his chest scared her.

"It's a demon mark. A favor owed that can be called due at any time," he said.

"You summoned a demon?" she asked, horrified. It was illegal, but most people weren't stupid enough to try it regardless. Summoning a demon was asking to get yourself killed.

Thallan grinned, a crazed look in his eyes as he stalked forward until he was standing toe to toe with Amber. "I was desperate to save my wife," Thallan explained. "Desperate enough to do anything."

Amber tried to keep her eyes from the mark, but she couldn't look away. She bit the inside of her cheek and forced herself to look into his eyes. "Then you should understand why I need you to be my sponsor. Tommy and Genevieve will suffer for the rest of their lives if I can't pass the Trials. They're my responsibility. I can't let that happen."

"Then take my mark," Thallan said, tapping the twisted, black scar again.

"What?" she asked, her eyes darting to the demon's mark.

"Take the mark and I will not only be your sponsor, I will also give you and your pack a place to live and hunt for as long as you need," Thallan said.

She stared at the mark. If it had been Dylan at risk, she wouldn't have even hesitated. She was out of options, and quickly running out of time.

"Fine," she said, determination settling in her gut. She would find a way to kill this demon if she had to. "How do I take it?"

Thallan pressed his hand to the mark and magic swelled between them. "That's all I needed to hear," he said. "But I can only give it to you if you are strong enough to fulfill the demon's wishes." He lifted his hand and the mark clung to his fingers like black tar.

"What happens if I'm not?"

"I remain stuck with my mistakes, and you get to walk away from all this," he said, his hand hovering between them.

She nodded. "Do it."

"A debt for a debt," he whispered as he pressed his hand to her chest, directly over her heart.

The magic burned through her shirt and into her flesh. She bit down on a scream, unwilling to show Thallan any weakness. The magic twisted into her, taking root. A dark awareness crept through her. The magic was vile.

Thallan lifted his hand and stepped backward. He stared at her for a moment before turning away. Even through the fog of pain, she could see that he looked guilty.

The wolf howled in her mind, as did every instinct she had, but it was done. She stared down at the demon mark that had buried itself in her skin. Cold radiated from it throughout her chest. She touched it hesitantly, and it twitched like it was alive.

"We're moving in tonight," she said, her voice hoarse.

Thallan nodded, then walked away.

CHAPTER 19

CERI

Ceri drove behind Amber's truck with Tommy and Woggy in the passenger seat. Genevieve was behind them in her car. The truck bed was packed full of disorganized boxes. Amber had said they didn't need furniture, and she didn't care enough about what she had to worry about bringing it or storing it somewhere. It wasn't worth anything anyhow; it had been bought used and then banged around in moves for the past six years.

"Is it weird to you that he suddenly agreed? Thallan seemed pretty adamant when we were there last that he had no interest in helping us," Tommy said. Woggy was running rampant over the dash of the car, but Tommy grabbed him every time he got in a precarious spot or tried to climb on the steering wheel.

She tapped her fingers against the wheel. It was suspicious, but she didn't want to give Tommy any reason to doubt Amber. "Maybe they worked out a deal. I think Thallan was more insulted I was trying to use my favor for it than anything. He can be such a prick."

Tommy snorted. "Yeah, I got that impression too. He seemed a little…self-absorbed."

"That's an understatement," she muttered.

"What's his deal? He's like some kind of Jane Eyre character holed up in a dying mansion." Tommy snatched Woggy from the gear shift, tutting at him. Woggy squeaked back imperiously, smacking Tommy's fist.

She looked at Tommy out of the corner of her eye. The more he relaxed and showed his personality, the more she wondered how he had ended up homeless. He was well-educated, kind, and very perceptive. Where were his parents?

She realized she'd been silent too long and cleared her throat. "Thallan lost his wife a few years ago. After that, he drove his daughter away, let the place fall into disrepair, and became a grumpy hermit. Losing someone you love can really change a person I guess."

Tommy was quiet for a moment, then whispered, "Yeah, it can."

The truck turned down the driveway. The gate swung open, beckoning the caravan inside. She followed, despite her misgivings. She wanted to catch Amber alone and demand some answers, but she had a feeling she wasn't going to get any no matter how hard she pressed. Her mother's voice echoed in her mind, suggesting a spell that would make Amber more honest, more likely to share secrets. She shoved the thought away. She was a white witch. Dabbling in magic that took away a person's free will was black magic. Plain and simple.

Amber drove straight to the guest house they'd seen on their first visit. Ceri was curious to see inside. She'd never been able to really explore the main house, much less the grounds.

The old house had two stories with a sharply slanted roof, and the outer walls were a cheery white with deep green shutters. She could have sworn the house looked drearier last time they were here. Perhaps it was eager to have new guests. Old estates could be funny like that. The longer magic infused a place, the more…alive it seemed.

They parked in the designated spots at the end of the driveway and clambered out of the car. Woggy was eager to run. He loved being outside.

"I'm going to go let Thallan know we're here, but he said the door would be unlocked. Y'all can go ahead and pick your rooms, there's more than enough for all of us," Amber said, already walking toward the main house.

"I call dibs on the upstairs rooms," Tommy said, hurrying toward the front door.

She smiled to herself. He was as eager to be here as Woggy. That was a big change from the boy that had his bags packed and ready to go that first day.

Genevieve ran after Tommy. "I want a room with an attached bathroom."

It was cool in the house, with the faint scent of mint in the air. It was elf-spelled to stay pleasant year round, warming itself in the winter and cooling itself in the hotter months. Not that it was ever *that* hot in Oregon.

Ceri took her time walking through the space. The entryway led right into the living area, which was open to the kitchen. It was very homey, with dark wood floors, bright white cabinets, and accents of orange. A leather sectional and two stuffed chairs sat in front of the fireplace. The back door was hidden behind the staircase, which was lined with a stately, carved bannister.

Tommy and Genevieve's footsteps thundered overhead as they raced around trying to find the best room. A little twinge of jealousy settled in her gut. This weird little pack had issues, but they were starting to trust each other. They *would* trust each other eventually.

Pausing in the doorway of a small room at the end of the hall, she leaned against the door jamb and sighed. The window had a perfect view of the backyard where it sloped down into the forest. There was a window seat and a desk in the corner of the room.

She walked further in and saw a bathroom on the right, and another room on the left. The door creaked as she pushed it all the way open and peered in the attached room. There were two work benches and an empty shelf. It was a spell room.

"This one looks perfect for you," Amber said, startling her.

She whipped around. "What?"

"If you ever want to stay over, or whatever. Or if you need a place to work. There's plenty of rooms. You should consider this one yours," Amber said with a shrug.

Her heart ached a little at the kindness. It was like Amber, or the house, had read her mind. "That would be really great. I really appreciate it. This place is so cool." A grin split her face. Magic had its ways, and it never ceased to surprise her.

Genevieve appeared in the doorway. Her buns had been knocked sideways. "My room is uh-mazing," she said with a huge grin. "Is this Ceri's or yours?"

"Ceri's," Amber answered. She pointed across the hall. "I'm taking that one. It has a good view of the driveway and the side of the house so I should be able to see anyone approaching. And someone would have to pass by my room to get upstairs."

Genevieve snorted. "Okay, whatever floats your boat, *alpha*."

Amber rolled her eyes. "Go start getting boxes."

Ceri followed them back toward the cars. Amber was already thinking like their protector, but she had a feeling the inexperienced alpha would be doing that even if she wasn't a wolf. Amber had a persistent air of worry about her. It was an almost pessimistic determination, which was an odd combination.

She ran her hand along the wall as she walked. This place...it felt like home. And she would do anything to help protect that. There was little enough good in this world sometimes.

Letting her eyes slip shut, she whispered a blessing, and a prayer to the goddess of life and renewal. Magic slipped from her fingertips, seeping into the wood and binding her to the house. If anyone with ill intent ever crossed the threshold, she would know.

⁓

TOMMY

Boxes were scattered around him and Ceri, but Tommy was focused on Woggy. Perched on a bottle of water, he was trying his best to get the cap off. He scrambled to one side then the other, back and forth. The pixie's long fingers dug into the grooves but he wasn't quite strong enough to make it move.

"Thirsty?" Tommy asked, signing as he asked the question aloud.

Woggy stopped and licked his lips, then tentatively repeated the sign. Close enough.

"I can't believe how quickly he's picking it up," Ceri said with a smile. She didn't have anything to unpack, so she had been helping him.

"We should be able to really talk to him within a couple of months, I think." Tommy picked up the bottle and nudged Woggy to the side as he opened it. The pixie wrapped his wide mouth around the opening and his tongue flicked down into the water like a frog.

"Gross. Guess that's your water now, buddy."

Thallan's voice echoed up from downstairs and Tommy froze, creeping toward his door. He listened carefully as the elf spoke. "Just keep your pack out of the main house. I don't care where else you go. The grounds are open to you."

"What is it?" Ceri asked, watching him tensely.

"Thallan is here," he replied quietly, pressing his finger to his lips and waving for Ceri to follow.

STEPHANIE FOXE

They slipped out of his room. Peeking over the bannister, he saw the elf standing by the front door facing away from him. Amber had her arms crossed, and her face was carefully blank. She looked like she resented Thallan for some reason. It made him even more curious what Amber had agreed to in order to get them this place. Surely it wasn't anything...shady.

Genevieve hissed Tommy's name, getting his attention. *Thallan?* she mouthed. He nodded, and she scurried over to his other side, crouching next to him. She looked as suspicious as he felt.

"Don't worry, we'll stay out of your hair," Amber said, her tone was half annoyance, half impatience. "Do you have any information on the Trials at all?"

"I'll look through the library. I wouldn't hold your breath though. I'm an elf, not a werewolf." He handed Amber something. "Here are the spare keys. If you actually need something, come yourself. I don't want the kid or the girl with the pink hair bothering me."

Amber rolled her eyes. "Don't worry, they don't want to talk to you either."

She was right about that. He had no intention of going in that house, or talking to that elf ever again if he could help it. *This* house, however, was awesome. There was so much room, and it felt like it wanted them there. The whole place smelled like magic, but it wasn't as weird as the stuff at The Market.

Thallan nodded and left the house. Amber's eyes immediately flicked up to their location. Panic clenched in Tommy's gut, but she just smirked at them. "Didn't anyone ever teach you not to eavesdrop?"

"We're werewolves, it's basically impossible not to hear," Genevieve said, unashamed at being caught.

The girls were starting to feel like the big sisters he'd never had. He smiled at Amber, and the irrational fear faded away.

"Get down here and help me cook dinner," Amber said, turning and walking toward the kitchen.

"Ugh, I hate cooking," Genevieve muttered.

"I don't mind," he said with a grin. Some of his best memories had been of cooking with his mother.

"Great, then I'm going to keep unpacking," she said, jumping up and heading back into her room.

He hurried down the staircase and caught up to Amber, who was putting away all the food she had bought. The kitchen was pretty big, probably built to cook for fancy parties at the now empty mansion.

"I just remembered I left something in the car, I'll be right back," Ceri said, leaving him and Amber alone in the kitchen.

His alpha shifted uncomfortably, then cleared her throat. "Sorry about...earlier. I'm not great at this, and I didn't...I just want everyone safe."

He shoved his hands in his pockets. If he was being honest, it had really freaked him out, but he could tell she was being sincere. "It's okay."

Amber's posture relaxed a little, and she gave him a half-hearted smile. "Great."

"Do you mind if I cook a family recipe? Butter chicken curry. My mom taught me when I was a kid."

Amber looked surprised, but she nodded. "Yeah, go ahead. Do we have everything for it?"

"Yeah, I…uh…dug through the spice cabinet and pantry while you were gone getting groceries. And you have chicken, and rice." He wiped sweaty palms on the legs of his pants. The wolf wanted to impress her, but he just wanted to a chance to cook in a *clean* kitchen again. Without anyone yelling at him to stop stinking up the house.

"Sounds perfect then." Amber smiled sincerely, relief clear on her face. "As you saw, I'm not exactly good at cooking, so anytime you want to take over, feel free."

He stepped into the kitchen and began gathering the ingredients. The knot of worry in his shoulders relaxed, and he forgot about everything with a knife in his hand and the warm scents filling the kitchen.

CHAPTER 20

AMBER

Amber sat up, going from dead asleep to awake instantly. Her nose twitched as the odd scent that had woken her grew stronger. She slipped out of bed, grabbing the baseball bat she kept nearby, and pushed open her door. She had told Tommy she didn't think Donovan would try to kill them, but she was seriously regretting that statement now.

Her feet pressed into the carpet without making a sound as she crept into the hallway. Carpet gave way to the wooden floor of the living room. Pausing, she drew in a long breath to taste the air. The scent kept changing directions. Whatever it was wasn't moving normally, like it was appearing and disappearing at random.

A chuckle made her skin crawl. She whipped around, swinging the bat, but all it hit was air. Panting, she turned in a circle. She had heard it. It was here somewhere.

"I'm outside," a male voice whispered. A sulfurous scent crept toward her from the door that led out into the garden.

She swallowed and glanced back down the hall. If she was smart, she'd wake the others up. But with the way the mark on her chest was aching, she had a feeling she knew who this was. If the demon was here to collect its mark, she wouldn't put the others at risk. Cursing herself for not asking Thallan how long she had before the demon came for her, she slipped outside, leaving the door cracked open.

Goosebumps rose on her exposed skin, and she shivered at the temperature change. It was cool. Way too cool to be walking about barefoot, in shorts that barely covered her ass, and a threadbare shirt that had seen better days.

The garden was just as well-maintained as the rest of the grounds. So, it was a tangle of overgrown bushes and vines that stretched across the walkways. She followed the scent, which was still moving away from her.

"How far are you going to make me chase you?" she hissed.

"Just far enough to talk privately," the voice replied. "I'd hate for your little pack to think you'd lost it, talking to yourself like this."

She paused, the cold seeping up from the stones into her feet. "What do you mean, talking to myself?"

"No one else can hear me," the voice whispered directly behind her.

She turned and struck out with the bat again. Laughter drifted toward her on the breeze.

"I suppose this is far enough," the voice said. "You're going to freeze to death in that outfit. And what exactly are *troll bangs*, by the way?"

She resisted the urge to glance down at her shirt. Her hand tightened on the wooden bat as the air shifted. A shadowy figure topped with horns formed right in front of her. She couldn't make out a face, or even his height. The thing had no legs, only a torso, a head, and the vague shape of arms. She jabbed it with the bat, but the weapon simply slipped through the apparition.

"That tickles," it said, amusement clear in its voice.

Amber frowned. "Are you a demon?" The shadow moved in a circle around her. She turned with it, not wanting the thing at her back.

"I am," it finally admitted, "and I was curious what sort of creature Thallan gave his mark to. It's not an easy thing to give away a debt like that." The demon surged closer, forcing her backward into a bush. "I must admit, you are not what I expected." His breath skated across her skin, hot and dry.

She cringed away from the demon's closeness. "What's your name?"

He chuckled. "Just telling you would be no fun," he said in a teasing tone. "Besides, I haven't told anyone my true name in almost fifteen years. Can't have you summoning me to the earthly planes then killing me to get rid of your mark."

"That would work?" she asked, narrowing her eyes at him.

The shadow swayed dramatically. "Already plotting my death? So callous," he said mournfully.

"What do you want from me?" She needed to get this over with. If it wanted something awful, she'd rather know now so she could figure out how to get rid of the mark or kill the demon.

"I'm not sure yet," the demon said, tapping a long finger against its chin. "I'll think of something eventually. Until then, you get to enjoy my occasional company."

"So you're basically going to haunt me?" There was a sinking feeling in the pit of her stomach.

"Haunt you? I prefer to think of myself as your guardian angel," the demon said, practically purring.

"I'm surprised you can even say the word angel without catching on fire," she muttered.

"The whole myth about us not being able to walk into churches *is* a myth. Not based in reality," the demon said with amusement.

Amber snorted and lowered the bat. "Alright, *Angel*. You really don't want anything from me right now?"

"This was more of a meet and greet, but if there's something *you* want, I can help you. For a price, of course," the demon said, drifting closer again.

The heat from his ethereal body took the chill out of her bare skin. "No," she replied quickly. "I don't need anything from you."

"You needed something," the demon said, his finger reaching out to press into the mark. She hissed as magic surged between them and tried to shove his finger away. Her hand swiped uselessly through the smoke. "What did Thallan do for you to get you to agree to take this?" the demon mused, finally removing his finger.

"None of your business."

The demon cackled. "Funny thing to say since I'm the one you owe the debt to," he drifted away. "But that's fine. It doesn't really matter except to satisfy my curiosity."

She stared at the demon for a moment then squared her shoulders and started back toward the house. "If that's all this is, then I'm going back to bed," she said as she brushed past him.

"Is that an invitation?" the demon asked.

Amber stopped and glared at him. "No, absolutely not."

A grin spread across the shadowy face, the only feature she could make out. "So grumpy, perhaps you do need to sleep."

"I thought demons were supposed to be menacing, not just annoying."

The shadowy figure tripled in size and loomed over her, flames pouring from his eyes. Long, black teeth stretched out of its gaping maw. "I can do menacing if you prefer." His voice boomed around them.

She stared back impassively. "So scary."

The demon shrunk back down. "You're no fun at all. You could have at least screamed a little. Flinched, perhaps."

"You'll have to try harder," she said, regretting the words as soon as they left her mouth.

"Challenge accepted," the demon said before disappearing with a pop.

She walked back to the mansion, gripping the bat tightly, and contemplated all of her bad life choices.

CHAPTER 21

AMBER

Amber tried not to scowl as Tommy trotted out from behind the house—understandably, he had refused to strip in front of the girls—fully shifted. She and Genevieve had been trying all morning and hadn't been able to.

Tommy sat down, his tongue lolling out of his mouth. If his wolf hadn't weighed two-hundred pounds and been the size of a small pony, he might have looked like a friendly dog.

She flexed her hand and tried to shift, but nothing happened. Now that she wasn't angry, she had no idea how to start it. She dropped her hand and looked back at Genevieve, whose head was bent over a book.

"Do those books say anything about how to shift when you're not about to lose control?" she asked, shoving a strand of hair out of her face. There was a nice breeze blowing through the backyard where they were training. Sundays had been tentatively declared "pack days," since the books recommended bonding for a new pack.

Genevieve looked up and blinked owlishly. "Yeah, actually," she said, tapping the red-leather bound tome she had last read through. "You have to connect with your wolf."

"What does that even mean?" Amber asked. She hated vague crap like that. There should be an on/off switch or a magic word.

"Maybe try talking to the wolf?" she suggested, twirling a lock of bright pink hair that had escaped from her bun around her finger. She propped her head up on her hand and turned her attention back to the other book Thallan had brought them.

As part of their bargain, Thallan was now her sponsor. Apparently, that included providing training for the budding alpha. Genevieve had volunteered to read through everything, which had been a huge relief for Amber.

Connect with the wolf...what a load of crap. Amber sighed. If Dylan had been here, he would have been dragging her to meditation classes and talking about living in the woods hunting bunnies.

"I'm going for a run," she said. They had run under the full moon once, and it had been exhilarating. Maybe running now would draw the wolf out. It had been quiet ever since she had taken the demon mark. It felt a little like it was giving her the silent treatment to punish her.

Amber jogged past Tommy. He had shifted back and re-dressed and was now busy teaching the pixie sign language. Since the job hadn't worked out, he was the *de facto* pixie babysitter.

"Woggy, focus," Tommy chastised, but the pixie was busy chasing a bug that had flown too close. It bounded around on shaky legs, hopping and trying to grab its prey.

Amber shook her head, a smile tugging at her lips as she passed into the trees. There wasn't a clear trail through the woods. No one had been out here in years. She pushed herself into a run, weaving around trees and jumping over fallen logs.

Her breath stayed steady and her legs felt like they could go forever. Being a werewolf had changed more than just her instincts. She was stronger, faster, and her senses were heightened. While she was in human form, she couldn't hear or smell as well as she could in wolf form, but it was still ten times as well as she could when she had been fully human.

Some small creature darted across her path, and the wolf stirred for the first time. Acting on instinct, she followed it. A flash of brown fur and a white tail bobbed through the underbrush. The wolf tried to hide its eagerness to hunt but she could feel it.

"Come on, what's your problem?" she muttered, bracing one hand on a large boulder as she leapt over it.

The wolf growled, and she stumbled as the mark ached fiercely. Stopping to lean against a tree, she rubbed the black scar. The wolf had tried to do something to it.

"I had to take it," she said, irritated with the wolf. "I had to protect them."

The wolf huffed, then pressed its claws into her mind. A sharp pain shot through her skull and she grabbed her head. Her fingers lengthened into claws and her muscles twitched as the wolf forced a shift. She ripped her shirt off over her head with a grunt and rolled onto her back to kick off her shoes and shorts.

The shift was faster this time than it had been on the night of the full moon. Fur rolled over her skin as her body reformed and grew. Rolling onto her feet, she shook out her fur and took in the scents around her. The first moment after the shift was always over-whelming. She tried to take a step forward, but her legs wouldn't move. Her muscles ached as the wolf fought her for control.

What are you doing? she demanded of the silent force in her mind. She couldn't help but think of it as a separate person. It didn't seem like it could speak, but it communicated how it felt well enough with feelings and instincts.

With one last trembling push, the wolf ripped away control and ran. It was disorienting to be the passenger in her own body, especially shifted.

The trees flashed by. Anger curled in her gut, but it wasn't her own. The wolf was pissed at her. Her legs flew over the ground. It was so much easier to run in this form. Four legs moved faster than two, and her claws dug into the soft ground, propelling her forward.

Something tickled the edge of her senses. The scent of another werewolf. She slid to a halt, sniffing the air. A breeze ruffled the fur on her face, and the fading scent of the intruder grew stronger.

Nose to the ground, she followed the smell as it grew stronger and stronger. The trail led her to a fence at the edge of the property. It was broken, falling down in places, and didn't have the same feeling of magic that the front gate had. It was unprotected.

The scent wasn't fresh anymore, and Amber had no idea when it was left there. Some parts of this were instinct, but being able to tell how old something was must come from experience. The scent was familiar though. Not the beta, but another werewolf from Donovan's pack that she had been near. They could have followed her to the property the first day she visited Thallan.

She wasn't sure if it was her or the wolf that initiated it, but she tilted her head back and howled. This was *her* home now, and she would not tolerate trespassers.

～

GENEVIEVE

Genevieve pushed the book away and rubbed her eyes, out of practice with all this reading. Thallan's books were helpful, to an extent, but they didn't have the details about the Trials that Amber needed. She had found some information she doubted Amber would be thrilled to hear. Honestly, she was starting to wonder if any of this was possible. Maybe they should have just taken Donovan's offer and dealt with a crappy pack. She was used to dealing with crap. It was better than uncertainty.

What made her the most upset was that Steven had the answers they needed, but he wouldn't return her calls after that disastrous attempt to talk to him at his dorm room. She stood, anger pumping through her as she kicked off her shoes and plopped down on the grass. Maybe she could figure out how to shift, since she apparently couldn't do anything else productive.

Connect with your wolf. That was what she had told Amber when she asked what the books had said, and like Amber, she thought it was a load of crap. She could feel something in the back of her mind now, but it wasn't like it had thoughts or feelings. It was just magic and instincts.

Her hand went to the scar on her thigh. She traced the jagged bite mark, remembering the pain and the terror she'd felt. Sometimes it was easy to forget she'd been changed, and then she'd feel the wolf in her head. It was so angry.

A howl erupted from the woods. Genevieve jumped to her feet. The sound cut straight through her, but instead of fear, it gave her a sense of determination. Belonging.

Tommy ran over, holding Woggy close to his chest. "Is that Amber? It...feels like her."

"Yeah, I feel it too," she whispered. "It's like she's claiming something."

They waited as the howl ended. In that place in the back of her mind, where the magic had settled after her change, she could feel Amber coming back to them.

"Should we go help her?" Tommy asked.

"She's coming back. I think we should just wait," she said, shaking her head.

The next few minutes were tense. She breathed a sigh of relief when Amber jogged out of the woods. Her bright red hair hung in tangled waves around her face. Dirt was smudged across her knees.

"Is everything okay? We heard you howl, but it just felt...annoyed? Or maybe territorial is a better word, so we thought we should stay here," she said, hardly taking a breath between words.

"One of Donovan's pack has been here, probably the same day I first visited Thallan." Her eyes still glowed with a hint of red.

"Do you think they'll come back?" Tommy eyed the forest warily.

Amber shrugged. "Maybe, maybe not. I'm going to ask Thallan why the wards aren't active in that area. He has most of this place locked down tight, it's odd that he would have missed a spot."

"Do we need to keep watch tonight?" Tommy asked. "I wouldn't mind."

Amber laughed. "I don't think we need to go that far. Donovan isn't trying to kill us, just make our lives difficult."

"Speaking of difficult," Genevieve said. She hated to bring it up at all, but she might as well get it over with. "I did find some information on the Trials."

"What did you find out?" Amber asked, her expression full of determination.

"The Trials have five parts. You have to pass at least three to become an alpha. The only part I could confirm is some kind of test of control." Genevieve walked back to the table and grabbed the book. She had stuck a leaf in between the pages to mark her place. She flipped to it and pulled the leaf out, tucking it behind her ear. "The Trials are designed to weed out the weak and the unworthy," she began reading. "It will test the potential alpha in every area in which they must excel in order to lead a pack." She lowered the book and looked up at Amber, who was grimacing.

"I guess I need to work on control some more," she said after a long pause. "My wallet is on the counter. Order something in for dinner, I'll eat anything with beef or chicken." Amber turned and walked back toward the woods, her shoulders tight.

"Do you think she can do it?" Tommy whispered.

Genevieve shut the book, but didn't respond. She didn't want to admit out loud that she didn't.

She had to talk to Steven. Amber needed more information if she was going to have any hope of passing the Trials. Tomorrow morning before everyone woke up, she was going to go back to Steven's dorm, and she wasn't leaving until he agreed to talk to her.

CHAPTER 22

AMBER

Amber couldn't sleep. Every time the old house creaked she thought the demon had returned to torment her for a second night. She'd given up on lying in bed about an hour ago and had been slumped in the armchair in front of the old-fashioned fireplace since then.

Her fingers idly tapped the bat resting against her knee. *Challenge accepted.* Amber wanted to slap herself. She should have just pretended to be intimidated, but of course, she had gone and taunted a demon instead.

A door creaked open in the hall, causing her heartbeat to kick into overdrive before Genevieve's scent drifted past her. She frowned. Genevieve had been disappearing a lot lately. The paranoid part of her brain wondered if she was meeting with Donovan and spying on the pack. Immediately, she felt guilty for even thinking it, but Genevieve was clearly trying to sneak out unnoticed.

She pulled her legs up into the chair to stay hidden from view and just listened. It didn't appear that Genevieve had noticed her. Her footsteps were almost too light to hear; she was still trying to sneak around. Amber wondered if her senses were stronger than Genevieve's, or if she was just too focused on listening for movement down the hall to realize that Amber was in the living room.

The front door opened and shut with barely a sound. Amber uncurled from the armchair and crept to the window. The lights on Genevieve's car lit up the driveway. She had parked as far away from the house as possible; Amber could barely hear her car start standing at the window. It wouldn't have woken her if she'd been sleeping.

She ran to the front door and yanked it open, then walked down the driveway as Genevieve's car backed out of its spot. She couldn't see her past the glare of the head-lights, but the car stopped abruptly.

The car door opened as Amber approached, and Genevieve climbed out, her face tight with irritation. "You're up early."

"Where are you going? You don't work until nine," she asked.

Genevieve rolled her eyes, but her knuckles were white she was gripping the car door so hard. "You're acting like I'm sneaking out of the house. I'm not sixteen, and you're not my mother. I don't have to fill you in every time I go somewhere."

"Until we know Donovan isn't going to do something else to try to hurt the pack, I do actually need to know," she said, resting her elbow on top of the door. "I'm not going to judge you if it's a booty call or something."

Genevieve shoved her arm off with a scowl. "You can just deal with not knowing."

"Why are you so intent on hiding this?" she snapped, the little patience she had left evaporating. She was tired, irritable, and worried all the time. The last thing she needed was a reason to doubt her own pack. "Or are you meeting with Donovan?"

Genevieve's face twisted in anger. She was close to shifting, Amber could feel it as sure as she could feel it in herself.

"You act like you aren't hiding things too!" Genevieve shouted back, balling her hands into fists as claws began pushing out of her fingertips. "You won't explain how you got Thallan to agree to be your sponsor and you haven't bothered to tell us that you can *feel our emotions*. So don't yell at me about hiding things! I have a right to a private life!" Genevieve's chest heaved with too fast breaths as she seemed to struggle for control.

Amber ground her teeth together. She had done everything she could to block out their emotions, but it had been impossible to do it completely. She hadn't mentioned it because she'd been afraid Tommy would freak out, and she hadn't anticipated how much it would upset Genevieve. "My bargain with Thallan isn't important right now. And I was going to tell you about the emotions thing when I figured it out!"

"You're a hypocrite!" Genevieve bared her teeth as a growl erupted from her throat. "And I would never betray this pack. Everything I'm doing is to help *you*."

Amidst the rage that hit her like a wall, there was also hurt. Embarrassment. Guilt. The emotions amplified what Amber was feeling. She squeezed her eyes shut and dug her claws into her palms to keep from shifting then and there.

She wanted to run away. It had been ridiculous to think she could be their alpha. She had no idea what she was doing, and she had no idea what she was supposed to be to them. Their friend? Mother? Captain?

"I'm not…good at this," she whispered. "I'm terrified the two of you will get hurt because I can't be everywhere. I can't take care of you. That witch attacked Tommy in broad daylight, in public. Donovan's men are stalking us." She forced her eyes open and looked at Genevieve. "I want to trust you, but before two weeks ago, we were strangers."

"We still are," Genevieve said, crossing her arms.

She dragged her hand down her face and took a deep breath. "I'm sorry I didn't tell you and Tommy about the emotions thing. I was worried it would freak him out especially."

Genevieve lifted her chin, but couldn't meet Amber's eyes. "Maybe I should have just told you what I was doing. I wanted to, but I was worried…" she huffed in frustration, rubbing her fingers over her eyes. "I know someone that can help us, help you, with the Trials, but he won't talk to me."

"Why not?" Amber asked, knitting her brows together.

"I kind of...dumped him a while back," Genevieve said, scuffing her shoe against the asphalt. "And then a few days ago kicked open his door and..." she sighed deeply, then continued, "and yelled at him a little."

"Okay, that's...uh..." Amber floundered before squaring her shoulders. "Well, maybe he'll talk to me. Would you mind if I came with you this time?"

"You're really asking?" Genevieve said, finally looking at Amber.

"Yes. If you want me to butt out, I will." She wouldn't like it, but she would deal with it to keep from driving her away.

Genevieve nodded as if that made the decision for her. "Sure, might as well try. He's getting his PhD in Magical Cultures and werewolves are his main focus."

"If you're still up for it, let's go convince him to help," she said confidently.

Genevieve hesitated and Amber could feel a confusing tangle of emotions warring in her, but she nodded, and a small smile crept across her face. "Let's do it."

~

Steven opened the door—and immediately tried to slam it shut when he saw Genevieve. Amber caught it with the flat of her hand and pushed it open. Steven's feet slid back on the concrete dorm-room floor.

"That's not very polite," Amber said, stepping into the room and forcing Steven to scramble backward.

Genevieve followed, trying to suppress a smile. Amber could be scary as hell when she wanted to be. She probably shouldn't enjoy it so much, but it was fun to watch her intimidate Steven.

"Who the hell are you?" Steven demanded, tucking his trembling hands under his arms.

"Amber," she said, sticking out her hand. Steven stared at it like it might bite him. She left it extended until he gave in and tentatively shook her hand. "I hear you're getting your PhD in Magical Cultural Studies." She put her hands on her hips and looked him up and down like she might try to beat the answers out of him.

Steven looked at Genevieve worriedly, but nodded. "Yeah, why do you care?"

Amber's eyes flashed red. Genevieve had to restrain the urge to submit. The impulse pissed her off a little; she wasn't a wild animal. She wasn't going to grovel at Amber's feet.

"I need information, and apparently you can get it for us," Amber said, looking over at her.

"That's what I was trying to tell you the other day." She crossed her arms. Amber had gotten them in the room, but it was awkward doing this in front of her. "We need your help. We were bitten, unwillingly, on the last full moon."

Steven's eyes went wide. "You're...both of you...oh my god..." he trailed off, staring at her like she might shift at any moment. He shook himself out of it and hurried over to his desk, grabbing his student ID and a couple of books. "I'll help you, on the condition that I get to ask you some questions for my thesis. I'll make sure you're anonymous, but this is exactly the topic I'm researching, and the opportunity to speak to a newly bitten werewolf is…it's…I can't pass it up," he finished, breathless. His eyes darted back and forth between her and Amber.

Amber looked over at her. "I don't mind answering your questions if you help us, but I can't speak for Genevieve."

She nodded. "I'll answer your questions too, but I doubt Tommy will want to."

"There's another?" Steven asked, his excitement ratcheting up another notch.

"Yes, there are three people in my pack, myself included," Amber responded.

"What exactly do you need information on? Werewolf laws? Customs?" Steven asked, hurrying back to his desk to grab a notepad and a pen. He awkwardly laid the books over his arm and the notepad on that, pen poised over the paper to take notes.

"I need to know about the Alpha Trials," Amber said. "I have two weeks left to prepare for them."

Steven's mouth opened, then shut, then opened again before he figured out how to talk. "Two weeks? Why isn't your sponsor helping you?"

"The sponsor is an elf," Genevieve said uncomfortably. "It's a loophole in the laws, but hardly anyone takes advantage of it because there's no one to teach you when you do."

"Wow. Okay," he said, rubbing the hand with the pen over his face. "We have to go to the library. I can get you all the appropriate information there, but it won't be complete. The Trials are shrouded in secrecy, and it's nearly impossible to get an alpha to talk to you about them." He stared at Amber, gnawing on the end of his pen. "Will you answer questions about that after the Trials? If you survive them, of course."

Amber's jaw tightened briefly. "Sure, as long as you make the information readily available to other werewolves in my situation."

Steven nodded hastily. "Definitely, I can totally do that."

"Let's go then, no time to waste," Genevieve said, grabbing Steven by the elbow and dragging him to the door.

"I can't believe you didn't tell me right away," Steven said as they hurried out of the dorm. "I would have helped if I had known it was about *this*."

Genevieve looked at the ground, her irritation making the wolf restless. "I tried."

Steven opened his mouth to argue, but Amber clamped her hand on his shoulder. "Give her a break, Steven," Amber said lightly, though the warning was clear in her voice. Genevieve frowned, she hated that Amber knew she was struggling for control.

Genevieve picked up the pace. Steven had to jog to keep up.

CHAPTER 23

AMBER

Amber walked down the narrow aisle between stacks, scanning the rows of books for the first name on her list. Genevieve and Steven were reading the first pile of books and debating everything they found.

It had surprised her how intelligent Genevieve was. Now that she thought about it, her assumption about the other woman was based entirely on her pink hair. It was dumb to assume based on something so superficial, but that was human nature.

GLENN, E., written in swirling gold ink on the spine of a book, caught her eye. She stopped and double checked the name of the book, then grabbed it off the shelf.

Smoke rushed out of the gap and hit her in the face. Stumbling back with a strangled yelp, she hit the bookshelf behind her, rattling the entire thing.

The demon formed above her, cackling loudly. Smoke drifted up from his bright red grin.

"What is wrong with you?" she hissed, glancing down the aisle to make sure no one had heard.

The demon drifted closer, stinking up the air around her face. "You should have seen your face." His hot breath tickled the skin of her neck. "That was priceless."

She pushed up to her feet and pinned the demon with a glare. "You are a menace."

His grin only grew wider. "Isn't that the purpose of a demon?"

With a huff, she turned and continued down the aisle. There were still three more books to find. The demon followed. "Are you stalking me now?" she asked.

"It's proving very entertaining so far. I see no reason to stop," he said, swooping through the air ahead of her. Every few feet he stuck his head in the books like he was sniffing them or peeking at the pages.

Amber bit the inside of her cheek, torn between trying to get answers and ignoring him. "Is this a normal demon thing? Harassing the people that have your mark?" she asked finally, giving in to the curiosity.

The demon shifted into a tiny red creature with a pointy tail. He was still slightly transparent, like he was made of smoke, and the edges of his form flickered. He flew over and landed on Amber's shoulder. She jerked away and tried to swipe him off, but her hand passed straight through him.

"I don't think there is a normal demon thing," he said, leaning back and settling against her hair. "What a way to stereotype."

Amber turned down the next aisle and spotted the second book immediately. She grabbed it and added it to the stack in the crook of her arm. She would have to ask Thallan about this next time she saw him. If the demon had haunted him like this too, she could absolutely understand why he had isolated himself in that mansion and gotten so grumpy.

"I don't suppose you know anything about the Alpha Trials?" she asked, deciding the demon might as well help if he was going to hang around bothering her.

He bounced off her shoulder and hovered in front of her, little red wings flapping excitedly. "Alpha Trials? Not a thing! I've had a few werewolves indebted to me before, but never an alpha. They're usually smart enough to avoid such things. Or at least too prideful to ask for help."

"Figures." She sighed and checked the name on her list again. The book should be here between Roberts and Roland, but it wasn't. Shrugging, she turned and headed back toward the others. The book must have been checked out already.

"Is that why you took Thallan's debt? Because you have to go through the Trials?"

"Go away, I have to talk to my pack." She tried to shoo him away, but the demon ignored her.

"I'm not going anywhere, this is fascinating. Best time I've had in years," he said, flying ahead of her.

With a sigh, she exited the stacks and headed back to the table. The demon zipped around Genevieve's head leaving a trail of smoke behind him. Neither she nor Steven were reacting, so they really couldn't see him. Amber ground her teeth together and steeled herself to ignore her stalker.

"I could only find two of the books," she said, setting them down between her study partners and handing Gen the slip of paper.

"That's fine for now," Steven said absently, gnawing on the end of his pen. "We can't read them all today anyhow."

"This one is very nerdy," the demon said, crossing his arms and hovering in front of Steven. He turned to Amber, thick framed glasses that matched Steven's sitting on his red face.

Amber had to press her lips together to hold in the sudden urge to laugh. He looked almost...cute. "Which one should I start with?"

Steven looked up, blinking owlishly, and pointed at the top book. "That one discusses werewolf culture fairly extensively. You need to know all of that regardless of the Trials."

"Alright." She grabbed it and sat down next to Genevieve. After nursing school, she hadn't wanted to even look at a book, much less read one for fun. This was giving her flashbacks to late night study sessions. She preferred hands on learning to reading until her eyes got blurry.

"An alpha must never show weakness to their pack," the demon read, settling by her hand. He looked up, adjusting his glasses. "I think you've already failed there."

Amber sighed. She couldn't even give the demon the retort on the tip of her tongue without looking crazy. It was going to be a long day.

CHAPTER 24

CERI

"That was not my fault!" Ceri yelled at her aunt.

The woman stood in front of her, face splotchy with rage, arms crossed. "I hired you as a courtesy to you mother, but you have been nothing but trouble! Coming in late, picking fights with customers. With the freaking *Blackwood Coven*."

"She dumped that potion on herself." She curled her hand into a fist. There were dozens of spells she could cast with a simple chant and the flick of her wrist to shut her aunt up, but none of them could fix this. She should have cursed Selena while she could.

"Enough!" her aunt screeched. "You're fired! Just get out!"

She twisted the fingers of her left hand and took a step toward her aunt. "As you have sown, so may you reap." The spell could be both a blessing, or a curse, but they both knew how it would end up. Karma was always fair.

Her aunt's face darkened. "The same to you."

She brushed past the old witch and left, slamming the door shut behind her, hands shaking with impotent rage. If she had fought back, it would look like she had attacked them unprovoked. She had hoped *family* would side with her. But, just like everyone else, her aunt loved power more than anything else. And anyone who wanted power in this city sucked up to the Blackwood Coven.

Her phone rang, the ringtone alerting her that it was her least favorite relative calling: her mother. Word traveled fast.

"Hello," she answered, voice curt.

"Enough is enough," her mother growled into the phone. "You have embarrassed us repeatedly. No matter how many chances I give you, you still manage to screw up. Your father and I are done supporting your immature decisions. Your things will be on the front lawn, and if you don't come get them within an hour, they'll be gone with the trash."

Every word felt like a knife in her gut. Of course her mother wasn't on her side. She never had been. Never would be.

"And you are not welcome in this house, or this coven. I don't want to see you–"

"Don't worry, you won't ever have to see me again." Rather than listen to any more of her mother's hateful ranting, she hung up the phone. She knew this would happen eventually, but for some reason that didn't make it hurt any less. As she walked to her car, it felt like she was floating. Like none of this was really happening. Perhaps it was all a bad dream.

She reached for the car door, but stopped short, alarm cutting through the mental fog. The beat up old car looked normal but she felt something *wrong*.

Crouching down beside it, she whispered a spell of revelation. The car lit up like a beacon. It was wrapped in dozens of curses, all nasty and meant to harm her if she touched it.

~

AMBER

Amber's phone went off, the loud jingle echoing through the library. She grabbed it and silenced it with fumbling fingers as every person in the quiet building turned to glare at her.

"Sorry, sorry," she said as she answered the call. "Ceri, what's up?"

There was silence, then a hiccoughing sound. She shot to her feet and grabbed her keys, immediately sensing something was wrong.

She covered the receiver with one hand. "Gen, I have to go. Steven, can you give her a ride back to the house?"

"What? Where–"

"Thanks," she said, hurrying toward the exit, leaving Genevieve to deal with Steven. Turning her attention back to the call, she asked, "Ceri, where are you?"

"Work, but...fired. Outside," Ceri said through her tears. "So stupid I'm crying, but they cursed my car, and I can't even get what I need to cleanse it. My mom kicked me out. I don't know what to do."

"I'll be there in just a few minutes, okay? Just stay on the line." As soon as Amber got outside, she sprinted for the truck. She knew exactly who had caused all this. Between the Lockhart pack and that stupid coven, there hadn't been a single day without someone being an asshole.

"I'm sorry. Didn't have anyone else to call," Ceri said quietly.

Amber had never heard her sound so defeated. She was usually optimistic. "You can call anytime. And you're staying with us, I won't hear any arguments about it. You already have a room, so it's a no brainer."

"But I can't stay forever—"

"Why not?" Amber demanded. She knew what it was like to have your own mother kick you out. Having the one person that was supposed to love you unconditionally push you away like that was a heartbreak not many people understood. "As far as I'm concerned, you can stay forever. You've gone out of your way to help us, and I'd like to think we're starting to become friends."

Ceri laughed, but there wasn't any real joy in it. "You're basically running a halfway house for misfits now. A wolf pack, with a witch, and a bunch of bitten werewolves."

She grinned, despite the sad truth of it. No one wanted them, but it didn't matter as long as they had each other. "Genevieve says we have to pick a pack name. Maybe we'll call ourselves the Misfit Pack."

That got a real chuckle. "I guess it's better to be a misfit than an evil dick witch."

"Dick witch?" Amber repeated with a laugh as she pulled up behind the cursed car. Ceri was sitting on the sidewalk, head resting on her knees.

"I stand by that insult," Ceri said before hanging up the phone. Standing, she walked over to the truck and climbed inside, wiping tears from her pale cheeks. Her messy blonde hair was even bushier than normal.

"It's a pretty good insult," Amber said reassuringly as she put the truck in reverse.

"What am I supposed to do now?" Ceri asked, staring at her hands.

Amber was quiet for a moment, trying to find the right words. "Tonight? Eat some ice cream. Watch TV. Tomorrow? Find a new job. We can look together."

"You make it sound so easy."

"It's not easy, but it is simple. You don't give up. When my mom kicked me out of the house I had nothing. I left the state, found a job at a mechanic shop, and went to night school, then eventually nursing school. All I could do was take it one day at a time. It sucks, but you will be okay," she said, reaching across the truck to squeeze Ceri's shoulder.

The witch gave her a wobbly smile. "This is probably for the best anyway. I was never going to be who my mother wanted. I'm not sure why I tried for so long."

"Because you love her," Amber said with a shrug. "And you always will."

CHAPTER 25

TOMMY

Tommy opened the oven door and pulled out the roast chicken. He could *smell* that it was cooked all the way through now. Every spice he had used, and the rich butter he'd stuffed under the skin, filled his nose.

Woggy poked out of Tommy's shirt, smacking loudly as he reached for the chicken.

"How are you always this hungry?" Tommy asked, picking off a piece of gristle for the pixie. The pot with the potatoes began boiling over, so he quickly handed the morsel to Woggy and hurried to pull off the lid and turn down the heat.

The door opened. He heard Amber's familiar heartbeat first, but the one that followed was too fast-paced.

"Damn, that smells good," Amber said with a smile as he turned around.

"What's wrong?" he asked, taking in Ceri's puffy red eyes.

"I got fired," Ceri said, staring at her feet. "So, of course, my mother kicked me out of the house as well."

His hand tightened around the handle of the lid. "Was it that coven again?"

Ceri straightened her shoulders and brushed her curls away from her face. "Yes."

"We have to do something," he said, throwing his hands in the air. This was how it always went. Bullies got their way, and people like him and Ceri got shit on. It wasn't fair. He was strong now, he should be able to fight back. The need to *do something* was pumping through his entire body. "We can't let them get away with it."

"We are doing something. We're helping Ceri. She's going to stay with us as long as she wants," Amber said, trying to placate him.

It was insulting. He didn't need to be pacified. The muscle in his jaw twitched as he ground his teeth together.

"That's not enough. The coven isn't going to stop just because they ruined her life. Why aren't you standing up for her?" His breath was getting faster, and he could hear his heart thundering in his ears.

Ceri shifted uncomfortably. "Tommy, there's nothing she can do. I didn't—"

"No! That's what everyone says. It's not true. There has to be some way to fix this!" He threw the lid across the kitchen as anger ripped through him. This was wrong. He couldn't allow it.

A growl erupted from his throat and his vision blurred. He didn't realize he was moving until Amber slammed him against the wall.

"Enough!" she shouted, her eyes bleeding red. The authority in her voice shook him back into control. She waited until his breathing slowed, then stepped back.

He stumbled away from her, panting. Keeping his eyes on the floor, he turned and walked back to the kitchen. A soft squeak reminded him that Woggy was still hiding in his shirt. He lifted out the trembling pixie.

"Sorry, buddy," he whispered, setting Woggy on the counter with shaky hands. He hadn't meant to lose control like that. He could have hurt Woggy, or even Ceri.

The pixie walked over to the chicken and pulled a piece free, but instead of eating it, he lifted it toward Tommy. Juices dripped down his spindly arms as he held the meat aloft.

"He wants to make sure you're okay," Ceri said, startling him. He hadn't realized she had followed him into the kitchen.

"I should be making sure you're okay," Tommy said, taking the proffered piece of chicken and eating it. Woggy looked very pleased and grabbed another piece, eating this one. Apparently food cured everything in a pixie's mind.

"I'll be fine, eventually," Ceri said. It seemed like she was being honest, but he still hated the whole situation.

He grabbed the pot of potatoes and dumped it into the strainer. They were over-cooked. Staring down at the steam rising from the uneven chunks, he felt helpless. He didn't want to feel that way anymore.

"It's almost Halloween," he said, looking up at Ceri.

"Yeah..." she said, dragging out the word curiously.

"Every Halloween the witches do those displays, showing off their power and skills, right?" he asked, his mind whirling with possibilities. "They got you fired. Maybe we can turn it around on them this time."

Ceri's eyes went wide. "That wouldn't be right—"

"Why not? It's just us finally fighting back. They're awful. Everyone should see who they really are."

Amber stood behind Ceri, her arms crossed. She looked angry and worried at the same time. "What exactly are you suggesting?"

"I don't know," he said, mirroring her posture. "Maybe we can sabotage them somehow?"

The door opened, and Genevieve walked in with some nerdy guy following closely behind her. She stopped in her tracks, taking in the tension in the room. "Hey...guys..."

The nerdy guy pulled out a notebook and started writing something down.

Amber cleared her throat. "This is Steven," she said, gesturing at the guy who waved absently. "He's helping out with research for the Trials."

"Why does Ceri look like she's been crying? More importantly, why is there a lid embedded in the wall?" Genevieve asked.

CHAPTER 26

AMBER

Amber groaned, putting her head in her hands. Once Genevieve had been filled in on what had happened, it had turned into a revenge brainstorming session. Ceri was perking up, but every new idea had made the knot of worry in Amber's stomach grow a little tighter. She wanted to help, but with the Trials so close, it felt risky.

"Well?" Genevieve asked, annoyed.

She looked up and realized they were all looking at her waiting on an answer. Steven was surreptitiously taking notes. She wanted to smack the pen out of his hand and kick him out, but they did still need his help.

"I want to help, I do, but maybe we should wait." As she spoke, Genevieve's face darkened in anger. She could feel the disappointment from each of her pack members. Only Ceri looked somewhat content with her answer, but Amber suspected she was disappointed in her too.

"Whatever," Genevieve said, turning away. "Dinner smells great, Tommy. Is it done?"

Amber felt them closing off. Her wolf whined, equally frustrated with her. It wanted to fight. It didn't understand what was at stake, though. Clenching her teeth tightly together to keep from yelling at her pack, she slipped out the back door and left them to eat.

"That could have gone better," the demon said as he formed in front of her. His smoky body bobbed in the wind.

"Shut up," she muttered, walking faster. They could probably still hear her this close to the house. The last thing she needed was them thinking she was an asshole *and* crazy.

"I'm surprised," the demon sighed. "I thought you were more of a go-getter than this."

"You don't get an opinion. You're not even really here," she said, swiping her hand through the demon's body.

He gasped, pretending offense. "So callous! I'm basically your only real friend right now."

"You're a parasite."

"I thought we'd established I was your guardian angel," he said swooping around in front of her. "And as your guardian angel, I am here to prevent you from making a terrible mistake."

She walked into the garden, feeling less exposed now that she was hidden behind the tall hedges. "What mistake is that?"

"Chickening out."

"I'm not chickening out!" she hissed, trying to keep from shouting. "Just because I'm not running out to pick a fight with some witches doesn't make me a coward. It makes me smart."

"Sure, just keep telling yourself that."

"Someone has to think about the good of the pack! If we get in trouble, we all pay the price. All this will have been for nothing."

The demon twisted into a new form, black wings unfurling behind him and a crooked, fiery halo settling on his head. "Cautious and prudent, the new alpha chose to retreat after an ally of the pack was attacked by witches," he said in a nasally high-pitched voice. "This was a good choice because, gosh-darnit, the odds just weren't in their favor. No one could *blame* her."

She glared at him and bit the inside of her cheek to keep from arguing. What she really needed was for him to go away so she could *think*. If only Dylan were here. He'd have known what to do. Hell, he would have been the alpha, not her. Dylan had been great with people. Everyone loved him. She had just tagged along, happy to bask in his light like everyone else.

"What would he have done?" Angel asked, his voice soft.

Her head snapped up. He couldn't read her mind...could he? "Who?"

"Your brother. He was your twin, right?"

"How the hell do you know about him? Are you reading my mind?" she demanded, advancing on the demon.

He raised his hands in surrender. "Only a little."

"Only a little?!" she shouted as she completely lost her cool. This couldn't be happening. She wanted him out of her mind. Sharing it with the wolf was plenty crowded already. "Stop it right now."

"I can't stop it. Believe me, it would be marvelous if I could, but the mark binds us together. I only get a sense of your strongest thoughts and emotions. Which you have a lot of." He changed back into the first form she'd seen him in as if he were trying to look non-threatening. "Especially when you need help. After all, I am here to serve."

"How do I get rid of the mark?" she asked, putting her hand over it and wishing that was enough to block the unwanted telepathy.

He was silent for a moment. "A time will come when you can repay the favor owed. After that, you can be rid of me."

The mark on her chest ached fiercely for a moment. This favor was going to come back to bite her in the ass, she was sure of it. But she hadn't had another choice. She hadn't had a choice about any of this.

She put her head in her hands and bit the inside of her cheek. She already knew what she needed to do, and she'd known all night. The only thing holding her back was fear. The voice in her head sounded exactly like her mother. Nagging, worrying, and fearful. Maybe she didn't deserve to be an alpha.

"This is going to be a disaster," she said, her voice muffled my her hands.

"I could make sure you succeed," the demon whispered in her ear, his voice velvety smooth.

She lifted her head. "Out of the goodness of your heart?"

He chuckled. "My heart is blackened and shriveled with pure evil, so, no. It would require a small price, just another mark."

"I'll pass," she said drily, trying to ignore how disappointed she was. He was a demon, not her friend.

"You'll pass on what?" Ceri asked, startling Amber.

She turned to the witch. "Sorry, just...talking to myself."

"Oh," Ceri said, looking around skeptically. "It sounded like you were having a whole conversation."

Shit. "Uh, sometimes it's like I can talk to the...wolf," Amber said, scrambling for a coherent excuse.

Ceri nodded, the tension in her shoulders relaxing just a fraction. "Look, I just came out here to apologize. I didn't want them to gang up on you like that. I think you're right, we should wait."

"No. I realized a couple of minutes ago that I was sounding like my mother. She worried over everything to the point that she never did anything. This is risky, but so was trying to fight off that werewolf. So are the Trials. That coven has hurt you and Tommy, and they're not going to stop just because we don't fight back."

The demon floated behind Ceri, settling with his elbow propped up on her shoulder. "She's much too nice to be your friend."

"Are you absolutely sure? Because it's okay if you're not," Ceri said, her brow still pinched with worry.

She laughed. "I don't think I'll ever be sure of anything again. Except for the fact that I'm going to do everything I can to protect my pack and my friends. And I'd like to think we're friends now."

"You were the person I called crying, so yeah, definitely friends." Ceri smiled and held out her hand. "Come on, there *might* still be some food left."

Her stomach rumbled in response. "God, I hope so."

They walked back inside. Genevieve and Tommy were sitting at the table, waiting expectantly. Steven must have left while she was outside having a mini-breakdown. Tommy's shoulders relaxed as soon as he saw them as if he could tell it had all been worked out just from a glance.

"We saved you some," Tommy said, nudging a plate toward her.

"Did y'all come up with a plan while I was out there?" she asked, pulling out a chair.

A blush colored Ceri's cheeks. "We might have."

"Good," Amber said with a grin. "Fill me in while I eat."

CHAPTER 27

AMBER

"What in the seven realms are you wearing?" the demon asked, drifting in a circle around her.

"I dressed up as Boggy Killspree," Amber explained, adjusting the tusks that now jutted out from her lips. They sparked as the charm settled into place.

She stepped back from the mirror and took in her outfit. Green skin, bright purple mohawk, shredded tank top, leather pants and bracers. It was spot on, and she was completely unrecognizable. "He's a troll. Lead singer of my favorite band."

The demon crossed his arms. "Aren't women supposed to use this holiday as an excuse to dress as slutty as possible?" he asked, sounding put out.

She rolled her eyes. "Don't be a perv."

"Just because I appreciate the confident display of a woman's body does not make me a *perv*," the demon huffed, a plume of smoke blowing from his nostrils.

"Can you even have sex?" She asked, gesturing at his lack of legs.

He chuckled, sending a chill down her spine. "Oh, I definitely can. Come to hell and I'll show you," he purred.

She grimaced. "Let's pretend I never asked that."

Grabbing her wallet, she stuffed it in her back pocket and looked around to make sure she hadn't forgotten anything. With one last admiring glance in the mirror, she went to the kitchen. This whole plan they had was a little insane, but Amber couldn't deny the sense of anticipation. The more they learned about the Trials, the more she doubted she'd survive them. This was something she could do.

She opened the refrigerator and stared at the mostly empty shelves. They went through groceries like they were starving lately. She had thought the increased appetite was only after shifts, but apparently, it was constant.

The demon's head popped out from behind a bottle of beer. She didn't flinch this time.

"I'll get you next time," he muttered, pouring out of the refrigerator. Even though he wasn't solid, she took a step back. She disliked it when he passed through her; it made the mark tingle oddly.

"What do you think?" Genevieve asked.

Amber turned around and found herself at a loss for words. Genevieve wore a bright red, spandex bodysuit. A tail waved behind her, the tip flickering with fake flames. She held a pitchfork in her left hand, and a red mask obscured her features. Her distinctive pink hair was black instead.

"Now *she* has the right idea," the demon said, a red smile appearing on his shadowy face as he circled Genevieve. She was oblivious to his presence.

Amber bit back several retorts, but only because she didn't want the others thinking she was crazier than she was.

"You look… striking," she said with a smile. Genevieve's petite frame was well-suited to the tight fabric. She didn't have an ounce of excess fat on her.

Tommy walked out, but if Amber hadn't been able to smell him she would have thought a stranger had strolled in.

"What the hell are you wearing?" she asked with a laugh as she took in the ridiculous costume. He wore a ratty gray wig topped with a pointy black hat. An old, lacy black dress was draped over his lanky frame.

"You think the witches will like it?" he asked, picking up and twirling in a circle with a smug grin that looked extra creepy behind the disguise. He paused mid-twirl and sniffed, his bulbous, warty nose twitching.

"What's wrong?" she asked.

He walked through the living room and the kitchen, still sniffing the air. "Do you smell that?" he asked, crouching down to peer under the table. "It smells weird, like smoke or sulfur. One second I get a whiff of it, the next it's gone."

She stiffened. "I haven't smelled anything weird."

Angel swooped around her, cackling. "The boy is perceptive."

She ignored the taunt and shouted toward the back of the house, "Ceri, you ready?"

"Almost!" Ceri shouted back. "I'll meet you at the truck!"

$\sim$

CERI

Ceri adjusted the fur sprouting from her jaw. She'd bought a bottle of Wolf Charm for the Halloween party. No one would be able to recognize her behind this disguise, which was important considering what they had planned.

The fur sticking out of her collar itched. Scratching it absentmindedly, she reviewed the plan in her head one last time. Amber and Genevieve were going to create a distraction, while Tommy would be her lookout. He'd make sure no one else came in until she was done with the sabotage.

That's where the hard part came in. She had no idea what they were planning for their display. Every coven guarded that knowledge like their life depended on it. No one wanted to risk being copied or shown up. Once she got in the room, she'd have to improvise.

She grabbed her phone and wallet, stuffing them in her pockets, and ran outside. They were all already in the truck. Tommy and Gen scooted over to give her some room on the bench seat, but it was going to be a tight fit. Especially with the pitchfork.

"The devil and a witch, huh?" she commented, smiling at Tommy's ridiculous costume. Snooty witches like the Blackwood coven hated ugly witch costumes. It was perfect.

Amber started the truck and backed out of the driveway. Woggy poked his head out of Tommy's wig, then squeaked in excitement. He scrambled over Gen's shoulder and launched himself at her. She caught him and helped him stand up on her palm.

"He missed you," Tommy said with a grin. "He's been signing for you all day." He leaned over and pointed at her. "Who is this?"

Woggy's long fingers formed a C that he placed over his heart. He held it there for a moment before pointing at Ceri and jumping up and down. The single remaining nub on his back wiggled as though he were trying to fly.

"That's how he says your name. He picked it out yesterday after I taught him how to say love," Tommy said.

She swallowed around the lump in her throat. "Thank you so much for teaching him," she managed, though her voice shook with emotion. She hated the witches all over again, especially Selena Blackwood, the asshole who had ripped off his wings. Tonight, she was going to pay for that. Turns out karma is a witch.

CHAPTER 28

❦

TOMMY

If they hadn't had a mission, Tommy would have been having the time of his life. This was almost better than The Market. The stately homes that filled the subdivision were lit up with magic.

They passed one house that looked like it was on fire, but the flames were cool to the touch. He wasn't sure if it was an illusion or some kind of fake flame. Kids ran in and out, shrieking in excitement.

For such a secretive bunch, he'd always found it odd how witches congregated together in these subdivisions. They must like to keep their friends close, and their enemies closer.

The busy street wound around, then dead-ended in front of the biggest house in the city. He didn't know much about witches, but *everyone* knew the Blackwood name. Blackwood meant power and money. After tonight, they'd know it for a different reason, too.

He'd already liked Ceri, but after the plan she'd come up with, he had a whole new level of respect for the witch. Her revenge was going to be public, and all the blame would be laid at Selena's feet.

"Where's Woggy?" Ceri asked, jogging up beside him.

"Last I saw he was in your hair. Here, let me look."

They stopped, and he dug through the thick, red hair. It was weird to see her without the blonde curls. She looked eerily like Amber in this costume. Woggy stuck his head out of the mass of hair and crawled onto his hand. "Here he is."

The pixie crawled onto Ceri's hand, immediately darting up her arm, trying to get back in her hair.

"Woggy, what is the matter with you," she said grabbing him. "I've never seen him this scared before."

Tommy looked around them. "Maybe he's scared of witches?"

"Oh, of course," she said, clutching the pixie close. He curled up in her palm, shivering. "I shouldn't have brought him here, but I worried about leaving him alone."

"He'll be okay. Just keep him with you and let him hide."

Amber walked over, followed by Gen, who was twirling her pitchfork like a baton.

"Should we go ahead and split up?" Amber asked. Despite the punk rock costume, she was still unmistakably herself. He was a little worried anyone that had met her would immediately recognize her.

"Yep, let's do it," Ceri said, adjusting her costume.

"Stay safe, okay?" Amber looked like she was barely resisting the urge to drag them all out of here. She was more mother hen than werewolf.

"We'll be fine. I won't let anything happen to Tommy, I promise," Ceri said, putting her hands on Amber's shoulders.

Amber nodded and grabbed Gen, walking toward the front of the big house. "You're going to hit someone with that thing."

"I haven't hit anyone yet!" Genevieve protested.

Ceri shook her head as they walked away. "She's going to have a nervous breakdown by the time we're done."

He laughed. "If she was going to have a nervous breakdown, she'd have already had it."

Ceri laughed at that and hooked her arm in his. They headed away from the crowd while doing their best to look nonchalant. His heart was beating a mile a minute but no one could tell underneath his costume.

It was hot and itchy, but the suffering was worth the offended looks on the faces of random witches. Some people didn't know how to take a joke.

They stopped at a hedge, and after a quick look around, jumped over it. Stooping down low, they ran behind the house. He gave Ceri a boost over a fence, then jumped over it himself. He didn't even have to use a hand. A *very* few things about being a werewolf were kind of awesome.

Three houses down was their target. It was quiet back there. The line of houses muffled the sounds of the crowd. Ceri held her finger to her lips to remind him not to speak and jogged ahead of him.

A few feet away from the property line, she stopped them. He looked around to make sure they were still alone as she knelt and pulled out a knotty wooden stick. She traced an intricate shape while chanting in a strange language. Magic tickled his nose, and he held back the need to sneeze.

The way she moved when she was casting was elegant. He'd seen a lot of witches do magic, but never like her. They were always so forceful and angry. She didn't try to force the magic; she just let it happen.

There was a light pop, and she stood back up, yanking him over the property line with her. "Sorry, we only had a few seconds," she whispered.

"It's fine. Let's get you inside. It's already a little later than we planned," he said, urging her toward the back door.

"This part is going to be a little harder. The wards on the backdoor are probably really intense," she whispered.

He nodded and stood beside her while she crouched in front of the door. She ran her hands an inch above the surface from the bottom to the doorknob, then frowned.

"What is it?" he asked.

She cocked her head to the side and repeated the motion, checking it from different angles. Her frown deepened. "There's no wards. How could they possibly leave the back door un-warded? It's so…arrogant."

"I think you just answered your own question," Tommy said as he knelt in front of the door. "But it makes it way easier for us, so I'm not complaining."

He pulled out his small lockpick kit. It wasn't exactly professional grade, but it always got the job done. He used to break into the school so he could shower and sleep in one of the classrooms.

This lock was a little trickier, but after a moment of wriggling, he heard it click. With all his senses focused on detecting any movement inside, he turned the door handle slowly.

The door swung open silently, and Ceri stepped inside. They both held their breath, waiting for a shout of alarm, but there was nothing. He followed her in and shut the door carefully behind him.

Woggy stuck his head out of her hair and squeaked in alarm. Tommy pressed his finger to his lips and signed for the pixie to be quiet. Woggy looked around with wide eyes, then retreated back into Ceri's hair. He knew the pixie had understood him. Hopefully he would listen and stay quiet.

They were in some kind of dining room. The pictures on the walls were of old men and women with stoic faces and dark eyes that seemed to follow them as they moved across the room.

This house was creepy. When they'd moved into Thallan's guest house, the place had seemed warm and welcoming. Coming in here was like walking into a coffin. His skin prickled with goosebumps, and he stayed as close to Ceri as he could.

She'd told him the entrance to the spell room would be obvious. Because it was Halloween, there were also going to be coven members inside. That's where Amber and Genevieve came in. Ceri had given them each a handful of what looked like marbles. Apparently, they blew up. Sort of.

All it took to set one off was a loud noise, then they'd start popping in a chain reaction. They couldn't hurt anything, but they were loud, and they'd rattle everything around them with a shock wave.

As they walked through the house, the dark feeling he'd noticed when they walked in increased. His nose twitched at the overwhelming scents. There was something rotting here.

Most of the coven members were outside, but they were drawing closer to two witches. He tapped Ceri's arm and pointed at the door ahead of them. She nodded and led him out of view of the door. They crouched behind a bookcase, and Ceri pulled out her phone and shot a quick text to Amber.

He heard the warning whistle from Amber and clamped his hands over his ears. One loud boom rattled the windows, followed by another, and another.

Two witches ran out of the work room as the explosions continued. One was Selena.

Her long black hair hung down her back, contrasting sharply with her bright green dress. The other witch was dressed in all black, so Selena must be the one presenting tonight.

He counted twelve of them then dropped his hands from his ears. Closing his eyes, he focused on the room behind them instead of the chaos outside. Once he was sure no one had stayed behind, he nodded.

Ceri ran inside. Full of misgivings, he pressed himself against the wall and listened intently for anyone other than Ceri. He really hoped she worked fast.

CHAPTER 29

CERI

They'd left the door standing wide open. *Idiots*, Ceri thought to herself. The coven must really think no one would dare try to break in. Or maybe they thought they were invincible.

The wards on property line were strong. Most witches wouldn't be able to get past them without their full coven, which would make it obvious.

She stepped into their sacred space and smiled. If only her mother could see her now. She'd be *so proud*. Actually, she'd probably be pissed.

Woggy poked his head out of her hair and tugged on her ear like he wanted to drag her out of the room.

"Sorry, buddy, I'll be quick," she said, hurrying forward.

It was obvious what they were prepping. The ingredients were all laid out, and the spell book was open to the recipe they were using. It was a summoning spell for a flurry of wisps. If successful, they'd bring good luck to everyone who saw them. Supposedly.

Her eyes scanned everything that was laid out. She had to think fast, but her mind had gone blank. Woggy climbed out of her hair and hopped off her shoulder onto the table.

She tried to grab him, but he darted under her hand and ran for a little pot of fine, white granules. She snatched him up just in time.

"That is not sugar, that's salt," she whispered disapprovingly. It looked exactly like sugar, but it was important to make sure you were using the right one. If you combined sugar with...she paused. "Oh my gosh, you're a genius."

She stuffed the pixie back in her hair and searched the room frantically. Over by the door was a spice cabinet. Sugar was used in spells often, as were other common spices.

She grabbed the jar of sugar and the little bowl of salt, searching for a place to dump the salt. There was a large furnace in the corner of the room. She yanked the door open and tossed the salt inside.

Replacing the bowl in its exact spot, she refilled it with sugar. Her hands shook as she poured, and a little sugar spilled next to the bowl. She grabbed Woggy out of her hair and held him above the spill like a vacuum. His tongue flicked out, cleaning up every grain.

"Good boy," she said, putting him back on her shoulder. He curled into her hair, smacking his lips in satisfaction.

She turned to leave but hesitated, her hand hovering over the spellbook. She could take it. Leave them crippled.

Shaking her head, she pulled her hand away. They'd come after her if she did that. There'd be no stopping them. Even without that, they'd be impossible to take on alone.

"Ceri!" Tommy hissed, appearing in the doorway. "Run!"

She ran back to the cabinet, shoved the jar inside, smacked the door shut, and then ran toward Tommy.

They sprinted out of the room and back around the corner. He clamped his hand over her mouth to muffle the sounds of her breathing, and they held perfectly still as Selena and the other witch hurried back into the spell room.

"I can't believe Erica didn't notice what was happening. They better find whoever caused those explosions," Selena said angrily.

Ceri shut her eyes and tried to slow her breathing. They hadn't caught Amber and Genevieve. Now they had to hope they could get our unnoticed as well.

Tommy pulled her to her feet and they crept toward the back door. Halfway there, he froze. Looking around frantically, he finally settled on a door next to them. He opened it and shoved her inside.

He pushed the door almost closed behind them and held his finger to his mouth to keep her quiet. She pressed her back against the wall and tried to breathe silently. Footsteps sounded in the hall a moment later.

"Where is Erica?" a woman asked harshly, pausing in front of the room.

Ceri looked at Tommy with wide eyes. If they came in this room, they were screwed. She looked around for a way out, but there weren't any windows or another door. They were trapped.

"I'm not sure, High Priestess, but I'll send her to you as soon as I find her," someone replied nervously.

"No, send her to the basement. If I see her now, she might not survive the encounter. We've been *humiliated*," the High Priestess said, taking a deep breath.

The door handle turned slightly, and Ceri tensed, her mind running through every defensive spell she knew. They'd have to blast their way out and hope they could run fast enough to get away.

"Madame," Selena said, interrupting the other two women's conversation. "We're about to begin."

The door handle turned back. "I'll join you then. We can't afford another mishap on a night like this."

Their footsteps led away, and Ceri slumped against Tommy in relief. He listened intently then nodded. They opened the door carefully and walked as quickly as they could toward the back door.

CHAPTER 30

GENEVIEVE

Genevieve took a few steps back as Selena climbed up onto the stage. Amber was on the other side of the yard, standing back in the crowd as well. They weren't sure exactly what Ceri had done to sabotage the coven's display, and she didn't want to be too close. Just in case. Ceri had promised she wasn't going to let any innocent bystanders get hurt, but accidents happened.

The witch lifted her hands, quieting the crowd. The conversations dropped off as everyone looked at her with a sense of anticipation. She'd gone all out with her outfit, wearing a bright green gown with an old-fashioned witch's hat perched on her head. Selena was the picture of elegance.

"On behalf of the Blackwood Coven, thank you for your interest tonight. In honor of this hallowed eve, we will display for you creativity, innovation, and power. The Blackwood Coven has long stood as a pillar of the community. We are ever ready to serve…"

Selena kept talking, but Genevieve tuned her out. This girl liked the sound of her own voice a little too much.

The girls in front of her were whispering about a spot where magic didn't work showing up right outside the city like it was a sign of the coming apocalypse. She leaned in, trying to hear the details. With all the upheaval, she hadn't exactly been paying attention to the news.

Trying to slip around the person in front of her to better eavesdrop, her tail hit someone in what felt like their nose. She turned to apologize and ended up face to face with a tall, hot guy dressed up as…well, she had no idea. He was just shirtless with pants that hung low on his hips.

"Hi," she whispered with a devilish wink.

He grinned at her and leaned in. "Hi."

"What are you tonight? Besides hot," she asked, letting the tip of her tail trace a line down his abs.

117

"Lust," he said, returning her wink. "One of the seven deadly sins. Fits perfectly with the devil, since you look pretty tempting yourself."

"Oh, you have no idea—"

A brilliant light flared behind them. She whipped around to face the stage. Selena was chanting, one hand held above a cauldron while she added ingredients with the other. Two more witches stood on either side of her, hands lifted. Their voices joined the chant.

"Tonight, we will summon an angel that will bless this night and this gathering." The crowd gasped as if on cue. Angels mingled with humans on occasion. They mostly hated any creature with magic, though no one knew why. To say that summoning an angel would be an impressive feat was the a huge understatement. This would draw national attention.

Genevieve grinned. Since it was about to fail in a big way, it would get even more attention.

Selena traced a symbol into the air with deft strokes. She picked up a small bowl and poured the contents into the cauldron as she began to chant, "Voco Ishim—"

A loud pop cut her off. The cauldron began to spark and shake. Based on how tightly her jaw was clenched, it wasn't supposed to do that.

Genevieve took a step back and bumped into the hot guy. He assumed she was trying to grind on him and started dancing. She went with it while looking through the crowd for Amber.

Selena stuck her finger in the bowl she held and tasted the remnants. Her eyes went wide and she looked back at the coven leader.

The cauldron shook harder and then it…burped. Green fog erupted from the surface and drifted toward the crowd. Screams began as it engulfed the people closest. Genevieve gagged as her sensitive nose picked up on the smell.

The people at the front began trying to run. Selena shouted something over the cacophony, trying to calm them. The cauldron rattled once more, then exploded, sending green slime in every direction. Her perfect dress and sleek hair were coated in the foul substance.

"What the fuck," hot guy said, horrified.

"I thought this coven was supposed to be good," she said, shoving him backward. She forgot her strength and sent him flying into the person behind him. "Oops."

He glared at her. "What the hell are you?"

"Umm, I…lift weights," she said with a shrug before darting into the crowd, trying to find Amber. It was definitely time to go.

She glanced back over her shoulder in time to see the coven leader backhand Selena across the face hard enough to knock her on her ass. Ouch.

There was a loud crack, and the cauldron caught fire. The awful smell only grew worse, and the flames spread from the cauldron to the porch.

Amber grabbed her arm and yanked her in a different direction. "Ceri said they're running back to the truck."

Genevieve followed Amber, looking back one last time. The whole coven was scrambling to put out the fire. A few of them stopped, gagging in the bushes due to the smell.

Whatever Ceri had done worked even better than they'd planned. Selena looked like an idiot.

CHAPTER 31

TOMMY

They'd done it. He'd wanted to try, but actually pulling it off surprised the hell out of him. When the coven leader had almost walked into the room they were hiding in, his entire life had flashed before his eyes.

Genevieve stood on the couch reenacting the final display with dramatic flair. "I have been sabotaged! My perfect life is *ruined!*" she shrieked, flailing around before falling off the couch.

Amber was laughing with them. Actually laughing. He hadn't realized she knew how.

"Tommy! You were genius!" Ceri exclaimed, wrapping him in a hug.

He laughed and picked her up, twirling her around. "Me? You were the genius! You and Woggy made Selena look like a complete idiot! And in such a simple way."

Woggy was laying on a chair stuffed full with all the chicken he'd been able to eat. His little gray tummy was distended with food. He looked smug about it.

"It's going to look like an accident, too," Genevieve said, climbing back up on the couch. "The more Selena tries to claim sabotage, the more desperate she'll look."

Shaking his head with a laugh, he walked into the kitchen. He shut the timer off with three seconds left and opened the oven. The sweet smell of apple pie filled the kitchen. The filling was bubbling through the criss-cross of crust he'd laid over the top.

"Oh my god, is that apple pie?" Genevieve exclaimed from the living room. There was a crash and Amber's exasperated warning to be careful.

He pulled the pie out of the oven and set it on the stove. It was perfect.

Amber joined him in the kitchen and pulled out some plates and silverware. "You did great today," she said as she set them next to the pie on the counter.

"Thanks," he replied with a grin.

She shifted uncomfortably. "I'm glad you decided to stay. It couldn't have been an easy decision."

He scratched the back of his neck, feeling awkward. They hadn't ever talked about it, even though he knew that she knew. "I'm glad you didn't sell us out to Donovan."

Opening the drawer to his left he pulled out Amber's old pie server. It was silicone, and the handle had fallen off. Cooking definitely wasn't her priority.

"Maybe it would have been better to join his pack, though," she said, looking unexpectedly vulnerable. She crossed her arms and leaned against the counter.

"Donovan would never have helped Ceri. He probably would have had us as the pack slaves or some crap like that. You made the only choice you could." He began cutting the pie, remembering the look on his stepmother's face when she used to yell at him to wash the dishes or clean up her vomit. "You care, you know? That's all that matters."

Genevieve burst into the kitchen, and Amber moved away, letting her and Ceri crowd around him.

Genevieve held up a plate and looked at him with pleading eyes. "It smells so good."

He laughed and scooped a big piece onto her plate. "How much do you want, Ceri?"

"Same," she said with a smile, holding up her own plate.

Amber slipped out of the back door. He watched her go, torn between following her and staying with the rest of the pack. But he knew she wouldn't relax if he did. She put up a front none of them could crack. With a sigh, he turned back to the others, resigned to letting her stew in all her worries.

～

AMBER

Amber stood in the garden, head tilted back, eyes on the stars. The moon hung in her periphery. No matter where she looked, it was always there. Taunting her. It grew larger every day, dragging her like the tides toward the thing she feared most. Failure.

"Tomorrow is the full moon," Angel said, twisting into a smoky imitation of the moon.

"I don't want you bugging me during the Trials. It's too important, okay?" she said, putting her hands on her hips.

He changed forms again, appearing as her demonic twin this time. "I could help you instead."

"No."

"You're very bossy," he said with a pout.

"Stop looking like me, it's creepy," she said, turning away.

"I could make sure you pass the Trials. You made one deal to gain your sponsor, I'm surprised you won't consider another," he said swooping around to hover in front of her again.

She looked down at her hands. A small, bitter part of her wished she'd just run when she'd seen that wolf attacking people. This wasn't what she wanted, but it was her life now.

"Ohhhh," Angel said, drifting backward. "I get it."

"Get what?" she asked.

"You actually want to prove yourself," he said propping his head up on his chin.

She rolled her eyes. "So what if I do?"

"It's fine, I suppose," he said with a shrug. "If you can manage it."

"You're real encouraging," she muttered.

"I'm a realist."

She heard the footsteps first, followed by the cloying smell of cigarettes. Angel went quiet, then waved goodbye and vanished.

Thallan rounded the corner, pausing when he saw her.

She nodded in greeting. "The garden is nice at night."

"Yes, though I'm surprised to see you out here with the noise coming from the house," he said as he walked up behind her. "You don't seem like you are in as *festive* a mood as the others."

He plucked a rose from the bush, knocking a petal off with the rough motion. Holding it close to his nose, he took a deep breath, his face softening as he smelled it.

The tense line of her shoulders grew tighter. She wasn't in the mood to deal with him right now. "I guess I'm just a party pooper. Kinda like you. Maybe it's a side effect of the demon mark."

"More likely a side effect of your desperation. It's hard to be carefree when you have to be realistic about the future," he said, motioning toward the house. Laughter drifted from an open window but was carried away by the breeze.

She pressed her thumb into the mark. "Did the demon ever...talk to you?"

"When it gave me the mark, yes. Why do you ask?" Thallan narrowed his eyes and took a drag from his cigarette.

"It never visited you after that?"

He tilted his head, looking at her curiously. "No, never." Silence hung between them for a moment, then he said, "Don't let it talk you into another deal. It will try, and you will not come out on top in a negotiation with a demon."

She shook her head. "I know. He hasn't tried, not seriously at least."

"He?" Thallan asked, taking another drag on his cigarette. The red glow of the ember reflected in his eyes, giving him a menacing look.

"The demon, well, I call him Angel. It's kind of a joke, but whatever," she waved away the over-explanation.

Thallan's hand curled into a fist, crushing the rose. "*It* is not a man. Or an angel. *It* is a demon, and it hates you. It wants to harm you." He got in her face, teeth bared and the vein in his temple throbbing in rage.

She put her hand on his chest and pushed him back firmly. "I don't need to be lectured about what he is or isn't."

"Apparently you do," Thallan sneered. "Have you already let it seduce you? Did you know they crave children just as much as the angels? I'm sure your child would be quite the anomaly, a demon wolf."

"I have enough to worry about without you accusing me of screwing a demon. Get the hell away from me." She turned to walk away, but Thallan grabbed her elbow. His fingers bit into her skin hard enough to bruise.

STEPHANIE FOXE

"I am going to kill it one day. Never forget that."

She believed him. His eyes shone with madness, and hate. He dropped her arm and walked slowly away. The rose lay on the ground where he had stood, its petals bruised and bent.

She knelt and picked it up. A sweet, bright scent filled her nose. It reminded her of home and her mother's rosebushes. She turned and headed back toward the house, her mind full of past failures and the challenges that grew closer every day.

CHAPTER 32

GENEVIEVE

Genevieve hissed as the piping hot coffee splashed out of her mug and stung her hand. They'd stayed up pretty late, and now she was running so late for work. Granted, she was running late most mornings, but since she intended to ask to leave early today, she figured she should at least *try* to show up on time.

Amber walked into the kitchen in her workout clothes. "Someone just drove up to the house."

"Just now?" She'd been in such a rush she hadn't even noticed.

There was a single hard knock on the door. Amber held a hand up, motioning for her to stay back. She ignored the command and followed instead. Neither she, nor the wolf, was willing to let Amber face the potential threat alone. Besides, it was no fun to hang back.

Amber checked the peephole then stepped back, frowning. "It's some werewolf in a suit."

"It could be a representative from the regional council," Genevieve said, eyes going wide. "They have to talk to you ahead of the Trials."

"She is correct," the man shouted through the door. "Also, I can hear you, since I *am* a werewolf."

A blush colored Amber's cheeks and she yanked the door open.

The representative nodded in greeting, clearly amused. He wore a suit, but it was clear that it wasn't his normal attire. It was freshly pressed, and Genevieve could smell the chemicals from the dry cleaner from where she stood. His dark brown hair was loosely tousled, and his eyes were so blue she wondered if he wore colored contact lenses.

"Sorry about that," Amber cleared her throat and stepped back to let him inside. "So, you're the rep?"

"Shane Weston," he said, extending his hand. "Can I assume you are Amber Hale?"

Amber nodded and shook his hand. "I am."

"And you are?" he asked, turning to her.

"Genevieve Bissett," she said, shaking his hand. This guy was smoking hot, and judging by the way he was looking at Amber, he had a thing for redheads.

"Your little pack has been hot gossip for the past couple of weeks," Shane said with a grin.

Amber looked surprised. "I didn't realize anyone knew we existed. Other than Lockhart, at least."

Shane chuckled. "You'll find that we're a very insular community, despite our separate packs. Gossip travels faster in the were community than at an all-girls high school."

"Greaaaat," Amber said, drawing out the word. Despite her tone, a smile played at her lips. It was almost...flirtatious. Now *that* was interesting.

"Perhaps sometime we can get together and I can fill you in on what everyone is saying about you. However," his demeanor changed to all business, "I am here to deliver a message from Alpha Clark Jameson, who will be presiding over the Trials on the next full moon. Two hours before sunset, myself and the betas of the other packs on the council will arrive to escort you to the Trials. Your pack, including your sponsor, must attend as well. If any one of them is not there, you will automatically fail."

Amber nodded her head in acknowledgment. "We'll be ready."

He hesitated for a moment then added, "Be careful to not let anything take you by surprise between now and then. Some of the gossip has been a little...heated."

"I hadn't realized how much werewolves resented bitten weres until I became one," Genevieve said, crossing her arms. This guy didn't seem like the bigoted type, but people could always disappoint you.

Shane managed to pull his eyes away from Amber to acknowledge her for a moment. "Not everyone shares that view, but I won't lie, most do."

"Is there a chance for me to pass the Trials, or will the powers that be not allow it?" Amber asked bluntly.

The smile returned to Shane's face. "You have the same chance as every other alpha that has gone through them. A born wolf doesn't have any advantage, other than an experienced sponsor perhaps."

"I don't suppose you can tell us what the Trials will entail?" Genevieve asked.

He shook his head. "I can't help or hinder you in any way. As Jameson's beta, I have to be completely neutral."

It sounded like he was telling the truth, but it was still total crap. Whoever made those rules wanted to maintain the status quo. It was ten times harder for a bitten wolf, despite Shane's claim that the Trials didn't give preference to anyone.

Amber pursed her lips and nodded. "Alright. Is there anything else you *can* tell us?"

"Trust yourself, and trust your pack. You'll need them." He patted Amber on the shoulder, his hand lingering a touch too long. *Definitely* flirting at this point.

Genevieve smiled to herself. Amber looked so awkward, like she wanted to flirt back but didn't know how.

"I guess we'll see you again soon," Amber said.

He nodded at the two of them. "Until then."

Amber shut the door behind him and Genevieve grinned at her. "He was *totally* into you."

"He can still hear you," Amber hissed, the blush returning to her cheeks. "And no he was not."

"Yes to both actually," Shane shouted from the driveway. They wouldn't have been able to hear him without the enhanced senses. Being a werewolf had *some* pros at least.

Amber stiffened, glaring at Genevieve.

She reached around Amber and pulled the door open. "I have to go to work."

"I'm going to murder you," Amber grumbled.

Shane's car started and he backed out of his spot, heading down the driveway.

"You have to wait until after the Trials," Genevieve said with a wink. "You should skip murdering me and just get his number."

She pulled the door shut before Amber could argue further and hurried to her car. Everything had been tragic and miserable since they were changed. It was nice to poke fun at Amber like they were still just *people*.

The warning Shane had given them made the feeling a little bittersweet. She didn't like the sound of being taken by surprise. Especially not with everything that had happened with the coven and with Donovan Lockhart.

CHAPTER 33

AMBER

Panting, Amber braced her hands on her knees and tried to catch her breath. She'd run flat out for two miles, but the wolf still didn't want to cooperate.

"How am I supposed to train if you keep hiding?" she asked the wolf out loud. There was no one around to hear and think she was crazy. Shockingly, the wolf did not reply. Sometimes the wolf seemed downright moody, which was odd for something that only existed in her head. It was annoying, too.

Huffing in annoyance, she jogged toward the house. If she couldn't shift, then all that was left to do was read.

Even though it was cool outside, stepping into the air conditioning was a relief. She opened the fridge and stood there, enjoying the cold air on her sweaty skin for a moment. Grabbing a bottle of water, she twisted off the cap and kicked the refrigerator door shut behind her.

Genevieve had left colorful notes sticking out of the books she was supposed to read. She eyed them as she quenched her thirst, not looking forward to an afternoon of study. Picking the thickest one up, she tested the weight in her hand. It must have been five pounds. With a sigh, she resigned herself to getting the worst one over with first. *Honoring the Wolf* sounded about as dry as it got.

A squeak from upstairs, barely loud enough to hear, made her pause. She held her breath as her senses rushed to high alert. A footstep. A heartbeat. There was someone, maybe two people, in the house.

Taking a slow step back, she glanced out of the kitchen window. The driveway was empty. Whoever was in the house had taken a different route.

Glass shattered as a canister was thrown through the living room window. Amber ran toward the back door, but a tall, muscled man wearing a balaclava that hid his features blocked her exit. She threw the book at him as hard as she could. It caught him square in the face as she rushed him and drove her shoulder into his diaphragm. The blow lifted him off his feet and they crashed through the door together.

The gas from the canister burned her nose and made her eyes water, but there was no time to hesitate. She slammed her elbow down on his face twice. Something cracked and he went still beneath her.

When in doubt, just pound their freaking face in, Dylan's voice echoed in her mind. She gritted her teeth, shoving away the memories. This wasn't the time.

Confusion filtered through the adrenaline as she looked around herself. They weren't outside. The living room was still behind her but...she was upstairs now. It smelled like Tommy's room. What the hell was going on?

"Where is she?" someone shouted downstairs.

"I hear her upstairs!" a gruff voice replied.

She shoved herself off the unconscious man and ran toward the door. The house was warded, but she'd never seen wards that could transport you around. She wasn't sure it was all that helpful, either.

A witch wearing a mask appeared at the top of the stairs. He lifted his hands and gestured as he began a chant. She turned and ran back to the room she'd come from when there was a loud thwack behind her.

Looking over her shoulder she saw the witch laying on the ground and the closet door slowly shutting itself.

"What the actual fuck," she muttered as she jumped into the room next to her. Everything blurred for a split second and she found herself back downstairs in the kitchen.

She dropped down behind the island, trying to catch her breath. Two of the attackers were headed away from her, but one of them was coming straight toward her. She sniffed the air and the scent of a werewolf filled her nose. It was familiar.

The steps grew closer. The other werewolf paused, inhaling deeply. "I can smell you," he whispered, as though he didn't want to draw the attention of his comrades. "Come on, Amber, don't you want to meet your maker?"

Her lip curled into a silent snarl. It was *him.* She could feel it. Something stretched between them, a strange bond that tugged at her. He had no power over her, but the connection was undeniable. She watched his reflection in the stainless steel refrigerator.

"You're an alpha now. I thought it'd be you after you jumped in front of the girl and tried to fight me off." He was full of nervous energy, bouncing on the balls of his feet as he picked at the seam of his pants. "Donovan knew I could pick the right three. He had no idea I could make such a strong wolf ,though. I *impressed* him."

A mix of joy, pride, and hate rushed through the connection. She wanted to recoil from his emotions, but she couldn't. She was trapped with them. Her lip curled back in a silent growl. The wolf was angry for different reasons, but they both wanted to rip him apart.

There was a scream upstairs, and she took advantage of it to dart out from behind the island and lunge at him. He didn't even try to block it or dodge the attack. Her fist hit his jaw.

Blood sprayed from his mouth as she knocked his tooth across the room. He turned his bloodied, yellow smile on her. "*So strong.*"

The kick came out of nowhere, catching her in the gut and driving all the air from her lungs. She growled at him and ran in swinging. This time he dodged, moving around each strike like she was moving in slow motion. He cackled as they danced around the room.

"Quit playing with her and grab her!" a woman shouted angrily from behind them. She tried to step into the room, but vanished as soon as her foot hit the floor.

The werewolf growled in irritation and lunged forward, wrapping her in a bear hug. She threw an elbow as best she could but he barely grunted. His arms tightened around her until she couldn't breathe.

Spots danced in her vision. There was no way she was going to die like this, though. She shifted into her wolf form in his arms and twisted her head around. Her long canines sunk into the side of his face before he shoved her away.

"You *bitch*," he growled, drool and blood dripping from his chin. Black fur rolled over his body, and he lunged at her. He hit her side, his teeth sinking into the thick muscles of her shoulder. She yelped and twisted away, snapping at his neck.

Anger and panic shot through the pack bonds. One of them was being attacked right now, and there was nothing she could do about it when she was struggling to stay alive herself.

Rage filled her and her wolf. He charged her again, and she ducked down then lunged upward, catching his throat in her jaws. Her teeth hit bone and cartilage. His flesh tore as he struggled, his claws digging into her legs and torso.

She wrenched her head from side to side, dragging him backward, and clamped down even tighter. Blood seeped into her mouth, coating her tongue. The warm liquid sent a thrill through the wolf, exultant that its enemy bled.

The other wolf's struggles slowed. His body grew weak as the supply of both oxygen and blood were cut off from his brain. She shook him viciously again. He had to be stopped.

Angel appeared in front of her and shouted, "Look out!"

She jumped away as a gunshot cracked through the air, striking the floor where she had been. It left a hole the size of a softball in the wood.

The witch held the gun with shaking hands. "Shift back, now!"

She shifted and stood naked before the witch, covered in the blood of the werewolf that had changed her. He was twitching on the floor, not quite dead.

Reaching behind her, the witch pulled out a pair of silver handcuffs. "Put these on," she said, tossing them at Amber. The handcuffs hit her leg, burning her skin and weakening her whole body for the instant it was touching her.

Someone stepped through the backdoor, but she couldn't see them. The witch shifted the gun toward them, then back to Amber. "Don't come any closer!"

"Don't worry, I don't need to," Thallan said, sounding bored. "Trespassers are not welcome. I'll give you one chance to leave."

The witch sneered at him. "We can take the girl and leave, or we can kill you and still do that."

"You will do neither." A smile spread across Thallan's face, and Amber was reminded of the demon's fiery-red grin.

"This isn't good," Angel said, startling her. "Thallan has a tendency to…overreact when he feels insulted."

She glared at the demon. Had he come to make jokes while she fought for her life? He wasn't even offering to help.

Thallan took a deep breath, then blew. Fire poured from his mouth like a dragon. Amber dove into the next room as bullets hit the wall behind her. She ended up upstairs again, in Genevieve's room this time. The witch's screams echoed through the house.

The werewolf was down. The witch was as good as dead. But there were still at least two more intruders in the house.

"You need to work on your fighting skills," Angel said, a hint of worry in his voice. "That was almost tragic. You know I lose out on my favor if you die, right?"

"I really don't care," she said angrily. "And fuck off if all you're going to do is mock me. My pack is in danger."

He lifted his hands in surrender and mimed zipping his lips. It was still a dick move, but at least he wasn't talking anymore.

She shifted back and crept toward the door. Her pack was headed toward her. She could feel it. The wolf urged her forward. The fight wasn't over yet; they had to protect the pack.

CHAPTER 34

GENEVIEVE

Genevieve dropped the file folder she was holding, scattering papers at her feet. Something was wrong. Very, very badly wrong.

"Karen, I've gotta go! Family emergency!" she shouted as she raced toward the door.

The need to shift and howl pumped through her veins. She barely heard the door slamming shut behind her. Her heels flew off her feet as she ran through the parking lot.

Ten feet from her car, she slid to a halt on the asphalt. A growl escaped from her throat as the smell of another werewolf and nicotine drifted toward her with the shifting wind. A man she didn't recognize stepped out from behind her car.

He took one last puff of his cigarette and flicked it on the ground. He didn't smile, just watched her, his hands hanging loosely by his side.

"You look pretty menacing," she said, sliding one foot back as she prepared for his attack. "I don't suppose you're standing next to my car by mistake?"

"No mistake." He grinned, all teeth. "You look small. This is going to be easier than I thought."

Donovan and his pack had ruined everything. They'd turned them, then tried to control and threaten them at every turn. She hadn't expected them to try and kill her, but maybe she should have.

Genevieve laughed, and it sounded hysterical even to her ears. She was scared, but she was also mad as hell. "For the last three weeks I've had to hold back. You're about to be my anger management therapy."

He rolled his shoulders. "Big words for such a little girl."

She bared her teeth at him. "I'm a woman, not a little girl. Asshole."

He snorted in amusement. "You're a waste of a bite."

The shift rolled over him, and his hands hit the ground as paws. His wolf was as tall as she was, with burning yellow eyes and massive canines. She'd frozen in the last attack, but she wouldn't this time. This time she was going to *fight*.

He dug his claws into the ground, leaping toward her. The shift ripped through her as she jumped, hitting him midair. His teeth dug into her shoulder. She dug her claws into his belly and twisted, snapping at everything she could reach.

She may not know any technical fighting moves, but she knew fury. *Finally*, she didn't have to hold back the violence that had been churning in her since the moment she was changed.

The wolf inside her took over. Warm blood filled her mouth and she tore through the fur and flesh. She knew she was hurt too, but the pain never reached her. He'd come alone, and that had been a mistake. Everyone underestimated her.

Someone was screaming in the distance. The sound was drowned out by their vicious growls. She jerked away and snapped at his face. Her canines drug across his eye.

He howled in pain and stumbled. She took her opportunity and clamped her jaws around his throat. Her teeth sunk in until they hit bone.

Wrenching her head side to side, she shook him like a rag doll. He fought back weakly, but he was half-dead already. She braced her feet on his body and ripped a chunk of flesh away.

Blood pooled around her feet as she panted. The wolf tilted back its head and howled in victory.

She could barely process what had happened. He'd tried to kill her. She knew she'd been justified, but the sticky warmth coating her paws made her want to vomit.

The jolt of alarm through the pack bond startled her out of her panicking. Amber was still in trouble. She backed away from the dead wolf, then turned and ran.

She didn't bother trying to shift back. There was only one thought in her mind. She had to protect her pack—and her alpha.

~

CERI

Ceri slammed through the gate. A chunk of metal flew off and cracked the windshield of her car. Magic sparked at her fingertips. She could see what was happening in the house in her mind. Strange people. Their menace and the threat of strange spells being cast in the house tingled along her skin. They'd jumped in the car as soon as they'd both felt the threat, Tommy through his pack bond, and her through the blessing she had left on the house.

Tommy opened his door and jumped out, shifting as he ran toward the fighting. She could feel the wards rising up all around them. Thallan must be helping. The doors and windows of the mansion were clanking in alarm. Screams were coming from the guest house, but it wasn't Amber. She hoped.

She slammed on the brakes, and the car slid to a halt right in front of the house. Without bothering to shut off the car, she leapt out and ran inside. As she stepped over the threshold, the house took her upstairs, to Amber, just like she wanted.

Amber was stuck between two witches. Her foot was frozen to the floor, and her tail was singed. The witch closest to her was preparing a big spell.

Ceri may not have liked her mother's lessons, but she remembered them. Speaking the spell inside her mind, she snapped her fingers. A small flash of light as loud as a firecracker snapped right next to the face of the witch closest to her. He flinched and faltered in his casting.

Before he had a chance to face her, she thrust both palms out. The wave of energy hit him in the back, launching him toward Amber. Distract, attack, keep them down. She refused to use the spells that would truly harm him, but she could incapacitate him without those.

Amber lunged forward and clamped down on his hand. He screamed in pain, and Ceri turned her attention to the other witch.

"Somnum!" she shouted, gesturing sharply. The blue spell raced through the air and hit the wall instead of the witch as he dodged it.

From his crouched position, he thrust his palm toward her shouting, "Ardeo!"

The spell rebounded on him, engulfing him in green flames. He fell to the ground rolling and shrieked in pain.

She ran forward, leaping over Amber, and dropped to her knees in front of him. "Glacio!" She repeated it over and over as snow poured from her hands. It blanketed the witch, snuffing out the flames.

The spell he had cast burned so hot. He was an idiot to cast something like that in a warded house. The more intense the spell, the more likely it was to rebound.

"Ceri, are you okay?" Amber asked, putting her hand on her shoulder.

She ignored the question as she brushed the melting snow off her attacker. "Was that all of them?"

"Yeah, I–I think so," Amber said, her voice unsteady.

The man twitched, covered in burns. His eyes were glassy. She began a healing chant. Her hands shook as she gathered the magic. Sunlight wound around her fingers like golden threads. She coaxed them down toward the man.

"What is she doing?" Genevieve demanded angrily behind her.

"She's healing him," Amber said. There was a brief scuffle that shook her concentration slightly. "She can't save him, but you're going to let her try! It's the right thing to do."

She wasn't so sure that it was the right thing, but she had to try. She'd never been able to turn away from someone that was hurting. The magic seeped into the man's chest. His eyes widened and he exhaled as the pain faded, but Amber was right, she couldn't save him.

His breaths became gasps. She continued the spell anyway, chanting faster and faster. If all she could do was dim the pain, then she would do that until the end.

The gasps grew farther apart and his unfocused eyes widened. She could take the pain, but not the fear. His hand twitched, brushing against her knee as he fought to hold on. But the injuries were too great. Another breath never came. He was gone.

She fell back onto her butt and put her head between her knees. Amber crouched next to her and rubbed a hand on her back. "It's not your fault, Ceri."

Amber was right. It was these witch's fault for showing up here at all. It was this dead idiot's fault for casting that awful spell. She forced herself to look up. "Are you okay?"

Amber nodded, but there was blood streaked across her face. Her hair was singed, and anger was still burning in her eyes. "Genevieve is hurt a little but nothing that won't heal. Other than that, we're all fine."

"Gen is hurt?" She scrambled to her feet. No wonder she'd been angry. "I'll heal her. I had no idea."

Genevieve was limping toward Thallan, shouting something about *shitty wards* and *idiotic witches*.

"She'll be fine," Amber said, grabbing her before she could run off. "I don't think you could get her to sit still long enough to help her right now." She paused looking back over her shoulder. "Could you sit with Tommy, though? I think he's a bit...shaken."

"Where is he?"

"Out on the front porch."

"Okay, I'll go see him. Let me know if you need anything else," she said.

Amber nodded. "Thanks. And I mean that, thanks for showing up. You didn't have to."

"That's what friends do," she said, plastering a smile on her face.

Ceri hurried downstairs and found Tommy sitting on the front step of the house. Woggy stood on his knee, petting his hair, but Tommy wasn't paying any attention.

Halfway to him, she heard sirens. Her shoulders slumped in relief. They'd gotten here late, but at least the police would be here to clean things up.

CHAPTER 35

AMBER

The flashing lights were beginning to give her a headache. Amber rubbed her fingers against her temples and sighed. The police had been here for over an hour. There'd been a hundred questions about what had happened. Who the attackers were, which she didn't know, and why they'd been targeted.

Worst of all, Peter, who she thought she'd killed, had disappeared. She was hoping the house had eaten him or something, but her gut told her he was still alive.

"Can I have a word?" Detective Sloan asked. He was a slender, unassuming man. His face didn't give away anything, and she wasn't sure if he thought she was lying or just didn't care.

She nodded and followed the officer away from the group. His shoulders grew tense, and his eyes kept darting around like someone might see them talking. He finally stopped once they were far enough away to prevent eavesdropping.

"Okay," he said, tapping his pen against his notepad. "Can you tell me again who you think is responsible for this attack?"

She dragged her hand down her face. This was the third time she'd explained this. "Donovan Lockhart somehow got a werewolf to attack myself, Genevieve, and Tommy. After that, he tried to coerce us to join his pack. I'm not sure why he wanted us. Ever since we turned him down, he's been trying to make our lives hell. I didn't expect him to try to *kill me*, but he did. I have no doubt he sent these people today."

"But you have no idea why he'd want you dead?"

"No. He wants something from me, but I don't know what," she said, crossing her arms.

"We'll look into it. However, we can't arrest anyone just because you're saying they don't like you," Sloan said.

She ground her teeth together. "That's not what I said. He's been threatening me."

The detective took a deep breath, then glanced around to make sure they were alone before continuing. "I'll be completely honest with you because I think you deserve it. Donovan Lockhart is respected and influential. My bosses won't let me talk to him as a suspect without rock solid evidence."

She curled her hand into a fist. "So that's it? You're just giving up?"

"It's not that simple—"

"Sure it is," she snapped. "You're either going to try to find evidence, or you're going to give up and walk away. Those are the only two options. It's pretty fucking black and white."

Genevieve's head popped up at the shouting and she walked toward them.

"This is my job on the line. I will do what I can, but I can't help anyone if I've been fired," he said, his face going red with anger.

"How many people has he done this to?" she demanded as Genevieve stopped beside her, glaring at the officer.

"I don't know," he said, his face going hard.

"Liar," Genevieve said, mirroring Amber's posture. "You're just scared."

"Look, I tried to help and be honest. If you can find any sort of hard evidence, here's my card," he handed it to Amber. "I *am* going to keep investigating. If I find a way to connect this back to Lockhart, I will. Going after him with a weak case will make me look incompetent, and it won't be enough to stop him. That's the truth, whether you want to believe it or not."

"Whatever helps you sleep at night," she said before turning and walking away.

Genevieve lingered for a moment before following her. "So they aren't going to do anything?"

"He's going to investigate, just like he said. And he isn't going to find any evidence, so yeah, they're aren't going to do a thing," she said from behind clenched teeth. The medics were carrying out a stretcher with a dead body.

Bile rose in the back of her throat. This wasn't how she'd wanted things to be. Tommy was barely seventeen; he shouldn't be fighting for his life. This was all wrong. She wanted to scream and rage against the injustice of it all, but it would be pointless.

Instead of protecting her pack, she was just dragging them into more danger. She had barely survived today. Tomorrow, she would probably fail the Trials. She shook her head. She couldn't even think about that. Failure was not an option.

CHAPTER 36

TOMMY

He should have run that first day. It had been insane to stay. They were going to get killed if they didn't get shipped off to the freaking werewolf prison.

"Tommy," Ceri said, placing her hand gently on his shoulder. "Are you hurt?"

He shook his head and dug his fingers into his shirt a little tighter. She was the last person he wanted to talk to, because he knew if he left, he'd miss her most.

His whole body was starting to shake, and he felt weirdly cold. He always felt like this right before a panic attack. Every time it felt like he was dying. He hated feeling like that.

She sat down beside him and wrapped her arms around him. The scent of her citrusy perfume surrounded him, blocking out the oppressive smell of death. He relaxed just a fraction and leaned into the embrace.

"It's going to be okay," she whispered.

"You can't know that," he muttered. "Unless you're psychic."

She snorted. "Psychics are all fake. But I believe in Amber, and in you."

"I learned a long time ago that things don't always turn out okay," he said, finally lifting his head. Woggy climbed up Ceri's hair and patted his cheek. The pixie signed his name a few times and he couldn't help but smile.

"You were homeless, right?" Ceri asked.

He nodded. "Yeah. After my mom died, my dad started drinking. He married this woman. She was a total bitch. If they weren't drunk, they were high. We got in a fight one day, and he kicked me out."

"Where are you now?" she asked, laying her head on his shoulder.

"Getting attacked by mercenaries."

She gave him a sad smile. "That's what happened, but that's not where you are. You have people that care about you like you're family. Amber would do anything for you. You have a home, friends, and Woggy."

"For now," he said, tugging on a strand of her hair.

"Everything is temporary. Happiness doesn't last forever, but neither do the bad days. Soon, this will be over. Amber will be your alpha, and you'll get to move on. Don't forget that, okay?"

"How can you be so optimistic?" he asked. In the next twenty-four hours, he'd either have everything he'd ever wanted, or lose it all. Again.

She sat up and turned to face him. "It's just a choice. You miss your mom, but I wish mine would drop dead. She's the only person, other than Selena I guess, that I've ever hated. I was angry when I was your age, but one day I realized that every moment I spent being angry was a waste. I was letting her win. She wanted me to be ruthless, so instead I chose compassion. She wanted me to be ambitious, so instead I chose generosity. I can't live my life expecting every day to be awful, so I look for the positive and I cling to it like a life preserver."

There was a lot of positive, if he looked for it. He got to cook almost every night. He had Woggy, Ceri, and his pack. Even if he had to run after this, at least he'd had a good month. He'd forgotten what it felt like to be safe.

He rubbed his hands over his face. That was probably why this had shaken him up so much. Every morning he woke up terrified he'd lose this all. Today, that nightmare had been perilously close to coming true.

Amber and Genevieve walked over toward them. They both looked upset. He stood abruptly and walked over to Amber, wrapping her in a tight hug.

She stood shocked for a moment before returning the hug. She was trembling. It was easy to forget she didn't know any more about this than they did. He couldn't imagine being in her position. The pressure had to be unbearable.

After a moment he stepped back awkwardly, embarrassed by the impulsive action. "Sorry, you just...I'm just glad we're all okay."

She gave him an odd look but smiled. "Yeah, we're okay."

"We should order pizza tonight," Genevieve said forcing her lips to turn up to a smile. "And we got stuff for s'mores. We could have a bonfire!"

He grinned at her. That's exactly what they needed. A celebration, and a distraction. "I love s'mores."

Amber laughed and punched Genevieve on the shoulder. "All you people ever think about is food."

"The beast hungers," Genevieve said, growling dramatically.

Ceri bumped his elbow and winked at him. He smiled back. This sucked, but he could be optimistic for one more night.

CHAPTER 37

AMBER

Amber licked the sticky marshmallow off her fingers and laughed at Tommy, who was just setting marshmallows on fire instead of roasting them now.

She'd done this so often with her brothers. It still wasn't exactly cool this time of year in Texas, but that hadn't stopped them from spending all their time outside. Bonfires, sneaking beers, and mudding in their trucks had been the best part of high school.

Grabbing a broken piece of chocolate, she retreated back into the house. Tomorrow was the day of reckoning. She wasn't ready, but these sorts of thing never waited for you to be ready.

She walked back to her room and plopped down in one of the chairs they'd found in the attic. It was red brocade and looked a little like a throne. Genevieve had left it in her room as a joke: red for the alpha. She'd been meaning to move it out but hadn't ever gotten around to it. There was always something more important to do.

Sighing, she pulled out her phone. Her hand shook a little as she dialed Derek's number. So much had changed since she'd talked to him last. It felt like a lifetime ago. It rang twice, seeming overly loud in her ear.

"Yo, this is Derek's phone," her eldest brother said, answering the call.

She considered hanging up right away and not speaking, but she couldn't bring herself to. "Heyyy, Jackson."

There was a pause and a shuffling noise. "Amber?"

"The one and only," she said, trying to sound like her old self, but it came off a little sad. She'd completely forgotten it was Sunday. The weekly family dinner must have continued. That shouldn't have surprised her. A little thing like your son dying and your daughter leaving shouldn't mess with such an important tradition.

Jackson cleared his throat. "How are you these days?"

"Fine, nothing special going on," she said with a wince. Palming her face, she was glad she was sitting in a dark room alone where no one could see her facial expressions.

"Right."

She wanted to demand he put Derek on the phone, but that would be a little insulting. This might be her last chance to talk to her brother. She and Jackson had never been close. He'd been half grown by the time she and Dylan were even born. When she was in high school, she'd jokingly called him Uncle J.

"How have you been? Still seeing…Mary? Or whatever her name was," she asked finally, uncomfortable with the silence.

"Maria, and no, we broke up four years ago," he said, a little bitterness leaking into his voice. The *you would have known that if you had called* hung unspoken between them. She didn't need him to say it out loud to feel the reprimand. "Derek is finally out of the bathroom. Here he is, I'm sure you don't want to talk to me anyway."

Before she could protest, the phone was handed off.

"Amber?" Derek said, sounding surprised.

"Yeah," she said shortly, uncomfortably guilty after the short conversation with Jackson.

"What's wrong?"

"Who said anything was wrong?" she asked, leaning back in her chair.

"*You* called *me*. That hasn't happened in at least six years." A door shut in the background of the call and gravel crunched under his feet. He'd always preferred to take his calls out in the shop, away from the ruckus of the family.

"I just…wanted to see how you were. Catch up, or something," she said.

He sighed. "Well, I'm still working for dad. I've been thinking about opening my own shop, but I'd have to leave town to do that. The old man would throw a fit if he thought I was trying to compete with him."

"You? Get out of town? Never thought I'd see the day," she said with a laugh.

"You aren't the only one that wanted to get out. I've been thinking about leaving for a while, it's just never seemed like a good time. Now dad is having problems."

"He's got three other kids to take care of him. You should go, if you want to."

"It might have been easy for you to leave, but it's not that simple for me," he said. His tone was normal, but she felt the verbal jab like a kick to the chest.

"No part of that was easy, but thanks for the reminder," she snapped, angry that the old wound still hurt so much.

Derek sigh. "Sorry, I just…it sucks. I wish you and mom would reconcile."

"This is why I don't call," she said, pushing out of the chair. She couldn't sit still when she was this agitated. "It's always a guilt trip. I can't check in on any of you without you giving me hell. None of you will let me forget what happened."

"Amber, come on, don't be like that—"

"No, you *don't be like that*. Just…I love you, okay? Give my love to the whole family, even Mom. I'll talk to you later."

"Wait—"

She hung up the call, breaths coming fast as tears stung her eyes. She hated crying. Hated this weak, guilty, helpless feeling that came with remembering what had happened.

Dropping to the floor, she buried her face in her knees. The wolf howled inside her. It wanted the pack and comfort. She refused to go to them. They couldn't see her like this.

CHAPTER 38

GENEVIEVE

Genevieve curled her hand into a fist to keep the shaking from being visible. The betas had shown up a few minutes ago. Thallan was watching the group, looking bored and smoking *in the house*. It was going to stink for days.

When Shane had greeted them this time there was no hint of flirtation, or even that he'd been to the house before. Tension was thick in the group of betas, which, as she'd read, was common when packs gathered. Everyone's instincts went a little haywire, and it was hard to hold back the need to compete for dominance.

"She is not a werewolf," a tall, lanky man with blond hair and a thick beard said, pointing at Ceri.

Genevieve tensed, ready to argue if needed. She had read *every* rule she could find. There was no reason they shouldn't be allowed to bring Ceri with them. Amber hadn't ever come out and said it, but it felt like she'd accepted the witch as part of the pack. Genevieve certainly had. Especially after what they'd done on Halloween. She'd go to bat for Ceri anytime, and she knew the witch would do the same.

"She's with us. With the pack," Amber said, stepping closer to the witch. "I'm not leaving her behind."

"It's Amber's choice," Shane said, waving away the other beta's objection. "Let's go."

They were ushered outside and piled into a van that Shane was driving. She crawled to the very back seat and squeezed into a corner. Shane stopped Thallan before he climbed in.

"No smoking in my car," he said, pointing at the smoldering cigarette in the elf's hand.

Thallan rolled his eyes and took a long drag before flicking it to the ground and snuffing it out with the toe of his leather shoe. He blew the smoke in Shane's face and climbed in.

A muscle in Shane's jaw jumped as he glared at the elf, but he didn't say anything. The blond werewolf joined them, sitting in the front seat, while the rest of the betas followed in a different car.

Amber sat in front of her, eyes fixed on a distant point. She was tense and it was making Genevieve anxious. She wanted to reassure her but she couldn't in front of these strangers.

These other wolves, even Shane, felt like a threat. Every instinct she had was screaming at her to fight and run. Instead, they were walking into even more danger. Willingly. Well...sort of willingly.

Shane drove them away from Portland. The woods grew deeper and darker as the sun slipped lower in the sky and the minutes ticked by. The only sound was the rumble of tires on asphalt.

She sighed in relief as as he turned down a long driveway. Crammed with Tommy and Ceri in the back of the van was an uncomfortable spot.

"This property is owned by the regional council," Shane said, breaking the silence. "It's used for events like this one, or for celebrations."

"That's useful," Amber replied.

"How long has the council owned it?" Genevieve asked, desperate to keep the conversation going. Silence wasn't really her thing. Especially tense, awkward silences.

"Since Portland was founded, but they've been using it since long before that," Shane said.

"This will only be the third time a bitten wolf has been tested here," Blondie said, glancing at them in the rearview mirror. She couldn't quite tell from his tone if he was happy about that or not. Shane had a good poker face, but this guy was completely unreadable.

The driveway forked off in two directions. Shane took the left path, and they arrived in a small clearing already packed with other vehicles. There must have been hundreds of people there. They parked near the front in a spot that must have been reserved for them.

Shane put the van in park and looked back. "Amber should answer any questions directed at your pack. Since you're bitten wolves, I'd like to remind your pack not to make eye contact with the other alphas. It could be taken as a challenge, and that's the last thing you need to deal with today."

Everyone nodded. She clasped her hands together anxiously. There was so much to remember. So many ways to screw up. Maybe they'd let her stay in the van.

They climbed out, and she stuck to Tommy and Ceri, taking comfort in their closeness. Before them was a wooden wall at least thirty feet high. The area felt a little like The Market, full of magic, and old.

They were escorted by the group of betas to the wide door in the center of the wall. Passing over the threshold, she suppressed a shiver as magical wards tingled over her skin.

She had to suppress another shiver when she saw the group of alphas gathered in front of them. The urge to challenge them was just as strong as the urge to roll over and show her belly. Behind them were dozens of packs. This must have attracted every werewolf in the area.

Ceri stiffened beside her. She followed her line of sight off to the side and found herself looking at the last person she expected to see there: Selena Blackwood. She'd managed to get off all the slime she'd been drenched in last time they saw her.

CHAPTER 39

AMBER

Shane gave Amber one last glance before leading the other betas to the side. She and her pack were left standing before the alphas, and that witch.

Selena only had eyes for Ceri. The witch's expression was cold and blank, but nothing could hide the rage in her eyes. Amber curled her hand into a fist and stepped in front of her pack, shielding them.

A grizzled, old alpha she assumed was Jameson stepped forward from the group. His gray hair was streaked with white, as was his thick beard. Three old scars stretched from his temple to his jaw where he must have been clawed years ago. Most injuries didn't cause scars on a werewolf; the cuts must have been deep.

"Amber Hale, before we begin the Trials, you have one last chance to consider the offer from Alpha Donovan Lockhart to admit you into his pack. If you accept, your alpha powers will be stripped from you and given to him, strengthening your new pack," he explained, his deep voice filling the space.

She ground her teeth together, refusing to acknowledge Donovan. "I decline."

A murmur went through the gathered crowd, but none of the alphas looked surprised. Jameson accepted her statement with a nod. "So be it."

"What is she doing here?" she asked, pointing at Selena. The witch's presence was gnawing at her. This was bad enough with one person here who wanted her to fail.

The old alpha's brows furrowed. "A member of a local coven assists with the Trials. Is that a problem?"

She didn't like the sound of that, but there wasn't much she could do to object. The only reason Selena had to hate her was because of what happened on Halloween, which wasn't exactly something she wanted to explain.

"I guess we'll find out," she said finally.

Jameson pursed his lips, looking annoyed by her response. He sighed and turned his attention to the elf standing to her right. "Thallan Firedale, as the sponsor for Amber

Hale, do you swear that she has maintained conduct becoming an alpha through the waning and the waxing of the moon?"

"I swear it," Thallan said drily.

Jameson motioned at Selena, who followed him as he walked toward the stone set in the center of the open area. He stopped in front of it and folded his hands in front of him, an air of ritual and formality settling over him. "Amber Hale, please come forward."

She took a steadying breath and joined them, standing on the opposite side of the stone. The top was discolored as if it had rusted. However, the old lingering scent of blood made it clear what had caused the discoloration.

"Once the Trials have begun, they cannot be stopped. Do you understand?" Jameson asked.

She looked up to his grizzled face and nodded. "I understand."

He pulled a small knife from his waistband. The handle was wooden, but the blade gleamed in the setting sun. "By the Moon, who gives us strength. By the Night, who gives us sight. By the Wolf, who gives us life. Let the candidate's worthiness be measured." He held his hand over the stone and drew the blade across his palm without flinching. Smoke curled up from the wound. The blade must have been silver.

He curled his hand into a fist and squeezed. Blood dripped onto the stone, and magic rose around them. It was invisible, but she could feel it like a cool breeze. Goosebumps erupted on her arms.

He handed the knife to her. She took it, willing her hands not to shake. Before she could think too hard about what she had to do, she extended her hand over the stone and cut her palm. There was no turning back.

It hurt more than she expected, but she kept the hiss of pain from escaping. As her blood hit the stone, the magic in the air shifted. It seeped inside her, and the clouds parted above them. Moonlight fell on them, and she turned her eyes to the sky. The moon was full and bright.

Just like that first night it sang to her, but she felt its call even deeper than before. She wanted to change. Run. Hunt. But first, she had to pass the Trials.

CHAPTER 40

AMBER

"The Trials test both your skills and your worthiness as a leader. You must display speed, cunning, strength, resolve, and control," Jameson said.

Amber nodded. They'd read that much, but that didn't actually explain *what* the trials were.

"The first trial is timed." Jameson stepped aside. "You will have four minutes to get through the obstacle course. You may use whatever form you prefer, shifting at any point throughout the course. We will watch from above, but no one is permitted to interfere or assist you," he said, casting a warning look at her pack. "Please strip down, then you can begin whenever you're ready."

She looked at the alpha, confused. "Strip down?"

Amusement flitted across his face before he schooled his features back to a neutral expression. "Nudity is a human concern. You'll become comfortable with it in time. If you prefer to shred your clothes during the shift, that is your choice. However, it might slow you down."

This was worse than those nightmares where you're naked in front of everyone you know…because it was real. A guy must have thought this up, because only a guy would insist you prove your worth by running naked through an obstacle course.

She yanked her shirt off angrily. No one reacted to the nudity except for Tommy, who turned his head away. He wasn't so embarrassed this time, just doing his best to be polite, which she appreciated.

Jameson took her crumpled bundle of clothes. She shivered in the cool night air. Not because she was cold, just out of sheer nervousness.

"The timer will begin as soon as you touch the wall," he said, pointing at the start of the course.

The first obstacle hid the rest. The wall was twenty feet tall. A rope hung down from the top, but she'd have to jump high enough to grab it without help. There wasn't a single handhold to grab and climb up.

Waiting any longer would just make the nerves worse. With one last glance at her pack, she took off at a run. Strength pumped through her as the wolf urged her on. She knew she shouldn't shift yet, but the wolf was eager to break free.

She jumped, weightless for a brief second before her hands wrapped around the thick rope. Her bare feet scraped against the wood as she hauled herself toward the top. She swung her right leg over first, then her left. From her perch, she took in the rest of the course. From here she had to jump across a small mud pit followed by a tunnel. It was hard to see what came after that.

Gritting her teeth, she braced her feet against the wall and launched herself forward. She flailed, trying to stay upright, then hit the ground. She landed on her feet. Barely.

The top of the tunnel came up chest high, but there was no way she could run through it without shifting. The change rolled over her as she ran toward the tunnel, completing just in time for her to duck inside.

It smelled like dirt and old moss. She'd expected a trap or a trick, but there was nothing special about this part of the obstacle course so far. It was a basic test. It proved she could shift, and that she was a werewolf, but that was it.

She darted into the tunnel entrance. The close quarters pressed in around her but her eyes quickly adjusted to the darkness. After a few turns, she reached the end. Slowing to a walk she stepped out cautiously.

The next obstacle was going to be a little trickier. She shifted back to her human form and looked up at the tall wooden posts that stood over the pit of spikes.

She'd already hesitated for too long. With a deep breath she ran for the first post, launching herself at it. She wrapped her arms around it and braced her feet against the rough wood. One step at a time she worked her way to the top.

The posts were spaced fairly close together. It was obvious the intention was for her to hop from one to the other. She could feel her pack. They were just behind her with the others, watching intently.

She jumped to the next post, wobbling slightly as she landed. Without pausing, she jumped to the next and the next, a wild thrill running through her. Maybe she could do this. Pass the Trials. Keep her pack.

The last pillar was a few feet away. She leaped for it, and for one elated moment, she was standing on it. Sudden pain lanced through her ankle, and it forcibly twisted. She pitched forward and fell.

Twisting in the air, she managed to grab the pillar before she hit the ground. Claws from her half-shifted hands dug into the hard wood as she held herself inches above the sharp spikes.

She dragged herself back up, cursing herself for her overconfidence. She'd been sure she'd landed that one. It had felt like something hit her ankle.

Ignoring the pain shooting through her leg, she jumped to the safety of the platform. In front of her was a doorway, and inside, it was pitch black.

She shifted, already feeling the wear of changing forms so many times in a row, and stepped over the threshold. The lack of light shouldn't have been a problem, but her eyes weren't adjusting to the darkness. She sniffed the air, and the unmistakeable scent of magic was present. This must be part of the test.

Letting her nose guide her, she took two cautious steps forward. With no idea how much time she had left, every second felt like an eternity. She picked up her pace and trotted forward. Underneath the other smells was the faint scent of Jameson, as if he'd walked this path earlier in the day.

That must be her clue. Nose to the ground, she moved even faster. Her tail hit something and she yelped in surprise but nothing happened. There must be walls around her, perhaps even a maze. The wolf grew impatient and urged her forward. It wasn't afraid. It had the scent and trusted it to lead them out of this darkness.

Giving in to those instincts, she let the wolf push them onward. The smell of magic grew stronger, almost overpowering Jameson's scent for a moment. She paused, one paw in the air, then sniffed carefully. Something popped and an awful smell filled the air.

In a panic, she fell backward, shifting to her human form. She covered her nose and mouth with her hands, wishing she had her shirt to breathe through. The smell dissipated almost immediately but the burning in her nose persisted.

She felt around on the ground for whatever had exploded but there was nothing. Reaching tentatively to the side she found a wall, and a foot above her, the ceiling. These tests had seemed simple but a trap made it more complicated. She wished she knew how much time she had left.

Shifting back, she sniffed the ground. The scent she'd been following might as well have been gone. She couldn't smell anything past the lingering burning in her nose.

With a huff, she rubbed it against her paw but that only made it hurt worse. Her bones ached from the back and forth of the shifts. And she was exhausted already.

"Amber, can you hear me?" Angel hissed in the darkness. "I can help you, if you want."

She shook her head vehemently, a motion that felt odd as a wolf, and glared in the demon's general direction. She'd been wondering when he'd show up.

"I could lead you out of here. You're running out of time," he said.

Ignoring him, she felt around for the wall, pressed her right side against it, and walked forward tentatively. No one could interfere so she had to get out on her own, no matter what. Making a deal with the demon wasn't an option.

The place felt like a maze. She ran faster as she started to panic. There couldn't be much time left. A flash of alarm startled her right before she ran smack into a wall.

"That looked like it hurt," Angel said. He was hovering close by, his warmth sinking into her fur.

Biting back a snarky response, she shook herself and tried to think through what had just happened. That hadn't been her emotion. It was from her pack. They must be able to see her still. She'd avoided using that bond because it felt intrusive but she hoped they'd forgive her for using it now.

A little more cautiously this time, she started walking again. As she moved she let the bond grow in her mind. There was worry, fear, and anger. She wasn't sure what that last one was about, but the others she expected.

She took off at a run again. When the alarm shot through her again, she slid to a halt and took a cautious step forward. Her nose bumped against the wall. She felt around until she had a clear path then took off at a run again. It wasn't as fast as following the scent, but it was all she had.

CHAPTER 41

CERI

It was like Amber had gone blind suddenly. She wasn't even trying to follow the scent anymore. It didn't make any sense, unless…

"Are there boobytraps in there?" Ceri demanded, her fingers gripping the wooden railing tightly.

Jameson, who stood a few paces away from her, frowned and shook his head. "The first test is simple. She had to follow the scent but it looks like she lost it."

She had thought she sensed a flicker of magic when Amber had stumbled on the wooden posts. But she was sure of it now. Someone was sabotaging Amber's Trials.

It wasn't a question of who; it was obviously Donovan or Selena, most likely both working together. It was a question of *how.* Jameson had made it clear he wouldn't allow interference. She had a good feeling about the old alpha, so she believed him.

Amber's pack was watching the proceedings intently. She had taken off at a run and it was obvious she was about to smack into a wall again.

"*Stop,*" Tommy whispered under his breath.

Amber slid to a stop, taking a cautious step forward.

Tommy looked up, shocked. "Did she hear me?"

Genevieve shook her head. "No, but I think she can sense our feelings."

"What?" Tommy looked alarmed.

"We'll talk about it later. Keep watching. Try to tell her where to go," Genevieve urged.

Tommy turned back to the course and focused all his attention there. With less than a minute left on the timer, it was looking less and less like she'd complete the first test in time.

Ceri stepped away from the group and looked over at Donovan. He stood with his betas, watching the proceedings and laughing at Amber's struggles. Selena, however, stood alone. She wasn't speaking to anyone and didn't seem particularly interested in the

Trials. As Ceri stared at her, the witch lifted her head and met her gaze. Hate burned in her venomous green eyes.

Whether the sabotage had been her idea or not, she was the one doing it. Ceri had to get proof, or there would be no way of stopping her.

Thallan stepped up beside Ceri, startling her. "I see you've noticed as well."

She nodded. "Any suggestions on how to handle it?"

He pursed his lips thoughtfully. "No good ones."

The pack would help any way they could if she told them, but she was a little afraid Genevieve might do something stupid. Like try to eat Selena.

Her attention was pulled back to the obstacle course as Amber finally made it out. She raced up the last portion, a steep hill, but the buzzer rang loudly when she was only halfway up.

Amber didn't stop running despite her failure but it was too late. Genevieve cursed and turned away, her dainty features contorted in anger.

Donovan laughed loudly, pointing at her and saying something she couldn't quite hear to his companions. She heard the word bitten loud and clear, though.

One of the betas, the hot one that had defended her coming today, looked back at her. He seemed concerned rather than smug about Amber's failure. Maybe...he would help.

～

AMBER

She shifted back, humiliation coursing through her. Donovan's jeers carried across the open space. Her hearing was unfortunately good enough to catch every word.

A door opened ahead of her and Shane stood in the space. He motioned for her to join him. She walked over silently, looking everywhere but him. Jameson was right. The nudity wasn't bothering her anymore. But the failure was.

"Chin up," Shane whispered as she fell in step beside him. "There's still four more chances."

"Was this the easiest trial?" she asked.

Shane hesitated, then nodded.

"Great."

They walked into some kind of arena. Her toes dug into hard-packed dirt as she followed Shane to the center of the space.

"Wait here," he said before jogging toward the side of the pit. He jumped up and grabbed the top of the wall, pulling himself up to join the others.

Jameson in the center of the group, her pack on his left. "In one minute, the doors below me will open. Wolves have no natural predators in the wild, but we do have one foe. A normal wolf would never be able to defeat this animal on their own, but we are not normal. We have been gifted with greater size and strength. As alpha, you must be able to defend your pack against even the most formidable threats. This trial demands you prove that you are capable of doing this."

She swallowed nervously. There was really only one thing that could walk out of those doors and she did not want to fight it. At all. "Do I have to kill it?"

Jameson nodded solemnly. "Yes. However, there is no time limit for this Trial. You will either prevail, or you will perish."

Well, shit. That wasn't exactly comforting. "Can I change now?"

"Yes, the doors will open in ten seconds," he said.

She shifted quickly, her heart pounding. When those witches had attacked, she'd only had time to react. Knowing what was coming filled her with fear. Having an audience didn't help much either. She really didn't want to be ripped apart in front of her pack.

Ceri leaned over the edge, making some kind of odd hand signal. She had no idea what to make of it but it felt like a warning. Since she knew she was about to have to fight something, that didn't make any sense. Was there something else going on?

The doors creaked open, pushing any thoughts of warnings out of her head. From the darkness came a huff and a rumbling growl.

She dug her paws into the dirt and crouched down, muscles tensed. One massive paw stepped into the fading light, then another. The bear's mouth hung open, saliva dripping onto the ground in long strings.

Thick brown fur covered the bulky animal. It padded out, watching her carefully. Once it was free of the confining room, it stood on its hind legs, and roared.

The challenge was clear. She lifted her head and howled, claiming the ring as her own.

The bear dropped down to four feet. Then it charged.

CHAPTER 42

CERI

Ceri's fingers dug into the wooden railing as the bear charged Amber. She wanted to look away but was terrified to. This was awful, all of it. There had to be a better way to prove Amber was worthy than killing some poor animal.

The crowd erupted in cheers as they crashed into each other, drowning out the vicious growling. Tommy wrapped an arm around her shoulders and she realized tears were streaming down her face.

Wiping them away angrily, she squeezed him back. She should be trying to take care of him, not the other way around. He wasn't even an adult.

The bear swiped at Amber, catching her in the shoulder. She was tossed back twenty feet and hit the ground limply. Tommy's fingers convulsed on her shoulder, but she was barely paying attention.

When the bear had struck her, for a brief moment, there had been a curl of smoke. It wasn't something you'd see if you weren't looking for it. But it had been there. Just like the last test, this one was being sabotaged.

She looked up and caught Shane's gaze. He glanced at Donovan and a muscle in his jaw jumped.

"I'll be right back," she said, squeezing Tommy's hand. He nodded and stepped away, eyes glued to the fight.

She tapped Thallan as she passed him. He followed her through the crowd and down the wooden steps that led back to the ground. She ducked under the scaffolding that supported the stadium seating and waited.

The elf leaned against the wall and crossed his arms, clearly bored. A moment later, Shane joined them. Lifting her hand, she cast a simple muffling spell.

"She's being sabotaged and we both know it," she said angrily.

"I know, but I can't be the one that protests. It has to be Thallan," Shane said, pointing at the elf. "Especially as Jameson's beta, I have to remain neutral."

"How does he protest it?" she asked.

Shane took a deep breath, rubbing his hand along his stubbled jaw. "Bring your proof to Jameson. Declare the interference, accuse who you suspect, and be prepared to prove it."

"How the hell are we supposed to get proof?" She threw her hands in the air, exasperated.

"I want to help you, but I can't. Try to think outside the box, okay?" he said, taking a step back. "I shouldn't have even come down here. And I can't stay."

"Fine." She turned away and pinched the bridge of her nose between her thumb and forefinger.

"Perhaps we just protest and figure it out along the way?" Thallan suggested, unhelpfully.

"That won't work and you know it."

He shrugged. "You think there is something on the bear's claws, right? If you demand they be examined, they'll find evidence of interference."

She shook her head. "It's probably gone by now. If I was doing this, I would have put just enough so that the first few swipes got it in her bloodstream, but it would be undetectable after that."

∼

GENEVIEVE

Genevieve looked behind her and realized Ceri was gone. So was Thallan. Shane walked past and gave her a strange look, almost guilty.

She grabbed Tommy and tugged his head down so she could whisper, "Do you know where Ceri is?"

He looked around, his eyebrows drawing together, then shook his head.

"Come on," she said, dragging him after her. Ceri was up to something, and there was no way she was going to leave them out of it.

She followed her nose. Thallan left a distinct trail that even a human could follow. It led through the crowd, then down the stairs.

There was a glimpse of white through the scaffolding that looked like Ceri's dress, but she couldn't hear them talking, or even their heartbeats.

She doubted Thallan and Ceri were just standing in there silently, so they were keeping anyone from hearing them intentionally.

"I think I see them," Tommy whispered.

"Me too."

They slipped under the scaffolding and walked over. Genevieve was turned away from Thallan like she was angry. The elf looked unconcerned, as always, but he was on his third or fourth cigarette. Even he didn't usually smoke that much.

Thallan looked up as they drew close but didn't say anything. Static zipped over her skin as she crossed some kind of invisible barrier.

She put her hands on her hips. "What the hell is going on?"

Ceri jumped and whipped around, her eyes bouncing between her and Tommy. "Umm, I just needed a minute...alone."

"Don't lie to us," Tommy said, sounding really hurt. He and Ceri had gotten pretty close over the last month.

"You either think Amber is being sabotaged or that she's about to die. Which is it?" she asked, wanting to get to the point.

Ceri swallowed uncomfortably. "Sabotage."

"Shane was down here, right? What did he say? Can we stop it?"

"Thallan has to protest it to Jameson, and then we have to prove that someone is interfering," Ceri said with a sigh. "We have a few minutes to figure something out, or Amber is going to die."

Genevieve crossed her arms, thinking. She'd been great in school debate competitions when she'd had to improvise but there had never been stakes this high before. "What if... we bluff."

Ceri looked up sharply. "Bluff?"

"Yeah, we know they're sabotaging her. Do you have any idea how?" she asked, trying to appear more confident than she felt.

"I know what I'd do," Ceri answered with a shrug.

"Then we go to Jameson, say what you think is happening, and point him toward something that would prove it. Is there anything that Selena or Donovan have done that would leave a trace?"

"When she was in the dark maze it looked like something blew up in her face. Could that have left a residue?" Tommy asked.

"It might have. It would be hard to detect, and it would be a very small amount," Ceri said.

"I could go look for it while you start the protest. If I find something, I'll bring it back."

Bluffing was risky but they didn't have many options. She might be able to pull it off just long enough for Tommy and Ceri to find something. "What should I tell them is in there?"

"Glass," Ceri said with a decisive nod. "If she left something, it would have had to be in glass. A very thin tube most likely, something that would shatter into pieces so small they're almost a powder."

"Do we even have time to find that?" Tommy asked.

"Probably not," Ceri admitted.

"Then we have to go with the silver. If Selena used it on the bear, then wouldn't she have some on her?" she asked.

"Yes, that stuff gets everywhere, like glitter," Ceri said, her tone going thoughtful.

"Are you thinking what I'm thinking?" she asked.

Ceri nodded. "Do you know how to do the protest?"

"Yes," she turned to Thallan. "Do I need to write this down, or can you remember it?"

"I think I'm capable of remembering it," he said, flicking his cigarette to the ground and snuffing it out with the toe of his shoe.

"Alright, then this is what you need to say," she said. Her heart was beating so fast she almost couldn't breathe. She hoped she remembered it correctly, or Amber was screwed. And it would be her fault.

CHAPTER 43

CERI

Thallan was walking too slowly. He had no sense of urgency at all, and it made Ceri want to strangle him. They had to squeeze through the crowd. Once they were back by the railing, she risked a glance down into the arena. Amber was stumbling around, barely dodging the bear's attacks.

"Alpha Clark Jameson," Thallan said, his voice booming over the noise of the crowd. "This sacred ritual has been tarnished by the actions of a coward. I name Donovan Lockhart as coward. I name Selena Blackwood as coward and mercenary."

Silence fell over the gathering. For a moment, the only sound was the huff of the bear.

"How dare—"

Jameson lifted his hand, cutting Donovan off. "In what manner have these Trials been sabotaged?"

"The first trial, through magic. A hex to twist the candidate's ankle, and a trap left to burn her nose. In this trial, through silver powder on the bear's claws."

Selena looked at Ceri directly. Her fingers twitched at her side like she wanted to throw a curse. She wouldn't be able to get away with it in a crowd like this, no matter how much the witch wanted to hurt her.

"Your protest is heard. Do you bring proof?" Jameson asked.

Ceri stepped forward. "Selena Blackwood will have silver on her body. Her hands, clothes, possibly her face. With a dust that fine, it's impossible to avoid getting it on you. If the maze were to be searched, you would find glass, but very little of it."

The old alpha waved the others back, parting the crowd. Selena stood a few feet away with her jaw clenched in anger. "How dare you accuse me of interfering in—"

"Occultatum fateor!" Ceri shouted, lifting her hand. The magic rushed between them, hitting Selena with a burst of light. Everywhere the silver had touched her glowed brightly. It was streaked across the hem of her dress and shimmering along the curve of her ear.

Jameson walked over to her and dragged his finger across one spot. Smoke drifted up from his finger. "Why is there silver on your clothes?"

"I work with silver often," Selena said, curling her hand into a fist. She held Jameson's gaze stubbornly.

"Please, stop the fight. Amber is being poisoned," Ceri begged. "You'll find silver residue on the bear's claws."

"This is a ridiculous ploy to save her friend," Donovan said, shoving forward to stand next to Selena. "A bitten wolf should never have been allowed to undergo the Trials in the first place."

Jameson pursed his lips. "If we stop this test, it must be counted as a failure."

"It's going to kill her if you don't stop the fight," she said, waving at the arena. "They've sabotaged her. You said we couldn't assist, but you also said no one could interfere."

"The sponsor must approve this action," Jameson said, looking at the elf.

Genevieve stepped up beside him, expression furious. "Do it. If she dies, it's a failure regardless."

"I approve, stop the fight," Thallan said, ignoring her.

Jameson nodded and waved at two of the alphas to follow him. The jumped down into the arena. Ceri couldn't wait for them to stop the bear, she had to get to Amber right now or the silver would keep weakening her.

∿

AMBER

Something was wrong. She shook her head but her vision swam. Her legs were weak. It wasn't from the pain, it was something else.

The bear charged in again. She darted under the first swing and bit its hind leg, wrenching it off balance. Frantically, she pulled on the pack bond. It was her only hope. Strength trickled through, and she had a brief burst of energy, but it was a losing battle.

She tried to lunge under the next swipe but her shoulder gave out and she hit the ground instead. It was numb now. Her good foot scraped against the dirt as she tried to force herself back to her feet.

The bear loomed over her, rising up to its hind feet. It roared and its paw came soaring toward her face. She couldn't move. This was not the way she thought she'd die, but maybe it was poetic justice that she die as a werewolf, just like Dylan.

Her eyes slipped shut, but she caught a glimpse of something hitting the side of the bear. Something large.

There was shouting. Someone shaking her. Pain. Bright light exploded in front of her. Ceri grabbed her and warmth rushed through her body, chasing away the bitter cold ache. She gasped for air and was finally able to take a full breath. The back of her hand scraped against a small rock and she realized she'd shifted back at some point.

"Keep still," Ceri warned.

"What? You can't—"

"There was silver on the bear's teeth or claws. Jameson stopped the test," Ceri said, pressing her hand against her chest. "Give me a moment and I'll have it purged from your body so it can heal."

"Am I going…to have to barf…again?" she asked as she panted. Whatever magic Ceri was using was *cold*. Her teeth clacked together as her body spasmed.

"Will she live?" Jameson asked, appearing near her head.

"Yes. I'm almost done, and then her body will take over the healing," Ceri said, shutting her eyes in concentration.

Amber's muscles twitched one last time, and then she felt her limbs fill with warmth. Pins and needles races down her arms as the feeling returned. Ceri removed her hands, and she pushed herself into a sitting position.

The wounds from the bear were stitching themselves back together, which was an odd feeling, to say the least. She watched one long cut close, pushing out debris as it went.

"Because this test had to be stopped, it must be counted as a failure," Jameson said, crouching beside her. "However, you can continue with the Trials, if you still wish to remain an alpha."

"So, even though someone interfered, they get rewarded, and I get punished?" she asked, anger clearing the shock.

Jameson's lips thinned. "They will be punished, but that will be separate from the Trials."

She sighed and let Ceri pull her to her feet. "I'll continue."

He nodded. "Take a moment with your friend while we prepare the next test. Then we will continue."

Ceri grabbed her arm and dragged her toward the room the bear had come out of. Once inside, she handed her a bottle of water.

"How'd you figure it out?" she asked before chugging half the bottle. It was cold and felt like heaven on her throat.

"It was mostly guesswork. How are you feeling?"

She shrugged. "Good enough. Just tired."

"Are Tommy and Gen okay?"

"Yes. Worried, but fine," Ceri said.

"I've failed two out of five of the tests. That means I have to pass the last three," she said, rubbing her hands over her face. They were still shaking, and she was so tired from the fight. "I can't do this."

Ceri grabbed her by the shoulders and shook her. "You can do it. You would have passed the first two if they hadn't sabotaged you. Even Donovan believes you can do this."

That comment brought a smirk to her face. "Well, when you put it like that."

CHAPTER 44

AMBER

The crowd was still gathered above the arena, but this time, Jameson and the other alphas were down there with her.

"I have personally inspected the weights. They have not been tampered with in any way," he said, pointing to the large boulder sitting in the dirt. There were three. The smallest one came up to her knee, while the largest would reach her hip. "You must lift them and carry them across that line. If you drop one, you fail the test and the Trials." About twenty feet away, a red line had been sprayed onto the dirt.

The outside of the boulders were mottled black and dirty as though they were coated in something. As she approached them, she realized where she had seen something like that before; her grandmother's old silver. Tentatively, she touched one. Burning pain seared her fingertips as her body weakened. The entire thing was shot through with silver. There was no way to pick the boulder up without touching it. Handling silver like this wouldn't poison her like it did when it had gotten in her bloodstream, but as long as she was in contact with it, she would be severely weakened.

She had failed the first two tests. That meant that she had to pass the last three or it was all over. In the previous test, while almost getting murdered by the bear, she'd felt something change in the bond. It was more than just sensing her pack's emotions—they had given her strength.

Taking a calming breath, she tried to think instead of react. This test had to be passable. The strength of an alpha lay with the pack. If she could use the bond to overcome the pain and the weakness the silver inflicted...that had to be it. It was the only way.

Please, help me, she begged the wolf internally. It looked out of her eyes, surveying the alphas watching. Donovan was grinning. He wanted nothing more than to see her to fail.

Walking toward the largest boulder, she crouched down and wrapped her arms around it. This was only going to get harder, so she wanted to get the largest one over with first. The wolf growled in her mind and the pack bond grew inside, stretching taut.

Strength that wasn't her own poured into her muscles. It couldn't stop the pain, but she could deal with that.

With a pained grunt, she forced herself to her feet. Claws extended form her fingertips, digging into the hard stone to keep it from slipping out of her hands. The pain was almost overwhelming. She could barely breathe. She took one wobbly step forward and almost toppled over.

The crowd gasped and began shouting. Half jeers, and half encouragement. She shut it all out and focused on the pack bond. She couldn't hear what her pack was saying but she could feel their strength. Tommy, the homeless kid with a heart of gold. Genevieve, an intelligent woman that hid her talents because she was afraid to fail. And Ceri, the white witch.

Her eyes snapped open. She wasn't sure when Ceri had become a part of the pack like that. There hadn't been a bite to bind her to them, but she could feel Ceri just like the others.

She took another step forward, then another, and another. The red line drew closer and she was filled with elation and determination from her pack. It mixed with her own, giving her a new kind of strength. She could do this.

The cheers increased as she drew close to the line, drowning out the boos completely. She picked up her pace. Her legs were shaking and it felt like she had no flesh left on her arms, but she didn't stop. Sweat rolled down her forehead and slipped into her eye. It stung and her vision blurred but she could still see that red line. Angel was floating behind it. He was shouting encouragement too, almost like he cared if she made it.

Grinding her teeth together, she took the final three steps to cross the line. She dropped the stone at her feet and turned back to the other alphas. Donovan's face was beet-red with fury, but Jameson was smiling.

Straightening her shoulders, she walked back to the next boulder. Success felt damn good.

CHAPTER 45

AMBER

"Kick this test's ass!" Genevieve shouted, leaning out from the crowd.

Amber winked at her with a smile as she followed Jameson into the squat building. The rest of the alphas, and Thallan, filed in behind them. The cottage consisted of a single room with roughly hewn floors and old wooden chairs set in a semicircle. It was dark and quiet, a stark contrast to the loud arena.

"Your physical body and your pack bond have been tested," Jameson said, folding his arms in front of him. "However, an alpha must also be in control of his mind. The fourth trial tests your mind." He opened the lid of an ornate wooden box and lifted out a smoking pipe. A rich, warm scent drifted toward her.

"Am I meant to say no to drugs?" she asked, raising her eyebrow.

A few of the alphas chuckled, and she even got a smirk from Jameson. "Aconite, or wolfsbane, is a poison that used to be used to kill wolves and werewolves alike in darker times. However, while searching for an antidote for the poison, the first Alpha discovered something. When combined with myrrh and dogwood under a full moon, it changes. Instead of killing you, it opens your mind to the wolf within. It allows you to face your inner demons."

She swallowed uncomfortably at the word demon. Hopefully Angel wouldn't be waiting for her in her mind. "Let me guess. If I fail to defeat my *inner demons,*" she used air quotes to emphasize the phrase, "I'll die?"

Jameson shrugged. "Not immediately. The ones that fail simply do not wake up."

"Will I be timed?"

He shook his head. "Not really. If you haven't woken by dawn, we'll assume you have failed, but most people pass or fail within less than a minute. Though, it will seem longer to you."

She nodded and shifted on her bare feet. The movement reminded her she was standing naked in a room full of strangers, but she shoved the embarrassment down. No one seemed to care; they were all focused on the Trials just like she was. "Okay, let's do this."

Jameson pulled an oddly shaped lighter from his pocket and handed her the pipe. "Three puffs as I light it."

She eyed the mouthpiece, hoping they washed it between trials, then put it in her mouth. It felt awkward, and she was sure she wasn't holding it right. Jameson clicked the lighter and passed the flame in a tight circle over the bowl of tightly packed herbs.

"Inhale," he reminded her.

She sucked in and her mouth filled with smoke, making her eyes water. She blew it out of the corner of her mouth and tamped down on the urge to cough. Whatever was in the smoke was making her tongue go numb.

Dutifully, she puffed twice more. Her entire body tingled. A loud ringing in her ears drowned out all sound. Gray seeped in at the edges of her vision. She pulled the pipe from her mouth and tried to hand it to Jameson but her body was numb and she was...she was...

CHAPTER 46

AMBER

"Amber!" Dylan shouted, wrapping her in a tight hug. "Tonight is the night. I can already feel the moon calling to me."

She rolled her eyes and slapped him on the arm. "No, you can't. Quit being so dramatic."

He grinned, his whole face lighting up. "I'm going to find a way to get you in the pack too, I promise."

"I'm not worried about it, okay? If they didn't want me, there must be a reason. Maybe I wouldn't be able to handle the change." She wrapped him in another hug. "I still think you should tell mom and dad. They're going to freak when they find out."

"That's exactly why I'm not telling them until it's done. They take bad news better once they can't do anything about it. Ask forgiveness, not permission. You know how it goes."

She snorted and buried her face in his neck. "That only works for you because you're their favorite."

"No, I'm not!" he protested, pushing her back.

Dark. Cold. Something growled behind her. She turned and found herself looking into the face of a large, ruddy wolf. Its eyes glowed red.

"Weak." It spoke without moving its mouth, but she knew the words came from it none-theless. With soundless steps, it prowled around her. "Angry."

"Who are you?" Her body trembled but she couldn't move. "Why are you showing me those memories?"

"You let your brother die," it said.

"No!" Her voice echoed around them, repeating over and over until it made her head ache. "I didn't know it would kill him. I didn't know."

The alpha held Dylan down, one paw on his back, then struck. His teeth sunk in deep. Dylan screamed. He wasn't supposed to scream. It wasn't supposed to hurt.

The werewolf jumped away, muscles tense. His tail drooped and he backed up, putting distance between himself and her brother. Then he lifted his head in a mournful howl. The pack's howls joined in.

Dylan screamed again, clawing at the bite wildly. She rushed from her place behind the pack and shoved her way through the circle. Dropping to her knees beside him, she tried to grab his arms, but his flailing limbs hit her. His eyes rolled back in his head and his body seized.

"Dylan!" She turned to the alpha. "What did you do? Help him! You have to help him!"

The alpha shook his head and turned away.

Crack. Dylan's arm snapped, wrenched to the side as his body tried to change but couldn't. Blood poured from the wound. From his eyes. From his mouth. Her hands hovered uselessly over his convulsing body.

More bones cracked and snapped as they were brutally twisted by magic gone wrong. His skin peeled away in random spots, replaced by mottled fur that grew straight out of the muscle.

"Am—ber—" he choked out, blood bubbling out of his lips. "Hel—p—hurts—"

"Someone help him!" she screamed, but the werewolves were all backing away...leaving him to die.

She wrapped her hands around her head, a guttural yell coming from her sore throat. It barely felt like she was the one screaming. The wolf huffed behind her.

Enraged, she turned and swung at it, barely registering that she could now move. "Stop showing me this!"

"You let him die, why shouldn't I show you your greatest failure?" the wolf taunted.

"I didn't let him die! I tried to save him. I would have done anything!"

The wolf's body slimmed, shifting back into a human form. Dylan's. Bloody, broken, and lifeless. His eyes opened slowly.

"Mom loved me best, and you let me take the bite even though you knew I might die. Why didn't you stop me?" he asked, lifting his broken and twisted arm toward her.

She took a step back and felt warmth seep through her shirt. "Get away from me."

"Don't freak out. It's just in your head," Angel whispered. Any other time she would have jerked away, but she was so relieved to not be *alone* with this horrible apparition that she leaned in closer instead.

"How do I make it stop?" she asked, voice thick with tears.

"Is what it's saying true?" Angel asked.

She shook her head. "No, I didn't know. I would have stopped him."

"Then convince it you're innocent," the demon suggested, drifting to her side and taking his warmth with him. "I can't help you in here, not even for a demon's mark."

"You blame yourself!" Dylan's ghoulish doppelganger screeched. "The guilt gnaws at you every day like cancer, spreading through your mind." It shifted back into the wolf, red eyes boring into her. "Why should I join my soul to such a pathetic creature? Even *you* don't think you deserve to be an alpha."

She took a step back. "You're...my wolf?"

The creature cocked its head and stepped closer. "Did you not recognize me?"

"No," she said as she lifted her hand toward it. She hadn't realized it was a completely separate creature. "I don't understand. I thought you were just...instincts. Maybe something more, but not like this."

"That is how we begin, but as you grow, I grow. You will not be able to see or hear me like this again for many years. If you even survive," the wolf said, circling her.

"Is the aconite killing me?" she asked.

The wolf huffed. "No, but I might."

She tensed, readying herself for an attack. "Why?"

It ignored her question and turned to the demon instead. "Why did you let the demon inside you?"

She glanced at Angel who was circling the wolf curiously now. "I had to in order to find a sponsor for these Trials."

The wolf watched the demon for a moment, then swiped at it. Angel shrieked and disappeared with a pop.

"What did you do to him?" she asked, alarmed.

"Just sent him away for a while. This is not for him." The wolf went back to circling her. "Why do you want to pass the Trials?"

"I have to protect Tommy and Genevieve. They're depending on me, and if I let them down, they'll be stuck in the System," she said, edging away from the wolf. It was too close; she wouldn't be able to move out of the way if it attacked.

"Would you defend them against anything?"

She furrowed her brows. "Of course I would."

"Even him?" the wolf asked, stepping aside to reveal an apparition of her brother. This time it was how she liked to remember him, young and smiling.

"Dylan is dead," she said, shaking her head.

"Yet everything you do is still centered around him. Your choice in career, your hatred of me, and your avoidance of your family. They were your pack once, but you abandoned them. Will you abandon this pack as soon as you make a mistake?" The wolf bared its teeth at her with its hackles raised.

"No!" she shouted, infuriated by the old memories and the accusation.

"Then choose. Your past, or your future?"

"What does that even mean?" She threw her hands in the air angrily.

The wolf vanished and Dylan's expression grew dark. He looked up at her with glowing red eyes. "I should have been the alpha and we both know it. So, if you want it, you have to defeat me and take it."

She bared her teeth at her twin, and for an instant, intensely hated every choice that had led her to this moment. Werewolves and their obsession with proving yourself, as if it mattered if she measured up to some stupid ideal. Donovan and his lust for power. And herself, for ever thinking she could do this.

Dylan lunged at her. She knew how he fought, and the wolf must have known, too. Or have been able to see it in her memories. She dodged the first punch and struck back. They threw elbows and kicks, and she bit him, even though they were fighting as humans.

She'd been running and shifting all day. Her body was exhausted, and so was her mind. Dylan caught her with an uppercut and she stumbled backward, spitting blood.

"Come on, little sister! You used to be tougher," he said with a sneer.

She growled and lunged at him, ducking down low at the last moment. Catching him around the waist, she lifted him from his feet and slammed him down. He wheezed as all the air was driven from his lungs.

He grabbed her hair and yanked her head to the side, but she dug her fingers into his face. He dropped his fistful of hair and tried to elbow her. She caught it and forced her way on top of him. Her elbow slipped through his defenses and cracked against his temple.

The strike dazed him, giving her the barest opening. She struck again, and again, bloodying his face. A vision of him dying, with blood bubbling from his lips, made her hesitate. He reared up and head-butted her.

Enraged, she punched him again as blood dripped from her nose and over her lips. He fell back and she pounded her fist into his face, his neck, anywhere she could reach. His struggles slowed until he lay underneath her, barely moving.

She stopped, horrified, and stared down at him.

His eyes opened, the red glow of the wolf shining through. "Finish it. Kill him."

"No," she sobbed, shoving off of him. "I won't kill my own brother. This isn't right. Why are you doing this?"

"Don't you want this? More than anything?" the wolf demanded, crawling toward her still wearing Dylan's face.

She shook her head. "I didn't want this at all. This was forced on me, and I'll do everything I can to be a good alpha, but no, I didn't want this."

The illusion fell away and the wolf sat before her. "You are strange."

She laughed, sounding hysterical even to her own ears. "You just had me fight my own dead brother, and you're calling me strange?"

The wolf huffed and she got the impression it muttered something unflattering under its breath. "Your pack submitted to you that day in the woods. To us."

She nodded. "Yes, I felt it. They chose me to be their alpha. That's why I can't abandon them."

"But you did not choose me," the wolf said. For a moment, she thought it sounded sad.

"No, I didn't," she said, honestly.

It rose to its feet. "Will you choose me now?"

She looked up, meeting its eyes in surprise. "Choose you?"

"Most werewolves do not know this, but while we're in this place I could leave you, turn you back to a human if I wanted. The first alpha didn't find an antidote to wolfsbane, he found a cure. You didn't want to be a werewolf, much less an alpha. I can give that choice back to you. Do you want to go back to being human and living your life however you choose, or will you choose to be the alpha?"

She froze, looking at the wolf in shock. A choice. It had been so long since she truly felt like she had one. "Why would you give me a choice?"

"Perhaps because it is the right thing to do," the wolf replied.

She looked down at bloodied knuckles and tried to think it through. But she realized there was nothing to consider, not now. She cared about Genevieve, Tommy, and Ceri. It wasn't just the wolf's instincts or the pack bond. She wanted to make sure they were safe.

Maybe a psychologist would say it was guilt from her brother's death motivating her, or the way her mother kicked her out. But those were the things that made her who she was today. The reasons didn't matter anymore.

She looked back up. "I want to be their alpha."

The wolf charged at her, hitting her like a battering ram. For a moment, she couldn't breathe, then everything shifted and power rushed through her body.

With a gasp, she awoke on the floor. The exposed beams of the cottage hung over her. Her body was trembling and she was panting as though she'd just run a marathon. Jameson was standing over her along with two other alphas. They looked extremely concerned.

"That was fucking strange," she said hoarsely. Grimacing, she sat up and rubbed her aching throat.

"We thought you were dying," Jameson said, handing her a bottle of water. "I've never seen anyone convulse like that and live."

She laughed. "I think I almost did die. The wolf…it…"

He nodded solemnly in understanding. "You are a vessel for two souls now. It changes you." He extended his hand, which she took, and pulled her to her feet. "It's time for the final trial."

She met his gaze, not terrified for the first time. "I'm ready."

CHAPTER 47

AMBER

"We will return to the altar for the final test."

Jameson led her outside. She saw Genevieve first, then Tommy, who slumped in relief upon spotting her. The pack bond was richer now, and she felt their worry and elation like her own emotions.

The crowd parted, then fell in behind them as they walked through a large, wide archway that led back to the beginning. Moonlight still shone on the altar like a spotlight.

They stopped a few feet away, and Jameson waited for the crowd to spread out around them. A few younger werewolves climbed up on the wall that had been the first obstacle in order to get a better view.

The tension within the crowd was palpable. Some of them wanted her to fail, some were just curious, but a few shouted encouragement. It was a relief to see that not every werewolf was a bigoted asshole.

The presiding alphas gathered behind Jameson, who turned to face her.

"As a werewolf, the rest of your life will be a struggle to balance your humanity with the soul of the wolf that now lives inside you," Jameson said, tapping on his chest over his heart. "You must be stronger than the wolf. You must stay in control. For this final test, you will take a potion that will force you to shift. In order to pass, you must keep from fully shifting for at least five—"

Donovan shoved his way forward, anger clear on his face. "I challenge her."

"I'd advise against doing this out of anger. You can't forget the unnecessary risk you are taking," Jameson said, folding his hands in front of him. "If you fail, your spot on this council will become hers."

Donovan sneered at the warning. "I'm not at risk of being beaten by a *bitten* wolf."

Genevieve stiffened at the insult, her lip curling up into a snarl, but she held herself still. Tommy moved a little closer and wrapped his arm around her. Even in the midst of all this, he thought about the people around him. He noticed everything.

"So be it. Your challenge is accepted. Please step down into the arena." Clearing his throat, he continued. "In normal circumstances, the test requires you to maintain control for five minutes. However, since you have been challenged, you must instead outlast Alpha Lockhart."

Amber kept her eyes on the stage as Donovan hopped down and walked over to stand beside her. His heart was beating as hard as hers. Every step of the way he had tried to make her fail. She was glad he was challenging her openly now. The strength of the wolf and her pack was pumping through her. He didn't stand a chance.

Jameson waved Selena forward. She approached, holding a large bowl. Leaning down, he inhaled deeply, then looked up at the witch. "If I find out that you have meddled with this potion in any way, you will answer to me. Your coven won't be able to protect you."

Selena's fingers tightened on the bowl, a slight tremor of fear running through her at the threat. "The potion is as it should be."

He took the bowl from her. "I will administer it to them myself."

Jameson hopped down as well and walked over to them holding two small cups. He handed one to each of us. "Dip the cup in here and drink the potion. It will force you to change. The challenge, laid out by Alpha Lockhart, is that you must resist the change longer than he does. We are werewolves, but we are human first. You must maintain control over yourself, and your wolf, for the rest of your life. If you want to lead others, you must prove today that you have that control."

She nodded, accepting the cup he handed her. Her pack was standing near the stage. Their presence was comforting, but it did add to the pressure.

Jameson lifted the bowl toward them. Inside was a strange, silvery liquid that smelled like grass after fresh rain. She and Donovan dipped their cups into the bowl in unison. Watching out of the corner of her eye to make sure he drained it completely, they both drank.

It was cool and almost sweet at first. As it slipped down her throat, it grew hotter and hotter, until it felt as if she'd drunk liquid fire.

Silently, Jameson directed them to sit across from each other next to the altar. She dropped to ground, crossing her legs and planting her hands on her knees. Donovan's eyes never left her.

"Remember, both of you will shift eventually," Jameson said.

Someone from the crowd shouted, "For the bitten!"

Cheers and boos fought for supremacy as some shouted encouragement to Donovan and some to her. She could barely make out what they were saying over the ringing in her ears.

The need to shift shot through her muscles. She ground her teeth together and fought against the urge. Nothing could make her give in.

Donovan sat across from her, his face red from the effort to control himself. Her muscles ached like they were cramping. Her leg twitched. The claws pressed against the skin of her fingertips. She curled her hands into a fist and sat up straighter, keeping her gaze locked on her foe.

He hated her. She didn't know why, but he truly hated her. She'd gotten involved in all this from bad luck. If it hadn't been her sitting here it might have been someone else. Or perhaps they would have fallen for his scheme. He might have gotten away with it. She'd make damn sure he never got a chance to do this to anyone else ever again.

"You will fail," he hissed at her, spittle flying from his lips.

"You don't really believe that," she shot back. "You were so afraid I'd succeed you tried to sabotage me."

He bared his teeth at her like a wild animal. "You should never have been allowed to participate in this ritual!"

"You should never have sent that omega to attack three innocent people. You brought this on yourself," she said, trying to calm down a little. The anger only pushed her closer to a shift. That was probably his plan for starting the argument in the first place.

He jerked and fell to the side, chest heaving as he gasped for air. His fingers curled inward and he shook, fighting so hard against the shift that his teeth clacked together.

The pain was growing worse. It spread out from her stomach like she might explode. Her head ached. Every muscle in her body seemed to have contracted. She dug her fingers into her legs to stay upright.

All around her, she could feel the pack bond. It could not stop this, but it gave her the strength to keep fighting. They believed in her. They needed her. And she had chosen them.

"You have no place in this world," he growled, a muscle in his jaw twitching.

"Yet, here I am," she said, leaning toward him.

Donovan screamed, his voice echoing through the arena. The crowd went silent. He arched back, and his clothes were ripped to shreds as he shifted.

The large black wolf turned his hateful eyes to her and lunged for her throat. Time seemed to slow as she gave in to the shift that she had been holding back for so long. She crashed into Donovan, and they tumbled to the ground.

His teeth dug into her chest, but she clamped her jaws around the back of his neck and jerked his head to the side. The challenge hadn't been enough. She knew it wouldn't be. She wanted to finish this now.

Strong hands grabbed her by the ruff of her neck and yanked her away. Jameson kept dragging her backward as three other alphas wrestled Donovan to the ground. He yelped as silver chains were tossed over his body to weaken him and hold him down. He howled, full of rage and pain.

Jameson slowly loosened his grip on her. "Shift back, if you can."

Her body shook with the effort, but slowly, she changed back. Panting, she turned on Jameson. "Why did you stop me?" she demanded with a growl.

"Donovan Lockhart has broken the sacred bonds of the Trial through interference and attempted murder," Jameson said, turning toward the crowd. His voice boomed throughout the space, silencing all the chatter. "His council spot is forfeit to you, and he will now answer for his actions according to the old laws."

Still shifted, Donovan growled and thrashed in his bonds. His pack was fighting in the crowd, but they were quickly subdued.

"Get them out of here," Jameson said. "It is time for a celebration as a new alpha joins our ranks. We are moon-blessed tonight, and we will *run*." The crowd erupted into cheers.

She was struck suddenly from the side and found herself in the middle of an enthusiastic group hug. Ceri was crying, Genevieve was shouting something, and Tommy was just hanging on for dear life.

"I'm okay, I'm okay," she repeated, trying to soothe the worry that was pounding against her mind through the bond.

Howls erupted all around them and the energy in the air changed. Everyone, even the ones that had wanted her to fail, were celebrating. People began stripping off their clothes and shifting. Wolves rushed past them, racing toward the forest.

Jameson walked toward them, eyes glowing bright red. "Run with us, and tomorrow we will talk about everything that has changed."

CHAPTER 48

CERI

Ceri stepped back from the group. She was so relieved Amber had survived and passed the Trials that she could barely breathe.

"This should be better than that first night," Amber said, nudging Genevieve with her elbow.

She laughed and pulled her shirt off over her head. Tommy blushed and turned away, stripping off in a more sedate manner.

Amber looked at her and held out her hand. "Will you join us?"

"I can't shift, and I'm not in the pack," she said, confused.

"You are, actually. I could feel it in the third trial. The bond isn't as strong as the others but I think it could be, even without turning you. Come with us tonight."

Her hand went to her chest, remembering the strange feeling she'd had throughout the Trials. She'd chalked it up to nerves and how much she wanted Amber to succeed. This whole part of the pack thing was something she'd have to talk to Amber about later, but like Jameson said, tonight was for running and tomorrow was for answers.

"I won't be able to keep up," she objected, not wanting to hold them back from enjoying themselves.

"I'll run with you," Tommy said, looking at her over his shoulder. "Please, come with us."

Even she could feel the excitement in the air. Shaking her head and smiling, she gathered her curls into a high ponytail. There was no reason *not* to go with them. "Alright. Let's do this."

Amber smiled at her and began to shift. Ceri bounced on her toes, excitement pumping through her. The energy around them was amazing. She'd never been around werewolves on a full moon. It was truly magical. She lifted her face to the moon and let the magic and the wonder sink into her.

Once all three of them were shifted they gathered around her and nudged her toward the woods. Amber ran ahead of the group, stretching her legs. She ran right behind with the others flanking her.

Amber lifted her head and howled. Her pack's voices joined the chorus. The sound awoke something in her, and she joined them. Any other time she'd be embarrassed to tilt her head back and howl like a wolf, but it felt right.

Genevieve raced up beside Amber, then started inching ahead of her. Amber seemed to take it as a challenge and they pulled away from her and Tommy. He chose to stay with her instead.

A gray wolf joined their race, and she smiled to herself. She guessed it was Shane, and based on the way he was chasing after Amber, Genevieve was right about him.

Tommy picked up his pace a little and she pushed herself to keep up. Her feet flew over the ground faster than she'd thought possible. She should have been tired already, but she knew she wouldn't tire for hours. Just like the pack bond had given Amber strength, it was giving her the same now.

CHAPTER 49

AMBER

Amber accepted the bottle of water Shane handed her gratefully. The run had been amazing, but she was thirsty, hungry, and exhausted now. He pulled out a slip of paper and scribbled something on it, then handed her that too.

"Here's my phone number. I hope you'll call soon," he said with a smile that was boy-next-door, apple pie, and *trouble* all rolled into one.

She took the card and fought to keep the smile off her face. "Just to chat?"

He tucked his thumbs in his belt loops. "I was thinking more like a date."

"A date?" she asked, raising her brows. "Is that...allowed?"

He chuckled. "This isn't the dark ages. We date who we want." He stepped in closer, his eyes hot on hers. "And I'm not intimidated by powerful women. I can handle you being an alpha."

She lost the struggle to keep the smile off her face and burst out laughing. "Sorry, I just...you were so serious," she said, gasping for air.

His face dropped for a moment, then he joined her laughing. "Damn, you are hard to flirt with," he said, still smiling.

She wiped the tears from her eyes. "My brothers scared off all the boys when I was growing up, so I never got much practice."

"How many brothers do you have?" he asked, looking alarmed.

"Four–I mean three. Just three, now," she said awkwardly.

"I'll see you around, Amber," he said, taking two steps backward like he couldn't tear his eyes from her before turning on his heel and walking away.

Someone whistled behind her and she turned around to find her entire pack had watched the exchange. Genevieve was laughing hysterically.

"It was not *that* funny," she said, rolling her eyes as she walked toward them.

"It so was," Genevieve said between gasps for air. She wiped her eyes and attempted to get control of herself.

"Joking aside, there is something I need to talk to y'all about," she said, smoothing her hair away from her face.

"What is it?" Tommy asked, immediately sensing how serious this was.

"During the fourth test, I spoke with…the wolf. My wolf," she said, tucking her hands in her pockets. Part of her didn't want to give them this option, it terrified her. But she had to. "I had to smoke this stuff…the point is that if you wanted, you could too, and it would be possible to cure you, in a sense. You could go back to being human."

Genevieve looked up sharply. "Are you serious?"

She nodded. "You have to know that you have a choice."

"That's crazy. How does no one know about that?" She threw her hands in the air and began pacing. "Do all werewolves know?"

"Just a few alphas, I think. The wolves know but they can't always talk to us."

Tommy, who had been silent thus far, looked up with tears in his eyes. "That means that you chose to stay a werewolf. Even though your brother…and even though you didn't want this."

"I chose the two of you. If being a werewolf is what I need to protect you, then so be it," she said firmly.

He crossed his arms. "I don't want to go back to being human. I want to be in your pack."

Genevieve kept pacing with her hands on her hips. "If I decided to go back to being human, it wouldn't be because I don't care."

Amber grabbed her, and made her stop walking. "You're right. It's your choice, I'd understand if you wanted to be human again, okay?"

"I should want to be human again," Genevieve said, her lower lip trembling. "But I don't, and I don't understand why."

"You don't have to decide today," Tommy said. He then looked at Amber. "Wait, she doesn't right?"

"Of course not. I know how it's done, so it doesn't matter if you decide tonight or in twenty years. You're not trapped in this pack, and you aren't trapped as a werewolf. I promise," she said.

Genevieve's whole body relaxed. "Then I don't want it right now. I want to stay in this pack."

CHAPTER 50

GENEVIEVE

"What are you getting all dressed up for?"

Genevieve turned and smiled at Amber, who was standing in her doorway. She twirled, her dress spinning around her. "You like it?"

Her alpha smirked at her. "You look like a fairy princess. It suits you."

"Steven wanted to go over the Trials since he couldn't attend, so he's taking me out to dinner," she said, turning back to the mirror and wiping at the corner of her mouth. Her lipstick was slightly uneven and it was driving her crazy, but it was the kind that lasted for twenty-four hours even if you went through an actual hurricane. There was no budging it now. She sighed, she'd just wanted to look...perfect.

"A date?" Amber asked, cocking her head to the side.

She stiffened and whipped around. "No, of course not. That's old news, we're just friends now."

"Whatever you say," Amber said, turning away with a laugh.

"Gen has a date?" Tommy parroted from his bedroom. "With Steven?"

"No! It's just DINNER!" she shouted back.

The doorbell rang, and for a half second, everyone froze. Then they ran for the front door. Amber was already halfway down the stairs, but she jumped off the balcony, landing past the couch. Genevieve sprinted for the door, throwing an elbow to keep Amber from passing her. When she tried to stop, her heel slipped on the new hall rug, and she slammed against the door.

Shoving off with a huff, she adjust her hair and plastered on a smile, then yanked the door open. "Steven, let's—"

He was standing on their porch holding...flowers. A lot of them. A whole freaking bouquet of a dozen different kinds of pink flowers.

He shifted on his feet and swallowed nervously. "You look really nice. And I, uh...got these. For you, of course. Not myself. That'd be weird."

She snatched the flowers out of his hand and stomped back down the hallway. After a moment he followed.

Amber was doubled over with silent laughter in the living room. When she heard Steven coming, she dropped down behind the couch. She could smell Tommy hiding back there, too. They were both nosy *brats*.

Realizing Steven was standing there looking like a kicked puppy, she sighed. "Thank you. They're nice."

He brightened. "For a second, I thought you were going to murder me with them."

She turned away to hide her grin and heard a snort from across the room. Steven turned around. "Is your pack—"

"Can you trim the ends for me while I find a vase?" she said frantically.

"Oh, sure," he said, hurrying over.

She handed him the scissors and positioned him in front of the sink. As soon as he wasn't looking, Tommy's head popped up. She gestured at him sharply, trying to get them both to *go away*, but he just grinned at her evilly. And to think she had ever believed he was a nice person.

"So, uh, the Trials. They went well?" he asked.

"Yep," she said, looking through a cabinet for a vase. She wasn't sure there even was one in the house, but she had to put the flowers in something, or Steven would get that look on his face. That look was the worst.

"Yesterday you said you were choosing to stay a werewolf? Why? I thought you hated it," he said, pausing in his snipping and turning to look at her.

She swallowed, uncomfortably aware the others were listening. She hadn't even told Amber yet, figured her alpha would just figure it out when she never asked for the cure. "Well, I like it."

"That's it? You *like* it?"

"Yeah," she said, turning away again. That wasn't the whole truth. The rest was... awkward to say aloud, but Amber deserved to know why. She cleared her throat. "Because I feel like I belong. I never felt that before. I don't have a sob story like them. I just—you know. I push people away. I don't want to push them away."

She spotted a big vase at the back of the cabinet under a dusty old waffle-maker. Reaching back, she grabbed it and pulled it out.

When she stood, Steven was giving her an odd look, like he hadn't expected her to share that much. "I'm glad you feel like you belong."

"Yeah, me too," she agreed with a smile.

CHAPTER 51

CERI

Ceri woke up in a cold sweat. She touched her fingers to her cheek and found them wet with tears. Rubbing her face with the palm of her hands, she tried to remember what the dream had been about. The details were already slipping out of her mind, but she remembered fear, fire, and a cool touch, like water in the desert.

She swung her legs over the edge of her bed and hopped down. These strange dreams had started the night she'd moved in. Sometimes they were scary, like tonight, but other times they just felt...important. Like someone was trying to tell her something.

Woggy was laying on her dresser in his favorite tuna can, which she had lined with felt, snoring. She watched him sleep for a second, then padded quietly out of the bedroom. It was always hard to get back to sleep after these dreams, and since it was five a.m., there was no point in even trying this time. Coffee would have to suffice.

Grabbing her book off the end table next to the couch, she headed toward the kitchen. The coffee pot was set to brew the coffee automatically at seven a.m., so she just hit the start button and got it started early.

Leaning back against the counter, she cracked open the book and scanned for the spot she'd left off. A sound from the door pulled her attention away from the novel. Using her finger as a bookmark, she shut it and crept around the island.

The front door opened slowly, and Genevieve walked inside, freezing when she saw her.

Ceri smiled and winked at her. "Did you have a good date?" she whispered.

Genevieve blushed furiously, but straightened and nodded. "I remember why I dated him for so long now."

She cocked her head to the side. "Ohhhh, is he...talented?"

"And imaginative," Genevieve confirmed with a nod. She sniffed once. "Is that coffee?"

She nodded. "Yeah, I didn't sleep much either. I'm going to need it."

"Perfect," Gen said, hurrying forward and dumping her stuff on the couch. "There's no point in going to sleep now. Coffee will have to sustain me."

They watched the coffee drip into the pot slowly. She yawned, then brushed her unruly curls away from her face. Most of them had come out of the braid she slept in. It never liked staying bound so she mostly let it do whatever it wanted.

"I know why I'm up so late...early, whatever. What's your excuse?" Gen asked, leaning against the counter and yawning.

"Just bad dreams," she said with a shrug.

Gen's brows pinched together, catching the undercurrent of her response. "Magical bad dreams? Or just normal nightmares?"

She shifted on her feet uncomfortably. She'd been avoiding asking herself that very question. "I don't know."

"But you're worried they are?"

"Yeah, it...sometimes curses are insidious. It could be something my mother is doing, but it doesn't feel like that. It could be nothing, but my gut is telling me that this is something...weird."

The coffee pot clicked over, and Gen poured them each a cup. "Is there anything you can do to stop them?"

Ceri accepted her cup and took a deep breath of the hot, rich drink. "No. It might be dumb, but I'm curious. If it's not malevolent, then I want to figure out what they mean."

Tommy walked down the stairs, bleary-eyed. His hair was sticking up in every direction. "What's wrong? Why is everyone awake?"

"Nothing's wrong," she said with a smile. "Gen just happened to wake up and we decided to get coffee."

Genevieve blushed and mouth *thank you.*

Tommy just grunted and flopped on the couch, falling back asleep almost instantly.

"He's like a puppy," Genevieve said looking at him fondly.

Amber's bedroom door opened and she trudged down the hall as well. "Is that coffee?"

Ceri nodded and poured her a cup. "Here, you look like you need it too."

Amber accepted the coffee, but got the milk out of the fridge and poured in so much you could barely tell it was still coffee. Then she added three spoonfuls of sugar.

"You could just eat the sugar straight," she teased.

Amber gave her a half-hearted glare then took a long sip, her eyes closing in satisfaction. "I prefer my sugar coffee-flavored, thank you very much."

She laughed and leaned back against the counter, taking in the group. In less than a month, four completely different people had been brought together by one man's power grab. They still weren't sure why Donovan had been so desperate to gain more power, but he was being punished, so maybe motive didn't matter.

Amber met her gaze and smiled. Some of the tension went out of her shoulders. Whatever these dreams meant, she didn't have to be afraid. Her pack wouldn't let her down.

$\sim$

TOMMY

Tommy did a fast walk to the dining room. The pot holder was too thin, and he'd taken this dish right out of the oven. Instead of using the big, formal dining room, they liked to eat in the smaller one. It had a round table just big enough for them to each have a seat and elbow room.

"Sunday family dinners should be a new tradition," Amber said as he set it on the table, waving his fingers around to cool them off.

"Just as long as someone else does the dishes." He'd left a huge mess behind in the kitchen, and there was no way he was cleaning it up alone.

"That seems fair," Amber said with a grin.

"Genevieve, food!" he shouted over his shoulder. Amber wouldn't let them eat until everyone was there, and he was starving.

"Sorry!" Genevieve shouted. She ran through the doorway and plopped down in her chair. "I just got off the phone with my new employer."

"New employer?" Amber asked, surprised.

"Yeah, I...I'm actually a lawyer. I passed the bar over a year ago. I just hadn't wanted to actually work as a lawyer because if you screw up, well, that's someone's whole life." She started picking at her napkin, tearing off tiny pieces. "But I really want to do it. I think I could help people."

"That's awesome," he said, beaming at her. Gen was wicked smart, but she normally played it down. She would kick ass in the courtroom.

"What will you being doing now?" Ceri asked, digging into the closest dish. Woggy hopped off her shoulder and pounced on the spoon. She dragged him off and set his serving on the small plate next to her to distract him.

"I'm starting out as part of a legal team that deals with inter-species disputes. Every race has their own rules, and trying to balance those with actual laws can gets messy. I really liked this firm because they make it a point to take on more than the minimum mandated pro bono cases per year," Genevieve explained as she buttered one of the fresh rolls he'd made.

"Have you thought any more about getting your GED, Tommy?" Ceri asked.

He nodded. "Yeah, I want to get it before the beginning of the year so I can start applying to colleges for the fall."

Amber visibly tensed, but took a deep breath and deliberately unwound her shoulders. "What colleges are you thinking about applying to?"

"Yale," he said with a grin, just to watch her freak out. She didn't disappoint. Her head snapped up, and that fake calm she tried to project shattered.

"That's on the other side—" she snapped her mouth shut when his expression finally registered. "You're just screwing with me, aren't you?"

He laughed and shook his head at her. "There's a college in Portland I'm applying too, but my first choice is in Seattle."

"Seattle is close! Barely a three hour drive away," Ceri said, beaming at him. There was a thunk under the table, and Amber flinched, then nodded.

"Yeah, that's great, super close," she said through gritted teeth.

He leaned over and fed Woggy a vegetable. The pixie got the whole bite in his mouth, then glared at him and spit it out. He signed *no*, which was his new favorite word.

"Oh, did you hear that they found another spot where magic isn't working in Portland?" Ceri asked, changing the subject. "There's one out near Tillamook, too. They think it might have been there for months before someone noticed."

"Are they sure the spots haven't always been there?" Amber asked.

"I thought that at first too, but they're popping up in places where people *know* magic used to work. It's super weird," Ceri said with a shrug.

Tommy shoved a forkful of food in his mouth, but worry gnawed in his gut. He was always a little worried in the back of his head that one day he'd lose this newfound peace. The no-magic spots could turn out to be nothing, but they gave him a sense of foreboding.

"Well, I'm sure every major coven is trying to figure it out and fix it. Not to mention the elves. This could be a natural thing," Amber said, reassuringly.

He wondered what would happen if a werewolf stumbled into one of those. The pack bond was magic, and the thing that allowed them to change forms was as well. Would it come back as soon as you moved out of the spot? Or was it permanent?

"How's your job search going?" Gen asked Amber.

She shrugged. "Not great, to be honest. But I'll figure something out after my trip."

Every time the trip came up, Amber got tense and quiet. He knew he bottled stuff up, but she took it to a whole different level.

"What's your family like?" he asked, pushing some food around on his plate. Maybe he shouldn't have asked. But he knew everyone was curious, and maybe if she wasn't trying to hard to avoid the topic, it wouldn't bother her so much.

Amber looked a little surprised by the question. She cleared her throat and shifted in her seat. "Well, I grew up with four brothers. I had a twin, Dylan. We were the youngest, so we were kind of spoiled compared to the others I guess. My dad owns a diesel mechanic shop, and we all grew up helping out there. Went to a small high school, small town, that whole stereotypical Texas thing."

"Had a twin?" he asked quietly. Ceri and Genevieve were listening intently, not saying a word, like if someone spoke too soon it'd shatter the moment.

She took a deep breath and nodded. "Yeah. Right after we graduated, we both applied to a local werewolf pack. He got accepted, I didn't." She set down her fork and stared hard at her plate. "It's rare. One in a million, but some people can't handle the bite. It kills them."

Genevieve's eyes went wide. "That's who you were talking about the night of the full moon when you said you knew someone that hadn't survived the change."

Amber nodded. "I guess I didn't handle being changed into a werewolf after all that very well. Thanks for sticking with me, even though I'm a little crazy."

That explained a lot. Everything, really. He wished she'd just told them earlier, but it looked like it was still hard for her to talk about.

"Sorry," he said.

She shrugged. "It's okay. Y'all needed to know."

"Did you like working with your father?" Ceri asked, changing the subject. Amber's shoulders relaxed slightly.

"Yeah, it was a pretty good way to grow up," she said with a smile. "Me and Dylan used to take our dog and go hunt squirrels. We tried to cook one once, and it was awful."

"What kind of dog did you have?" he asked.

Amber shrugged. "A mutt we got for free in the supermarket parking lot. My parents didn't believe in paying for pets."

"I never had a pet," he said. His mom had said she'd get him one before she got sick. But after that, well…lots of promises got broken.

"We should get a dog!" Genevieve announced with a grin. "Maybe a cat *and* a dog. I like cats better."

Amber looked horrified. "What? No!"

"There's a rescue shelter in town that's waiving adoption fees right now," Ceri said, jumping on board just like he knew she would.

He grinned at Amber. "You know you've already lost, right?"

She groaned and put her head in her hands, but he could tell she was hiding a grin. "Y'all are going to be the death of me."

"Pshh, you love it," Genevieve said, smiling with a mouthful of food.

"I *guess*," Amber said, dropping her hands and looking at the pack fondly. She stood and picked up her beer, lifting it in a toast. "To our pack, our future, and happiness."

He lifted his glass and let himself feel optimistic for the first time in years.

CHAPTER 52

AMBER

"Are you sure? I can always wait until next month, or—"

"Oh my god," Genevieve exclaimed, cutting her off. "Go. Get out. We're going to be *fine*. It's a week. We are adults, and we will not starve to death, I promise."

Amber sighed and let Genevieve shove her out of the front door. Ceri was already in the truck, waiting to take her to to airport.

"Have fun!" Tommy shouted from the couch. He was more concerned with his tv show than with her leaving. It was *almost* insulting, but she was just glad he had gotten so comfortable. The days of worrying about him leaving were long gone.

Ceri honked and rolled down the passenger side window. "Come on, we're going to be late!"

"Fine," she said, throwing her hands in the air. She jogged to the truck and tossed her backpack on the floorboard before climbing inside. Looking at her friend, she sighed. "This is a terrible idea. What if something happens while I'm gone?"

Ceri leaned over and put her hands on both sides of her head. "Then we will handle it, and you will come back early."

"Ugh, fine."

Laughing at her, Ceri dropped her hands and put the truck in reverse. "Now, Tommy might come pick you up from the airport—"

"Tommy?" she asked, alarmed. "He doesn't even have his driver's license yet!"

"He's getting one while you're gone," Ceri beamed. "Genevieve has been teaching him, and he's going to take his test tomorrow."

She slid down in her seat and let her head fall back. "Y'all waited for me to leave to plan this, didn't you?"

"Absolutely. You were freaking him out with your *lessons*," Ceri said, raising an eyebrow at her.

"There's nothing wrong with learning evasive maneuvers," she muttered.

"He should probably learn how to parallel park first, though."

She sighed and rubbed her hand over her face. Sure, she was committed to being their alpha since the Trials, but that didn't mean that she didn't have days where she doubted herself all over again. It made the wolf moody.

"So, you've been a little...on edge the past week. You're worried about seeing your family again, right?" Ceri asked hesitantly.

"My brothers are all mad at me, my mom hates me, and my dad, he just...ignores me. I don't know why I'm even doing this."

"It's been a long time. It's not crazy to think you might be able to repair those relationships. Maybe your mom has been scared to call after so long," Ceri suggested.

She shrugged. "I just hope the rest of them have forgiven me."   •

Ceri reached over and grabbed her shoulder as she drove. "There's nothing to forgive. Your brother made his choice, and he died, tragically, because of that choice. All the arguments that you could have stopped him are crap."

"I just want to stop being angry about it," she said with a sigh.

"Let me know if you figure out how to," Ceri said with a laugh, lightening the mood. They'd bumped into her mother a few days ago, and...it had not gone well, to say the least.

"You promise to call me if *anything* happens, right? Even if someone stubs a toe?" she asked, still feeling antsy.

"Absolutely not," Ceri said firmly. "I will call you if something bad happens, or if something good happens. But I am not going to call you over something silly. Stop fretting. You're going to drive yourself batty."

She sighed. "Fine. I don't like it, but you're right."

"Such sweet words from my dear alpha," Ceri said with a laugh.

She stuck her tongue out at Ceri and crossed her arms. "No one shows me any respect around here."

Ceri busted out laughing, and Amber couldn't help but join her. It eased some of the ache in her chest.

~

The rental car agency had given her some elf-spelled electric, eco-friendly car. She wasn't sure it would hold together long enough to make it down the gravel road that led to the house. Her brothers were going to have a field day mocking her car and asking if she was a hippie now. If they spoke to her at all.

She rolled down the windows and let the brisk air flow through the car, whipping her hair around her face. Now that she was a werewolf, she could smell so much more. Pine trees, cow manure, and a hint of exhaust from a truck that must have passed this way recently.

She'd missed Texas but less than she expected. It felt like home, but the country was prettier than she'd ever imagined. People were still polite in other states and still willing to lend a hand if you needed it. The weather was way better. Even now, her shirt was starting to stick to her skin from the humidity.

After a curve in the road, she saw the beat up old mailbox with HALE in black, boxy letters on the side. Her stomach did a weird flip that she did not appreciate. She took a deep breath and turned down the driveway. A couple of dogs ran around from the back of the house, barking to announce the intruder. She didn't recognize them, which meant Rusty and Princess had passed while she was gone.

She parked next to her dad's truck and climbed out. The dogs slid to a halt a few feet from her, tails drooping as they recognized the predator that now lived in her.

"Hey, guys, I'm friendly," she said, trying to sound nice. The white dog yelped and ran for it. After a moment, the other dog followed suit.

Hoping that wasn't setting the tone for the next reunion, she straightened and looked at the house she'd grown up in. Two story brick house with a wrap-a-round porch that had hosted many a summer barbecue. Her dad had cooked in an old metal barrel, cut in half lengthwise and converted into a charcoal grill.

She couldn't see her room from there. The window had overlooked the backyard and the pond, where she and her brothers had spent most of their time playing. The sun was setting behind the house, casting the whole thing in a warm glow.

With a deep breath, she shook off the nostalgia and walked up to the porch. The wooden steps creaked under her feet, and the noise startled her so badly she almost bolted. She rubbed her hand down her face and tried to slow her heartbeat. Even during the Trials she hadn't been this nervous. She wanted to throw up or run away. Maybe both.

With a shaking hand, she knocked twice on the old red door. She heard footsteps, a heartbeat drawing closer.

The door opened and Derek stood in the doorway. His eyes went wide.

"What the hell are you trying to do, air condition Texas? In or out!" her mother shouted from behind him.

He stepped back, opening the door wider. Her mom was sitting on the couch in her favorite pair of stained jean shorts. She must have been out in the garden earlier.

"Hey, mom."

Her mother looked up, face going pale as her hands fell into her lap. Her mouth worked for a moment, no words coming out, then Derek dragged Amber inside. He wrapped her up in a hug and squeezed so tight she thought he might break a rib. She hung on tightly, trying to crush the disappointment she felt at her mother's reaction. At least one person was happy to see her. That was enough. It had to be.

Even a thousand miles away, she felt the pack bond next to her heart. It beat strong and steady. Even if this went badly, she still had them. They might be misfits that didn't fit in anywhere else, but they had chosen her, and she had chosen them.

She buried her face in her brother's shoulder. "I missed you."

"Missed you too, little sister."

MISFIT ANGEL

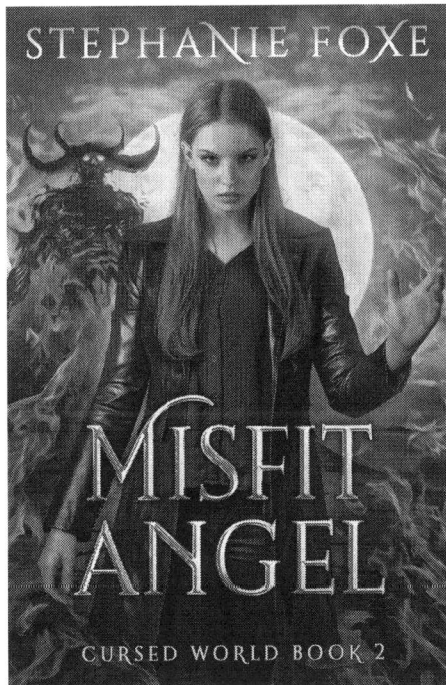

To my husband

Who helps me through my bad days
And celebrates my good days

I love you!

PROLOGUE

ELOISE

Eloise yawned as she tapped another piece of the puzzle into place. It was still dark outside but she was already awake. The older she got, the harder it was to sleep through the night. She supposed it was insomnia. Or too much coffee after dinner.

Her seventieth birthday was in less than a month. The number galled her, so she refused to think about it. Her body was aging faster than her mind, and it was annoying, to say the least.

There was a quiet creak and she turned around expecting to see Evangeline coming down the stairs, but the stairway stood empty. Knitting her brows together, she reached toward the curtain to peek outside. The back door crashed open at the same moment as a flaming bottle flew through the kitchen window. It shattered against a cabinet and burst into flame.

Eloise jumped up from her puzzle and ran for the antique buffet where she kept her pistol. Just before she reached it, thick arms wrapped around her from behind and lifted her off the ground. She kicked wildly, hoping to catch his knee or something more sensitive.

The man grunted and slammed her against the wall. He grabbed a handful of her hair and yanked her head back sharply. "Where is the demon spawn?"

She bared her teeth at the intruder. "I'm looking right at him," she said right before she spat in his eye.

He reared back in anger and disgust giving her enough room to kick him square in the balls. Without hesitating, she lunged for the drawer again and ripped it open. As her fingers closed around the pistol as he yanked her back by her arm.

She pointed the gun at him, but he shoved her arm up and the first shot went wild. Her ears rang from the deafening blast of the Colt 45 and she prayed to God she hadn't hit Evangeline. She had to have heard the fight. Eloise hoped she had run.

The man's fist connected with her face and she felt her knees give out as her vision exploded into stars. She was too old for this, but she wouldn't let them hurt her daughter. She kicked blindly and kept a firm grip on the gun. It was her only chance.

As her vision began to clear, he swung her around and her back hit the bookcase. Something cracked, most likely a rib, and breathing became painful. Books toppled down onto both their heads. She lunged forward and sank her teeth into his meaty forearm. He slammed her against the bookcase again and she cried out in pain.

When he slammed her against it a third time, the whole thing swayed forward. He jumped back to avoid getting crushed, half dragging her with him. She pulled in the opposite direction then yanked her arm free. Aiming the gun right at his chest, she pulled the trigger as the bookcase crashed down on top of her.

Pain like she'd never felt throbbed through her leg where the heavy bookcase had her pinned. The intruder lay dead in a pool of blood across from her. She'd barely been able to shoot him before he killed her. His face was still contorted with rage and malice, but his eyes were empty.

Smoke filled the home she had lived in for thirty years. Flames licked up the wallpaper, turning the delicate flowers black. The air was thick with the scent of gasoline.

Her daughter stumbled down the hallway, clutching her pillow. Her face was pale from weeks of illness, and now this.

"Just run," Eloise choked out, willing her daughter to get out before they found her. Another bottle crashed through the window, shattering and igniting the carpet.

"I won't leave you!" Evangeline cried, limping toward her. As she drew closer, the flames lapped at her legs, but they didn't hurt her. They couldn't, because she wasn't human. Her daughter knelt down by her and pushed futilely at the heavy bookcase she was trapped underneath.

These bastards had managed to kill her, but not Evangeline. That was all that mattered.

"Eva, baby, you have to run before they find you," she said, forcing her fingers to release their tight grip on the gun. She wiped away the tears streaming through the ash and grime on Evangeline's face.

"I can't leave you!" Evangeline sobbed, banging her fists against the bookcase.

"You can't move it--"

The demon mark on Eloise's chest tingled and he appeared, looking as he always did, like an old man cloaked in shadows.

"Why are you still here?" the demon demanded, surging toward Evangeline. "Get out before it's too late!"

"No!" she snapped back, slashing her hand through his smoky form. "Help her!"

"You know I can't," he growled. "But you can if you just stop suppressing your magic!"

For a brief moment, Eloise wondered if the demon had arranged this just to force Evangeline to accept her demon side, but she dismissed the thought. She didn't think he would truly risk her being harmed.

The demon leaned in, whispering something in Evangeline's ear. The fire was drawing closer and Eloise could barely catch a breath. Evangeline couldn't be hurt by the fire and smoke, but she could be hurt by whomever was outside.

Evangeline's scream of anguish cut off her words. Her black hair lifted from her shoulders, floating around her head. With a scream, wings of fire burst from her back. She sat there panting, then looked up. Her eyes were black as night.

Eloise gasped as she took in the transformation. She'd known from the day she found the baby abandoned in the woods and the demon had appeared to her, what Evangeline really was. She'd also known that people would hate her, and she'd protected the child as long as she could.

Her daughter lifted her shaking hands, tears still streaming down her face, grabbed the bookcase and threw it across the room. She blinked, delirious from the lack of oxygen. Her daughter scooped her up carefully but she still had to bite her tongue to keep from crying out as pain shot through her legs and her side. She wouldn't have to hold it back long though, her vision blurred as her mind tried to protect itself by sliding into unconsciousness.

Evangeline walked to the back door and kicked it open, then flew into the night. Cool air stung Eloise's burned skin as they raced through the sky.

CHAPTER 1

AMBER

Three days earlier...

Amber's hand tightened on the armrest as they hit another patch of turbulence. She ground her teeth together and pretended the plane was just bumping down a gravel road and that they weren't thirty thousand feet in the air. There was nothing to worry about. Nothing at all.

"Are you sure there's room? I could camp in the woods if I had to," her brother, Derek said, for the tenth time.

"Dude, there are two extra bedrooms even with four of us staying there. It's fine."

"And your pack won't mind? I won't be intruding on your new family, or whatever?"

She punched him in the arm, maybe too hard judging by his flinch. "They're not my new family. Stop saying it like that. And they're alarmingly excited to meet you."

The pilot announced the plane was beginning its descent. She double-checked her seatbelt and leaned back in her seat.

Her visit had ended up with a big family fight, of course, but Derek had decided he wanted to open his own mechanic shop after all. Since doing it in the same town as their father was out of the question, he'd asked to come to Portland with her. That had caused another family fight when he'd told their parents, but she just didn't care anymore. Derek had been fed up with it as well and stormed out.

She needed a job, he wanted a fresh start, and it seemed like the perfect opportunity for both of them. When she'd told her pack their plans, Tommy had volunteered immediately to help out, eager to have a job again himself. He was always fretting about helping to pay the bills.

As the plane bounced onto the ground, the demon mark on her chest twinged painfully. She rubbed it. It had been aching a lot like that ever since the wolf had somehow banished Angel during the fourth trial to prove her worthiness as an alpha. She kept expecting the demon to show back up that day...and the next...but he never did.

She had no idea how the wolf had done it, but she was insanely glad Angel had been absent while she had visited her family. Though, the temporary peace was probably going to come at a high price.

Everyone stood and crammed into the aisles, but Amber just relaxed in her seat. She'd wait out the crowd and avoid the mad rush for the exit. She didn't have a connecting flight to make and ever since she'd been changed being shoved around by strangers made her irrationally angry. It was better for her sanity and everyone else's health if she just waited. The wolf huffed in agreement in her mind.

"Who did you say was picking us up?" Derek asked, turning his cellphone back on.

"Ceri, she's a witch in my pack."

"That's so weird," he said, shaking his head. "How does that work?"

She shrugged. "I don't know, it just happened. I'm not convinced anyone actually understands how magic works."

"No kidding, there's no explaining how my baby sister ended up an alpha werewolf." He snorted in amusement.

She glared at him. Maybe she *hadn't* missed having her brothers around. "I could always beat you up."

"You could not!" he objected as she finally moved out into the aisle and grabbed her backpack from the overhead bin.

All her luggage fit in a backpack. Derek had chosen to only bring a carry-on as well, having mailed the stuff he wanted to bring to the house. He'd said he didn't have much in the way of furniture and hadn't thought it valuable enough to bother bringing with him to Portland, especially since there wasn't anywhere to put it.

"Just keep telling yourself that," she said with a smirk.

They finally got off the plane and a knot of tension unwound from her shoulders. The wolf had not been a fan of flying, and she wasn't exactly a nervous flyer, but she was a grumpy one. The combination hadn't been fun.

Her phone buzzed about ten times, finally receiving all the messages that had been sent while she'd had it turned off. She skipped all the ones from her pack and found Ceri's name.

"Ceri is here already and waiting for us at the terminal," she said, shoving the phone back in her pocket and picking up her pace. It was weird since she hadn't had many close friends in her adult life, but she missed her pack.

They passed through baggage claim, then headed outside. It was chilly out. She tugged her jacket a little closer around her and adjusted the backpack on her shoulder. The wind shifted and she caught Ceri's scent.

"This way," she said, hurrying in the direction the scent led without waiting to see if Derek actually followed.

When she spotted Ceri, the wolf practically howled inside her. Before she realized what she was doing, she'd run over and wrapped her friend up in a tight hug, inhaling her scent deeply. Blonde curls covered her face and drowned out all the other smells. It was nice.

"Hey there, missed you too," Ceri said with a laugh, hugging her back just as tight.

"Felt wrong to be gone," she muttered, feeling a blush grow on her face.

"Yeah, it did. Gen has been grumpy as a hungry pixie since the day after you left."

Amber forced herself to let go and moved back. She jabbed her thumb over her shoulder at her brother as he jogged up behind her. "This is Derek."

"Hey, I'm Ceri," the witch said, stepping forward with a bright smile and wrapping him in a hug as well.

Derek looked surprised and patted her back awkwardly, getting a face full of curly, blonde hair. "Nice to meet you."

Ceri let go of him. "You too! I expected you to be a redhead like Amber though."

He grinned. "Our oldest brother is the only other carrot top in the family. Other than Mom."

Amber rolled her eyes. She hated being called carrot top. "My hair is auburn, not orange. I'm not a carrot."

Derek slung his arm around her shoulder. "Whatever you say, alpha."

"Oh, shut up," she said, shoving his arm off. "Let's get out of here. I don't like the way it smells."

CHAPTER 2

TOMMY

Tommy gnawed on the end of his pencil as he stared at the problem. He'd been good at math, but after over a year off, he was rusty. Deward had taken away his formula cheat sheet and insisted that he work from memory. He glanced at the troll, wondering if he could wrestle it away from him and deciding against it. Deward was taller, buffer, and had probably been wrestling since before he could walk.

It had been Ceri's idea to hire the troll as his GED tutor. Deward was insanely smart, but he wasn't really the best teacher. If Tommy didn't understand the first explanation, he'd just shake his head and mutter something about humans, then tell him to try it anyhow.

"Don't forget the power rule," Deward prompted. "It tells you how to differentiate––"

"Yeah, I remember," Tommy interrupted with a sigh. "It's just all running together in my brain. Maybe we should have started with algebra."

"A challenge will strengthen the mind faster," Deward said, adjusting his glasses.

That was apparently the troll's favorite saying. Tommy rubbed his eyes and tried to refocus. If he knew the rule, he should be able to do the math.

An enraged squeak broke his concentration and he looked up, realizing Woggy was no longer in his box. "When did he get out?"

Deward looked in the box as well and frowned. "I don't know, I didn't notice either."

Tommy jumped to his feet and looked around, his ears straining to tell where the noise had come from. There was another squeal, then a shriek of pain. He took off at a run, headed straight for a bush near the edge of the house. As he rounded the corner he saw a swarm of pixies throwing small pebbles.

Woggy was on the ground, hopping and waving a stick furiously. The wingless pixie managed to deflect a few of the pebbles but most hit their target.

"Ah, a territorial fight," Deward said, sounding unconcerned.

Tommy darted in and grabbed Woggy to the displeasure of the attacking pixies. "Well they can buzz off, this is Woggy's yard," he said, swatting at them to try and shoo them away.

The little monsters swarmed him. One of them bit his neck while three more attacked the hand that held Woggy. He yanked the one off his neck and threw it away. The pixie managed to get its bearings and fly back toward him. Their teeth might be small, but they were sharp. He shook his arm to get them off, belatedly realizing that was probably really jarring for Woggy.

Deward finally stepped in and plucked the pixies off, tossing them over his shoulder. He managed to throw them hard enough that they hit the ground. One struggled to its feet and stumbled around in a daze.

"Don't hurt them," Tommy said, watching them struggle back to their feet.

"If you take that disabled pixie away, they'll feel they've won. You either have to kill them, or cede the yard to their control," Deward said, crossing his arms.

He took a deep breath to keep from snapping at his tutor. "I'm not going to kill them, but I'm not giving up that easy either." A pebble thunked against his cheek and he scowled at the attacking pixies.

Woggy was trying to escape from his hands, ready to fight to the death for his territory. The pixie reminded him of Amber. Fearless and full of rage. Unlike Amber, though, Woggy wasn't strong enough to fight off his enemies.

Tommy could relate to that. When he and Ceri had arrived at the house while it was being attacked, she'd run inside. He had tried to help. Despite the wolf's instincts, he simply hadn't known what to do. Of all of them, he could shift the fastest, and had the most control. Maybe too much control. He wasn't sure he *could* fight, even if he had to.

Deward shrugged. "Suit yourself, however, I consider it a waste of time."

"Noted," Tommy said drily, heading back toward the table where they'd left all their books.

Deward followed and began picking up his things, tucking them neatly away in his backpack. "My father suggested it would be polite to invite you over for dinner tomorrow evening."

Tommy glanced at the troll, raising his brow. He wasn't sure if that was an invitation, or if Deward was just letting him know his father had suggested it. Either way, he had no interest in going. "We have pack dinner tomorrow, if that was an invitation."

"Of course it was," Deward said, frowning at him as he slung his backpack over his shoulder. "I'll let my father know and confirm a different time that will work for my parents."

"Great," Tommy said, already thinking up various excuses to get out of going. He had a feeling Deward would trap him eventually. Trolls were too smart to be fooled forever.

Deward nodded his head farewell and headed toward his car. It was pretty small for such a big troll, but Deward said it got excellent gas mileage which allowed him to save more of his tutoring income.

That reminded Tommy that he still needed to find a way to pay Gen back for his tutoring. Somehow. Without a job. Hopefully Amber's brother would want to hire him.

The pixies started gathering together, looking like they were about to swarm him again. He piled his books in his free arm and jogged inside before they had a chance to attack. He checked on Woggy briefly, and the pixie was worse off than he thought.

He pulled out his phone and called Ceri, guilt already curdling in his gut for not watching the pixie closely enough.

CHAPTER 3

GENEVIEVE

Genevieve pinched the bridge of her nose between her finger and thumb and thanked every deity that her boss couldn't see her face. She'd taken this job because she thought this law firm cared more about pro-bono cases. She didn't understand why her boss was fighting her so hard on this potential case.

A bitten werewolf had been attacked at a bar. When he'd defended himself, he'd put the other guy in the hospital. Because he was bitten, it was being called a 'failure to maintain control', which meant he could end up in the System even though he had a pack. She couldn't let that happen.

"Look, I'm not saying we can't take it on, but I think you misunderstand how the pro-bono cases work. If you think this is a worthy cause, then take the case. Do the work. However, you have to keep up with all your billable hours as well."

"Is that even possible?" she asked.

"Of course it is, you'll just have to work weekends. That's what this job is, if you haven't figured that out yet. It's actually a good opportunity to prove yourself if you're interested in becoming a partner in the next few years," Susan said, typing in the background. That woman never sat still. She was always doing two things at once and expected the same of every other employee. Especially the lowly associates.

Genevieve paused for a moment to steel herself for taking on another challenge. "Alright, I'll do it."

Susan shouted something at someone in the background, though the words were muffled. "Great!" she said, returning to their conversation abruptly. "Send Jorge all the information you find. The client interview needs to be done by Sunday evening, and then we can get into the rest Monday morning. Go ahead and come in early, maybe around seven a.m., so you can catch me up before the rest of the partners arrive."

"Alright, I can do that." She wasn't actually sure she could, but she had to try. She didn't want to spend the rest of her life getting people out of parking tickets. She wanted to actually help people. Besides, if she couldn't do this basic grunt work she'd never make it as a lawyer.

When she gotten into college she'd chosen law because her dad had always called her his little lawyer. She argued her way out of every punishment and had enjoyed debate in high school. This was nothing like she pictured.

Susan ended the call without saying goodbye. Genevieve tossed her phone down on the table and put her face in her hands thinking, once again, that this had been a huge mistake. Someone's well-being depended on her ability to do her job. She had no idea how surgeons functioned. Hell, she wasn't even sure how Amber walked around all day like everything was fine when the pack's safety depended on her.

The door opened and she looked up. Tommy walked in with his arms covered in tiny cuts. They were already healing, so they must have been way worse a few minutes ago.

"What happened to you?" she asked in alarm.

He muttered something even her enhanced hearing couldn't make out.

She got up and walked over, grabbing his arm and inspecting one of the bloody spots. It looked sort of like a bite. "Did Woggy bite you?"

"No, but it was a pixie," he said with a sigh, lifting his other hand to show her Woggy. He was badly beaten, his gray body mottled with purple bruises. The tip of the pixie's ear was torn. "A whole swarm of them. I think Woggy started the fight, and by the time I got there and got him out, he was already in bad shape."

The pixie rolled over in Tommy's hand, whimpering. He opened his big, watery eyes and gave them an utterly pathetic look.

She wasn't as enamored with Woggy as the others, but even she felt bad seeing him like this. "Did you call Ceri?"

"Yeah, she said to give him meat and that if he's breathing without trouble to wait on doing anything else until she gets back. They're almost here by the way," Tommy said, heading toward the kitchen.

Genevieve started packing up all the paperwork spread over the coffee table. She was a little embarrassed how excited she was to have Amber back but was trying to learn to accept the odd instincts that came with being a werewolf. She could take the cure, but...she felt braver when she was with the pack. If she left, she knew she'd just go back to avoiding her responsibilities and never challenging herself.

"What do you think her brother is going to be like?" Tommy asked from the kitchen as he cracked open a can of pre-cooked chicken. It was normally a treat they gave Woggy at dinner to keep him from trying to get into their food.

She zipped up her briefcase and snorted at his question. "Bossy, probably."

He grinned at that. "As long as he doesn't run around worrying about everyone constantly."

"Oh my god, that would be miserable," she agreed with a laugh.

Tommy paused. "Do you think she'll be mad about...you know," he asked, gesturing down the hall.

"She's going to rage about it and demand to know who did it, and then whine about it, for days possibly, but she's going to be secretly thrilled."

He looked unconvinced. "I'm telling her it was your idea."

"You picked--"

They both stopped, their heads cocking toward the front of the house as the sound of tires on gravel drifted toward them from the driveway.

"They're here!" she said, running for the door. Tommy followed and they tumbled out onto the porch.

Ceri parked and the door to the truck opened. A tall man with dark brown hair, a thick beard, and a shirt that said It's Bigger Down South stepped out. She sucked up the drool threatening to escape her mouth as he hoisted a backpack onto his shoulders and smiled at her.

Amber hopped down from the truck and Genevieve forgot all about the newcomer. She ran forward, Amber meeting her halfway, and slammed into her alpha. Tommy got there a half second later and wrapped his long arms around both of them, turning it into a group hug.

"You're finally back!" Genevieve squealed, her words muffled by Tommy's forearm and Amber's shoulder.

Amber laughed and squeezed them a little tighter. "I'm glad to see I was missed. I was worried I'd get back and you'd all be gone."

"Never," Tommy objected.

They pulled back, but Amber grabbed her and sniffed her again, carefully. "Why do you smell like...I don't even know what it is." She paused, a low growl rumbling in her throat as her eyes flashed red. "Who marked you?"

Genevieve busted out laughing. "Don't worry, whatever you're thinking is wrong."

CHAPTER 4

AMBER

This was so much worse than what she'd been thinking. This was very, very bad. She was never leaving the pack unsupervised again.

The mangy, one-eyed cat hissed at her again, arching its back to make its already massive form look bigger. The thing had to weigh at least forty pounds. It was possible it was mostly fluff though. It had long, ratty gray fur that probably needed to be shaved off. The animal was filthy.

Genevieve pet it soothingly. "It's okay Captain Jack, she's not as mean as she looks. Her face just does that naturally."

"What the hell is that?" she demanded after a few moments of stunned silence.

"It was Gen's idea," Tommy said hastily, crossing his arms and taking a step back.

Genevieve glared at him. "Tommy picked him out."

Amber turned to Ceri, who was feeding Woggy little pieces of chicken. "Why didn't you stop them? And I thought y'all were planning on getting a *dog?*"

"Well, we saw this old guy in the shelter, and he'd been there for over a year," Ceri said, her blue eyes getting watery, like she might start crying. "We couldn't just leave him."

Amber put her face in her hands and muttered threats she knew she wouldn't follow through on. This was all part of her cosmic punishment for the bad things she'd done in her life. That was the only explanation.

She dropped her hands and faced the cat again. It was licking its leg now and ignoring her. Tentatively, she patted its head. It looked up at her and hissed. "Great, we're friends now," she said, wiping her hand on her leg.

Genevieve rolled her eyes and picked the cat up. Its legs hung down to her hips. She nuzzled her head into its fluff, which explained the smell on her, and the cat began to purr like a motorboat. "Captain Jack is the best cat ever."

Derek clapped his hand on her shoulder. "At least it won't bark. Now, where's my room?"

"There are two free rooms upstairs, pick whichever you like," she said, gesturing toward the stairs.

"So inhospitable," Derek joked as he headed toward the stairs.

"I'll show you around," Ceri offered.

"That'd be great," he said, his face lighting up in a smile.

Amber grimaced. She should have just done it. Genevieve caught her eye, then looked pointedly at Ceri and Derek heading upstairs. Genevieve's smile grew, clearly amused by the obvious chemistry between the two.

Her stomach growled, distracting her from all that. "What's for dinner?" she asked, looking at Tommy hopefully.

"I ordered pizza," Genevieve said. "Tommy had tutoring with Deward today, so he didn't really have time."

"Sorry," Tommy said, looking chagrined.

"Pizza sounds great, nothing to be sorry about. How's tutoring going? Did you get your driver's license?" she asked, eager to catch up.

"Yeah," he said with a grin, finally straightening his shoulders. "Passed with flying colors."

Amber heard someone turn down the driveway and tilted her head toward the noise. "Pizza guy?"

"What? Oh, I hear it now," Genevieve said, hurrying toward the door. She grabbed her wallet from her purse and yanked the door open before the guy had a chance to knock. The smell of pizza filled the house.

"You aren't too mad about the cat, are you?" Tommy asked, tugging his beanie down nervously.

Amber shook her head and looked at the beast. "No, I'm not mad. He's probably the perfect mascot for us."

Tommy laughed. "You've got that right. He's definitely not your average cat."

"Is he getting along with Woggy?" she asked.

"Yeah, surprisingly. We actually took Woggy to the shelter with us. He climbed on Captain Jack's back and the cat just sniffed him, then laid down."

"Huh, I would not have guess that'd be the cat's reaction. Glad to hear it though."

Genevieve walked back into the living room with the pizza. "DINNER IS HERE!" she shouted in the general direction of upstairs.

"Be right down!" Ceri shouted back.

Amber smiled to herself, she was glad to be home. Even if the cat was currently stealing a piece of pizza straight out of the box with its filthy paws.

CHAPTER 5

CERI

The house had gone quiet, and Ceri should be sleeping, but between the odd dreams and the anxiety she'd had since the Trials...well, she wasn't. Instead, she'd been living on caffeine and naps. Sleeping during the day seemed to result in fewer dreams.

Covering a yawn with the back of her hand, she shuffled into the work room. She'd been investigating the wards on the house to keep herself from brooding over everything that had happened. It was fascinating how the house had moved them around during the attack. She'd never seen magic like it before. It was almost as if it had been left alone and gotten unruly, coming up with its own ideas about how to protect itself. The only thing she knew for sure so far was that gaining new inhabitants had strengthened it and made it happy.

She lit a bundle of sage and began walking the perimeter of the room. Waving the smoldering herb gently, she directed the smoke with her free hand as she cleansed it methodically. It was important to make sure the space was clear of negative energies and spirits before she opened her mind to the magic of the house.

There were spirits in this world, born of pure magic, that were both good and bad. This was another thing her grandmother had taught her, all the while cursing people that lived their lives with a black and white view of good and evil.

Ceri rolled her eyes at the memory. Her grandmother had been wise, powerful, and vicious. And just as disappointed in her daughter as her mother was in her. Her grandmother had had such high hopes for her. She was probably rolling in her grave watching her now.

Setting the still smoldering bundle of sage in a bowl on the floor in the center of the room, she sat down in front of it. The scent surrounded her and cleared her senses. She crossed her legs and rested her hands on her thighs.

Her senses reached out and sank into the walls, the floor, and wards that were a part of the house. It looked back at her and she felt the air around her shift slightly.

The house was excited she was acknowledging it, almost like a happy puppy. The floorboards under her creaked and trembled slightly. A barrage of images flashed through her mind, too fast to process. A glimpse of the kitchen. The back door. The porch. The attic. Then, in a blinding burst, the wards themselves came into focus.

Her breath caught in her throat. Woven into every board, and into the air itself, were golden threads of elven magic. They burned as bright as the sun. Whoever had created them had been pure of heart and had poured love and creativity into them. She mentally snorted. That ruled out Thallan, the house's owner.

She lifted her hand, eyes still closed, and tentatively touched a spot where she knew one of the threads laid. The magic was warm at first but quickly became too hot to touch. She yanked her hand away with a pained hiss, sucking on the burned finger.

The house groaned in alarm. The curtains fluttered behind her and the light fixture overhead began to sway. It was then that she realized that she could see everything around her. She could even see herself.

"Shhh, it's okay. You didn't mean to hurt me," she whispered, trying to soothe the agitated house.

It seemed to huff at her as it curled around her once again. Emotions that weren't her own bounced through her. Worry, shame, fear...and hope.

She smiled and did her best to send back contentment, curiosity, and forgiveness. The trembling of the room stopped and she was filled with warmth.

Another image appeared in her mind. It didn't change abruptly this time, instead, it slowly came into focus, showing her Derek standing in front of the kitchen counter. She nudged it and found she was able to move slightly to see better. He was stirring honey into a mug of tea.

She almost jumped when he picked it up and turned around, then laughed to herself. He couldn't see her. She pressed her hand into the floor by her foot to ground herself. Despite what she could see, she hadn't moved. The house was simply showing her what *it* could see.

Instead of walking upstairs to his room, Derek headed out of the kitchen and down the hall that led to her and Amber's rooms. She expected him to knock on his sister's door, but he passed it up, and stopped in front of hers.

That was surprising. Though...perhaps it shouldn't be. She thought he'd been flirting most of the day, but she never liked to assume that sort of thing. She was a very friendly person, and he was new to the house.

Derek lifted his hand, then hesitated and turned around, walking away. Then he stopped and shook his head and walked back to her door once again. He squared his shoulders and knocked lightly.

She grinned to herself. He was nervous. He seemed so confident in all their other interactions, it was endearing to see him fretting about bringing her a cup of tea. It also made it clear that he *was* wooing her. While flattering, her stomach twisted with misgivings.

This was Amber's brother, and someone that now lived with the pack. They could date, but if either of them broke it off, it could get very awkward. She wasn't one for casual relationships either. She knew she always fell in love first, and way too fast. She'd never understood how people held their hearts back.

With a sigh, she released her connection to the house and stood. Derek knocked again, a little quieter this time. She hurried toward the door, pausing to take a breath before she cracked it open.

"Derek?" she asked in fake surprise, not wanting him to know she'd been spying on him.

He lifted the steaming mug of tea. It smelled like lavender and chamomile. "You said you'd been having trouble sleeping," he said. His smile drooped. "Aw hell, I didn't wake you, did I?"

She shook her head and opened the door wider. "No, you didn't. I was researching something."

"Oh, okay, that's good." He extended the cup of tea toward her. "I've heard this tea stuff can help you sleep, and you mentioned you'd been having some insomnia lately. I thought this might help."

She accepted the cup with a smile. "Thank you, it smells wonderful. And I love honey in my tea."

"How'd you know there's honey?" he asked, confused.

"Oh, I can smell it," she said, swallowing nervously. She wasn't quite ready to let anyone know the house let her spy on them. That was a conversation to have with Amber first, anyhow. She blew gently on the tea, then took a sip. Her eyes fell shut. He'd put in just the right amount of honey. "That's perfect."

Derek cleared his throat and rubbed a hand across the back of his neck. "That's great," he said in a slightly strangled tone. "Glad you like it."

"Stop flirting in the hallway. It's gross!" Amber whisper-shouted through her closed door, sounding like they'd woken her up.

Derek turned bright red and took a step back. "Hope it helps you sleep."

Ceri grinned at him. "Thanks for thinking of me."

That got his smile back. He glanced at Amber's door and mimed zipping his lips shut, then winked at her, and walked away.

She stayed standing in her doorway for a moment, sipping the tea, and chastising herself for flirting back. The tea *was* really good though.

CHAPTER 6

AMBER

Amber hopped down from her truck and looked at the rundown warehouse in front of them. The windows were broken with old, dusty glass still clinging to the weathered frames. It was made of brick but looked like a stiff wind might blow it over. On the side of the dilapidated building was an overhead door that was so badly rusted there were holes in it. "Derek, are we about to get murdered by a man wearing a mask made of someone else's face and wielding a chainsaw?"

"Nah, I'm getting more undead-welder-with-a-grudge vibes from this place. So, a blowtorch maybe?" he suggested with a shrug of his shoulders.

She rolled her eyes. "Who are we supposed to be meeting here?"

The door the warehouse opened and she flinched slightly. Derek snorted in amusement and shook his head, walking over to meet the guy heading toward them.

The guy didn't look like a serial killer. In fact, he looked like an old hippie. He had on cut-off jean shorts that showed an awful lot of thigh for an old man. He'd topped that with a tie-dyed shirt and a vest made of some kind of weird, faux-leather looking material.

"Good to meet you in person, Mr. Suthersby," Derek said, greeting him with a handshake.

"You too, my friend, but call me Bernard. We're all brothers on this great, green ball of life," he said, dragging Derek into a brief hug. Her brother grimaced and patted his shoulder awkwardly, pulling away as soon as he could.

Amber hid a smile behind her hand. Derek was getting ambushed by a lot of hugs recently. Served him right for bringing her to this creepy place. When he'd said he had a potential shop already lined up, she'd imagined something nicer. Something *useable*. This place would take weeks of work just to clean up, much less to get it ready for customers. Her savings account was dwindling fast just trying to keep everyone fed. Genevieve had insisted on covering things while she was gone, but it frustrated her to not be able to provide for her pack, or at least contribute more.

"Is this your sister?" Bernard asked, turning his attention to Amber.

"I am," she said, walking forward and shaking his hand as well. Instead of letting go, he wrapped both his hands around her and looked deep into her eyes.

"You're a werewolf," he stated. It wasn't a question, she could tell he was absolutely sure of it.

She inhaled carefully, but her first impression was right, he was human. She glanced at Derek, but he shook his head. He hadn't told Bernard. "Yeah. Is that a problem?" she asked, already feeling herself stiffen. If he was going to reject them because of what she was, then she wanted to know right now. "I'm bitten, too."

He smiled gently and patted her cheek. "Thought so. Mother Earth has blessed you with her magic, what is there to have a problem with?"

She raised a brow. "Everybody else seems to come up with a list of concerns."

He waved his hand at her and shook his head. "Ignorance leads to anger, which leads to hate. They need to smoke a little weed and meditate. Can't force a person to choose happiness though."

Well, this guy was nuts, but at least he wasn't a bigoted asshole. She managed to extract her hand from his and nodded. "You sure can't."

"Now," he said, rubbing his hands together. "I'm sure you'd like a tour. I know she looks rough on the outside, but my inspector promised she's safe to enter."

Amber groaned internally. 'Safe to enter' was a very low bar. Derek happily followed Bernard to the front door though, no hint of concern on his features. Maybe Ceri was right and she did worry too much.

She began to follow them, but her phone rang. Glancing at the caller ID, she saw it was Shane, the werewolf contact who'd helped her through the alpha trials, and quickly answered it.

"Alpha Hale," she answered with a smirk.

Shane chuckled. "Like the way it sounds?"

"Yeah, actually, I do," she said, unable to keep a smile from forming on her face.

"You might like it a little less after your first council meeting."

She groaned internally. Jameson, Shane's alpha, had originally planned on getting her up to date before she left on her trip, but ended up postponing it, though he wouldn't say why. "Is it going to be that bad? I'm not going to have to fight a bear again, am I?"

"Nah, nothing that easy. You instead get to learn about all your new responsibilities. I'll be picking you up at six a.m., by the way."

"No one should ever have to be awake that early," she muttered. "I hate Donovan. Have I mentioned that recently?"

He cleared his throat uncomfortably. "About Donovan…"

"What?" she prompted when he didn't continue.

"He disappeared from the cell the council was holding him in, then turned up dead a couple of days ago. Well, his head turned up. The police haven't found the rest of him."

She froze, her heart hammering in her chest. "What? Who killed him?"

"They don't know. I think you should expect a visit from the police soon, though. Your issues with him were pretty well-known. Honestly, he's lucky he got off with decapitation. His punishment was going to be way worse."

"Shit," she said, beginning to pace. She had an air-tight alibi, but Donovan's murder couldn't be good news. She wasn't exactly sad to see him go, but she had a bad feeling about this. Her wolf growled in agreement.

"Yeah, that's one word for it," Shane agreed.

"What about Peter, the werewolf that turned us? Any sign of him yet?" she asked.

"No, we never did find him," Shane said. "Look, I can't discuss this any further over the phone, but Jameson will tell you more tomorrow. Just be ready to go at six a.m. sharp."

"Alright."

"Talk to you soon," he said before ending the call.

She dropped her hand to her side and rubbed her hand against the demon mark. It was aching again, as if it was responding to her emotions. She was going to have to get the pack together this evening and let them know what had happened.

"Amber!" Derek shouted from the doorway of the warehouse. "Get in here and check it out. This place is awesome!"

She mentally shook off the worry and jogged toward her brother. "I'm coming, don't get your panties in a twist."

~

One hour, two hugs, and three large rats later they were heading out. Derek was thrilled with the warehouse. All she could see was the mess, but her brother was more of a visionary like Dylan had been. They saw the potential in broken things, and had the patience to try and fix them.

"Replacing the door will be the biggest expense," Derek said, scrolling through a web page on his phone. "Other than tools, obviously."

"A month ago, I'd have been able to offer a little more help with all that," she said, her hands tightening on the steering wheel.

"Don't worry about it, you're going to be free labor until we start earning enough to cover all the expenses. That's gonna save me a ton of money," he said, waving her misgivings away.

"Well, now I feel taken advantage of," she said, grinning at him.

"Tommy said he wanted to help, too. I'll work out a way to get him a little cash."

"Just make sure he always has time to study. He's trying to get his GED soon."

"Did he not finish high school?" Derek asked, looking up from his phone in confusion.

She shook her head. "Ran away from home when he was sixteen and dropped out of school."

"Damn, you really did find yourself a weird little pack."

"It wasn't his fault," she said, frowning at him. She didn't like him calling her pack weird, even though it was. They might be an odd group, but they'd managed to accomplish a lot.

"I didn't mean that in a bad way," he said, nudging her shoulder.

They fell silent for a few minutes as they drove; Derek lost in his research, and Amber lost in her thoughts. The song on the radio ended and the DJ's started talking about the new spots that had popped up where magic didn't work. Apparently, they were blaming overuse of magic now. She rolled her eyes and changed the channel. There was always a new conspiracy theory about what had caused it, but the truth was no one knew.

Her phone buzzed and she glanced at the screen. It was a short text from Ceri. She'd figured out something weird but cool about the house that she wanted to show her later. That reminded Amber of last night.

She turned back to Derek and narrowed her eyes at him. "What exactly are your intentions with Ceri?"

He looked up slowly. "That was out of nowhere."

"Answer the question, buster. All I remember from high school is that you brought a new girl home every week," she said accusingly.

"Geez, I'd forgotten how protective you were," he muttered. "It's been six years, and I've grown as a person, thank you very much. I'm not planning our wedding or anything, but I like her. She's all bohemian and cool, not to mention really nice. I don't know, I just couldn't help but flirt, and maybe I do want to date her. Or something."

Amber sighed at him. "Or something? That's the best you've got?"

"I'm being honest here. Do you want me to lie to make you feel better?"

"No, just don't screw her over, alright? She's in my pack, and I won't ask her to leave if you hurt her and make things awkward."

Derek looked offended at that. "Why do you assume I'd be the one to screw it up?"

She rolled her eyes. "You've met Ceri, I don't think she's capable of hurting anyone. For any reason."

He crossed his arms, still looking annoyed. "I'm not planning on screwing things up. Don't go all mama bear on me over it."

She knew she was being slightly overprotective. They were both adults after all, but all her instincts were going haywire over it. Learning that Donovan was dead was only making it worse.

"If she breaks your heart, I'll...ground her or something," she said finally, winking at her brother.

He snorted. "Thanks, that'll really show her."

"Bros over hoes."

He busted out laughing. "Your jokes are so bad, they're *almost* funny."

She reached over and punched him in the arm. "I'm hilarious. You're just jealous I'm the funniest one in the family."

"Oh please. Everyone knows I'm the funny one. You're the grumpy one."

CHAPTER 7

TOMMY

Tommy was bored. Amber and Derek were off looking at a place for their mechanic shop, Ceri was napping with Woggy, and Genevieve was working. He wasn't sleepy, but he definitely wasn't interested in studying anymore.

He rummaged through the refrigerator until he found stuff to make a sandwich and slapped a couple together. He scarfed down the first one standing there but took the second with him. The estate was huge and he hadn't explored any of it yet. When Amber had been preparing to take the Trials, they were all he could think about. Now, he was curious.

He left out the back door and wandered in the direction of the main house. There was no way he was going inside Thallan's creepy, old mansion, but there was no harm in checking out the gardens around it.

The garden by their guest house was decently well-maintained, if a little overgrown, but the closer you got to the main house, the worse shape everything was in. It was like the place was cursed and slowly killing everything around it.

He headed toward the back of the mansion, chewing as he looked around. There were remnants of wooden archways and a crumbling stone path. A big willow tree drooped over a scummy pond that was only half full. The narrow stream that used to feed it was dry. Weeds grew up through the cracks now. This place was probably really pretty once. It smelled weird around here, too. It wasn't exactly *bad*, but it definitely wasn't good. He sniffed the air, trying to parse it and got some combination of wet dirt, cut grass, and old fish.

He wondered what had made Thallan hate it so much that he'd let the place rot. The only thing elves loved more than themselves was nature. Their gardens were usually a little wild, but this was just…in ruins.

Shoving the rest of the sandwich in his mouth, he ducked under the drooping branch of an old tree and rounded a curve in the pathway. He caught a glimpse of a pixie in the shrub next to him and walked a few paces forward to try and get a better look. He needed to figure out a way to run them off, or gain their trust, so they didn't hurt Woggy.

"I was promised you wouldn't come snooping around the house," a gruff voice said from right behind him.

He jumped, not having seen Thallan when he was walking up. The creepy elf was sitting on a stone bench that was half covered in vines. He should have smelled the elf, but the scent of cigarettes wasn't noticeable until after Thallan had spoken.

"I'm just looking around. I didn't go in your house," Tommy said, backing up a step.

Thallan exhaled smoke through his nose and turned his eyes back to the overgrown rose bush in front of him. "Don't come lurking through my gardens either. You and your pack get the guest house, and the lands. But not this. That was the deal."

"Got it. Sorry." Tommy turned to go back the way he'd come.

"Has Amber been acting odd in any way since she got back?" Thallan asked before he'd even taken a step.

He paused and looked over his shoulder. "No. Why?"

Thallan shrugged. "No reason."

Tommy waited for some kind of explanation, but the elf just took another drag of his cigarette and stared at nothing. He decided to leave before he got asked anything else.

The question had unsettled him though. Amber never had explained how she got Thallan to agree to letting them live there, or to be her sponsor. Now the old creep thought there was a chance she might start acting weird. He wasn't sure if that's because he'd cursed her, or if there was some other reason.

When he made it back to the pack house he saw Amber's truck was back in the driveway. He frowned thinking he should have been able to hear them arrive. Maybe the garden had some weird wards on it that had prevented it.

The back door opened as he approached it and Amber visibly slumped in relief. "Are you okay? You just felt really...disturbed for a moment."

"Oh, yeah. I was just wandering around and Thallan startled me," Tommy said with a shrug. He didn't want to talk about it yet. He wanted to bring it up with Ceri first, and see if she knew anything. "Did the place Derek found work out?"

She groaned. "He seems to think so."

"Just because there are a few rats and cobwebs doesn't mean it isn't perfect," Derek shouted from inside the house.

She turned back to her brother and Tommy followed her inside. "I can help clean up," he offered.

"That'd be great!" Derek said. "I was actually going to talk to you about your pay. I can give you fifty bucks a week for part-time work until the place opens, then I'll see about a raise. Until then, I thought maybe we could work something else out. Maybe teaching you how to work on the trucks so you can help out as a mechanic eventually?"

Tommy hesitated, the gears in his head turning, then tugged his beanie down farther on his head. He had something else in mind, but he wanted to talk to Derek about it in private. "Sure, sounds good. I'll just be glad to have something to do. I can only study so much."

"Perfect," Derek said, rubbing his hands together. "Studying is overrated anyhow."

Amber rolled her eyes and punched him in the shoulder. "Don't even start."

Derek just punched her right back, starting an impromptu wrestling match. Tommy grinned. It was good to see someone giving his alpha crap. She looked more relaxed than she had since…well, since he'd met her.

CHAPTER 8

GENEVIEVE

The werewolf was younger than Genevieve had expected. He was a skinny, blond college kid, and he looked scared out of his mind.

"I was out for my twenty-first birthday with my human friends and this group of guys started picking on a girl. I was feeling cocky, because what can they do to me, you know? So, I stepped in. I didn't think I was going to hurt him that bad. He threw the first punch and I didn't lose control. I didn't. I just hit him back and he crumpled," Davie said, his hands shaking as he rubbed them over his watery eyes. "I'm screwed, aren't I?"

"You should never have been arrested," she said firmly, reaching across the table to squeeze his arm. Her wolf was furious, all her protective instincts were raging inside her. If she'd been in his situation she might have actually lost control and ripped the dude's arms off. "My firm has agreed to take on the case, free of charge. We're going to get these charges dismissed."

"Really?" he asked, not looking like he believed her at all. "My alpha said it was a lost cause."

"No offense to your alpha, but that's bullshit," she said, pausing to take a deep breath. "What pack are you with? I'll need to talk with them."

He sniffled and wiped his nose on the back of his sleeve. "The Lockhart Pack."

Her pen snapped in her hand, ink soaking into her fingers. She quickly dropped it on the table. This werewolf belonged to Donovan's pack. There was no way she could just stroll up and talk to Donovan. He might kill her, or refuse to help just to spite her.

"You okay?" he asked, confused.

"Yeah, just fine," she said, clearing her throat and curling her stained fingers into her palm. "I'll be back to see you tomorrow, okay? Keep thinking about the details, and anyone that can vouch for your character. Especially any humans."

"Okay."

She got up and rapped on the door to let the guard know she was done. The guard opened the door to let her out, but she paused in the doorway. "Keep your chin up, okay Davie? It's going to work out. I promise."

Davie nodded, the tense line of his shoulders loosening just a little. "I'll try to believe that."

"Thanks," she said with a nod to the guard as she slipped out of the room. Her fingers tightened on the handle of her briefcase. Being in the jail made her skin crawl. She'd come so close to being in this place herself. It hadn't seemed real until she'd walked in here today, though.

She made it out of the building and to her car before before the tears of frustration welled up in her eyes. She wanted to strangle Donovan. He'd abandoned his pack member so easily. She couldn't fathom doing that. Even now, she could feel the pack bond stretching between her, Tommy, Ceri, and Amber. It thrummed in her gut, a warm reassurance. How could an alpha turn their back on that?

She rested her forehead against the steering wheel and took a deep breath. Maybe, she could have one of the other associates talk to Donovan and convince him to give Davie the support he needed.

The only issue was if she could do it in less than a week. She'd spent the entire morning prepping to go to the jail and most of the afternoon interviewing Davie.

She checked her phone and saw an invitation from Steven to dinner, which she quickly replied to with a rejection. The last thing she had time for was a date. Her mother had also texted her now, which meant a phone call was imminent if she didn't reply. She opened the message and saw that her parents wanted to have dinner and catch up. That meant they'd probably heard something about her getting bitten. She wondered who had ratted her out. It was probably her sister, the little snoop.

She didn't hate her parents or anything. It was the opposite actually. They were frustratingly perfect. They never pried and always supported her. Her dad used to take off work to come to all her softball games. He'd cheer when she struck out and tell her *better luck next time, princess*. She knew he'd probably been embarrassed though.

Dropping her phone in her lap, she groaned in annoyance. Her mother would probably love Amber, want to adopt Tommy, and think Ceri walked on water. Logically, she knew it was a dumb thing to be frustrated by, but all she'd ever done was let them down. She'd graduated college only to avoid using the degree they'd paid for as long as she could. She was in her mid-twenties now and hadn't had a serious boyfriend yet. Unless you counted Steven, but they didn't know about him, and she still wasn't sure she wanted that to be serious.

She needed, desperately, to be able to help Davie. She wanted to prove she could do something right, and do it well. That, and she couldn't bear the idea of letting an injustice like this happen.

Angry, she threw the car into reverse and backed out of her parking spot. It was time to hunt down an alpha. She should probably let Amber know what she was doing first. And call Steven and see if there was any etiquette she needed to follow since she was also a werewolf.

"It just has to keep getting more complicated," she muttered to herself.

CHAPTER 9

CERI

Ceri parked her car a few blocks from the store and climbed out. The wind whipped around her legs, scattering leaves across the sidewalk. She pulled her cardigan a little closer around her. It was time to start wearing leggings under her dresses again.

She hadn't wanted to come into the city. Despite its size, the chance that she'd run into either a family member or someone from the Blackwood coven was high. Witches ran in small circles, and the things she needed to get today took her right into the midst of them.

She was going to have to look into getting another job soon. Amber had told her not to stress about it, but there was no way she'd just mooch off the pack forever. Even if all she could do was contribute to the grocery bill, she would. There were things she could do to make the wards on the house stronger if she had the right supplies. With a little time and money, she thought she could actually improve the wards on the entire property. They just needed a little TLC.

A little bell tinkled overhead as she walked in. Pausing just inside, she scanned the sections for hyssop elixir and powdered pennyroyal. A sign in the back corner of the store pointed out what she needed. She wound through the aisles, refusing to look at the little jars that held pixie parts and other magical creatures. It had always bothered her, but now that she had Woggy, it made her nauseous to even think about it.

As she neared the back of the store, the scents of sage and other cleansing herbs made her nose tickle. She grabbed a few sticks of sage since she had a feeling she'd be using a lot of it in the coming weeks, then continued toward the back.

She paused in front of the shelf that had it and picked up two brands, comparing the strength of the ingredients versus the price. Despite preferring to use the more concentrated version, she was probably going to have to settle for the cheaper one and hope the strength of her magic could make up the difference.

"Ceridwen," a deep voice said behind her. Her heart immediately kicked into overdrive as her gut twisted in worry. He shouldn't be here.

She turned slowly to face her father. He was only slightly taller than she was and almost as slender. He had thin strawberry blond hair and a baby face that made many people underestimate him. Her mother was their coven leader, but he was her second. They'd married for no other reason than to combine the magical potential of their families. It had paid off with powerful and talented children.

"Father," she said, meeting his eyes despite her unease. *Don't show fear. Don't show weakness. Don't ever turn your back on an enemy.*

"Your mother is surprised you haven't come back," he said, rubbing his hand along the stubble on his jaw.

"But you're not."

He shook his head. "You've never been willing to commit to the coven. It was only a matter of time before you found a reason to leave permanently."

There were many reasons she'd stayed for so long. Wanting her parent's approval, fear of striking out on her own, and knowing that if she joined another coven they'd consider her an enemy. This meeting wasn't a coincidence. Her father had come specifically to speak with her. Perhaps to threaten her.

"I don't want to hurt other living things just to gain more power," she said, repeating the beginning of an old argument.

He shook his head in exasperation. "You've made that very clear."

"Why are you here then, if not to talk me into returning to the coven?" she asked.

He lifted his head and spoke formally, "You weakened the coven when you left. Normally this would justify retaliation."

She stiffened, preparing for an attack. Her mind went to the pack, praying they were still alright. She hadn't even considered that her family might move against them after her mother kicked her out, but she should have.

"However," he continued, "your actions at the Alpha Trials, and on Halloween, severely weakened our enemy, the Blackwood Coven. Your mother has chosen, as a final act of mercy, to accept this as an offering that balances out your transgressions. You are persona non grata with the Gallagher Clan from this day forward. Under the rules of coven engagement, we will not act against you unless you first act against us."

She had no idea how he knew about Halloween, or if he just suspected it had been her. Perhaps it had been a simple matter of deduction. Not many witches could get past the Blackwood wards.

"The Hale pack will not threaten or harm the Gallagher clan unless you first move against us," she said, echoing his words as the formal declaration demanded.

Her father nodded, then turned and walked away. Her heart was racing and, now that he wasn't looking, her hands shook slightly. That was it. She had no family anymore. Her mother had kicked her out before, but she had always come back. That wasn't a choice this time.

Relief and sorrow warred inside her. Her parents were cruel, but she hadn't seen that as a child. She didn't want to see it now.

Shaking off the self-pity, she straightened her shoulders and steeled herself. Enough was enough. She'd made her choice and she didn't regret it. Amber was her alpha now, and she was a good person. Tommy was like a little brother already, and Genevieve could be the sister she always wished she'd had. Her actual siblings were...like her parents. They'd never gotten along.

She grabbed the last thing she needed from the shelves and walked to the register, paying as quickly as she could. She knew her parents hadn't done anything to the pack or her father wouldn't have said what he did. Still, she'd feel better once she was back there and could confirm it in person.

"Thanks, have a good day," the cashier said cheerfully.

"You too," she replied, though her smile in return was wooden.

She grabbed the bag the cashier handed her and hurried out the door, almost running into someone trying to enter. With a muttered 'sorry', she sidestepped around them. She wished she'd parked closer now. Parking down the street had obviously done nothing to help avoid running into someone she knew. It took all her self-control, and the knowledge that her father or someone else might be watching, to walk and not run.

Finally, her car came into view, but...an owl sat on the roof. Her blood ran cold. Owls were ill omens. They portended death, misfortune, and illness. This was the last thing she needed right now. Running into her father had been enough of a bad sign. She didn't want another.

Glaring at it, she walked up to her car and waved her hands at the unwelcome creature. "Shoo!"

The owl flapped its wings and hopped out of her reach but didn't fly away. It hooted at her softly.

"Go away," she hissed.

It hooted again and walked sideways, hopping down onto the side mirror. Its eerie, orange eyes fixed on her. She tried to shoo it away again and it nipped at her finger, drawing a little blood.

She hissed in pain and shook her finger. Seemingly pleased with itself, it took flight. Instead of going over her head, it almost collided with her. She ducked to avoid it, then turned to glare at the persistent bird. It was sitting under a tree looking quite smug.

She thought about throwing something at it when she saw what was growing next to its foot. It had barely sprouted out of the ground. If the owl hadn't been practically standing on it, she never would have seen the slight, purple glow.

Crouching down, she cautiously reached for the little mushroom near its foot. The owl hooted happily and shuffled to the side. She brushed the dirt away and, sure enough, there was the beginning of a Fairy Ring. It was a super rare mushroom that had all but died out due to over-harvesting. It was useful in all manner of spells, as well as meditation. There were rumors it could help a powerful enough witch catch glimpses of the future, or at least its possibilities.

She brushed the dirt a little farther away and saw that there wasn't just one. There was a circle of seven little, purple mushrooms. That was a lucky number, and meant that she could collect the whole bundle and use them to grow more.

She looked at the owl again, suspicious now. It cocked its head at her as though it were analyzing her right back. This wasn't a normal animal.

"Thank you," she whispered.

It hooted, then took off, flying over her head and into the sky. She was going to have to do a little research, perhaps they weren't always ill omens.

Turning her attention back to the Fairy Ring, she quickly dug around it and pulled out a whole chunk of dirt. With nowhere else to put it, she opened her purse and set it carefully inside. It'd wash.

CHAPTER 10

AMBER

Amber sat next to Ceri on the porch swing sipping coffee. She was tired, and the demon mark was throbbing like a headache. That couldn't be a good sign.

Mentally, she prodded the wolf, asking what she'd done to the demon. Amber got back a strong impression of smugness, but nothing else. She sighed. She didn't like being caught between the wolf and Angel.

Ceri shifted around, yawning. The witch had been in a weird mood since she got back yesterday, and she hadn't been sleeping much since the Trials. It was starting to worry Amber, but she knew Ceri would just say she worried about everything.

"I saw an owl yesterday," Ceri said, her tone suggesting that meant something important, and possibly bad.

"Are you allergic to them or something?" she asked.

Ceri snorted in amusement. "No, well, figuratively I guess we all are. They're considered ill omens."

"Great," Amber muttered before chugging the rest of her coffee. "Just what I needed to hear right before this meeting."

"Well, that's the thing," Ceri said thoughtfully. "It led me to something really good. Those mushrooms I told you about yesterday evening –– which I planted in the garden by the way. Anyhow, my gut is telling me it wasn't an ill omen, that it's something else instead. I just have to figure out what, exactly."

"You're probably turning into some kind of animal whisperer," Amber suggested. "All the forest creatures are going to start flocking to you. Witches don't ever join packs. It was bound to do something weird to you."

Ceri laughed, then sat up straight, her eyes going wide. "Amber, you're a genius."

"What?" she asked, confused.

"An absolute genius," Ceri said, jumping to her feet and running inside, slamming the door shut behind her.

"Well, okay then." She'd have to corner Ceri later and get an explanation, but she'd take being called a genius for now. She glanced at her phone. Shane was two minutes late. The bastard.

Leaning her head back against the back of the swing she let her eyes slip shut. Maybe there was time for a short nap. Of course, that was when she heard a car turn down the driveway.

She peeked her eye open and saw it was the same suburban he'd driven to pick her up for the Trials. She stood and hurried back inside to dump her coffee mug in the sink, then walked back out to the porch.

Shane hadn't bothered to get out to greet her; he just flashed his headlights impatiently. He had some nerve.

She yanked the car door open and glared at him. "You're late."

"I know, get in," he said, motioning for her to hurry.

She hopped up into the passenger seat and buckled her seatbelt. "Is something wrong?"

"Not really, it was just a late night last night. Since Donovan was ousted from the council, and you haven't filled his spot yet, Jameson has been handling all his duties. Which means I've been dealing with a lot of petty crap as his beta," Shane said tiredly.

"Great," Amber said with a sigh.

"Don't worry, I won't let them throw you to the wolves. Jameson is going to let me assist you for a while. He knows you're clueless," Shane said with a smirk.

"Gee, thanks."

"Oh, come on, you know it's true."

"I'm not *completely* clueless, just slightly under-educated," she retorted. He was right though. She'd be lost without help. "Thanks for the help though. I'd prefer to not screw everything up my first week on the job."

He chuckled. "Maybe you can take me out for coffee to pay me back."

"I don't know if it's appropriate to date my coworkers," she said, looking out the window to hide the slight blush on her cheeks. She really needed to date more if this was how she reacted to a little light flirting. This was just embarrassing.

"Think of us more as allies," Shane said, nodding to himself. "No rules against allies dating."

Shane had a lot of things going for him. He was attractive, confident, and best of all, he was straightforward about what he wanted.

"Fine, let's do coffee in a few days. I need to make sure you earn it before I take you out," she said, crossing her arms.

"That won't be a problem."

It turned out that Jameson only lived twenty minutes away. The drive passed quickly and Amber had to fight down the nervous energy that was about to make her sweat through her shirt. She hated not knowing what to expect, and this was all brand new. The wolf was pacing in her mind too, which didn't help calm her down at all.

They turned down a street that led into a small subdivision.

"Do these homes all belong to pack members?" she asked, looking at the rows of houses. The lawns were neat, and no cars were parked in the street clogging up traffic. It looked like any other human subdivision.

"Pack and their families," Shane confirmed with a nod. "There's another community about a mile north of here that's bigger. I live out there since Alpha Jameson wanted a high-ranking pack member in the neighborhood to keep the peace, and protect the pack."

"How big is Jameson's pack?" she asked in surprise. She'd always thought of packs as small, with ten to twelve members. Maybe that's just how it was in the South.

"He has fifty registered members. It's a big pack, which is part of why he's the head of the council. Not many people could keep a pack this big together."

"That's a lot of people to keep track of," she said, shaking her head in disbelief. She couldn't fathom what it would be like to be connected so intimately to so many people. How did he not go crazy feeling them all the time? And the strength she got from the pack bond was already crazy. Being able to draw on fifty people would make you insanely powerful.

Shane pulled into a driveway in front of a two-story house. It wasn't the biggest, or grandest house on the block. There was nothing to make it stand out at all other than the cars in the driveway and parked along the street.

"Before we go in, just remember, you're their equal. You don't have to be submissive to them," Shane said in a whisper.

She nodded. "Got it."

They climbed out and headed toward the door. She could smell the other alphas now, and recognized their scents from the Trials. It was odd to have some of her senses enhanced so dramatically, but she was getting used to it. Slowly.

Jameson greeted them at the door, waving them inside. There was none of the formality of the Trials this time. He was barefoot in a pair of cargo shorts and a t-shirt.

"Alpha Lawrence is running late, but we're getting started without him," Jameson said as he let them through the house. "Need coffee?"

"I already had some, thanks though," Amber said as she looked around curiously. There wasn't anything unusual about the place. He had family pictures on the wall. The living room was a mix of new furniture and a bookshelf that looked like an old, family antique.

She could smell that dozens of weres had passed through, but it seemed like only his immediate family actually lived here. She was glad her pack could all live together, for now at least. It still made her skin crawl to think about being separated. Maybe that was something that lessened in time.

"We have these meetings bi-weekly unless something is going on," Jameson explained as they walked. "We get them done early so everyone can be to work on time."

"What do you do outside of being an alpha?" she asked, curious.

"My wife owns a hair salon, and I'm mostly in real estate. I own a strip center in Portland, and a couple of apartment complexes."

"You don't own Rosewood Lake Apartments, do you?" she asked, narrowing her eyes at him.

"No. Why?" he asked, pausing to turn and look at her.

She shrugged. "I got evicted for being bitten. Just making sure it wasn't you."

"Ah," he said, looking annoyed. "The laws make it harder on bitten weres than it needs to be. They tend to have less control at first, generally speaking. You certainly proved that wrong. Humans worry too much, and have to regulate damn near everything."

They walked out the back door and she was hit with the scent of other alphas, and a sense of something *other*. Of magic. She hadn't noticed at the Trials. Maybe the ritual changed her somehow, or maybe she could just sense more as the wolf settled into her mind.

She could feel her eyes shifting to red as she surveyed the other alphas. Currently present were a man and a woman she recognized from the Trials.

"This is Alpha Salazar," he said, pointing at the woman, who nodded in her direction.

She was Hispanic with short, black hair. She wore a pantsuit with a bright teal shirt underneath the jacket. To be honest, she kind of looked like your average real estate agent.

"And this is Alpha Bennett," Jameson said, finishing the introductions.

This guy looked like he worked with his hands. He was a textbook burly, mountain man with a plaid shirt, worn jeans, and a bushy black beard that stretched halfway down his chest. A knit cap hid his hair. He inclined his head slowly, his eyes never leaving hers.

They didn't seem particularly welcoming, but no one was trying to bite her head off. She'd call that a win.

"Nice to meet you," she said, nodding at them in return. It was difficult, but she pulled the wolf back, and willed her eyes to return to normal. There was no need to piss off anyone with some kind of inadvertent werewolf challenge the day she met them.

Jameson plopped down on the porch swing and gestured at the chair next to Salazar. "Grab a seat, this is going to take a while."

Shane chuckled as he moved to stand behind her. She noticed he didn't sit, and Jameson didn't ask him to. There were several places he could have sat, so it must have been intentional. She crossed her arms and leaned back in her seat, unsure of how she felt about that. All this posturing didn't come naturally to her. Born wolves did have that advantage over the bitten wolves like her.

Jameson leaned back and pushed the swing with his foot. "As you all already know, Alpha Donovan Lockhart is dead. However, about a half hour before you two arrived," he nodded at Salazar and Bennett, "I found out some more information. The police found his body." He paused, as though collecting himself to deliver bad news. "His heart was gone."

"Shit," Bennett said immediately, running his hand down his face. "How was it removed?"

"Obsidian blade. He was bound with silver. And he was definitely alive when it was cut out," Jameson said, shaking his head in disgust.

"Wait, someone cut out his heart?" Amber interjected, both horrified and confused.

"A sorcerer," Salazar said, speaking for the first time. "Witches sacrifice animals all the time; cut them up into little pieces to fuel their magic. Sacrificing a werewolf or human? That's sorcery. It's as dark as magic gets."

"We have to assume that every alpha in the area may be a target next," Jameson said.

"I hope the bastard tries to take me," Bennett grunted.

Salazar scoffed at his comment. "You've obviously never fought a sorcerer then."

The door opened and a reedy man with thick, black-framed glasses hurried over to join the group. "Sorry I'm late."

He must be Alpha Lawrence. Despite his nerdy appearance, his rolled-up sleeves revealed wiry muscles. His eyes flicked to her and he nodded briefly, returning his attention to Jameson.

"You say that every meeting," Jameson said, raising a brow.

Lawrence shrugged and smirked at the older man. "Maybe we should have them in the evenings instead."

Jameson shook his head in annoyance, then continued the meeting, "With Donovan dead, his pack is in turmoil. Over the past two days, there have been five challenge fights." He turned to look at Amber. "This will be a good situation for you to learn what this council does. We are not here to try to tell the other packs what to do, but we are here to make sure they don't get out of control in these sorts of situations."

She forced herself not to fidget as the eyes of every alpha landed on her. "Alright. What do I need to do?"

"Go meet the current alpha, and register the names and positions of all the pack members. With every challenge, record the name of the winner, loser, and any other changes in rank. Someone has to be the alpha for one cycle of the moon, or they can't go through the Trials. Anything that can be done to calm down the situation would be better for everyone involved. I've seen packs completely unravel after losing their alpha if there wasn't a clear successor. If that happens, we'll have dozens of omegas in the region that we'll either have to take into our packs, or risk starting this whole process over again," Jameson said with a sigh.

Amber felt a headache forming behind her eyes. "So, babysit their pack while they fight over who becomes the new alpha?"

A smile tugged at the corner of Jameson's mouth. "Yes."

"They won't try to challenge her, will they?" Lawrence asked, pointing at her.

Jameson frowned. "We've never had that issue before."

"Never had a bitten wolf on the council before either," Lawrence said with a shrug.

"I beat their alpha, why would they bother trying to challenge me?" Amber asked, irritated at the implications. Shane had warned her not to let them treat her like she wasn't their equal. If this guy had a problem with her, she was going to settle it right now.

"You beat him in a test of control, not a fight. Some idiot might want to see if they can take your pack instead," Lawrence replied.

"If I'm going to be a part of this council, they'll all have to learn to respect me eventually," Amber said, relaxing slightly. It sounded more like genuine concern than him trying to put her down. She turned back to Jameson. "If I hide behind the council it'll make me look weak. I never wanted Donovan's place here, hell, I never wanted to be a werewolf, but I'm not going to shirk my duties out of fear. If this is what I need to do, then I'll do it."

"No one else wants to do it, that's for sure," Salazar said under her breath.

Bennett didn't comment, but he did look like he thought she'd fail.

"I agree," Jameson said with a nod. "Shane will be there to back you up. I don't foresee any problems coming up that you can't handle. Honestly, if you can't deal with them, you aren't fit to be on the council."

Bennet snorted at that and muttered something that sounded like 'natural selection'. She ignored him and did her best to take in all the information Jameson shared during the meeting.

It turned out babysitting Donovan's pack was only part of what she'd have to deal with now. Who knew being a werewolf would come with so much paperwork?

CHAPTER 11

TOMMY

Tommy scooped the cheesy omelet out onto a plate and inspected it. It wasn't burned, hadn't broken when he flipped it, and it had just the right amount of gooey cheese. It was perfect.

Derek was sitting at the table oblivious, but perked up when he set the omelet down in front of him. He looked at the omelet, then looked at Tommy. "Why do I feel like this is a bribe?"

"Because it is," Tommy said, crossing his arms.

Derek picked up his fork and took a big bite. His eyes widened as he chewed. Swallowing, he said, "Okay, it worked. What do you want?"

"Could you teach me how to fight?"

"Shouldn't you ask Amber for that kinda help?" Derek asked, scratching the back of his head.

"Yeah, probably," Tommy said shoving his hands in his pockets. "But I don't want her to think I'm completely incompetent. I'd like to learn a few things first. Even Genevieve can hold her own. I've lost every fight I've been in."

Derek shrugged like that made perfect sense to him. A mischievous grin spread across his face. "Alright, I can show you how to punch and I'll show you a few wrestling moves that always used to work on Amber."

"That would be awesome," Tommy said with a huge smile.

"But you're not allowed to use your werewolf strength while I'm showing you things. I don't need my arm getting accidentally broken or anything stupid like that," Derek said, pointing his finger at him.

"No werewolf strength," Tommy said, lifting his hands in surrender.

Derek nodded, then scarfed down the rest of the omelet. "Dude, where did you learn to cook like this?"

"My mom I guess, but most of the time I just follow the recipes," Tommy said. He hadn't enjoyed cooking so much when he'd been a kid. Now, it was one of the few things that could relax him when he started feeling anxious. He didn't have to go hungry anymore. He had a place to call home, and a makeshift family.

"Do you know when Amber is supposed to be back?" Derek asked, glancing at his watch.

"No clue, but I'll hear her coming before they even reach the driveway," Tommy said, tapping his ear. "Shane's suburban makes a weird noise."

"Oh, that's right, you can hear super well. That's going to come in handy when I start teaching you how to work on cars," Derek said as he stood, walking the plate over to the sink and quickly washing it. "Let's do what we can today before Amber gets back. There's no telling when else we'll have time."

"Sounds great," Tommy said, practically bouncing with nervous energy. He needed this, but he couldn't say he wasn't still worried. Like he'd told Derek, he'd lost every fight he'd been in. Before he was bitten, he was scrawny and weak. He had muscles coming in now, but he didn't know what to do with them.

"Let's go out back," Derek said.

They headed out the back door and behind the house. It was shady and grassy with plenty of room to move around.

Derek nodded in approval, then turned to him. "Okay, throw a punch."

Tommy curled his hand into a fist and swung his arm as hard and fast as he could. The momentum of the punch drug him forward and he stumbled slightly as his feet twisted in the grass. When he looked up at Derek to see how he'd done, the man had one hand covering his face.

"Okay, so...that was...completely wrong in every way," he said, taking a deep breath before looking up. "Come here. Let's start with how to make a proper fist. Never, ever stick your thumb out like that. You're just asking for it to get broken."

Tommy sighed. He knew he sucked, but he'd hoped he wasn't *that* bad.

CHAPTER 12

CERI

Ceri flipped through her old spellbook, filled with notes from her grandmother's lessons, until she found it. She hadn't remembered her grandmother had even talked about it until Amber had said "animal whisperer". Her old notes were there, written in glittery pink ink and uneven letters.

"A witch belongs in a coven, lassie. There should be at least three, but a coven of seven or thirteen will be stronger. The number of witches must always be a prime number, so the coven cannot be divided. Always an odd number for luck," her grandmother said as she dissected the remains of the pixie.

Ceri kept her eyes on her notes so she didn't have to see. "Can't a witch be alone?"

"Pah, she could, but then she'd be vulnerable. Limited. This family is meant for powerful magic, not tricks a human could do."

She kicked her legs, trying to think of another question. She only got the knowledge she asked for, that was the rule. Sometimes it was risky to ask, because the lessons were...unpleasant. But her grandmother said not to let fear rule her.

"Has a witch ever been part of a pack?" she asked tentatively.

Her grandmother stopped cutting and glared at her. "Why would ya want ta consort with a bunch of flea-ridden weres?"

She lifted her chin stubbornly. "Never said I did, I just wondered if it had ever happened. Werewolves can't even control their magic. I'd never want to be one of them."

Her grandmother didn't speak immediately. She weighed Ceri with her gaze, as though she could see a lie written on her face. "If ya let a pack suck ya in, you'll turn into a pathetic little shaman. You'll end up spending all your time outside talking ta birds like you're some kind of animal whisperer. Shamans think every little bug that crawls the earth has a spirit inside it. They use soft magic."

Saying someone had soft magic was the highest insult her grandmother could give.

Ceri snapped out of the memory. Shaman. Her grandmother was probably rolling in her grave right now.

She'd never heard anyone else talk about shamans. Human magic users were either witches or sorcerers. Good or bad. Though she knew how often those lines got blurred.

This was something she needed to figure out, then talk to Amber about. Sooner rather than later. She wasn't sure if anyone outside the pack should know. They'd thought it odd Amber was claiming a witch as part of the pack, but everyone seemed to think it was in name only. It had surprised both of them to discover it wasn't.

She closed the book and grabbed her sage. It was time to figure this out. She walked the room as she usually did, but hesitated by the window. She'd always left the curtains shut, but this time…she needed something different.

She yanked the curtains open and lifted the window. The screen was awkward to pop out, but she got it and set it aside. Taking a deep breath to re-center herself, she moved the sage around the edges of the window. Nothing could come in that meant her, or her pack, harm.

Placing the sage in a bowl in front of her, she sat cross legged in the center of the room. She closed her eyes and instead of focusing on the house, she turned her attention inward. The pack bond was intertwined with her own, innate magic now. She turned her hands upward and recited a spell for clarity. The energy in her body moved, shifting to her head and her heart.

A noise at the window startled her, and her eyes snapped open. Big orange eyes stared back at her as the owl she'd seen the day before settled itself on her work table. She forced herself to examine it rather than just shoo it away out of fear.

It was large, at least two feet tall. The tawny feathers were striped with black and brown. Two tufts that looked like ears sat above the round face. The creature's vibrant orange eyes watched her patiently as she inspected it.

"Umm, hello," she said quietly.

It hooted, fluffing its feathers out and shifting closer to her.

As she looked into its eyes, she felt like she was being tugged forward, but her body wasn't moving. She exhaled, letting the magic flow through her without struggle. The orange eyes grew larger in her vision until it was all she could see…and she was falling.

The warm glow of the owl's eyes grew, and it didn't stop. The warmth became heat. It grew hotter and hotter until it felt like she might suffocate.

Darkness. Fire. Screams. Pain.

The visions rolled over her so fast she couldn't process them. There were only glimpses. They terrified her. Strange magic pounded against her mind. This creature didn't just use magic, it *was* magic.

Help me.

The desperate plea for help washed over her, bathing her in someone else's terror. Her heart pounded in her chest and she struggled against the magic holding her in the vision. As though sensing her distress, the owl blinked and everything stopped just as abruptly as it had begun.

Ceri's eyes snapped open. Her hands shook as she pushed her hair back from face. She was sweating and her hands were trembling. She had no idea how long it had been, but her body ached from sitting in one position for so long.

She looked up, relieved to see the owl was still there. "What are you?"

The owl hooted, then turned and flew out of the open window.

She couldn't bring herself to stand, or move at all. Whatever she'd just seen was bad. Someone was in danger, though she had no idea if it was happening in the past, present, or future. It had been vague and confusing, but she had felt the darkness.

Something was coming and it was powerful. She pressed a clammy hand to her cheek and closed her eyes. Whatever it was, it was evil.

CHAPTER 13

AMBER

Amber waved goodbye to Shane. They had to go see Donovan's old pack later that evening, but they both had things to do before that.

She headed inside, her brain hurting from all the information she'd absorbed this morning. For every answer she'd gotten, she'd ended up with five more questions. She had a list of things to ask Steven, Genevieve's boyfriend. He'd been peppering her with questions for his thesis lately as they'd agreed to when he'd helped her prepare for the Trials, so she didn't feel bad using him for research. It made her life easier and made him happy as a clam.

She walked inside and saw Tommy and Derek standing in the kitchen. Looking *guilty*. Tommy's hair was standing on end and the side of his neck and face was all red. Derek's shirt had a tear under the sleeve that she knew hadn't been there before.

"Why are you both so sweaty?" Amber asked, her nose twitching as she looked between the two miscreants.

"We were...cooking," Derek lied, gesturing at the stove.

Amber was about to retort that he hated cooking and he would never, ever do it under any circumstances when Derek winked at her. She sighed. He was asking her to drop it. It looked like they'd been wrestling, so she doubted it was some kind of bad secret. Derek would tell her if it was important. She hoped. "Whatever. Has anyone heard from Gen?"

"Nah, but I think she should be home—" Tommy stopped abruptly, his head tilting toward the door.

Amber heard it then too; the car turning down the driveway. That wasn't Genevieve or anyone else she recognized. "I'll see who it is."

She looked out the peephole and saw an unmarked police car parking in front of the porch. The detective she'd met after those mercenaries had attacked her stepped out.

"It's the police. Stay inside, I'll go talk to him," she said, barely suppressing a growl. She knew he was probably here about Donovan. Luckily, she had an airtight alibi for his murder, but that wouldn't necessarily stop her from being a suspect.

She walked outside, shutting the door firmly behind her, and waited for the detective on the steps. Tommy and Derek were whispering inside. Tommy was probably explaining what had happened. She hadn't actually told Derek about all that yet. She glossed over the Trials too, making the whole ordeal sound easy. He was probably going to have a ton of questions now.

Detective Sloan stopped in front of her. He had bags under his eyes and looked even skinnier than last time she'd seen him, like he hadn't been eating or sleeping. "Ms. Hale," he said in greeting.

"Detective," she said, nodding her head at him. "How can I help you?"

"I'm sure you've heard about Donovan Lockhart's murder."

"Yes," she acknowledged, seeing no reason to lie about it.

"I've already looked into your whereabouts around the time of the murder and you aren't a suspect. I just came to warn you," he said, running his hand through his light brown hair. "I spoke with a friend that works up near Seattle. There were two alphas killed the same way out there."

She frowned. Jameson hadn't mentioned that. Maybe he didn't know. "Like a serial killer?"

Sloan nodded. "That's my suspicion. It looks like they might be working their way south."

"Do you have any idea who's behind the killings?"

"No. So be careful, and let me know if you see or hear anything odd. We have reason to believe there may be more than one person involved in the killings. I know you weres like to handle things on your own, but this may not be something you can stop." He pulled his card out of his pocket and handed it to her. "Call me if you have even the slightest suspicion you're being targeted."

She took it with a nod. "Alright."

Sloan turned and headed back to his car. She waited until he was leaving the driveway before going back inside. Derek was standing in the living room, arms crossed, jaw set with anger.

"Don't start," she said, shoving the card in her pocket.

"What the hell, Amber? Don't start? You nearly got killed, on more than one occasion!" he shouted at her, throwing his hands in the air.

Tommy backed up so fast he was almost running backward and disappeared into the kitchen with a guilty expression.

"There was no point worrying anyone!" she shouted back, her eyes flashing red.

"You don't just keep something like that from your family," he insisted, jabbing his finger at her. "And now there's a serial killer after you? Would you have told anyone about that if we weren't here listening in?"

"Of course, I would have," she ground out. "This puts the whole pack at risk. I'm not gonna call Mom and tell the whole family though, if that's what you're asking. She made it clear I still wasn't welcome."

"The rest of us care though! She doesn't speak for the whole family."

"Look, you know now. Just let it go. This was the worst possible thing that could have happened to me at the time, but I got through it, and we're all going to be fine," she said, her breaths coming hard as she fought against the sudden, overwhelming emotions. She wanted to shift and run away. The wolf wanted to make her brother submit.

Ceri appeared in the hallway. She hadn't even realized the witch was home.

"Is everything okay?" Ceri asked quietly as she approached.

The mark on Amber's chest throbbed. She doubled over in pain, unable to catch her breath as it seemed to make every muscle in her chest contract. *No, not now. She couldn't deal with this right now too.*

Captain Jack rose from his spot on the couch and hissed at her angrily before fleeing the room entirely.

"Amber?" Derek asked, worry clear in his voice. "Tommy, get back in here. Is she about to lose control?"

Pain turned to agony and the wolf howled in her head. She could feel it struggling against something, fighting back viciously.

"What are you doing?" she demanded between gasps.

The wolf howled. Amber screamed.

CHAPTER 14

AMBER

The room grew dark and her vision swam in front of her eyes. Claws pressed out of her fingertips, scoring deep lines in the floor. She gritted her teeth and refused to shift.

Tommy was close. He was shouting something at Derek. A cool presence drew close. Ceri. Hands touched her face and she realized someone was pushing her backwards. The room spun and she shoved them away. They needed to leave.

"No, run, please go," she gasped, clutching at the mark on her chest.

Her hands were ripped away and her shirt tugged down. Ceri would know what it meant. Then they'd all know. The whole pack. What had she done? She shouldn't have trusted the demon.

A roaring sound overtook the buzzing in her ears and her muscles twitched. The war in her head raged on but she could feel the tide shifting. The wolf was being forced back. The shields it had erected against the demon were cracking. Pain engulfed her entire body as they gave way.

Darkness rushed out of the mark, pushing Ceri and the others back forcefully. Angel had never been solid before. Instead of his usual, small form, a massive demon filled the room. His dark body blocked out every bit of light, except for the flames that burned behind his eyes. Horns curled from his head and smoke poured from his nostrils.

"How dare you attempt to block me from your mind." Angel's voice shook the entire house and pounded against her eardrums.

Amber forced herself upright, bracing herself against the arm of the couch. "I didn't do it--"

"Shut up!" Angel shouted, growing even larger. Her nickname for him felt so wrong now. He wasn't an angel. He wasn't innocuous. He wasn't *funny*.

"Amber, what the hell is going on?" Derek asked, trying to edge toward her.

"She made a deal with a demon," Ceri said, her face pale and angry. Her hand curled into a fist and light flickered from inside the closed hand.

"Don't even think about it, witch," the demon snarled. "You can't force me out. Not when she's invited me in."

The demon turned to her and surged in close. She forced herself to hold his gaze. This hadn't been her fault...well, it had been. She made the deal with Thallan to take on his debt. The wolf had just made the demon angry. She had gone quiet now, and Amber was a little worried the demon had done something to her in retaliation.

"Leave them out of this," she said, pushing up to her feet. "What do you want?"

"I'm calling in your debt. Now."

The words made her heart sink into her stomach. She wasn't ready for this moment to come, but she had no choice. "What do I need to do?"

"Amber, don't--"

Ceri clamped her hand over Derek's mouth. "She has to fulfill her end of the bargain, or her soul is forfeit. She'll die."

The demon looked deep into Amber's eyes. "There is a girl outside of Timber, Oregon, lost somewhere in the woods. Find her, and her guardian, and protect them. If she dies, I'm holding you responsible."

"Where is she, exactly?"

"She's lost, that's why you need to find her. I'll give you three hours."

"It'll take us an hour just to get there," she objected.

"Then you better drive fast," the demon said, before disappearing with a pop.

Amber stood there, staring at the space he'd left behind. A thousand thoughts were racing through her mind. She could still feel his presence too. He wasn't really gone, just invisible.

"Why the hell did you make a deal with a demon?" Ceri demanded, startling her. She'd never seen the witch this mad before.

She looked up, forcing herself to meet Ceri's eyes. "I took the demon mark from Thallan in exchange for him being my sponsor for the Trials and a place to stay."

Ceri shook her head, pressing her lips tightly together. "You *idiot*."

"I was out of options," Amber said angrily. "You can stand there and judge my choice all you want, but we'd be in the System and you'd be homeless if I hadn't done something."

Ceri's pale face went red. "That doesn't make this right."

"I'm going to go deal with this. Stay here. Someone find Genevieve and make sure she gets back to the house as soon as she can. No one leaves until I say so," Amber said, ignoring her last comment.

"You can't just order everyone--"

"I can," Amber snapped, drawing on the pack bond roughly. The power she rarely used burned behind her eyes. "And I will."

"I'm going with you," Tommy said, stepping out from behind Ceri.

"What?" she asked in surprise.

"You need to find this girl, and fast. I tend to notice things before you, and we can cover more ground if we both go and split up."

"This is dangerous," Amber objected.

"Everything we've done since we were bitten has been dangerous. I don't care. Losing our alpha to a demon because she couldn't find someone fast enough is more dangerous than whatever might be in those woods," Tommy insisted.

She wanted to turn him down and make him stay, but he was right. She needed to be practical. If she died, the pack may not be safe. "Fine, let's go."

Amber turned and headed toward the door. She didn't have time to argue, or to over-think any of this. She hadn't even had time to take her jacket off when she got home before everything went to crap.

Tommy followed her outside. She could feel his anticipation, worry, and frustration through the pack bond. It was Ceri's anger that beat against her mind like a drum though. She wished, yet again, that she could block how much of her pack's emotions she felt.

Halfway to the truck, the door opened behind them and Ceri jogged out. She had her bag slung over her shoulder and had to hold it down as she ran.

"I'm coming too," she said, jaw set stubbornly. "I don't like this, but I like what would happen if you failed even less. Derek is staying behind to wait for Genevieve."

Amber nodded, and climbed in the truck. The day had started off bad enough, but now it had completely spun out of control.

CHAPTER 15

TOMMY

Tommy sat between Amber and Ceri and kept his eyes forward. Amber was driving like a crazy person, passing every person she got behind on the narrow, two-lane road. Ceri was *stewing* in anger.

He got why Ceri was freaked out, but the anger really surprised him. It's not like Amber had summoned a demon for fun. She hadn't even been the one to do it. Thallan had. Amber had been protecting them when she took the demon mark.

Amber had driven straight here without directions. He looked around the cab of the truck again, but didn't see any hint of the demon. Something told him it was still here, though.

His nose twitched as the scent of smoke washed through the truck through the open windows. "Do you smell that?"

Amber nodded, then pointed off to the left. "There's smoke over there. Looks like a house fire, it's all black."

They turned down a short, gravel road which seemed to lead straight toward the house. The smell grew worse and he noticed a strong smell of gasoline as well.

Amber slammed on the brakes and turned down a dirt driveway. She drove just far enough that the truck wouldn't be visible from the road, and parked.

"Is this it?" Tommy asked.

"No," she said, opening her door and hopping out. "This is just as close as it's safe to get in the truck. The demon thinks there's still a threat at the house. And he doesn't want us drawing attention to ourselves."

Tommy nodded. He was conflicted about this whole thing. He'd never heard of a demon demanding protection for someone before. Then again, the only thing he knew about demon marks were from tv shows. In those, it was always about murder and chaos. There was something odd going on here. The demon had scared the hell out of them all and hurt Amber, but it had seemed almost...fearful.

"We're a half mile away. We're going to go that way, quietly," Amber said, pointing north, deeper into the woods.

The trio walked quietly, each of them watching the woods intently for any sign of movement. All of Tommy's senses were on high alert. He could hear people in the distance, but he couldn't make out any of the conversations yet.

The smell of smoke grew stronger as they drew closer to the house. He focused on trying to catch the scent of a person underneath it all, but no one had come this way recently.

Soon, the charred skeleton of a house was visible through the dense forest. All that was left of the house was a crumbling shell of still smoldering beams. He could hear faint voices now, and put his hand on Amber's shoulder, then tapped his ear to let her know.

Amber nodded and motioned for them to slow down. They crept in a wide circle around the house until they could see the people that were talking.

There were two men. The one Tommy had heard first turned out to be on the phone. He had long, blond hair tied back in a ponytail and wore some kind of linen suit. He looked like he belonged on a yacht or something, not standing in ash. The way he moved was graceful, unnaturally so. His skin almost glowed with health, and that was when Tommy realized what he was. He was half-angel.

They weren't common, but every single one of them was beautiful and talented. They were always models, actors, or singers. Everything they did seemed effortless, and they were even more beautiful than the elves.

The other guy was no angel, that was for sure. He wore dark jeans and a long sleeve shirt. The sleeves were pushed up, exposing strange tattoos and old scars. His hair was buzzed short making his face look harsh. He walked a short distance away from the half-angel and crouched down in front of the house.

Tommy tensed when he drew a knife from a sheath in the back of his pants. The man curled his hand into a tight fist, then drew the blade over the back of his forearm, leaving a fairly deep cut. Blood dripped into the ash and dirt as he began to chant.

Ceri grabbed Amber's arm and motioned for them to move back. They retreated a decent distance back into the trees where they could talk.

"If you want to find this girl, you have to do it now," Ceri whispered urgently. "That's a method for tracking someone. It's an insane method, but extremely effective. It will also hurt her."

"How long do we have?" Amber asked.

"Fifteen, twenty minutes tops," Ceri said, glancing back at the house. "I might be able to buy you more time, but you have to hurry. Does the demon have any idea where she is?"

Amber glanced to her left, then shook her head. "No."

"Find her, and get her to me as fast as you can. I can protect her, but I need her blood," Ceri said, grimacing slightly.

"We have to split up," Tommy said, already pulling his shirt over his head. He knew he could cover more ground in wolf form.

"Be careful," Amber said, her eyes flashing red like it was an order.

"I will be," Tommy said before turning around to shuck off his pants. Nudity still made him intensely uncomfortable, but they didn't have time to worry about that right now.

The shift came easier every time he did it. The wolf grew in his mind as he dropped to four feet, his paws forming before he hit the ground. He shook out his fur and panted for a moment, processing the changes. The acrid scent of the smoke made his nose burn.

He turned around and saw that Ceri was already headed back toward the house. Amber nodded at him, also in wolf form now, and took off at a run. He went in the opposite direction, skirting around the side of the house, heading into the densest section of the forest.

He ran until he could smell something other than burnt, then paused to take a deep breath. He sniffed the ground, getting a nose full of pine needles, but nothing that smelled like a person. This might be harder than he thought.

CHAPTER 16

CERI

Ceri's blood was boiling with rage. Amber had been an idiot. This demon had led them into extreme danger because that was what demons did. She hated that Tommy had come. If she'd known there was going to be a sorcerer here, she would have made him stay at the house.

Blood magic was one of those things you rarely saw used. There were so many other ways to enhance your magic. Sacrificing your own lifeblood to power a spell damaged you. It twisted something inside of you and left a dark mark on your soul.

The owl was perched on a branch above her. She didn't have to look up to know it was there. This was what it had been trying to warn her about. In some ways, she had been right. It was an ill omen, but if it hadn't warned her she would have been even more unprepared.

Ceri crouched behind a tree and lifted the strap of her purse over her head. She had what she needed to slow the sorcerer down. Stopping him was borderline impossible. The raw power needed to do that was beyond her without a coven. Luckily, he was alone, or she wouldn't be able to do a thing.

She lifted out her spellbook first, then her little tin of mugwort. The plant was helpful in protection against a psychic attack, which was, at its heart, what the sorcerer was casting. It attacked the natural mental protections of the target. The spell could leave physical wounds as well, depending on the strength of the caster.

Finding a decent branch nearby, she grabbed it and drew a circle of protection around herself. She added a triangle with a second horizontal line that cut through the bottom third of it. Invoking the element of air to give her strength and embrace its energy.

Most witches viewed these rituals as weak and unreliable. Her grandmother had hated them. Without a coven, and without a living sacrifice such as a pixie or other animal, it was all she had.

She crossed her legs and dug her fingers into the earth to ground herself, literally and figuratively. The magic inside her would have to be enough to slow this sorcerer down.

"Spiritus defendat," she chanted softly. Magic welled up within her. Instead of sinking into the ground, it lifted up from the top of her head. A breeze picked up around her.

Her eyes slipped shut and her other senses came into focus. The sorcerer's magic was hot and dark to the west. It crept through the forest like a hunter after its prey. Though it passed her by, she felt its attention turn toward her briefly, inspecting the competing magic. The sorcerer would know she was here, but he would not attack her until he'd accomplished his task.

The owl flew down and stood at the top point of the symbol she'd drawn. It twisted its head, picking at its feathers until one came loose then dropped the feather, which floated down onto the symbol. She felt a surge of energy and clarity.

In her mind, she saw her magic flare up, cutting through the darkness that pressed around her. The sorcerer's spell shuddered. Her hair lifted off her shoulder as the breeze tickling her skin grew stronger. It was tinged with magic, both hers and the spirits. The owl was aiding her. The strength of help that was freely given could never be matched by a sacrifice ripped from the animal's body.

The darkness around her shifted as the wind pushed against it. She continued chanting to give herself something to focus on. The wind lifted the words from her lips and carried them like daggers through the forest. Her magic cut through the sorcerer's spell. It groaned and shuddered.

She could feel the sorcerer's attention turn to her briefly. He didn't falter in the pursuit of his target, but she could feel his anger growing in the darkness like a storm.

The pack bond shifted inside her and she felt a *push*. Instead of drawing strength from her, it was being poured into her. Amber was helping, the only way she could. A smile spread across Ceri's face. This was the strength of the pack, of being a shaman.

The wind howled like a hurricane, whipping her hair up into a frenzy. The trees around her strained against the onslaught. A branch cracked and snapped off the trunk, flying through the air like a missile. Her magic pushed against the sorcerer's spell, slowing its progress and stripping away its power.

Lifting her face to the sky, Ceri poured every ounce of her strength into the battle. She would not falter. She would not show fear. She was strong enough.

CHAPTER 17

AMBER

It was an odd sensation to be sending the strength of the pack to one of the pack members instead of drawing it into herself. The wind buffeted Amber as she jogged through the forest. There was magic in the air, both Ceri's and something that smelled like blood and fire.

The demon drifted beside her, glaring at the forest around them. He hadn't spoken. Just watched. Every few minutes he'd float away until she felt a strange tug in her chest, then he'd reappear. It seemed like he was tethered to her.

A sound behind her, muffled by the wind, made her pause. The scent of metal and gunpowder had her dropping to her stomach. Splinters exploded from the tree trunk in front of her as a bullet impacted it. Her ears ached from the loud crack of the gunfire.

Not wanting to be a stationary target, she darted to the side, running as low as possible. Her first thought was that she had to get to Tommy, her second was that they were all screwed. Two more shots cracked through the air, one hitting a tree, the other striking the dirt right in front of her.

She zig-zagged as best she could, but she had to get to the shooter fast. If those were regular bullets, she could afford to get hit. It would hurt but she could deal with that. If they were silver...she didn't want to have to draw on the pack's strength. Ceri needed it.

"He's moving that way," the demon said, pointing in the same direction she was running. "There are two, I think."

She changed directions to try to get behind him. Her heart was racing in her chest and the wolf was finally fully awake.

There was another shot. The pain didn't register until she stumbled. Her shoulder burned and blood seeped into her fur. Growling in anger, she pushed herself to go faster. She didn't know anything about the girl lost in this forest, but she couldn't imagine a good reason for her to be hunted like an animal.

She ran recklessly, no longer worried about being shot. The wound hurt, but it wasn't silver. It would heal. Over the rush of the wind, she heard the man's footsteps. Smelled his cologne. His fear. He was right to be afraid.

The wolf pushed her even faster, thrilled to be chasing prey. The wolf's instincts over-rode her fear and worry. There were two of them. She was closing in on the first, but the other was coming up behind her.

The demon surged ahead of her and she heard a scream. She pushed herself to go faster and a man hit the dirt in front of her, scrambling on hands and knees trying to get away. The demon loomed over him, larger than he'd been even in the house. He backed right into a tree and was left with nowhere to run.

She lunged for him as he lifted the gun, aiming it with shaking hands at the demon. Her teeth closed around his forearm and the bone snapped in her powerful jaws. She shook viciously and the gun fell to the ground. The man's head hit the tree with a crack and he fell limp.

She wasn't sure if he was dead, and she didn't have time to worry about it. Three fast shots rang through the air, but the other man was shooting at the demon as well. They didn't realize he couldn't touch them.

"Charlie!" the other attacker shouted behind them in alarm.

Amber turned and ran toward him. He swung his gun toward her as she leapt. The bullet hit her in the gut and knocked her to the ground. She scrambled to her feet, but her legs were like jello. She couldn't breathe.

"Who the hell sent a damn werewolf out here?" the man shouted as he fumbled to reload his gun.

Her body was already healing, but it was slower than she'd expected. She drew on the pack bond for one moment, just to give herself strength, then charged the man.

He locked the slide in place a half-second before she collided with him. It wasn't a clean takedown, she'd missed his throat. The pain had been greater than she'd expected. He scrambled for a place to grab her as they hit the ground. His fist connected with the bullet wound and she yelped, tearing at him with her paws. One of his hands wrapped around her throat, holding her at a distance.

She yanked her head away, then snapped at his arm. Her teeth tore into his skin and he screamed in pain. It made him slow, and her jaw closed around his neck. One bite was all it took. His throat collapsed under the pressure. The scream abruptly cut off.

Excitement pulsed through the pack bond from Tommy as she stumbled away from the body. She could barely process it as she looked at the carnage at her feet. Bile rose in the back of her throat and she vomited as she backed away. She'd had to kill him. She hadn't had a choice...but it was awful. There was so much blood.

The excitement from Tommy changed to fear and her head snapped up. He had found them.

CHAPTER 18

TOMMY

He took a winding path through the woods, trying to cover as much ground as possible. They had two hours left. He was pretty sure bloodhounds got to smell something that the person they were tracking owned before they were sent out to find them. It would have been really helpful to have *something*. Instead, he was just wandering aimlessly hoping to get lucky.

At the back of his mind, the wolf seemed unconcerned. It was patient. Tommy huffed in annoyance and picked up his pace. He was afraid to run in case he missed something, but he wasn't making enough progress.

His ears twitched as he took in the sounds of the forest. It was surprisingly noisy now that he could hear for miles in every direction. Wind ruffled his fur lightly and he reveled in the cool breeze. In this form, he'd found it was easy to feel overheated.

The wind grew steadily stronger, making him pause. He looked around and saw the trees waving wildly. The steady breeze shifted, buffeting from different directions. A particularly strong gust hit him in the side and he stumbled from the force of it.

Magic tickled his nose. He lifted his face toward the sky as the wind howled through the trees. It smelled like magic, and Ceri. He hoped this meant she was winning.

The pack bond began to grow inside him like it did whenever Amber pulled on it. Ceri must be fighting the sorcerer, or Amber was in danger. He shifted anxiously on his feet, but there was nothing he could do to help except find the girl. He hoped Ceri could slow the sorcerer down. And that she could stay hidden. He knew she could probably fight way better than he could, but he still didn't like her being alone out there.

He took off again, moving at a steady trot this time. A faint scent whipped past him and the wolf woke up inside of him, going from patient to excited. He changed direction, following where his instincts led him despite the scent fading. It wasn't exactly human, but it wasn't an animal. It reminded him of the strange, sulfur smell he'd noticed around the house. And the smell in the truck when the demon had been there.

He followed the trail with his nose to the ground. The wind shifted, swirling around him like a tornado, and for a split second, he almost lost the trail. A branch snapped off a tree overhead and he dropped to the forest floor, ducking underneath it just in time.

Taking off at a run, he stopped hesitating. The girl had to be somewhere in this direction. The wind was blowing so hard now that he had to lean his head down just to run.

He heard her before he saw her. She was crying and shouting curse words at the wind. He slowed his pace, creeping up slowly toward the sounds. At first, he wasn't sure where he was, then he saw a glimpse of pale blonde hair through the underbrush. She was crouched behind a tree.

The smell of blood and burnt flesh hit him and he froze. Then he realized there was someone with her. They weren't moving.

He ran toward the two of them, his heart racing with excitement. Her head snapped toward him when he got close and she jumped up, her eyes going wide with fear. Slowing down to a walk, he stepped toward her trying to look friendly.

She grabbed a fallen branch off the ground and ran at him, holding it like a bat. Her long blonde hair swept behind her like a veil and he was momentarily mesmerized. Until she swung the branch at his head.

He dodged the attack and skittered backward. Maybe he hadn't fully thought this plan through. He'd been so focused on finding her that he hadn't thought about how she'd react to a wolf showing up.

"Get back!" she shouted again, swinging the branch at him. The harsh wind kicked her blonde hair into her face as she tried to fend him off. She was wearing pajamas and didn't even have on shoes.

He ducked underneath it and yipped, trying to look more like a puppy than a wolf. She swung the branch again viciously. Well, that didn't work.

Backing off, he ran behind a tree. She didn't follow, staying in front of her tree holding the branch like a shield.

He shifted, feeling very vulnerable standing naked in the woods. "I, uh, come in peace," he said, sticking his arms out from behind the tree. The wind was blowing so hard now he had to shout.

"Wait, you're a werewolf?" the girl asked, lowering her weapon. She didn't drop it though.

He peeked his head out from behind the tree, keeping himself carefully hidden. "Yeah, we were told you were lost and sent to find you."

Her blue eyes narrowed as she brushed her hair out of her eyes. She pressed her lips into a thin line. "Who sent you?"

"Well…just someone that was….concerned," he deflected. The demon hadn't told them if she knew who he was, and she looked pretty suspicious. He wasn't sure admitting it was a demon was the best move.

"It was Kadrithan, wasn't it?" she demanded, anger leaking into her tone.

"If Kadrithan is a demon, then…yes?"

She snorted in derision. "How in the hell did a scrawny teenager like you get a demon mark?"

"Oh, I don't have the mark. My alpha does, but I wanted to help."

"Great, an idiot has come to rescue me," she muttered, dropping the branch and walking back to her hiding spot. She paused and looked back over her shoulder. "I don't suppose you have pants anywhere close, do you?"

"Not really close, no," he said. A noise caught his attention. He wasn't sure if it was a branch hitting a tree or a footstep.

She sighed and rolled her eyes. "Well, I can't carry her, so you're going--"

"Be quiet," he said urgently, interrupting her. The wind had shifted and he'd smelled something out of place. Another person.

She opened her mouth -- probably to tell him not to talk to her like that -- when a gunshot cracked through the air. Her eyes went wide as she hit the ground.

Tommy ran for them, shifting as he went. He didn't know what to do. He could smell her blood. He should have just taken them and run, but he'd been standing around like an idiot chatting.

His paws dug into the dirt as he sprinted toward them. As soon as he was close enough, he launched himself toward them, landing right behind her facing the direction the shot had come from. He couldn't see anyone. The wind was blowing too hard for him to hear or smell them properly. Were they moving?

He backed up until his hind foot bumped into the girl. She groaned and scooted away. He sighed in relief. She was alive, for now.

Amber had to have felt his panic. He thought he could feel her headed his way, but it was hard to focus on the pack bond right now.

A man stepped out from the trees a few yards away. He had a shotgun held up to his shoulder and pointed straight at them. Tommy growled and took another step back, standing over the girl to protect her. He was tempted to charge the man, but he could hear two other people closing in from either side. They were surrounded.

CHAPTER 19

EVANGELINE

Another gunshot blasted through the air, making her ears ring. Evangeline curled over her mother as the werewolf leaped over her. The first shot had only grazed her arm, but it still stung like a bitch.

She could barely hear anything over the panicked beating of her heart. Blood from the werewolf's wound dripped down onto her, staining her pajamas. The second shot had hit him. He'd thrown himself in the path of the gunfire to protect her, which was insane, and further confirmed she was being rescued by idiots.

The wind was blowing so hard her hair was practically standing on end. It whipped up dirt and leaves around them like a tornado.

Her mother was deathly still beneath her. She was breathing, but it was labored. Evangeline cursed herself for not trying harder to get her to a hospital. She'd never forgive herself if her mother died out here in the woods. It was her fault she was hurt in the first place. This was all her fault. She tightened her grip on her mother's arms and tried to convince herself to just end all this. But…she didn't want to die. Even if she did deserve it.

She looked back over her shoulder, weighing her options. During the day, her demonic side slept. She couldn't use the fire magic at all. Instead, her other side awoke. It wouldn't be much help here though, it wasn't the type of magic you could use in a fight, especially with the talismans hanging around the men's necks. She was as helpless as a human.

Scooting forward, she dug through the leaves until her fingers hit a rock. The werewolf howled as two men circled around them. Another shot rang out and the wolf flinched from the impact but didn't flee. He pressed down closer against her as he howled again, hopefully calling the rest of his pack. Werewolves weren't her favorite -- they tended to be arrogant blowhards -- but she'd welcome a whole pack of them right about now.

A ruddy wolf appeared out of nowhere, ripping out the throat of one of the men. Evangeline flinched as blood sprayed from his neck, soaking into the leaves. It didn't seem like any of this could be real. She'd always known what she was, but she'd been able to ignore it all her life. She'd never seen someone die.

The black wolf ran toward the ruddy wolf and they attacked the second man together. Evangeline frantically pulled at the rock buried in the dirt. A twig snapped in front of her and she looked up, straight into the eyes of a third attacker.

He lifted his gun toward her. It felt like everything was moving in slow motion as she ripped the rock free. He peered down the sight of the rifle. She threw the rock, a scream erupting from her throat. The rock hit his gun, knocking it off just enough that the shot went wide.

A red blur flew toward him, hitting him so hard his neck snapped to the side. The gun flew form his hands and the werewolf's jaws clamped around his throat. She squeezed her eyes shut, not wanting to see what happened next.

Something nudged her shoulder. She peeked behind her to see the gray werewolf looking at her expectantly. He nodded, as if to say *yes, it's safe now.*

Hesitantly, she sat up and looked around. The bodies were still there, laying in growing pools of blood. Bile rose in the back of her throat and she forced herself to look away.

The ruddy wolf shifted into a woman as she approached. Her wavy red hair fell down over her shoulders but did nothing to hide the fact that she was buck ass naked. Or the blood dripping from her chin and slipping down her neck in little rivulets.

Evangeline's eyes were immediately drawn to the black demon mark on the woman's chest. It twitched as her uncle appeared behind the woman. It wouldn't be visible to everyone but she could see those sorts of things.

"If you want your mother to live, go with them," Kadrithan said, still scowling at her from their last argument.

She didn't want to go with these people, but, once again, her uncle had outmaneuvered her. It was easy when he had all the information and she had none of it.

"We have to go, can you walk?" the woman asked.

"Yeah, but my mother can't."

"I'll carry her," the woman said, brushing past her and kneeling at her mother's side.

"Be careful!" she warned, hovering over them.

The woman glared at her. "Obviously."

With more tenderness than she'd expected, the woman eased her arms under her mother's knees and shoulder. She lifted her like she weighed two pounds. It was effortless. Damn werewolves and their superhuman strength.

"You could be stronger too if you would just give someone a mark," her uncle whispered in her ear as though he could read her mind.

She pressed her lips together in annoyance and ignored him. She jumped when she felt fur brush her hand. The other wolf, the guy, was standing next to her looking around warily. His ears were perked up, twitching this way and that.

He huffed softly and the woman nodded. "I know, let's go." The woman turned to

Evangeline for a moment. "We're going to go as fast as you can. If we get in trouble, Tommy is going to shift and carry you on his back."

Evangeline nodded and started walking. Her feet ached and she was so thirsty it felt like her throat was cracking, but none of that mattered. They had to get her mother to safety.

CHAPTER 20

CERI

The strain of channeling so much magic was beginning to wear on Ceri. She pressed her fingers deeper into the dirt but she couldn't feel them anymore. They'd gone numb. Sweat dripped down her forehead as she struggled to breathe past the burning in her lungs.

Wind swirled around her in a funnel that grew narrower and narrower. Darkness pressed in from all sides invisible to the naked eye. She could see it though, even with her eyes shut.

"You can't win this battle." The sorcerer's voice drifted past her. The wind tickled her neck as though it was his breath.

She ground her teeth together. He was getting closer to the girl, but he hadn't found her yet. She was slowing him down more than she had thought possible. He could taunt all he wanted, it was merely a sign of his frustration.

"Neither can you," she whispered back.

Amber and Tommy had to be close to finding her. She'd felt something through the pack bond. A tug. It had almost made her falter, but it had been brief, and she'd held onto the spell through it. If Amber could get to the girl first, Ceri could protect her.

The owl squawked and her eyes flew open in alarm. The large bird fell back, wrapped in ropes of darkness that threatened to crush its wings. She lifted one hand and a gust of air rushed past her, hitting the bird and the dark magic and loosening the bonds just enough for the owl to struggle free. It lifted into the air, circling overhead.

"Just go!" she shouted, fear sinking into her. The darkness was closer than she realized. The sorcerer's magic was closing in around her and she was about to lose this fight. He was too powerful.

The weight of the magic slammed into her. She fell back, pinned against the ground, unable to move. It felt like her teeth were going to crack as her jaw clenched tight. Breathing became harder with every breath as her lungs tired.

Something wet touched her face. After a moment, she realized it was a tongue. The weight of the magic lessened, but she felt fur pressing against her neck and arms. Another lick, then warmth enveloped her. The darkness vanished.

With a gasp, her eyes flew open. Genevieve was looking down at her in wolf form, whining softly.

"How the hell did you get here?" she croaked.

The wolf rolled her eyes and scooted back far enough that she could sit up. Blood dripped from Ceri's nose and she coughed, tasting it on the back of her tongue as well.

Genevieve was looking around them warily. She stood abruptly, her ears perking up as she looked to the west. A moment later, Amber burst out of the trees, naked, and carrying an old woman. Ceri wasn't sure the woman was alive. She was badly beaten, and had severe burns on the lower half of her body.

Behind Amber was Tommy, in wolf form, and a blonde girl that looked around his age. Her bare feet were torn up and her pajamas were filthy from the run through the woods. Tommy quickly grabbed his and Amber's clothes, carrying them in his mouth.

"Run," Amber said urgently.

Her legs wobbled underneath her as she turned to flee, but Tommy was right there, supporting her. She wound her fingers into his fur and let him drag her forward as she attempted to keep up. The blonde girl kept her eyes glued to the woman Amber was holding.

"You're jostling her too much," the girl hissed, trying to grab Amber's arm.

"She's unconscious, she can't feel it," Amber snapped. "Stop complaining and run."

As Ceri grabbed her bag, she could still feel the sorcerer's spell pressing down on them. He would find the girl any second now. They needed to go faster. She was exhausted, but she had to save what strength she had left to protect the girl once the spell found its mark. She would have one chance to fight him off then.

The forest thinned slightly and Amber's truck came into view. Genevieve had parked behind the truck and left her clothes in a pile by her driver's side door, which was hanging open. She'd been in a hurry.

Amber ran to the passenger side of the truck and the girl yanked the door open. She laid the woman down on the bench seat.

"Has that sorcerer done whatever to the girl yet?" Amber asked as she grabbed the clothes Tommy had dropped next to her. "Tommy, go with Gen, there's no room," she shouted over her shoulder.

Genevieve, who was hopping on one foot trying to get redressed, shouted back, "When is someone going to explain what the hell is going on?"

"When we're back, just take Tommy and drive home as fast as you can," Amber said, running toward the driver side of her truck.

The girl was already sitting in the truck with the old woman's head in her lap. Ceri jumped in the passenger door and crouched on the floor. She dumped half the contents of her bag out between her legs, scrambling to find something that would help the old woman until she could properly heal her, or get her to a hospital.

Amber started the truck and threw it into reverse. The truck whipped around, slinging Ceri into the dashboard. Amber gunned it toward the main road, gravel flying from under her tires.

The girl glared at someone Ceri couldn't see and flicked them off. "This is all your fault anyhow!"

Amber rolled her eyes. "Do you know who is after you?"

"No, I don't know, and I don't care," the girl snapped. "I--" Her eyes rolled back in her head and a red glow thrummed around her body. Her muscles rippled under her skin as she began to shake.

Ceri grabbed the bundle of herbs she'd been putting together and shoved it in the girl's mouth, holding her jaw shut.

"What the hell is that?" Amber demanded.

"The sorcerer," Ceri said, pushing up onto her knees so she could get a hand around the back of the girl's neck. This was going to be tricky, but lucky for her, psychic attacks were one of her family's specialties.

"Custodiat cor tuum. Custodiat animam. Custodiat cor tuum." Ceri's fingers dug into the girl's neck as she repeated the chant. There was magic inside her, and it was helping Ceri fight back. It was hot and uncontrolled. Whatever this girl was, she was completely untrained.

The sorcerer's spell worked by using the blood in its victim's body to force them to return to the sorcerer, by any means. If the spell couldn't be stopped before it reached its target, the only option was to change the victim's blood. Ceri abhorred what she had to do, but the only way to fight the sorcerer's blood magic, was with more of the same.

The darkness lashed at the truck. There was no time left. Ceri looked up at Amber as fear curled in her gut. If she didn't do something to stop this, Amber would die. Just like that. All because she was doing the only thing she could to protect her pack. Ceri couldn't let that happen.

Never hesitate.

Fuck you, grandmother, she thought as she squeezed her eyes shut and grabbed the blessed knife from the pocket in her bag and drug the tip along the back of her arm. There was only one other scar there from years ago. It had almost faded completely. It would have a twin now. Two times Ceri hadn't been able to find a way to avoid using black magic. Two failures.

Sorcery was dark magic, but she wasn't strong enough to fight back with only white magic. As the blood seeped from her palm, she swore to herself to find a way to do so in the future without having to resort to this. The pack bond curled around her but she wanted to shove it away. This was going to leave its mark on her and the pack.

The blood seeped out of the wound, writhing on her skin instead of dripping. She began chanting again, calling on her own magic, and whatever she could drag from the pack bond. Flipping the knife around, she sliced through the sleeve of the girl's pajamas, opening a small wound at the same time. The girl didn't even flinch, too lost in the haze of the sorcerer's spell.

Her blood stretched toward the wound and sank into it. Ceri's gritted her teeth as she forced herself into the girl's body and mind.

"Ceri, what the hell are you doing?" Amber asked as she skidded around a turn.

"Saving this girl's life so you don't die," she replied quietly. The dark magic pulsed around her as her magic blazed to life. It was always warm and comforting, but this...this was different. This was like standing on the surface of the sun. It didn't hurt her, it raged inside of her with an addictive thrill. This was the rush of heroin and crackling energy of cocaine. Sorcerers weren't just power hungry. They were addicts. She was going to regret this.

The spell she was using wasn't straightforward. It was an off the cuff combination of a white magic spell of psychic protection with the power of a blood sacrifice. Her family had always been inventors and creators. They twisted magic in new ways. Ceri had always excelled at this. She was the only one of her parent's children to truly match her grandmother's talents. Some days she hated it.

She pushed the old guilt away and plucked at the threads of magic weaving around her and the girl. Ceri cocooned her in blood, magic, and the pack bond. It wouldn't make her pack, but it would let Ceri use the strength of the pack and her own magic to protect her from the sorcerer's attack.

Amber swerved sharply, her breath coming in pants. "How much longer?"

"Shut up, I need to focus," Ceri said sharply, forcing her mind back to the task at hand. It was uncomfortable, but it wouldn't truly harm Amber. The still angry part of her mind considered this Amber's penance for taking the demon's mark in the first place. This was affecting the whole pack, not just her.

Something in the girl shifted, as though it was coming awake. The hot tendrils of magic inspected Ceri. They poked and prodded, searching for a threat, but when they found none, retreated. Ceri's hands shook as the nature of the magic finally became apparent.

Ceri's protective spell slid into place, locking around herself and the girl. They were tied together until she released the spell. Ceri opened her eyes and pressed herself back against the dash, horrified. If Amber's life hadn't been at stake she would have ripped the spell away and thrown the girl out of the car.

"What's wrong? Is it over?" Amber asked, still breathless.

"She's...a demon, but..." There was something else, but it didn't make sense. Ceri looked up at her alpha. "She's part angel as well."

"That's impossible," Amber said, eyes going wide.

CHAPTER 21

AMBER

Amber thought she might be sick. She could still taste the blood that had coated her tongue. It was drying on her skin and it made her want to bathe in acid. She wasn't sure she'd ever feel clean again.

They'd tried to kill that girl in cold blood. They'd deserved to die, but for some reason that didn't take away the guilt she felt. She'd seen the fear in their eyes when she'd killed them.

Angel appeared behind her just as she was about to take off her shirt. "We need to talk."

Angry that he couldn't leave her alone for ten damn minutes, she ripped her shirt off over her head anyhow, not caring what he saw. She'd been wandering around the forest naked. It didn't matter at this point and she needed a shower. Now.

"Then you can talk while I shower," she said, throwing her clothes straight in the trash.

"If her guardian dies, Evangeline will become completely unmanageable," Angel said testily, following her into the shower and hovering above the soap dish. He kept his head turned slightly away as if he cared about her modesty. She knew better. He didn't care about anything except himself.

"She's not going to die. Ceri said she can heal her, without a hospital, just like you wanted," she replied before dunking her head under the hot water. It stung, but she reveled in it. Needed it. She groped blindly for the shampoo, then poured a large amount into her hand.

"She needs to be monitored closely. We can't risk any complications," Angel insisted.

Amber leaned her head out of the flow of water and slathered the shampoo into her hair, scrubbing furiously. "Ceri is not going to let the woman die. Stop harping on it."

The demon snorted and mumbled something she couldn't understand, then said, "You have no idea what's at stake here."

"Are you going to explain it?" Amber asked, peeking one eye at him.

The demon sneered at her. "No."

She rolled her eyes and began rinsing out the shampoo. The water swirling around her feet was pink from all the blood. The need to vomit roiled up in her gut and she squeezed her eyes shut again, breathing through her nose. Her enhanced senses weren't helping right now. She could smell it like it was fresh, and she hated it.

"Who is this girl anyhow?" she asked as she lathered up the rag.

"You don't need to – –"

"Just answer the damn question. I already know she's part demon, and part angel, so that cat's out of the bag."

He grew in size, filling up one corner of the shower. His burning eyes fixed on her face. "You don't get to demand anything. Not after that stunt you pulled. You're lucky I've left you alive. I'll tell you what to do, and you will obey. That's the bargain."

Turning away she began scrubbing at the blood again. She wished she could scrub away the demon mark. Or punch Angel in the face.

He vanished, finally, and she slumped against the wall of the shower. Tears burned at the back of her eyes but she didn't deserve to cry. This was all happening because she thought it was the only choice she had. It *had* been her choice.

Everyone was waiting for her to come out and explain herself and fix everything. She didn't want to. She wanted to curl up in bed and hide but she couldn't. That was never an option for her.

Straightening back up, she finished scrubbing off all the blood and sweat, then climbed out of the shower. She could break down when this was all over, but until then, she had to put her pack first.

CHAPTER 22

GENEVIEVE

Genevieve sat on the couch with Captain Jack and watched the argument unfolding in front of her. She'd been furious they'd gone off on some half-cocked rescue mission without her, but now that she knew why...well, she was still furious.

Derek was yelling at Amber, for the third time, that it was total crap she'd let him come out here to start a business without telling him about the whole demon mark thing.

"I would have still come but I can't believe you'd keep something like that from me!" he said, slamming his fist onto the coffee table for emphasis.

"I was trying to figure out what it meant!" Amber shouted back.

Ceri finally stood. "Both of you, just shut up."

Genevieve raised a brow at her tone. Little Miss Sunshine was angry too. That meant things were probably about to get ugly. She glanced at Tommy. He was hiding in the kitchen with Woggy trying to ignore the whole argument.

"Amber, is there anything *else* you haven't told the pack?" Ceri asked, crossing her arms.

Their alpha's face reddened to match her hair. "No," she ground out.

"Alright. Then enough with the whole conversation. The two of you can argue about it later. We have a severely injured woman and an unconscious, half-demon, half-angel teenaged girl to worry about. Along with a sorcerer who has apparently already killed one alpha werewolf." Ceri, looking exhausted, sat down on the couch next to her and crossed her arms.

"Do the police know about the attack today?" Genevieve asked, speaking for the first time since they'd gotten home. She hadn't been able to get a word in edgewise once Amber and Derek had started arguing.

Amber rubbed her hand over her face. "The police weren't there when we arrived, so I doubt it."

"Is there any reason we can't report it to the police? Or that you didn't call the police when you got there?" she asked, raising a brow.

Amber shook her head. "We didn't have much time to find the girl. Now, I have to protect her and the older woman."

"Protect them until what?" Genevieve asked.

Amber looked at her, brows furrowed. "What do you mean?"

"Protect them is super vague. There's no end to it. How long do you have to protect them?"

Amber turned to her right, facing no one. "Well?"

Everyone looked at the blank space uncomfortably. Only Amber could see or hear the demon most of the time. And right now, she didn't like what it was saying.

"I think you're lying," Amber said, crossing her arms.

"I want to talk to this demon," Genevieve said, frustrated at being left on the outside of all this. Everyone else had been here when the demon had appeared. She was the only one that hadn't seen it. The others all seemed to be afraid of it, but she knew a little something about demons. Theoretically.

They had a reputation for murder and mayhem, but when you looked at actual events of a demon appearing, the facts showed something different. Sometimes bad things happened, but sometimes they didn't.

Amber flinched, her hand flying to her chest. The air next to her twisted and a shadow grew, enveloping that corner of the room.

Horns extended from the creature's head. Its face was a cross between a bull and a dragon. Smoke curled from its nostrils and mouth, which was curled into a menacing, fiery grin. His dark form seemed to suck all the light from the room. "Speak then, mortal."

Everyone else took a step back, but Genevieve rolled her eyes. If it was trying to intimidate her, then it needed something from them. Badly. That was something she'd learned from Donovan. They still hadn't found out why the dead alpha had needed Amber's power, but he had desperately wanted it for some reason.

"How can Amber fulfill the bargain she made with you and have your mark removed?" Genevieve asked, walking slowly toward the creature until she was standing beside Amber. It seemed that the demon was taking something from her in order to appear like this. She couldn't feel anything odd in the pack bond but that was probably because Amber wasn't pulling on it.

The demon shrank until he was more or less her same height and began to float around her. She let him, choosing instead to inspect her nails. She wasn't concerned about him being at her back.

"As I told her, I need her to protect the girl," the demon said.

"And as I said, that's too vague. You have to be more specific, and it has to be possible for her to succeed, therefore, there has to be a way to measure that success. What is she protecting the girl from? And for how long?" Genevieve asked, placing a hand on Amber's shoulder. Immediately, the pack bond grew in her chest. She let it draw strength from her and give it to her alpha. Of course, Amber-the-stubborn had been holding back doing so.

The demon sneered at her. "You don't get to negotiate for her. Amber has to do it herself."

"I can negotiate for her if she asks me to," Genevieve said, gently squeezing Amber's shoulder to prompt her.

"I want her to," Amber said, glaring at the demon. "You haven't exactly been straight with me."

The demon changed shape. His smoky form was dressed in a suit, but his head remained the same. "You are very bossy. I guess I shouldn't expect any less from a lawyer."

Genevieve snorted. He had no idea. "What do you want?"

"Someone is trying to kill Evangeline," the demon said, striking a relaxed pose. "I will consider the obligation of the mark fulfilled if Amber can find out who, stop them, and ensure Evangeline's safety until that is done."

"Do you already know who is trying to kill Evangeline?" she asked, narrowing her eyes at the demon.

A smirk lifted the corner of his mouth. "No, not for sure."

"Who do you suspect is behind it?"

"The angels."

Genevieve pinched the bridge of her nose and held back a sigh, with effort. "Sarcasm isn't helpful."

"Who said I was being sarcastic?"

She looked up at him, suspicious. "Why the hell would *angels* try to kill someone?"

"There was a half angel at the house when we got there. He was working with the sorcerer," Ceri said, speaking up for the first time since the demon had appeared. "And the girl is half angel."

The demon turned his attention to Ceri. "Who told you that?"

"No one had to, I sensed it when I was protecting her from the sorcerer's spell. She's half angel, and half demon," Ceri said, walking toward them. "Which shouldn't be possible, but I know it's true. Is that why you're protecting her?"

The demon snorted and turned back to Genevieve. "You know as much about who is trying to kill Evangeline as I do. My offer remains the same, and is more than fair. Take it, or leave it."

"We'll accept it on one condition," Genevieve said, stepping up to the demon to make sure he understood she was serious. "You help in any and every way you can, and share any new information you discover about who is trying to kill Evangeline with us."

The demon stared at her, and she got the sense he would have set her on fire if he could have. Lucky for her, he couldn't.

"It's a deal." He moved in closer, his red eyes flickering with dark amusement. "You looked good as a demon, by the way."

He must have been here on Halloween, watching them. She leaned away from him. "Stop being creepy."

The demon vanished and it felt like a weight had been lifted from the room. Amber groaned, bracing her hand against the wall so she could stay upright. "I hate that," she muttered, rubbing the spot on her chest where the demon mark must be.

Genevieve walked toward her and stood over her alpha, hands on hips. "I can't believe you didn't tell us you made a deal with a demon. But what really makes me mad, is that you didn't even try to negotiate with him. You were just going to let him walk all over you!"

Amber squinted at her. "I didn't know it was negotiable!"

"Everything is negotiable," she said, crossing her arms. "Also, my parents and my sister are coming over for dinner tomorrow evening to meet all of you. I don't want them to have even the *slightest* clue that something weird is going on," she said, glaring at each of her pack mates in turn, finishing with her alpha. "My sister is nosy. She's going to ask intrusive questions if she thinks anything might be amiss."

Amber looked worried. "This isn't really a good time, can they come some other week?"

"No," Genevieve said, crossing her arms. "That will worry them."

CHAPTER 23

CERI

Demon. The word repeated over and over in Ceri's mind. She should have noticed sooner. Magic that dark should have been apparent, but she hadn't sensed it at all.

She smoothed her hair back with angry strokes and bound it into a loose bun on top of her head. A few curls spilled out, tickling the back of her neck. For a split second, she was tempted to shave it all off. She took a steadying breath, then grabbed her supplies.

The girl's guardian, a woman named Eloise Berger, was injured, but not enough that required a hospital, luckily. She'd treated her share of smoke inhalation –– witches tended to get into all sorts of trouble as kids, and telling their parents they were hurt meant getting grounded –– and it had been simple to fix once they were somewhere safe.

She'd sedated the woman simply so she didn't have to deal with her, but now they needed to wake her up. Ceri wanted a couple of minutes alone with her before she called Amber in. She needed to know if the girl was a danger.

Coming out of the sedation, she'd be loopy, and more likely to be honest. Ceri made sure her bedroom door was shut then knelt by the cot they'd made from a few blankets they'd found in a closet. She pressed her hands tightly together and spoke the words for silence and privacy. The sounds from outside her room became muted and she felt the spell press around her. Until she broke it, the pack wouldn't be able to eavesdrop on her. They'd only hear muffled sounds.

She unstoppered the bottle of Perk Up and waved it under Eloise's nose. The woman's eyes flew open and she jerked with a gasp.

"Shhh, calm down," Ceri said, pressing her back against the blankets to keep her from hurting her ribs any worse. "You're safe. The girl is safe."

Eloise's eyes were wide with confusion as she looked around the room. "What happened?" Her voice was hoarse and thready.

"You were attacked by someone. Your house burned down, but somehow you and your...daughter ended up in the woods. My alpha has a demon mark. He sent us to find you and the girl, and protect you."

Eloise instantly relaxed. Her eyes fluttered shut and she covered her face with her hands. "Oh, thank goodness."

Ceri sat back, completely surprised by her reaction. Normally saying demon wasn't cause for an 'oh thank goodness'.

"You, uh, know this demon?" she asked.

"Of course," Eloise said, dropping her hands. "He's Evangeline's uncle." She said it so casually. She had no idea what this demon really was, or how dangerous he could be.

"Has Evangeline ever hurt anyone?"

Eloise's eyes narrowed and she pressed her lips into a thin line. "No, and she wouldn't. She is harmless."

"How can you be sure?"

"Because I know her. I raised her from a baby. I taught her how to walk and how to read. She used to rescue insects that got into the house and carry them out to the garden. Wouldn't let me squash them. She's a good girl."

The door opened and Amber walked in. Ceri subtly canceled the muffling spell and nodded toward her alpha.

"Eloise, this is Amber. She is the one that rescued you," Ceri said as Amber sat down on the bed on the other side of Eloise.

"The demon mentioned you. He said a red-headed woman would help me," Eloise said with a smile. "Where is Evangeline? Is she okay?"

"Yeah, she's upstairs. I'll bring her to see you in a few minutes," Amber said, returning the woman's smile tensely. "Do you have any idea who attacked you?"

"They were humans, at least the one that got in the house." Eloise's hands shook slightly in her lap. "I knew they'd come one day, but I didn't think it'd be so soon."

"You knew they'd come one day?" Amber asked, her brows drawing together in confusion.

"Not them specifically, but someone. I've been so careful to make sure no one found out what Evangeline is. I never let her go out at night, she never had friends. Kadrithan told me that there have been others like her, and they'd all been killed. None of them made it past infancy, but they hid Evangeline better. They'd learned from their mistakes."

Ceri sat back in shock. How many had there been? Were they conducting some kind of experiment?

"Kadrithan...is that the demon's name?"

Eloise nodded. "It's not his real name I suspect. Not the one you'd use to summon him, but it's the name he gave me."

"How long have you been raising Evangeline?" Amber asked.

"Since she was a baby."

"Did the demon give her to you?"

Eloise nodded. "He's been with us since I found the girl. She was laying in the woods outside my house still covered in afterbirth. I have no idea how she got there, but he asked me to care for her."

"You have a demon mark, what deal did you make with him?" Amber asked, crossing her arms.

Eloise blushed, the color stark on her otherwise pale face. "Money. He gave me money in exchange for caring for her. My husband had died and I was about to lose the house." She looked up, meeting both their gazes. "I loved her right away though, treated her like my own child. I didn't care about the money, but I needed it. I needed it to care for her and to pay the bills."

Ceri sighed, brushing her hair back again. The wind had tangled it hopelessly and it was a huge mess now. She couldn't blame the woman for taking the money, and she obviously did care for Evangeline. It was just...the girl was a demon. At least half a demon.

She considered herself open-minded and non-judgmental, but demons and sorcerers were the exceptions. The things sorcerers did were evil and wrong. She'd always believed that demons not only committed evil acts, but were evil. Inherently.

"And that's all the demon wanted? For you to care for Evangeline?" Ceri asked finally.

Eloise nodded. "Care for her and keep her safe. And, of course, keep the secret. I've had to be strict with her because of that, and she hasn't been able to make many friends. I always regretted that, but there was no way around it."

"Why not? Were you worried she'd tell someone?" Amber asked.

"Not exactly. When it's daytime, Evangeline looks like a normal, pretty girl. When the sun sets though, she...changes. Physically. If anyone were to see here at night it would be obvious she was a demon."

"Does she act differently?" Ceri asked, glancing out the window to see the sun was already low in the sky.

"Not in the way you might think," Eloise said, shaking her head. "When she was a little girl, there was no change. But, as she got older, she started to understand it made her different. She hates it, so she gets all moody and irritable." Eloise paused then, hesitating.

"What is it?" Ceri prompted. They needed all the information they could get.

"She's been sick lately. Kadrithan knows why, but won't tell me, and neither will she. Every day it seems she gets weaker, and now sometimes, the-- she'll pass out or throw up. I just want to help her, but she won't tell me what's wrong." Eloise wrung her hands together, clearly upset.

"We'll keep an eye on her while y'all are staying here too, okay?" Amber said, trying to reassure the woman.

Ceri, however, had no interest in doing that. Eloise was acting like these were just normal teenage issues. The girl was a *demon*. Whatever was happening to her could have serious repercussions for her, and everyone around her.

"Can I see her?" Eloise asked.

"Yeah, she's been wanting to see you to. I'll go get her," Amber said, glancing at Ceri to make sure that was okay.

Ceri nodded and rose to her feet. "Just a quick visit. I need to sedate you again, Eloise, to help you heal. Your body can recover faster when you aren't moving or exerting yourself."

Amber knelt by Eloise to offer her more reassurances, but Ceri was done for now. She needed a break. Derek was standing in the hall when she walked out. He looked as angry as she felt.

"You okay?" he asked as she approached.

"I'm fine, what do you need?"

He glanced at the closed door and shook his head as if he disapproved. "Is this demon girl going to be safe to have here?"

Ceri thought about his question before answering. She felt even more confused now than she had before they'd talked to Eloise. "Yes and no," she said honestly. "She's not going to hurt us, as far as I can tell, but whoever is after her might try to, if they find out she's here."

Derek took a deep breath and nodded. "I have to go to the mechanic shop. *Call me* if something happens."

"I will," she said with a tight smile. She probably wouldn't until it was over, but if it made him feel better to hear it, she'd reassure him. Humans weren't completely defenseless, but with a sorcerer threatening them, he'd be safer far, far away from the fighting.

He lifted his hand and squeezed her shoulder, but didn't pull away. "Thanks for looking out for my sister. Lord knows she doesn't think things through sometimes." He dropped his hand and took a step back. "I'll see y'all this evening for dinner. Try not to summon any more demons while I'm gone."

She snorted. "We'll do our best, but no promises."

"Oh, and you might want to check on Tommy. Apparently, he got shot while he was out there, but didn't tell anyone."

Her heart plummeted. "Thanks for telling me. Dammit, I can't believe he didn't say anything."

"He's a teenage boy trying to look tough, what do you expect? I think he's okay." He flashed her a charming grin that, for a second, lifted her spirits. Then, he was walking away and she was left with nothing but anger for Amber and the situation she'd drug them into.

CHAPTER 24

TOMMY

Tommy was halfway through his third sandwich when Ceri stomped into the kitchen. She looked even angrier than she had when she'd found out about the demon mark. "What's wrong?"

"You didn't tell me you were shot," Ceri said as she grabbed his arm and spun him around, looking for injuries.

"Because I'm fine. They healed," he protested.

"Do you know for sure that every bullet was pushed out and not just healed over?"

"Well, I don't know, but I feel fine," he said, batting her hands away.

"Where were you shot? Show me," she said, finally letting go and putting her hands on her hips. Her hair was even frizzier than normal and her fingers were white she was digging her fingers into her waist so hard. He didn't *want* to get checked over right now, but decided she needed it.

"Fine," he said with a sigh. "Left leg and my side, right here." He lifted his shirt and she began carefully palpating the area.

"Are you okay? I know it healed, but being shot had to hurt," she asked quietly.

He hesitated before answering. "It doesn't seem real. I don't know, I'm not freaking out, but maybe I should be. I'm more worried about Amber. What she did was brutal, and she's had this *look* on her face ever since."

Ceri snorted. "Amber will be fine."

He didn't like the tone in her voice, but he wasn't sure what to say. "Why are you so mad at her?"

She paused and looked up at him. "She put the whole pack in danger."

"There wouldn't be a pack if she hadn't made that deal."

Ceri straightened and crossed her arms, looking away. "We could have found a different sponsor. She shouldn't have done that without telling us."

Tommy shook his head. "It's easy to say that looking back, but we barely knew each other when she did that. And I don't think we could have found a different sponsor. Just, I don't know, give her a break. Derek is all over her about leaving him out of the loop, and now you are too. She actually listens to you. She needs you."

Ceri glanced toward Amber's room where Evangeline was laying, still sedated. "Easier said than done."

He shook his head, still confused. "What are you *actually* mad about?"

Her eyes snapped to his and she gnawed on the inside of her cheek. "I'm worried we're going to fail."

Tommy looked at his feet. He hadn't let himself think about that yet. Failure just wasn't an option. "We can't, so we won't."

"Since when are you so optimistic?" Ceri asked with a short, humorless laugh.

"Since some wise old lady told me it was just a choice, or something silly like that," he said with a grin. "She also told me to believe in myself, and my pack."

Ceri pressed her lips together, failing to completely hide her smile. "You're not supposed to use my advice against me."

Genevieve strolled into the kitchen. "Did you eat all the bread again?"

Tommy grabbed the bag and tossed it at her. "Nope."

"He's right, by the way, you're the only one Amber really listens to," Genevieve said as she fished a piece of bread out.

"She listens to --"

Genevieve cut her off with an unimpressed look. "And then does what she wants. *You* can change her mind when you need to. You are the alpha whisperer."

Ceri laughed, finally relaxing a little. "What a grand title."

The tension bled from the room and Tommy took a deep breath. Just being with pack like this had a way of calming him. It was a sense of safety he hadn't felt since his mother died. He'd do anything to keep them safe, and to keep the pack together. Even help a demon.

He just had to find a way to get stronger. He'd frozen in the forest, and he couldn't afford to do that again. Amber couldn't fight every fight for them. She needed them just as much as they needed her.

CHAPTER 25

EVANGELINE

Evangeline grasped onto consciousness and forced her heavy eyes to open. She was inside. An old-fashioned light fixture cast yellow light on the white ceiling. She rolled her head to the side and saw the woman with red hair who had found her in the forest. The woman was sitting in a chair, watching her.

"Are you feeling okay?" the woman asked. Her eyes were freaky, like all alpha werewolves. They were tinted with red from the magic that flowed through her.

She forced herself to sit up, though the movement made her arm ache. "I'm thirsty."

The woman leaned down and grabbed a bottle of water, then carried it to her. Evangeline took it and drank from it, swallowing as quickly as she could. Her throat felt like sandpaper, but the water soothed it.

"My name is Amber, by the way," the woman said. "And as Tommy told you, the demon I owe a favor to sent me to find you and protect you."

She nodded and swung her legs over the edge of the bed. "Yeah, I got all that."

Amber crossed her arms. "Any clue who attacked your house? Did you see anyone?"

Evangeline fiddled with the bottle cap and shrugged. She didn't want to rehash all of this with some stranger, especially one stupid enough to take a demon mark. Anyone working for her uncle didn't have her best interests at heart. "Where's my mother? I want to see her."

Amber looked annoyed for a moment, then took a deep breath and headed toward the door. "Come on, she's in the bedroom across the hall."

She scrambled to her feet, ignoring the wooziness that hit her as soon as she stood, and followed Amber. As they passed through the hall, she caught a glimpse of three other people watching them expectantly. The witch, and the two other werewolves who'd been in the forest earlier.

Her mother was laying on a cot on the floor. Her eyes popped open as soon as they walked in. "Oh, Eva," she said, lifting her arms for a hug.

Evangeline ran toward her and buried her face in her mother's neck. Distantly, she heard Amber saying she'd give them a minute, then the door shut again and they were alone. She knew the werewolves would still be able to hear them, but at least they weren't staring at her.

"Are you okay?" she whispered.

Her mother smoothed her hand down her back. "I've felt better, but that witch is healing me. I'm going to be just fine."

She sat back and wiped a tear from her cheek angrily. She hated crying in front of people. "Are we going to have to stay here?"

"Yes," her uncle answered, startling her.

She turned and glared at him, not realizing he was in the room. "I wasn't asking you."

"You will stay here and stay hidden as well as you can, or you will be killed. As I keep reminding you, all I'm trying to do is keep you alive," he sneered.

"I believed that when I was five, but I know better now," Evangeline hissed, glancing toward the door suspiciously. She didn't really want anyone listening in on this conversation.

"Don't worry, they can't hear us," the demon said.

"If you wanted to keep me alive then you would have warned us those people were coming to kill us, but you weren't even there!" she said, all the pent-up anger from the last twelve hours spilling out.

He ground his teeth together and glared at her. "If I'd known they were coming, I would have gotten both of you out days before. Someone found out you exist, and when I find out how, I will punish whoever screwed up appropriately. However, until then, you have to stay here, and stay safe."

Evangeline wanted nothing more than to just run and disappear, but she could never escape her uncle. He'd dug his claws into her mother long ago with a demon mark she could never be rid of as long as she lived. He knew she loved her mother, and so she was trapped.

"How are you feeling today? You used magic to get the two of you to safety," he asked, floating over to the bed.

She felt sicker than ever and weak. Her bones ached and she knew it would only grow worse when the sun set. "I feel fine."

"You can keep lying to yourself, and to me, but eventually it will break you," he sneered.

"Kadrithan, leave her alone. She'll come to the decision in her own time. I told you I wouldn't tolerate you trying to scare her into it," Eloise objected.

"She should be scared. If she doesn't do what she needs to, she will die." He stepped over her mother and got in her face. "If you die, then Eloise has failed. I'll take her soul."

She jumped to her feet. "You can't do that!"

"I can and I will! Come to your senses and stop putting off the inevitable."

She curled her hand into a fist and yanked the bedroom door open. Amber, who had been waiting just down the hall jumped, clearly startled. "I'd like to go back to sleep."

"Okay, we have a room for you upstairs," Amber said, pointing toward the stairs.

Evangeline nodded, then turned back to her mother for a moment. "Love you, and see you in the morning."

Her mother smiled, but it didn't have the usual joy behind it. "Love you too, sweetie."

CHAPTER 26

AMBER

"How's your arm? Ceri said you'd probably need to change the bandage when you woke up," Amber asked as they walked upstairs.

The girl looked angry, and Amber had felt a slight tug on her demon mark while she was alone in that room with Eloise. She wondered what the demon had said to her, if anything. Or if he'd just been lurking and eavesdropping.

Evangeline pulled her sleeve up and shrugged. "It's only bled through a little bit."

"Here," Amber said, making a quick detour to the upstairs bathroom. Ceri had left a first aid kit on the sink with a big band-aid set on top. She picked it up and showed Evangeline. "You don't need the full bandage anymore."

Evangeline didn't respond, just pushed the sleeve of her hoodie up and started unwinding the bandage. She hissed in pain as she started to peel the gauze away from the wound. It had bled a little and then dried, which made it stick.

"I can keep that from sticking if you want," Amber said, reaching for the bandage.

"Don't touch me," Evangeline snapped, flinching away from her outstretched hand. "I can do it myself."

Amber lifted her hands in surrender. "Fine. You should change the band-aid every morning and evening." She picked up a little tub of ointment Ceri had added to the kit. "And smear a small amount of this on it. Ceri said it should help it heal within a few days."

It wasn't hard to believe this girl was a demon. She was rude, ungrateful, and looked like she wanted to punch anyone that came near her. The angel part seemed to have only affected her appearance.

"Great," Evangeline said, grabbing the tub opening it. She dabbed the ointment on while standing as far away from Amber as physically possible in the small bathroom.

The band-aid made it onto her arm but it was crooked and only partially covered the wound. Evangeline tossed the trash, most of it making it in the actual trashcan, the rest falling on the floor. Angered by its apparent uncooperativeness, she bent down and picked up the pieces, throwing them in one at a time.

Amber crossed her arms and waited. When Evangeline was finally done, she tried to leave the bathroom. She grabbed the girl's uninjured arm. "We need to talk."

"Why? You're supposed to keep me alive, not get to know me," Evangeline said, flipping her long hair over her shoulder.

Amber's eye twitched. She wondered if shaving the girl's head would count as 'harming her'. "Did you see any of the people that attacked you?"

"Only the one my mom killed, but he was already dead," she said, turning her head away. But she couldn't hide the slight tremble of her lips.

"Have you seen any other half angels around recently? At school? Following you?" Amber asked.

Evangeline shook her head. "People like that don't come to Timber. It's in the middle of nowhere. They would have stuck out."

"Has anything weird happened around you recently?"

"Yeah," Evangeline said, shrugging her shoulders. "But everybody already knows about that."

"Well *I* don't. What was it?"

"A no-magic spot showed up right outside our school," she said, crossing her arm and looking uncomfortable. "There was a rumor going around that it must be demon related."

"Is it?" Amber asked bluntly. That earned her another glare, but at least Evangeline didn't look like she was about to cry anymore.

"No. At least not anything *I* did. I don't know what Kadrithan gets up to in his spare time."

Amber's phone buzzed with a message. She pulled it out and saw Shane's message letting her know he'd be there in ten minutes. "Shit."

She'd completely forgotten he was going to pick her up this evening to go visit Donovan's old pack. The timing couldn't be worse.

"What?" Evangeline asked, eyeing her suspiciously.

"I need you to stay in your room and stay *quiet*. There's another werewolf from the council stopping by." She shoved Evangeline out of the bathroom and pointed toward the spare bedroom she'd be staying in.

"That I can do," Evangeline muttered. She hurried into the room, slamming the door shut behind her.

Amber put her hands over her face and cursed Angel, demons, and teenagers. She was never, ever having kids.

She left the first aid kit where it was so Evangeline could find it later and hurried downstairs. The pack was in the kitchen and...they were laughing. She stopped in the living room and just watched for a moment, completely confused. Less than an hour ago they'd been at each other's throats. Well, they'd been mad at her. Not each other.

"Hey, Shane is on his way here. I completely forgot he was coming by this evening to pick me up. We have to go to Lockhart's old pack to check in on things and see if they have a new alpha yet," she said, feeling strangely left out for the first time.

Genevieve immediately perked up. "I need to go with you."

"Why?" Amber asked, frowning.

"I wanted to talk to you about it earlier today, but..." she waved her hand around to indicate the chaos that had taken over the afternoon. In some ways, it felt like it had been days since the demon had appeared in the living room and called in his debt. "Anyhow, I have a new client. He's a bitten wolf, and about a week ago he was charged with loss of control. He was attacked in a bar, and when he defended himself, he hurt the other guy pretty badly. Without his alpha to vouch for him, they won't even consider letting him out on bail."

"It may be a while before the pack accepts a new alpha," Amber warned. She hated the injustice, but she had no idea if they'd be able to help this bitten wolf anytime soon.

"That's okay, I just need to talk to *someone*," Genevieve said. She grabbed a slice of bread from the bag she was holding, then retied it and tossed it at Tommy. He caught it easily thanks to his werewolf reflexes.

"Alright, when Shane gets here I'll make sure it's not against some kind of rule, but it'd be good to have more backup there." She dragged her hands through her hair. "I think it's best if no one knows we have guests."

"I definitely agree," Ceri said with a gentle smile that took Amber off guard. The witch had been pissed last time she saw her. "I'll make sure he can't smell anything out of place. How long do I have?"

Amber glanced at her phone. "Maybe ten minutes, but I wasn't going to let him inside."

Tommy started cleaning up the kitchen and Genevieve ran up to her room to grab something.

Ceri walked over and put her hand on Amber's arm. "After you get back, we need to talk about that whole animal whisperer thing."

"Okay," Amber said, her eyebrows drawing together. "Is everything okay?"

"Yes. There's just a lot to explain, and we need to start figuring out how to track down whoever is trying to hurt Evangeline."

"As soon as we get back, I'm all yours."

Ceri smiled and squeezed her elbow lightly. "Be safe."

~

Amber finished tying off her braid when Angel appeared at her shoulder. Her phone vibrated on the counter and she saw Shane's message on the screen letting her know he was in the driveway.

"You don't have time for these sorts of distractions," he said, blocking her view of the mirror. He had reverted to his little red devil form, but his humor still hadn't returned.

"If I don't take care of this, Shane and the council will be suspicious," she said, grabbing her jacket and hurrying toward the front door. "Just stay out of it and let me get it over with."

She hurried for the front door, shouting for Genevieve over her shoulder. Angel followed her as well, much to her chagrin.

Amber plastered a smile on her face before yanking the door open. Shane froze, his fist still in the air, ready to knock.

He lowered his hand. "Everything okay?"

"Yeah, sorry, running a little late. Also, Genevieve is coming with us," she said, slightly breathless from scrambling to get ready. "She's representing one of members of the Lockhart pack. She needs to talk to whoever the alpha might be right now and see if they can help the werewolf. I'm bringing her along if that isn't against some kind of weird werewolf code of conduct I don't know about."

He raised a brow, but didn't object. "Fine with me. She'll need to be careful not to challenge anyone and stay by you."

Amber nodded. "That shouldn't be a problem."

"I didn't realize she was a lawyer."

"No one ever does," Genevieve said, popping up behind Amber. "Are we going to leave, or just stand in the doorway all evening?"

Amber threw a glare over her shoulder. Genevieve winked at her.

Shane just laughed and swept his hand to the side. "Ladies first."

She headed toward the suburban, walking a little fast so she could get shotgun and make Genevieve sit in the back. It was uncomfortable leaving Evangeline with the pack, but she knew Ceri could take care of her and protect the rest of them if needed.

Angel settled on the dashboard as they climbed in the suburban. He glared at Shane and Amber found herself glad she was the only one that could see him, even if it did make her feel a little crazy sometimes.

The drive was uneventful. Shane spent most of it asking Genevieve how she'd ended up a lawyer, and all about the bitten wolf that had been arrested. Amber had trouble focusing on the conversation. Angel kept making snide comments she couldn't respond to.

That wasn't what really bothered her though. Her heart was beating faster than normal and her palms were sweaty. She felt a strange disconnect from everything around her. It didn't seem possible that earlier today she had killed four people. It had been in self defense, but the memories of the violence made her skin crawl. And now she was just going on an errand for the council like nothing had happened. Maybe she was going crazy.

The wolf felt nothing but fierce pride over the kills. She rubbed the hem of her jacket between her fingers to ground herself. She had to calm down before they saw the other pack or she'd end up setting someone off. Or letting someone get to her.

Genevieve's hand landed on her shoulder and squeezed. Some of the tension bled out of her as the pack bond wrapped around her. She forced herself to turn her attention back to the conversation. In just a couple of hours this would be over, and she could go take care of what really mattered. Her pack.

CHAPTER 27

AMBER

Amber grew tense as they pulled into the driveway of Donovan Lockhart's house. It belonged to the pack now, according to his will, and would house whoever managed to claim the title of alpha. It was a nice house, though a little gaudy for Amber's taste. It was a mix of five different architectural styles, all mashed together in an attempt to make it look expensive.

Cars and trucks were parked in the driveway, with the overflow spilling into the side yard. Even from inside Shane's suburban, she could hear shouting and growling in the distance.

"They must be in the middle of a challenge," Shane said as he parked next to the car farthest from the house.

"After all these years you'd think they'd move to some kind of election-based system instead of literally fighting for the position," Genevieve muttered from the backseat.

Shane shook his head. "The wolf in us would never respect something like that. We could never follow someone weak."

Amber would never admit it out loud, but a small part of her craved the chance to fight off a challenger and prove her worth to her pack. Being a werewolf didn't change who you were, exactly, but it did give you new instincts. She wasn't alone in her head anymore.

"Wolves are savages. You should know that, Amber," Angel purred, twisting around her shoulders.

She glared at the demon as they climbed out of the suburban, but couldn't respond. He seemed pleased to have gotten a reaction.

They headed toward the sounds of fighting. The wolf peered out of her eyes and took it all in. There was a sense of excitement in the air. She could smell it.

"Stay calm, and don't make eye contact for too long," Shane cautioned, for a third time,

STEPHANIE FOXE

as they walked toward the crowd gathered in the backyard. "The pack has no clear leadership right now and everyone is keyed up from the fighting."

"Shane, you worry more than Amber, and that is really alarming," Genevieve said, patting him on the shoulder.

Amber snorted in amusement, but tried to hide it behind a cough.

Shane gave them both a dirty look. "See if I try to keep you from getting in a fight ever again."

"You know you will," Amber said with a grin that didn't feel entirely forced. "You want to hand off these crappy duties too bad to let me get hurt or killed."

He sighed dramatically. "That and you are still supposed to buy me dinner."

Genevieve made a gagging noise. "Please don't flirt in front of me. I *just* ate."

Amber was about to make a smart remark back when she saw the fight. She stopped in her tracks and just stared.

To say it was violent would be an understatement. The two wolves were huge. One was dark gray, and the other a muddy mix of red and brown. Their lips were curled back revealing long, sharp teeth streaked with blood. Their fur was matted with dirt and grass that had been torn up by their sharp claws.

The wolves collided with a furious snarl. The gray one bit into the thick muscle of the other wolf's shoulder. The brown wolf yelped and twisted, clawing at the gray wolf's gut. The snarls were almost drowned out by the jeers of the crowd as they shouted insults and encouragement.

Amber couldn't tell who they wanted to win, or if they even cared. It seemed like they were caught up in the thrill of it. The whole thing made her sick, but the wolf was merely curious. It looked at the two fighting as potential challengers. They were slightly bigger than she was, but they fought recklessly, depending on their size and strength to dominate the other.

The wolves broke apart and circled each other slowly. Genevieve pressed against Amber's side. She was just as tense as Amber felt.

"You can't tell me this isn't barbaric," Angel whispered. "But people fear *demons*."

She wished her wolf could banish Angel again, even if it was just for a few days. He needed to shut up. This was awful enough without his commentary.

The gray wolf lunged, jaws open, but this time the brown wolf didn't meet his charge. He skittered backward, then ducked underneath the attack. His jaws clamped around the gray wolf's neck and he dragged him to the ground, managing to twist at the last moment so that he ended up on top.

"That's a common move," Shane said, whispering directly into Amber's ear. Despite the current situation, she felt a shiver go down her spine as his breath tickled the skin of her neck. She glanced back and caught his gaze. He was standing very close. Close enough to touch.

"The gray wolf seems like the better fighter, but not by much," Amber replied quietly.

Shane nodded. "He's a little older. Jameson expects him to end up as the alpha. He was one of Donovan's gammas, but he was dominant enough to be a beta at least."

Amber looked around at the crowd. There must have been thirty people here. She

296

recognized a couple from the night they'd been changed, but they weren't paying any attention to her. They were completely focused on the fight.

The former beta whose ass she'd kicked when he'd showed up at her apartment to gloat over her eviction was watching as well, though he had a sullen expression on his face. He must have tried to take the position early on and lost.

A sudden cheer from the crowd brought her attention back to the fight. The gray wolf had the brown wolf's ear in his mouth. He jerked his head viciously and ripped the ear off, taking a hunk of fur with it. Bile rose in Amber's throat, but she forced it down and didn't look away.

He attacked again immediately, forcing the brown wolf onto his back with his jaws clamped firmly around his neck. The other wolf struggled for a moment, but it was clear he couldn't breathe.

"He'll forfeit now, don't worry," Shane said, touching her back briefly. True to his word, a moment later the brown wolf shifted back to human form. He lay still underneath the gray wolf who tilted his head back and howled in victory. She had hated Donovan, but she hated this more. There had to be a better way. A less violent way.

The gray wolf shifted into human form and glared down at his defeated opponent. His body was streaked with sweat and the wounds from the fight were even more obvious on his bare skin.

"Do you submit?" His voice carried over the crowd, silencing every conversation as the pack waited for the response.

The other man kept his eyes on the ground, but his body was shaking with anger, or embarrassment. She wasn't sure which. "Yes."

The pack erupted into howls, celebrating their newest alpha. A few of the men and women watching didn't join in though. Amber looked at each of them in turn. The wolf thought they were potential challengers, and she agreed. At the very least they didn't like their new alpha.

"You look disgusted, but I can sense your strongest emotions. You wish that was you," Angel said, morphing into a vicious looking wolf with a pointed tail and horns.

She took a deep breath and sent all the hate she could muster at the demon. If he could sense her emotions, then she hoped he suffered.

He wagged his tail at her. "You can do better than that. I know you have a lot of anger and hate in that savage, wolfy heart."

Shane tapped Amber on the arm and motioned for her to follow him. She turned her back on Angel and tried to put him from her mind. Engaging with him never turned out in her favor.

The winner was exiting the circle and accepted a pair of loose shorts handed to him by another pack member. He paused to pull them on, then continued to a table where he grabbed a pitcher of water and downed it. The water spilled over his jaw and chest, washing away some of the blood.

"Congratulations, Kevin," Shane said, raising his voice loud enough to be heard at a distance.

The man lowered the pitcher and nodded toward Shane, though he didn't look excited to see him. "I didn't expect the council to show up so soon."

"We waited a few days to show up, but you know how the government gets. They want their paperwork," Shane said with an easy grin, completely ignoring the tension in the other werewolf. "Alpha Hale is with me. She took Donovan's position on the council."

Kevin turned his dark eyes to her and she felt her skin crawl. "I know who she is." He seemed to bite back something he wanted to add on to that statement.

Amber took her cue from Shane and simply stared at him impassively. The wolf rose up in her mind, hackles raised and red bloomed along the edges of her vision. She would tolerate a certain amount of attitude, but she wasn't going to cower in front of him.

"We need to record the names and rank of every pack member. Are you going to help, or do you want your beta to do it?" Shane asked. "Assuming you have someone in mind for the position."

Kevin pointed at the man who'd handed him the shorts. "He'll do it."

Shane nodded and headed toward the guy, but Amber walked over to Kevin. Genevieve followed her.

"What do you want?" he asked, looking her over. It wasn't sexual though, it was fear, which surprised her for a moment. She had defeated his alpha in the Trials though, something no one thought possible.

"Genevieve is representing one of your pack members that has been arrested. She has some questions, and needs your help. Are you willing to talk to her?" Amber asked, holding his gaze. Shane had said no prolonged eye contact, but she wasn't going to act scared. Kevin could look away first if he didn't want another fight on his hands.

"Sure, but she needs to make it quick." Kevin opened up an ice chest and grabbed a beer, cracking it open and chugging half of it immediately.

Amber turned to Genevieve for a moment. "I'm going to go help Shane, and make sure the other guy is alright. If you need help, just let me know."

Genevieve patted her arm. "I'll be fine."

Amber nodded and caught up to Shane, cursing Donovan in her head for being stupid enough to get murdered.

CHAPTER 28

GENEVIEVE

Genevieve locked gazes with the interim alpha. He hated her. And the feeling was mutual.

"Davie is a little shit and I'm not bailing him out of trouble," Kevin growled, his eyes flashing red like that could make her cower. This asshole wasn't more dominant than she was. He had won that fight but he was nothing special. He'd be knocked out of his position by tomorrow, if not sooner.

"You are worthless," Genevieve said quietly, leaning in slightly and baring her teeth at him.

He sneered at her. "Unless you intend to challenge me, you better keep that pretty little mouth shut. Insult me again and it might start a fight you can't win."

She rolled her eyes and grabbed her briefcase. This conversation was going nowhere. Absolutely nowhere. This pack was in shambles, and every single member was going to suffer until someone managed to come out on top.

Genevieve stood and glared down at him. "I won't have to challenge you, you'll be ousted by the end of the day."

He growled and made a move like he was going to lunge at her, but Shane appeared out of nowhere and slammed him back down in his chair.

"Let it go, Kevin," Shane warned. "You try to challenge her, you'll have to go through me."

The werewolf sneered at them, but didn't make another move. Genevieve turned and walked away, heading back toward the car. Amber was off to the side talking to the werewolf that had lost the fight. She looked back over her shoulder to make sure Genevieve was alright. She nodded at her alpha and kept going.

This entire pack were idiots. All of them. She tightened her grip on her briefcase and thanked every deity she could think of that Amber had been there the night they were attacked. If it had been someone else…she may have ended up in the System. Or worse, in this pack.

Halfway through the impromptu parking lot she noticed a man with light brown hair underneath a well-worn ball cap leaning against the side of his car. She couldn't quite pin down his age. He wasn't young, but she didn't think he was middle-aged yet either. He was dressed casually in jeans and a white t-shirt. He had a bag of donut holes in one hand but wasn't eating them.

She paused when she felt his eyes on her. It felt like he was waiting for her to show up. He wasn't checking her out and he didn't look nervous. His expression was more...expectant. She changed directions and headed straight for him.

He waited until she was about a foot away to lift the bag in her direction. "Hungry?"

"Always," she said, extending her hand for a treat.

He picked out three donut holes and placed them in her hand before grabbing one for himself. She wasted no time scarfing down two of them, eyes slipping shut as she enjoyed the melt-in-your-mouth glaze and the soft dough.

"Who are you and why are you handing out donut holes?" she asked, holding her hand in front of her mouth as she continued chewing.

"My name is Paul Greer, and I have a proposition for you."

She narrowed her eyes at him. "Alright, Paul Greer, let's hear it."

"This pack has gone to shit," he said without preamble. "And it's going to stay that way until the idiots get done fighting amongst themselves. I intend to claim it; however, I've been waiting for the right moment. No matter how good of a fighter I am, I can't defend three challenges a day for very long."

She nodded. "Yeah, that'd be pretty insane."

"I've heard a lot about your alpha, and I was there for the Trials, watching." He opened the bag again and ate another donut hole, chewing it thoughtfully. "It's weird seeing a bitten wolf pull something like that off, but I think I like it. Werewolves have been getting complacent in recent years. Getting humanized, and acting like they don't have to prove themselves if they were born that way." He shook his head in disapproval.

"What are you planning on doing about that?" She wasn't sure if she should be creeped out by his little speech or not. He didn't give off crazy person vibes, but there was something...wild about him.

"Not much," he admitted with a shrug. "But I'll run this pack differently, and I think I'll get along well with your alpha. If I win my challenge, I want her as my sponsor."

Genevieve's jaw dropped, but she quickly clamped it shut. A sponsor would need a certain amount of money, and she wasn't sure Amber could come up with it. "Ooookay, why aren't you talking to her about this?"

His mouth quirked up into a smile. "It's tradition to contact the alpha's beta first, which I assume you are. It's meant to be an introduction. Tell her what you think of me." He pulled a slip of paper out of his pocket. "This is my contact information. I'll be challenging whatever knucklehead is the alpha in a few days, on the night of the Full Moon. Then, I'll come call on Alpha Hale. If you have any questions for me between now and then, let me know."

This was completely unexpected, but the wheels in her head were already turning. She wasn't even sure if she *was* Amber's beta. The pack had never talked about pack ranks since there were so few of them. They just worked together and didn't overthink it.

She wanted to ask Paul to swear to help out Davie before she passed along his info to Amber but decided against it. This guy seemed like he was fairly honest and blunt. She didn't want to try to manipulate him. He couldn't do anything for Davie right now, so she would wait until he become the alpha to present the case to him. There were a few details she needed to figure out anyhow, since it was starting to look like Davie wasn't being entirely honest with her. She had wanted to get him out on bail but that just wasn't an option anymore. The Full Moon was in three days. Davie could wait until then.

She put the paper in her briefcase and nodded. "Alright, I'll be in touch."

"Have a good day," he said, tipping his head toward her. He pushed off the car and strolled back toward the area where the pack had congregated.

She watched him go as she stuffed the last donut hole in her mouth. They were really good.

CHAPTER 29

CERI

Ceri handed Derek a mug of tea. "You look like you could use something to relax. A friend recommended this to me recently, and it was very effective."

He smiled for the first time in twenty-four hours as he accepted her offering. "Your friend sounds smart."

Leaning back against the counter she picked up her own mug of tea and took a sip. The lavender and honey tasted like heaven and she felt her muscles slowly un-tensing.

The house was quiet. Eloise was still sleeping off the sedative, and Evangeline had no interest in talking to or seeing anyone from the pack. It was almost blissful. Ceri knew she was an introvert, but sometimes she forgot just how draining other people could be. The magical battle had drained her too, and was still draining her. She needed to talk to Amber about that as soon as she got back.

"Am I being too hard on Amber?" Derek asked, startling her out of her thoughts.

Ceri blew on her tea, taking a moment to think. "I think we both are. Maybe. She knows she should have told us sooner. I'm done being mad at her, it doesn't help anything."

Derek nodded in agreement. "I can't really blame her for keeping it to herself, I guess. She was real messed up after Dylan died. We weren't there for her. I think that kind of thing could make a person forget they can actually turn to family for help."

"She's mentioned that her mom blamed her for what happened, but she doesn't talk about it much."

He sighed and shook his head. "Yeah, mom definitely blamed her. It was stupid, but Amber just always took care of Dylan. Kept him out of trouble. He was the risk-taker. It caught us all off guard that they'd both tried to join a pack. It's something I would have expected her to talk him out of, but I guess she wanted it too." He cleared his throat. "But enough about all that. How'd you end up in the pack?"

Ceri laughed. "That's not any less depressing. My family kicked me out because I won't join the coven properly."

"Why not?" Derek asked. His blue eyes watched her over the brim of his mug with genuine interest. It made something warm curl up in her gut to see. All her dating prospects had always been other witches, and they only saw her family name, and her reputation as a tree-hugging disappointment.

"The magic witches use is based on a trade. You have to sacrifice something. A plant is a small sacrifice. It's alive, but its life force doesn't hold the same...oomph that something sentient does. A pixie, like Woggy, is a common ingredient." She looked down into the amber liquid of the tea, her fingers tightening on her mug. "No one talks about it, but they'll do bigger animals too. Cats, dogs, horses. It's all about power."

"The elves don't have to do that to work their magic, why do y'all?" he asked, looking a little disturbed.

"They tap into something else. Some theorize there's a type of spirit realm, or that magic is in the air we breathe but that not every race can access it," she said with a shrug. "Hard to say, really. These spots where magic doesn't work might give us some insight though."

A loud squeak caught her attention and she looked down to find that Woggy had escaped from his box yet again. "Are you hungry?" she asked, signing along as she spoke just like Tommy had taught her.

The pixie squeaked and signed back with a very emphatic yes.

"Is that sign language?" Derek asked.

Ceri nodded. "Tommy suggested it. It's completely brilliant, and I'm mad I didn't think of it first."

"And he really understands it?"

"Yep. Woggy is learning more every day too." She grabbed a can of tuna from the pantry, opened it, and sat it on the floor. Woggy dived into the meat immediately, eating with gusto. And making a mess. "We're working on teaching him to clean up after himself too, but he hasn't been very interested in that lesson."

Derek snorted. "Of course not."

The front door opened and Genevieve walked inside yawning. She grimaced. "We have got to get Woggy something other than tuna. The whole house reeks all the time now."

"Better than just smelling like cat," Amber said, appearing behind her and glaring down the hall. Captain Jack appeared, his tail swishing behind him. He made a beeline for the tuna, but Woggy turned and hissed at him, hugging the can of fish close to his chest.

"Captain Jack does not stink," Genevieve said, picking up the giant cat. "He's very cleanly."

Amber rolled her eyes and muttered something about putting him outside to catch rats. Ceri hid a smile behind her tea. It was refreshing to see them arguing about something normal.

But, there were still things to discuss before the night was over. She caught Amber's gaze and nodded toward the porch.

Derek seemed to understand that they needed to talk. "Gen, did that alpha end up agreeing to help you get that bitten wolf out on bail?"

Genevieve groaned and launched into a long explanation. Ceri took the distraction and headed toward the porch with Amber. It was cool outside, borderline cold, now that the sun was down.

"This has been the longest day in history," Amber said, plopping down on the porch swing. She held it still so Ceri could sit, then pushed off the ground with her toe, rocking them gently.

"Yeah, it has been," Ceri agreed. She was tired down to her bones. They sat quietly on the porch swing and enjoyed the breeze for a moment before continuing. "What you said the other morning reminded me of a conversation with my grandmother. She was a nasty piece of work, but I learned a lot from her. Have you ever heard of a shaman?"

Amber shook her head. "Is that some kind of witch?"

"Technically, yes." She pulled her foot up onto the porch swing and hugged her knee to her chest. "When a witch joins a pack, it can change her magic. That owl I was complaining about the other day wasn't just an owl. It was a spirit. I don't know what it wants, but it helped me when I was fighting that sorcerer. Without it, and the pack bond, I would have been completely outmatched."

Amber ran her hands through her hair and pulled her feet up on the swing as well. "What does that mean for you? It doesn't sound bad, but you didn't exactly sign up for having your magic changed."

Ceri rested her chin on her knee and stared out at the night sky. "I don't know what it means, but it definitely isn't bad. I've always hated how weak white magic is. This...was different. It was more powerful."

"More powerful is better, right?"

"Mostly, but more power generally requires a greater sacrifice. At least for a witch. I shouldn't be able to just tap into the source like an elf." She rubbed her temples, wishing she had answers for herself and Amber. "The second time this owl visited me, right before the demon called in his favor, I had a vision of fire, pain, and darkness. Then the demon showed up and we rescued Evangeline. I don't know if I was being warned she was in danger, or being warned that *we* were because of the demon." The vision had been gnawing at her ever since the demon had appeared.

"In some ways, I guess we both are. Whoever is hunting Evangeline is a threat to us now. Too bad this shaman stuff doesn't come with a guidebook," Amber said with a snort.

"No kidding. That'd make our lives so much easier," she agreed with a laugh. "Speaking of no guidebook, I might have done something kind of risky."

"Risky?" Amber asked, sitting up straight.

"To stop the sorcerer, I had to kind of...create a shield for Evangeline," she said, twisting her fingers in the hem of her sweater.

"Ceri, just spit it out," Amber said, frustration evident in her voice. Her whole body was tense, like she was ready to fight someone.

Ceri sighed and dropped her head back to her knees. "My magic is shielding her. We're kind of tied together until I undo the...well, it's basically a psychic shield. But it's the only thing keeping the sorcerer's spell from killing her."

Amber put her hand over her mouth, her fingers digging into her cheeks slightly, then dropped her hand. "Can it hurt you?"

"It's not likely."

"Why doesn't that sound very reassuring?" Amber asked, making it sound like an accusation.

She wanted to say *because it shouldn't*, but Amber had enough to worry about. "We have to find this sorcerer and stop him. But I'm more worried about the demon than I am the sorcerer. Does he know anything about who is hunting her?"

"Not much. I think we may know more than Evangeline or the demon at this point. The blond guy was a half angel, and he has a sorcerer working with him. Maybe we can start asking around. Would a sorcerer leave any signs if he showed up in town?" Amber asked.

"They tend to fly under the radar. It's technically illegal, after all. But...they might buy supplies wherever they end up," she said, her mind racing. The black market for magical supplies was alive and well in Portland. There were a dozen people the sorcerer could contact, but it was somewhere to start. "I know a few people that my family used to buy from when we needed something not on the record. We can start by talking to one of them."

Amber nodded immediately. "How soon can we talk to them? Is it like a night time only thing?"

Ceri laughed. "They're not vampires, well, not all of them. There's someone we can definitely talk to tomorrow before Gen's parents come over for dinner."

"Ugh, don't remind me. They couldn't be coming at a worse time," Amber groaned, putting her head in her hands.

"When it rains it pours," Ceri agreed. Part of her was glad though. She wanted to cling to every bit of normalcy as tightly as possible. A gentle hoot caught her attention and she saw the owl, her near constant companion, sitting in a tree near the porch. She twisted her fingers tighter in her sweater and tried to ignore the sense of doom she hadn't been able to shake since the vision.

Amber shifted on the swing, starting up the rocking again. She cleared her throat, like she was gearing up to say something, but only ended up chewing her nails.

"What is it?" Ceri asked, nudging her gently.

"I'm sorry I wasn't honest with you," Amber said quietly.

Ceri turned her head to rest her cheek on her knees instead and reached her hand out, entwining her fingers with Amber's. "I know. And it's okay. No one is perfect, not even a woman who's only been an alpha for just over a month and who had no idea she was about to be dumped into a dangerous, magical world."

Amber glared at her, but there was no heat behind it. "Are you mocking me while I'm trying to apologize?"

"Only a little," Ceri said with a grin.

Amber shook her head, but she was smiling now. "Everyone in my pack is a jerk. That is my karmic punishment."

Ceri laughed, and it felt good. She felt lighter than she had in days. "Oh, that reminds me...our house is kind of sentient."

"What?" Amber asked in alarm.

She grinned and launched into an explanation. Freaking Amber out with magic was the best form of therapy.

CHAPTER 30

GENEVIEVE

"You promised you could get me out!" Davie said, his voice cracking. "Come on, I can't stay in here."

"Listen to me," Genevieve said, leaning forward. She was about as frustrated as he was, but all this panicking didn't help anything. "I am going to help you, but until an alpha is chosen, there's nothing we can do. Do you know Paul Greer?"

Davie wiped his nose on the back of his sleeve and nodded. "Yeah, why?"

"He's going to try to take the position on the night of the full moon, and I think he would help," she said, sitting back in her chair.

He snorted and shook his head. "No way. He's just some quiet loner, he's not gonna be able to win a challenge."

She pinched the bridge of her nose between her thumb and forefinger. "Well, you better hope he wins, because if Kevin keeps it, he won't vouch for you and we'll have to try a different strategy. What I need you to do for me now is *stay out of trouble*. I can't believe you got into a fight in here."

Davie looked chagrined. "They told me bitten wolves might as well be puppies."

"So what? They're just trying to get a rise out of you. If you can't show some semblance of control while you're waiting for your hearing, there's no way the judge is going to let you out on bail no matter what your alpha says." She was starting to think Davie *did* have a problem with control. He definitely had an attitude problem. Someone like him should never have been bitten, but from what she knew of Donovan's pack, he hadn't exactly chosen the most upstanding citizens to bring into the fold.

"I'll try, okay? Just please get me out of here as soon as you can," he begged again, giving her puppy dog eyes.

"That's my job," Genevieve said as she rose from her chair. She had so much paperwork to do today for other cases. This visit had been a last minute decision after she'd gotten a phone call from Davie where he'd been sobbing about a fight he'd gotten into.

She rapped on the door for the guard to let her out. He opened the door and she hurried down the hallway. She wasn't sure if it was a good sign or not, but she was getting used to coming here.

Halfway back to her car, her phone rang. She saw Steven's number and almost ignored the call but a twinge of guilt stopped her.

"Hey," she said, tucking the phone between her cheek and shoulder while she unlocked her car.

"Finally," Steven said, irritation clear in his tone.

"I'm sorry, it's been a really weird couple of days." She climbed into the car, tossing her briefcase in the passenger seat.

"You could at least text me back. It takes two seconds."

"I know, I know. I said I was sorry." She backed up quickly and checked the time. She was going to be at least thirty minutes late getting to the office, and she'd missed the morning meeting completely.

"Can you come over tonight? It's been a week since we've had dinner."

"I can't, my parents are coming over for dinner to meet the pack." She mentally groaned. It was the last thing she wanted to deal with right now, but she'd put them off even longer than Steven. When he didn't reply, she checked her phone to make sure the call hadn't dropped. It still showed connected, but he was completely silent. "Steven?"

"You know we dated for a year and you barely even mentioned your parents, much less let me meet them."

"We weren't...it just didn't seem like the right time," she said, cringing as the words came out of her mouth.

"Genevieve, why can't you just be honest? You were never serious about our relationship, and still aren't," he said in clipped tones.

She sighed and ground her teeth together. Normally, this was the part where she just agreed, and they broke up for a few weeks before they got back together. "Then just come tonight."

As soon as the words left her mouth, she wanted to drive her car into a telephone pole. It wasn't that she didn't want to be with Steven, it's just that the idea of forever made her skin crawl. She didn't want everyone to think they were madly in love and then be disappointed if they broke up. So, she'd just...not told anyone. It was easier that way. For her at least. It obviously wasn't easier for Steven.

"Are you serious?"

"Yes," she said hesitantly. She couldn't tell if he was still mad, or excited.

"Are you going to introduce me as your boyfriend or try to pretend I'm just part of the pack?"

"As my boyfriend," she said, exasperated at him now. "Look, I'm not good at this stuff. You know that. Just take the invitation and stop making me repeat it."

He sighed. "Fine, but we're going to hold hands, and sometime in the next month, we're going to have a dinner with just us and your parents. No hiding behind the pack."

"Fine. Look, I'm almost to work, I really need to go."

"I'll be at the house at four this evening, unless they'll be over earlier?" he asked.

"No, they're coming around five."

"Okay, see you then. Have a good day at work, bye," he said, sounding a little more chipper.

"You too. Bye," she said, hanging up the phone. As soon as she tapped end, her heart dropped into her stomach. "Ah, hell."

She'd completely forgotten about Evangeline. She still hadn't told Steven about her, and he would know something weird was going on. With a sigh, she picked up her phone again, and texted Amber.

She was so busy now that she was working all the time, she felt like she'd abandoned the pack. Ceri, Amber, and Tommy had run off to rescue Evangeline without her and she hadn't gotten there in time to help. She left before everyone was awake, and barely made dinner most nights.

Taking on this case felt like a mistake but if she hadn't, then Davie would just rot in prison. She wished she was smarter and had a way to help him *now*. Paul Greer might be able to help but the full moon was still two days away. She also had no guarantee he'd want to help Davie either, especially as a new alpha.

Her fingers twitched on the steering wheel as the sudden urge to shift and run flowed through her. The wolf was restless and tired of being restrained. The more frustrated she got, the harder it was to stay in control. None of the others struggled with it as much as she did.

After the Trials, she'd thought she could just turn her life around and *do something*, but it was silly to assume she'd be able to succeed just like that. Maybe it had been silly to try at all.

She parked the car on the far end of the parking lot in the only space left and shook her head at herself. She couldn't even manage to get to work on time.

CHAPTER 31

CERI

Ceri had a headache, and this downtown traffic wasn't helping. "Oh my god, learn to use your accelerator," she muttered as she changed lanes to pass a slow driver.

Amber looked askance at her. "I never suspected you'd have road rage."

"I don't have road rage!" she objected, glaring at the road. "Normally. I might be a little hungry and tired."

Amber smirked and propped her foot up on the dash. "Who are we going to see today?"

"My cousin. And, just be warned, she's awful. She actually managed to get kicked out of the coven for using too much black magic. Well, for getting caught using it by the wrong people." She twirled a curl around her finger. That had been a huge mess. Her mother had done a lot of damage control, but it had been yet another step on her coven's downward spiral into oblivion. Her grandmother had probably been rolling in her grave.

"Is it common for so many covens to use black magic whenever they can get away with it?" Amber asked. "I didn't know that many witches back in Texas, or here for that matter, but I thought it just wasn't done anymore."

"It's probably fifty-fifty," she said with a shrug. "Newer covens are more likely to be completely legal, but the older covens gained their power through spells that no one could consider white magic. They aren't about to give that up just because the laws have changed, and no one is going to rat them out."

Her cousin worked at a beauty shop owned by some elves that sold elf-spelled cosmetics in the front, and more interesting things in the basement, if you had the money. It was in a nice part of town; the kind of place you felt comfortable letting your kids run around alone. And, to be fair, it was safe for them. You only got into trouble if you pissed someone off, and then it wouldn't matter where you were.

The shop had a big parking lot filled with new, shiny cars. Ceri parked near the door, but didn't get out immediately.

"What?"

She sighed and yanked down the visor to use the mirror. "You can never tell anyone about this, but if I walk in there without looking perfect, we're just going to spend the whole time with her insulting my hair."

Amber raised a brow. "What's wrong with your hair?"

"Nothing," she said as she pulled a small tub of Friz-B-Smooth out of the center console. She scooped the smallest amount possible out and rubbed it on her hands. "But she's a pompous turd-face. If we didn't need information, I wouldn't bother, but I'd rather spend as little time in there as possible."

Magic tingled on her palms. She waited for it to feel warm, then vigorously brushed her fingers through her hair. The curls detangled easily, then popped back into shape perfectly smooth and shiny. Her blonde hair practically sparkled in the sunlight.

"Will you hate me if I say that's actually kind of awesome?" Amber asked, leaning over and sniffing slightly. "You smell like fruit."

Ceri arranged the curls in the mirror and examined the final results. It *was* awesome. "I love the stuff, but it's expensive so I save it for special occasions. I don't need to look perfect all the time, and besides, any spellwork will make it fall out right away. This kind of elf magic is delicate." She nodded into the mirror and steeled herself for a miserable conversation. "Alright. Let's do this."

They hopped out of her car and headed inside. The first thing that hit her was the impossibly fresh scent of the store. It was spotless, as always. The shop was to the right and the salon area was to the left.

A tall, willowy elf with pastel pink hair was shampooing a customer's hair. Her hands danced through the air as she guided the water -- spelled to the perfect temperature of course -- over the woman's scalp. Elves used an elemental type magic and could manipulate the base elements, like water, fairly easily. The stronger and older they were, the larger quantity of the element they could manipulate. Even an elvish child could do what she was doing though.

"Welcome to Glow Up," a cheery saleswoman said, appearing from behind one of the shelves. Her ears weren't as pointy as an elf's usually were, so she probably had some human in her heritage. "How can we help you today?"

"Hi, I needed to see Siobhan," Ceri said, forcing herself to keep her hands where they were and not fidget with her hair. "I heard she has something in stock for discerning witches."

The saleswoman's smile stiffened slightly. "Of course! Come right this way."

Amber stuck close to her as they followed the woman through the shelves filled with glittering potions and spells that promised beauty, happiness, and confidence. It all worked, but it was also all very expensive. Witch's potions could do many of the same things, but anyone who could afford it used elf products instead. They were just classier. And tasted better if they were the sort you had to drink.

"If you can wait right here I'll see if she's free," the saleswoman said, gesturing toward a plush, red velvet couch. "Can I get your names?"

"You can tell her that her favorite cousin is here," Ceri replied with a smile. She didn't want anyone here having their names, it was bad enough they'd had to stop by.

"Alrighty, be right back!" The woman hurried through the 'Employee Only' door a few feet away, letting it swing shut behind her.

"Why do I feel so...refreshed?" Amber asked, sniffing slightly. "The air smells odd."

"They spell a little more oxygen into the air to give you an energy boost every time you visit the shop. It's all part of the experience."

Amber wandered toward the shelves and picked up a little vial that promised to change your eye color. She coughed when she saw the price tag on the bottom and quickly set it back down. Shaking her head, she walked back over to Ceri, putting her hands in her pockets.

"That cost more than I made in a month as a nurse," she said with a shudder.

Ceri laughed. "It takes them almost two weeks to make, and it's permanent, unlike most cosmetic spells. This is why elves have money coming out of their long, pointy ears."

The door the saleswoman had disappeared through reopened and she peeked her head out. "Siobhan will see you now."

They followed her into the back room. It looked completely normal. Concrete floors, stacks of boxes, and a small table for the staff to eat lunch at. The door that led to the basement was easy to miss. It was tucked behind some industrial shelving in the corner of the room.

"Go ahead," the saleswoman said, pointing at the door. "You can leave out the back when you're done, please."

Ceri nodded and took a brief second to compose herself before pulling the door open. Soft, flickering light shone at the bottom of the stairs. It was warm and inviting, but she knew that was all an illusion. Siobhan was as mean as their grandmother, but not quite as talented, which had made her bitter. It was an unfortunate combination.

The stairwell led them down into a cozy room. The light came from a fireplace, but the room wasn't hot like it should have been with a huge fire in one corner. Siobhan stood over a large cauldron stirring what smelled like chicken noodle soup. Knowing her, it could be anything.

Her long, red hair cascaded down her back in perfect, effortless waves. She turned to them with a welcoming smile that made her baby blue eyes sparkle. Nothing about her was real anymore. She'd darkened the red of her hair, lightened her eyes, erased all her freckles, and doubled the size of her boobs.

"Ceridwen! It's been too long," she exclaimed, hurrying over for a hug. Ceri endured the brief hug, patting her once on the back, before untangling herself from Siobhan's grasp. The witch's eyes turned to Amber, examining her intently. "Who is this with you? You've never brought company here before."

"This is my friend, Amber," Ceri said.

"Hmm, the rumors said she was your alpha," Siobhan said, cocking her head to the side. She walked toward Amber and held out her hand, which Amber shook firmly, never dropping her cousin's gaze. "You're definitely a werewolf, and surprisingly an alpha. I guess the rumors are true."

"That's not why we're here." She didn't want to spend forever down here discussing her personal life with the town gossip.

315

Siobhan turned back to Ceri and rolled her eyes. "Are you here to finally get that hair under control? The Frizz-B-Gone can only do so much, sweetie."

"Oh, come on, Siobhan. You can do better than that. Where are the insults about me getting kicked out of the house?" Ceri asked with a grin.

"That's too easy of a target, besides, your hair always bothered you more whether you admit it or not. Why else would you try to fix it just to see me?" She sashayed back to her cauldron, her tight pants accentuating her curves.

"I thought Ceri was exaggerating, but you really are a bitch," Amber said, crossing her arms.

Siobhan looked back over her shoulder with a smirk. "It's a family trait."

"Speaking of family traits, have you been selling supplies to any sorcerers lately?" Ceri asked.

Siobhan stopped stirring and turned around, raising a brow. "Not since Grandmother died, may her soul burn in hell." She narrowed her eyes at the two of them. "Why?"

"If you do, be a good cousin and let me know, please," Ceri said with a smile.

"Why should I? You aren't even in the coven anymore," she said, cocking her hip out to the side.

"You still want the spell, don't you?"

A muscle in Siobhan's jaw jumped as she ground her teeth together. The pleasant facade dropped from her features and she glared at Ceri. "She did not give it to you."

Ceri grinned, taking sick satisfaction at finally putting her cousin on the defensive. "I was her favorite. That's why you always hated me."

Siobhan's hands curled into fists. "I want it now."

"Grandmother would come out of her grave and strike me down if I just *gave* it to you," Ceri said, shaking her head. "You can have it for information. The name and the location of the sorcerer that just showed up in the area. I *know* you've heard something."

Siobhan's fingers twitched like she was considering throwing an attack. She straightened her shoulders instead and turned back to her cauldron instead. "I'll be in touch."

"Always a pleasure seeing you," Ceri said with a smile while nudging Amber toward the stairs. Siobhan didn't bother with a reply, she just glared at them while they headed back up to the storefront.

Ceri's hands were shaking by the time they made it outside. They hurried through the parking lot and climbed back into the car.

"What the hell was that about?" Amber demanded as soon as both doors were shut.

She sighed and rubbed her hands over her face. "My grandmother left me a spell that isn't in the family spellbook. It's something she created, one of dozens of powerful spells actually. The family thought she died without sharing them with anyone, but she gave them to me. All of them."

Amber sat back in shock. "Why you?"

She picked at the seam of her dress. "When I was around seventeen, I made a conscious choice not to follow in my family's footsteps. Before that, I was my grandmother's favorite. And her experiment, most likely. I got all the attention, all the lessons, and it made the rest of my family jealous. But, anyhow, I have the spells, and there's one that Siobhan has always wanted."

"What does it do?"

"It binds a demon to your control for one night," Ceri said quietly. "It's supposed to be a way to get what you want from a demon without having to pay the price."

"Shit," Amber said, sitting back in her seat.

"It doesn't..." Ceri hesitated, shaking her head. "It doesn't work. My grandmother died trying to use it, but, uh, no one knows that."

"Did they think she just fell over dead?"

"No, I made it look like an attack by another coven," Ceri whispered, her hands shaking. She'd never told anyone this before. That one little lie had launched a war between their covens. The Blackwood coven had been trying to ruin them before that, so they'd been the perfect cover. "I hated my grandmother, but watching that demon kill her was terrifying. And I blamed myself for a while even though it was my grandmother's own fault. What she did was insanely stupid, but she thought she was invincible."

"Seeing that demon show up in our house must have been a shock then," Amber said, staring out the passenger window with a guilty expression.

"It was, and I still don't trust him, but he'll abide by the bargain," Ceri said with a shrug. "When my grandmother tried to bind the demon, it pissed it off. This is a different situation."

Amber laughed humorlessly. "Pissing them off is definitely not a good idea."

"Yeah," Ceri said with a weak smile.

"Well, let's get that stuff Tommy wanted for dinner," Amber said, visibly shaking off her thoughts.

Ceri nodded and put the car in drive. They'd keep searching for the sorcerer, but Siobhan's contacts were their best bet for finding him before he found them.

CHAPTER 32

TOMMY

Tommy signed *no* emphatically, then crossed his arms. Woggy's bottom lip trembled and he signed *outside* again before throwing himself down on the floor and squealing.

"What the hell is that noise?" Derek shouted from the living room.

"Woggy," Tommy shouted back. He headed toward the kitchen with a sigh. He was going to have to bribe the pixie with chicken again to get him to calm down. Woggy hated being cooped up inside, but if he let him out, he was going to get attacked by the other pixies that had moved into the yard.

"Did you pinch him or something?" Derek asked walking up next to him at the end of the hallway where Woggy was having his temper tantrum.

"No, I just won't let him outside," Tommy said tiredly, tugging his beanie down on his head.

"Because of those other pixies?"

"Yeah."

Captain Jack peeked around the corner, watching the scene disdainfully with his one good eye. He prowled toward Woggy, sniffed him, then planted his paw on the pixie's head. Woggy's squeals were cut off and he flailed, trying to get free.

"No, bad kitty," Tommy said firmly, pushing his paw off of Woggy's head.

The cat swished his tail and gave him a dirty look.

"I think Captain Jack had the right idea. You're encouraging Woggy if you keep giving him treats when he acts like this." Derek took another bite of the bread he was holding. "Why don't you just get the other pixies out of the yard?"

"I'm not sure how to do that without hurting them."

"Then Woggy is just going to be stuck inside," Derek said pragmatically. "You want to get a little training in while Amber and Ceri are out?"

Tommy nodded. He'd been feeling especially useless lately. Amber had asked him to stick around the house while they were out so Evangeline and Eloise weren't left alone, but it felt more like she was just worried about taking him somewhere potentially dangerous.

He sighed. At least everyone liked his cooking. Maybe he'd just be a werewolf chef. Make food, not war.

"Yeah, let's go ahead and train. I just need to go check on Eloise real quick," he said, pushing himself back up to his feet.

He hurried upstairs and knocked on the door to the room right next to his. Eloise spent all day with Evangeline in their room resting. She was recovering, but still too sick to do much more than sleep all day, and Evangeline refused to leave her side.

The door opened, but Evangeline didn't open it wide enough for him to come in. "What?"

"Do you need anything? I'm about to go outside for a little while." Every single interaction with Evangeline had gone the same. She glared at him. He felt awkward. Then she slammed the door in his face.

"You brought up a gallon of water and two plates of food an hour ago. We're fine," she said sarcastically.

"Great––" The door shut in his face right on cue. He pressed his lips together and turned on his heel, hurrying back downstairs.

"She seems friendly," Derek commented, nodding his head toward her room.

"She's grumpier than Amber," Tommy muttered as he pulled on his shoes.

Derek shuddered in mock horror. "That's terrifying."

～

He tried to punch quickly, but not too hard. Derek slapped it out of the way and he stumbled forward a half step. Derek's leg hit the back of his knees and swept his legs out from under him. He hit the ground hard and all the air rushed from his lungs.

"You alright?" Derek asked, staring down at him with concern.

Tommy let his head fall back against the grass. "I think I'm getting worse. How is that even possible?"

Derek scratched his jaw. "I'm probably not teaching you right. And you're too worried about hurting me. It might be time to talk to Amber."

He groaned. "I'm not ready for that kind of embarrassment." A car turned down the driveway and he scrambled to his feet. "That's them."

They both hurried back inside and Tommy met them at the door. Ceri walked in, her arms full of bags.

"How much did you get?" he asked as he took in the huge haul of groceries.

Amber walked in behind her carrying just as much and kicked the door shut. "Way too much probably, but Genevieve texted us with a bunch more stuff she wanted."

Tommy scratched the back of his head. "Well, I guess we'll have lots of leftovers."

He followed them into the kitchen and began unloading the bags, trying to organize by item.

"Do you know when Gen is supposed to be back?" Amber asked as she dumped a bag of pears into the fruit drawer in the refrigerator.

He shook his head. "She just said before dinner, which based on her usual schedule, means after we've all eaten."

"Something tells me she's going to be here two hours early this time," Ceri said with a snort. "I'm starting to worry her family is awful and judgmental."

"Did you find anything out about the sorcerer?" Tommy asked. Neither of them looked particularly upset, so they probably hadn't found anything useful.

Amber waffled her hand. "Ceri asked her cousin to let us know if she hears anything. If that doesn't pan out in the next couple of days I might go back to Eloise's house and see if I can find something. For now though, Evangeline is safe, so that's all that matters. No one knows where she is. We can take our time figuring this out."

Tommy had a feeling Evangeline wouldn't be so patient, but he kept that thought to himself. "Are they joining us for dinner?"

"Not sure. I asked Eloise earlier and she said she'd love to if she was awake, but Evangeline didn't look enthused about it," Amber said with a shrug.

There was a knock on the door and Amber frowned, then recognition dawned on her face. "Why is Steven here?"

"No clue," Ceri said.

Amber hurried over to the front door. "Hey, Gen isn't here, but you can come in while you wait for her."

Steven sighed deeply. "She didn't tell you, did she?"

Tommy had to clamp his hand over his mouth to suppress his laughter. Ceri caught his eye and turned away, her shoulders shaking slightly. Steven was a nice guy, but he and Genevieve were a mess as a couple.

Steven followed Amber into the kitchen and she wrapped her arms around his shoulders. "Steven is meeting Genevieve's parents tonight!"

He was blushing furiously and looked like he might be sick. His skin definitely wasn't that shade of pale green normally.

"That's awesome!" Ceri exclaimed.

"She was supposed to be here by now though. She said she'd be home by four," he said, adjusting his shirt, which had come untucked.

Tommy laughed. "She's always late, don't worry about it," he paused, cocking his head to the side. "She's actually coming down the road right now."

Steven's nervousness immediately fell away and he pulled out a notepad. "How far away is the entrance exactly? Have you noticed your hearing getting better the longer you've been a werewolf?"

Amber backed away with a smirk and gave him a thumbs up for distracting Steven. He glared at her and whispered, *"Traitor."*

"What was that?" Steven asked, looking up and adjusting his glasses.

"Nothing," Tommy said quickly. "And no, not really. It's just easier to sift through all the noise now. It was just chaos for a while."

Steven nodded and scribbled down his answer. Tommy sighed and pulled out a cutting board. So much for getting to relax while he cooked.

CHAPTER 33

GENEVIEVE

Genevieve tucked her hair behind her ears and tried to smooth a wrinkle out of her shirt.

Steven grabbed her by the shoulders and turned her away from the mirror. "You look beautiful, quit fussing. Is your family really so bad?"

She sighed and dropped her head to his shoulder. "No, they're just...freaking perfect all the time. And I'm not. I'm a mess."

"Were they really hard on you growing up?" He wrapped his arms around her and she let herself enjoy the comfort, even though she knew she was overreacting.

"No, I mean actually perfect. They're super supportive and want me to follow my dreams and be happy. But I keep screwing everything up. I barely got a job with the degree they paid for, and I don't stay in touch even though they invite me to everything. I'm such an asshole."

"That sounds like it'd be nice. Why are you freaking out?" he asked, pushing her back slightly so he could look at her face.

She glared at him. "Will you just let me be irrationally freaked out without trying to fix it?"

He looked completely baffled by that request. Steven was logic personified. He was a fixer of problems and a scientist at heart. Emotions were not his strong suit.

"Gen, how did you want these place settings again?" Amber shouted from downstairs.

"Ugh, I should go help her," she said, pulling away from Steven and hurrying toward the stairs. He followed, and she knew he was shaking his head at her, but he hadn't had to grow up with her parents.

Amber was in the dining room examining the table. It was already filled with food and each place setting was neatly arranged. They'd busted out the good china they'd found in one of the cabinets for the occasion.

"It's perfect," she said as she hurried over to straighten one of the spoons.

"Uh huh," Amber said, raising a brow at her.

The doorbell rang and her heart stopped for a split second before jumping into over-drive. She started to scramble for the door, but Amber grabbed her, forcing her to be still.

"Calm. Down." Her alpha's eyes flashed red like it was an order, and, despite herself, her muscles un-bunched slightly.

She took a deep breath and nodded. "I'm calm."

"That's a lie, but at least you're trying," Amber said, shoving her toward the door. "If they're mean, I'll kick them out."

"They're not..." she sighed. "You'll see."

Bracing herself, she walked toward the door. Each step made her heart stutter. It had been over six months since she'd seen them. She'd been dodging dinner invites and coffee dates with increasingly weak excuses, but she hadn't wanted to update them on her lack of a life. At least now she had a job to talk about.

She opened the door and was immediately tackled and wrapped up in a hug so tight she could hardly breathe. Blonde hair tickled the bottom of her nose and she realized her sister was here.

"Susannah? What are you doing here?" she exclaimed, hugging her younger sister back. "I thought you were still in Washington."

Her sister stepped back, beaming at her. "I flew down to see you after mom told me you were a werewolf now! That is *wicked* cool."

"Are you gonna let us in, kiddo?" her dad asked, holding up a pie dish.

"Oh, yeah, sorry," she said, opening the door wider and stepping back. Her dad and sister filed in, looking around the entry way curiously. "Where's mom?"

"She's grabbing something from the car, she'll be right in," her dad said. "Now, where can I put this?"

Amber walked into the living room just then with Tommy trailing nervously behind her. "Hi, Mr. Bisset, my name is Amber, I'm Genevieve's alpha."

They started the introductions, and Tommy took the pie dish from her dad. Genevieve watched it all in a slight daze. Seeing her family here with her pack was like two alternate realities colliding.

"I see your hair is still pink," her mother said from right behind her, startling her.

"Yeah, the law firm didn't..." She stopped when she saw her mother. She was wearing a wig. No. That wasn't a wig. She'd dyed her hair pink. And she was wearing a shirt that said *Bitten = Born* in...glitter. "What. Are. You. Wearing."

Her mother beamed at her and struck a pose. "I made it myself."

"Why is your hair pink?" Genevieve could feel herself becoming slightly hysterical. Her voice cracked as she attempted to keep from shouting.

"I retired from my job! My last day was Thursday, so I went to the salon, and got my hair dyed. I just thought it'd be fun, it always looked so cute on you," her mother said, her smile faltering slightly at Genevieve's expression.

She put her hand over her mouth, completely taken aback, then burst out laughing. There was nothing else she could do. She pulled her mother with a big hug. "You are so ridiculous."

Her mother laughed, clearly relieved, and hugged her back. "I'm too old to be not-ridiculous."

She should have known her mother was going to show up and do something like this. That was how she showed her love. She threw herself behind you one thousand percent. That made it all the more awful when you failed, but she'd never known how to tell her that.

Pulling away from the hug she turned toward the pack who were watching with varying degrees of shock and amusement. "Mom, this my pack."

"You must be Amber," her mother said, walking straight toward Genevieve's alpha.

"I am," Amber confirmed with a smile.

"Thank you for saving my daughter." Her mother wrapped Amber up in a big hug then stepped back, keeping both hands on her arms. "Not many people could have done what you did. Or would have even stepped in that night to help a stranger."

Amber looked intensely uncomfortable with the thanks, which made Genevieve relax even further. At least she wasn't the only one overwhelmed by it all.

Steven shuffled forward, looking at her expectantly, but before she could introduce him her father approached him and crossed his arms.

"You're dating my daughter," he stated without preamble, staring Steven down.

"Uh, yes, yes, he is," Genevieve said, hurrying over and linking her arm with his. "Dad, this is Steven, Steven, this is my Dad, Levi Bissett."

Her dad shook Steven's hand firmly. "My daughter can take care of herself, but you should know that she has me for backup. And I'm not scared to go to jail."

Steven swallowed, his face paling. "I would never hurt--"

"Ooookay, let's not do this," she said, pushing her dad away. "No threats, just get to know him."

Her dad's face split into a grin. "Oh, come on, I totally had him going. It's my right as a father to terrorize your suitors."

Steven relaxed slightly, but she could still hear his heart beating so fast she thought it legitimately might explode.

Her mother whacked her father on the arm. "Be nice or we won't get invited back for dinner."

Ceri appeared at the top of the stairs with Eloise, thankfully interrupting the conversation. Evangeline was on the woman's other side and they gently helped her walk down. She had a hoodie on with the hood pulled so far forward you could hardly see her face. Talk about anti-social.

"This is Eloise and Evangeline," Amber explained to her parents. "They're staying with us for a while. Eloise was in a...car crash."

Amber could keep a secret, but she was a crappy liar. It seemed like those were the same thing, but Genevieve had learned they were two very different skills. Her sister raised her brow, but neither she nor her parents called Amber out on it. Genevieve sighed in relief. Maybe her parents had gotten better about being too nosy.

The whole group filed into the dining room and sat down. Susannah grabbed the chair right next to her while her parents took the two seats across the table. Steven managed to get the seat on her other side, leaving her completely boxed in as the center of attention.

Amber smirked at her from the head of the table, clearly able to read all her emotions. Genevieve cursed the pack bond and its lack of privacy.

"I kind of thought you might look different, but you don't," Susannah said, inspecting her closely. "What does your wolf look like?"

"It's black. I'm not as big as some werewolves, but I'm fast," she said.

"Can you shift for us later?" Susannah asked, her eyes going wide with excitement.

"That would be awesome to see," her mother agreed. "I don't think I've ever seen a werewolf shift in person before."

"Uh, sure," she said hesitantly. "Well, I'll show you my wolf. I'm not stripping down naked in front of you."

Steven wrapped his arm around her shoulders. "She is a very beautiful wolf."

Her mother practically melted at that, looking at the two of them with so much hope in her eyes. Genevieve forced a smile onto her face. Tommy really needed to get the rest of the food out here soon so she could distract herself.

CHAPTER 34

AMBER

Amber grabbed the mashed potatoes and handed them to Mr. Bissett, or Levi as he had insisted they call him.

"These are excellent, Tommy," Levi said, scooping a third serving onto his plate. "Genevieve never ate this good at our house growing up. She was forced to survive off sandwiches and frozen dinners."

"Oh, stop it," Genevieve's mother said, smacking his arm. "She got overcooked meatloaf every Sunday too."

Tommy blushed under all the praise, but he was happier than she'd seen him all week. Amber had been worried this visit would be awkward, and it was a little with Evangeline sitting at the end of the table looking miserable, but it was also nice. The problem was, she hated it.

Amber had started questioning whether or not she was a good person about two minutes after she watched her brother die, but now she knew it for sure. Genevieve's family was basically perfect. Maybe a little too enthusiastic to the point where they might smother you if you let them, but they loved her. She'd never been so jealous in her life.

Derek caught her eye and she knew he could tell what she was thinking. Clearing her throat, she put down her fork and excused herself to the kitchen. She'd find something to bring back to cover her absence, but she needed a minute alone or her feelings were going to flood the pack bond and freak everyone out.

She'd learned to control that on her trip back to visit her family right about the time her mother had ordered her to leave as soon as she'd walked through the front door.

Derek released her from the tight hug and she shifted on her feet, waiting for the rest of the family to react. They never got a chance.

"Get out," her mother said, her voice cracking. An angry red flush was crawling up her neck and her jaw was clenched so tight Amber wondered how her teeth hadn't cracked.

"Miranda, that's enough," her father said gruffly, striding into the room.

Her mother glared at him, then turned and walked away, disappearing into the hallway. Amber watched her go and wondered how fast she could get back to the airport. She clamped down on the pack bond so tight she could barely feel the others at all.

"I know what you're thinking," her father said, walking up and grounding her with a hand on her shoulder. "But you ain't leaving yet."

"Why the hell shouldn't I?"

"Because I said so. Your mother is just shocked, that's all. She'll come around by tomorrow."

She hadn't come around. Her mother had stayed as far away as she could the whole week until the day she was leaving; when she'd found out Derek was planning on going back to Portland with her.

Amber yanked open the freezer and pulled out the ice cream. It needed to thaw a little before they ate it with the pie the Bissett's had brought.

She heard the chairs in the dining room pushing back, and something about starting a bonfire. The air shifted behind her and she heard, and smelled, Derek walking up behind her. She was starting to get used to the enhanced senses, but being able to *smell* someone coming was probably always going to be strange.

"You okay?"

"I'm great," she said turning around with a smile plastered on her face. "I take it everyone is headed outside to start a bonfire or something?"

"Yeah, nothing like a fall night outside under the stars," he said, still looking at her with concern. "We used to do that all the time when we were kids."

"Dylan always tried to set the grass on fire," she said, looking down at her feet.

"And you always stomped it out before it could spread." Derek sighed and shoved his hands in his pockets. He was silent for a moment, but finally looked up at her with a determined expression. "Mom is just...she's being an asshole."

Amber's eyebrows shot up in surprise. Everyone always danced around the issue, talked about how she was grieving. "What?"

"She's being an asshole. Dad lost a kid too, and we all lost a brother. You lost your other half. I mean, you two were never apart when you were kids," he said, shaking his head. "She has no right to blame you for what happened, and we've all let her get away with it for too long because we didn't know how to handle it either."

She gnawed on the inside of her cheek to keep from crying. She hated crying, and she certainly didn't want to cry at the dinner party for Genevieve's parents. "I just can't stop wishing she'd forgive me."

Derek dragged his hand over his mouth. "I'm sorry. Me too."

The others could probably hear them even though they were outside, but no one was coming inside to bother them. An unspoken rule had developed that they just didn't comment on things they overheard. Privacy had become difficult with their enhanced senses, so they tried to just pretend it still existed.

She took a deep breath and opened a cabinet, pulling out some paper plates. "Let's take the pie out there so we can enjoy it by the fire."

Derek nodded and came to help her, letting the conversation drop. Sometimes, certain things just couldn't be fixed, and she didn't want to wallow in it. Her mother had stolen enough of her happiness. She had a new family now, and her brother was here. They were going to build something together that she was excited about. She wouldn't let the past keep her from enjoying what she had now. Dylan wouldn't have wanted that.

They headed outside, their arms full of plates, forks, and desserts. Genevieve's mom had an arm around Tommy and her dad was helping Ceri start the fire.

Amber smiled. "Ceri, can't you just do that with magic?"

"No, no," Levi said, waving his hand at Amber. "We're going to do this the hard way. It's more satisfying."

Ceri shrugged and kept helping him place little twigs in a tee-pee formation. Amber set her pile of things down and went to join them.

CHAPTER 35

AMBER

Amber pulled on her softest flannel pajama pants and her favorite worn shirt. She'd eaten too much pie and was ready to face plant in her bed. The pack was still wired but the noise wouldn't keep her up tonight. It was comforting.

She pulled her covers back and slid in between the freshly washed sheets. They were a little cold, but she ran hot these days. With a happy sigh, she tugged the comforter up to her chin and squished the pillow up so that it cradled her head perfectly. Her eyes slipped shut and she felt her entire body relax into the soft mattress.

Genevieve's shout echoed down the hallway. "Amber, we have a problem!"

A spike of panic shot through the pack bond and she jolted upright, all remnants of sleepiness vanishing immediately. She jumped out of bed and ran out of her room. Her fluffy socks slipped on the hardwood floor as she rounded the corner and she had to grab the wall to keep from falling.

The pack was gathered in the living room, their eyes glued to the television. The first thing she saw was Evangeline's picture. Bold red text cut across the bottom of the picture, "DEMON THREAT?". Her heart dropped into her stomach and the demon mark on her chest flared to life.

Genevieve turned up the volume and the reporter's voice filled the room.

"The areas where magic does not work have been growing. Early this morning, one of those spots was discovered in downtown Portland. Before today, something like this hadn't been seen outside of rural areas. Mr. Hudson, a representative with ATD, an organization devoted to stamping out black magic, is here with us today claiming he has information on what is causing these spots to pop up," the reporter turned in her chair and the camera shifted, another face popping up on the television.

Amber recognized him immediately. He'd been there when they rescued Evangeline, but it wasn't the sorcerer, it was the half-angel. This wasn't good. The demon materialized next to her, drifting toward the television.

"Thank you for having me, Ms. Laramie," Mr. Hudson said with a brilliant smile.

The reporter blushed slightly before responding. "Mr. Hudson, you're claiming that demons are behind the destruction of magic in these areas?"

"I am, however the threat is even more insidious than that," he said, his flirtatious grin turning serious. He looked directly into the camera, every word intent and clear. "The demons have always been a threat against humanity and the supernatural races. We used to be protected from them because even a summoned demon that has escaped will be banished back to their realm when the sun rises. However, they have found a way to walk among us by creating hybrid demonic abominations through mating with humans, witches, and other supernatural races. These creatures are now using their infernal powers to consume magic, which is part of the very fabric of our world."

"These are very serious accusations. Do you have any proof?" the reporter asked.

It was absolute crap, but everyone was going to believe it. Evangeline was kind of moody, but she wasn't doing anything nefarious. She couldn't use magic at all as far as Amber could tell, much less eat it. Amber had to wonder if Angel would do something like that though. She glanced at him. He looked angry, offended even, but he didn't look guilty.

"I do. However, I must warn your viewers that what they are about to see is disturbing," Mr. Hudson said, shaking his head slightly.

A "Viewer Discretion is Advised" warning flashed on the screen before a video started playing. A house was engulfed in flames. A figure burst up into the air, and appeared to be holding someone. Through the smoke you could make out horns and fiery wings, but their face was obscured.

The video ended abruptly and switched back to the reporter, who looked truly alarmed, and Mr. Hudson.

"This was a recent attack by the demon. It has been masquerading as a human teenager named Evangeline Deschamps from a small town less than an hour from Portland, called Timber. As you know, another town recently had an area appear where magic no longer works. We believe this demon fled to Portland, and this morning, another spot appeared. The pattern is clear."

"Where is this demon hiding in Portland? There haven't been any sightings of a fiery winged creature flying over the city," the reporter said, chuckling nervously.

Mr. Hudson's frown deepened. "My organization believes she is being harbored by a werewolf pack. We're not sure which pack, but we *will* find them."

A picture of Amber in wolf form appeared next to Evangeline.

"Shit," Amber said.

Genevieve looked at her with wide eyes. "That is an understatement."

CHAPTER 36

EVANGELINE

Evangeline stopped at the bottom of the stairs. Her face was on the tv screen. The witch looked back at her with a worried expression that made her want to shrink back into the woodwork.

"Have they found us?" Her question seemed to startle the rest of the pack, who apparently hadn't noticed her walking down the stairs. That wasn't a good sign. She tugged the hood of her jacket down a little farther to make sure they couldn't see her hair. She wouldn't have even come downstairs after sunset but she'd heard them freaking out and had to know what was going on.

"No," Amber, the alpha, said. She tried to say it like it was a fact, but Evangeline could hear the *not yet* that she hadn't spoken aloud. They had her freaking picture on the news.

"But they're going to," she said angrily. The least these people could do was be honest with her. Kadrithan never was -- he wouldn't even tell her his *real* name -- but she'd expected better from the pack for some reason.

"Until we track down the sorcerer and this pretentious blond dude you'll have to stay in the house, but that's doable," Amber insisted. Tommy nodded along eagerly, but he always did that when his alpha spoke.

The witch, at least, didn't look convinced. Evangeline got the impression Ceri hated her, but she'd saved her mother's life. So, she didn't hate her enough to hurt her. Maybe just enough to not worry about her *feelings.*

"They have a picture of you, too," she said, pointing at the television. "They're going to look here eventually." She was half expecting someone to knock on the door right then.

"Can they identify you by a picture of your wolf?" Amber's brother asked, casting a suspicious glance at her. She wasn't surprised a human would be wary. They tended to be warier of anyone supernatural that might be a threat.

"I...don't know," Amber said with a frown. "I doubt it. It's not like it's on file somewhere."

Genevieve shook her head. "Everyone saw you at the Trials though. Like, every were-wolf in a hundred square miles."

"Freaking out isn't going to help anything," Ceri said, finally stepping into the conversation. "They can't prove it was Amber based off a fuzzy picture."

She felt the air shift at her back and looked over her shoulder. Her uncle was there, watching the drama, as usual.

"I won't let them take you," he said, watching the news play on impassively. He didn't speak out loud, just in her mind. It was something he didn't do often because she tended to ignore him when he did it.

This time she didn't. "You couldn't stop them when they attacked the house. Why would next time be any different?" she replied silently.

Amber glanced at them, her eyes lingering on Kadrithan before her brother drew her attention again. Other than Eloise, she was the only one that could see him when he showed up like this.

"They revealed their hand and lost their greatest strength. The element of surprise. Now, if you would just accept your heritage and ––"

"SHUT UP," she shouted mentally, as loud as she could. "I won't do it."

He shook his head. "You will, and dragging it out is just a waste of time."

And that was why she normally just ignored him. It was like talking to a brick wall. Only that brick wall thought it knew everything.

The pack could debate whatever useless plans it wanted, but it was all pointless. She turned away and walked back up the stairs as quietly as she could. No one tried to stop her. Her uncle just drifted down the stairs, probably to go bother Amber again. She should probably just keep walking right out of the house and disappear forever.

She shoved her hands into the pocket of her hoodie and curled them into fists. Her mother wasn't going to be healed enough to leave anytime soon, but even if she was, as long as she was with her, her mother would be in danger.

At some point she was going to have to really leave. Maybe the pack could fix all this in another couple of days, but if they couldn't...She had to protect her mother. She wouldn't let them hurt her again.

CHAPTER 37

AMBER

Amber stood in front of the pack and tried not to look as nervous as she felt. Her mind was whirring through all the possible catastrophes that might be headed their way. No one knew Evangeline was with them yet, but it was only a matter of time.

Everyone would be looking for her now, and Zachariah knew a werewolf pack and a witch had rescued her. It wouldn't take them long to connect the dots once they started asking around. Word had traveled fast about her odd little pack.

Angel was floating around her brother, but he wasn't being silly, he was just watching them. The demon's sense of humor hadn't returned along with him. Instead, he was everything she had expected a demon to be. Demanding. Mean. Dangerous.

Clearing her throat, she decided to just get this over with. "When I took the mark from Thallan, I didn't think I would have to pay the debt anytime soon. He'd had it for years. I was just…fed up that day. I'd been fired and evicted, and we were running out of options." She paused, dragging her hands roughly through her hair. "Anyhow, it was a decision I made without y'all, so, if you want out, I'll find a way for you to join a different pack. And, of course, I can try to cure you."

Genevieve immediately stood and put her hands on her hips. "I'm not going anywhere. You risked all of this for us, the least we can do is support you now that you have to deal with the fallout."

Tommy nodded along. "I'm not leaving. We're in this together."

There was a long silence, and Ceri stayed still, staring at her hands. Amber's heart dropped into her stomach. She could barely breathe at the idea of losing one of her pack, and Ceri was special. She understood Amber better than Tommy and Genevieve did. Amber curled her hand into a fist as she waited for Ceri to say what they all knew she was thinking.

Genevieve looked back at her and broke the silence. "If you're going to bitch out, then just say it and leave."

Amber's eyes grew wide. "Gen, don't say that. She's allowed to leave if she ——"

"I can speak for myself," Ceri interrupted. She rose from the couch and glared at Genevieve. "I'm not sure what we're doing is right."

"So, you don't want to help this girl?" Genevieve demanded, looking sincerely offended.

"She's a demon," Ceri said, exasperated.

"She's also an angel. And from what I've seen, she's just your average teenage girl who's done nothing wrong, but people are trying to kill her because she's different. You lose your shit if someone tries to kill a pixie, but you'll let them kill her?"

Ceri stiffened. "I'm not saying she should die, but——"

"I don't want to hear the *but*," Genevieve snapped. "She either deserves to die, or she doesn't. There is no caveat."

"Evangeline is scared," Tommy interjected, finally speaking up. "She's terrified that someone else is going to get hurt because of her. How could we turn our back on her even if there wasn't a demon mark involved?"

"I want to help Evangeline, I just don't want to help *him*," Ceri said angrily. Her face was flushed with anger. "This demon is using Evangeline somehow, and we're letting him. Helping him even. We have no idea what the consequences might be."

Amber looked at the demon. He looked back, his expression neutral. Nothing Ceri said seemed to have bothered him. She had the same concern as Ceri, she just hadn't wanted to think about it too hard.

"Well I'm not willing to let Evangeline die just to keep a demon from possibly carrying out a nefarious plan," Genevieve said, crossing her arms.

Ceri pinched the bridge of her nose and sighed. "I'm not either. I just hate this."

"So do I," Amber admitted, shoving her hands in her pockets. "I'm sorry."

Ceri dropped her arms and pushed back her shoulders. "I've waffled enough. After everything you've done for us, there's no way I'd ever leave. We're in this together, whether it's good or bad. We'll get through this, and then we'll be free from the demon."

Angel drifted behind Ceri, invisible to her and grinned darkly. "You'll never be free of me, Amber. Not if I get my way."

She ground her teeth together and ignored the taunt. "You can always change your mind, any of you."

Genevieve marched over and wrapped Amber in a hug. "Shut up."

She let the warmth of the pack bond soothe her for a moment.

～

Amber was bone tired. Tommy had passed out on the couch after their conversation. Ceri and Gen were outside on the porch talking about something just quietly enough that she couldn't hear. She grabbed a blanket and laid it carefully over Tommy. He didn't stir.

Sleeping like this, he looked so young. He *was* young. And she'd drug him even deeper into a dangerous world. She dragged a hand down her face as she walked down the hall. Maybe tonight she'd be able to just sleep.

Evangeline was upstairs. She could still hear her heartbeat, so she hadn't run off. Yet.

Eloise was up there with her, sedated once again so she could finish healing. Amber pushed her bedroom door open and caught a whiff of cat.

Her eyes adjusted to the dark room and she saw a fluffy lump on her pillow. She ground her teeth together in irritation. The last thing she needed was a mangy cat sneaking into her room. She must have forgotten to shut her door in her haste to get out to the living room to see what was going on.

She walked over and picked him up, dumping him unceremoniously on the floor. "Shoo," she said, waving her hands at him before climbing in bed.

"Mrow," he said irritably.

"I don't care, get out," she said, pointing at the door. His tail swished unhappily.

Her sheets were still cool, but they didn't have that same super fresh feel and the cat had squished all the fluff out of her pillow. She smacked it a few times to get it back to normal and laid down with an angry huff.

Captain Jack hopped back up on the bed, walked over her legs, and curled up against her knee. Sighing, she scooted farther down in the bed then flipped her pillow over to the clean side and curled up under the covers. Her movements disrupted his position. She felt him circle a few more times before curling up against her back.

Despite herself, the warmth and steady, slow beat of his heart made all the tension bleed out of her shoulders. He was still annoying, but he could stay for the night. As long as he left her alone. Her eyes slipped shut and she fell asleep.

CHAPTER 38

CERI

The snow was feather soft and freshly fallen. She curled her toes into it, expecting to feel icy cold seeping into her skin, but there was nothing. Neither heat nor cold. Her entire body felt...neutral.

The sparkling powder stretched out in every direction as far as she could see. The wind had blown it into drifts like sand dunes, but there was nothing to break up the endless white. No trees. No people. No life.

She took a deep breath and felt her lungs and chest move, yet, when she looked down, she was nothing more than a formless shadow. It was a surreal mix of real and not real. She lifted her ghostly hand and moved her fingers one by one. The shadow shifted, showing glimpses of the hand she knew was there, but couldn't quite see.

Content she wouldn't float away, she started walking. She didn't have a particular destination in mind but felt the urge to move. This was a time to let her intuition guide her, rather than her logical mind. She had no idea why the spirit had brought her here.

As she walked, she realized she was headed uphill. She paused and looked behind her. It looked like that way led up as well. Shaking off the dizziness that caused, she turned back around and continued. There was no point in trying to make sense of it.

The powdery snow firmed beneath her feet as she walked, then gave way to rock. Wind tugged at her hair and whipped her skirt around her legs. She blinked and found herself at the top of a mountain on a narrow ledge. Despite knowing this was only a vision, her heart caught in her throat as she looked down from the dizzying height.

She picked up her pace, hugging close to the cliff face. The wind blew harder and harder. Her footing slipped and she dug her fingers into the rock, but the wind only grew stronger. A sudden gust lifted her from her feet and tossed her into the air.

A scream caught in her throat as she grasped uselessly at the air. Another current of wind caught her and she was flung upward toward the top of the mountain. Tears stung at her eyes from the force of the wind. She forced herself not to look down again.

The wind shifted and she was thrown forward, landing in a pile of snow that went up her nose and blinded her for a moment. She pushed up to her hands and knees and shook her head to clear it, coughing slightly.

"Oh, sorry about that," a melodic voice said, drifting past her like a breeze. "You're heavier than I expected."

Ceri looked around but didn't see anyone. "Where are you?"

"I'm right here," the voice replied as a breeze danced through her hair.

She lifted her hand and trailed her fingers through the wind. It felt almost solid. "Are you...air? Or wind?"

"I am not all of it, only my part," it replied.

"Are you a spirit?"

It swirled around her as though it were thinking. "That's a good word for it in your language."

"Have you been visiting me through the owl?" she asked as she finally pushed to her feet, brushing the snow from her ethereal body.

"Yes," it replied, sounding pleased she recognized it. "I saw you through the veil like a beacon and felt you calling to me. You need guidance."

"Something bad is coming, isn't it?" she asked.

A shimmery creature with a body like a ribbon formed in front of her. Its body drooped forlornly. "Something very bad."

"Is it the sorcerer?"

The spirit shook its head. "He is only the beginning."

"Can I stop it?" she asked, the sense of doom growing in her chest.

The spirit drifted closer. "I don't know. No one can tell the future. I can only warn you."

"What is the sorcerer trying to do?" She turned in a circle, trying to keep the spirit in sight. It floated around her, it's body undulating like an eel.

"It's not about him, he's just the beginning. A tool," the spirit said again.

"Who is he working for?"

The spirit charged at her and she fell back, sinking into the snow. It covered her chest and her legs, then her face.

She was falling again. Through darkness and absolute silence. Then, there was fire. The flames roared, reaching out across the inky blackness, but it was met with bright, searing light. The two collided with a deafening crash.

She jerked with a gasp and found herself back in her work room, breathing like she'd just run a race. Her head was spinning and for a moment, it was hard to tell which way was up. She wiggled her feet to ground herself and forcibly slowed her breathing, letting out a slow exhale.

As the room came back into focus, she saw Derek was sitting in front of her. He looked worried. He reached out like he wanted to touch her, but kept his hand hovering in the air. "Ceri, can you hear me?"

She blinked a few times and unclenched her fingers. "Yes. Sorry. How long have you been sitting there?"

He still looked skeptical that she was alright. "About ten minutes. I was about to call

Amber."

She looked up at the clock. Only an hour had passed since she entered the vision. It had felt like longer. "It's okay, I mean, you can tell her, but I'm okay."

"What were you doing?"

She uncurled her legs and grimaced at the pins and needles feeling in her foot. Next time, she needed to just lay down. There was no way she could explain what she'd just seen. It hadn't made any sense. "It was a vision. I know it sounds crazy, even for a witch, but being a part of this pack has changed my magic a little. I have a stronger connection to the spirit world, and one of them sent me a vision."

"A vision of what?" he asked, brows furrowed tightly together. He and Amber had similar eyes, but his were piercing. The way they contrasted with his dark brown hair made it hard to tear her eyes away from his face.

"I'm not sure. It was another warning, but either the spirits don't know, or can't tell me, exactly what is coming." She rubbed her fingers over her temples. Her head ached slightly, but that was to be expected with the amount of magic she was using lately. Maintaining the shield that protected Evangeline was a constant drain.

He extended his hand and helped her to her feet. "Do you think someone's going to try to hurt the pack?"

"Yes and no. I'm not sure it's about us, in particular, just that we're going to be caught up in it. My instincts are telling me Evangeline is involved, but I'm not sure how," she said with a shrug. "I'll talk to Amber about it whenever she gets back. There's not much we can do until we find this sorcerer."

"He's working for Zachariah, that guy from the news, right? Maybe you can track him down and find the sorcerer that way," he suggested.

The vision of fire and light colliding flashed through her mind again at the mention of Zachariah. She frowned and rubbed her temples again, trying to ease the headache. "Maybe. We'll have to be careful though. Zachariah wants Evangeline dead, too. The sorcerer must have convinced him that she was to blame for the magic disappearing."

"Are you okay?" Derek asked, his fingers brushing over her shoulder. She melted into the touch and he dug his thumb into a knot. "You've been really tense."

"I'm just not sleeping well," she said, rolling her head forward to give him better access. If he came and gave her a back rub, she'd probably sleep like a baby. He dug his thumb in a little deeper and she almost let out a groan, which sent her thoughts racing in an entirely different direction. She felt her cheeks heating and pulled away, smiling at him awkwardly. "Thanks, that helped a lot."

"Anytime." He was still standing close. She could smell his cologne and the shampoo he used. They locked eyes and her heart skipped a couple of beats. "Maybe you can take a break, and we could go get dinner tomorrow evening," Derek said, holding her gaze. "And I mean a date, just to be clear."

She swallowed and stared back dumbly for a moment. They'd been flirting, but for some reason she hadn't expected him to ask her out so soon.

He ran his fingers through his hair and started to look nervous. "That looks like a no."

"I don't...think it's a good time," Ceri said quietly. She wanted to say yes, but she had to put the pack first. If things went bad with Derek, it could hurt Amber. The pack couldn't afford any more conflict right now, not with a literal demon in their midst.

Derek shoved his hands in his pockets and nodded. "I can take no for an answer," he said carefully. "I'd still like to be friends, especially since we live together, so don't take it as me pushing you if I'm still friendly."

Ceri smiled at him. "Of course not, we can certainly be friends."

He turned to leave, then paused, clearing his throat. "If you change your mind though, just say the word. I won't wait on you or anything pathetic like that, but if the timing changes..." he shrugged. "Just say something."

She nodded and he left. It had been a perfectly polite exchange but she felt sick to her stomach. This was the right choice, she knew it was. Dating in your friend group was tricky, and dating your alpha's brother was just asking for a disaster. Especially in the middle of all this chaos.

It had been the right choice. She curled her hand back into a fist and willed it to be true.

CHAPTER 39

TOMMY

Tommy tried to focus on the problem in front of him, but Deward was staring at him intently, and it was unsettling.

"Is there something on my face?" he asked finally.

The troll frowned. "No."

"Then what ––"

"Why are you hiding bruises? They're fresh, and you winced when you picked up the books," he said, suspicion and concern clear on his face. "If you are being hurt by your pack, my family would be willing to assist you. Just because you can heal quickly does not mean abuse is justified."

"Oh, it's nothing like that," Tommy said, finally understanding. "I'm trying to learn how to fight. Apparently, the bite doesn't automatically impart that knowledge."

The troll continued to frown. "Who is teaching you? Your alpha?"

Tommy shook his head. "Nah, I don't want to embarrass myself in front of her yet. Her brother Derek is trying to help me, but I can't use my werewolf strength on him because he's human, and I suck, so I keep screwing up."

"You should not be fighting humans. You will never learn how to fight if you are constantly holding back. You will only learn how to hesitate, and therefore fail. That builds bad habits that are hard to break." Deward's frown deepened, as if he was unhappier with the idea of bad training than abuse.

Tommy snorted. "Well, I don't exactly have any other options."

Deward picked up his phone and started typing a message. Tommy turned back to the problem, assuming the conversation must be done. He'd learned the troll was generally very abrupt, not bothering with small talk. Their culture tended to be blunt like that. Trolls got straight to the point and didn't tolerate bullshit.

"I have received permission to bring you to our training grounds this afternoon," Deward said, startling him.

"Wait…what?" Tommy stared at Deward with his mouth hanging open.

"I told my father of your predicament, and he has invited you to train with us," Deward repeated, slower this time.

He cleared his throat nervously and eyed Deward's biceps. The fabric of his button-down shirt was straining against the bulging muscles. "Umm, how much?"

Deward waved his hand at him. "Free. Trolls do not charge for training, ever. It is as important to us as air or water, and always freely given. Only a dishonorable coward would try to demand payment for such knowledge."

Tommy pursed his lips, considering. On one hand, he might get crushed if he went. On the other…Derek was trying, but Tommy wasn't improving with his help. It was starting to feel pointless. He knew what he wanted to say: no. But he also knew what Amber would say if she was given an opportunity like this.

Curling his hand into a fist to suppress his nerves, he nodded. "Okay, I'll do it."

A rare smile crossed Deward's face, revealing teeth sharper than humans, and making his tusks look even bigger. "I look forward to testing your courage."

All Tommy could think was, *what the hell have I gotten myself into?*

∿

Deward pulled his shirt off over his head and folded it neatly, laying it on the bench. Tommy stared at the rippling muscles and felt…small. He had filled out quite a lot since being bitten, but all that meant was that he was now lean with muscle, instead of just lean.

"So, is shirtless a requirement?" he asked.

Deward nodded. "It will likely be ripped if you don't remove it anyhow."

The last thing Tommy wanted was to ruin the clothes Amber had bought for him. Reluctantly, he removed it, folding like Deward had, and setting it on the bench. He crossed his arms over his chest and stood there, practically shivering with nerves.

"This way." Deward led him out into a large, circular room. The walls of the building were concrete, but the roof was wooden. It arched up, creating a vaulted ceiling that made the place feel even bigger than it already was.

It had a dirt floor with two traditional style boxing rings and three matted areas to their left. Heavy weights and what looked like a troll-sized jungle gym took up the right side of the training area.

"This place is huge. Did your parents build it?" Tommy asked, looking around in awe.

"The tribe built it. We use it as a community center on the weekends, and for training during the week," Deward said, rolling his head around in a circle to loosen up. The muscles in his back flexed with every movement. "We should start with a light sparring session to see how you move."

Tommy scratched the back of his head and shrugged. "I'm not even very good at punching yet, but I guess I can try."

"Just fight, and we will go from there." Deward waved away his concerns. The dirt floor was cool under Tommy's feet as he followed Deward to the closest mat. "No hits to the groin and no eye gouges. I will start light, then match the power of your punches, so you get to decide how hard you are hit."

"Uh, great," Tommy said, cringing internally. Deward was assuming he'd be able to land a punch, which so far in his training was only a fifty-fifty shot.

Deward shifted into a fighting stance. His right foot moved back and he brought his hands up in front of his face. The muscles in his shoulders bunched up as he began to move a little, advancing on Tommy, who quickly brought his hands up as well.

He had no idea what he was doing, but it seemed like Deward wanted him to attack first. Swallowing down his nervousness, he threw a punch. The troll didn't bother moving, but his fist still didn't hit anything but air.

"You need to hit *me*, not the air in front of me," Deward said with a hint of confusion in his voice. "I promise you cannot hurt me if that is your concern."

Tommy grimaced. "I just…missed."

Deward took a step forward. "Try again."

He sighed and adjusted his feet. This was going to be just as humiliating as he'd feared.

CHAPTER 40

GENEVIEVE

Genevieve was sprawled on Steven's futon with an empty box of pizza to her left and a watered-down iced coffee on the floor to her right. She'd spent the past two hours looking at case files and making notes. Her brain was fried and all the caffeine in the world couldn't resuscitate it right now.

She sighed, rolling over onto her side and pulling out Greer's card. It had been two days since she'd spoken to him and she still didn't know much about him. Or how to deal with his request. Or if she was even Amber's beta.

Steven closed his textbook and leaned back in his chair with a groan. "I should have just been an accountant."

"Don't be ridiculous," Genevieve scoffed. "You'd have hated it."

He sighed, dragging his hands down his face. "Yeah. I would have."

"Hey, in all that research we did about sponsors, did you find anything on how the sponsor decides if they're willing to vouch for a potential alpha?" she asked, tapping Greer's card against the palm of her hand.

Steven shrugged. "Probably, why?"

She hadn't talked to Amber about it yet, and she really needed to, but it felt like her responsibility to figure this out first. "Well, this werewolf, from the old Lockhart pack, approached me when I was there trying to get help for my case. He wants Amber to sponsor him."

"Why?" Steven asked, looking somewhat alarmed.

"I don't know. I think he might want to shake things up a little. It seemed like he was impressed by her performance at the Trials. He said he wanted to run things differently once he became alpha." He'd also said werewolves had become a little too humanized, which she wasn't sure she agreed with, but she kept that little tidbit to herself.

"That is an interesting perspective." Steven got up and started digging through a box of his whole notepads. He wrote everything he learned down in them, then stacked them, organized by date, in various boxes around his room. She'd tried to talk him into putting it all in his computer, but he had insisted handwritten notes helped him think.

He pulled out a notebook and flipped through it before stopping on one page. "Here it is. Actually, I still have the book. Keating's *Politics of the Wolf.*" He leaned over and grabbed a thick book out of the stack next to his desk.

Genevieve grabbed it and flipped to the table of contents. It looked like it had five chapters on alphas, with one that focused entirely on an alpha's rise to power. "This is perfect."

"I made a few notes on how the sponsor chooses an alpha just in case Amber had needed to try to convince someone. Most of it appears to be centered around future alliances, favors, and sometimes even a payment. Though that 'paying your sponsor' is a new thing. It's looked down on."

"This guy wouldn't want to do that. The alliance though...he'd probably be interested in something like that."

"You'd have to be careful not to be taken advantage of when negotiating a deal," Steven said, flipping to the next page in his notebook. "He'll probably press for whatever he can get. It's a natural part of the process. A sort of dominance game."

"Would I negotiate, or would Amber?" she asked.

"You would start the negotiations, with your alpha's permission, but Amber would have to have the final discussion with him. That's the most important conversation where last-minute concessions or demands are made." He lowered his notebook. "You need to know what he wants, and why he wants Amber as his sponsor."

"I know. We can't negotiate with him until I know what he's hoping to get." She leaned back on the futon again. It was time to get creative.

CHAPTER 41

TOMMY

"You're still holding back," Deward said with a grunt, flexing as he paced in front of him. "Where is the wolf? The hunter inside of you?"

Tommy ground his teeth together, tempted to shift and show him exactly where the wolf was. They'd been at this for over an hour. He'd finally figured out how to hit Deward, but his attempts at sparring were still pathetic.

"Maybe bitten wolves *are* weaker," Deward taunted, dropping his hands like Tommy wasn't even the slightest threat.

Anger rose in his chest, pushing power into his limbs. He charged the troll, slamming right into him. Deward dropped his hips, stepped, and pivoted. He flipped Tommy over his hip in a blinding fast move and let him fall to the mats.

"Anger is better than apathy, but you must focus it!"

Tommy groaned from his place on the ground, but Deward wasn't having it this time. The troll grabbed his arm and yanked him back up to his feet, giving him a slight shove backward to create space.

"We're going to do this again, and you're going to fight me. No more training, no more sparring. You either fight, or I will beat you until you can no longer lift a hand to defend yourself," Deward said, his eyes flashing with irritation.

"Wait, wha––" His question was cut off with a sharp jab that snapped his head backward and blurred his vision. Tears stung at his eyes from the impact on his nose. He bobbed under the next punch, just barely avoiding catching another blow with his face.

The pace of the fight had changed. They were no longer student and teacher. They were opponents. Tommy felt it in every fiber of his being. The drive to fight. To win.

The wolf peered out of his eyes and the instincts of a predator took over. There was nothing to fear. His body would heal. The nervous energy he'd been stuck under for so long began to lift.

He struck back with two fast strikes to stop the barrage Deward had been throwing.

He threw all his power behind a third punch. It only grazed Deward's ribs, but he had been close.

The troll was stronger, taller, and heavier, and that wasn't going to change anytime soon. But Tommy wasn't by any means slow. His speed was the only thing that saved him from the surprise uppercut. He threw himself backward, tripping over his own feet, but avoiding the knockout blow.

Deward's foot slammed into his solar plexus, driving all the air from his lungs and picking him up off his feet. He hit the ground at least a yard away and immediately tried to roll back to his feet, but two-hundred fifty pounds of troll landed on top of him before he could move. Deward's first punch hit his jaw, the second his nose.

Feral rage rose up inside of him. He was tired of being beaten. Tired of losing. He'd frozen when those men were shooting at him and Evangeline. He didn't ever want to freeze again.

He swung his fists wildly while bucking his hips in an attempt to throw the troll off. It wasn't even close to the technique Deward had shown him earlier, but he wasn't just going to lay there and take it. He reached up blindly. His fingers caught on a tusk. He grabbed it and wrenched Deward's head to the side as hard as he could.

The troll roared in outrage, hitting Tommy even harder as he attempted to pry Tommy's hand off his tusk. Tommy pulled even harder. Deward's weight shifted slightly and he bucked his hips again. The troll was thrown just far enough to the side that he was able to get the leverage to shove him completely away.

He immediately lunged at Deward, tackling him and driving him back down to the mat. He rained punches down on the troll's head. Deward shielded his face with one arm and drilled two hard punches into Tommy's unprotected side. The first one hurt, the second cracked a rib.

Breathing suddenly became extremely difficult. He tried to keep punching, but he could barely move his left arm through the fog of pain. Deward threw another punch, his fist narrowing in on the injury mercilessly. Tommy crumpled and Deward flipped him over with ease.

It only took on more punch and then everything went dark.

～

Tommy came to what felt like hours later. Deward's father was crouched over him with a look of concern.

"You should not have injured him," the older troll said and he snapped his fingers in front of Tommy's face. "Can you hear me?"

His mouth didn't want to work and it felt like he was outside of his body watching all this happening from above. "Whaaa..."

"He needed to be pushed, father. He was still holding back," Deward protested, only looking slightly remorseful.

"Am fiiiiine," Tommy said, waving away their concern. He wasn't sure he was fine, actually, but he wasn't dying. His ribs felt weird. It hurt, but there was magic rushing through the bones and muscles healing them. "Healin' jus' fine."

"Is his alpha here yet?" Deward's father asked. He was taller, bigger, and nerdier than Deward. Black, thick-framed glasses were perched on his nose and gave him a scholarly look...if you ignored the bulging muscles and the long tusks.

"Almost, she'll be here in about five minutes," Deward replied.

Tommy's eyes went wide and he suddenly felt much more awake. "What? Alpha?"

"Deward called your alpha as soon as you were injured. She'd be able to sense it, of course, so it was proper to call and reassure her that you were safe. Allowing her to believe you were under attack by an enemy would be irresponsible and callous to her responsibility to protect you." Deward's father narrowed his eyes at Tommy, then at Deward. "She should have been informed before the sparring even took place."

"Ah, well," Tommy said, trying to push up to a sitting position. "I didn't want to worry her."

"Foolish and immature," the old troll said, shaking his head. He extended his hand and, very gently, helped Tommy to his feet. "You will apologize when she arrives."

Tommy swallowed, feeling embarrassed. "Yes, sir."

"Wait for her, I will get refreshments for our guest," Deward's father said before turning and walking away, leaving them alone.

Deward shifted on his feet, looking properly chastised. "Are you okay?"

Tommy grinned at him. "I feel awesome."

Deward looked up, his green face a picture of shock. "What?"

"I lost, but...not because I gave up. I've never done that before. I've never stuck it out," Tommy said, rubbing the back of his head awkwardly.

"Well, you're not dead." Amber's voice cut through the training center. He looked back in surprise, he hadn't felt her coming. She didn't look particularly mad, just curious. She'd kicked off her shoes by the door and was strolling toward them, her hands in the pockets of her jeans.

"I must apologize for the liberty I took in fighting one of your pack without speaking to you first and obtaining your permission," Deward said with a short bow of his head.

Amber raised a brow, glancing at Tommy before responding. "Uh, that's fine. Assuming this idiot agreed to receive a beating?"

"Yeah, I did," Tommy said quickly.

Amber shrugged. "You and Derek have been beating on each other all week. This seems like it'll be more effective. It's no big deal."

Tommy's mouth fell open in shock. "You knew about that?"

She laughed. "Of course I did. You think I don't know when my own brother is hiding something from me? That and the bruises you both had, and pretending nothing was going on every time I got home even though you were both panting? It was either that or a torrid love affair and we both know Derek has the hots for Ceri."

Tommy crossed his arms, feeling even more idiotic for thinking he was hiding it from her. "Well, I guess we were kind of obvious."

She patted him on the arm, then turned back to Deward. "Do you want to keep training him?"

Deward looked between them, then nodded. "If Tommy is amenable."

Tommy nodded quickly. "Yeah, this is great."

Amber shrugged. "Then feel free to keep knocking each other out."

Deward's father returned at that moment carrying a tray of sodas with a glass of ice in front of each one. There were also two beers on the tray.

"Alpha Amber Hale, welcome to our home," he said with a polite smile.

Amber returned it. "Thank you for welcoming me and Tommy here."

Deward pulled Tommy aside while they continued to exchange small talk and apologies. "Did you mean what you said? That this was helpful?"

He nodded. "It was. I need to know how to fight." Evangeline had brought a new kind of danger to their pack. It felt like he was running out of time, and if he didn't learn fast, he might end up dead. Or someone he cared about would.

This also gave him an idea for how to help Woggy. He'd have to talk to Ceri and make sure it was okay, but he was pretty confident she'd be on board.

"Can you start coming here for tutoring? We can do that first, then train. Most evenings my friends come over to train as well. It would do you good to fight different people so you can see the different strengths and weaknesses we have."

"I'll be over here as often as you'll have me," Tommy said.

Deward slapped his hand on his shoulder. "Then I'll see you tomorrow evening."

CHAPTER 42

AMBER

Amber walked back inside to a disaster. A loud shriek split the air and a grey blur streaked past her, headed toward living room. An angry, yowling mass of fluff followed close behind as Captain Jack pursued the pixie. His hair was mussed and streaked in... grape jelly?

"What the hell..."

"Dammit Woggy, get back here!" Ceri shouted, stumbling after them as the caboose in the crazy train. She lunged for the cat, but at that moment Woggy took a sharp turn and the cat darted after him. Ceri tripped over the hem of her dress and was sent sprawling onto the floor.

Amber couldn't help but laugh. "Graceful."

"Quit laughing at me and help!" Ceri demanded as she untangled her legs.

Tommy hurried around to the other side of the couch and grabbed Woggy just as he shimmied out from under it. Purring loudly, and completely failing in his attempt to look innocent, Captain Jack curled through Tommy's legs. His one eye was locked on the tasty treat Woggy still had clutched in his hands.

Evangeline was peeking over the balcony upstairs to see what was going on, but she disappeared as soon as she noticed Amber looking at her.

Amber walked over and gave Ceri a hand up, which she took with a sigh. "I see you're having a good day."

Ceri just glared at her. When she saw Tommy though, her eyes went wide. "Tommy, what the hell happened to you?"

He grinned, making his bruised eye close completely. "Trolls."

"He fired Derek as his trainer and is now letting Deward beat him up," Amber said cheerfully.

"That actually makes sense. Do you want a poultice to help it heal quicker?"

Tommy shook his head. "It should be fine by dinner. I've noticed bruises heal within a few hours."

"I'm going to go take a shower," Amber said. She'd spent the day at the warehouse cleaning –– until she'd gotten the call from the troll –– and she was filthy. Derek had shown up about an hour after she'd gotten there, and he'd been in a rotten mood, but wouldn't say why.

She and Ceri had both agreed they shouldn't go around asking questions the day after a picture of her had been on the news, even if it was just her in wolf form. But she needed something to keep herself occupied, so murdering spiders it was.

"Same. I'm covered in Deward's sweat." Tommy sniffed his arm, then grimaced. "Sweaty trolls don't smell great."

"I'm going to clean up the *giant mess* these two knuckleheads made." Ceri grabbed Captain Jack and lifted him with both hands. He meowed mournfully. "No complaining. You're getting a bath."

Amber snorted and headed toward her room before Ceri could rope her into helping bathe the vicious beast.

As she dropped her things on the dresser next to her bedroom door, the faint scent of cigarettes drifted toward her. Frowning, she looked for the source and noticed a single, folded sheet of paper sat on the dresser where she'd just dumped her keys. She grabbed it, Thallan's scent filling her nose.

Come see me, alone.

Alarm bells went off in her head and she crumpled the paper in her hand. He must have seen the news like everyone else. He'd know why she was involved.

Only Ceri was still in the living room when she walked back through. She could hear Tommy upstairs in the shower. Eloise and Evangeline were talking quietly.

"What's wrong?" Ceri asked.

Amber handed her the note, worst case scenarios running through her head. Would he try to hurt Evangeline? Or kick them out? They'd be screwed if he told them to leave. "I'm going to go see him and get it over with."

"Maybe I should come with you."

Amber shook her head. "I don't want to piss him off. This could already be dicey."

Ceri looked hesitant.

"If he tries to murder me, you'll feel it through the pack bond. I'll be fine."

"Fine. But you're coming straight back here and explaining what's going on."

"I'll be back as soon as I can," Amber agreed with a nod.

She left out the back door and jogged across the lawn. The wind had picked up since they got home. It smelled like rain.

Thallan's house looked ominous in the moonlight. It would be a full moon in a few days, but the heavy clouds were blocking most of the light tonight. She hopped up onto the porch and let herself in through the front door.

Her footsteps echoed through the empty house. It really was like a tomb in here. It even smelled like death. Like something rotten. She wrinkled her nose and hurried to the study she knew Thallan was hiding out in.

The door was open and warm light spilled into the hallway.

Thallan stepped into the doorway, a disturbing excitement on his face. She'd never seen him look so alive, but the tension in his body worried her. "I told you it wasn't your friend."

"What's your point?" she asked.

He turned away and vanished into the office. Rolling her eyes, she followed. He was pacing the length of the room puffing on his cigarette like he needed the smoke to live.

"You wanted to talk?" she prompted, feeling a strong urge to leave. He looked completely manic.

His head snapped up and he pointed the glowing end of the cigarette at her. "The demon has called in its mark."

She nodded impatiently. "Yes."

He took one last drag on the cigarette then flicked it into the hardwood floor, grinding it out with his foot, not caring about the scorch mark it left on the wood floor. "Is it here?"

"No, not that I can see." Her hand went to her mark automatically. The sensation she'd come to associate with Angel's presence was gone, for now.

"Then we have to talk, quickly. We won't have many chances to execute my plan," Thallan said, a dark grin spreading across his face.

"What are you talking about?"

"I'm going to kill it."

Amber's gut twisted. Angel was a threat to her. She shouldn't care, but she did. The idea of just murdering him made her skin crawl. "What? Why?"

"Because he killed my wife!" Thallan shouted, spittle flying from his lips. He advanced on her, forcing her to move backward until she hit the bookshelf. "He's a liar and a murderer, and I swore I would have my revenge!"

"He killed your wife? Is that why you have the mark?"

Thallan turned away, disgust clear on his face. "I made a deal with the devil. Traded my soul. All I wanted was for him to heal her. For two months, I thought he had done it, and that my sacrifice was worth it." He lifted his face toward her. "Then she was killed in a car accident. I know he did it. That monster manipulated me and stole the only thing that mattered. He killed her!"

Amber swallowed and pushed herself off the bookshelf. She wasn't sure if she should believe Thallan or not. Why would the demon kill his wife? But if he had, would he betray her too?

"What's your plan?" she asked. If he was going to do this, she at least needed to know what he was thinking.

Thallan straightened slightly and walked over to his desk. He opened a drawer and pulled out a long, flat box. Lifting a thin, silver chain from around his neck, he pulled a key out of his shirt which he used to open the box.

He picked up a thin, white blade. It glowed as though it were filled with light, casting a strange pallor over his skin. He rotated it slowly and it pushed back the shadows of the room.

"This," he said, his eyes fixed on the shimmering metal, "can kill a demon."

"What the hell is it?" Amber whispered.

"That doesn't matter. All I need is an opportunity. The demon must be visible to the physical realm, not just the apparition you sometimes see. It will be at its most vulnerable then." He tightened his grip on the knife. "That will be my moment to strike."

"I can't do this," Amber said, shaking her head.

Thallan's lips peeled back from his teeth and he advanced on her, reminding her of the two wolves she'd seen fighting for alpha. He looked feral. "You don't get to say no."

"Your wife died in a car wreck. Why do you think it was his fault?"

"It's the only explanation!" Thallan shouted at her, spittle flying from his lips. "She was my light, and that bastard killed her! I know he did, even if no one believes me."

He was insane. She'd always suspected it, but she hadn't realized how bad it was. His insanity was infecting everything around him. The house, the grounds...they were rotting from the inside out because of the hate he held inside him.

"I can't just summon him," Amber said, trying to deflect.

"The witch knows how. She used to dabble in black magic." Thallan sneered at her. "Find a way. Before you fulfill the bargain."

She ground her teeth together. There was no way she was going along with this plan, except as a last resort if Angel tried to kill her. She still had a hard time imagining he would despite how much of an asshole he'd been lately.

"I have to talk to my pack."

Thallan snorted. "Talk to the witch. She'll know how to get the demon at his most vulnerable. If nothing else, he wants to protect this girl you have stashed away in my guest house."

"You're not hurting her," Amber said, immediately angry.

"That's up to you," he said with a mock bow.

Amber turned and left, her mind racing. She wouldn't let him hurt Evangeline, but he could be unpredictable. If he thought she wasn't going to help him, he might try to do something on his own.

There was so much to do. And so many ways it could all go wrong. She stopped in the middle of the grounds and kicked off her shoes, then stripped her shirt off over her head. She couldn't think right now.

The shift rolled over her like a wave and she dropped to four feet. Normally, she tried to maintain control while she was shifted. This time, she just let go.

The wolf shook out its fur and trotted toward the woods.

CHAPTER 43

CERI

Ceri had waited over an hour for Amber to return, and had started getting a little nervous that something was wrong. But the pack bond stayed calm, so she forced herself to sit and wait instead of marching over to Thallan's house to demand to see her alpha.

She sighed and started the porch swing rocking again. It was getting too cold to sit outside but she didn't much feel like sleeping either.

A pair of bright red eyes appeared in the darkness right in front of the porch and she tensed up. "Amber?"

The wolf stepped into the light, holding her clothes in her mouth. She nodded her head.

"Where have you been? You were supposed to come talk to me."

Amber sighed and looked away guiltily then trotted up onto the porch where she shifted. Ceri looked away while she pulled on her clothes, waiting to glare at Amber until she sat down on the porch swing next to her.

"Well?"

"Sorry," she said, crossing her arms. "I needed a minute to clear my head."

"That bad?"

Amber nervously picked at the hem of her shirt. "Thallan wants me to kill the demon," she whispered, glancing around like the demon might pop out at any moment.

Ceri was quiet. She just stared down at her hands. A thousand thoughts raced through her mind in an instant. None of them good.

"You can't seriously think I should go along with his plan."

Ceri knew she expected her to be her sounding board. The voice of reason.

"I mean...it would free you," Ceri said hesitantly, barely able to meet her eyes.

"And what would it mean for Evangeline? He's protecting her." Amber crossed her arms.

"That's what he's told you he's doing, but it could be a lie. He's a *demon* for heaven's sake. They *lie*," Ceri said, exasperated.

"There's something else going on. I just don't know what yet."

"Honestly, my biggest issue with it is just that it's risky. If we can get through this and free you from the mark, that's better than trying to kill...you know who." She drained the last of her tea, grimacing as she swallowed down the dregs at the bottom.

"Do you think Evangeline is evil?" Amber asked, turning to look at her.

Ceri gnawed on the inside of her cheek as she rolled the question around in her mind. She'd been avoiding this question, so of course Amber had to bring it up. "She's not really a demon."

Amber gave her an unimpressed look, raising one of her eyebrows.

"She's not," Ceri insisted. "The angel side of her changes things."

"Before the whole incident with Angel, he really seemed just like any other person. Maybe a little bit of an asshole, but so are most humans."

"And when you crossed him he threatened your life and put everyone in danger." Ceri sighed, rubbing her temples. The headache was back. "I'm not saying you should do it, but I wouldn't exactly cry. Do you think Thallan will try without you?"

"Probably. I want to keep an eye on him. He's not exactly...stable."

"That's an understatement."

Amber glanced at her. "What was that favor you did for him before? The one you thought you could trade for the whole sponsor thing."

"Ah..." she grimaced at the memory. "I tracked his daughter down for him. She disappeared after he went all crazy after his wife died. He didn't know where she was or if she was okay, and she refused to speak with him."

"I really can't picture him as a father."

Ceri snorted. "She said he was a good one, before his wife died. Grief makes people do awful things sometimes."

Amber's face fell. "Yeah, it does."

Ceri reached across the bench and grabbed her hand. "I'm sorry."

She wished she could fix all of this. Maybe killing the demon was the only way. It scared her how deep he had his claws in Amber already. Amber always wanted to see the best in people, and sometimes, it just wasn't there.

CHAPTER 44

EVANGELINE

Evangeline grabbed the shower handle, turning on the water just in time to drown out the sound of her throwing up her dinner. The room spun as her stomach heaved. Her skin was clammy all over. It had been all day and she had thrown up every time she'd eaten.

She yanked some toilet paper off the roll and wiped her mouth, then sat back, leaning her head against the wall. Her skin ached, especially where the boils had started popping up. She thought she'd have more time, but using her demon side's magic the other night seemed to have accelerated the illness.

She lifted her hoodie a little and saw that the boils had grown even larger. The skin around them was red and inflamed.

There was a soft knock at the bathroom door and she froze. "I'm busy."

"I heard you throwing up. Again," Tommy said quietly, just audible over the noise of the shower. "Are you okay?"

"I'm fine," she said, glaring at the door and cursing werewolf hearing. She'd hoped the shower would drown it out. It had always hidden it from Eloise.

"Even if I couldn't hear your heartbeat stuttering all over the place, it'd be obvious you were lying."

"I'm fine is code for go away," she snapped, pushing up to her feet. Her vision blurred from the sudden movement and she had to pause to catch her breath. She tried to take a step forward, but her legs buckled.

Instead of hitting the tile floor, she landed in Tommy's arms. She hadn't even heard the door open, but somehow, he was in the bathroom. He lifted her like she weighed nothing then set her down gently, with her back propped up against the wall.

"Are you sick? You smell like...I don't know what. It's really weird though," he said as he smoothed the hair back from her face.

Her eyes popped open and she pushed his hand away but it was too late. Her hood slipped back and she felt him freeze, his eyes locked on her head. She knew what he was seeing. Black hair, and her least favorite part...

"Are those horns?"

"You cannot tell anyone," she said angrily, pulling her hood back over them. They'd gotten bigger over the years and she hated it.

"Did they just grow or something? Your hair was definitely blonde before too." He sat back, watching her curiously. She felt like a zoo animal.

She stared at the floor so she didn't have to see his expression. "They grow when the sun sets. My demon side comes out. I don't like to talk about it."

He shrugged and stood up, grabbing one of the disposable cups they kept by the sink. "You should drink some water."

"I'm not thirsty."

"You've thrown up three times today. You're bound to be dehydrated. I know you want to be left alone, but don't be dumb." Tommy thrust the little cup of water toward her. She wanted to knock it out of his hand and run away, but he was right. She needed whatever she could manage to keep down.

"Fine," she said, taking the cup and draining it quickly. It still made her stomach churn but she didn't vomit right away.

"This isn't the flu, is it?" Tommy asked, crossing his arms.

She looked down at her hands. "No."

"Does Eloise know what's going on?"

Her head snapped up and she glared at him. "Do not tell her."

"Why are you hiding it from her?"

"Because she already has enough to worry about and I don't want to make it worse. There's nothing she can do anyhow."

"We could take you to a doctor."

Evangeline snorted at that. "Hey doc, this half demon recently accused of eating all our magic is sick. Can you help? Yeah, that's going to go over real well."

"What about Ceri? She knows how to help with most things."

She wrapped her arms a little tighter around her herself. "I don't want her help. There's nothing anyone can do about it anyhow. It's...genetic." That wasn't exactly a lie. Maybe not the whole truth, but the curse was woven into her genes in a manner of speaking. Her biological mother had passed it on to her just like every other demon.

"Are you dying or something?" he asked, his brows knitting together in concern.

"No," she said, rolling her eyes. "I'm just sick. I'll be fine."

Unless she never did what she had to in order to make the sickness go away. Some days she thought it might be better if she didn't. Kadrithan acted like everything depended on her staying alive, but she didn't want that responsibility. Certainly not for the demons. Anything they wanted from her couldn't be good, and he wouldn't explain it.

Tommy shifted on his feet as the silence became awkward. She wanted to just leave, but she didn't have the energy to get off the floor right now.

"I'm going to ask Ceri if she has anything for nausea," he said finally.

"I don't want––"

He cut her off with a glare. "I'm going to, and then you can stop throwing up all the delicious food I make."

"Why are you such a mother hen?" she muttered, twirling the cup in her hands.

"Why are you so determined to keep feeling like crap?"

"I'm not, I just don't want everyone fussing over me." She tossed the cup into the trash and pushed herself off the floor. Slowly.

"If you just told Ceri you needed something, she'd give it to you, and then no one would worry. You're seriously overthinking all of this," he said, catching her arm as her legs wobbled again and pulling her upright.

The front door opened and Genevieve walked in. "Please tell me you saved me some dinner this time, Tommy," she shouted as she dumped her stuff on the couch.

Evangeline jerked away and slipped out of the bathroom. She knew he meant well, but she just wanted to be left alone. She'd disappear if she could. Sometimes she thought she *should*. She was evil after all. Or at least half evil.

She shut the bedroom door behind her and shuffled over to the bed. Her mother was already asleep as she slid under the covers and curled up behind her. At least while she was sleeping she didn't have to think.

CHAPTER 45

AMBER

Amber parked in front of Jameson's house and frowned. She wasn't late, but the others were already here. The wolf perked up in her mind as a feeling of dread settled in her gut. She'd been slightly worried about this meeting, but maybe she should have been *really* worried about it.

She hurried to the front door and let herself in. Jameson said he knew everyone by the sound of their vehicle, so driving up was as good as knocking. The house was quiet except for the sound of voices coming from the gathered werewolves.

Shane was waiting outside. He looked up, and she stopped in her tracks. He was furious. Wordlessly, he opened the door to the room and motioned for her to enter ahead of him.

Part of her was tempted to run, but the stubborn, alpha side of her refused to do that. She was going to deal with this.

Everyone was silent as she stepped into the room. Salazar was watching her curiously, but Bennett's expression was one of disgust, and hate. She didn't bother going to the one empty seat at the table. Instead, she just looked to Jameson.

"Do you have Evangeline Deschamps?" he asked without preamble. She could at least appreciate that he didn't beat around the bush and draw this out.

"She's not responsible for the magic disappearing," Amber replied, crossing her arms and holding his gaze.

"I'll take that as a yes," Jameson replied, rising from his seat. "We have a rule. We don't report other alphas to the police, no matter what the infraction is. If it's serious, we simply take care of it ourselves. If you believe this girl is innocent, then I will give you the benefit of the doubt."

"You can't be serious––"

Jameson cut off Bennett with a glare. "I lead the council. It is my decision, and without definite proof, I'm willing to acknowledge the girl may be innocent." He turned back to Amber. "You have a week to prove this demon-child isn't responsible."

"Or what?" Amber ground out.

"Or the council will come get her ourselves, and you will be punished as I see fit."

One week. Amber curled her hand into a fist and nodded. She was lucky she got that much based on the way Bennett was looking at her. "Can I trust that no one will come looking for trouble during that week?"

Jameson nodded. "You have my word."

Amber nodded. "Then I guess we'll talk again in a week."

"You're relieved of your council duties until this is resolved, and you won't be needed for this meeting," Jameson said, turning away in a clear dismissal.

"Just a word of warning. When I rescued Evangeline, there was a sorcerer there. He was trying to kill her. He's probably the same one that killed Lockhart," Amber said.

Jameson looked back at her. "I'll look into it."

She nodded, then turned around and walked out of the room. Shane shut the door behind her and followed her. They were silent as they left the house and walked back out to her truck.

Pausing by the driver side door, she crossed her arms. "Spit it out."

"What the hell are you thinking?" he demanded, just as angry as she expected. "You're a brand-new alpha whose reputation is already shit, and now you're harboring a demon? That's not just irresponsible, that's insane."

"You have no clue what you're talking about," she snapped, her eyes flashing red. "All of you idiots saw a man on the news making crazy claims, and you what? Just believed him? That asshole burned down an old woman's house, then sent men with guns into the woods to hunt down a seventeen-year-old girl. If she is part demon, no one knows what that means. You can't execute her without giving her a chance."

"You don't have the right to risk the safety of an entire city just because you feel bad for her," Shane snapped back. She could see the struggle not to flinch back under her gaze, and any other time, she'd feel bad for using the dominance that came with being an alpha like this.

"I'm not going to sacrifice my conscience because some people are afraid of anyone that is different," she ground out. "I'm going to find out what the hell is actually going on, and kill the sorcerer that's behind all this. I don't miss Donovan one tiny bit, but a sorcerer killed him and cut out his heart. Something everyone conveniently forgot today. Jameson might be next, but sure, let's worry about the girl that hides in her room all day because she's terrified someone is going to find her and hurt her mother again."

Shane finally looked away. "If, in a week, you discover this girl is responsible, what will you do?"

Amber knew he could hear a lie just like she could. If she said she'd just hand the girl over that wouldn't be the truth. She couldn't. Not without dying. But if the council was going to come after her pack she might not have a choice.

Thallan thought he could kill the demon, but something about that plan made her skin crawl. If it came down to it though...she couldn't let Angel take her soul for failing to fulfill her end of the bargain.

"I don't know," she said finally.

He shook his head in frustration. "Sometimes I wish you'd just lie and tell me what I want to hear."

She shrugged and climbed into her truck. She didn't have time to sit here and baby Shane.

"Wait, I'm coming with you," he said, heading around toward the passenger door.

"What? Why?"

He hopped up in the truck. "You're going to go try to figure out what's going on, right?"

"Yes."

"Then I'm going to help." He pressed his lips into a thin line. "So you don't get yourself killed."

She sighed and cranked up the truck. "Do you know anyone that might know where to find a sorcerer?"

"Actually, I do."

She backed out of her spot and headed out of the subdivision. "If you try to screw me over, or hurt Evangeline, I will rip you apart. Just so we're clear."

He looked at her from the corner of his eye. "I never doubted that for a second."

CHAPTER 46

AMBER

"His name is Bram? Seriously?" Amber asked, raising her brow.

"He's older than the other guy. And he's very sensitive about those sorts of jokes, so just…don't bring it up." Shane pointed at the light ahead. "Turn here."

She did as instructed, nervously checking the rearview mirror to make sure they weren't being followed. It was completely paranoid, but she was starting to feel justified in her paranoia. The council had connected the dots after seeing the news report, there was no reason someone else couldn't have as well.

"How old is this vampire, exactly?"

"I have no idea. Old enough to be a little crazy," Shane said with a shrug.

"How do you know him?" she asked, glancing at him curiously.

"I was an omega briefly when my original pack fell apart. I ended up in a less than savory crowd. We used to get things for him." Shane's shoulders tightened at whatever memories that question had brought up.

"Ah," she said, letting the conversation drop. He was already pissed enough at her without her pressing him on an obviously sensitive topic.

"It's that gate."

A chain link fence topped with barbed wire protected an old, brick building. It was unmarked, and every window had been boarded up. A man in a hoodie with his face and hands covered lounged near the gate, watching them. She turned into the short driveway and stopped, rolling down her window.

The man strolled over, tugging down the bandana that covered his face a little. He was pale, his eyes were a light almost golden color, but the teeth were what really gave it away. When he grinned, his sharp incisors were impossible to hide.

Vampires could go out in the sun with the right spell to protect them, but they'd still get a nasty sunburn in about an hour if they didn't keep their skin covered.

"Shane Weston, it's been a few years," the guard said, resting his forearms on the window ledge and leaning farther into the truck than Amber was comfortable with.

"Yet, you're still out here doing the grunt work," Shane said, returning the smile. All the tension was gone from his posture now. Even his heartbeat was slower. She had no idea how he did that, but she needed to learn that trick.

The vampire, of course, had no heartbeat which was creepy as hell now that she was used to hearing them.

"Ah, you know how it is. I like to party, and Bram doesn't like it when I party."

"Is that what you call those ragers? Parties?" Shane asked, raising a brow.

"Psh," the vampire said, waving a hand at Shane. "Semantics. Anyhow, you didn't come by just to see me. What do you need today?"

"I need to talk to Bram."

The vampire glanced at Amber. "Her too?"

"Yes," Amber said, answering for herself.

The vampire shook his head with a laugh. "Your funeral." He pushed off the truck and walked over to the gate, unlocking with a key he kept in his pocket.

"What does he mean 'your funeral'?" Amber asked, looking at Shane suspiciously.

"He's just goading me. Mostly. Bram can be weird about new people. He's slightly obsessed with...blood," Shane said, grimacing.

"Aren't all vampires?" The gate slid open and she drove through, parking in the only open spot.

"Not like this. You can tell him no when he asks for...well, you'll see..." he trailed off with a guilty expression, "but he will definitely be more cooperative if you say yes."

"You could have told me that before you brought me here," she said, a little angry that he hadn't warned her before they were driving through the gate.

"I had a lot on my mind," Shane said sarcastically.

They climbed out of the truck and she followed him toward the front door, where another guard sat. This one wasn't a vampire though. She was a werewolf.

The woman rose as they approached and opened the door. "I'd say it's good to see you again, Shane, but since you're just here for business..." She shrugged and gave Amber a curious look.

"Sorry, Bella, I'll try to make one of the game nights sometime. Being Jameson's beta doesn't leave me with a whole lot of free time."

"Excuses, excuses," Bella said, waving them inside. "Have fuuuun."

Amber stepped into the dimly lit building and almost gagged as the scent hit her. Blood, both old and fresh, was all she could smell. Her hand shook as she covered her mouth and nose, trying to breathe shallowly.

Her ears buzzed with the pop of gunfire and Tommy's frantic howls. She tasted blood in her mouth. Felt it dripping from her muzzle. Red tinted her vision as she lunged at the last attacker.

"Are you okay?" Shane asked, pressing his hand against her back.

His touch shocked her out of the flashback and she forced herself to focus on the concrete under her feet and the light scent of his cologne.

"I'm fine," she said sharply. She wasn't. She needed to get out of here, but running away wasn't going to make those memories go away. "Let's just go."

Shane kept his hand on her back, something she would have objected to at any other time. Right now, it was the only thing keeping her from bolting.

The hallway led into the open lower floor of the building. It had been some kind of manufacturing business in the past, but all the machinery had been taken out and replaced with clutter. Couches were placed haphazardly around the room. Most looked like they'd been reclaimed from dumpsters. A few people were sleeping on them, curled up without a blanket or pillow.

There was a huge flat screen tv hung from one of the walls. A troll rugby game, that was playing silently on it, was the only source of light down here.

She expected Shane to lead her toward the rickety stairs that led up to the second level, but he took her down instead.

"In the basement? Really? That's borderline cliche," she muttered as they descended into the narrow stairwell.

"It's easier to block the light down here."

"Is he that worried about a sunburn?"

"Bram refuses to use the protective spells," Shane said, his voice suggesting this was an old argument he'd had many times.

There was a chuckle ahead of them and the door at the bottom of the stairs opened, revealing a tall, thin vampire -- there was no doubt in her mind that he was a vampire, even without the teeth visible -- wearing a pair of black leather pants and...nothing else.

"I'm a vampire. Why would I want to prance around in the sun like some sparkly elf?" He waved them down, his ropey muscles flexing under skin so pale it was almost white.

"No one is suggesting you go sunbathing, Bram, but knowing that you won't burst into flames at the first lick of sunlight is a nice reassurance for most vampires."

Bram pulled Shane into a hug at the bottom of the stairs. Amber kept her distance. It was obvious Shane liked the weird, old vampire. He seemed eccentric, but not too dangerous.

"Come in, then you can introduce me to your friend," Bram said as he waved them inside.

Amber walked in and looked around. The place was covered in paintings. They were all the same color, a kind of sepia-toned red. Bram seemed to have an obsession with portraits. All of the faces stared out at her. Some angry, some happy, some terrified. She walked over to one still sitting on an easel and leaned in for a better look. That's when she realized...it wasn't paint that he used. It was blood.

"Beautiful, aren't they?" he whispered from right behind her.

She jumped and whirled around, coming face to face with the artist himself. "You paint them with blood?"

"Yes, their own blood. Art is a kind of magic all its own. The sacrifice makes it even more special," Bram said with a grin. His eyes were so light that his iris blended into the rest of his eye at the edges.

Shane cleared his throat. "This is Amber. She's --"

"The bitten werewolf who became an alpha. I know." Bram finally turned away. He walked over to a long workbench piled with supplies and picked up an apron. It used to be white, but was now streaked with red. "I am curious what she might need from me though."

"What do you know about demons?" Shane asked.

Bram looked thoughtful, and slightly surprised at the question. "Not terribly friendly, similarly afflicted to not walk the earth while the sun is up, and rather long-lived. They've also been recently accused of destroying magic, though I doubt that." He grabbed a packet off the workbench that Amber immediately recognized. It was a blood draw kit.

The vampire walked toward her, watching her expression carefully. "I think I know what you're concerned about, and I'm happy to answer your questions, and keep the knowledge that you were here to myself, if…"

"If I give you some blood," Amber finished for him.

He smiled. "I simply want to do your portrait."

She ground her teeth together, but nodded. It was creepy, but it's not like it would kill her. He directed her to sit down in an armchair next to a table, then sat across from her and opened the kit. She laid her arm on the table and tried to focus on slowing her heart rate, but this whole process made her feel slightly ill.

He pulled out the needle and adjusted the angle of her arm.

"I'd rather do it myself, actually." She snatched the needle from his hand and clenched her hand into a fist to make the vein on the inside of her arm pop, then slid it in smoothly.

He watched her, swaying slightly as the blood began to pump into the tube. His eyes were locked onto her arm as though he were hypnotized. "This is even better, you doing it yourself."

"Do you realize how creepy you sound, or do you just not care?" She switched to the second vial. Only three more to go.

"Oh, I just don't care." His lips curled up into a smile and he dragged his eyes away from her arm to look at her. "You don't strike me as a drug addict. How did you learn to do this?"

"I'm a nurse. Or was. I got fired after I was bitten."

"Ah, yes. Those are some silly laws. I'm surprised they haven't been overturned yet."

She switched to the third vial and Bram grabbed the first two, carrying them over to the long, paint-splattered bench near the wall. He dumped the contents into a small bowl, using a thin piece of plastic to carefully scrape out every last drop.

Amber glanced back at Shane, who had on a neutral expression. How many times had he watched Bram do this? Had he let Bram do it to him?

Bram hummed happily as she disconnected the final vial. There was a band-aid sitting on top of the other supplies. She grabbed it and opened it with her teeth, then quickly slipped out the needle and tried to put on the band-aid, but it went crooked.

Shane startled her when he grabbed it. "You looked like you could use a little help." His hands were steady as he pressed the band-aid on.

"Thanks."

Bram collected the other vials and dropped them in the pocket of his apron. He looked more like a butcher than a painter splattered with all that blood.

"What do you know about Zachariah Hudson?" Amber asked, sitting on the edge of the armchair. She felt restless and wanted out of this room.

The vampire adjusted his canvas and began painting. "Well, he's a half-angel that works for the angels as far as anyone can tell. Their organization is perfectly above board in all their dealings, which I find terribly suspicious. No one is that perfect."

"Have any new sorcerers showed up in town recently?"

He switched brushes, dipping it in water this time before adding the blood. "Hmm, I'd say so. Lockhart having his heart cut out was a dead giveaway," he said, smirking at his own pun.

"Do you know where the sorcerer is?" Shane asked, pacing the edge of the room.

"I find it interesting that you ask about demons first, then an angel, then a sorcerer. It's as if you think they're all connected," Bram mused, ignoring Shane's question.

Amber resisted the urge to roll her eyes. "Maybe they are. Have you ever talked to a demon?"

"Yes, a few times. We used to summon them for fun." Bram switched paintbrushes again and leaned in close to the canvas. "They're very interesting. Determined to get you to agree to a favor, of course, but not nearly so menacing as most people would have you believe."

Summoning demons for fun...who the hell was this guy? Amber dragged her hands through her hair and shook her head in disbelief. "Have you ever heard of someone that was only half demon?"

"I've heard rumors, but I've never met anyone that was that sort of hybrid. It kind of makes you wonder though, doesn't it? There are so many half angels running around, but no half demons," he mused.

"This sorcerer, do you know his name?" Amber asked.

"Interesting you'd assume it was a man," Bram said, his eyes flicking to her for a moment.

"I saw him in the woods. I know he's a man."

"Ah, of course, my mistake. I believe he goes by Caligo. Sometimes they leave their real names behind in order to seem more mysterious, or simply to maintain their anonymity."

Amber narrowed her eyes at him. It felt like he meant something else. She didn't think there were two sorcerers. Donovan had been killed right before this guy had showed up. It had to be him.

"Have you sold anything to him?" Shane asked.

Bram shook his head. "No, not directly at least. It's possible some of my regular clients worked as a middle man." The vampire looked at Amber again. "Siobhan, for example. She also recently started asking around about a sorcerer. I believe she's your witch's cousin, right?"

Amber nodded. This guy seemed to know everyone. "I saw her yesterday."

"It was a smart choice to speak with her. She might be able to find him faster. A lot of paranormals owe her favors these days." He switched brushes again, a disturbing smile forming on his face.

"You never did answer my question about where the sorcerer is. Do you know?" Shane pressed. He looked as impatient as she felt.

"It makes you uncomfortable, doesn't it?" Bram asked with a broad grin. "You look like you'd rather rip off my head than stay in this room for another minute."

Amber curled her hand into a fist. "The thought has crossed my mind."

Bram threw his head back and laughed. "Shane, you can't handle this one, but I like her."

Amber glanced at Shane, who looked slightly embarrassed. He crossed his arms and sighed. "Can you answer our questions, or not?"

"Still so impatient," Bram grumbled. "And of course I can, however, I doubt you'll like my answers."

"Why is that?" Amber asked, trying to encourage the crazy old bat to get to the point.

"Because it won't help you." He dabbed the paint brush into the little cup of blood and added a final flourish to his macabre painting, then spun it around.

Amber stared at her likeness, painted in her own blood, and felt sick. Her eyes were striking, probably more so than in real life. Her face was tight with repressed anger and he'd made her hair look like flames wrapping around her head. She looked dangerous.

"What do you think?" he asked eagerly.

"It's the most awful thing I've ever seen," she said bluntly.

"You have got to be kidding me," Shane mumbled, dragging his hand down his face.

She glared at him. If Bram hadn't wanted her honest opinion, he shouldn't have asked. He didn't seem offended though, if anything, the answer had delighted him.

"It is awful to see yourself through the eyes of another, isn't it?" he purred, gazing at his own painting with adoration. "I'm sure that if you could paint me, my portrait would be just as horrifying to me."

"Somehow I doubt that," Amber said tiredly. "Look, if you don't want to give me the answers we came here for, then just say so. But I'm not staying any longer and playing these weird games with you if you can't tell us anything."

Bram looked up at her and grinned, revealing twisted yellow teeth. "Of course, of course. I've had my fun." He hopped up from his stool and grabbed a slip of paper. "I don't know where the sorcerer is staying, but I can tell you exactly where Zachariah Hudson is, and that he purchased a large amount of very odd ingredients from me recently. He wanted it off the record, but he failed to pay the full amount, so I consider any expectation of confidentiality void."

"What did he buy?" Amber asked as she accepted the note from Bram.

"It's all in the note, but I found the items particularly interesting. They are all things that could be used in spells, but they are not common ingredients. They're also normally bought by a witch. Interesting coincidence, don't you think?"

"Yeah, I do," Amber said, staring at the list. She looked up, that stupid painting catching her eye for a moment before she forced herself to look at Bram instead. "Thanks for your help."

He nodded. "You're welcome. Would you like to keep the painting?"

"Hell no."

He grinned. "Perhaps you should come back some time, when you hate yourself less. You might find that it has changed."

CHAPTER 47

CERI

Ceri parked next to Shane's suburban and hopped out of her car. Amber had texted her a half hour ago and nearly given her a heart attack.

> The council knows I have Evangeline. We're in deep shit if I can't prove she's innocent in a week.
>
> Going to a no magic spot with Shane. Need to see it for myself.

Announcing that the council knew they were harboring a demon in their house required a *phone call*. That was not a text-and-then-not-respond-to-any-replies kind of situation.

She jogged into the woods, following the path worn by investigators and probably tourists that wanted to see the freaky place where magic didn't work.

There was police tape around the area, but there weren't any guards. I guess they figured no one would want to come here. Being near it made her skin crawl. There was something off about the air. A strange smell that made her want to turn and run away. Every instinct she had was warning her against getting any closer.

Amber and Shane were waiting for her right next to the affected zone. Her alpha looked particularly grumpy, which she'd expected. She'd never seen Shane look so irritable though. He'd always been sunny and happy, even before the Trials.

"Took you long enough," Amber said as she approached.

"I can't believe you didn't call me. And what is he doing here?" She jabbed her thumb at Shane, then felt bad. "No offense, it'd be good to see you under different circumstances."

"None taken," he said, nodding in greeting. "And I volunteered to help since Amber is stubborn and won't just hand the girl over."

So, the council didn't know everything. That was probably for the best.

"We met with this old vampire named Bram, and he said he sold a bunch of stuff to Zachariah Hudson, that half angel we saw." Amber handed her a list scribbled down on a piece of paper. "He bought it all before the attack on Evangeline's house."

She read the list quickly, her brows knitting together as she thought about the supplies. They had to be for multiple spells because she couldn't think of anything that would require all this. Some of the ingredients would even work against each other. Then the name of the vampire registered and she looked up sharply, glaring at Shane. "You took her to see *Bram?*"

He lifted his hands and took a step back. "She was safe, Bram trusts me."

"You have got to be kidding me. That guy is insane. He *uses* people."

"He was a little weird but he didn't seem that bad––"

"You don't know his reputation," Ceri snapped before turning her glare back to Shane. "Are you actually trying to help or are you just here to keep an eye on her for the council?"

"I think Amber is being an idiot, but I'm trying to help."

Well, that sounded honest at least. "Fine. Let's get this over with."

It was impossible to miss the spot. She'd seen the pictures on the news, but nothing could prepare you for the wrongness of it. She braced herself and ducked under the police tape. It was a perfect circle about ten feet across where all the light and life seemed to have been stripped away.

Amber leaned in toward it and Shane grabbed her arm, yanking her back a step. "Don't step inside it!"

Amber batted his hand away. "I'm not an idiot. I'm just trying to smell it."

Ceri rolled her eyes. They were like children. "Sniff it from farther away. We can't risk you tripping into it. They're not sure what it would do to a werewolf."

She crouched down and opened her bag. Dozens of witches, elves, and other magic users had done tests to try to find out how these spots were made, and if they could be fixed. None of them had come up with anything, but she had something they didn't.

Her owl flew down from the tree and landed on the ground next to her, startling both the werewolves.

"Where the hell did that thing come from?" Shane asked, eyeing it warily. "I didn't hear it."

"Guess you should pay better attention," Ceri said, smirking at him. It was fun to see him a little freaked out, and she didn't want to explain the owl anyhow.

Amber simply looked at it curiously. She knew what it was now, though she'd never seen it up close.

Her bag was a mess. She'd dumped everything in it in a hurry so that she could meet them here. After digging around for a moment, she brought out the sage and a little vial of holy water. She knew she had some lavender in there too but––

Her hand hit something warm and wiggly and she shrieked, almost falling backward as she jerked her hand out of the bag. Woggy was flung through the air, shrieking as well.

"Oh shi––"

Shane grabbed the back of Amber's shirt as she reached over the no magic spot, catching Woggy before he could fall into it. Shane yanked them both back and Amber toppled onto her butt, holding the pixie close to her chest.

"Well, that was close," Amber said drily.

Ceri put her head in her hands and tried to get herself under control. She was *not* going to cry. "That's it. Woggy is grounded."

Shane laughed. "Is that pixie some kind of a pet or something? I thought witches just used them for parts."

Ceri lifted her head and glared at him. "They're sentient. He's not a pet, he's part of the pack."

"Oh...okay." Shane glanced at Amber as if expecting her to tell him that was just a joke, but Amber was busy making sure Woggy was alright. The pixie seemed rather excited actually and was signing something at her about *outside* and *happy*.

Taking a deep breath to shake off the trauma of nearly dumping Woggy into a no magic spot, she found the lavender and set it next to the sage. This was a chance to see if demons were actually involved in the creation of these spots, something that had been bothering her since it had come on the news.

She didn't trust Zachariah. The way he'd acted at the house that day, and on the news, set off warning bells in her head. But just because he couldn't be trusted didn't mean he was entirely wrong. Evangeline didn't seem to be the culprit, but that didn't mean Amber's demon wasn't doing something shady on the side.

Shane crouched down near the edge and sniffed it carefully. "It's weird that magic doesn't work inside it since it smells like magic."

"It smells like death and decay to me," Ceri said as she lit the sage stick. She pushed up to her knees and waved it gently around the edge of the no magic spot. The smoke curled around it, and drifted upward, but couldn't seem to pass over the edge. She frowned and blew gently, trying to coax it into the circle. It simply spread even further in either direction, none of it able to drift forward.

"Is there some kind of barrier?" Amber asked. Woggy was struggling in her hands, so she set him on her shoulder. He liked to climb in everyone's hair and hide in it, which he promptly did, disappearing into Amber's.

Shane grabbed a stick and tossed it into the circle. It passed through unimpeded and landed on the ground. Nothing seemed to happen to it. "Not a physical one."

"Whatever spell created this was evil. The sage won't touch it." Ceri set the bundle of sage next to her, letting it smolder. Having it nearby was calming. It afforded her a little protection against any evil spirits that might be lingering nearby.

The owl shuffled closer, climbing onto her knee. She pet it tentatively. It had never let her touch it before, and she wasn't sure why now was different. It seemed content just to sit on her knee for now though.

She grabbed the holy water and whispered a quick incantation —— infusing the water with her magic to give it a little more oomph —— then squirted some into the circle. The droplets hit the ground and...did nothing.

She frowned. "If this had been created by demons, the holy water should have done *something*."

"Could it be a natural phenomenon?" Amber asked.

Ceri shook her head. "No, there's something very wrong about it. It feels the opposite of natural."

The owl turned its head to face her and she met its deep, orange eyes. All the sounds around her faded away, including Shane and Amber.

The ground shook. Red eyes glowed in the darkness, surrounded by magic. A voice chanted, growing louder and louder, but she couldn't make out the words. Only the feel of them. They were wrong. Cursed. Hollow.

The owl blinked and she snapped out of the vision.

"Ceri?" Amber prompted again, looking a little concerned.

"Sorry, what?" she asked, rubbing the back of her hand over her eyes.

"I think I hear someone coming down the road, we should go."

Ceri nodded and began gathering up her things. The owl hopped off her knee, then launched into the air, disappearing into the trees. Shane watched it go suspiciously.

"I think that whatever answers we're looking for, we won't find here," she said as she pushed up to her feet. "I don't know what the council wants as proof, but I don't think any demon did this."

Shane shoved his hands in his pockets. "Jameson will stand by his word if you can prove it, but I don't think he knows what he wants to see either. The biggest issue is just disproving Hudson publicly. If it gets out that the council was protecting you, it won't matter what the truth is. It'll be a shit show."

"We'll figure something out." Amber untangled Woggy from her hair. He'd fallen asleep and simply rolled over in her hand. She walked him over to Ceri who took him and set him back in her bag. "I have to take Shane home. I'll see you back at the house."

Ceri nodded and hurried back toward her car. The more they learned about all this, the more it bothered her. Something wasn't adding up. They were missing something important.

She followed Amber's truck back to the main road. As they turned onto the highway, a sleek black sedan turned down the gravel road. She thought she saw a glimpse of blond hair through the tinted windows, but she couldn't be sure.

CHAPTER 48

GENEVIEVE

Genevieve's favorite part of her job was research. Digging into a client's past and finding every skeleton was important for a defense lawyer. She had to know her client's weaknesses better than the prosecution. If she got blindsided by evidence or something they'd done in the past, the client was screwed.

Finding out everything she could about Paul Greer was probably an abuse of power. After all, she had access to information most people didn't. She didn't feel the slightest bit guilty though.

"Here's your waffles," the waitress said cheerfully as she slid the plate in front of her.

"Thanks," Genevieve said with a smile.

The waitress set Paul's food in front of him –– steak with a side of mashed potatoes –– then hurried away to the next table.

He picked up his fork and knife and raised an eyebrow at her. "Aren't waffles normally a breakfast food?"

"They're delicious, therefore they're breakfast, lunch, and dinner food." She grabbed the blueberry syrup and poured a liberal amount on top of the perfectly golden waffles. This was going to hit the spot. "Thanks for meeting with me on such short notice."

"It was no problem. I was surprised to receive your message, actually. Many new alphas aren't interested in taking on the responsibility of sponsoring someone, especially for a pack that has caused them trouble." He cut into his steak and blood leaked out. In the past that would have grossed her out, but now it just looked good. The wolf was jealous he had steak and she didn't, but she pushed the urges down.

"It is a lot of responsibility, which is why I'm interested in negotiating a few things before I approach Amber. I guarantee she'd turn you down without hesitation if we can't work out something that will help her before I bring it up." She watched his reaction closely. He did look a little surprised. Perhaps he hadn't expected her to be so prepared.

He finished chewing his bite, then set his fork down and clasped his hands together in front of him. "Alright, that seems fair enough. What do you want?"

She smiled, expecting the question. "I think we should start with what you want. Seeking out Amber is an odd choice. Most potential alphas would go to someone like Jameson first."

"You haven't been a werewolf long, so you haven't seen the way things have changed in the past decade," he said, his eyes going distant. "Some of the packs are becoming more like gangs than a werewolf pack. We're meant to be family, not mercenaries for hire. The alphas also try to suppress the instincts of their pack members so much that they end up acting out like rebellious teenagers."

"There has been a rise in gang violence associated with werewolf packs," she agreed with a nod. "Especially in cities."

"Born or bitten doesn't matter to me. If anything, the bitten wolves help the packs. Their issues with control remind us that we aren't human. We aren't tame. There is a balance between control and accepting the wolf that lives up here." He tapped a long finger against his head. "Lockhart never got that. He never accepted how much the wolf drove him, and he became mean. And selfish. He wouldn't allow challenges within the pack and simply chose his favorites for various positions. No one respected his beta or gammas as a result."

"They were definitely assholes," Genevieve muttered, sopping up some more syrup with an already soggy piece of waffle. "How does Amber fit into all this?"

Paul smiled at that. "She didn't give a fuck about what people thought. She demanded their respect, and found a way to not only enter the Trials, but survive them. I have changes to make in this pack, and allying myself with someone like Amber sends a message not only to my pack but everyone else as well."

"It doesn't also have to do with the fact that Jameson refused to sponsor you once before?"

Paul sat back, a smile forming on his face. "You looked into my past in more detail than I expected."

"I might be recently bitten, but I wasn't born yesterday. You might want to send a message, but I knew that couldn't be it." She took a drink of water and waited for him to explain. She already knew the gossip, but hearing from him why he'd been turned down was important.

"My original pack fell apart. I was the beta, and I expected that I'd be able to take control and move on. I expected it to be simple, but I made a mistake." He sighed and tapped his thumb on the table, an almost nervous gesture. "I didn't gain the pack's respect. A few of them broke the rules, went out on a full moon and got drunk, and someone got killed. It was my fault. I'd seen the signs and thought simply forbidding it was enough. I'd barely been alpha for a day but thought my word was law. It was naive."

"What should you have done?" she asked curiously. Amber never really told them what to do, but with such a small pack, they hadn't had any issues with idiotic pack members.

"Watched them. One of them showed disrespect when I gave the orders, but I didn't want to be too hard on them since their alpha had just died. I should have challenged him and forced his submission, for his own good. He was wild with grief. His wolf wanted a fight and I could have given it to him." He rubbed his hand along his jaw with a sigh. "Instead, he is spending life in jail. That is my fault."

"Well, we all make mistakes. Sounds like you've learned from yours," she said, setting her fork to the side. It was time to get down to business. "So, Amber is a bit of a last resort for you. All the risk is on her if she does this for you. What can you offer to my pack?"

He leaned in and rested his arms on the table. "I think the first thing we should discuss is an alliance. However, I would also like to offer to cover the sponsor's fee. From what I understand, Amber doesn't necessarily have the funds for it."

Genevieve nodded. "That sounds like an excellent start."

She smiled as they got down to the nitty-gritty. This was something she was good at. Hopefully, Amber wouldn't be pissed about it, but this could be really good for the pack. Right now, no one really respected them. It would only cause problems in the future if that wasn't remedied. Even if Amber asked Ceri to be her beta instead, she wanted to do this for her.

CHAPTER 49

AMBER

Amber rubbed the demon mark. Angel had been mysteriously absent today. Normally, he followed her around trying to ruin her mood. The absence made her suspicious, but perhaps he was spending his time harassing Evangeline instead. She'd seen him talking to her the night that half angel had come on the news.

"Is the mark hurting?" Derek asked, sipping on a beer. He'd been at the warehouse all day, and she felt bad about not helping, but everything had gone downhill fast after that council meeting.

"Yeah, I just haven't seen the demon in a while. Makes me antsy," she admitted with a shrug.

Eloise grunted as she sat down on the couch. They'd decided to include her and Evangeline in tonight's conversation. They needed to know about the most recent issue, and Amber was hoping they might be able to remember something helpful from the night of the attack.

Ceri handed Eloise a small vial to help with the pain of her healing ribs, then turned to her and Derek. "You ready?"

"Yeah, let's get this over with." She headed into the living room and plopped down in the armchair she'd dragged into the room just for this.

This needed to be a pack meeting, not just her standing in front of them telling them what to do, and she thought sitting might help with that. Genevieve and Ceri sat on either side of her, while Tommy took the last seat on the couch next to Evangeline.

With a sigh, she leaned forward, bracing her elbows on her knees. "This morning when I arrived at the council meeting, they demanded that I hand Evangeline over to the police."

Eloise visibly tensed, her hand going to her daughter's arm. "You can't--"

"I know," Amber said, waving her concerns away. "I wouldn't do that, and I can't anyhow with the deal I've made with the demon, Kadrithan. Fortunately, they're willing to give me a week to prove that Evangeline isn't the one destroying magic."

"Only a week?" Tommy asked, his face pinched in concern.

She nodded. "Ceri's cousin is looking for the sorcerer, and I talked to someone else today who gave me some interesting insight into that guy on the news, Zachariah Hudson. I have an address for him, and I think I should go see him tomorrow."

Ceri and Genevieve turned on her in sync, each of them in varying states of shock.

"You can't be serious," Ceri choked out.

"I'm not going to say I have Evangeline, but I want to try to figure out what he's after, really. He's working with the sorcerer, so he has to have a different reason for wanting her dead."

"That is the worst idea you've ever had. Hands down," Genevieve said, shaking her head. "If you go try to talk to this guy he's going to show up here with the police, and they're going to find Evangeline."

"We can't just sit here and wait for something to fall in our laps." Amber crossed her arms and sat back in her chair, exasperated.

"What if you just send me away somewhere?" Evangeline suggested. "If I leave, then everyone will be safe."

As if summoned by the utterance, Angel appeared. "She's not going anywhere until I figure out how she was found in the first place. I won't risk sending her into greater danger."

Amber met Evangeline's gaze. The girl looked as furious as she felt. They didn't have much in common but they both hated Kadrithan's constant interfering.

"If you're going to barge into our pack meetings, you should show yourself," Genevieve said, glaring around the room.

The demon obliged, pulling strength from the demon mark to appear to them all. He'd taken on his red devil form again, only bigger this time, and sneered at Genevieve. "Better?"

"It'd be better if you disappeared forever, but yeah, I prefer getting to hear both sides of the conversation," she snapped.

"And you wonder why I don't hang around for chats," Angel muttered as he arranged himself on the arm of the couch.

"Maybe you just need to find the sorcerer, then call the police," Derek suggested. "No matter what else is going on, he is breaking the law. You don't necessarily have to do this all on your own."

Amber stared at her knees. He wasn't wrong, it'd just be tricky. "We still have to find him."

"Siobhan should be getting back to me soon. She can talk to people we can't. She'll find him." Ceri seemed confident, and Amber hoped she was right.

"I hate waiting around," Amber said, dragging her hands down her face and taking a deep breath. "Okay, we wait to hear from Siobhan, but if she hasn't found him in two days, I'm going to have to do *something*."

No one seemed particularly enthused with the plan, but it was all they had. Amber felt completely out of her depth. She wasn't a detective or a bodyguard. She probably shouldn't be an alpha either at this rate.

CHAPTER 50

CERI

Ceri sat across from Woggy, who was watching her hands intently. She was trying to expand his vocabulary now that he'd adapted to using sign language every day. He always enjoyed the lessons, but that was probably because of the treats he got.

She began signing *chicken* when pain shot through her head. It was so intense her vision blurred and for a moment, she thought she might vomit.

"Evangeline..." she gasped out as she collapsed to the floor. Her magic flared out from inside her, trying to defend her against the sudden attack. Gritting her teeth, she forced herself to shout, "EVANGELINE!"

Footsteps sounded on the stairs and through the tears of pain she caught a glimpse of the girl kneeling over her. She looked frantic. "What's wrong?"

"Call...Amber...attack," she managed to force out. Each word was a struggle. Her muscles began to seize as magic flowed through her. She shut her eyes and pulled desperately on the pack bond. It came alive and poured into her, giving her just enough power to let her breathe again.

She'd known this was coming, but she'd hoped she had more time. That maybe they'd find the sorcerer first.

Her fingernails scraped against the wood floor and she felt the house come alive around her. It groaned, panicking at the rage and pain it felt in her.

Please help me, she begged.

All around her, the wards burst to life. The house's magic unfurled and lights danced behind her vision as she opened her mind to it.

The painful sensations racking her body faded away as her mind linked with the house. The sorcerer's attack was all around them, pounding on the windows, curling through the rafters, and seeping under the door.

The house roared, sounding like a dragon in her mind, and light burst from it, driving the darkness back. Her view shifted and she saw Evangeline shaking her limp body. It was odd to see her own face staring blankly at the ceiling.

"What do I do?" Evangeline begged as tears slipped down her face.

She drifted toward her, trying to be comforting, but the girl shrieked as she mentally touched her, whirling around like someone had touched her. "Who's there?"

The air shifted to Ceri's left and she saw the demon appear. He looked straight at her as though he could see her even though Evangeline couldn't.

"What's happening?" he demanded.

"I don't know! She said something about an attack, then just stopped moving! She said to call Amber, but I don't have a phone!"

"Use hers," the demon said, keeping a suspicious eye on Ceri's ethereal form.

"It's in the pocket of my cardigan," she said, finding her voice suddenly.

"Check the pocket of her cardigan," the demon passed on, drifting toward her body.

Evangeline dug through her pockets and found her phone. She never kept it locked with a password, so the girl was able to unlock it and find Amber's number with shaking fingers.

"Hello? Amber? Something is wrong...I don't know...Amber? AMBER?" She dropped the phone and put her face in her hands.

"What's happening?" the demon demanded.

"I don't know," Evangeline sobbed. "I think something is attacking them. We're screwed."

Ceri's heart fell out of her chest. The sorcerer wasn't just attacking her, he was attacking her pack too. The house felt her fear and wrapped around her, pulling her out of the living room.

Her view changed and she saw everything around the house as though she was sitting on the roof. The house was an island in a sea of darkness. The black magic churned around it like they were in the midst of a hurricane.

Ceridwen Gallagher, a voice said, sliding around her like a snake. *I told you I'd find you.*

The flap of wings startled her and she looked up. Her owl was flying toward her but a gust of hot air knocked it aside, sending it careening toward the ground.

"No!" she cried, reaching out with her magic to protect it. The sorcerer's magic whipped upward and wrapped around her ankle, yanking her from her feet. Cold seeped into her leg as it dragged her toward the edge of the roof.

The spell had grown in power tenfold. She could feel the sorcerer's evil intent in the very air. The house groaned beneath her as it strained against the relentless attack.

Inch by inch the spell dragged her to the edge. She looked over her shoulder and saw the darkness waiting for her. Its maw stretched wide open, sharp teeth and a swirling, fiery throat that eagerly lifted toward her.

How many people did you have to kill to steal this power? Ceri demanded as she held onto the roof with aching fingers.

A chuckle floated past her. *Are you jealous?*

No, I pity you.

A vicious jerk ripped her hands free and for a moment she was falling. Her view shifted once again as the house dragged her inside to protect her. Her body was shaking now, teeth chattering as her head rocked from side to side.

"It won't work!" Evangeline shouted at the demon, hands curled into tight fists.

"Try it regardless! Or would you rather die crying in the corner?" He sneered at her. "Don't be *pathetic.*"

A window shattered, glass spraying over the carpet. Ceri rushed toward it, chanting a spell of protection, but without her physical body, she was struggling to use her magic. If the spirit had been able to make it to her, she might had had a chance.

"Evangeline," Eloise said from the top of the stairs. "Look at me."

The girl turned toward her mother, eyes red with unshed tears. "I can't do this."

"Remember that lullaby I used to sing to you? The one about the castle. Sing that for me, just shut your eyes, and sing." With a pained grunt, Eloise lowered herself down to the floor and leaned against the banister, a gentle smile on her face.

Evangeline nodded tremulously and, keeping her back to the demon, began to sing. "Ah! Mon beau château…"

Her voice lifted all around them, twisting through the air as if it were pure light. Ceri had never seen anything like it, then again, she'd never watched an angel sing from the spirit realm. This was powerful magic, though not the type most people would understand. It wasn't a simple spell. It was life…power…and beauty. It was everything the sorcerer's spell wasn't.

Evangeline's magic, which was tied to the protective spell Ceri had cast, surged through their shaky bond. Her white blonde hair lifted from her shoulder and her pale skin glowed with a light that pulsed inside of her.

The lyrics didn't matter, they were nothing more than a focus for the magic inside of Evangeline. With renewed determination, Ceri took hold of the strength Evangeline was giving her, and opened the front door.

I'm going to kill you! the sorcerer howled, the darkness whipping into a frenzy.

Not today.

She lifted her hands and light poured forth.

CHAPTER 51

AMBER

Amber smashed another spider with the end of the broom. "We will, we will, smush you," she sang along with the radio, changing the lyrics to suit her current activities.

The warehouse was starting to look less like a haunted house and more like a place someone might actually want to leave their truck to have it fixed. They'd already cleared out all the trash in the main area where they'd work. She was tackling the office today.

There was a crash and she poked her head out. Tommy was sprawled out in front of a stack of now broken wooden pallets and Derek was cackling. "Told you that was too many."

"I almost had it!" Tommy hopped up to his feet and brushed the dust off his shirt.

She rolled her eyes but smiled at their antics. Her brother and Tommy got along great. He had a knack for bringing out Tommy's adventurous side that she appreciated. Between her brother and Deward, Tommy was really coming out of his shell.

Crouching down, she swept the dirt into the dustpan then headed outside to dump it. Derek had forgotten only one thing. A trash can. So, they had to get creative until he had time to go to the store and grab one.

She tossed the dirt and turned to head back inside when her phone rang. Tucking the dustpan under her arm, she pulled out her phone.

"Hey Ceri, what's––"

"Something is wrong."

Her fingers tightened on the phone as every sense jumped into high alert. That wasn't Ceri. "Evangeline? What's wrong?"

The wind shifted and the smell of something wrong blew past her. It smelled like fire and death. She stepped back outside and saw something moving in the trees. There was more than one of them, whatever they were, and they were big.

"I don't know," Evangeline said sounding frantic.

Amber felt Ceri pull on the pack bond and desperately sent her every ounce of strength she could. At the same time, a monster burst out of the trees. It wasn't like anything she'd ever seen. It was as if the earth itself had spit the thing out. Thick arms made of dirt and debris from the forest dragged along the ground as it lumbered toward her on thick, tree trunk-like legs. The thing had no eyes, but its wide, gaping mouth roared as it charged toward her.

She dropped the phone and shouted over her shoulder as she ran toward it. "Run!"

She didn't hesitate to shift. Her clothes tore and fell away as her body changed. The wolf came alive inside her, ready to fight. The creature was faster than she expected and it caught her midair with a swing of its massive fist.

Disoriented from the blow, she hit the ground and slid. With an enraged howl, she leaped back to her feet and raced after the thing. It was headed for the warehouse. Derek stood right in its path, a look of shock on his face. She wanted to scream for him to move, but she couldn't.

The creature lifted its fist, swinging it at her brother. Derek was shoved to the side and Tommy caught the blow with his side, stopping the creature's momentum completely. His teeth were bared, and a wild look was in his eye as he shoved the arm away, then shifted and lunged at its face.

Amber jumped on its back as it roared its displeasure. It reared up, trying to grab her. She dug her claws into the dirt that made up its body and bit into the back of its neck. Her mouth filled with soil and rocks and the sickly taste of magic. She spat it out and struck again, biting and tearing.

The ground shook as it stomped around, swinging its arms wildly. With one particularly vicious shake of its head, it threw her off. She hit the ground on her feet this time but was frozen in place for a moment.

Emerging from the trees were two more.

CHAPTER 52

TOMMY

Tommy saw the other two charge out of the forest and he wanted to run. There was no way they could defeat all three. They hadn't even managed to hurt the first one. There had to be something they could do to slow it down, but it wasn't made of flesh and bone. It was dirt and rock and magic.

A gunshot rang out and he dropped to the ground in a panic before he realized it was Derek. He racked his shotgun and fired again, hitting the first monster in the face and knocking it back. It seemed to stun the monster more than their attacks had.

He darted in and bit a chunk out of its ankle before hurrying back out of the reach of the thing's huge arms. It was slower than they were since it was big, but it was still faster than he'd expected. Faster than something that huge should be.

Amber charged toward the two new monsters, trying to get their attention. They roared and began following her, almost stumbling into each other in their haste to attack her. She wasn't going to be able to keep them running in circles forever though. They had to kill these things.

Derek shot the first one again, this time in the chest, and that's when Tommy saw it. There was something glowing inside it. If they couldn't damage the creature's themselves, maybe they could destroy whatever was powering them.

He yipped at Derek to get his attention so he didn't get shot, then ran toward the first creature. As soon as he got close enough, he bunched his legs up underneath himself and jumped. The force of his impact knocked the creature back slightly. He tore into its chest, ripping away chunks of dirt until he saw it.

Stars exploded behind his eyes and he felt himself flying through the air. He wasn't sure what hit him, he hadn't seen it coming. All the air rushed out of his lungs as he hit the ground, but he rolled immediately and forced himself back up to his feet.

"Stay down!" Derek shouted, reloading his shotgun as he ran. Sliding to a stop not far from Tommy, he swung the gun up to his shoulder and fired another shot. This one hit the glowing, red spot in the monster's chest.

It stumbled back, its arms flailing in panic, then it exploded. Dirt and debris flew in every direction and Tommy's ears rang painfully. He couldn't hear anything around him anymore, just his own panicked breathing.

Derek had been thrown onto his back, but he pushed himself upright and climbed back onto his feet. "Holy shit that worked. Amber! There's something in their chests!"

Tommy howled in victory, adrenaline rushing through him as he regained hope they could stop these things.

He and Derek worked like a well-oiled machine as they attacked one of the two chasing after Amber. She kept their attention, attacking as needed to make sure they kept following her.

Tommy darted in, his ears still ringing from the sounds of gunfire. He launched himself onto the back of the closest one and bit down hard on the back of its neck. It leaned back, trying to grab him as expected. Running into range, Derek swung his shotgun up to his shoulder and shot it in the chest twice, drilling a hole into the dirt.

Tommy leapt away and Derek fired again. The shot hit the thing in its chest and it exploded, tossing him a little farther than he'd expected with the resulting shockwave. The last creature turned, roaring its displeasure, and ran for Derek.

Derek, using common sense, took off at a run toward the warehouse. Amber leapt on the thing's back, but it immediately grabbed her and tossed her aside. A pulse of magic glowed within the creature, growing brighter and brighter as it ran.

As Derek ran into the warehouse, it launched itself after him in a leap that left craters behind in the soft dirt. It hit the front of the warehouse, its massive head catching on the top of the already broken roll-up door.

With one final, bright pulse, it exploded. A fireball erupted from the center of it, engulfing the front of the warehouse in flames.

Amber raced toward it, jumping through the fire without any concern for herself. Tommy followed close behind, his heart beating a million miles a minute. As he skidded through the smoke inside the building he saw Derek running for the fire extinguisher. He had survived.

∼

Tommy couldn't stop shaking even though it had been an hour, but he knew it was just the after effects of all the adrenaline that had been pumping through his body. That made it a little better, knowing that he wasn't just trembling in fear. The monsters were gone and they had all survived.

"It's a perversion of a golem." Ceri's face was drawn and pale. Dark circles stood out in stark relief under her eyes. She'd come as soon as she'd heard about the attack and filled them in on what had happened to her. "They're usually peaceful. Whatever magic was used to create them was twisted and filled with malice."

"The sorcerer did this, right?" He wrapped his arms a little tighter around his chest.

He'd started keeping a pair of shorts in Amber's truck but apparently, he needed an entire spare outfit.

She stared at the pile of rubble, her eyes unfocused. "It could be. There's just something that bothers me about it. This sorcerer is all about psychic attacks. The whole time I was under attack at the house, he was taunting me, but he never mentioned this."

The sound of an unfamiliar voice startled Tommy. He looked over his shoulder and saw a black sedan had driven up. The detective that had come by their house after the attack there was talking to Amber in the driveway. He didn't look happy. Then again, neither did she.

"I think the same sorcerer that killed Donovan did this," Amber said, hands on her hips. She was still streaked with mud. None of them had had a chance to clean up.

Ceri nodded her head toward them tiredly. "Let's go help her out."

He nodded and trailed after her. The blackened front of the warehouse loomed in front of them. So much damage had been done. The fire hadn't spread far, but it hadn't needed to.

Derek hauled a pile of charred debris out of the warehouse. His eyes flashed with anger as he tossed it onto the growing pile. He'd been mostly silent since the attack. This place meant everything to him. Having it damaged like this had to be infuriating.

They'd almost lost everything. He couldn't imagine something happening to Ceri. He curled his hand into a fist and cursed the demon and the sorcerer.

CHAPTER 53

GENEVIEVE

It had happened again. Her pack had been fighting for their lives while she was miles away, unable to get to them in time to help. She'd just hurried back to the house to find Ceri having convulsions on the living room floor. Then she'd had to stay behind to protect that demon girl while Ceri had gone to see Amber and the others.

Genevieve bit another hunk of chicken off the sticky drumstick in her hand and glared at the wall as if it were to blame.

"Did you eat that entire chicken?"

Amber's voice startled her out of her angry thoughts. She looked down at what used to be a rotisserie chicken and sighed.

"Apparently I did. Guess I'll order pizza for dinner." She tossed the bone onto the now ravaged carcass and threw the whole mess away. "Is Ceri feeling better?"

Amber shrugged. "Yeah, she's just...angry. Everybody is on edge. Evangeline is scared out of her mind."

"Tommy said he thinks she's going to try to bolt." Genevieve walked over to the fridge and pulled out two beers. If any conversation required alcohol, it was going to be this one. With all the chaos going on, it was even more important to get the stuff with Greer nailed down. And it made her feel like she was actually contributing instead of just goofing off while her friends nearly got murdered.

"She probably will. He's keeping an eye on her. As is the house," Amber said, looking around like it might hear her.

It probably could. It probably watched them all the time. She was glad it decided it liked them because living in some kind of sentient house that had it out for you was her worst nightmare.

"It's kind of cool it can do all that. Makes me wonder who put all that magic into it." She looked up at the ceiling curiously. The house was older, but it wasn't anything too special design-wise. She took a sip of her beer, then decided to get the awkwardness over with.

"So..." she paused and tried to remember how she'd wanted to phrase this. "When we were visiting the Lockhart Pack, or whatever the hell it's called now, one of them approached me. They want you to sponsor them if they can take the pack on the next full moon."

"Seriously?" Amber looked about as surprised as she'd felt that day. "Why? Not that I have the money anyhow."

"Well, I had dinner with him yesterday and asked him that very question," she said nervously.

"You're taking this request seriously?" Amber laughed and took a long drink of her beer.

Genevieve's fingers tightened on the icy cold bottle she was holding. "Yeah, I am. It's actually a really good opportunity for the pack, especially since you are on the council. We're a little bit of a target right now. I mean, honestly, we're lucky no one has come to challenge you yet."

That sobered her up a bit. "Is that common?"

She nodded. "Smaller packs don't tend to last long."

"I still don't see how I could sponsor this guy, and there's no guarantee he'd help us after we did regardless."

"According to the deal I've begun negotiating with him there..." Genevieve began, pulling her notes out of her pocket.

"You started negotiating without even talking to--"

"Slow your roll," Genevieve said, holding up her hand. "So, traditionally, a potential alpha approaches the beta of the alpha they want to sponsor them. He, uh, assumed that was me."

"Oh."

"And nothing is set in stone, these have all been preliminary negotiations. It's all part of the game, basically. I told him it wasn't even worth bringing up to you if I couldn't show you that it would help the pack in some way. And I was right," she said, giving Amber a look.

Amber snorted. "Ok, fine. I'm cynical and suspicious. What can he give us?"

"First, he will cover the sponsor fee, and we will return the funds to him if he passes the Trials. Second, a basic alliance. He won't act against us, and we won't act against him. Third, he will, personally, come to your aid any time you call to fulfill a single favor." She smirked at her alpha. "I took a little inspiration from the demon for that one."

"Lawyers, demons, same thing really," Amber said with a smirk.

"Hey! I'm trying to help here and now you're insulting me?"

Amber threw her head back and laughed. "Sorry, it was too easy."

Clearing her throat, she folded the paper back up and shoved it in her pocket. "Anyhow, that's what I have for now. You have to do the final negotiating if you agree to meet with him. And...you should also choose who is your actual beta. Though, since I started the negotiations it's probably best if I just finish it with you."

She crossed her arms and stared at Amber, waiting for some kind of response.

"This is a trap, isn't it?"

"It's not a trap. You just have to tell me who your beta is." Genevieve shrugged like it didn't matter.

"I don't know. I've never thought about it." Amber looked like she wanted to bolt. "This is worse than trying to pick your maid of honor for your wedding. Maybe I should make y'all fight for it."

Genevieve glared at her. "I'm not fighting for anything. Just pick."

Amber shook her head, her lips pressed firmly together. "Nope, not going to happen. You can deal with this little sponsor issue, then we'll just go back to normal. Nobody needs a rank."

She then fled to the living room while shouting for Ceri.

"This conversation is so not done," she muttered as she dialed the nearest pizza place, knowing full well that Amber could still hear her.

CHAPTER 54

AMBER

Rain pattered against the window in a soothing rhythm. Amber yawned as she stared absently at the gray fog outside. Maybe she could get to bed early for once.

The mark moved under her skin and she felt the demon now known as The Asshole behind her. "I see you're hard at work staring out a window now."

She rolled her eyes and turned to face him. "When are you going to stop being a dick? You were almost pleasant when you first showed up, but now you're acting like an angry sixteen-year-old girl who lost the title of Prom Queen to her little sister."

He sneered at her. "I had every right to kill you for what you did when you banished me. I'm surprised you would complain about my *tone*."

"I didn't ask the wolf to do that or help her do it. She just did it on her own! So quit fucking blaming me for it!" Amber shouted at the demon, fed up with the attitude and constant digs. Red bled into her vision as she glared at him. The urge to shift and rip something apart crawled under her skin. "If you had told me a young girl was going to be killed for being half demon, I would have helped without the damn mark. We saved her. She's here, safe and sound, and she's going to stay that way. Quit being a damn drama queen about it!"

"You have no idea how important she is!" Angel shouted back. Flames shot from his mouth and he doubled in size, as he always did when he got pissy.

"So tell me, you stubborn asshole!"

He solidified for a split second and knocked a pile of books off the table, sending them scattering across the floor. His chest heaved as he panted from the exertion of affecting the material world. He shrank as he turned away and crossed his arms. "She's my niece, as you know."

Amber sat down in her armchair but didn't reply. This had been a long time coming, and she didn't want to interrupt. She pressed the palms of her hand into her eyes until she saw stars. She *was* sorry the wolf had banished him. He had completely overreacted though, and it was hard to trust him now.

Angel floated toward the fireplace and settled in front of it, a smoky chair appearing behind him. He grew legs and sat down, crossing them at the ankle as he stretched out. He looked mostly human in this form. His face wasn't fully formed, just shifting shadows. She caught a glimpse of a strong jaw, eyes that burned red, and aquiline nose. She wondered if this was close to what he really looked like, or if it was just another illusion.

He sighed before finally speaking. "My sister, the idiot that she was, fell in love with an angel. It was a real Romeo and Juliet situation. And everyone knows how that ended."

He fell silent again and Amber looked down at her hands. She knew the pain of losing a sibling. It was something most people didn't get.

"Angels hate us. Well, everyone hates us. We're monsters. Tricksters that are after your soul." He snorted and shook his head. "Nobody knows or cares about the truth."

"Are you saying you aren't after people's souls?" Amber asked, skeptical. It was indisputable that a deal with a demon came at the price of a demon mark. If you failed to fulfill your end of the bargain, you died. What happened to your soul was debatable, but she doubted it was good.

"It's complicated," he said, waving away her question. "Evangeline was never supposed to be born. She's an embarrassment for the angels. There have been others like her in the past, but none of them ever made it past infancy."

She looked up sharply. "The angels killed them?"

He nodded slowly. "Killed them and their parents. That threat is enough to deter most romances, but not all of them. Some people are too stupid to be helped."

"Why do the angels hate you so much?"

Angel stood and ignored her question for a second time. "I have things I need to do. Get some sleep."

"Why can't you just be honest with me?" she asked quietly. She wanted him to give her a reason not to kill him. The thought of it still made her sick to her stomach, but she didn't know if that was because he was manipulating her, or if it was because her instincts about him were right.

He paused, glancing back over his shoulder. "It's for your own good."

CHAPTER 55

TOMMY

Tommy had been paying attention, and he knew what she was going to do. It's what he would have done in her situation, what he almost did. If Amber hadn't come back early that day he'd be wandering in the woods somewhere as an omega.

He stood outside her window and waited quietly. Evangeline was zipping up the backpack she'd taken from his room earlier that day. He had no clue why she thought she could get away with it, but she seemed more stubborn than smart. She was too angry to think anything through clearly.

The window slid open and the screen flew out, follow by the backpack, then her foot. He crossed his arms and waited for her to hop down. She straightened her jacket, pulling her hoodie farther down over her face, and picked up the backpack.

"Nice backpack," he said in a normal tone.

She jumped with a strangled yelp and whipped around to face him. "What the hell are you doing out here?"

"Convincing you to not run away and getting back my backpack. Not gonna lie, it was a little crappy of you to steal it after I took a bullet for you."

Her eyes flashed with anger and she didn't look the least bit remorseful. "Just buy a new one. I'm not staying, and neither is your backpack."

"No, you need to stay here and stop being an idiot."

"I'll be better off alone, and everyone will be safer with me gone. Get your fake mom to buy you a new backpack," she said with a sneer.

"You're going overboard with the whole tragic, teenager thing," he said, shoving his hands in his pocket.

"Excuse me?"

He shrugged. "You're a demon, and you don't have any control over that. But the whole woe-is-me act is getting old."

"Woe is me? Seriously? I have people actively hunting me because one of my dead parents was a demon, and you're mocking me? You have no idea what it's like--"

"We're a brand new pack that everyone already distrusted simply because we were bitten and not born. I know exactly what it's like to be an outcast. And now, I have a monster in my head that likes the taste of blood, and every time I get angry, I think I might lose control." His voice rose with every word until he was practically shouting. "You've been a total ass to every single person around you since we rescued you. We're all having a shitty week. Do you think anyone wanted to deal with this? "

"So just let me leave!"

"If you leave and get hurt, not only will it devastate Eloise, but it will *kill* Amber."

Evangeline yanked the backpack off her shoulder and threw it on the ground. "What am I supposed to do then? Just sit in my bedroom and hope for the best?"

"Yes. Stay optimistic, help your mother heal, and learn how to control whatever magic you have. And maybe try admitting that you're sick."

She looked at him, expression furious with her lips pressed into a thin line. "It's not that easy."

"I never said it was easy, but running away isn't going to help anything. It's just going to get someone hurt and break your mother's heart. Did you even think about how she'd feel when she woke up in the morning and you were gone?" She had no idea how lucky she was to still have her mother. He'd never left his mother's side when she was sick. He'd stayed as her hair fell out and her skin grew pale. He'd stayed when his dad escaped into the bottle. He'd stayed until she took her last breath. There was no way he'd let Evangeline run away from this when she still had a chance to be with her mother.

"You don't understand what Kadrithan wants from me," Evangeline said quietly.

Tommy sighed. "Then tell me."

She looked away and shook her head. "Can I at least sit outside for a while? I'm going stir crazy in there."

He wanted to shake the truth out of her, but if he pressed now, he knew she'd just clam up. She was stubborn like that. "Fine, but I'm staying with you."

She turned on her heel and walked toward the porch without responding. He followed, shoving his hands in his pockets and wishing he was a mind reader instead of a shifter.

CHAPTER 56

GENEVIEVE

Genevieve's palms were sweating, but she was managing to keep her face straight at least. Having to sit here silently while Amber negotiated this part was killing her. Maybe she should have taped her mouth shut before they started, just to remove the temptation.

Amber didn't look nervous at all. If anything, she looked bored. "Honestly, if I came here just to quibble over the details of an alliance, I will consider this time wasted."

She had to actually bite her tongue after that comment. Cool and untouchable was good, apathetic was not. They had talked about this beforehand, but Amber was already striking out on her own and *improvising*.

Greer snorted and shook his head. "You're too impatient. The details are what matters in this agreement, unless you want to end up having to take over my pack in the event of my death?"

"Then let's make this clear and simple." Amber grabbed a fresh sheet of paper and numbered it one through three. "First, I don't act against your pack, and you don't act against mine. Second, if I have any knowledge of someone that intends to harm you or your pack, I tell you. You do the same. Third, in the event of my death, you agree to sponsor my chosen successor if they successfully claim the position, and vice versa."

Amber pushed the paper toward him and leaned back, crossing her arms. Paul reread each of the points, tapping his finger against his cheek thoughtfully. This was exactly what she and Amber had talked about earlier. The alliance would help them, without requiring them to exert much time or energy. It was the perfect balance for a small, isolated pack like theirs.

This all depended on Paul now. She couldn't quite read him despite the research she'd done. He kept a cool, thoughtful expression on his face, making him look almost bored at some points in the conversation. The only time she'd gotten him to break was the other day when she'd brought up his last try at being an alpha.

His eyes flicked up to hers, then he turned his attention to Amber once again. He extended his hand toward her. "I accept."

Amber shook his hand firmly, sealing the deal once and for all. Werewolf agreements were always sealed with a handshake. If you couldn't be trusted to uphold your word, then you were worthless in the werewolf community.

"Is that it?" Amber asked.

Genevieve nodded. "Now Paul just has to win his challenge, and pass the Trials, of course."

"I'm not concerned with either," he said, rising from his seat.

"Glad we worked this out. You aren't half bad, Paul," Amber said with a smile.

He chuckled as they all headed out to the parking lot. "You're just as determined as I expected."

As they exited, Genevieve paused in front of the door. "Thank you for reaching out, and for meeting with us today."

Paul looked at her, a genuine smile turning up the corners of his mouth. "It was a pleasure."

"See you around," she replied with a self-satisfied smile.

"Absolutely."

She turned and headed toward the truck, jogging to catch up to Amber. Maybe she wasn't really Amber's beta, but for today she had been, and she hadn't let her down. The pack was better off than it was the day before and it was because she'd figured out what needed to be done and had helped her alpha. She could get used to this.

CHAPTER 57

AMBER

High on the thrill of actually accomplishing something as an alpha, Amber wrapped Genevieve up in a big hug. "We did it!"

Genevieve stiffened with surprise for a moment, then returned the hug with gusto and actually lifted Amber off her feet, swinging her around in a circle. "You owned that negotiation! Even though you deviated from our plan of attack which you *specifically* agreed not to do." Genevieve lost her grip and Amber almost tripped over her own feet trying to save herself from falling.

"I'm the alpha! I'm supposed to negotiate!" she objected. "I get no respect around here. Bunch of unruly werewolves."

Tommy walked in at that moment and stopped, looking at them suspiciously. "Why do you two look so happy?"

"Something has gone right for a change," Amber said, heading toward the kitchen. She was pretty sure Tommy had been stress baking again, so there should be more pie. As suspected, a fresh one was on the stove, still cooling. "Oh, did you make apple this time?"

"Yeah, but what happened?"

Ceri walked into the kitchen carrying Captain Jack who was straining to reach Woggy on top of her head. The pixie had ahold of her hair like reins and was taunting the cat by staying just out of reach.

Amber waved a hand at Genevieve. "You explain."

Genevieve happily launched into an explanation of not only the meeting they'd just had with Paul Greer, but also everything that had led up to it. Amber dug out a piece of pie and listened contentedly. She'd been worried about Tommy after the fight at the warehouse the day before, but with all them together right now, the pack bond was practically purring with contentment. Her pack still felt safe together.

Derek had borrowed her truck and met Bernard for coffee this afternoon to discuss the damage to the warehouse. She took a big bite of pie to distract herself from thinking about that anymore. She was furious that someone targeting her had damaged something so important to her brother. He'd taken a huge risk coming out here with her to start a business, and so far, it wasn't exactly paying off.

The road that went past their house wasn't very busy, but a few cars still drove by every hour. She had learned to tune out the noise unless one slowed, or turned down their driveway. She frowned as a vehicle that definitely was not her truck slowed and drove into their driveway.

"Who is that?" As soon as she spoke, she realized there was more than one car. There were at least three.

Tommy frowned. "I have no idea. It's not Deward."

She set her pie down and walked to the living room, peeking out the window. Her heart dropped into her stomach. "The police are here."

Ceri dropped Captain Jack and ran upstairs. "Give me two minutes before they come in!"

Amber turned back to the others and tried to remember how to breathe. They had to be here for Evangeline. "You two should leave. Go out the back. Can you carry Eloise?"

"I'm not going anywhere. And they aren't coming in this house without a warrant," Genevieve said stubbornly.

There was a bark from outside and Amber cursed, looking outside the window again. They'd brought a K9 unit. There's no way they could sneak Eloise and Evangeline out the back now, the dogs would notice immediately. Ceri had better be working some serious magic up there.

The demon mark twitched under her skin and Angel appeared. Because, of course, this needed to become even more complicated.

"Why are the police here?" the demon demanded.

She glared at him. "If I knew that, we would have been gone before they showed up."

"Are you talking to the demon again?" Tommy asked, staring hard at the air next to her.

"Yes." She let the curtain fall back as Detective Sloan stepped out of the first car. She was starting to get sick of this guy showing up. It was never good news.

"That is so creepy," Tommy muttered.

"What do I do?" Amber asked, looking at Genevieve.

"Answer the door like normal. If he asks to come in, ask for a warrant. Be polite."

Amber nodded and took a deep breath to steady her nerves. She really should have asked Shane how he slowed his heart rate like that. This would have been a great moment to look perfectly calm.

There was a brisk knock at the door. "Police, open up!"

"You cannot let them in! Evangeline is just upstairs. Why haven't you gotten her out?" Angel demanded as she walked toward the front door.

"Shut up and trust me."

She opened the door wide, but stood in the center of the doorway and crossed her arms, looking Detective Sloan in the eye. Behind him, six other officers were waiting, one of them heading toward the side of the house with his police dog.

"I would ask if there's been another alpha death, but something tells me you didn't bring all these people with you just to update me on the case," Amber said drily. Her heart was pounding in her chest.

"An anonymous tip was called in, naming you and your pack as harboring Evangeline Bissett. I have a warrant to search the house." He lifted an official looking piece of paper to emphasize his point. "Please step aside, I don't want this to get ugly." The detective looked run down. His suit was wrinkled and the lines around his eyes had deepened since the last time she'd seen him; when he'd been warning her about Donovan's murder.

"You can let him in now," Ceri whispered from the bottom of the stairs, just loud enough for her enhanced hearing to pick up.

"It's not going to get ugly, but I would like to see that warrant," Amber said, stepping back and inviting him inside. She had to trust Ceri right now. There was no time for arguing or worrying. The police were coming in whether she wanted them to or not.

"If they find her, you are dead," the demon threatened, furious at her compliance.

She ignored him and waved the detective inside. "We have nothing to hide."

Angel practically growled at that remark. He circled the detective as he walked in, trying to read the warrant over his shoulder.

"I'd like to see the warrant," Genevieve said, holding out her hand. She and the detective stepped to the side, and he handed over the piece of paper.

Ceri grabbed Amber's arm and dragged her back a few steps. "The house is helping."

"What?"

"Shh, just...act normal. The house won't let the police find them," Ceri whispered quickly before walking away and joining Genevieve and the detective.

Amber stood off to the side watching two officers head upstairs, with Angel following close behind, her heart pounding in her chest. How the hell was she supposed to act normal in the midst of possibly breaking her deal with a demon?

She heard her bedroom door open and had to dig her nails into her palm to keep from running over and demanding they get out. She'd always hated people going into her private spaces, but that feeling was amplified by the wolf's instincts. Everything inside her was screaming that there were intruders in her home. Her den. The wolf snarled impatiently as she stared down the hallway.

"What the hell is that?" One of the officers demanded, sounding alarmed.

"Oh crap, Woggy." Ceri jogged toward her room. "Do not hurt that pixie!"

"No, the...is that a cat?" he sounded even more appalled.

Captain Jack hissed loudly before being shushed by Ceri.

No one upstairs was shouting yet, so that must mean they hadn't found Evangeline or Eloise. She focused intently on her hearing and realized she couldn't even hear their heartbeats anymore. What the hell had Ceri, or the house, done with them?

Amber was distracted by the sound of her truck pulling into the driveway. She wanted to pull out her phone and warn Derek, but she thought it would look suspicious. Frustrated, she headed toward the front door so she could at least meet him outside so he didn't panic.

He parked haphazardly in the middle of the driveway and jumped out of the truck. She jogged toward him and managed to intercept him before he made it to the porch.

"What the hell is going on?" He was practically shouting. So much for not panicking.

"They have a warrant because someone claims we have that demon girl they were talking about on the news in our house. It's total bullshit, but I had to let them in," she said, trying to sound as exasperated as possible.

A muscle in Derek's jaw jumped as he ground his teeth tightly together, but he stopped freaking out. "Who is trying to pin this on you?"

She shrugged. "No clue, though I could probably make a couple of guesses. One of the council members has been kind of pissy since I made it through the Trials."

Detective Sloan walked out of the front door and headed over to them. He held out his hand to Derek. "Detective Sloan, I don't believe we've met."

"Derek Hale," her brother said shortly as he shook the man's hand.

"I need to talk to your sister alone for a moment," Sloan said, putting his hands in his pockets.

Amber almost agreed but decided that with Derek's current level of anger, it might be better if he stayed. "My brother can hear anything you might have to say, if it's all the same to you."

Derek looked surprised at that.

Sloan shrugged. "Alright." He sighed again and scratched his bristly jaw. "I didn't want to run this warrant. The tip that got called in was clearly from someone that had it out for you, in my opinion, but it wasn't my decision to make."

"Who was it?"

He shook his head regretfully. "I can't tell you that. Just keep an eye out, alright? I shouldn't be warning you about this at all, but my investigation into Lockhart's death is turning up some weird inconsistencies with the other murders. I don't think they're connected, but I can't prove it. Yet."

"There's a second sorcerer?" she asked in surprise.

"I think so."

"Are they working together?" Derek asked.

The detective shrugged. "I don't know. Sorcerers are generally loners, but they could be working together for a time. It's impossible to tell right now. Just watch your back, alright?"

She nodded. "Thanks for the warning. You keep going out of your way for me, and I appreciate that."

He smiled ruefully. "My sister was bitten, like you. I wish she'd managed to find an alpha."

"Is she an omega?"

"No, she killed herself before they could put her in the System." He nodded and walked off, his shoulders hunched with exhaustion.

Amber watched him go, her arms wrapped tightly around her. "We should get back inside."

"How--"

"Later," she said sharply.

They walked silently back toward the house. In her peripheral vision, she saw a curl of smoke drifted up from Thallan's porch. She almost hadn't seen him watching from the shadows.

She frowned. Maybe she was wrong about who had called in the tip. The alpha council and Selena Blackwood weren't the only people with reasons to hate her. Thallan wanted to punish the demon and didn't care who got hurt in the meantime.

CHAPTER 58

CERI

Ceri almost walked into a wall. The house was showing her everything all at once, laid over her own vision, and it was extremely disorienting.

Hiding Evangeline and Eloise had been fairly simple, but it definitely wasn't easy. The house's wards had come alive as soon as the police had pulled into the driveway. It sensed their intent and had reacted to protect them. With only a little coaxing, the room Eloise and Evangeline were in had simply...disappeared. They were still here, but they also weren't. She wasn't sure where the house had put them and was trying not to think too hard about it.

The police had been here for almost an hour already. Most of the nerves had faded into frustration and boredom. She was also tiring from the effort of maintaining a connection to the house, but she couldn't risk letting it go.

Amber had planted herself in the middle of the living room and was simply glaring at everyone touching all her things. Genevieve was following Detective Sloan around prying for further information. She glanced over at Tommy. He was holding up surprisingly well but had hidden in the kitchen with Woggy and Captain Jack. That was probably for the best.

One of the officers walked down the stairs, then waved Sloan over. "They're not here. We've searched the place up and down. Carter even cast a finding spell and she came up empty-handed."

Ceri could barely contain her sigh of relief. Now, if they could all just leave she could finally release the magic.

The front door popped open and Detective Sloan looked back at it, brows furrowed.

"Oh, sorry, it does that," Ceri said with a slightly hysterical laugh as she hurried over to close it. "So windy out here."

"Windy. Right," Sloan said skeptically.

The house pouted a little and she tried to send reassuring thoughts. It had only been trying to help, but that was only going to cause more questions.

She surreptitiously patted the wall behind her back like she was soothing a nervous dog. Sometimes the house felt a little like a dog. Eager to please, extremely social, and boisterous. The more she connected to it, the more alive it became as well.

"Alright, make sure you put everything back where you found it, and let's get back to the station. We all have a lot of paperwork to do tonight," Sloan said loudly.

The officers started heading outside one by one until only Sloan was left. Thankfully, they hadn't torn the place apart completely. They had been thorough, but under Sloan's watchful eye, each of them was considerate about the way they conducted the search.

Sloan paused in the doorway and nodded in Amber's direction. "I hope I don't see you again anytime soon."

Amber snorted. "Likewise. Have a good day."

He walked out and the door slammed shut behind him. And locked. Ceri cringed, but Sloan didn't turn around. He seemed as eager to leave as they were to have him go.

"What the hell was that?" Genevieve whispered.

"The house is...eager for them to be gone," Ceri said quietly. "Amber, can I let Eloise and Evangeline out yet?"

"Wait for them to be off the property," Amber said, listening intently to the cars drive away with her head cocked to the side.

It was a painfully long minute as they all waited with bated breath for the last car to drive away. As soon as Amber nodded, Ceri darted upstairs and pressed her hands against the blank wall where their room used to be. It was simply gone as if it had never been built. The magic was similar to The Market, the way it compressed space without the slightest consideration for the laws of physics.

"Where is their room?" Amber asked in alarm.

"One second," Ceri said, panting with exertion as she coaxed the house to release them. It was a little nervous, and required some reassurances, but finally it groaned and everything snapped back into place.

She stumbled back and finally dropped the connection to the house. Her vision cleared and she blinked rapidly, feeling disoriented all over again.

The door to the bedroom flew open and Evangeline burst out of the room panting, her hair wild. "Never do that again."

Ceri rushed over. "Where were you? Are you hurt?"

"We were...flat. It's like it just...squished us. But it didn't hurt it just...mush..." Evangeline could barely speak, she just kept bringing her palms together like she was crushing something between them and shaking her head.

"This house is weird," Genevieve muttered, looking around suspiciously.

Ceri glared at her. "It saved all our asses today, be nice. Tell her she did a good job."

"Are you serious?"

"Yes."

Genevieve sighed but looked around with a softer expression. "Thank you."

Ceri felt the house perk up. The picture frames in the hall all jiggled happily, which made Gen's face go pale.

"She's happy," Ceri said gently. "She likes it when we talk to her."

Genevieve gave her a fearful look and nodded, then hurried back downstairs.

"Do you want some pie?" Tommy asked tentatively.

Evangeline gave him a hateful look. "Don't even talk about food to me. I think I'm going to barf."

Ceri laughed and glanced downstairs, realizing Amber had disappeared. She was arguing quietly with someone only she could see. Fear twisted in her gut even though the danger had passed. This had been close. Too close.

CHAPTER 59

⊗

CERI

Ceri hadn't slept in almost twenty-four hours. Her body still ached and every sound and shadow made her twitchy. She couldn't relax until this sorcerer was gone.

Which was why she was standing on the sidewalk outside of a nightclub at one a.m. Her cousin, Siobhan, was holding court in there, and had summoned her here with promises of information. This wasn't the type of place she wanted to bring Amber, or any of the rest of the pack.

She'd gotten the message when everyone was asleep, and had used a spell to leave without anyone noticing. Derek might have seen her leave, but he hadn't said anything if he had. The thought of Derek made her head hurt even worse. She just needed to find out what Siobhan knew, then she could head back to the house and tell the pack. The note on her nightstand let them know where she was just in case something went wrong. But that was unlikely.

She sighed and headed toward the back door of the club. Her hair was a frizzy, curly mess, and she was wearing leggings under an old, beige cardigan, but tonight she did not care. Siobhan could mock her all she wanted as long as she told her where the sorcerer was so she could end this nightmare.

The back door was the employee entrance, but it wasn't locked, as usual. One of the shot girls looked up curiously, but didn't ask any questions. People were always coming and going back here, and she didn't look like someone trying to sneak into the club.

Bass thumped overhead, a never-ending beat since the club never closed. Vampires had lobbied hard for that win years ago. After all, two a.m. was just the middle of the day for them. They owned most of the nicer clubs now and found both their living and their daily meal in them.

She pushed the door that led from the break room into the club open and the music grew louder. The neon, flashing lights hurt her eyes as she looked around, trying to remember where the VIP section was. She'd always come here already drunk when she was younger, so some of her memories on the layout were a little fuzzy.

An argument just loud enough to carry over the DJ caught her attention and she saw a group of three, well-dressed young women getting turned away by a bouncer. Behind him was a short staircase roped off from the rest of the place. It led up to the VIP section that had the best view of the peasants that couldn't afford to gain access to it.

Wading into the crowd was like getting sucked back in time. She brushed off the memories and walked faster, using her elbows as needed to get people out of her way. No one was paying attention to anything other than their drink or potential one-night stand. Or their next meal.

As she brushed past the girls that had gotten rejected by the bouncer, she heard one of them giggling about her outfit. The bouncer also raised an eyebrow when he saw her approaching, but that she expected.

She stood on her tiptoes and shouted into the bouncer's ear. "Siobhan sent for me."

He nodded and lifted the velvet rope, allowing her to pass.

"Are you serious? You're letting *her* in?" the giggler from before complained.

The bouncer ignored her and placed the rope back in its place. They were lucky they couldn't get in. Maybe one day they'd realize that, but until then, a little disappointment on a Friday night wouldn't kill them. Unlike what was up here.

This place was owned by Bram -- another reason she was pissed Shane had taken Amber to see him -- but he didn't bother running it. He left that to his lackeys and just raked in the money. Siobhan was a staple here, and in most of the vampire's bedrooms. She didn't care about that though; her cousin could sleep with whoever she wanted. It was the drugs she sold to naive college students that made her mad.

She reached the top step and paused to look around. Everything was cast in shadow up here. Even the music wasn't quite as loud, though it was still enough to keep anyone from overhearing your conversation.

In the far corner she spotted her cousin sitting in the lap of a vampire. Siobhan noticed her at about the same time and whispered something in her conquest's ear, then stood. The vampire left and Siobhan sat back down on the loveseat alone. Ready to get this over with, Ceri marched over to her, trying to ignore the ever-increasing headache.

Siobhan draped her arm over the back of the loveseat and watched her approach, looking elegant as always. She had on some sparkly black number that was just long enough to qualify as a dress. Barely. "Dear cousin, I thought you'd never get here."

"You're lucky I came at all at this hour," Ceri muttered, inspecting the other two chairs for signs of bodily fluids before picking the one closest and sitting down.

"Don't be silly, I know you're desperate." Siobhan shifted her weight and swung her legs off the couch.

She wanted to punch her in the face. Maybe she could beat the information out of her. "Get to the point, Siobhan."

"I think I like watching you squirm." Siobhan grinned, something manic glinting in her eyes. "I can't believe you got in here wearing that atrocious cardigan. I mean, honestly. You could have thrown on a dress."

"Yes, I'm sure it's truly shocking. You'll live," she said shortly, rubbing her fingers against her temple. She was surprised her cousin hadn't gone after her hair first. Siobhan knew that was a sore spot. She'd said as much the last time they saw each other.

"I think I should get my payment first," her cousin said abruptly, leaning back and crossing her arms.

Ceri raised her brow. "No way in hell. Tell me where he is and then I'll give you the…" she hesitated, just for a moment, a gut feeling of worry cutting through the mental fog. "I'll give you the spell my mother made."

Siobhan sighed, pushing out her bottom lip in a pout. "Fine, but only because you're too much of a goody two-shoes to screw me over."

She forced herself to keep a blank expression on her face, but her heart started pounding in her chest. This wasn't her cousin. Not only did she know that Ceri would screw her over given even half a chance, goody two shoes or not, Siobhan knew the spell she wanted was made by their grandmother. That's not a slip of the tongue she would have ignored.

"Well? Where is he?" Ceri asked, quickly pulling magic into the palm of her hand. She'd have to fight her way out of here somehow. If she could manage a diversion, she might have a chance of succeeding.

The woman who was not her cousin looked at her carefully, her smile growing wider. The pretense fell away and she changed her posture, crossing her legs and sitting up straight. "You know I'm not going to tell you that."

"Who are you?"

"Someone you shouldn't have screwed over," the impostor said with a vicious grin.

The attack didn't come from across from her, it came from behind. A quick prick against the back of her neck before a defensive spell could leave her fingertips. Everything went black.

CHAPTER 60

GENEVIEVE

Genevieve pulled up a fifth news report but it didn't have any new information. What she really needed was the actual police report. There was no way she could get her hands on it though. She didn't know any of the officers well enough to get a favor like that.

Detective Sloan had told Amber he didn't think the same sorcerer had killed Donovan that had killed the others. That begged the question of whether the sorcerer they'd been fighting had killed Donovan, or the others. Or both. Sloan could be wrong after all.

She yawned, covering her mouth with the back of her hand, and wondered how her life had come to this. Awake early on her day off investigating a murder. The house was quiet. Tommy, Amber, and Derek were asleep. Ceri must have gone somewhere early this morning, because she was already gone when Genevieve woke up. Sometimes she disappeared into the woods on a walk when she couldn't sleep, something about *communing with nature*.

A door upstairs opened and someone started down the stairs. She glanced over her shoulder when they stopped.

Evangeline stood at the bottom of the stairs and looked around uncomfortably. She tugged down the hood of her jacket. "Have you seen Ceri?"

"Not recently, why?"

"She comes every morning to give my mom her pain meds and she hasn't shown up. Mom woke up and she's really hurting now."

Genevieve frowned. That wasn't like Ceri. She was a total mother hen as soon as someone got hurt.

"Maybe she's in her room," Genevieve said. She suspected that Ceri occasionally soundproofed her room with magic. There were times where her heartbeat would vanish abruptly or a conversation would end mid-sentence. It was subtle, but she paid attention.

Knowing how sleep-deprived Ceri had been recently, she very well could have fallen asleep with the spell up, or be in one of her weird visions and lost track of time.

She set her laptop aside and uncurled from the couch. Evangeline followed her to Ceri's room. She knocked twice and waited. There was no response.

Frowning, she pressed her ear to Ceri's door. The witch wasn't in there but she could hear Woggy snoring.

"Is she there or not? My mom needs another dose of that pain medication she makes," Evangeline repeated impatiently.

"I heard you the first time, give me a minute." She pushed the door open and looked around, sniffing the air. It smelled so much like Ceri in here it was hard to tell how long she'd been gone. Nothing seemed out of place, just the normal clutter. Except for the note on the bed.

"What's going on?" Tommy asked, appearing in the doorway behind her.

Genevieve ignored him and grabbed the note. It had been written quickly and was almost illegible.

Going to Redrum, a nightclub in town. Siobhan called. Will be back by three a.m.

Her hands shook as she reread the note again, hoping she'd misunderstood. But she hadn't. Ceri was supposed to be home five hours ago.

"Gen, what's wrong?" Tommy demanded, shoving past Evangeline into the room.

She thrust the note at him then ran to Amber's room, banging her fist on the door. "AMBER!"

The door flew open a second later and Amber stood in the doorway, wild-eyed, wearing her pajamas. "What's wrong?"

"Ceri isn't here, and she left a note saying she was going to go see someone, her cousin I think, last night, but she'd be home by three a.m. She isn't here. She's gone." She stood there panting with her hands shaking. This couldn't be happening. She didn't want to believe it but every instinct she had was screaming at her that something was wrong.

Amber's face went hard and she ran back into her room, quickly changing clothes. "Where did she go to meet Siobhan? I don't feel her through the pack bond. Like nothing. I didn't notice until you said something."

"Someplace called Redrum, I don't know. She said it was a nightclub?"

"We'll go there first." Amber ran out of her room and shouted for Derek.

Genevieve's head was spinning as she ran to the front door and pulled on her tennis shoes. She was wearing shorts and a tank top but there was no time to change. If the sorcerer had taken Ceri she may not even be alive. The fact that Amber couldn't feel her through the pack bond made her want to vomit. She couldn't be gone. She just couldn't.

Tommy was standing in the middle of the living room with his hands balled into fists. She realized he was about to lose control and ran over, wrapping him in a tight hug to ground him.

"We're going to find her. I promise," she said, squeezing him even tighter.

"You can't know that. She could already be--"

"Shut up. She's always saying to be optimistic. So do that for her, okay?"

Tommy nodded, and his breathing slowed a little. "Okay."

Evangeline was hovering awkwardly behind him looking both terrified and angry. She couldn't blame her.

Derek barreled down the stairs holding a shotgun. Another pistol was tucked in the waistband of his pants and his other hand held a massive tire iron. "I'm going with you and I'm not going to argue about it. You'll need help, and if you say a human won't be able to help, I'll deck you."

"What about Eloise and Evangeline?" Genevieve asked as she stepped away from Tommy.

Amber dragged her hands through her hair. "Tommy, I need you to stay."

"You can't be serious!" He looked angrier than she'd ever seen him before, but Amber was right to choose him. He was the best one to stay here. Evangeline trusted him more than the rest of them.

"We cannot leave her alone. If this is a trap, they may come here, too. I need you. Please," Amber pleaded, desperation clear in her eyes.

Tommy still looked unhappy but nodded reluctantly. "Fine, I'll stay."

"Thank you." Amber jogged over to the front door and grabbed her keys, then headed outside at a run.

Genevieve and Derek ran after her, but pausing at the front door, Genevieve looked back at Tommy. "Call Deward. If you think he can be trusted. I don't like you being here alone."

He nodded. "I will."

Genevieve pulled the front door shut and ran after Amber and Derek. As soon as they piled into the truck, she pulled out her phone and texted two people. Amber would probably kill her for this, but this was their chance to prove to the council what was happening.

Shane replied right away.

CHAPTER 61

CERI

Ceri woke up choking. She rolled to the side only to be stopped by arm restraints. Pushing up as far as she could, she vomited over her shoulder. It hit the floor with a wet splatter. Her chest heaved as she tried to catch her breath.

They'd dosed her with something at the nightclub to knock her out, which explained the vomiting. Her magic was trying to purge the poison from her body to protect her.

Wherever she was, it was dark. She couldn't see anything, not even her hand where it was tied to the cold, stone slab she was laying on. Closing her eyes to block out the oppressive darkness, she wiggled her toes just to make sure they were there, then did a mental check on the state of her injuries.

Everything still ached and she somehow felt even more tired than before, but whoever had taken her hadn't hurt her more. Yet. Lying there, alone in a cold, dark room, the fear began to creep in. Her imagination filled in all the ways they could hurt her. All the things a sorcerer might do before taking her heart and killing her. Pain and blood powered their black magic spells and it was easier if they could use someone else's.

Frustrated tears rolled down her cheeks. She should have seen this coming, but she'd walked right into the trap. She'd gone to see Siobhan without her pack, like an idiot. Though, part of her was thankful Amber hadn't come. She probably couldn't have stopped them either. Maybe it was better if only *she* died.

She had to get out of here. There were spells she could use, though they were harder tied up and weakened like she was. Giving up just wasn't an option. This was not how she was going to die.

Gritting her teeth, she pulled magic into her hands. Unlocking whatever held her wrists was step one. If she could get her hands free, she could find her way out.

"Conminuo," she whispered, pushing her magic into the shackle. It grew warm, struggling to hold its shape under the pressure of the spell. Using a spell like this without a ritual or any spell ingredients was extremely difficult. It would take time and patience.

She repeated the spell and pushed harder the second time, regaining a little of her energy. Whatever they'd dosed her with was continuing to wear off. She pushed, and rested, over and over. Finally, the hinge creaked slightly.

Hope bloomed in her chest. She almost had it, and they didn't know she was awake. Perhaps the drug had worn off faster than expected. She began pooling the magic in her palms once again, focusing hard on drawing enough to finish the job.

"Conmi--"

Agonizing pain exploded over her arm and chest. She screamed, jerking away from the green fire spreading over her body. It illuminated the room with a sickly color, revealing a figure standing in the corner.

Ceri thrashed under the attack, trying to get away, and unable to focus her magic to stop whatever was happening to her while in so much pain. The figure threw their head back and laughed, then the fire vanished, disappearing without a trace.

"You were so close. I could practically see the hope on your sniveling little face," the voice from the darkness hissed. "That makes failure all the more painful, doesn't it? Being so close you can practically taste it, then having it all ripped away."

Ceri ground her teeth together and glared in the direction the voice had come from. "Who the hell are you?"

"I already told you. Someone you shouldn't have screwed over." A light flicked on overhead, casting light throughout the room. Selena stood before her, clutching a wooden wand. Her long, beautiful black hair had been shaved off. Her delicate features were sallow, as though she hadn't been getting enough food or sun. Gone was the glittery black dress she'd worn in the club. It was replaced by dirty jeans and a threadbare shirt that hung off her frame. "You have no idea what you did to me, do you?"

Selena prowled closer, holding the wand in her hand. Ceri's eyes followed it fearfully. The witch stopped a few feet away, green eyes boring into her.

"I thought at first that you were doing it for your coven. That you thought it was a way to reclaim the prominence your coven had once had, but then..." Selena laughed hysterically, but there was no humor on her face. "Then I realized it was all over a stupid, fucking pixie. You ruined my life over a pest."

"You got me fired and tried to kill--"

"SHUT UP!" Selena pointed the wand at her again and the green flames spread over her stomach, eating through the fabric of her shirt.

Ceri held back the scream by sheer force of will. Her teeth dug into her inner cheek and her mouth filled with blood as the pain coursed through her. As abruptly as it started, it stopped, and she was left panting.

"I was showing you your place in the world! You had overstepped, and you should have known better. You don't cross the Blackwood coven." Selena took three quick steps toward her and grabbed a handful of her hair, wrenching her head up harshly. She leaned in close, her face flushed with anger and hate burning in her eyes. "Did you think I wouldn't come after you for what you did?"

Ceri spat in her face. The resulting slap rocked her head back against the stone slab and stars exploded across her vision. She tasted blood.

"I am going to watch you scream while Caligo cuts out your heart and I won't feel anything but glee," Selena sneered, wiping her hand off on her dress. "Or maybe we'll make you watch Amber die first. She's a pathetic excuse for an alpha, but you're the real embarrassment here. I didn't think even *you* were pathetic enough to join a werewolf pack. You've sunk so low."

Blinking to try and clear her vision, she tried to make sense of what Selena had said. "You're working for him?"

"No, I just sold you. I'll get a bonus if your pack comes for you and then I can buy my way back into my coven. Money covers a multitude of sins," Selena said with a particularly nasty grin. "And as a free perk, I get to make you suffer."

"Where is my cousin?"

Selena dug the wand into her cheek and pushed her head in the opposite direction. The sight that met her eyes made her want to scream, or cry. She had no love for Siobhan, but this was too awful to wish on anyone.

The long auburn hair she'd loved so much had been hacked off. Her eyes were gone and her mouth was locked in a silent scream. She was dead now, but she hadn't been when her eyes were taken. She'd been alive when they'd cut out her heart. When they had ripped her magic from her body.

"It's horrible, isn't it?" Selena whispered directly into her ear.

Ceri jerked away from her, looking at the woman in horror. "You're sick."

"And you're going to die." Selena lifted the wand again and Ceri braced for the pain, wishing she was already dead.

CHAPTER 62

AMBER

Amber grabbed the bouncer by his jacket and jerked him forward so hard he lost his footing. "You either let me in, or I'm going to rip off your arms and beat you to death with them you piece of shit––"

Genevieve got in between them and shoved her back, and kept a hand on both of them to hold them apart. "My packmate disappeared from here early this morning, around one a.m. We need to talk to someone, or look at video surveillance."

He shoved Genevieve's hand away angrily and sneered at her. "We don't have video surveillance. And you're sure as hell not walking in there now. You can leave or I'm calling the police and pressing assault charges."

Amber growled and her vision bled red. She was two seconds away from shifting right there and forcing her way inside.

"Amber, enough!" Angel shouted. He swooped in front of her, blocking her view of the bouncer and Genevieve. "Ceri is counting on you, if you lose your shit in public, she will die."

"They can help us!"

Angel rolled his eyes. "You don't need him. All you need are your senses. Find her scent. Her car is parked right over there, so you know she made it here. Stop and think."

She jerked around, seeing Ceri's car for the first time and felt like an idiot. Dragging her hand down her face, she forced herself to breathe.

"The sorcerer most likely took her to lure you into a trap," Angel said, drifting around her. "While I wouldn't normally recommend walking into a trap, I think this one is unavoidable. This is a chance to kill him."

"Shut up and let me think," she said angrily as she walked over to Ceri's car. Pausing next to the driver's side door, she shut her eyes and inhaled deeply. The wolf, already at the front of her mind, sifted through the scents until it found the one that was distinctly Ceri. Citrus, lavender, and magic.

She followed it across the street, though it was faint beneath the smells of exhaust and other people. Instead of leading to the front door, it led around back. Derek hurried after her, while Genevieve followed a little slower, still apologizing to the bouncer.

Ceri's scent led in through an employee's only door, but it also led back out. Not back to her car though, it led into the alley, then...vanished.

"It ends here," she said, dropping to one knee and inhaling deeply to draw in as many scents as she could.

"If someone took her here, perhaps you can get their scent."

"Dozens of people have been through here. I'm not a bloodhound, I don't know what to follow." Amber pushed back up to her feet angrily. This couldn't be a dead end. There had to be a way to find Ceri.

"Can you use the pack bond somehow?" Genevieve asked.

"I can't feel her at all," Amber said, pacing nervously.

"Perhaps you should try again," Angel suggested, swooping in front of her to force her to pay attention. "You don't know as much about the pack bond as you should, but it's not something that can be completely severed unless she's dead. If she is alive, no matter how they're blocking it, if you are strong enough you can find her."

"How the hell do you know all of this?"

Angel rolled his eyes. "I'm extremely intelligent and well-educated. And I've known more werewolves than you, Miss Recently-Bitten."

"What is he saying?" Derek asked impatiently.

Amber turned back to them. "That if I focus hard enough, and I'm strong enough, that I'll be able to find her." She paused, swallowing down the lump in her throat. "If she's alive."

"Then do it." Derek balled his hands into fists as though he were expecting the worst news. She couldn't even consider that as a possibility.

Footsteps from the end of the alley startled her and she looked up only to see Shane walking toward them.

"What the hell are you doing here?"

"Genevieve texted me," he said.

Genevieve immediately lifted her hands. "We need help, and we need someone else from the council there if we do find the sorcerer. They may not take our word for it. Shane was the only option I could think of."

Amber ground her teeth together but nodded. Genevieve was right and was thinking of all the things she hadn't.

"I'm here to help," Shane said firmly. "If Ceri has been taken by a sorcerer, I don't want to see her dead either."

"Does Jameson know you're here?" Amber asked.

He scratched the back of his head and pursed his lips. "Not yet."

"Will you get in trouble if he finds out you helped us?"

Shane shook his head. "That's for me to worry about, not you." He held his hand up before she could object. "I may be his beta, but I'm not his slave. That's not how this works."

She pulled back all her questions and worries and nodded, accepting that he could decide for himself. "What do you know about pack bonds?"

~

Amber sat sideways in the driver's side seat with her feet resting on the running board. Her hand was wrapped tightly in Genevieve's and she was trying to breathe deeply while she focused on the pack bond.

"This will be as natural as breathing one day, but for now, let the wolf guide you," Shane said slowly.

She tried to picture the wolf as she'd seen her that day during the Trials. Perhaps it was her imagination, but she thought she could see red eyes looking back at her. She focused on the pack bond strumming between herself and Genevieve.

Her pack's fear and worry rushed over her like a tidal wave. It was hard not to pull back just to protect herself from their emotions, but she couldn't do that. The wolf pushed her deeper, not caring what she felt. The sounds of traffic and Derek pacing impatiently began to fade away as other senses came into focus.

Each of her pack members felt like another heartbeat in her chest. She could sense where each of them was. The wolf looked around, touching each bond in turn. Genevieve. Close. Tommy. Far. She held her breath and she sank farther into her mind.

Ceri had to be there, she couldn't be dead. As she drifted deeper, she felt something dark slither across her mind. The wolf growled in her mind and crouched down. There was something pushing back. Trying to hide.

With a glimmer of hope that Ceri may actually be alive, she pushed back against the shifting shadows in her mind. The wolf howled and the sound grew louder and louder, making her head ache. She gritted her teeth and kept pushing. Angel said she just had to be stronger than whoever was trying to hide the bond from her. There was no power in heaven or hell that could keep her from Ceri.

She pulled strength from the pack and tore through the darkness. The bond that tied her to Ceri throbbed weakly in the back of her mind. She dug her fingers into Genevieve's hand so hard she had to be bruising it as she desperately reached for the bond. Ceri was alive.

"I can feel her," Amber gasped. "She's pretty far, not within the city limits."

"Where?" Derek growled.

"I don't know, but I can get there."

"I'll text Tommy," Genevieve said as she hurried around to the passenger side of the truck.

"I'll follow you," Shane said, before running back to his suburban.

They piled into the truck and Amber cranked it up with shaking hands. They had a chance if they could just get there in time. Ceri was alive, but she was in pain. And she was afraid.

CHAPTER 63

TOMMY

Witch's Castle in Forest Park. Call the police if I don't text back in one hour.

Tommy dropped his phone in his lap and buried his face in his hands. The wolf was raging inside of him. He couldn't just sit here and wait.

"Is she alive?" Evangeline asked quietly, stopping her pacing abruptly.

"Yeah. For now."

She started pacing again. He wanted to tie her to a chair and make her stop. It was driving him nuts.

"What if..." she hesitated, picking at the hem of her jacket. "These people hurt my mom, and they're not going to stop until we're dead. What if we go help?"

"And leave Eloise here alone?" He couldn't believe she was even suggesting it. He wanted to go get Ceri back more than anything, but he understood why Amber had asked him to stay.

Evangeline groaned in frustration. "I don't want her to die, but I couldn't live with myself if Ceri died either."

Tommy looked down at his hands. He couldn't even think about that. Ceri was the one that had convinced him to stay. She'd given him hope. He didn't want a life without her in it.

The floor near the balcony upstairs creaked and Tommy's head snapped up. Eloise was leaning against the banister looking down at them.

"Evangeline, you should go help them," the old woman said, her face set in determination.

Evangeline stared at her in shock. "You can't be serious."

"And why can't I be? Haven't I taught you to help people when they need it?" Eloise asked, her hands gripping the banister tightly to stay upright.

"But you know what this means. What it requires," Evangeline said quietly.

"I do. In fact, I think I know better than you," Eloise replied, giving her a serious look. "I won't tell you what to do, but I will give you permission, since it seems like you need it." With a final nod, Eloise pushed off the banister and began hobbling back toward the bedroom.

Tommy heard Deward's car turned into the driveway.

"What is she talking about?" he asked as he rose from the couch.

"She's talking about my demon side. The way that I saved her that night we were attacked." Evangeline dragged her hands down her face.

"Didn't you fly away with your mom or something that night? Can you do that now?" he asked, a plan forming in his mind.

"There's only one way I can do that right now," Evangeline said, her expression pained.

"How?"

"As a favor."

"I don't understand." They didn't have time for this. Tommy could feel the panic coursing through the pack bond. "A favor?"

"As part of a demon mark." Evangeline blurted out. Her hands trembled as she pushed her hoodie back. Her hair was blonde, like it had been the day in the forest. She'd grown paler though and had dark circles under her eyes. "The demon magic is limited during the day, but if you accept my demon mark in return for my help in getting you there and defeating the sorcerer and Zachariah, then I can use it."

"Then let's do it," he said without hesitation.

"You'd be indebted to me. How can you be so casual about it?"

"Are you going to demand I do something terrible?" he asked.

"No, I would never––"

"Then what is there to think about? I trust you, and I need your help. Please stop hesitating. We have to do something."

Evangeline looked stunned, but nodded. She lifted her hand. "Come here."

He walked up, standing within reach. She placed her hand over his heart. Heat rushed between them and her eyes lit up with power. "A debt for a debt."

The magic burned. He ground his teeth together to keep from reacting as the magic forced its way under his skin. She yanked her hand away like she'd been burned and took a step back but it felt like she was still touching him. Like she was part of him now.

"That wasn't so bad," he said despite the sudden dizziness at the loss of contact.

She held her hand to her chest and looked out the window. "I'm a parasite."

"Barely."

Eva glared at him, but the corner of her lip turned up in a half smile. "You're an idiot."

As she stood there, color bloomed in her cheeks. Her blonde hair darkened from root to tip as the horns grew from her head. Blue eyes became black. The effervescent glow of her skin became warmer. Healthier.

"Was that why you were sick? Because you wouldn't give someone your mark?" he asked, understanding dawning on him.

"Yes. It's a curse. A demon will die without at least one mark, and the more we have the more powerful we become." She glanced around the room furtively. "Don't tell anyone I told you that. Please."

He nodded, though he would have to tell Amber. Right now, he needed Evangeline focused and an argument would distract her.

There was a knock at the door and he rushed over, yanking it open.

Deward looked startled. "What's wrong?"

"Deward, I need to ask you to do something both dangerous and possibly stupid." He stepped back and waved him inside, shutting the door behind them.

The troll raised an eyebrow, but didn't immediately object. "What is your request?"

"Ceri has been kidnapped by a sorcerer. My pack is about to try to rescue her, but they need all the help they can get. There is..." he hesitated, then decided Deward would appreciate the truth more than anything else. He pointed at Evangeline. "She is the girl on the news. The demon they are stupidly blaming for the no magic spots. It's a really long story, but her mother was hurt when the sorcerer and this half angel tried to kill her. She's upstairs, and we can't leave her defenseless in case someone comes here trying to hurt her, but I can't let my alpha fight alone."

Deward crossed his arms and looked at the floor, thinking. He tapped his long green fingers against his arm. Tommy knew better than to interrupt, but it was hard.

Finally, he looked up. "I see your dilemma, and I am willing to protect the woman. Perhaps this is reckless, but I find myself inspired by your fervor. I will do it."

Tommy sighed in relief. "Thank you."

"Also, just so you know, the house is kind of...sentient." Evangeline said hesitantly. "If someone tries to hurt you it may help. Trust it. And talking to it may not be a bad idea. It likes compliments. Isn't that right, Mr. Cottage?"

The cabinets flapped happily, and Deward jerked in alarm. "That should *not* be possible."

"Well it is, good luck," Tommy said, grabbing Evangeline by the arm and dragging her outside. The front door shut on its own and he heard all the locks click into place. The window shades dropped one by one and a wave of magic passed over the house as it turned itself into some kind of fortress.

He turned back to Evangeline. "Okay, how do we do this?"

"Um, just step back." She pulled off her hood and shook out her arms. Her horns, normally black as her hair, began to glow red. With a rush of magic that almost knocked him back, fiery wings exploded out of her back. Her eyes were completely black and her hands changed, claws extending from her fingertips.

He looked at her in awe. "That is badass."

"Shut up and get over here, teen wolf," she hissed, her voice changed by the sharp teeth in her mouth. He walked over and she awkwardly wrapped her arms around him. "Arms around my neck, and hold on tight."

Standing this close, for a split second, all he could think about was kissing her, but thoughts of what Ceri might be going through killed that as soon as it began. He wrapped his arms tightly around her neck and she kicked off the ground. They shot straight up and he squeezed his eyes shut, focusing on the bond and not the fact that he was flying through the air with a demon that had no clue what she was doing.

CHAPTER 64

AMBER

Amber stared at the old ruin. The roof of the house had rotted away long ago leaving only the skeletal stone structure behind. Moss grew on the exposed edges, dripping down the sides like mold. Deep in the forest, The Witch's Castle was rumored to be haunted but still attracted tourists daily.

Strangely, no one was here today. Perhaps they'd felt the ominous chill in the air. She shuddered as the wind picked up slightly.

"I can try to convince Jameson to come help if you wait," Shane said quietly.

"No. Ceri doesn't have much time." She scanned the ruins for any signs of life but the whole area was still. "It doesn't look like there's an entrance but I know she's here somewhere."

She walked into the ruins with Genevieve and Shane close behind her. Derek pushed ahead of her, jogging into the main room of the old house. They spread out slightly as they searched for whatever room or basement they had Ceri in. The pack bond throbbed painfully in her chest almost robbing her of her breath.

All her senses focused on the area around her. She thought she caught a whiff of Ceri but it faded quickly. It had rained sometime last night -- the forest floor had still been soft and damp -- and washed away the trail.

A loud crack startled her and she whipped around ready to fight, but it was just Derek. He'd kicked in an old cellar door that had been hidden under a pile of wet leaves and was peering inside. He nudged the now broken lock away with the butt of his gun.

"I saw a footprint near it," he said, waving Amber over.

She sprinted to him and helped him pull open the splintered door. The pack bond twisted inside of her, abruptly growing even stronger. The underside of the cellar doors had symbols drawn in what looked and smelled like blood. It had been blocking the bond.

Genevieve jogged up behind her, almost bumping into her. "Is this it?"

"Yes." Desperation filled Amber's heart as she felt the full extent of Ceri's suffering. She stepped down into the darkness without hesitation. The pain Ceri was in was almost overwhelming even through the bond. Her friend's fear screamed at her to move faster.

"Amber, we should make a plan," Shane said, trying to grab her arm.

She jerked it away and glared at him over her shoulder. "The plan is to rescue her and all get out alive. Don't you dare try to stop me. You don't have to come if you don't want to."

Shane's lips thinned in frustration, but he nodded. "I'm calling Jameson then I'll catch up."

Done waiting on him, Amber walked carefully into the cellar. The wooden steps creaked under her feet. She had to blink for her eyes to adjust to the impenetrable darkness. It smelled like earth, moss, and rat droppings down here. Ceri's scent mingled with all of it. She'd been brought this way.

"I can smell her," Genevieve said quietly from somewhere behind her.

"Me too."

"Is she close?" Derek asked. He had one hand on the wall guiding himself. She'd almost forgotten he wouldn't be able to see in the dark down here.

"Sort of. We're headed in the right direction, but she's still a good distance away." She picked up her pace, wanting to get to the bottom before the others, just in case.

The stairs led down into a what looked like an old wine cellar. Old, wooden racks rotted with age stood empty on either side of the room like sentries. Cobwebs draped over the aged wood. Even those seemed to be covered in dust. The floor was carpeted in a layer of grime that had been recently disturbed. A trail led through the center of the room to a door. It was propped open with a chunk of wood.

A strange smell drifted from the doorway. There was a hint of decay, but also of magic, and something else. Blood.

"Do you smell that?" Genevieve asked nervously.

Amber lifted her hand and motioned for the others to stop. "Yes, be careful. Derek, did you bring a flashlight? You need to be able to see now."

There was a click and light flooded the room as he pulled his headlight onto his head. He swung the shotgun up to his shoulder and aimed it at the door. Leave it to her brother to be prepared even in a crisis.

The smell grew stronger and there was a strange clicking noise, like claws on stone. Pale fingers wrapped around the door. They weren't human, exactly. The claws of a wolf extended from bony, human fingers. Fur grew in mangy patches on the knuckles, extending up to the wrist.

With a groan, the door was pushed open, and a horrible sight met Amber's eyes. She recognized this creature, or at least who he used to be. It was her maker. Peter.

His eyes were all white and his sallow flesh was spotted with rotten, black holes. He was hunched over like he had been caught mid-shift. Teeth too big for his mouth dug into his gray lips. He wasn't breathing. His heart wasn't beating.

The door swung all the way open, rattling as it hit the wall. Peter stepped into the room, stretching up to his full height, and howled.

CHAPTER 65

GENEVIEVE

Genevieve's heart skipped a beat as the howl echoed around them, signaling their presence here. This thing wasn't alive but it was walking and howling. Using magic for something like this was sick.

"Peter," Amber said, her voice shifting into a growl.

"Who is Peter?" Derek demanded.

"The wolf that bit us and changed us against our will. He used to work for Lockhart." Amber was shaking with anger. She could feel it pulsing through the pack bond, filling her with strength.

"I bought silver bullets after the issue with those golem monsters," Derek said, keeping his shotgun pointed at Peter. "Will they help?"

"I hope so." Amber took a step back and glanced at her. "Don't let him get near Derek."

"No shit." She hoped Shane would get down here soon. He had to have heard the howl.

"I don't have time for this. I need to get to Ceri," Amber said in frustration.

"I'll try to distract him so you can get past," Genevieve said, pulling her shirt off over her head. She was faster as a wolf, and she had a feeling she'd need all the speed she could get.

Peter cocked his head at them and curled his lips up into a twisted version of a smile. His muscles twitched slightly, then he exploded into motion. Amber ducked under the first swipe of his claws without shifting.

Genevieve launched herself toward him, shifting mid-air and ripping her pants to pieces. She caught his arm in her jaws and yanked him away from her alpha. A gunshot blasted through the room and the bullet hit Peter with a dull thunk, punching a hole straight through his chest. Viscous blood seeped from the wound but he didn't even flinch.

Peter slashed at her with his other arm and she ducked under it, scampering back a few steps. The gunshot hadn't slowed him down at all. If anything, he was getting faster.

Amber raced for the door. Peter tried to follow but Genevieve grabbed his ankle and bit down hard enough to crack the bone.

There was a loud smack and a grunt. Amber flew back from the door just as she tried to cross the threshold. She hit the floor and slid toward the stairs, stunned. A woman with red hair that looked like it had been hacked off with an axe stepped out. Her lips were sewn shut and her eyes had been cut out, leaving bloody holes in her face. Like Peter, her body wasn't right. Magical symbols had been carved into her bare arms and magic drifted up from them like black smoke.

The woman shambled toward Amber, who shifted, her clothes tearing away. Shane finally appeared at the bottom of the stairs, already in wolf form. He was snowy white and his eyes glowed bright yellow. With a growl, he launched himself over Amber and collided with the zombie. She grabbed him by the ruff of his neck and threw him to the side.

Genevieve danced in and out of reach as Peter slashed at her with his clawed hands. Her ears rang painfully as another shot echoed through the small room. It hit Peter in the leg this time, almost severing the limb. She watched in horror as the wound began mending immediately. The hole in his chest was almost filled in as well. The silver wasn't having any effect on him at all.

A scream split the air, coming from the direction of the door. Genevieve's heart clenched in her chest. Ceri.

"CERI!" Derek yelled, desperation clear in his voice. He tried to run for the door, but the zombie woman caught him with a kick, crumpling him. He rolled onto his back on the floor and swung his gun toward her, pulling the trigger. The blast hit her straight in the face, blowing out the back of her head and reducing her features to bloody gore. She faltered, legs wobbling underneath her.

Peter turned toward the sound of gunfire, distracted for a split second. Genevieve jumped and bit down on the back of his neck. His spine cracked between her jaws. She dug her claws into his back and ripped her head from side to side viciously, trying to tear his head off.

His hands grasped at her fur and ears. Sharp claws cut into her skin, but she didn't let go. They were hurting Ceri. They had to get to her now.

CHAPTER 66

CERI

The blast of gunfire shocked Ceri awake. A wave of pain hit her as her muscles protested the sudden movement. The light overhead made her head ache.

"They shouldn't be here yet," an unfamiliar male voice said, sounding very annoyed.

"I told you they might arrive early. It doesn't matter," another responded. This voice was familiar and unmistakable. It was the sorcerer. "They won't make it back here before we are ready considering the welcoming committee I left for them."

The sounds of fighting drifting down the hallway were faint. She craned her head trying to see the two men but they remained just out of sight. The other man was likely Zachariah Hudson, the half angel they'd seen on the news. She still didn't understand why he would be working with a sorcerer, even to kill a demon. Half angels tended to be somewhat rigid about black magic use.

"Ah, our sacrifice is awake." The sorcerer drew closer. His aura was oppressive, as though a black cloud of magic followed him wherever he went.

He came into view and grinned at her, revealing yellow teeth and a scarred face. The freshest of the scars was on his cheek and looked like he'd stitched the wound closed himself. As she stared into the face of evil, despair grew in her chest. Her pack had walked into his trap with her as bait.

"Ceridwen, you don't look pleased to see me," he cooed, stroking her cheek.

"Is anyone ever pleased to see you?" Her voice cracked as she forced the words out of her bone-dry throat. She'd almost lost her voice from screaming before she'd passed out.

He cackled, then backhanded her so hard she lost consciousness again for a moment. "This might be even more satisfying than my other kills. I was supposed to get Donovan after he failed to deliver me the alpha I paid him for, but Selena got to him first." He grabbed her cheeks. "Now that is an interesting woman. She's everything you could have been. It's almost sad to see your potential wasted, but your magic will only make my spells that much more powerful. Already your pain has provided enough to——"

"Will you shut up," Zachariah hissed. "You talk too much."

The sorcerer sneered at the other man, anger contorting his features. "Talk to me like that again and you'll regret it."

"I'm paying you to do a job, not fuck around with this bitch." He sighed, beginning to pace the room. Even in the midst of all this filth, the half angel was still beautiful. The darkness didn't seem to touch him. "Can't you just kill her already so we can get on with this?"

Panic curled in Ceri's gut. She didn't want to die here like this, her magic warped and used for evil.

"I'll kill her when *I* am *ready.*"

Zachariah huffed in annoyance. "I'm going back upstairs. This better be done when I get back."

They kept sniping back and forth at each other, arguing about the timing of their plans.

Ceri looked around for Selena as she tested how tightly her arms were bound. Her earlier magic use had weakened them, but it would take another two or three attempts to break free considering how weak she was now. An offensive attack against the sorcerer was out of the question too. All she'd manage would be to piss him off. Selena's absence gave her a little hope though. Maybe she had a chance if it was just him.

A gentle breeze brushed up against her hair and she jerked her head around but no one was there. Frowning, she looked around carefully. It happened again, tickling her foot and she felt a gentle touch against her mind.

The room drifted away and the pain lifted from her mind like a fog clearing. It remained dark, but it felt different. This was just the absence of light rather than the stifling feeling that came with black magic.

Ceridwen, the voice whispered.

Can you help me?

There was a sense of uncertainty followed by determination. *I will try.*

Pain jerked her back into the room and she couldn't hold back the scream that wrenched itself out of her throat. A knife was buried up to the hilt in her leg and the sorcerer looked furious.

"That's not going to work again," he sneered.

Selena walked into the room just then. "I see you're getting started without me."

CHAPTER 67

TOMMY

They landed silently a few feet away from the ruins of the old stone house. Tommy was grateful to have his feet on solid ground again. Despite the awesome views of the city, he never wanted to do that again.

Evangeline took a deep breath and her hair faded back to blonde as the horns simply disappeared. The fiery wings drifted into ash that she brushed off her shoulders. "Do you know where they are?"

He shook his head. "I can tell they're close, but I don't know exactly where they are. I think they must be underground though. If they weren't we'd be able to see them."

They walked quietly toward the stone house. He kept his ears peeled for any hint of movement as he sniffed the air, hoping to pick up their scents. As the wind shifted, he thought he could smell Amber but he couldn't tell exactly which direction it was coming from. She must have walked all around this area.

A few broken beer bottles were strewn around on this side of the house. This was probably the favorite spot for the local kids to come drink, smoke, and get laid. He stepped over the glass and walked around to the other side of the house. A doorway stood empty, the door having rotted away long ago.

The ground looked slightly disturbed here and there was the slightest hint of someone unfamiliar lingering on the stone wall, as though they had brushed against it as they walked through the opening. He stepped over the threshold and looked around. The roof was missing so the room was lit by the afternoon sunlight that made it through the thick clouds overhead.

"Do you see anything?" Evangeline asked in a whisper.

He shook his head. "I smelled something though. Maybe the entrance is hidden."

Slowly, they paced the inner perimeter of the room, pressing on random stones and scuffing up the dirt on the stone floor to check for seams. Just as he was about to give up and look elsewhere, he heard a scraping noise and jerked around, motioning for Evangeline to be quiet.

The wall swung open, revealing a hidden door, and Zachariah stopped in his tracks, looking as surprised to see them as they were to see him.

"You bastard!" Evangeline shouted, flames bursting to life around her as she drew on the demonic power that coursed through her. Her hair turned black and the horns returned as her fiery wings flared behind her. The mark on his chest twitched and he felt the magic moving under his skin as if she were drawing strength from him.

Flames streaked from her hands. They crashed into Zachariah like waves breaking against the shore, rolling over and around him without harming him.

He sneered at her. "Your disgusting magic cannot touch me, demon."

"I bet my teeth can." Tommy shifted and charged the pretentious asshole that had tried to ruin all their lives out of blind hatred. Zachariah's eyes widened in fear as he frantically scrambled backward, hands grasping at thin air.

Just as he was about to collide with Zachariah, a flash of light blinded him. He hit something solid and searingly cold that threw him back with a wave of magic.

Shaking off the blow, Tommy looked up to see the half angel now held a shield that seemed to be made of pure magic and a strange sword that crackled with energy.

Zachariah shifted his feet into a fighting stance and turned his cold eyes to Evangeline. "I'll probably get a commendation for killing you myself."

"I'm going to rip you apart for hurting my mother."

A malicious grin spread across his face. "Your adoptive mother is nothing more than collateral damage. Killing your actual mother was a pleasure though."

Evangeline shrieked with rage as she launched herself at him, her wings propelling her up above the walls into the space the roof should be before angling down. Tommy forced himself back to his feet and raced toward the half angel as well. Zachariah moved his left foot back and held his shield up at an angle, his sword concealed behind it. He was going to skewer her.

Howling in warning, Tommy leapt as she sped down at him. His teeth closed around Zachariah's arm, wrenching the sword to the side just in time. Evangeline collided with him and they went down in a tangle of limbs.

Zachariah threw her back with a well-placed kick, then struck him with the shield. The magic flared painfully against his skin and knocked him off Zachariah's arm. He skittered back just far enough to avoid a swipe of the sword, but his skin went numb from the close proximity to the insanely cold magic.

He couldn't let it hit him or he wouldn't be able to walk. Flattening his ears against his head, he growled at Zachariah. The wolf was furious but also exhilarated by this opponent.

Flames rushed toward Zachariah again, but just like before, they washed over him ineffectively. If they were going to stop this guy, Tommy was going to have to do it himself. The half angel looked away for a split second and Tommy darted in, running behind Zachariah out of range of that sword. He nipped at his heels, his teeth tearing at the back of his ankle and drawing blood.

Zachariah shouted in pain and jerked around, swinging wildly in an attempt to hit him. The first two strikes missed, but the third came worryingly close as Tommy found himself backed into a corner. Tommy could smell the blood seeping into the fabric of his pants. He'd wounded him more than he'd realized.

Bunching his legs underneath him, he prepared to charge straight in, sword be damned. But then the air around them twitched and his legs faltered underneath him as gravity suddenly doubled. All three of them were knocked to the ground.

Zachariah looked up, straining against the overwhelming pressure, with a satisfied grin. "You're too late."

As abruptly as it had started, the pressure vanished. Zachariah jumped to his feet and ran. Evangeline turned to follow and he ran after her, but only made it two steps.

The ground split wide open right underneath Tommy's feet. Evangeline screamed but she was too far away to stop him from falling. A terrible feeling washed over him, stealing his strength. The wolf went silent in his head and he felt suddenly very empty. A shout tore from his throat as he fell into the gaping chasm.

CHAPTER 68

EVANGELINE

Evangeline watched Tommy fall in horror. A massive shockwave of magic lifted her from her feet and threw her back. She caught herself with her wings and shot up above the destruction. A chasm three feet wide and twenty feet long had rent the earth open.

As she drew closer to it, she felt the wrongness of it. It was the exact same feeling she'd noticed when she'd secretly visited the no magic zone near her school. She couldn't enter it even if she wanted to. She'd tried that day, but it had repelled her like a physical barrier.

Gritting her teeth together, she pounded her fists against the invisible wall. Tommy wasn't dead, but he was probably hurt, and there was no telling what effect it was having on him. Furious, she turned around, searching the forest for the angel. Tommy had taken the mark so that they could stop Zachariah and the sorcerer. She couldn't let him escape.

He still had his shield and sword which lit him up like a beacon even in the daylight. She dropped to the ground just outside of the house and grabbed a stone about the size of a softball. Her magic may not be able to touch him, but as Tommy had proved, he wasn't invincible. It was time to see if she still remembered how to throw that fastball that had been her signature when she'd played softball in junior high school.

She launched herself back up into the air and flew toward him as fast as she could. Her speed surprised her, she barely remembered fleeing with her mother, just racing against the sunrise. She didn't have to worry about the sun now.

Zachariah came into view once again and she flattened her wings against her back, racing toward him as she wove between the treetops. He was almost back to his car. She adjusted her grip on the first stone and threw it at him as hard as she could. It hit the back of his skull with a loud crack and sent him sprawling onto the ground.

She was on him in the blink of an eye. Every point of contact with him burned like she was touching an open flame. She faltered for a moment and he twisted, throwing her off. His shield blinked out of existence, but he kept the sword.

He swung it, slashing through her wing as she raised it to protect herself. Cold, burning pain rushed through her and it felt as though he'd severed a limb. She shrieked in rage and kicked out, catching his wrist, flinging his arm and the sword backward. It fell from his hand, rolling away on the forest floor.

He turned and scrambled after it. She jumped on his back and grabbed two handfuls of his hair. It hurt and her hands began to go numb, but she refused to let go this time. She slammed his face into the ground as he struggled underneath her, still trying to get to his sword. Her arms grew weaker the longer she held on. With a furious shout, Zachariah yanked one of her hands away and pulled her off balance.

Right next to the sword lay the rock she'd thrown at him. Dropping the other handful of hair, she launched herself at it, her fingers closing around it right as he grabbed his sword. She grabbed his wrist to stop him from stabbing her again and slammed the rock down on the back of his head. The blow dazed him and his body went limp for a moment.

She brought stone down on his head again and again, screaming in rage. Power flowed through her as his skull cracked under her attack. Rage, glee, and hate fueled her, replacing the strength his cold magic had stolen from her.

Memories of the pain in her mother's eyes as the fire had crawled over her legs, the exhaustion as she struggled to heal from the injuries, and the constant fear they'd both had to live with blinded her with rage. He was already dead, but she didn't stop until there was nothing left of his head but a mess of gore.

She paused panting, and that's when she heard it. A twig snapped and she looked up in alarm. A group of werewolves stood all around her, and they did not look friendly.

One of them stepped forward, an older man with a gray beard and a scar across his face. He looked at her, and the lifeless body in front of her. "Why have you killed Zachariah Hudson?"

She raised her bloody hands but otherwise stayed perfectly still so as not to startle them. "He was working with the sorcerer. He tried to kill me, and Amber's pack."

The old alpha looked her over critically, giving nothing away with his expression. "Show us where the sorcerer is. If you try to hurt one of my pack members or flee, I will kill you."

Swallowing down the fear curling in her throat, she nodded and pointed behind her. "They're at the Witch's Castle, the old stone house. I think they're somewhere underground in the new no magic zone."

Jameson's face hardened at the mention of a no magic zone. "Let's go."

CHAPTER 69

AMBER

Amber tore another chunk of flesh from the zombie's arm but she knew it would just grow back. They were fighting a losing battle and she was beginning to tire. No matter how they hurt them, the zombies simply healed. They couldn't tear them apart fast enough to disable them.

A blast shook the walls of the cellar, threatening the cave the whole thing in. Amber dropped to her stomach, ready to run for the stairs if needed, but the walls and ceiling held.

The zombies went strangely still, the unholy light behind their eyes dying. Siobhan stuttered, the symbols on her body flickering before snuffing out completely. She collapsed into a heap on the floor, lifeless once again. Peter fell as well, the half-shift vanishing and leaving him fully human, and fully dead, on the ground.

Amber took a step back, looking around in disbelief. They couldn't have just given up. These twisted creatures must have only been meant to delay them.

"What the hell was that?" Derek asked, leaning against the wall and panting as he tried to regain his breath.

She walked hesitantly toward the door, peering down the short hallway it led to. Light flickered in the distance casting strange shadows, beckoning her. Glancing back over her shoulder to ensure the others were following, she crept carefully down the hall.

There were three heartbeats in the room. She could hear Ceri's labored breathing, but the other two people in there were waiting for them silently. She paused, looking into the pack bond, then realized why she felt so strange. Tommy was gone. She couldn't feel him at all.

Fury rushed through her. She refused to consider that he might be dead. They must have taken him too, somehow. A growl escaped her throat as she wrapped what was left of the pack bond around herself and rose up to her full height, letting it burn in her eyes before rounding the corner and facing them.

The sorcerer stood in the center of the room, blocking her view of Ceri. In the corner, half hidden in the shadows, stood the last person she expected to see. Selena. The witch grinned at her, tapping a wooden wand against her thigh. She barely looked like herself. Her hair had been buzzed off and she looked ill.

Behind them, it looked as if the earth itself had split apart. A chasm filled with rubble stretched farther than she could see away from them.

Caligo grinned, spreading his arms wide as though he was welcoming them. "When Selena said she knew how to deliver you to me, I must say, I was skeptical. It looks like I was wrong to doubt her."

"Werewolves are utterly predictable," Selena said, her manic grin matching his own.

They were both insane. Amber lowered her head and growled. Ceri was so close, but she wasn't moving and her eyes were shut. She could smell her blood from here.

"Ah, I see you don't want to talk," Caligo said, throwing his head back with a cackle. His eyes were solid black when he looked back at her. "I guess it's time to finish this."

The rumble of falling rocks startled them both and Caligo took a step back so he could see behind himself while keeping Amber in his view.

Tommy stumbled out of the chasm in human form, but completely naked. He kept one hand on the wall to keep himself upright as he looked around the room. Amber wanted to howl in relief. When he took a step out of the opening, she felt the pack bond snap back into place. Tommy shuddered and seemed to instantly regain his strength. His eyes flashed yellow.

"The whole pack is here. How sweet." Caligo lifted his hand toward Tommy, magic pooling in his palm. Amber wasn't about to let him hurt Tommy. She raced toward him with Genevieve close behind.

CHAPTER 70

AMBER

At the last moment, Caligo turned the spell on her. A black blur shot in front of her, blocking the attack right before it could hit her. Genevieve crashed to the floor, yelping in pain and black flames burned away her fur. She rolled, smothering it against the floor.

Amber howled in rage and ducked down, charging at him low. Her claws scraped against the stone as she launched herself at him. He yelled something in Latin and swiped his hand across her path. Her vision went completely dark for a split second and she was thrown to the side.

She hit the ground as gunfire cracked through the air. Her vision returned, though it remained slightly foggy. Derek shot at Selena again, driving her back as Tommy circled behind her, now in his wolf form. There was blood on his muzzle and dripping from Selena's arm.

Amber tried to stand but her muscles only jerked erratically. The floor under her was slick with what smelled like blood. As she twitched, the red stains grew darker, glowing with an unholy light. The spell seeped into her body, twisting dark claws into her mind. Her front paw moved, claws sliding against the stone. She hadn't moved it. She couldn't.

A growl came unbidden from her throat as she stood. Foreign rage filled her. The wolf howled, eager to kill. She screamed inside her mind, trying to wrestle back control of her body, but it did no good.

Caligo's voice whispered through her mind. *Kill them all.*

Amber's head swiveled around to face Genevieve, who was back on her feet and watching her carefully. Her lips curled back over her teeth and she growled at the small black wolf.

Kill.

She charged at Genevieve, her powerful muscles propelling her across the distance in the blink of an eye. Her jaws snapped close on air as Genevieve ducked underneath the initial attack, darting away to her left.

Kill.

Her next strike caught Genevieve's leg and blood filled her mouth. Genevieve yelped and tried to jerk away, snapping at her shoulder when she couldn't pull her leg free. Amber used her weight to shove Genevieve off balance then lunged for her throat. The smaller wolf twisted out of the way, putting space between them. They circled each other, heads low and ears flat against their head.

There was a loud crash as Selena threw Derek back with a wave of her hand. His head struck the wall and the shotgun clattered to the floor as he lost consciousness. She turned her wand on Tommy who yelped in pain. Green flames engulfed him as he writhed on the floor, twisting in a frantic attempt to get them off of him.

Kill.

Amber charged Genevieve again. They collided in a tangle of limbs and teeth. Her teeth sunk into Genevieve's shoulder, ripping away a chunk of flesh. She yelped in pain and struck back with two vicious bites that grazed Amber's side, cutting almost down to the bone of her ribs.

Shane was circling Caligo, attempting to get close. The sorcerer held his hands out wide as if welcoming an attack. "Perhaps you should help Amber. It looks like she's having a little trouble controlling herself."

Shane growled and took another step forward, all his muscles tensed for an attack.

"The longer you wait, the less likely it is she'll--" Caligo's words were cut off by Shane's attack. The sorcerer brought his hands together with a loud crack. A shockwave caught Shane and tossed him back. He slid across the floor and hit the wall. As he scrambled back to his feet, a brilliant, shimmering cloud engulfed him. His legs collapsed beneath him and he clawed against the ground, trying to get away from the powdered silver.

Genevieve clawed at her gut and pushed her snapping jaws away with her other paw. She bit down on the leg, and the bone cracked. Genevieve yelped in pain but didn't stop fighting back. Amber had to jerk away as the other wolf snapped at her throat.

Something heavy hit her in the side, knocking her off Genevieve completely. She struggled against the arms that wrapped around her, trying to cut off her air supply.

Kill.

She snapped at the hand that held her, grazing it and drawing blood. Derek refused to let go but she was stronger than a human. Getting leverage with her back legs, she jerked free and turned on him, forcing him to the ground.

"Amber, look at me!" Derek shouted, pinned beneath her weight. "Don't do this! Fight back!"

"Am...ber..." Dylan choked out, blood bubbling out of his lips. *"Hel...p...hurts..."*

The memory crashed over her mind like an ice bath, shocking her into stillness as her jaws closed around her brother's neck. She trembled as the urge to bite and tear coursed through her. Something wasn't right.

Hands sunk into her fur, the touch gentle. "It's okay," Derek whispered. "If you remember this later, I forgive you."

Kill. The command came again. She hesitated, trembling under the weight of the magic.

No. It couldn't happen again. Amber whined and tried to let go, but her body was fighting her. She squeezed her eyes shut and sunk into her mind, searching for the wolf. The angry, hateful thing howling in her mind was all wrong. It wasn't the creature whose soul had joined with hers.

Wind ruffled her fur, bringing with it the sweet scent of Ceri's magic. Amber growled and fought back against the black magic that clung to her mind. Slowly, the wolf's power joined hers. The pack bond reignited inside her and she wrapped herself in its protection. Turning toward the darkness in her mind, she shredded the spell.

Her jaws released and she jerked away from Derek, chest heaving. He looked at her wide-eyed, staying perfectly still as if he was afraid to set her off.

The breeze blowing through the room turned into a sudden gale, almost knocking her off her feet. The sorcerer shouted in rage and turned toward Ceri with a furious expression. Her eyes popped open and she ripped her arm free of one of the restraints.

Shane was the first to move this time, though he was slow from the silver he'd inhaled, attempting to draw Caligo's attention away from Ceri. He darted in, barely dodging the first swipe of the sorcerer's blade, then latched onto the arm that held the dagger. Caligo didn't even hesitate. He flipped the dagger to the other hand and stabbed it into Shane's back, then kicked him away. Shane fell to the ground and didn't move.

Caligo ran toward Ceri, who had one hand stretched out toward Selena. The witch clawed at her own throat, choking as though she couldn't breathe. Ceri curled her hand into a fist, her face set in determination. Selena's lips began to turn blue as she was deprived of oxygen.

The sorcerer cast a spell that hit Ceri with a flash of light. Her spell faltered and she slumped back to the table, her body shaking erratically. Selena, freed from the spell, took off at a run. She disappeared through some door that hadn't been visible before.

Enraged, Amber howled as she charged the sorcerer. Her legs were shaky but they were responding to her once again. This bastard was hurting everyone she cared about, and for what? Power? Money? Nothing could be worth this amount of suffering.

Amber ran as fast as she could toward him, her heart pounding in her ears. Caligo slid to a stop next to Ceri and lifted the knife high overhead, his eyes locking with Amber's.

She launched herself at him, but it was too late. The knife plunged into Ceri's chest and she convulsed, her one free hand clawing uselessly at Caligo's arm. He ripped the knife free in a spray of blood in the same moment that Amber clamped her jaw around his throat.

She ripped out his throat with her teeth. Caligo crumpled to the floor as blood poured from the wound. Pain shot through Amber's chest as the demon mark dissolved, but she didn't care. All she cared about was Ceri.

Amber shifted back and pressed her hands against the wound in Ceri's chest. Her blood ran freely under Amber's hands. She'd seen wounds like these before in the emergency room. The victim was normally dead by the time they got to the hospital. She just had to stop the bleeding. She had to. Somehow.

Ceri gasped, blood bubbling up between her lips as it filled her lungs. Her eyes were wide with fear, but she still lifted a trembling hand to Amber's face, her mouth opening and shutting around words she couldn't quite form.

"Please don't die," Amber begged. She couldn't watch someone she loved die again. She wasn't strong enough for that. "Just hang on. I'll stop the bleeding."

Desperately, she pushed all the strength she had left through the pack bond, trying to give Ceri a little more time, but she was bleeding out so fast. The pack bond was a mess of pain and fear. Every single member of her pack was hurt. They had no strength to give. Ceri gasped for air she could no longer take in. Her lung had probably collapsed.

"Ceri!" Derek shouted, running over. Horror spread across his face as he took in the extent of her injuries. Looking up at Amber, he asked. "Can you save her?"

She stared back at her brother, tears slipping from her eyes. She couldn't say it out loud. She refused to.

Angel appeared in front of her, near Ceri's head. He was barely visible, just an apparition. "I can heal her."

"How?" she asked, pressing down so hard she feared she'd break one of Ceri's ribs. The witch didn't even flinch, she was too far gone to feel pain and barely conscious.

"Take another mark from me. I can't act without it."

Amber hesitated, hands trembling. She couldn't think, not with Ceri laying here like this.

"Amber!" he shouted as his body began to fade even further. "Take the mark or I cannot help you!"

His face flickered, shifting from the demonic to something almost...human. Amber reached her hand up, trailing her fingers across his cheek, then grabbed his hand and placed it against her chest. "A debt for a debt."

As painful as the first time, the magic seared the skin under his hand, burying itself in her chest where the other mark had been. She could feel him once again. His eyes met hers and she saw the satisfaction there.

She knew he hadn't planned this but he had found a way to take advantage. Dropping his hand, she put pressure on the wound once again. "Help her."

CHAPTER 71

CERI

Magic burned through her body like a lightning bolt. Ceri gasped as she was finally able to take a full breath. Every wound and ache was gone. For a brief moment, she wondered if she'd died and gone on to the afterlife, but then Amber was above her, tears dripping from her cheeks.

"Ceri? Can you hear me? Please say something, please," Amber gasped, shaking her lightly.

"What..." she blinked, still disoriented. What had happened? She remembered the knife. The pain. And darkness overtaking her.

Derek shoved his way in close and wrapped her in a hug. He was shaking and she felt still-wet blood in his hair when she put her arms around him.

Her eyes met Amber who was standing a few steps away. She was pale and looked like she was trembling as well. Amber's eyes strayed to the left and she nodded.

Ceri frowned. Caligo was dead at her feet. The demon's mark should be dissolved now.

Derek released her slowly, gently pushing her sweat-soaked hair back from her face. "Are you okay?"

"Yes, but I shouldn't be. What happened?" she asked, eyes flicking between Derek and Amber.

"I took another demon mark," Amber said, her lips pressed together into a thin line. "I couldn't watch you die, I'm sorry."

Ceri's face softened and she rubbed her hand over the place the knife had sunk in. She could be angry or blame Amber for making a foolish choice, but the truth was she was thankful she was alive. Amber hadn't had many choices. She met her alpha's eyes and said, "Thank you."

Amber's shoulders slumped in relief. "Get her off that stupid slab, I'm going to go check on the others."

Shane, who must have been the white wolf she'd seen, was slumped in a corner panting. As Derek helped her sit up, she saw that Genevieve was helping Tommy sit up with one arm. The other was cradled against her chest. Tommy's skin was red and angry from Selena's attack with the wand. Seeing his injuries only reminded her of the torture she'd endured.

Her fingers dug into Derek's arm as she struggled to keep from panicking. He pulled her into a tight hug and she buried her face in his shoulder, letting the scent of his sweat and cologne fill her nose, blocking out the rest of it. His touch grounded her and she slowed her breathing. Even though the physical wounds had healed, she couldn't escape the mental scars this day had left behind.

As Derek helped her off the slab she saw Amber and the others tense up. Amber walked toward the door, her hands clenched into tight fists.

Shane limped after her, catching her arm. "He's not going to hurt you," he croaked, still struggling for a breath.

"I'll believe that when I see it," Amber said shortly.

Jameson walked into the room, followed by a blood-soaked Evangeline and his pack. Evangeline looked basically unharmed, but the way her eyes were darting around betrayed her nervousness.

"You wanted proof, here it is," Amber said, sweeping her arm toward the sorcerer's dead body and the destruction behind them.

Shane locked eyes with his alpha. He was practically swaying on his feet but seemed determined to stand with Amber. "I saw the sorcerer attempting to kill them."

"And the creation of the no magic zone?" Jameson asked, nodding toward the rubble-filled chasm.

"We were fighting in a different room."

Amber gave him a withering look. "The sorcerer did it."

"It opened up underneath me when Evangeline and I were fighting Zachariah," Tommy said, walking up to stand beside Amber.

Jameson sighed and dragged his hand down his face. "Alright. I think it's obvious that neither you nor this girl is responsible for the no magic zones. You'll still need to keep her hidden or get her out of town. Hudson made too big an impact for her to go walking around without causing a riot."

"That won't be a problem. We'll be finding a safe place for her soon," Amber agreed with a nod.

Ceri slumped with relief. It was over, for now at least. With the new demon mark, they wouldn't be truly safe, but they had a chance now. Her eyes felt heavy. More than anything, she just wanted to sleep.

CHAPTER 72

AMBER

It was still daylight outside and that felt wrong considering the darkness they'd just endured. Amber looked at the sun where it hung low in the sky, partially blocked by clouds and tried to still the trembling in her hands.

She'd come so close to losing someone else, someone she'd come to think of as a sister, all because of a demon's mark. She'd hurt Genevieve and almost killed her brother. All she'd wanted was to protect them but she'd put them all in even more danger instead by dragging them into a fight with an evil sorcerer.

Angel was still floating around, observing Jameson and his pack as they milled around discussing what had happened. Maybe Thallan was right and she should kill him to protect everyone else.

Shane walked up beside her, startling her. "Sorry," he said, touching her arm gently. "Didn't mean to scare you."

"It's okay. I'm just jumpy right now."

He gave her a wan smile. "Understandable."

"What now? Is the council still going to try to punish me or something?" she asked, wrapping her arms around herself. She felt cold down to the bone.

"No. Jameson asked for proof, and you managed to give it to him." He hesitated. "Some of them may trust you a little less, or be assholes, but they can't do anything to you without risking punishment themselves."

She snorted. "That's comforting. I see how well that went last time."

"Jameson is on your side." Shane squeezed her shoulder gently. "I have to go. I inhaled a lot of silver earlier, and while the pack bond is keeping me upright, I really need to get treated."

She nodded. "Of course. I'm sorry you got drug into all this."

"No one dragged me into anything. I wanted to help because I care about you and this sorcerer needed to be stopped. Don't fret about it, okay?"

That was easier said than done. "Sure."

"I'll see you soon." He headed back toward Jameson. Ceri, Derek, and Evangeline were still talking to the old alpha, trying to work out how exactly the sorcerer had created the no magic zone.

She tuned them out and looked around for Tommy and Genevieve. They were sitting out of the way. Both looked exhausted. Genevieve met her eyes and she had a strong urge to turn and just run but she swallowed down her fear and guilt and walked over.

She nervously crossed her arms and stared at her bare feet that were now completely filthy. It finally occurred to her that she was still naked, but it seemed they were all past being concerned about modesty. "Is your arm okay?"

Genevieve sighed and pushed up to her feet. Amber watched her warily, expecting a punch or accusations. Instead, Genevieve dragged her into a one-armed hug.

"It's healing, and if I hear one word of you blaming yourself for what happened, I'll break my other arm."

Amber laughed, though the sound was a bit hysterical. "I tried to kill you."

"The sorcerer tried to kill me." Genevieve stepped away and met her gaze, eyes narrowed. "Unless you've secretly wanted me dead all along?"

"Of course not!"

"Then why are you acting like you did it on purpose?" Genevieve demanded, jabbing her in the arm with her finger.

"I fell into his trap, I should have seen——"

"Blah blah blah." Genevieve rolled her eyes. "We're all alive, and the sorcerer is dead. We can analyze our strategy some other time."

Tommy snorted in amusement. "Gen, you may not be the best at comforting people."

"I'm excellent at it. You hush."

Amber shook her head. No matter what happened, they didn't lose their sense of humor. Frowning, she looked down at Tommy.

"How the hell did you and Evangeline end up here? You were supposed to stay home." She crossed her arms and glared at him.

"About that..."

A hand on her shoulder startled her, but she looked back to see it was Ceri, her brother, and Evangeline. She avoided eye contact with Derek. That was a conversation she was not ready to have, not if she wanted to keep her shit together until she had a chance to be alone.

"Is everyone doing okay?" Ceri asked, leaning in to take a closer look at Genevieve's arm.

"As well as can be expected," Genevieve said, waving Ceri away. "You can look at it later. Let's go home."

Amber agreed with a nod. Nothing sounded better.

CHAPTER 73

EVANGELINE

Evangeline couldn't believe her good luck. When those werewolves had shown up, she was sure she'd be killed. The fact that they'd given her the benefit of the doubt after they'd watched her literally beat a man's head in with a rock was insane. Maybe there was a chance she could have a normal life after all...or at least be safe for a while.

They climbed out of the truck and she was tempted to run inside and tell Eloise they were safe now, but she held back and walked next to Tommy. It was strange how aware of him she was now. Kadrithan had dozens of demon marks at least but he'd never talked about how close you felt to the person that wore it. She felt Tommy's fear and pain as he'd fought, and she felt his exhaustion now. His strongest emotions were like a heartbeat at the back of her mind.

Ceri paused in front of the door. "There's something wrong. I should have noticed sooner, but I thought it was just because of the fight."

"What?" Evangeline asked, shoving in front of Tommy. "What's wrong?"

"There is a threat inside the house. The wards are activating."

Evangeline yanked the door open, but Amber's grip on her arm kept her from entering. "Get off of me!"

"Slow down. You can't help Eloise if you walk into a trap."

"Deward is supposed to be there with her. Can you see him?" Tommy asked nervously from behind them.

There was a strange thunk from upstairs and Amber rushed inside with Evangeline close behind her. She ran in front of the alpha and looked up toward her mother's room. An elf was facing off with Deward, the troll that always tutored Tommy, and his features were contorted with rage.

Deward's shirt was singed and he was standing in front of her mother who was slumped against the wall with a baseball bat in her hand. She could barely stand but her mother wasn't the type to go down without a fight.

"Get out of my way or I'll kill you too!" the elf shouted.

"Move, Deward," Eloise growled.

"I refuse."

"Get the hell away from my mother!" Evangeline yelled, wishing she could draw on the demon's power again. Now that she'd fulfilled Tommy's request, she wouldn't be able to access it until the sun set.

The elf's eyes turned to her and hate filled his face.

"Thallan, what the hell are you doing?" Amber asked, her tone even and calm like she was trying to talk down a hostage situation.

"I waited but as expected, the demon has you wrapped around his little finger." He drew a gleaming blade from his belt. "SHOW YOURSELF KADRITHAN OR I'LL KILL THEM BOTH."

Thallan walked toward the stairs, the knife held in his hand like a shield. There was a strange, glowing sphere in his other hand. He lifted it and his eyes darted around the room. "I can kill them all. I know you've seen one of these before."

Amber stepped in front of Evangeline, shielding her with her body. A useless gesture if that was a firebomb. Evangeline eyed the door to her mother's room, trying to find a way to get to her and run before it was too late.

Her uncle appeared, looking at the elf with a bored expression. "This is beneath you, Thallan."

The elf sneered at him. "You murdered my wife."

Kadrithan raised his brow. "Your wife was killed in a car accident. I know you've always irrationally blamed me, but this is taking things a bit far."

Evangeline knew that tone. Her uncle was pissed. If he'd been able, he would have killed the elf right then and there, but of course, he couldn't.

Thallan's fingers tightened on the firebomb and Amber tensed like she was going to try to make a leap for it. If she missed, the whole house would blow.

Evangeline stepped around Amber and walked straight toward him, her hands held out to her side to show she had no weapons. "Stop it. If you want revenge, just kill me."

Thallan's eyes flicked over to her.

"Kadrithan wants me alive. He'd be devastated if I was killed. So, if you think you need some kind of revenge, then just kill me. Leave everyone else out of it." She took another step forward. "I'm sick of everyone around me getting hurt trying to protect me, so just hurt me instead."

"Evangeline, get away from him and stop being stupid," Kadrithan demanded.

Amber was trying to edge toward her and she could feel Tommy panicking. She didn't care anymore. She thought she'd done enough when she had killed Zachariah but they'd come home to another threat. It would never end, not as long as she was alive.

"Evangeline, no!" her mother screamed from upstairs. Her shout made Evangeline look up and she saw horror on her mother's face, but she couldn't turn back now. This was the only way to keep her safe.

Thallan adjusted the grip on his knife, then moved toward her like a flash. She lunged at him at the same time to stop Amber from getting in the way, but they never collided.

Blinking she looked around and found herself...upstairs. Deward looked just as surprised as she did to see her standing next to him.

Her mother limped toward her and yanked her into a hug. "What the hell were you thinking?"

"I had to..." her thought trailed off as a woman appeared in the midst of the living room. Pale green hair fell over her shoulders in loose curls, framing a delicate face. She was beautiful...and transparent.

Thallan, whose legs had sunk into the floor like it was quicksand froze, his eyes going wide.

"Illya?" he whispered reverently as if he were looking at an angel.

She drifted forward, her ethereal feet not touching the floor. "I waited for you," she whispered. "Day after day, but everything around me grew dark. What have you done?"

Tears slipped out of Thallan's eyes and slid down his cheeks. "I was trying to find a way to avenge you. The demon, he took you from me. I didn't know you were here."

She shook her head, a frown marring her perfect mouth. Gently, she tried to stroke Thallan's cheek, but her hand passed through him. "It was an accident. Simple bad luck."

Her mother's hug tightened around her as if the mention of death scared her. It scared Evangeline too. Her mother was old. If she was attacked again she probably wouldn't survive. They might have gotten through this but all hope of feeling safe seemed laughable now.

"No," Thallan insisted, cringing away from her. "No, I can't..."

Illya leaned in close. "Stop looking for someone to blame. The man who killed me is already dead."

Thallan's body shook with grief but he couldn't look away from the woman.

Evangeline glanced at the others to see if they had any clue what was going on, but they all looked just as confused as she was, except for Ceri, who looked about as awed as Thallan.

"What is she?" Amber asked nervously.

"An echo," Ceri said in awe. "She poured so much magic into this place that a little piece of her stayed behind. The house isn't sentient, she is."

Illya moved away from Thallan, shaking her head in disappointment.

"You will not come here again until you hold no more hate in your heart," she said, lifting both hands. The house groaned and everything shifted, rolling in a dizzying blur, and then Thallan was gone.

The woman, Illya, glanced back at Evangeline and smiled brilliantly at her. She felt herself relax slightly.

"Don't be so hard on yourself. I can see the good in you." As quickly as she had appeared, Illya vanished, disappearing back into the house.

Evangeline looked down at the pack, stunned. "That was weird, right?"

"Extremely," Deward said, crossing his arms and shaking his head. "This pack is very strange."

CHAPTER 74

TOMMY

They'd all searched the yard after the incident with Thallan, but hadn't been able to find him. Amber had decided that they were safe enough in the house for now and she'd deal with him later.

Tommy pressed the palms of his hands into his eyes until he saw stars, then took a deep breath and headed over to talk to Deward. Amber had spent the last ten minutes apologizing and thanking him while also chastising him for going along with their plan even though it had worked.

He stopped awkwardly in front of the troll and scratched his head. "Sorry about that."

"I've never been called irresponsible or idiotic before," Deward said with a frown.

"I can't believe she said that." Tommy covered his face with a groan. "I really am sorry, I shouldn't have--"

"Do not apologize," Deward said, lifting his hand. "I think, perhaps, I did act rashly. Something I've never done before, but the result was satisfying. Despite your alpha's doubts, you joining the fight did seem to make a difference."

He wasn't sure how to respond to that. "Well, yeah, it did."

Deward nodded. "Then I shall take that conversation simply as a sign of concern from your alpha."

"Probably a good idea."

Captain Jack walked through the living room and pawed at Amber's leg, meowing loudly. Deward eyed the cat warily.

"I did notice something while you were gone. There is something wrong with your cat."

"Did he throw up or something?" Tommy asked, concerned.

Deward shook his head. "No, but before your ghost appeared, its eye was glowing. It looked as if it were about to attack. No one seemed to notice since they were focused on the demon and the elf."

Tommy looked at Captain Jack, brows pinched together. "Glowing?"

"Glowing green. It's possible the adrenaline caused me to mistake what I saw, but I'm almost positive that I remember correctly."

"Weird. I'll keep an eye on him."

Deward nodded. "I should return home now to give your pack privacy and discuss all this with my father."

"He won't tell anyone about Evangeline, will he?"

"No. My father never believed demons were responsible for the no magic zones. He will not betray your pack's confidence."

"Great," Tommy said with a huge sigh of relief. "So, I'll see you in a few days for more tutoring?"

Deward shook his hand firmly, and pulled him in, pressing their foreheads together briefly before stepping back. "Yes. See you then, brother."

Tommy blinked, not sure what had just happened. It kind of felt like Deward had just declared him an ally or best friend or something. "Yeah, uh, see you then...brother."

Deward grinned and headed toward the door, waving his goodbye to the rest of the pack.

"Are you two dating now?" Evangeline asked drily, appearing next to him.

Tommy shrugged. "Maybe." He had managed to find pants shortly after they'd dealt with the Thallan crap, but no one had had a chance to clean off yet. He felt grimy but Evangeline was covered in blood. "Are you okay?"

She looked down at her hands. "I guess."

"I take it you killed that half angel?" He probably shouldn't be asking but he thought avoiding it might not be healthy either.

"I beat his head in with a rock."

"That's intense." He took a deep breath. "And kind of awesome."

She looked up at him and raised a brow. "Awesome?"

He nodded, trying to convince himself as much as her. "He tried to kill you and hurt your mother, and you protected her. That's brave."

She laughed. "Is it awesome that I liked it? That I reveled in crushing in his skull?"

Tommy shrugged. He'd been asking himself the same thing. When Amber had ripped the sorcerer's throat out, he'd been happy. He'd wanted to kill Selena and he'd wanted her to suffer when he did it. "Maybe it's normal for us. Demons and werewolves aren't...human, exactly. We're both predators. As long as you don't go full serial killer, I think you're good."

"That's real comforting."

"Just being honest," he said with a grin.

"Hey, Tommy, can you order pizza?" Amber asked from across the room.

"Absolutely." Today sucked, and nothing could change that. Food could make it better for a little while though.

CHAPTER 75

AMBER

A text from Shane popped up on her phone, confirming he was back to full health. Amber dropped her phone on her bed and sat down, unwinding the towel from her head.

Angel formed right across from her sitting in a black chair. He looked more solid than normal. There was no silly form this time either. She suspected this was his real face. It looked close to the glimpse she'd seen other day; the sharp jaw, aquiline nose, and tousled black hair.

"You better not intend on demanding I fulfill my mark right now," she said as she squeezed water from the ends of her hair with the towel.

He smirked at her. "Did you know Tommy bears Evangeline's demon mark now?"

She sighed, annoyed that he'd reminded her about that little complication. "Yes, did you come to gloat?"

"No, I came to tell you that I've found a safe place for Evangeline to stay. Someone will come to pick her and Eloise up in a couple of days."

"Did you ever find out how they located her?" Amber asked, surprised. She'd expected to have to keep Evangeline forever.

"Yes. It's been taken care of."

That sounded ominous and Amber decided she didn't want to know any details. "Great. Will handing her over to them fulfill my new demon mark?"

Angel threw his head back and laughed. "No, it's not nearly enough. Besides, I know you'd do it anyhow, so there's not much incentive for me to waste a favor on it, is there?"

Amber wished, once again, that she could punch him. "You're an ass."

"And you're a soft, squishy, easily-manipulated marshmallow." The smile on his face made him look easy-going but she couldn't forget the satisfaction she'd seen when he'd trapped her with another mark. She'd never forget that. Thallan was crazy, but he was right about the demon.

She got up and pulled her warmest pajamas out of her drawer. "Great talk. I'm going to bed now. Make yourself scarce."

"It was impressive what you did," Angel said, standing from his chair and prowling toward her. "Killing a sorcerer isn't easy."

"No, it wasn't."

He stopped right in front of her. Close enough to touch and leaned in. "You should be proud of yourself."

He lifted his hand like he meant to touch her face but she caught it and was surprised to find his fingers were solid.

"What are you doing?" She tightened her grip on his hand. His eyes strayed to her lips for a moment and she could practically feel his intent. She shoved him away. "Don't even think about it."

His grin widened. "Sleep well, Amber."

He vanished and her demon mark returned to its dormant state. She pressed her hand against it, wishing for the hundredth time she could cut it out of her chest.

Angry, she yanked on her pajamas and crawled into bed. Of course, that asshole had to come piss her off right before bed. The cherry on top of a terrible day.

She tugged the covers up to her chin, then grabbed a pillow and held it. That was still uncomfortable so she flipped to her other side and tried to squish her pillow into a better shape.

After five minutes of tossing and turning, a gentle knock at her door startled her. She sat up and heard Ceri just outside. Crawling out of bed, she hurried to the door.

Ceri stood in the doorway with a pillow tucked under her arm and tears streaming down her face.

"What's wrong?" she asked, pulling her into a hug.

"Can I sleep with you tonight? I know it's dumb, I'm not a two-year-old but--"

"It's not dumb. What's wrong?"

Ceri took a shaky breath. "I can't stand being alone right now. Every time I close my eyes I'm right back in that room."

Amber kept an arm around Ceri and walked her over to the queen-sized bed. "Come on. Just don't hog the covers."

They curled into bed together and Amber stroked her friend's hair gently. She would never admit it aloud but she was glad to not have to be alone tonight either. Small feet walked over her leg and a warm weight settled in the crevice between her and Ceri. Captain Jack's rumbling purr mingled with Ceri's heartbeat and slow breaths. It was comforting. She pressed her head against Ceri's back and counted the steady rhythm until she drifted off to sleep.

CHAPTER 76

GENEVIEVE

Genevieve hurried toward the rest of the old Lockhart pack. The challenge had already begun. Greer hadn't given her much warning. Part of her didn't want to watch this but part of her needed to. She wanted to see Greer win.

"Gen, wait up!" Steven huffed as he tried to catch up. He wasn't much of a runner. He'd stayed over because of the whole near-death experience thing, which he was still upset about.

"Walk faster, I want to watch," she said, not slowing down to wait.

She slipped through a hole in the crowd and stood at the edge of the circle they'd formed. Kevin, the temporary alpha she'd met at the last challenge, was already limping. The other wolf, a tall black wolf with a white patch near his nose who she assumed was Paul, stayed still as Kevin circled around him.

"There are so many werewolves here. Are they all part of this pack?" Steven whispered in her ear.

"Yes, but hush and watch," she said, pushing her fingers against Steven's lips. He sighed in annoyance but she didn't care. The only thing that mattered right now was this fight.

When Kevin charged, he moved so fast he was a blur. He went straight for the neck but Paul was ready. Ducking down and catching him under the jaw, Paul rose up on his hind legs and forced Kevin onto his back. Furious snarls filled the air and Kevin scrambled to get back up as Paul tested his defenses.

The sound made the hair on the back of her neck stand on end. When Amber had turned to her, eyes bright red, and attacked she'd thought it had to be a dream. A nightmare. But the pain had been all too real.

It felt like the pack bond had been ripped away the moment Amber's teeth had sunk into the flesh of her leg. She hadn't wanted to fight back at all but she'd known from the first instant that she *had* to. That Amber would never forgive her if she let her kill her. Amber would rather die herself. So, she had fought back...and lost.

Paul's jaws closed around Kevin's throat. The other werewolf thrashed underneath him but Paul had every advantage and the struggle was futile. Slowly, the thrashing stopped and Kevin shifted back to human form, staying submissive with his face against the ground.

After releasing his grip on Kevin's neck, Paul shifted and stood over him. "Do you submit?"

Kevin's eyes flicked up toward Paul, then he twisted sharply, throwing dirt into Paul's eyes. He stumbled backward and Kevin jumped to his feet, landing a single punch. Genevieve's heart stuttered fearfully and she curled her hands into a fist.

Paul rolled with the punch, then whipped around stomping down on the side of Kevin's knee. A scream of pain tore from Kevin's throat as his leg crumpled. With two quick steps, Paul got behind him, back to back, and wrapped his hands around Kevin's head. With his shoulder, he lifted Kevin off the ground, then brought him down sharply. A loud crack echoed through the silent crowd as Kevin's neck broke. He went limp and Paul tossed his body to the ground.

"I will not tolerate cowardly, dishonorable actions in this pack," he shouted at the shocked onlookers. Everyone shuffled nervously in place looking at the people standing next to them in disbelief. Then, Paul tilted his head back and howled.

The sound resonated in Genevieve's chest. This was power. This was pack. Maybe Greer was right and werewolves had become too tame recently. She might hate that people had to be hurt, but she couldn't deny how this made her feel. The pack would follow Paul now.

"That was intense," Steven said, already scribbling down notes.

It annoyed her to see him doing that, as if the werewolves were zoo animals he was studying. He might think what he'd just witnessed was "intense" but he hadn't felt it. He had no idea how powerful it really was.

"I'll be back, I need to go talk to him about my case."

"What?" Steven's head snapped up, his eyes focusing on her finally. "I'll go with you. I'd like to see--"

"No. This is pack business, it's not appropriate for you to tag along. Just stay here and don't bother anyone," she said, barely keeping from snapping at him. It wasn't really Steven's fault she was upset with him. She'd just been having a bad week and didn't have the patience for his quirks today.

"Okayyy, fine," he said, looking put out.

She hurried toward where Paul was standing, talking to a few of his pack members. They looked completely awed by their new alpha. Paul had always exuded a cool, give-no-shits vibe but he was standing straighter now.

As she approached, he turned and caught her gaze, then said something to the others before heading toward her. He was still completely nude but that didn't faze her anymore. She kept her eyes firmly on his face though.

They stopped in front of each other and Paul grinned at her. "I didn't expect you to come."

"I wanted to watch you win. Congrats by the way," she said, returning his smile.

He nodded his head in thanks. "Now I simply have to maintain the position for a month."

"Something tells me you won't have a problem after how...decisive your victory was." Her eyes strayed to Kevin's corpse. They hadn't moved him yet. If her research was correct, they'd wait for a council member to come and record the death, then turn his body over to the authorities. She thought she should feel bad for the guy but he had been an awful alpha and person.

Paul snorted. "It wasn't what I intended but I will gladly use it as a teaching experience for the rest of the pack. But I know that's not why you're here. What do you need?"

She turned back, slipping into her business mindset. "Davie Johnson is sitting in jail, unable to be released on bail until his alpha vouches for him."

He sighed and scratched the back of his head. "I thought it might be about him."

"He never should have been arrested. The fight was started by someone else, he just happened to finish it."

"Davie is an idiot and a troublemaker, and he has been since the day he was turned. He was one of Lockhart's poorer choices."

"He may be an idiot, but he needs help. Maybe a respectable alpha to show him the error of his ways?" she prodded, trying not to be too blunt about bringing up his past mistakes.

Paul smiled and shook his head. "You certainly know how to guilt a man into doing what you want."

She shrugged and did her best to keep the smile off her face. "Just doing my job."

"I'll be there. You can text me the address." He nodded goodbye, then headed back to his pack.

Genevieve watched him go and felt...satisfied. She had done it. It hadn't gone how she'd hoped, exactly, but that didn't matter. In the end, she'd succeeded.

"Hey Gen, you ready to go?" Steven shouted from across the yard.

"Yeah, I am." She headed back to her pack and felt a little lighter on her feet. It was time to celebrate.

Today was Tommy's birthday –– the butthead had tried to hide the date but she'd found it out just in time –– and then tonight was the full moon. They hadn't run together as a pack in forever. She was looking forward to it.

CHAPTER 77

TOMMY

A chest plate crafted from one hundred percent tuna can. A helmet made from a measuring cup. A slingshot of rubber bands and chopsticks. And a saddle that was carefully sewn together from only the finest tire scraps.

"There's no way he can do it," Evangeline said, eyeing Woggy's get up.

"Quit being so pessimistic. We've been training for this. He can do it." Tommy adjusted the little helmet, strapping it securely under the pixie's wide chin. Woggy smacked his hands against it and almost knocked himself over but it stayed in place.

"I agree, the chances of success are low despite extensive preparation," Deward chimed in unhelpfully.

Tommy glared at him. "That's enough from both of you. You should be encouraging him, not assuming he'll fail."

Ceri knocked on the door to his room, slightly breathless from jogging upstairs. "Is he ready? The pixies are swarming out front."

Tommy looked down at Woggy who stared up at him with a determined expression. *Outside?* he signed.

The pixie nodded resolutely and signed, *outside* and *mine*. Standing there in his armor, he looked like a little warrior. It still pained Tommy to think of the pixies fighting since someone was bound to get hurt, but Woggy needed his yard. He couldn't live in fear.

Tommy handed Woggy the slingshot and the little bag of pebbles they'd chosen for this battle. With weapons in hand, Woggy marched over to Captain Jack. The cat paused, looking up from his belly licking, and seemed to sense that it was time. The two of them had a strange connection, and sometimes Tommy wondered how smart the cat was, exactly. Especially after the whole glowing eyes thing Deward had mentioned.

Once Captain Jack had rolled to his feet, Woggy climbed up the makeshift saddle, settling in place. The bag hooked over the front of the saddle, keeping his ammo within reach. Rubber band stirrups hung down from each side to brace Woggy's feet and help him hang on. Watching them race around the house for the past week had been hilarious. Even Captain Jack seemed to enjoy his role as the pixie's noble steed.

Riding with his head held high, Woggy pointed toward the door and squeaked twice, signaling Captain Jack to head in that direction. The procession that led downstairs was somber, marred only by Amber giggling hysterically.

Derek clamped a hand over her mouth but that quickly devolved into a wrestling match.

Tommy walked ahead and grabbed the door handle, ready to open it, but he hesitated. "Maybe I should go out there with him. Just in case--"

"You can't," Ceri said firmly. "We talked about this and Deward is right. Woggy has to win their respect to reclaim the yard if we don't want to murder them all."

He sighed and nodded his head. They'd talked this over a dozen times. It was the only way. "Okay."

Stepping back, he pulled the door open. Woggy put a pebble in the slingshot and adjusted his position in the saddle. Captain Jack meowed loudly. And then they were off.

The cat could move fast when he wanted to. The crazed duo shot out of the door, both of them letting out a ferocious battle cry.

Their fearless charge startled the swarm of pixies currently hovering in the bushes near the porch. They scattered like a flock of startled birds, shooting into the air with a frantic flapping of their wings.

Tommy shut the door and hurried over to the living room window. Each window had the eager faces of the pack pressed up against it. Watching and waiting.

"Yes! That was the perfect shot!"

Tommy shoved his way in next to Evangeline and watched as Woggy unleashed his fury over the rival swarm. Pebbles sped out of the slingshot, each one hitting its mark. A pixie crashed into the bushes, another onto the walkway that led to the porch.

As a few of the pixies began to fight back, Captain Jack darted here and there, dodging the rocks they threw. He caught one with a swipe of his paw and knocked it into the porch banister.

"Oooh, Jack is helping him," Amber said excitedly.

Tommy curled his hands into a fist and watched with bated breath. The scattered pixies were starting to regroup. They were flying at him now in groups of two or three trying to snatch him out of his saddle. They knew he couldn't fly. If they knocked him off...he'd be vulnerable.

"He's running low on ammo already," Deward said, watching intently. The troll tried to pretend he didn't care about this whole thing, but Tommy knew he wanted to see Woggy win. The pixie had a way of winning even the most cold-hearted over.

Woggy launched a pebble at a group of three pixies speeding toward him. He caught one in the head, but the other two grabbed his helmet and yanked. With an angry squeak he was dragged backward off the saddle, then tossed onto the porch. He hit the ground and rolled a ways before coming to a stop. For a moment, Tommy was afraid he wouldn't get up, but he did, shaking his head as though the blow had knocked him senseless.

The remaining pebbles had been scattered across the porch when he'd fallen. Woggy stuck his hand in the little bag and pulled out the last one. He loaded it into the slingshot and pulled the rubber band taut as he turned in a slow circle, searching for the next attack.

Captain Jack yowled and charged at some of the pixies, forcing the majority of the swarm back. One of them got through. This pixie was different from the others. He wore a paperclip necklace with a leaf dangling from it and had a distinctly fierce look about him. He swooped toward Woggy, zig-zagging in the air to make himself a harder target.

"He's only got one shot left," Ceri said, her face practically pressed against the window. "The odds of him making the shot are——"

Tommy elbowed Deward. "Good. They're *good odds.*"

The pack went silent after that, watching the pixie close in with bated breath. Woggy pulled the rubber band back as far as was possible without snapping it. His big, bulging eyes narrowed as he focused in on his target. The old pixie darted left then right, then shot up into the air.

Woggy followed the quick movement, moving his left leg back to brace himself. With a rage-filled squeak, the pixie flattened his wings to his back and dove. Woggy released the pebble.

Tommy's fingertips dug into the window-sill as he watched the pebble fly up, up, and smack dab into the center of the attacking pixie's forehead.

The old pixie dropped like a stone as Woggy leapt out of the way, hitting the ground with a thud and lying still in a small, gray heap. Woggy froze, watching him with his slingshot clutched to his chest. After one breathless moment, the pixie's leg twitched and he jerked back to consciousness. He pushed himself upright slowly, keeping an eye on Woggy.

The old pixie was a darker gray than the others. A scar slashed through his wide lips and his wings were notched and torn from old battles. He rose and limped toward Woggy, who brandished his empty slingshot like a sword. Then, he did the last thing Tommy expected. He yanked the leaf off his necklace and dropped it at Woggy's feet with a firm squeak. Woggy stared at the leaf, then looked at the other pixie, big eyes widening in surprise.

Woggy lowered his slingshot, then signed *friend.* The other pixie cocked his head in confusion, but awkwardly repeated the motion. The leader then turned to leave but Woggy squeaked, stopping him in his tracks. He turned back in confusion and Woggy signed *friend* again, then grabbed the leaf and ripped it in half.

All the gathered pixies squeaked in shock and horror, their wings flapping excitedly. The leader's lips curled back in a growl until Woggy held out half the leaf to him. He looked at the leaf, then looked at Woggy, who signed *friend* for a third time.

Something like understanding dawned on the old pixie's face and he took half the leaf, clutching it to his chest. He limped forward and Woggy held still, holding onto his own leaf. The old pixie squeaked, then very carefully licked the top of Woggy's head.

"Ew," Genevieve muttered.

Ceri smacked her on the arm. "Shhh, this is a beautiful moment."

Woggy returned the gesture, his long, slimy tongue wiping away the blood on the pixie's head. The leader repeated the sign for *friend*, seeming to finally get the connection.

Behind them, the other pixies began squeaking and swooping through the air in celebration. The ones that could still fly at least. Many of them were a bit worse for the wear.

Tommy let out a breath he hadn't realized he'd been holding. This was the best birthday present ever.

CHAPTER 78

DEREK

Derek had never really looked at the moon before, not like they did. Whatever their connection to it was, it seemed worshipful. All day they'd been full of energy and talking about their run that night.

He watched them shift while trying real hard not to think about the fact that his sister was naked. It was easy to watch Ceri instead. She was currently twirling in the middle of the yard, her face turned up toward the sky, and her skirt billowing around her. It was the first time he'd seen her *really* smile since she had been taken.

"Come on," Ceri said, holding her hand out to him with a brilliant smile.

"What?"

"Come run with us!" She started walking backwards toward the pack and they all looked at him expectantly.

"We can't keep up with them." He felt out of place. He wasn't part of the pack. They had welcomed him but it wasn't the same.

"You can keep up with me," Ceri insisted.

The wind danced through her curls and the moonlight highlighted the soft curve of her cheeks. She was looking right at him, into him. There was no way he could say no to her right now. Probably not ever.

He set his drink down and jogged after her. Amber took off at a run toward the tree line, a howl rising up that each pack member echoed. Ceri grabbed his hand and dragged him after her. She lifted her head and howled too, completely carefree.

He laughed and tried to howl too, but it came out more like a strangled yell. She laughed anyhow and tightened her grip on his hand. Their feet flew over the forest floor as the pack darted around them. Tommy was like a puppy, yipping and tripping over things. The black wolf, Genevieve, was so fast he could barely see her sometimes. She raced ahead with Amber, winding through the trees.

Something stirred in him as he ran with them. It was faint, but it felt like family. Ceri looked back at him, her blue eyes sparkling with pure happiness, and he knew he wanted to stay with them forever.

CHAPTER 79

CERI

Ceri stared at the ceiling and wondered what the hell she'd been thinking. Well, she knew what she'd been thinking. She'd nearly died, been tortured, and had almost given in to the dark side. That and the full moon had made all sorts of things seem like a good idea.

Derek's snore turned into a snort and he shifted in his sleep, throwing his arm over her chest and burying his face in her neck. She sighed. Last night had been nothing short of perfect but now she had to deal with the consequences. Maybe they could try this... whatever it was. The damage was already done so she might as well enjoy it while she could. Or maybe that would make it worse.

She wished she could just go back to sleep and be blissfully unaware of all of this but sleep was no longer an option, not with her mind running through worst case scenarios like a hyperactive hamster on a wheel. Maybe if she got up and hid in the bathroom he'd just go back to his room and they wouldn't even have to talk about it.

"I can feel you overthinking this," Derek said. His voice was rough from sleep. He smoothed his fingers through her hair and the tension in her muscles relaxed slightly.

"I just––"

He quickly put his fingers over her lips, then pushed up on his elbow so he could look at her. "You don't owe me anything because of last night. I'm not going to pressure you. You said you didn't want to date me, so unless you decide you've changed your mind, let's not rehash all that."

She pulled his hand down so she could reply. "You're being way too accommodating."

He grinned and tugged on a lock of her hair, winding the curl around his finger. "I learned the hard way that there's nothing worse than chasing after a girl that doesn't want to be with you. I'm not doing that again. However, if you just need a distraction every now and then, I can certainly *accommodate* that."

She smacked him but couldn't help but grin. "This is a slippery slope. It's going to end in disaster."

He flopped back down on the bed beside her and dragged her over on top of him. "Then we should have fun along the way."

Winding his hands through her hair, he tugged her down for a kiss. She quickly pushed her hand in between them, covering his mouth, and wiggled her fingers, casting a quick spell. He flinched and grimaced at her.

"What the hell was that?"

"Breath freshening spell." She grabbed his head and closed the distance between them, letting his lips distract her from the worries in her mind. As his hands slid down her back, she melted into his embrace, letting her fingers trace the muscles in his arms. He was already in her bed after all, she might as well enjoy him while she had him close by.

CHAPTER 80

EVANGELINE

Her life fit into a backpack. The one she'd tried to steal that Tommy had instead given to her when he'd heard she was leaving.

"Are you okay?" her mother asked, putting an arm around her shoulders.

"Is it weird that I'll miss them?"

Her mother smiled and tucked a loose strand of hair behind her ear. "Not at all. I think it's the closest I've seen you come to having friends."

"Oh gods, don't make me sound so pathetic," she said, zipping up her backpack and swinging it over her shoulder.

"Then don't look so pathetic," her mother said, clapping a hand on her back. "We're getting a fresh start and you know they'll stay in touch however they can. Especially that *boy.*"

She glared at her mother and held her finger up to her lips emphatically, shushing her. "They can *hear you.*"

Her mother laughed as she hurried out of the room, cheeks flushed with embarrassment. As she headed down the stairs the front door opened. Kadrithan was hovering behind Amber in his ridiculous little, red devil form.

A man and a woman walked in. The man was tall and lanky with a slight stoop to his shoulders. He had on a baseball cap that was pushed back with black curls spilling out beneath the brim.

"Ms. Hale, Asshole Demon," he greeted the two of them in turn with a nod. His wife or whoever she was, smacked him on the arm.

Evangeline had to hide her laugh behind her hand. She already liked them. Anyone who literally called her uncle Asshole Demon was her hero.

"I'm Katarina, and this is my idiot lover, Charlie," she said, shaking Amber's hand. Her accent was Russian but she looked like she was half elf. Her ears were lightly pointed and her hair had a hint of pastel blue to it.

"Nice to meet y'all," Amber said, shaking her hand with a smile.

Eloise walked past her and hurried over to meet their new hosts. They were apparently being driven over the border, then flown to somewhere in South America, the location to be disclosed once they were there. Her uncle had promised her beaches and no strangers, so she hadn't complained. Honestly, it sounded like a paradise right now.

A mass of blonde curls suddenly blocked her view as Ceri wrapped her up in an unexpected hug. "I know we weren't all that close, but I wish you well."

"Thanks," Evangeline said, pulling away. The rest of the pack gave her a brief hug as well, wishing her luck.

Charlie grabbed her mother's suitcase and headed out toward the car.

"We'll see you at the car," Katarina said with a gentle smile. She had a calming air about her that Evangeline had come to associate with elves. Except for Thallan. That asshole was insane.

Kadrithan followed Katarina outside, discussing some detail about their journey with her. Evangeline sighed and followed. As she stepped outside, Tommy stopped her, shutting the door behind him. He looked a little awkward. She could actually feel his nervousness through the mark, which was an odd sensation.

"Do you know how long you'll be gone?"

She shrugged. "No clue."

"Alright, well, keep in touch."

Acting on impulse, she put her hand over the mark on his chest and looked up. "I'll see you again, don't worry." She felt like an idiot right away but it was too late to take it back.

He smiled and placed his hand over hers. "Maybe you can come visit every now and then like your uncle."

Shuddering in horror, she shook her head. "That's way too creepy. I'll just text."

He laughed and dragged her into an unexpected hug. "Ok, that works."

They parted and she hurried to the waiting car, looking back over her shoulder one last time. The pack had not been what she'd expected. They'd been good, even to someone like her who didn't fit in anywhere.

CHAPTER 81

AMBER

It was almost Thanksgiving. The leaves had all fallen from the trees and it was getting genuinely cold at night. Amber curled her arms around her legs and stared up at the moon. It was waning now, but she could still feel the pull of it in her blood. The wolf shifted in her mind, watching alongside her.

The door opened and she jumped, still easily startled after the week they'd had. Derek walked out and shut the door behind him.

"I've finally caught you alone," he said, raising a judgmental brow.

"Has it been that obvious I've been avoiding you?" she asked ruefully.

"Yes." He walked over and sat down on the porch swing next to her, making the chains clank. "I talked to Bernard and he's not going to evict us. Insurance will also cover the damage to the warehouse. We should be able to open the mechanic shop only two weeks later than planned."

Amber's shoulder slumped in relief. "Glad to hear it. I'm sorry it's been nothing but trouble since you got here. I really thought we could just get to work and not have all this drama."

He raised his brow at her. "I don't think your life will ever be drama free again. But that's okay. We've got this, sis."

"I really hope so but sometimes I wonder." She rubbed her forehead and sighed. "The no magic zone is different from the others. It's still expanding, which is freaking everyone out. Selena is still out there, probably murdering people as we speak."

"I know. We'll find her and stop her. The police are blaming her and the sorcerer for the no magic spots, so you'll even have help for once."

"They still don't understand how the no magic spots are created or why. Detective Sloan also said the sorcerer we killed couldn't have been responsible for them all." She shook her head, frustrated. They may have saved Ceri but the sorcerer had still succeeded.

He'd left his mark on the pack too. Ceri still woke up with nightmares. If Amber moved too quickly, sometimes Genevieve would flinch. She always tried to laugh it off, but Amber knew she had hurt her. Tommy spent every free moment training with Deward like he expected them to go to war at any moment. This wasn't what she wanted for them.

"What are we becoming?" she asked quietly, regretting the words a little as soon as they left her mouth.

"You're still who you were before you were bitten. You're just stronger, faster, and hairier now," Derek said with a smile, trying to lighten the mood.

"Am I though?" she asked, turning to look at her brother. "I've killed people, and enjoyed it. I almost killed *you*. Whatever this is, it's changing me. Maybe it's impossible to keep from becoming...evil."

Derek sighed and the smile fell away. He looked out over the yard and pursed his lips thoughtfully. "You're not a bad person, no matter how much you think you've changed. We both saw *real* evil that night. The wolf inside you is a predator, but you control those urges, and most importantly, you still control your own actions."

"If there ever comes a moment where I'm not in control anymore you have to promise me that you'll stop me," she said, holding his gaze.

"You have me and the whole pack watching your back, Amber. We won't let anything happen to you."

She rubbed her hand against the demon mark absently and forced herself to smile at her brother. "I know."

CHAPTER 82

KADRITHAN

"Is the girl safe?" Zerestria demanded.

"She is, and she has embraced her potential, finally. She gave one of the wolves her demon mark," he said, careful to keep his tone even and respectful.

Zerestria slumped back in her chair in relief. She was old, one of the few still left that remembered what it had been like before the Fall. Before the curse. "The girl's stubbornness was infuriating, but in some ways, I respect her resisting as long as she did."

"It was foolish. She is the key to breaking this curse, and she put that all at risk just because she didn't *like* what she had to do." He paced the length of the room, only looking up when he noted that Zerestria hadn't responded yet.

She looked at him with amusement, raising her brow.

"Oh, shut up, she's nothing like me," he said, rolling his eyes.

"She has your stubbornness and her mother's temper. It's a miracle she's still alive," the old woman said, shaking her head with a laugh.

"She might be my niece, but sometimes she's an asshole," he said grumpily.

"That's the angel half of her," Zerestria said with a smirk as she rose from her chair. Her back was slightly stooped with age, but the magic that kept them alive strengthened her frail body. Her long, silver hair fell over her shoulders like a shawl.

As she rummaged through her desk, he wandered toward the window. It used to be beautiful. It had been a paradise.

Now bare trees covered the barren hills, their arms stretching toward an orange sky. The air was dry and still. There was no breeze. The seasons never changed. When their magic had been stripped from them, it had destroyed this realm.

He closed his eyes, and for a moment, let himself remember their glorious past. His mouth watered at the thought of the sweet fruits he used to pick from the trees. The gardens had been bursting with flowers. He and his sister had spent every afternoon swimming in the cool, clear lakes.

"Kadrithan, we need to get in touch with the others. I need to know if your cousin managed to get a mark on someone actually useful," Zerestria said, interrupting his pity party. She sealed the envelope and set it aside.

"I'll go ask in person, I've been meaning to check with my cousin as well," he said, extending his hand for the letter.

Once the dust had settled, a resistance had grown within their ranks. It had been scattered and ineffectual for centuries, but slowly, the elders had begun to work together instead of against one another. A plan had been formed. They hadn't realized someone like Evangeline would have to play a role until she was about five years old. They'd initially kept her alive just because of how badly the angels wanted her kind dead. His gut had told him she would be important.

Amber was both a complication, and possibly, an unexpected help. She didn't trust him at all now, but he could fix that eventually. She was driven by a sense of justice, and she had a thing for helping the underdog. If all else failed, he could make her help. She wore his mark.

That had been a bit of quick thinking. He smiled as he strode out of the tower. He wasn't really a demon any more than the angels were really angels, but he could play the part. He was good at it. Amber's mark was one of a hundred he wore. All different pawns in this centuries long war. He had more marked souls than any of his brethren.

One day, he would be rid of them all. His hand tightened on the envelope, crinkling it. One day, he would be free.

MISFIT FORTUNE

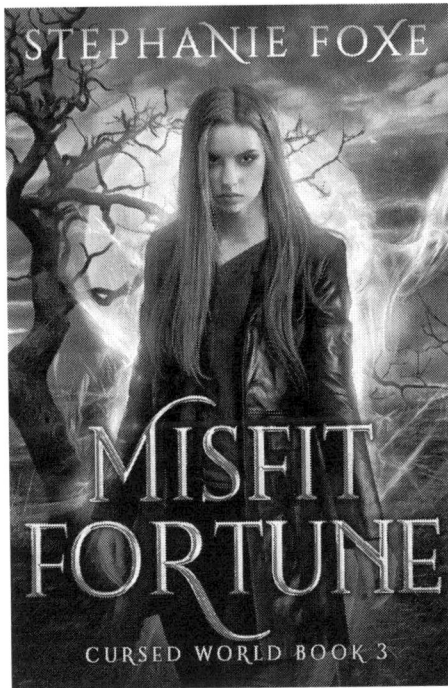

"You guys might not know this, but I consider myself a bit of a loner. I tend to think of myself as a one-man wolf pack. But when my sister brought Doug home, I knew he was one of my own. And my wolf pack... it grew by one. So there... there were two of us in the wolf pack... I was alone first in the pack, and then Doug joined in later. And six months ago, when Doug introduced me to you guys, I thought, "Wait a second, could it be?" And now I know for sure, I just added two more guys to my wolf pack. Four of us wolves, running around the desert together, in Las Vegas, looking for strippers and cocaine. So tonight, I make a toast!"

- Alan, The Hangover

To growing your wolf pack, overcoming fears, and finding your way in the world!

AROOOOOO!

PROLOGUE

It buzzed in the air, crackling and scraping against the small chamber that confined it. The elf bit her tongue until blood filled her mouth, but she couldn't stop it. The truth had to be released.

Bubbling up her throat like acid, it spilled through her teeth and past her lips in a scream. Even if she hadn't been alone, no one would have been able to understand her. The words tumbled over each other too fast and out of order. There was too much that had to be said and seen. It had been so long since the truth had been spoken. Perhaps centuries.

Cassandra writhed on the ground, grime caking the strands of her white-blonde hair. If she could have seen it she would have recoiled in disgust, but her eyes were focused on something far away.

On blood and flame that fell from the sky.
On light and darkness.
On death.

The curse burrowed into her soul and latched onto her magic like a leech. For years she had searched for this. She'd thought it was a gift, but she had been wrong. So very wrong.

Hours, or perhaps days, later she stilled. Her eyes remained unfocused, a strange white fog obscuring her vision. Her blood-stained lips twitched as if they were still trying to speak truth.

Tears slipped from her eyes as she rolled onto her knees but she ignored them. It was clear now what she had to do. She hadn't known or understood before.

"The angel...the angel..." she whispered as she crawled forward, ignoring the filth under her hands.

CHAPTER 1

❧

AMBER

Amber wiped a trickle of sweat threatening to roll into her eyes and accidentally smeared oil across her forehead. With a sigh, she tried to rub it off with the rag tucked in her pocket but it was a lost cause.

"I see you still can't stay clean when you're under a truck," Derek said, kicking her foot lightly.

"Like you do any better. Only Dad and Jackson ever managed that." Her old truck had been in desperate need of a tune up. Today was a slow day in the shop, so Derek had told her to bring it in and work on it. Of course, he'd added that she probably needed the practice, and she'd punched him in the arm too hard. Ceri had been mad at her for that, which had made Derek smug. Older brothers were a pain in the butt.

Derek chuckled. "Maybe they made a deal with a demon."

"Ha. Ha." She stuck her hand out. "Give me the 10mm socket."

The tools clanked together as he dug through the box. It had been organized, but that had only lasted for one day.

"I can't find it."

"Of course you can't. I swear that one has legs and just walks off."

"I'll check the office. I know I saw it somewhere weird." Derek's footsteps headed toward the back of the shop where his office was. The place was a lot less creepy now that they'd cleared out the dirt, cobwebs, and chased out the rats.

Rolling herself out from under the truck, she came face to face with her own personal demon. She jerked in surprise and almost hit her head.

A satisfied grin spread across Angel's face. He'd made it his life's mission to scare her whenever he could. Taunting him during that first meeting had backfired badly.

"I seriously need to put a bell on you," she muttered, waving him away so she could sit up.

Angel snorted and transformed into a cowbell with an ominous pair of red eyes. He swung side to side and a low gong echoed through the shop. "Is this better?"

"That might actually be creepier."

He reverted back to his usual shape –– a small, red demon complete with a spiked tail –– and hovered by her shoulder. "Have you found anything out yet?"

"No, have you?"

Angel crossed his arms. "Nothing helpful."

They'd been looking for anything that might prove that the sorcerer, who had been destroying magic all around Portland, wasn't acting alone. Zachariah, the half angel Evangeline had killed, had worked for a powerful organization. They had to have known what he was doing. They'd likely been helping. What Amber couldn't figure out was why.

She also couldn't figure out what Angel really wanted from her. The threat of him calling in the new demon mark hung over her head like a storm cloud. More often than she'd like to admit, she'd realize that she was rubbing it absently as though it ached. The habit bothered Ceri most of all.

Derek stepped out of the office with an irritated expression. "Are you talking to yourself or...Kadrithan?"

That was one of the demon's names, though she knew it wasn't his summoning name. Kadrithan wouldn't explain the difference. No one else liked calling him Angel, though the nickname had stuck for Amber.

"Kadrithan," Amber said, walking away from the demon who seemed lost in thought.

"So creepy," Derek muttered, shaking his head. "I found the 10 mm socket hiding under the paper towels, but can you come look at this invoice? I can't read your handwriting. You got grease all over it too. You need to be more careful, I don't want everything getting trashed constantly."

Amber raised a brow at his tone. "Alright, grumpypants."

He sighed. "Yeah, yeah, just stop messing up the invoices. We kinda need these to get paid."

"I guess that's important," she muttered, snatching the invoice out of his hands, getting more grease on it. Maybe he did have a point. She sighed at the smudged writing. "I'll redo it. I remember this customer, but I can't read it either."

"You are an extremely messy person," Angel observed as he followed her toward the makeshift front desk they'd set up to handle customers. They didn't have a ton of them yet, but there was at least one or two every day. Enough to pay rent and get her a paycheck that was big enough to start covering groceries again.

"And you're annoying." She squirted some anti-grease soap Ceri had made the day before last in her hands and started scrubbing. Her fingernails seemed permanently stained, but the witch-made soap was helping. Slowly.

Angel snorted. "I am wise, cunning, and devastatingly handsome."

"You're two feet tall and look like a cartoon."

The demon tutted at her. "Perhaps one day I will permit you to look upon my true form. I'd show you now but I can't risk you swooning over me when there is so much work to be done."

He was right about the work part at least. Ever since the fight with the sorcerer it had felt like there was no time to rest.

They'd talked with the werewolf council, the police, and had been forced to ward the property against reporters. When the first group had managed to pop up at the front door, she'd nearly bitten their head off. Luckily Genevieve had been there to smooth things over and tell them *politely* to go the hell away.

If that wasn't enough, her council duties had become even more annoying. The paperwork was already miserable, but the torture she was going to be put through in a few days was...well...going to be torture.

She wished Donovan Lockhart was still alive just so she could kill him again before he stuck her with this crappy job.

The sink cracked under her grip and she realized she'd just been staring into the mirror growling. With a guilty glance over her shoulder, she dried her hands and grimaced at the state of the sink. At least it wasn't completely broken. Maybe Derek wouldn't notice.

"Amber, are you done yet?" Derek shouted from the other side of the shop. He was starting to get irritated. He'd had a short fuse for the past week.

"Almost!" She sighed and headed back to the desk to rewrite the invoice.

It was obvious something was bothering him, but she'd already asked once and he'd nearly bitten her head off. He was even more allergic to chatting about his feelings than she was apparently.

Wait for them to come to you. If you nag them to come to you every time they're upset, then they'll really start hiding things. Trust them to know when they need help. And that includes me.

She'd promised Ceri she'd take her advice, but it went against her instincts. She was their alpha. How could she protect them if she didn't know what was wrong?

"Well, this has been great fun, but I'll have to leave you for now." The demon yawned mockingly, then disappeared in a puff of smoke.

Amber snatched a new invoice from the paper pad and grabbed a pen. After this, she was spending the rest of the day under a truck. They weren't complicated and moody. If there was a problem, she just found it and fixed it. No stupid emotions necessary.

CHAPTER 2

⚜

GENEVIEVE

"Amber is so not ready for this," Genevieve said, dropping the book on the bed and putting her head in her hands. "This is all about politics and kissing ass. The two things she sucks at the *most*."

Steven, who was sitting cross-legged on the other end of the bed, grimaced. "But she has to do it, right?"

"Yeah, she has to." She flopped back and stared up at the ceiling, tracing the old water stains with her eyes. There was no way out of this. It wasn't something they could run from or avoid. Amber, as an alpha on a council, had to show up at The Gathering –– the colloquial term for the National Gathering of Werewolves.

It was a huge conference that hosted hundreds of packs. Luckily, it was held in Seattle, otherwise they'd be forced to fly to wherever it was. Last year it had been in New York City.

Supposedly, the idea was to make sure laws and rules were being enforced, put new rules to a vote, and introduce new alphas. In practice, there was a lot of posturing. Alliances were forged among the more powerful packs, of course. On the other hand, there were challenges. Some alphas lost their packs. It was rare but it made her nervous nonetheless.

She dragged her hands down her face with a groan and tossed her feet in Steven's lap. He absently massaged one with his free hand, nose still stuck in a book.

"When are you meeting with Shane?"

"Ah, crap." She scrambled for her phone, fumbling with it to turn on the screen. "In five minutes. I've gotta go."

Steven frowned as she jumped out of bed. "I thought we were going to get lunch."

"Shane had to move up the meeting. Sorry I forgot to tell you. I obviously forgot myself." She shoved her feet in her black boots and yanked on her jacket. "We'll reschedule."

Steven sighed, curling back up and staring down at his book. He was mad. Again.

Antsy to leave, she didn't have time to coddle him right now. "Look, we'll reschedule soon, okay?"

"Sure," he said tightly.

With a sigh, she left. Things had been getting awkward between them. He wanted more attention than she had time to give. Work and her duties as Amber's beta took up all her energy. Sometimes she thought she should just break up with him and save them both the pain but she couldn't bring herself to do it. Not again. If she was honest, she didn't want to either. She just didn't know how to make it work.

Traffic worked in her favor, but she was still ten minutes late by the time she jogged into the restaurant. She followed the distinctive scent of Shane's cologne to a table near the back.

"Sorry I'm late," she said as she hurried toward the booth.

He waved away her apology. "I know you well enough now to not expect punctuality."

"Glad to know I've made a good impression," she muttered as she plopped down across from him.

The corners of his mouth lifted as he picked up his menu. "You're a good beta. Amber is lucky to have you."

"Darn right she is." She picked up the menu. "What's good here?"

"Steak, rare, with a side of shrimp."

She nodded and set the menu aside. Ever since they'd learned about The Gathering, she'd been full of nervous energy. Today was no different. She couldn't stop her fingers from drumming against the table and she had an urge to shift and growl at the people that kept walking too close to their table as they passed by.

"Having a bad day?" Shane asked, eyeing her suspiciously.

"Have you been to The Gathering?"

He nodded. "Five times since I became Jameson's beta."

Genevieve curled her hand into a fist to keep her fingers from acting on their own. "I've been doing a lot of research on it, and it's looking more and more...risky."

Shane frowned and leaned back against the gaudy red pleather that lined the booth. She was picking the restaurant next time.

"Jameson's pack is well-established, so we've never had issues. I've never seen such a new pack attend since it normally takes a long time to acquire a council seat. So yes, it is a bit of a risk for your pack, but you won't be alone. Jameson has your back."

"We don't have an alliance with Jameson."

"Not everything is alliances and politics. He's a good guy and he's not going to let some other pack do anything stupid."

"That's easy to say now. In practice, these things are always messy. Amber is a bitten alpha. There are rumors flying around about my pack's involvement with the sorcerer and demons. This isn't going to be your typical Gathering."

Shane sighed. "I guess I can't argue with that."

"I have to be as prepared as possible. I need to know *everything* about *everyone*. Alliances. Enemies. Alphas that just hate each other on principle. And I want to know which packs are more sympathetic towards bitten weres."

Shane shook his head but had a smile on his face now. "They're not going to know what hit them."

She grinned unapologetically. "That's the idea."

"I take it back, Amber isn't lucky to have you, she's *incredibly* lucky."

"As I said, darn right she is." The nervous energy faded a little as they got to work making lists and plans. Working behind the scenes was where Genevieve shined, and she knew it. Amber was the brave one, and she was their leader. As her beta, Genevieve could use her cunning to give Amber the edge she needed over those born alphas. They wouldn't go into this unprepared.

CHAPTER 3

TOMMY

If he hadn't been a werewolf, Tommy would have been cold. As it was, the afternoon sun beating down on his back was enough to make him sweat.

His muscles burned as he completed his fifth set of pushups. Deward had decided to combine studying with exercise and, possibly, a murder attempt. At least that's how it was starting to feel. The troll seemed particularly determined to make him stronger and faster than ever. If it were anyone else, Tommy would think they were worried about some kind of imminent attack.

"Pause," Deward said, stopping his own set of pushups and grabbing the flashcards.

He held them up, giving Tommy only three seconds to blurt out the right answer before he'd set it in the 'needs work' pile. Every card in that pile meant another set of some kind of exercise. Tommy was highly motivated to get the answers right.

His GED test was in a few weeks and he'd thought he was ready but Deward was still pushing him. Deep down, he was thankful. Very, very deep down.

Deward put the final card in the 'known' pile and crossed his arms. "You're still weak in history."

"That's because it's boring," Tommy said, still panting slightly. "What's next?"

Deward's green face twisted in shock and dismay. "No area of learning and knowledge can be described as boring. You should look for what interests you within the subject. History is one of the most important——"

"Dude, calm down, I know. We've been over this before."

Deward scoffed and turned away, smoothing down his bright blue hair which was sticking up because of the vigorous exercise. "Obviously the lesson hasn't settled in."

Tommy stood, stretching his sore muscles. To his eyes the demon mark Evangeline had given him stood out in sharp contrast to his brown skin. No one else could see it though. He rubbed it absently. It didn't quite ache, but he could always feel it. Amber did the same thing, always looking guilty when she realized what she was doing. It bothered Ceri but he understood the impulse. It wasn't about the demon, really, it was just that it was *there*, all the time, like an itch.

"Does it hurt?" Deward asked curiously. One of the things Tommy liked about the troll was that he was the least judgmental person he'd ever met. Deward was driven by curiosity, not by a need to feel morally superior. Unless you were factually wrong, of course. Or neglected your education.

"No," he said, pressing his fingers into the mark again. "I'm just always aware of it. It was worse when it was fresh, but it's getting less…annoying."

"I've been reading up on demon marks, but have found it difficult to separate fact from fiction."

"I'm sure most people with a demon mark don't want to talk about it. It's not entirely legal, and it comes with a big stigma."

Deward nodded, then rubbed at the base of a tusk with a grimace.

"What's wrong?"

"Growing pains," Deward grumbled. "My tusks will shed soon and the new ones will come in. I will become a man."

"Oh, that's kind of cool. I didn't realize they did that," Tommy said, surprised.

"We don't speak of it to outsiders often. It's a sacred time."

"Is it okay to tell me then?"

Deward slapped a strong hand on his shoulder. "You are my brother now. Of course it is okay."

Tommy still wasn't sure *exactly* what that meant and he had been hesitant to ask for some reason. "About that…"

Ceri walked out just then, interrupting the conversation.

Deward nodded to the witch in greeting. "Ceridwen, how are you?"

She still had dark circles under her eyes, showing she hadn't been sleeping, and had a scowl on her face.

"I have to go deal with…well, you know," she said, waving her hand at them.

"Do you need help?" Tommy asked, crossing his arms. He didn't like her dealing with it alone but she kept insisting on it.

"No, I'll be fine. It's easier when it's just me." She sighed at his expression, her stance softening slightly. "I really will be fine. It's not dangerous."

"You keep saying that, but I don't buy it," Tommy muttered.

"I can take care of myself," Ceri said with a bemused smile.

"The point of a pack is that you don't *have* to. Aren't you always saying it's okay to accept help?"

"I have to stop giving you advice you can use against me," she said with a laugh, already walking away. "Maybe next time. It really is easier with just me though. I promise."

He watched her go with a sigh.

Deward stepped up beside him. "What is she doing that is so dangerous?"

Tommy stared across the yard at the old mansion. Grass wouldn't grow around it anymore. The now-rotting garden was brown and dry despite the recent rain. "Making sure Thallan doesn't kill himself."

"Ah," Deward said, his jaw clenching in anger. He wasn't any more fond of the crazy old elf than Tommy was.

Tommy turned his back on the shrine to Thallan's mental instability and cracked his knuckles. "Let's get back to work."

CHAPTER 4

CERI

The smell of alcohol and vomit hit Ceri as soon as she pushed open the front door. Thallan hadn't even bothered to fully shut it whenever he last stumbled back in.

She surveyed the entry way. It had never been clean but this was beyond even that. This was *disgusting*. He'd trashed half the mansion after his dead wife, Illya, had kicked him out of the guest house, and now he seemed determined to make the biggest mess possible. Especially on days when his therapist was supposed to show up.

They'd gone through five. Only one had attempted more than one appointment. Considering Thallan had tried to set that one on fire, she couldn't blame them for quitting.

The agency she was working with insisted they had found the perfect fit for him this time. Ceri was here to make sure Thallan was at least awake and not covered in his own vomit when the therapist showed up.

Some days she thought she might as well just let the elf give up and die. He seemed determined to do so after all, but...between Illya and her own conscience, she just couldn't let the idiotic elf hurt himself like this without at least *trying* to help.

She stepped over some vomit that had been smeared across the wooden floor. It was red, which had been worrying the first time she saw it. Now she knew that just meant he'd been out getting half-priced watermelon margaritas. The sickly sweet smell of it almost made her gag.

There were two spots in the house Thallan seemed to prefer passing out in. The first was in the tower, but based on the damage she was seeing, she doubted he'd made it that far. She headed past the study and library to the master suite.

The bedroom was shrouded in darkness. She flung open the curtains, letting the sunlight pour in. Thallan's bare foot protruded over the threshold to the bathroom.

She sighed. If he was naked again, she was just leaving.

Bracing herself for the worst, she walked over and looked in the bathroom. He'd managed to get his shirt off, but his pants were still in place. Soaked with piss, but at least his...bits...were hidden.

Despite only being forced to see that once, the image was forever burned into her brain. It would probably show up in her nightmares too if she ever managed to sleep again. Even curling up in bed with Derek or Amber wasn't doing the trick anymore. She'd have to resort to a sleeping potion soon, but she hated how foggy they made her feel when she woke up.

And how they could leave you trapped in nightmares until they wore off.

Grabbing the rubber band off her wrist, she tied her mess of curls into a bun on the top of her head. Hands on her hips, she went through the spells she'd need.

First things first, something for the smell. She pulled the sage stick out of her bag and lit it. After one quick wave around the door frame, she set it on the edge of the vanity where it could continue cleansing the air.

Stepping around the unconscious elf, she hurried over to the bathtub and turned on the water, plugging the drain. Magic was easier when you used the resources around you.

She placed her palms together and chanted quietly in Latin, "*Aer et aqua. Spiritus et vita. Hac tum praetoria nave emundate.*"

The water lifted from the tub and arced through the air before crashing into Thallan. He slid and rolled, slamming into the wall. The impact jarred him awake. Icy water rushed around him in a spiral, stripping away the filth.

"Wha...the...f..."

She hit him with a breath freshening spell, which had the added bonus of momentarily shutting him up. The sobering spell hit him even harder and he groaned, holding his head in his hands.

"I see you've been at happy hour again."

Peeking from under his arms, he scowled at her. "Nothing happy about it. The drinks are terrible."

"I'm sure it's truly terrible for you. Must be why you drink so many of them."

Thallan rolled up to his knees, glaring at her all the while. "I don't need *your* judgment. You're just their pet now. It's pathetic."

Ceri laughed aloud, startling herself and Thallan. It was ridiculous to hear him calling her pathetic when he had been laying in his own piss and vomit just a few minutes before. "Yeah, I'm the pathetic one. Get up and change clothes."

Thallan pushed up to his feet and half-stomped, half-limped toward his massive closet. There was nothing to distinguish the dirty piles that littered the floor of the walk in from the clean ones, but he seemed to know which to grab from. Or didn't care if the clothes were clean.

She sent a freshening spell at the shirt he picked up, just in case.

"Which method of harassment have you chosen for today? A sniveling psychotherapist? An idiotic, crackpot psychic?" Thallan yanked the silky black shirt on over his head without trying to unbutton it first. By the time he had it pulled down, his fine, white-blond hair hung in tangled, wet strands that stuck to his jaw. The twisted scar that cut through his patrician features reddened as a flush spread across his face from the exertion.

Ceri rolled her eyes. "At this point, I hope they just send someone who can shake some sense into you."

The doorbell rang discordantly through the house and she flinched. It had not sounded like that last time it rang. Somehow, Thallan had managed to break that too.

"I'm not answering it," Thallan growled as he brushed past her. "Tell whoever it is to go away and leave me alone."

Ignoring his whining, she headed toward the front of the house. As she stepped around the red vomit stain, she hoped the new therapist had a strong stomach.

"The things I do in the name of compassion," she muttered to herself with a sigh. She knew why she kept trying to save Thallan though. It was the only thing keeping her from collapsing. Every time she looked at him laying on the floor it reminded her to not give up. Gallaghers didn't crumble.

Steeling herself for another disaster, she opened the door, then froze.

The person she was seeing standing in front of her didn't make sense. This guy...there was no way he was a therapist. The chances were much higher that he was part of a motorcycle gang and was here to rob them.

"Are you..."

"Dr. Gunner Stone," he rumbled, his voice a deep bass, as he extended a scarred hand for her to shake.

She shook it absently. Dr. Gunner Stone was at least fifty years old but he looked like he'd lived a dozen lives in that time. Deep frown lines were carved into his tanned face. Thick, grey stubble grew on a boxy jaw. A leather vest covered in patches covered a sleeveless button up shirt, leaving his arms bare. His terrifyingly muscular arms.

This guy really *could* shake some sense into Thallan. Literally. She wanted to watch if he did.

"Sorry, come in," she said, stepping back and pulling the door open. Sunlight illuminated the dust in the entryway.

"Yes, I am a therapist." Dr. Stone said, walking further inside and looking around with a neutral expression. That was a feat in and of itself. It was hard to keep a straight face while looking at...all this.

"Oh, no, sorry, I believed you," Ceri said, a blush creeping up her neck. It must have been obvious by her expression how taken aback she was.

Dr. Stone waved away her explanation. "I don't wear suits and walk around looking like a prissy quack. Throws people off."

"Right. Well, um, would you like me to take you to Thallan?" she asked, feeling very thrown off indeed.

"I'll find him," Dr. Stone said, cracking his knuckles. He paused, humming curiously. A small wobbly, ball of light bloomed in front of him. He dipped his hand into and pulled out a thick card about the size of his palm.

She felt the hum of magic in the air and a wave of it passed through her. It felt...interested. "What was that?"

Dr. Stone extended a thick card toward her. The back was dark blue with a simple, symmetrical swirl in silver. "This is yours."

"What?" She stared at it, unwilling to touch anything magical when she had no clue what it was or why it was being given to her.

"The tarot card. It's yours," he said with a shrug. "I use them for my work, but every now and then I run across someone that needs to know something, and this one showed up for you."

"No offense, but tarot just really isn't my thing," Ceri said taking a step back and raising her hands. All fortune telling was complete crap. Tarot was no exception. She preferred real, solid magic. The card wiggled in his grip like it was trying to get to her.

"Well, you're going to have to take this one. If you don't, it's just going to follow you. They're very stubborn."

"You're talking about it like it's alive or something," she said with a nervous laugh.

He nodded thoughtfully. "They might be."

"Look, I really don't--"

There was a loud crash and the smell of smoke blew down the hall toward them.

Dr. Stone let the card go and it zoomed at her, hovering eagerly right in front of her face.

"I'll go deal with this nutcase. Good luck, and a bit of advice, don't avoid it too long or it will make itself real annoying."

With that, the doctor just walked off.

Ceri glared at the card jiggling in front of her and batted at it. It tried to grab her hand and she stumbled back with a shriek. "No! Bad tarot card!"

The corners of the card drooped as if she'd hurt it's feelings. The manipulation almost worked, but instead of falling for it, she turned and ran.

Sometimes it was simply the best course of action.

CHAPTER 5

AMBER

Amber stood next to Tommy at the window, watching the pixies intently. After the battle -- which Woggy had decisively won -- they had settled into a truce. It was tentative at first, but lately they'd been interacting a lot more.

The other pixies couldn't quite understand why Woggy couldn't fly. They'd look at his back and inspect the nubs where his wings used to be. It clearly disturbed them.

One of the pixies, who Amber was fairly certain was a girl, had tried tying two leaves to his back. Woggy had tested the contraption valiantly by jumping off the porch banister...and falling straight to the ground.

She was glad they could let Woggy outside without having to worry about him constantly though. Birds and other predators were still a concern, but since he hung out with the swarm, he was relatively safe. The swarm's leader seemed especially protective of him. Ceri said it was because he owed Woggy his life after Woggy had spared him in the battle.

Woggy had a group of pixies around him right now. He signed *food* and they all imitated the movement.

"Is he still trying to teach them sign language?" Amber asked.

"Yeah, and they seem to be making up their own words now. That's one of the cool things about sign language, it evolves based on the culture of the people using it. They've all given each other names and I *think* they are insulting each other as well."

Amber laughed. "Insults, huh?"

Tommy nodded solemnly. "My best translation of their most dire insult is *fruit sniffer.*"

"Ooooh, that's harsh."

"They really hate fruit."

"I've noticed. It's the only thing Woggy won't try to steal and eat." Amber's nose twitched at an acrid scent. "Is something burning?"

"Crap!" Tommy turned and sprinted back into the kitchen, muttering something about his onions.

"I chopped those carefully, you better not have wasted them!" she shouted after him.

Recently, she'd started helping him when he cooked, but he'd only let her do so much before he shooed her out of his kitchen. That didn't bother her in the least. Cooking was not one of her strengths.

Besides, she was just glad Tommy didn't cower or hesitate anymore. It was satisfying to see that she hadn't completely screwed up at least one of her pack members. Genevieve was still a little jumpy around her when she was shifted after the sorcerer had mind-controlled her. And Ceri...well, she was just in pain.

Right now, though, they were all together and as happy as she'd seen them. Pack dinners had become something of a ritual for them. They ate together often but the nights leading up to the full moon always felt different.

The wolf peered out of Amber's eyes and huffed in agreement. She wanted to shift and stretch her legs. Maybe they should run after dinner to work off the tension from the upcoming conference. The Gathering had them all nervous.

Amber glanced at her phone, looking for a text from Derek to let her know he'd be late and miss dinner. He'd skipped the last two, claiming he had paperwork to finish up. She wished he'd just come home and stop being grumpy, but the text was there just like she'd expected.

Genevieve picked up Captain Jack and almost tripped over his dangling legs.

"Did...is he bigger?" Genevieve asked, trying to lift the cat's back paws off the floor, and failing.

Ceri looked up from the book she was reading on the couch. "He can't be. He was full grown when we got him." She shook her head as if that could make it not true.

"I used to be able to pick him up!"

"Maybe you're shrinking?"

Genevieve narrowed her eyes at Ceri. "So that's possible, but the cat growing isn't?"

Amber walked over and crouched down, sniffing the mangy cat suspiciously. "He's definitely bigger. The greedy old fart hasn't gotten into your potions, has he?" she asked, looking over her shoulder at Ceri.

"Definitely not. I keep my room warded and locked. Besides, I would have noticed if there was a mess in there. You remember what he did to that lasagna."

Amber's face darkened. "Don't remind me." She stood and put her hands on her hips. "Maybe we should take him to the vet?"

"He isn't sick," Genevieve said, exasperated. She set the monster down and scratched underneath his jaw, making him purr like a chainsaw. "He's just our big, growing boy. Yes, he is. So strong and fierce."

Rolling her eyes, Amber walked back to the cabinets and pulled out dishes to set the table. "That thing is going to eat us all in our sleep one day."

"Not all of us. Just you," Genevieve shot back with a smirk.

As Amber tried to close the cabinet door something flew out and smacked her in the face. She dropped into a crouch and growled, whipping around to try and find where it had gone.

Tommy was by her side in a split second, claws growing from his fingertips.

"What is it?" Genevieve demanded as fur crept along her jaw.

Ceri sighed dramatically. "It's nothing, calm down."

A thick, black card bounced off her blonde curls, then did a little shimmy that looked suspiciously like some kind of mating dance.

"What the hell is that?" Amber demanded, not willing to relax quite so soon.

Ceri crossed her arms and thrust her chin out stubbornly. "A tarot card."

"Tarot cards don't normally attack people and fly around." Amber took a few cautious steps forward, ready to dodge if it attacked again.

"Don't be so dramatic. It didn't attack you, it just…" she threw her hands in the air. "It can't hurt anyone, okay?"

Despite her remaining hesitation, Amber relaxed and retracted her claws. "Why is it so attached to you?"

It clearly wanted the witch's attention. Badly. It hadn't stopped trying to get her to look at it, alternating between exotic shaking and forlorn little waves.

"I can set it on fire," Genevieve offered, producing a lighter out of nowhere.

"No," Ceri said quickly. "I think that would be a very bad idea."

"Why?" Amber asked, getting frustrated with the deflections.

Ceri sighed and glared at the card. "Thallan's new therapist sicced it on me. Apparently it won't go away until I look at it."

Amber stared at her, baffled. "Then why haven't you just looked at it?"

"Tarot is complete crap! It can't actually tell me anything!"

"And? You don't have to do anything about whatever it shows you, but if you look at it, then it'll go away."

"Fine." With a deep breath and a shaking hand, Ceri snatched the card out of the air. Light erupted from her hand and the card in a brilliant display. It wound up her arm and enveloped her body before disappearing with a soft chime.

"That was pretty," Tommy said, walking over to her. He leaned in, inspecting the card. "Does that say Devil?"

"Yes," Ceri said quietly.

"Does it being upside down mean something?"

"Probably, but I don't know. I don't mess with this crap." She handed him the card and plopped back down on the couch, picking up her book.

Tommy shrugged and handed the card to Amber as he hurried back to the stove.

She turned the card over in her hands. Despite the skill of the painting, it wasn't pretty. A fat creature that looked to be half-goat and half-man with long curved horns and the wings of a bat perched on a stool. A naked man and woman, chained by the neck to his seat, stood on either side.

The image was ominous and dark. She flipped it upside down trying to see if it made more sense that way, but she still had no idea what it meant. "You said the new therapist gave this to you?"

Ceri nodded and flipped a page in her book without looking up.

"Are you going to ask him what it means?"

"No, I don't care." Ceri paused for a moment. "I know you're going to go ask him yourself now, but don't come running back to me with whatever insight that quack thinks he has. I don't want to hear it."

Amber raised a brow at Ceri's tone but didn't argue. "Alright."

She absolutely was going to talk to this alleged therapist. For one, she didn't like him making the card follow her packmate around, but she also didn't like the look of this card. If it did mean something, she wanted to know what.

"Dinner is almost ready!" Tommy shouted.

Captain Jack meowed enthusiastically and trotted toward the dining room. Amber watched him go. His back was as tall as the seat of the chairs now. He really was growing.

She frowned and followed him.

CHAPTER 6

KADRITHAN (ANGEL)

Kadrithan stared at the prostrate man. The sort of people that were willing to take a demon mark fell into two categories. Desperate and prideful. This imbecile was desperate, and even worse, pathetic. At least some of the people he had marked didn't cower in fear every time he appeared.

"P…please don't hurt me. I swear I won't screw it up again," the man keened, a high pitched whine escaping his lips as snot dripped from his upturned nose.

"Get up, you sniveling little rat, or I will hang you up by your toes and eviscerate you." He took a deep breath to rein in his anger. This particular mark was becoming more trouble than he was worth.

The man rose on shaking legs and shuffled backward, pressing his back against the wall. "I swear, I swear I can do it."

"You have one last chance," Kadrithan said, pressing in far closer than he wanted, to put just the right amount of fear into the man. "Do you understand how much it will hurt if I take your soul? They call it the greatest agony a man can know. Some even say the torture is eternal."

That was total crap. No one ever said anything about it considering they were dead afterward, but this idiot didn't need to know that.

The man trembled, his face going pale. "I swear I'll do it."

Kadrithan took an abrupt step back. "You have thirty-six hours."

Darkness rose from the ground, enveloping his body and he disappeared from the man's view. He could still see him, however.

The man slumped in relief, rubbing the demon mark on his chest like it ached. It probably did considering how much energy he'd drawn from the idiot in order to strike the proper amount of fear into him.

They always thought he couldn't see them once the demon mark went dormant, but that was a misconception. He didn't often linger and spy on them since he generally had something better to do, but sometimes he did.

His thoughts strayed to Amber. The betrayal the elf had planned had been a surprise. If it hadn't been for the complication with Evangeline he would have been following the alpha werewolf, and he would have discovered the half-baked plot. Luckily, Amber hadn't seemed to intend to follow through with it.

Still, he should probably keep a closer eye on her. Something told him she would have a greater role to play than any of them could guess. One of his many talents was being able to see who had the greatest potential. Amber and her little pack of misfits were a group to pay attention to, and he never neglected his duties.

For now, though, he needed to rest. Closing his eyes, he focused on his physical body. While his spirit could travel anywhere, his actual body was trapped in a realm far removed from this one.

With close attention to the rhythm of his breaths, he pulled his spirit back. Every inch was painful but he had grown used to the ache. It was no worse than a migraine. The backlash was what was really annoying. For a few minutes after returning, he would be vulnerable. Even more so if he had pushed to take on a solid form in the human realm.

The toll that took on his body and magic was extreme. Of all the indignities the *angels* had forced upon his race, this one galled him the most.

His breaths grew deeper as he slowly settled back into his body. Sweat trickled down his brow and he forced his eyes open. The ceiling was blurry until he'd blinked a few times. With a crack, the last of his spirit snapped back into place. Magic rushed through him, stealing his breath for a moment.

Once it had passed he forced his body to move and sat up, curling his stiff fingers into a fist. His joints ached from laying in one position for so long but it was easier to visit all his marks at once rather than making several trips a day.

"You look rather worse for the wear, cousin," an unwelcome voice said from his study door. A door that *had* been locked.

"You'd look the same if you were doing your job," Kadrithan snapped as he pushed off the chaise lounge and stood to face his unwanted guest.

He'd intended on meeting the ingrate in a more neutral location, but of course the idiot knew how much he hated people being in his study. His cousin would never pass up an opportunity to needle him. Jealousy and ineptitude had made him petty.

Venali adjusted the lay of his cuff, as if bored. He wouldn't have to constantly tug at it if it hadn't been poorly made, but he didn't have the money for anything better. "You summoned me, what can I do for my dearest cousin?"

Kadrithan wandered over to his desk and poured a finger of his third-favorite elven whisky. He was out of all the rest with no way to get more. It was possible to move an item from this realm to the human realm, but the reverse was beyond his power. For now. "Tell me that you've completed the simple task given to you nearly a fortnight ago."

The other demon scoffed. "Simple? It is everything but simple. All the intel I was given on the target has been wrong."

Kadrithan took a sip before turning back to face Venali. The cool facade was gone and he looked petulant and scared. Some days he wished he could just cut him loose, but they couldn't afford to lose even one more of their army.

"Wrong? I hadn't heard anything about this. Did you report it?"

"Of course I did! The captain you so graciously put in charge of me wouldn't listen though. He's ignored everything I've told him."

The amber liquid swirled in the bottom of the glass as he tilted it back and forth to calm his irritation. "I'll deal with him. Tell me, now."

Venali was agitated, and when he got agitated, he rambled. Leaning against the edge of his desk, Kadrithan listened and tried to parse through the whining to find the important information as his cousin paced back and forth in front of him.

His head snapped up when Venali mentioned something that caught his attention. "Stop."

"What?" Venali asked, freezing mid-step.

"You said a name. One of target's acquaintances that wasn't in the file. Repeat it."

"Rafael Vida," he said slowly, confusion apparent on his face. "That's hardly the most important issue here. Your intel people said he took lunch at the country club on Tuesdays, but clearly, it's Thursdays. He also likes cigars, not cigarettes."

"Shut up," Kadrithan said, turning back to his desk. That name. It meant something. He'd heard it before.

If Venali was right, and this person was involved, it changed everything. This was no simple target. This was the key to their success, or downfall.

.

CHAPTER 7

AMBER

Amber flipped the card over in her hand, inspecting the details critically. There was no way she was leaving for The Gathering with something like this hanging over Ceri's head.

Ceri had gone inside to get Thallan cleaned up and insisted she wait outside. He didn't like any of them, but seeing her sent him into a rage because she reminded him of the demon.

The rumble of a motorcycle drifted down the driveway. She rose from the front steps of Thallan's dingy, old mansion and watched the strange therapist park a few feet away. His scent was nearly buried under gasoline and leather, but what she could smell indicated he was a human.

However, humans couldn't use magic on their own. They could use some enchanted items, like elf-spelled air conditioners, but the magic had to come from somewhere else.

The doctor pulled off his helmet and set it on the front of the bike. It was an old Harley but it was in perfect condition. The fender gleamed glossy black. Even the tires had a shine to them.

"Dr. Gunner Stone?" Amber asked, approaching him slowly.

He nodded. "You must be that witch's alpha."

"Who told you that?" she asked, stopping just out of reach. Dr. Stone didn't actually give her any bad vibes but he was a burly guy. One she could probably pick up one-handed, but still, it was better to avoid a fight with a human since she was a bitten were-wolf. Genevieve had had a hell of a time getting that kid out of jail after he'd gotten in that bar fight.

"The crazy old coot holed up in that shack," Dr. Stone said with a shrug. "At least that's what I made out amongst the angry shouts. He isn't what I'd call…forthcoming."

"Ah." She extended her hand. "Amber Hale, and the witch's alpha like you said."

He shook her hand firmly while meeting her eyes without a hint of contest. A lot of men had trouble with that. They either tried to crush her hand or went completely limp.

STEPHANIE FOXE

"Dr. Gunner Stone, as you already know as well. How can I help you?"

She held up the card. "What is this?"

"Ah, she looked at it. I thought it'd take longer," he said, looking a little bemused.

Amber frowned, biting down on the urge to growl at him. This wasn't *funny*. "It flew out of a cabinet and attacked me, then wouldn't leave her alone."

"Oooh, she must have really pissed it off. That one can be especially temperamental."

"Dr. Stone." Red leaked into her eyes, tinting her vision slightly. She was all out of patience. "Why did you make a tarot card harass my pack member?"

He looked even more amused at her reaction but raised his hands in surrender. "I don't actually control them. It's a long story, that started with a curse ––"

"Is she cursed?" Amber demanded.

"No, definitely not," Dr. Stone said, waving her concerns away. "I was the one cursed but I broke it. Well, bent is probably a better way of putting it. The cards are attached to me. I can use them now for my therapy but a side effect of the curse is that they will also appear for anyone that truly needs their insight."

Amber frowned at the card, the fat devil staring back at her. "Why would she need the Devil?"

"The Devil is part of the major arcana. It has several meanings that I can explain to you. However, the only person that will really know what it means is Ceri. It's a message for her," he said with a shrug.

"Is it some kind of threat? Or warning?"

He looked down at the card and shook his head. "Was the card upright or reversed when she finally took it?"

"Reversed, if that means upside down."

He nodded. "This card isn't a bad omen but it does signify the person that drew it is troubled. Something is holding her back, most likely something unhealthy, perhaps even just fear. There will be things she will have to confront whether she wants to or not. She may be feeling guilty, ashamed, or have some secret she can't share. The Devil does signify a struggle, but it also signifies an *opportunity*. It's calling her to overcome something."

"I see," Amber said, feeling even more worried about her friend. Ceri had been insisting she was fine despite all the evidence to the contrary. She also insisted Amber let her work through it alone. With a sigh, she extended the card back to Dr. Stone. "Well, thanks for the explanation. Here's your card back."

He shook his head. "It'll come back when it's ready. I've learned not to rush them."

She shrugged and tucked it in her back pocket. "Thanks for the help then."

As she was turning to leave he stopped her.

"Well this is odd," he said, a frown tugging at his mouth.

Amber turned back around to ask what he meant when she saw a strange light growing near his head.

"The cards haven't ever been this active between two closely connected people before." He reached into the light and pulled out a second card, holding it out toward her. "You can run from it like she did, but if you take it now I can explain it."

She bit the inside of her cheek but nodded and stepped forward to accept it. Of course, that was when Angel made an appearance.

"Dabbling in the fine arts of fortune telling. How unlike you," the demon crooned, floating around Dr. Stone curiously. "And with such a strange fortune teller."

She ignored him, which was all she could do with the therapist standing right in front of her. He was the last person she needed thinking she was insane. Or demon marked.

When her fingers closed on the card, the same light she'd seen envelop Ceri enveloped her. It washed through her in a strange wave of emotions. She blinked, trying to clear her thoughts.

"That was not normal. What the hell did you just touch?" Angel hovered by Dr. Stone's head, frowning at her. "I can't believe you took a magical item from a stranger."

She was surprised at the demon's anger but would have to deal with it later. Turning the card over, she was confronted with something much more worrying.

A man hung by his foot from a tree. The other leg and his arms were crossed behind his back. A golden halo shone from behind his head that was almost beautiful, but she couldn't get over how vulnerable the man looked.

"Is this one reversed too?" she asked.

"No, the Hanged Man is simply upside down on the card."

"The Hanged Man? That doesn't sound positive."

Angel swooped over to look at it. "It certainly doesn't. I'm glad you're intelligent enough to recognize that, at least."

She glared at him before remembering not to react.

"This card is all about surrender. You need to look at things from a new perspective and make some changes. That could mean letting go of old beliefs or behaviors. It's different for everyone. You should take the card with you and do a little research. The answers are most clear when you find them yourself."

Her head snapped up. "That's sounds like absolute crap, you know that right?"

Dr. Stone grinned at her unapologetically. "Yet, it is true. Good luck, alpha."

He headed toward the mansion and the door opened a moment later, revealing an aggravated looking Ceri.

Amber shoved the new tarot card in her back pocket, hoping Ceri hadn't seen it while her attention was focused on the therapist.

"Keeping secrets are we?" Angel whispered in her ear.

"Shut up."

CHAPTER 8

TOMMY

Tommy opened the front door and saw Derek coming down the driveway. It was just past nine pm, which was late even for Derek.

Instead of hurrying to the woods like he'd planned, he jogged toward Derek. The guy's dark brown beard was out of control now. He looked like he was either a mountain man or a hipster.

"Hey, Tommy." Derek nodded in greeting. "Any leftovers?"

He snorted. "Only because I hid a plate in the microwave. Hopefully Woggy didn't find it. He's gotten really good at climbing lately."

"I'll take what I can get," Derek said with a laugh, walking toward the house.

"You aren't avoiding the pack are you?" Tommy blurted out. He hated asking questions like this but no one else was.

Derek stopped, scratching his head uncomfortably. "Maybe a little. Not really the pack though."

"Ceri?" Tommy suggested. "You know we all know about the…thing."

"It's not because of…that." Derek shook his head firmly. "I'm not really an emotions guy. If there's a problem, I want to just fix it. But Ceri's not okay and I can't fix her. Maybe the pack can help her."

He kicked at a loose rock on the ground. "I mean, you're part of the pack."

"Nah kid, I'm not. I know y'all like having me around, but that's different." Derek shrugged. "It's no big deal. Anyhow, I need to eat and crash. Early day tomorrow, and I've got some work for you if you're up for coming in around eight with Amber?"

"Sure thing," he said with a nod. "It'll save me from another full day of studying." The thought of that made him shiver involuntarily. Despite his increased healing and strength he was still sore from today's tortures.

Derek laughed. "See you then."

Tommy watched him walk away for a moment before realizing he was running late.

Amber knew he'd been going into the forest every few days and hadn't tried to stop him or question him about it. It wasn't about keeping it a secret, it was just the only way to get any privacy around a bunch of werewolves that could hear *everything* in the house.

He ran toward the forest, easing into a sprint. It felt good to stretch his legs like this. The wolf loved it too.

He'd been trying to listen to the wolf more lately. It was dumb considering the wolf was literally part of him, but he envied the wolf's confidence.

Through practice, he'd found that he could tap into the wolf without a shift. The shift was a physical change, and it gave the wolf greater influence, but that didn't mean the wolf was dormant when was he was in human form. It shaped his instincts, emotions, and reactions now. Becoming a werewolf had changed him through and through. For the better.

As the trees whipped past, he reveled in the scent of the forest. Somewhere in the distance was a creek. Water bubbled over rocks and the branches overhead creaked as the cold, evening wind blew through the trees.

"Lost in thought?" an amused feminine voice asked from just behind him.

He slid to a stop, kicking up dirt and debris. Panting, he looked up at Evangeline with a smile. "Just lost in the run."

She laughed, the shimmery swirl of lights that she had appeared as jiggling. Kadrithan, Amber's demon, was always shadow and flame, but when Evangeline had first come to him she'd been like this. Pure light. They'd guessed that was due to her angelic side.

He sat down on an old moss-covered log, digging his toes into the cool earth. "How's the beach?"

She sighed. "*Sunny.* It's relentless. There's sand everywhere. And mosquitos."

"I'm sure it's awful." He couldn't resist smirking at her. Only she could manage to hate the beach.

The light puffed up in annoyance. "I was going to show you something I've been working on, but I'm not going to if you keep mocking me."

He lifted his hands in surrender. "Alright, I apologize. What have you been working on?"

The light twisted. Slowly the loose specks of light condensed into an opaque form. Legs stretched down toward the forest floor pushing away the shadows. Wobbly arms extended to either side and something sort of like a head perched on top. She had comically large eyes that were brighter than the rest of her form.

He pressed his lips together to keep from laughing, then cleared his throat. "That's great progress!"

The bright eyes narrowed. "I'm still working on it."

"Of course," he said, still just managing to suppress the laughter.

She sighed and popped back into her original form. "It's harder than I expected."

"Has Kadrithan been helping you with it?"

"Not really. He says you can only learn by doing. He gave me the basics, but I've been on my own since then."

"Have the boils and stuff finally gone away?"

"Yeah, that's all gone completely now." She didn't sound entirely pleased about it.

"But?"

The light shifted grumpily. "But I can feel the demon side getting stronger."

"Yeah? Can you do anything new?"

Evangeline was still bitter about being half demon but they'd been working on acceptance. There was no changing it, so she kind of needed to learn to deal.

"Has anyone ever told you how obnoxious your optimism is?"

"Yeah, you. Last week," Tommy replied with an unabashed grin. "Oh, watch this."

He jumped up and stepped into a handstand. Finding balance in this position had been hard at first but now it was easy. Holding his legs in just the right positions, he lowered himself until his nose was almost touching the dirt, then pushed back up.

"Why couldn't I have been a werewolf?" Evangeline muttered.

He dropped his legs and dusted his hands off. "I'm pretty sure you're just as strong as I am. Besides, even humans can do that. It's just a matter of balance and a little upper body strength. Why don't you try it?"

"Maybe I will later."

He padded back over to the log but sat on the ground this time, letting his head fall back against it. It was a clear night so the stars were bright, blinking in and out as the branches waved in the breeze.

"Has Kadrithan talked to you any more about what it is he wants from you?"

She sighed and pooled on the ground next to him. "Not directly. He obviously thinks I'm going to have to do some fighting eventually. I'm working on using both kinds of my magic even though he looks kind of...murderous when I'm using the angelic spells."

"Did he answer those questions about your parents?"

She snorted. "No, and he said it didn't matter. He was completely dismissive."

"Maybe there's someone else you can ask."

"Maybe."

She shifted closer and her light warmed him, taking the chill out of the air.

"How long can you manage this time?"

"At least another ten minutes. It gets easier every time."

He sat up abruptly. "Want to have a race? That's bound to help make you stronger."

"You're turning into Deward."

Before he could object, she zipped away. He jumped to his feet and raced after her.

CHAPTER 9

AMBER

Amber did her best thinking in wolf form these days. Her paws dug into the dirt and she let the wolf take over, retreating into her mind. The nip of cold air against her snout was energizing and the thud of her heart in her chest grounded her.

There were myriad things to think about. The strange tarot cards was one, but those seemed like the lowest in priority. Shane was another, but again, that whole *thing* wasn't a priority. He couldn't blame her for not following up on that promised date after everything that had happened.

The thing she needed to sort out was The Gathering. Paul, the alpha that had asked her to be his sponsor, was going to go through his Alpha Trials during the conference. Having that happen during such a prominent event filled her with unease, not that it'd be any better without that. After the sabotage she'd endured she couldn't bring herself to trust the supposedly honorable werewolf community.

Tommy's scent flooded her nose but she immediately realized it wasn't fresh. She snickered in her mind. This must be where he snuck off to chat with Evangeline. The memory of the half demon made the wolf growl -- she disliked the girl even more than Amber.

If it had been anyone other than Tommy, Amber would have worried they were being corrupted, but he seemed immune to that kind of thing. He was probably slowly reforming that bratty demon somehow.

She wasn't sad Evangeline was gone. Her presence had put everyone at risk. It also reduced the chance that Tommy would get an even bigger crush on the girl. Possibly.

A low howl echoed through the forest and she slid to a stop, cocking her head to the side. It sounded again and she recognized the wolf. It was Shane. She must have been running longer than she realized. Or they were early.

Lifting her head, she howled back in welcome, then started running in his general direction. A few moments later, she spotted his snowy white fur between the trees. He was beautiful in this form. Her ruddy fur looked dirty in comparison.

She yipped in greeting as he trotted toward her, sniffing the air curiously. Crouching low, she wagged her tail playfully. They couldn't talk but she was pretty sure he got her intention when he also tensed.

She charged him, changing directions at the last moment and racing back toward the house, laughing inside. He barked, half-annoyed and half-amused.

The wolf could tell what every yip and bark meant and she'd gotten used to communicating like that when their pack went on runs.

She pushed herself to run almost as fast as she could. Her competitive side and alpha instincts wouldn't allow her to let him win the impromptu race.

He was quite a ways behind her to start but was slowly gaining. She waited until she burst out of the tree line to put on more speed, leaving the white wolf in the proverbial dust.

Leaping over the porch banister, she slid to a stop, nearly crashing into the swing. Her claws left gouges in the wooden planks.

Panting happily, she sat down and waited for Shane. He arrived much more sedately, trotting onto the porch as if he hadn't just lost badly.

The front door snapped open and Genevieve stuck her head out. "Seriously?"

Amber huffed in reply.

"Get in here, everyone is waiting on you."

Feeling pretty pleased with herself, she brushed past Shane and Genevieve and headed to her bedroom to shift back and put on clothes. No matter how comfortable werewolves were with nudity, she was not going to prance around naked in front of other people unless she had to.

Shane followed, hesitating at her door until she nodded her approval for him to come inside as well. He immediately turned and faced the other way as he began to shift. Tearing her eyes away before she saw anything private, she shifted as well.

"You need any clothes?" She yanked her jeans on quickly despite knowing he wouldn't peek.

"Gen said I could leave them in here, so I'm good, thanks."

Amber pulled on a shirt that had *BITE ME* emblazoned in red across the front, then turned around. Shane was fully dressed, but waiting respectfully to turn around.

His hair, normally artfully tousled, was a bit of a mess. It made her feel better that she wasn't the only one that ended up looking crazy after a shift.

"I'm good."

He turned around and met her with a smile that turned into a grin when he saw her shirt. "You should bring that to the conference."

She laughed and shook her head. "I think Genevieve would burn it if I tried that."

"It would be so entertaining though," he said with a wink.

"Maybe I'll try to sneak it in my suitcase."

He dragged his hands through his hair in an attempt to smooth it. "I was surprised to hear you were going on a run just for the hell of it. You weren't thrilled about the whole werewolf thing at the beginning."

She shrugged. "I've accepted it. Anyhow, we shouldn't keep them waiting."

He nodded in agreement and opened the door for her. She grabbed a hairband off her dresser, then headed out.

As they walked back into the living room, she saw Paul -- the alpha she was sponsoring that had taken over the Lockhart Pack -- glaring at Captain Jack, his arms crossed.

"What is that?"

"A cat," Genevieve said with a broad grin, crouching down to pet the beast.

"I'm pretty sure it's some kind of mutant," Amber muttered, pulling her hair up into a loose bun. It was hopelessly tangled and she wasn't going to waste everyone's time trying to fix it.

"It smells weird," Paul insisted, his nose twitching like he smelled something bad.

"He *stinks*," Amber agreed. Something about the cat's scent set her on edge as well. Mostly though, he just smelled like cat, and the wolf hated it. "Anyone want anything to drink? There's sweet tea in the fridge, we also have sandwich stuff and fresh cookies."

Shane's mouth twitched. "I could get used to southern hospitality."

"I'll take some tea and cookies," Paul said, finally tearing his eyes away from Captain Jack.

The cat prowled ahead of them into the kitchen, watching Amber intently as she picked up the platter of cookies. She flashed her eyes at him, but his only reaction was to swish his tail in annoyance.

Tommy was at the mechanic shop with Derek today. He'd chosen to stay there and keep helping her brother since, of course, they'd had three people show up needing help right as she was planning to leave for lunch and this meeting. It was a good sign for the business but bad timing since she was about to be gone for a few days.

Ceri shuffled into the kitchen wrapped in a fluffy blue robe. Amber subtly scented her and was frustrated to find that she even *smelled* tired today.

"You joining us?" she asked.

"I have some other stuff I need to work on actually. Do you need me in there? I wasn't sure since I'll be staying here with Tommy instead of attending The Gathering." Ceri asked, putting a mug of water in the microwave.

Woggy was snoozing on top of her head, strapped down by some curls he had braided together. In the wild, pixies wove beds like that in the trees from grass and vines. Apparently he'd applied the same principle to Ceri's crazy curls.

"No, if you're busy that's fine," Amber said with a smile. "Let me know if you need anything, all right?"

Ceri nodded absently, eyes unfocused as she stared across the kitchen. The emotions coming from her through the pack bond were as muted as her expression. At first, Amber had thought that meant she was getting better, but she was starting to wonder if that was true.

With a sigh, she joined the group in the dining room. Once everyone had a snack and a drink, Amber leaned forward and rested her elbows on the table. It was time to get down to business.

"We leave tomorrow at noon. Shane, is Jameson still alright with us joining his caravan?" she asked, drawing everyone's attention.

Shane nodded. "Yes. He agrees that it's important to have that show of support from the beginning. Our packs may not have a formal alliance but he does stand with you, and all bitten werewolves."

Unease drifted from Genevieve but she wasn't speaking up.

"Any concerns about that, Gen?" Amber asked, unable to ignore the emotions she was getting from her beta. She *needed* to know if there was going to be an issue.

Genevieve twirled a strand of bright pink hair that had fallen from her bun around a finger. "It makes a big statement right off the bat. Part of me hoped we could fly under the radar for this thing but I know that's not realistic."

Paul chuckled and leaned back in his chair. He took off the baseball cap he always wore and smoothed down his light brown hair. "Your pack made a statement the day you were formed. If you start trying to turtle now, they'll all just see it as a sign of weakness."

She knew he was right, but she didn't like it any more than Genevieve did. "Do we have any reason to believe someone will try to interfere with Paul's Trials because of that?"

Shane's face darkened with anger. "No. Interference is almost unheard of. Underhanded crap like that goes against our nature. What happened to you was an anomaly."

She doubted that was true but kept her opinion to herself. Bitten werewolves probably didn't get sabotaged simply because most could never make it to the Trials.

Amber looked to Paul, who shook his head.

"No threats. Plenty of people who think I'm an idiot for choosing you as my sponsor, but they're going to show up with popcorn to watch me fail, not sabotage me."

"Alright, what else do we need to prepare for?" Amber clasped her hands in front of her, looking to Genevieve first.

"Other alphas or betas trying to annoy you into losing control or challenging someone. There's always a bit of posturing and some scuffles from what I've seen in my research, but only the truly stupid, or very well prepared challenge another alpha at The Gathering," Genevieve said, flipping through her notes.

Shane nodded as he took another bite of a cookie.

"Everybody acts like they've got something to prove when they're at The Gathering," Paul added. "Keep a cool head and you'll be golden."

"There will be a chance to form some alliances, or at least start discussions with other packs while we're there." Genevieve slid a binder with colored tabs toward her. "This is a detailed list of every alpha in attendance. I have more information on some than others. The most important ones to familiarize yourself with are the ones with the green tabs –– bitten-friendly packs, and the red tabs –– bigoted assholes who think they're better than everyone else."

Amber took the binder and flipped it open, slightly overwhelmed at the amount of information. "This is definitely going to be valuable."

"I have it in a spreadsheet as well, which I emailed to you so you can access it on your phone. Sorry I couldn't get it to you sooner. It took longer than I wanted."

"This is awesome, don't worry about it. Did you already send Paul a copy?"

Genevieve pulled out her phone. "Doing that now."

"So, the Trials, challenges, potential alliances." Amber leaned back, tapping her fingers against the table thoughtfully. "Not as bad as I thought."

Her beta grimaced. "Well, there are the rumors."

Amber shut her eyes for a moment. "The sorcerer?"

"And the demon," Shane added. "No one knows what really went down but they like to think they do. Some of the packs will just be curious, some are ready to pass judgment. There will be questions."

"We'll stick to the same answers we gave the police," she said firmly. The questioning they'd had to endure after that had been annoying, but Genevieve's law firm had stepped in and taken the pressure off them. They had told the truth about everything they could.

Because of the demon mark, they had to keep Evangeline's involvement under wraps. Jameson's statement had been that his pack had briefly seen the demon standing over Zachariah Hudson's body, but she had fled before they could do anything. She'd been surprised that Jameson had been so ready to lie to the police, but Shane had explained that werewolves took care of each other first. Laws were more of a thing to work around than follow absolutely.

She rubbed her temples, trying to fend off the headache building in in her skull. "Paul, you up to date on all that?"

He nodded. "Genevieve filled me in. I've got your back."

"Then I guess we're as ready as we'll ever be."

Shane's phone rang. He glanced at the caller ID, then excused himself and headed toward the living room.

Paul pulled out his phone and walked around the table to sit next to Genevieve instead of across from her. "I have a few things to add to this spreadsheet that may be helpful later."

The two of them got to work and Amber's focus drifted. The incident with the sorcerer had attracted a lot of attention. After all, the no magic zones threatened everything. Finally having proof that they weren't a natural phenomenon had further unsettled the general public.

"Do you ever wonder how werewolves went from savage infighting to holding conferences in hotels?" Angel asked, appearing in front of her as a little red devil in a puff of smoke.

She snorted before she could catch herself. Genevieve and Paul were too absorbed in their conversation to pay any attention to her though.

Without bothering trying to interrupt Genevieve and Paul, she got up from the table and headed out the back door to get a little privacy. It was insanely irritating to not be able to talk back to Angel.

Once the door was shut firmly behind them, she turned to the pesky demon. "Did you come to harass me, or do you have any news?"

He crossed his tiny arms and nodded. "In a way."

She waited for a moment, then gave up. "Well?"

"I have reason to believe that your defeat of the sorcerer has managed to make some of our enemies nervous. Some people that haven't moved openly in a very long time are doing some unexpected things."

She curled her hands into a fist, nails biting into her palm. Yet again, he was being infuriatingly vague. "What does that mean, exactly?"

A puff of smoke erupted from his nose as he sighed in irritation. "Just watch your back for unexpected threats. Nothing may happen, or someone may come after you. If I knew who or what *exactly* we wouldn't even be having this conversation because I would have already taken care of it."

"How comforting," she muttered.

"It should be. You're important enough that I would actually be annoyed if you died."

After he'd given her the second mark, Amber had never doubted her *importance*. It was easy when he was floating there looking ridiculous to forget for a moment that he was using her and her pack, and would continue to do so.

"Thanks for the warning, you can leave now," she said irritably.

"I actually plan on being around a lot more often, especially at the conference. Someone has to watch your back."

Amber crossed her arms. "Genevieve has that covered."

"More backup is always better. Speaking of, Shane is watching you talk to yourself and he looks *very* worried."

She jerked around and saw Shane looking through the window in the back door. He did look worried.

With a sigh, she nodded and waved in what she hoped was a reassuring way. It's not like she could convince Shane that Angel was safe. He wasn't. It was still annoying to have to hide her conversations with the demon constantly just to keep everyone from worrying.

Sometimes she wished Angel would just appear in a way that allowed everyone to see and hear him but she suspected that exhausted the demon. She wasn't going to ask anyhow. He'd probably just end up insulting her openly instead of privately.

Shane opened the door and stepped outside. "Everything okay?"

"It's fine."

Angel snorted. "You lie a lot."

CHAPTER 10

GENEVIEVE

Genevieve did a double-take. She'd been reading up on old werewolf traditions, just to have some context for current behaviors. This was not something she'd expected to find. Picking up the book, she raced downstairs to Ceri's room.

"Ceri! I know you're up, let me in!" she whispered loudly, tapping softly on the door. Everyone else was asleep so she didn't want to wake them.

The door cracked open and Ceri glared at her. "I was in the middle of something."

"I don't care, this is important." She shoved her way inside, ignoring the witch's eye roll. Ceri might be grumpy now but she'd be thanking her in a moment. "So, I was reading this book on old werewolf traditions and it has a few things that pertain to shamans."

"What? Let me see," Ceri said reaching for the book.

She hopped back and held it just out of reach. "Only if you promise to actually *discuss it* and not just zone out and run off with it."

"Fine, hand it over." Ceri wiggled her hand demandingly.

She gave it to Ceri and watched her face eagerly as she skimmed the page. It was obvious when she got to it.

Ceri's blue eyes went wide and she looked up in shock. "This..."

"I *know*," Genevieve agreed smugly. "I had no idea."

"How does no one talk about this anymore? Maybe they're mistaken."

"Witches probably buried it. You said your grandmother would have had a fit knowing you'd joined the pack if she'd still been alive."

Ceri sat down heavily on her bed, resting the book on her knees. "It would benefit the pack and the coven so much though. Both would be stronger."

Genevieve shrugged. "Witches are generally control freaks. No offense."

"No, you're right. They are secretive, selfish, control freaks."

They were silent for a moment, thinking through what this meant. How it might change things.

"We have to talk to Amber about it before she leaves. Your role in the pack needs to be kept under wraps as long as possible. I don't want someone thinking we're a threat," Genevieve said seriously, her mind running through every worst case scenario and how to avoid them.

Ceri glanced at the clock on her nightstand. "We should just wake her up then. She won't want this dumped on her an hour before she leaves."

"Agreed. I'll go get her."

Ceri nodded and started reading through the book.

Genevieve hurried across the hall and opened Amber's door, which immediately woke the alpha up. Her eyes flared red in the darkness.

"What's wrong?" Her voice was still rough with sleep.

"I found something interesting about the shaman stuff. Ceri and I need to talk to you."

Amber nodded dutifully and slid out of bed, upsetting Captain Jack, who meowed moodily and padded up to her pillow. Genevieve had wondered where he'd been sleeping when he wasn't with her. She would not have guessed with Amber.

"I knew you secretly loved Captain Jack," she said with a sly smile.

Amber glared at her. "I really, really don't."

Laughing, Genevieve followed her across the hall to Ceri's room. She was torn between excitement at the discovery and trepidation at how it could change things. Despite all that, she was so glad they'd found this out now.

Jameson's pack knew Ceri was considered part of the pack. They knew Amber had been able to track her through the pack bond, but they'd never said the word shaman around anyone else. It hadn't been discussed, they'd simply all kept it to themselves by some unspoken agreement.

Amber shut the door behind them and crossed her arms. "Alright, what did y'all find?"

Ceri sighed, lowering the book to look at her alpha. "We already knew my magic was changing due to my joining the pack."

Amber nodded.

"Well, it's also changing the pack," Ceri said quietly, reaching up to push back a curl that was brushing her cheek.

"Not necessarily in a bad way," Genevieve added quickly.

"Just explain," Amber said, dragging a hand down her face.

Ceri took a deep breath, as though steeling herself. "What I'm reading here isn't super clear, but it does say that your wolves will grow stronger. It suggests that they may change somehow but I don't recognize the term they're using."

"It also said you're going to get stronger as the alpha, though it wasn't specific with how," Genevieve added.

"Yes, it talks a little more about that a few chapters later," Ceri said, flipping to that section. "You will get physically bigger, apparently. In wolf form at least. I think."

"I better not end up seven feet tall," Amber muttered.

"The last thing it mentions is that the pack bond will slowly grow. It could eventually become more than just a one way thing. We might be able to communicate through it somehow," Genevieve said. That had been the one thing that interested her the most. Being able to actually talk through it, even if it was just images or impressions, would be very useful.

"None of that sounds bad. Why do you look worried...ah," Amber said, understanding dawning on her face. "The other packs won't like this."

"We're already breaking their social norms, this will be even more threatening to the unenlightened among them," Genevieve said with a sigh.

"Not many people know about this though, right?" Amber asked, looking between them.

Genevieve shook her head. "Not as far as I know. Ceri hadn't heard about it. If witches don't know, or don't talk about it, then it stands to reason it's been mostly forgotten, if not entirely."

"I agree," Ceri said with a nod. "There are probably a few older packs that have the knowledge, but I've never heard even a rumor about something like this."

"Alright, then all we can do is keep it quiet and try to figure out what else might change."

Amber was taking this better than she expected. Something had shifted in her after the fight with the sorcerer. She was calmer and less pushy. A better alpha.

After a moment's thought, Genevieve asked. "Is it alright if I ask Steven for help?"

Amber looked to Ceri for input. "What do you think?"

"I don't think he'd intentionally say anything but he can be a little...thoughtless when he gets excited about something," Ceri said hesitantly.

"Yeah, you're right," she agreed with a sigh. And she didn't want to say it out loud, but if they broke up it would be better if he didn't know. "Pack only. And Derek, he should know."

Amber nodded, frowning slightly as if something about what she'd said had bothered her. "Sounds like a plan. I'm going to go ahead and wake Tommy up so he doesn't feel left out in the morning."

Genevieve cringed a little. She hadn't exactly forgotten about Tommy, but she hadn't thought to wake him up for this too. She should have. The pack needed to discuss these things together. He was still young but he wasn't stupid.

"I'll grab Derek, too," Ceri said, rising from the bed. "No point in going over this three separate times."

While they went to get the others, Genevieve picked up the book and flipped through it, tracing her finger over the single drawing included. A woman wreathed in flame hovered between two people, their hands linked. Shadowy wolves sat at the feet of the two people on the side, their heads lifted in a howl.

CHAPTER 11

CERI

Ceri tucked the covers closer around Derek's shoulders. He'd stayed after the others had gone back to bed and ended up falling asleep after a long conversation. They hadn't chatted about anything important, really. Both of them had avoided everything to do with her becoming a shaman and the sorcerer. It had been nice. She'd even managed to sleep for a couple of hours after as well.

Then the usual dream had woken her up.

She wrapped her robe a little tighter around her waist as she padded to her work room. The door creaked as she closed it but it didn't seem to wake Derek. He was a heavy sleeper.

The room was a bit of a mess. She'd been studying old family spells and brewing almost non-stop since they'd taken down the sorcerer.

Rubbing the sleep from her eyes, she picked up her spellbook and plopped down in a chair. The old thing was starting to fall apart. She really needed to remake it –– organized this time –– before she started losing pieces of paper out of it.

She flipped to the place she'd left off the night before and resumed reviewing all the spells she learned over the years. The only thing that would keep her and the pack safe in the future was if she could become more powerful. More prepared.

They needed salves and potions for injuries, amulets of protection, better wards. All of it. She might not be able to sleep but she could do this.

Turning the page, a spell caught her eye. It was a variation of the spell the sorcerer had cast to track down Evangeline. Blood magic. The darkest of the dark.

Her fingers tapped restlessly against the page. She could use it to find Selena. She *knew* the witch was out there still plotting against them. They had no way of knowing when she'd strike next but she would. She'd seen the hate in Selena's eyes. That wasn't some-thing anyone would just put aside and forget about because they'd lost one fight.

She scanned through the ingredients. Blood of the witch. Snake eyes. When she saw the third ingredient she slammed the spell book shut. Ten hearts of a pixie.

A year ago, she wouldn't have hesitated. Even now she was tempted. It was sick and twisted that she could be tempted to do this, but she was so scared. Maybe it would be worth the sacrifice if it would protect the pack. Were the lives of ten pixies worth those of her friends?

Something tapped against her window and she almost jumped out of her skin, dropping the spellbook on the floor. It fell open, crumpling some of the pages.

"Dammit." She knelt down and tried to smooth it out before closing it. The tapping started again, more earnestly this time.

She was pretty sure it was her spirit guide, but just in case it wasn't actually the helpful owl spirit outside, she grabbed a bundle of sage and began cleansing the room. It was always better to be safe than sorry.

Learning the new ways the pack could grow as her magic changed only made her more paranoid. Power like that had a way of drawing things to it.

The piney scent of the sage cleared her mind and the last vestiges of sleepiness faded away. She set the bundle down in a bowl near the window then drew the curtains open.

It wasn't yet dawn but the moon was nearly full. Soft, silvery light filled the room and she found her gaze drawn upward. Perhaps it was her imagination because of what they'd discussed last night, but she could have sworn she felt something move inside of her. Something that delighted in the pull of the moon.

Shaking off the strange feeling, she lifted the window and whistled softly. With a whoosh, a tawny owl landed on the window sill. It's big orange eyes glowed brightly. She'd just left the screen off the window now that it was visiting regularly. It was a pain to put it back on.

"Welcome back," she said with a smile. Being near the owl filled her with a sense of well-being, especially after the help it had given her when she had been...well, that didn't bear thinking about anymore. Now or ever.

The owl hooted in greeting, puffing its feathers up as it settled itself on the windowsill.

After a few interactions with the spirit, she'd learned to just go ahead and lay down so she didn't end up with weird bruises. It waited patiently for her to get comfortable.

She relaxed into the little cot she'd made of blankets, pressing one hand against the floor. The house -- it was still hard to think of her as Illya -- warmed in greeting and strengthened her wards. Illya would keep watch while she was unconscious.

With deep, even breaths, she met the owl's eyes and sunk into the spirit realm.

～

The snow was deeper than usual today. Dark, heavy clouds drifted overhead, dimming the normally bright sky.

"That can't be good," she said with a sigh as her ethereal feet moved over the snow.

Just like last time, she traveled up for a while before the wind grabbed her and carried her to the top of the mountain. She shut her eyes and let it carry her. Looking around while she was flying just made her dizzy.

She landed in a soft pile of snow. A breeze ruffled her hair in greeting.

"You were much braver this time," the spirit said in amusement.

Ceri smiled. "I'm getting used to it. I can't get hurt here, can I?"

A shimmery creature with a body like a ribbon materialized in front of her. "You certainly can but I would never hurt you."

"Ah," she said, looking over her shoulder with worry. Of all the things, she hadn't really considered that coming here might be dangerous. She'd blindly trusted the spirit.

"No need to worry yet. I'll let you know if danger is coming."

"Alright," she said, still skeptical. "There isn't another sorcerer, is there?"

"There are many, but that isn't why I brought you here today." The spirit unfurled and swam through the air away from her. "Follow me."

Ceri hurried after the spirit. They stopped at the edge of the mountain. A sheer cliff extended what must be thousands of feet downward. They were above the clouds so she couldn't see the ground.

"Why are we here?" Ceri asked, staring down at the dizzying height.

"There's something you need to get that I can't get for you," the spirit said forlornly.

"What is it?"

"The missing half of something."

That wasn't what she expected. It was also vague. "The missing half of what?"

The spirit shuddered and floated a little closer. "I can't say," it whispered.

"How far is it? My pack will worry if I'm gone a long time." She was putting off the inevitable but the darkness down there scared her. It felt *alive*. The last time she'd sensed something similar, the sorcerer had been attacking the house.

"It's not that far, but it will be very hard to get to. The darkness doesn't want you to reach it."

"Will I have to fight something?" Ceri pressed, determined not to walk into some kind of trap.

"I don't know."

This was stupid. Possibly suicidal. But she had to at least get closer and feel it out. If she needed to leave she could jump back to her body at any time. "How do I get down there?"

A gust of wind hit her back and flung her off the cliff. A scream tore from her throat before she could stop it. Abruptly, her descent slowed. The wind tearing at her hair and ethereal body disappeared and she found she was floating down slowly now.

Blinking rapidly to try and clear the tears from her eyes, she saw the darkness wasn't as dense as it had looked from the mountaintop. It was also growing warmer the farther down she got. Snow was replaced with dense, green foliage. They weren't so much trees as they were very large plants that parted as she drew near, pushed aside by the wind that carried her.

The warmth down here didn't seem to reach her, much like the cold. There was also something...disquieting about the silence. She landed near a tall, narrow plant with a trunk similar to a palm tree. However, instead of rough brown bark, the trunk was a deep, emerald green.

As she walked farther into the strange jungle, uneasiness crept up her spine. Her movements slowed until it felt like she was trying to swim through molasses. Walking had never been difficult in this place.

She stopped and looked around. There was no magic holding her back that she could sense.

"Hello?" she whispered, her voice shaking a little.

There was no response but the pressure around her increased. Her vision swam and she tried to move away but found herself stuck.

"What are you doing to me?" she demanded, hoping she sounded more confident.

A shudder ran through her physical body as her spirit was squeezed. There was nothing attacking her and it wasn't painful, she was simply crumbling. She lifted her hand and watched it fade away in confusion. Her arms followed and the forest began to fade from sight.

Weak, a deep voice whispered, the word floating through her as if to emphasize its point.

"No," she retorted through gritted teeth, but it was too late. The last of her ethereal body faded and her eyes snapped open in her work room, breaths coming in sharp pants. She smacked her hand against the floor angrily. "Dammit."

The door to the room flew open and a bleary-eyed Derek stood in the doorway. "What's wrong?"

"Nothi––" she stopped herself from dismissing his question and pushed up into a sitting position. It wasn't fair to him, and the pack would need to know what the spirit had asked of her. They'd also need to know she'd completely failed at it. "I'm fine. Not hurt or anything, just frustrated."

"Ah..." Derek wavered for a moment before walking in the room and claiming the chair by her desk. "With what?"

She glanced at the window, not surprised to see the owl was gone. He came and went as he pleased, and whatever he'd wanted to share with her had already been shared.

"The owl –– the spirit that's been helping me –– took me to the place it always has, but this time told me there was something in the spirit realm I needed to get. Something important –– it said was the missing half of something." She ground her teeth together as she stared blankly through the window. "I went to the bottom of the mountain but I didn't even get close to finding it. There's some kind of...darkness down there. It ripped through me. I just disintegrated and got tossed back here, into my body."

"You're sure it didn't hurt you?" Derek asked, his shoulders almost hunched over with tension.

"No, just pissed me off. I don't usually fail like that. I didn't even get a chance to fight back."

He was quiet for a moment as he thought something over. She could see the wheels turning in his mind. "Could the pack bond help? Hasn't Amber used it to make you more powerful before?"

"Maybe. I'll have to ask. I'm not even sure when I'll have a chance to go back." She shivered a little at the thought of returning and tucked her arms around herself. "It'll have to wait until after The Gathering. Honestly, I should have bailed before even attempting it with Amber leaving this afternoon. This isn't the week to take risks."

Derek chuckled. "Not sure the pack has had a week where it was a good time to take risks."

She couldn't help but smirk at that. "That is so true. It's been one thing after another, hasn't it?"

"Yeah, it has," he said softly. "You're...not really doing well are you?"

"I survived. We survived."

"You died."

His words made her want to throw up. She'd wondered then if she'd actually died, or if the demon had healed her before she had passed. She chose to believe the latter for the sake of her sanity. "Almost died."

"Close enough to be terrifying, and I wasn't even the one laying on that slab."

She curled her hands into fists. "What do you want me to say? I'm not doing well. I can't sleep. I have nightmares. I'm terrified that demon did something to me when he healed me that I don't know about. Happy?"

"I'm happy you've finally admitted it." Derek stood, his expression conflicted. "Are you blocking your emotions from Amber?"

She snorted. "As much as I can. I don't want to be distracting."

He dragged his hands down his face, for a moment looking as tired as she felt. "After The Gathering, talk to her. Please. I don't know how to help, and I don't think you even want me to try. But stop lying to her."

Ceri stared at his chest, unwilling to look him in the eye right now. She didn't want to see his worry. "What can she do?"

"I don't know, but she always seems to figure something out. Maybe that's why she's the alpha and none of us are."

"Okay."

"You mean it?"

"Yeah."

CHAPTER 12

AMBER

Amber had ended up in a car with Shane, alone, while Genevieve had gleefully skipped off to Paul's truck. She could still feel the smugness in the pack bond over two hours later.

Rain splattered against the windshield as they sat in traffic on the highway that led toward downtown. Despite her irritation with the delay, she knew it was probably her last moment of peace for the next two days.

"Have you ever been to Seattle?" Shane asked, fingers tapping out an impatient rhythm on the steering wheel.

"Nope. Portland was as far north as I made it. I meant to find a job in Los Angeles when I graduated nursing school actually, but it didn't work out."

"It's a pretty interesting city. Elliot Bay is full of mermaids. They have a floating market out there."

"Huh, that would be interesting to see. The mermaids in the Gulf were pretty antisocial."

"Maybe we'll have time after the conference to visit it," Shane said with a smile.

She leaned against the window, watching him out of the corner of her eye. He'd dressed up a little today. Nothing crazy, but his hair was tamed with something that smelled elf-made and he was wearing a button up shirt over his jeans instead of a plain t-shirt.

Attraction curled in her gut and the wolf didn't seem to mind her choice. They'd chatted off and on during the drive. Her favorite part had been the comfortable silences though. It was hard to find someone where lack of conversation was just as good as the conversation itself.

Her phone buzzed and she pulled it out to find a text from Tommy.

We're going to some kind of super secret troll thing the day of the full moon?? Some kind of coming of age ceremony. Idk. Don't freak if you get weird vibes through the bond. I get the feeling I might be involved somehow.

She snorted. Of course Tommy was going to be involved somehow.

Don't let Deward knock you out again. Have fun.

"Everything okay?" Shane asked, glancing at her phone.

"Yeah, it's great. Tommy is just going to a party the day of the full moon and didn't want me to worry." She put her phone away. "We almost there?"

"Actually yes." He pointed straight ahead to a massive building that towered over the street. "That's the hotel The Gathering is always hosted in."

"Will the Trials be held in there too somehow?"

"Nah, they do that a little ways out of the city in one of the national parks. It's not really something that could, or should, be done indoors. Just feels wrong."

The wolf stirred grumpily inside of her at the idea of having to shift and run indoors, away from the sky. "It really would."

There was finally a break in the traffic and they made it to the hotel. Their caravan drove down into the parking garage. The whole council had decided to arrive together. She and Genevieve had carpooled with Jameson's pack, but Alphas Lawrence, Salazar, and Bennett, as well as their betas, had all driven their own vehicles.

Packs were limited to three members; the alpha and one to two betas. That had been a relief to her since she hadn't wanted to have the whole pack in one place like that. Especially a potentially unwelcoming place.

A valet met them and they hopped out of the car. Amber bristled when she saw someone was already pulling her bags out of the trunk but resisted the urge to growl. It was technically nice of them, but she didn't like people touching her things, and she could carry it just fine without help.

Shane chuckled at her. "It's supposed to make you feel pampered you know."

"Well it doesn't," she muttered, following close behind the bellboy who had her bags on a cart.

He laughed and shook his head. "Try not to eat anyone. I have to go meet up with Jameson."

She waved him away. "I'm not feral. Go take care of your alpha."

There was a line to check in, so Amber filed into place at the end of the line and looked around the room. She'd been so distracted walking in that she hadn't noticed how grand the place was. The atrium was dozens of stories high. If it had been sunny, the tall windows would have flooded the place with light.

Even without that, the slick marble floors and elegant gold decorations left her feeling very out place. This explained why the rooms had been six-hundred dollars a night even with the conference discount rates. They were normally double that.

Over the cleaning products and perfumes, she could smell the other werewolves. Some were in line ahead of her and others milling around chatting.

The pack bond warmed as Genevieve drew closer. She looked over her shoulder and nodded at her beta who quickly joined her in line.

"Good drive?" Genevieve asked nonchalantly.

She rolled her eyes. "It was *fine.*"

Her beta only pouted for a moment before grabbing her arm. "Up ahead and just to the right is Ellie Parker. She's bitten friendly. I think her beta is bitten, actually. If the rumors are right, it was her childhood friend that she turned after they got sick."

"Seriously? That's normally a death sentence," Amber said with a frown. Ellie Parker was a little taller than average with slightly broad shoulders. She was talking to someone with a smile that lit up her face.

Genevieve shrugged. "I guess if you're terminal, it's worth the risk."

They lapsed into silence and Amber waited impatiently. She recognized a lot of people from Genevieve's binder, though she couldn't remember all their names.

Her wolf abruptly rose up in her mind and it took all her control to keep her eyes from turning red. They were being watched.

Slowly, Amber turned to her left. The man staring at her hadn't shown the same control, and she met blood red eyes from across the room. His lip curled in distaste and he turned away with a huff, walking away with his companion.

He looked like a grumpy Viking with his shaggy blonde hair, massive build, and permanent scowl.

"Who is that?" Amber asked quietly, nudging Genevieve.

Her beta looked up and immediately frowned. "Bad news."

"He was staring at me."

"His name's Jason Carter and he is the alpha of one of the few packs to not have a single bitten member. He's all born, all the way. Avoid him if you can."

As Amber watched, he paused and glanced back over his shoulder, a sneer still on his face.

"I don't think that's going to be possible."

CHAPTER 13

AMBER

Amber tossed her and Genevieve's stuff in a pile on one of the beds. Genevieve had decided to hunt down dinner for them from a restaurant Steven had recommended, which she had encouraged. A little time alone to get her bearings was much needed.

One consolation for the exorbitant price was that the rooms were really, really nice. Unlike your average motel room there was space to walk around, a closet, and both a bathtub *and* shower in the bathroom. It also smelled insanely clean. Whatever they used had removed the previous customer's scent entirely. It had to be magic-based, probably elf-made. She grabbed the pillow and sniffed it carefully, but there was nothing. Not even the smell of cleaning products.

"I need to get some of this for home. Maybe that'd solve the cat smell," she muttered to herself.

"Talking to yourself even when I'm not here now?" Angel said humorously from behind her.

She tossed the pillow back on the bed. "I'm starting to think you're always here."

"If only you could be so lucky." Shadows merged into a human form against the wall and the demon pulled a chair out of thin air, settling in it and crossing his legs. His features were a little clearer today. Red eyes gleamed in a handsome face with a sharp jaw line and aquiline nose. His hair was smoothed back in a polished style.

"What do you want?"

"Perhaps I'm just checking in on my favorite werewolf," he said with a grin.

"I doubt that." She grabbed her bag and started unpacking the stuff she'd need in the morning. Hopefully they had an iron. Her shirts had wrinkles despite the short drive.

"This conference is going to be pivotal for your pack," Angel continued, unabashed.

"Yes, I'm aware."

"People will have questions about what happened with the sorcerer."

She stopped what she was doing to look him in the eye. "Kadrithan, get to the point."

He sighed, inspecting his nails like he was bored. "You need to speak with Alpha Vernier and get her on your side before the end of the conference."

That wasn't a name she recognized from Genevieve's binder. Then again, she didn't exactly have them memorized. She pulled it out and flipped to the back of each section, looking for her name. There was a small yellow section near the back labeled 'Unknown'. Vernier was the last entry with very little information. "Why is she important?"

"You're very uncooperative for someone with my mark," Angel said with a sigh.

"Considering I didn't tell you to shove it instead of asking for an explanation, I'm being *very* cooperative. I know this isn't you calling in the mark, so if you want my help, tell me why."

"Vernier is quietly influential. She was childhood friends with Ito, who, as everyone knows, runs the biggest and oldest pack in this hemisphere. Anyone smart enough to stay out of the limelight while still wielding that much power is someone you want on your side."

"How do you know all this if everyone else here doesn't? Surely she's going to get swamped with people wanting to be her friend at an event like this," Amber said skeptically as she hung her last shirt up.

"Werewolves are often blinded by displays of bravado. The loudest voice gets heard and the rest are drowned out."

Amber pulled the rubber band off the end of her braid and started unwinding it so she could shower. "Do you know what she wants? Is she fighting for werewolf rights or anything helpful?"

Angel shrugged. "I'm not sure, which is why it would be so helpful if you found that out."

"Great. If she turns out to hate bitten wolves, I'm firing you as my advisor."

He chuckled. "You could try."

She grabbed her bag of toiletries. "Time for you to go, unless you have something else to talk about?"

"Nothing else, but I do have a gift for you," he said, standing and walking toward her.

"A gift?" she asked, raising an eyebrow. "Why does that sound so ominous?"

"Because you are overly suspicious of everyone and everything, a trait I heartily approve of." He snapped his fingers and a book appeared in his hand. The shadows that formed it coalesced and darkened until it looked completely real.

"What's the catch?" she asked, staring at it like it might bite her.

"No catch. No strings attached. A gift without expectation of reciprocation." He extended it toward her.

Still hesitant, she took it. The cover felt like real leather and smelled like it too. Hopefully it wasn't made from anything gross.

He stepped in closer and smiled, his face a little more clear at this distance. "Enjoy."

With that, he disappeared in a puff of smoke.

She stood there confused and conflicted for a moment before opening the book. It was old but well-kept. Her fingers tingled from the magic that coated the pages. She'd heard of spells that protected them from decay and hoped that's what she was feeling.

Flipping to the title page, she saw the book was about tarot. That...actually would be helpful.

With a sigh, she set the book on her nightstand. Leave it to Angel to be confusingly nice again. She reminded herself that she couldn't trust him. Not now, and not ever.

This would serve him somehow, she just didn't know how yet. Maybe the whole reason was to make her trust him more. After all, he needed her to cooperate with his suggestions, like the one to seek out Vernier. She was going to talk that over with Genevieve before she did as Angel had asked. He wasn't wrong when he'd said she was suspicious.

CHAPTER 14

GENEVIEVE

In the back of the main conference hall, there were dozens of small alcoves. They were pretty swanky, with plush high back chairs and mahogany tables. It was quieter sitting in one since, unlike the main hall, the floor was carpeted.

Genevieve had settled in one to get a feel for the room before she tried to strike up a conversation. It had worked out even better than she'd planned.

She leaned against the wall, chewing her bite of pastry slowly as she tried to listen in. It was hard to hear over all the other chatter but she was close enough to make out the gist of the conversation.

What she was hearing didn't improve her mood any. A group of some no-name packs were discussing how embarrassing it was for a bitten alpha to be on a council and how Amber had probably been working for the sorcerer. That part just didn't make any sense. The sorcerer had literally tried to kill them.

"Your face is going to get stuck like that," Paul whispered from the entrance to the alcove. He'd obviously been trying to sneak up on her but she'd smelled him coming ages ago.

Turning her frown on him, she took another bite. "Good, maybe people will leave me alone," she said around the food in her mouth.

Paul maintained a blank face but she could see the amusement in his eyes as he walked over to her. "That strategy might work." He held up a small plate with two more pastries. The one closest to her was a chocolate donut. "I brought you a bribe."

"Where did you get this?" she demanded, grabbing the donut. "They were out when I got down there."

"I got there earlier and grabbed one," he said, raising an eyebrow as she scarfed it down in three bites.

"Alright, what do you want?" she asked, thinking she should have figured out what he was bribing her for *before* eating the bribe. Too late for regrets though.

"Come and let me introduce you to a few people," he said, sedately taking a bite of his own pastry.

"Who?"

"The people you're eavesdropping on."

Her eyebrows shot up. "Why?"

"It's easier for them to gossip about people they don't know. Once you are standing in front of them, it's no longer a hypothetical pack, it's *you*. Make an impression and put some of the rumors to rest." He shrugged and put his hands in his pockets. "I won't force you to do it, it's just a suggestion."

She sighed. "I hate you."

This was why they were here though, no matter how much she disliked it. She'd had to burn vacation time for this conference. She couldn't waste the opportunity just because she didn't enjoy it.

"Let's go," she said, marching out from around the corner ahead of him.

He jogged to catch up and walked next to her toward the little group of gossipers. They all turned and looked at them. She could see them wondering if she'd overheard what they'd said and plastered a smile to her face. Let them wonder.

"Barry, good to see you again," Paul greeted one of the men with a nod. "This is Genevieve Bisset, Amber Hale's beta."

Barry scratched the back of his head awkwardly as he returned the nod. "Barry Goodman, beta to the Perry pack. Nice to meet you."

Genevieve shook each of their hands, recognizing all the names from her binder. Most were from packs that didn't like bitten wolves, though one she had down as neutral. She'd have to make a note that their beta, at least, was an ass.

She spotted Amber across the hall and nodded toward her. Amber nodded back and followed Jameson and the other council alphas toward a meeting room. It looked like she was stuck in an even worse situation.

Genevieve ground her teeth together and forced herself to focus on the conversation. It was time to dazzle these idiots with her brilliance and control until the panel *Betas in Today's World* started.

CHAPTER 15

AMBER

She'd made it through the day. Somehow. Amber rubbed her temples absently. Her head ached from the information overload, not to mention the stack of paperwork now sitting on the nightstand. The panels had been repetitive, grating, and only vaguely helpful. She suspected the real purpose of these conferences was *networking*, but she had no interest in that.

Worst of all, she was being forced into fancy clothes for a formal dinner. For a culture that opted for nudity as often as they did clothes, they were awfully obsessed with dressing up for no reason. Half the attendees had been in suits all day.

"Amber, you ready?" Genevieve asked from the bathroom.

"Sure," she replied, glaring at the dress laid out on her bed.

Genevieve poked her head out of the bathroom. "Don't make me put it on you. Because I will. I did not spend all that time doing your makeup and hair just to have you wimp out now."

She'd let her beta pick the dress out to avoid having to shop herself, which in hindsight, had been a bad idea.

There was no avoiding it now though. Grumbling to herself, she tossed her robe on the bed and pulled on the dress. Thankfully, Ceri had spelled the bodice to adhere to her skin so she didn't have a nip-slip. It made the whole thing feel more secure but dressing up like this still made her feel like a little kid who'd gotten into her mother's closet.

"What do you think?" Genevieve asked as she walked out of the bathroom.

Genevieve looked elegant and more grown-up than she'd ever seen her. The heart-shaped neckline and three-quarter length sleeves suited her perfectly. The whole dress was made of black lace, with a high-low skirt that was layered to just the right fullness. Her pink hair was down for once, cascading over her shoulder in soft waves. She was the picture of elegance.

"You look amazing," Amber said, a little awed.

"Thanks," Genevieve said with a big grin. "I've had this for a while and nowhere to wear it."

"I suppose we actually have to go down there now?" Amber asked, holding out for the tiniest bit of hope that the whole thing would end up canceled.

Genevieve put her hands on her hips. "Yes. You're showing off that dress."

There was a tug on the demon mark as Angel formed behind her. She turned around in annoyance. Of course he'd show up for this.

He was in a human form again. He strode toward her, abruptly stopping short, mouth agape.

"You're gonna catch flies if you leave your mouth hanging open like that," Amber said sullenly. It wasn't *that* shocking to see her in a dress. She glanced in the mirror. Maybe it was a little tight.

She'd almost killed Genevieve over the plunging neckline, but at least it covered most everything else. It had long sleeves with lacy gold embroidery at her wrist, shoulder, and waist that took it from plain to pretty. The slit was a little too high, reaching up to mid-thigh, but she wouldn't be accidentally flashing anyone. Her hair looked fiery-red against the stark black.

"What are you wearing?" he finally asked, still frozen in place.

She crossed her arms. "It's a dress, Kadrithan. It's not that shocking. Do I look stupid or something? Someone tell me if I look stupid."

Genevieve snorted and opened the door. "I'll see you down there when Kadrithan gets some blood flow back to his brain."

Amber glared at her until she left with a smirk, then turned back to Angel. He was still looking at her with an odd expression.

"You don't look stupid." He strode past her toward the still open door. "We should get down there. There is fashionably late, and then there is just...late."

"Fine," she mumbled, pushing her shoulders back and walking out with as much confidence as she could fake.

Shane was stepping out of the elevator as they rounded the corner. Genevieve hopped on and pressed the door close button, leaving him stranded with her and Angel. Shane had no idea Angel was there though and greeted her with a smile. He couldn't quite keep his eyes on her face. She found she didn't mind with him.

"You look nice," she said in greeting. And he did. His suit fit perfectly and the soft gray made his eyes an even brighter blue than normal.

"And you are breathtaking," Shane said with a hint of heat in his voice.

Angel snorted. "How unoriginal."

She ground her teeth together and bit back a retort. "Thanks."

The elevator door slid open and they walked inside. Angel stood in front of the doors, facing the wrong way, and glared at Shane. This was going to be an extremely uncomfortable elevator ride.

"You seemed to get through the day just fine," Shane said, shifting to stand closer than was strictly necessary. His fingers brushed against her but she couldn't bring herself to hold his hand with Angel staring them down like some kind of aggressive chaperone.

"It was boring, which I won't complain about. I expected more drama," Amber admitted, trying to focus on Shane instead of the grumpy demon third-wheeling her moment with the guy she was interested in.

Shane chuckled. "Boring is definitely good at this sort of thing. Tonight...probably won't be. The alcohol will be flowing. Open bar."

"Great." A drink didn't sound bad, actually, but combining alcohol with a bunch of posturing alphas was a recipe for disaster. She was starting to wonder if that wasn't part of the point. This conference gave everyone a lot of opportunities to screw up.

"Is Paul ready for the Trials tomorrow?"

She nodded firmly. "He is as ready as he can be. I've told him everything I know and he's been working with his pack to strengthen the bond." She paused, hesitating over her next question, but decided to just go ahead and ask. "Do you know Alpha Vernier?"

Shane frowned. "The name doesn't sound familiar, but I can ask around."

"That'd be great, thanks." She avoided looking at Angel. He was probably smug. As usual.

The elevator finally reached the top floor and the doors slid open. Amber practically ran out, passing straight through Angel which sent a shiver of heat over her skin. He always felt warm to her. She had no idea how other people didn't notice that when he was near them.

The banquet hall was massive. Large, circular tables with sweeping crystal center-pieces dominated the center of the room. Small groups were gathered around tables while others milled around the hall.

There were three bars to accommodate the high demand for drinks. A large number of werewolves were gathered around each.

Tall windows provided a view of the city which looked amazing from this high up at night. The golden lights that blanketed the ground twinkled as far as she could see. There was a balcony out there as well, which she intended to slip out to if she had a chance.

She spotted Jameson just as he waved her over.

"Duty calls," she said with a sigh.

"I'll grab us both a drink. What would you like?" Shane offered.

"With that dress, you need a Scotch neat." Angel drifted around her, now in a more defined human form wearing a deep-black suit with a gold handkerchief that matched her dress perfectly.

"Cranberry vodka," Amber said with a strained smile.

Shane nodded and hurried away.

Angel snorted. "Cranberry vodka? Have you no dignity?"

"I have tastebuds," she shot back and she headed toward Jameson, hoping no one could overhear her.

"Tastebuds are required for appreciating a good scotch, they are *not* for slamming back a cranberry vodka like you're at a sorority party."

"Why do you care what I drink? And why do we match now?"

"Second-hand embarrassment, and we match due to my innate sense of style."

"No one can see you, you weirdo." She had to cut off any further retort as she approached Jameson and the other werewolves at the table.

If she'd been paying attention, she would have realized sooner it wasn't the rest of the council like she expected. The people Jameson was talking with were unfamiliar. Except for one.

"Amber, good of you to join us," Jameson said in greeting. His gray hair was slicked back and he looked as polished as was possible for the grizzled old alpha. "This is Alpha Carter, Alpha Ivanov and his beta, and Alpha Yang."

She recognized all their names from the red tabs in Genevieve's binder. Carter had been the one glaring at her during check-in and it didn't look like his opinion of her had changed much. It appeared Jameson was throwing her in the deep end.

"Good evening, nice to meet you all," she said with the smile she normally reserved for patients that threw their food at her when she'd worked in the hospital.

Alpha Yang gave her a short nod, but the others gave no indication they'd even heard her speak.

"Jameson, you've been busier than usual the last few months," Carter said, finally deigning to glance at Amber. His dark brown eyes shone with intelligence and a hint of cruelty that made her wolf draw up tight in her mind. "You've been quite…philanthropic, taking charity cases under your wing and what not."

"I prefer to think of it as fostering the potential for the next generation of leaders among us," Jameson said with a sharp smile.

"Oh, interesting. Are you angling for New Alpha of the Year, Miss Hale?"

"Please, call me Alpha Hale," Amber said, meeting his eyes. Miss was something you called little girls, not a grown woman who was your peer. "And no, I'm not interested in awards."

A muscle in Carter's jaw jumped as he ground his teeth together. "What are you interested in then, *Alpha* Hale?"

She cocked her head at him curiously. "I want my pack safe and happy. I'm sure as we grow, we'll set new goals, but as a new alpha my focus is on security."

"A wise choice for a bitten wolf," Ivanov said drily. "Though you will always lack the security you could have had if you had simply joined an already established pack instead of striking out on your own."

"Considering it was an established pack that ordered one of its members to change me without consent, I doubt that," she said as Shane joined them, offering her the bright red drink she'd requested.

"This is getting rather tense," Angel said, walking over to stand near Carter. "He is getting angry, I can feel the wolf close to the surface. His control is abysmal."

She did her best to ignore the commentary as Yang turned the conversation back to Jameson, asking him how many new members he was expecting to add in the next year, if any.

Shane was tense next to her. He must have heard Carter when he was walking up.

A spike of annoyance followed by panic shot through the pack bond from Genevieve. "Excuse me," Amber said to whoever might care she was leaving as she headed immediately toward her beta.

She couldn't see her yet, but the bond drew her toward Genevieve like a magnet. Finally, she spotted her in the crowd. There didn't seem to be an immediate threat. She was standing with Paul and a few others.

Genevieve looked over her shoulder and saw her approaching, then whispered something to Paul and broke away from the group.

"What's wrong?" Amber asked quietly, trying to look unconcerned. It felt like everyone was watching her constantly.

Genevieve smoothed her hair down nervously. "Nothing."

"Genevieve, that was not nothing."

"It's stupid, okay? Not safety related. Can we talk about it later?"

Amber took a long drink of her cranberry vodka. Screw Angel, this stuff was amazing. "Sure, as long as you're actually okay."

"I am."

She drained her glass, then set it on an empty table next to another glass for one of the waiters to pick up. They had been appearing and disappearing like ninjas to keep the dirty dishes cleaned up. "I'm going to get another drink."

Genevieve smirked at her. "Isn't that Shane's job?"

"Shut up." She turned and headed toward the bar, a stupid smile tugging at her lips. It was nice to have a guy pursuing her. It was even nicer that he was responsible, unlike the last few guys she'd tried dating in college. That had been a disaster.

The crowd grew more dense near the bar. She stepped around a small group with a polite murmur.

"Watch out," Angel hissed urgently as he flew at her, startling her into taking half a step back. That was the only thing that saved her from getting a glass of whisky in the face.

She couldn't avoid the mess entirely. The amber liquid splattered against her chest, soaking into her dress and dripping down her cleavage.

The woman Carter had *accidentally* bumped into smirked at her before disappearing into the crowd.

"My mistake. How clumsy of me." Carter said, extending a cloth napkin out toward her like he was going to try to pat her chest dry.

She grabbed his wrist before he could touch her. "Very clumsy of you."

He tried to push his hand in for a moment, but he couldn't overpower her without making it obvious. "Napkin?" he offered, as if he had just been trying to hand it to her the whole time.

"Thank you," she said, calmly taking it before letting his wrist go.

Carter watched her dab away the whisky with a smug expression. She was pretty sure he was trying to bait her into losing her temper but she wasn't sure why he looked like he'd accomplished something.

Sure, she was going to smell like alcohol the rest of the night, but half the room had seen his sad attempt at subtlety. People were whispering around them and what she could make out didn't sound like it favored Carter. The word caveman was used several times.

"Behind you," Angel said again.

She stepped to her left and Ivanov stumbled past her previous position. He'd been trying to shoulder check her from behind.

Fury rose up in her. They were working together, circling around her because they thought she was weak. If Angel hadn't been helping, they would have caught her completely unaware.

"Seems your friends are clumsy too, Carter," she said flatly, letting none of the anger leak into her voice.

"Two more coming up behind you," Angel said urgently. "Wait, don't move."

She held still, lifting her gaze to Carter's. Trusting Angel was the only option right now.

"Barry, I've been looking for you!" Genevieve said happily behind her. She'd been so mad she hadn't noticed her beta's approach, but it seemed Genevieve had cut them off.

Carter's smug expression turned furious. "You think you belong here, but you don't."

"Why not?" she asked, taking one step toward him.

"You are weak," he snarled, red pooling in his irises.

The same old, tired argument. She bit down on a sigh and tried to think of how Genevieve would handle this. Her beta was better at the political crap than she was, but she was the alpha, and she had to be the one to speak now.

"I passed the same Trials as every other alpha here. Why do you assume I'm weak?"

Carter snorted in derision. "Passing the basic threshold for being an alpha does not mean you aren't lesser in every way. I was born into this, chosen by the wolf in my mother's womb. You are an imposter."

"So your plan for proving that is throwing alcohol on me and getting your friends to bump into me?" she asked, raising an eyebrow. Political or not, she preferred to be blunt.

"You're going to need to do better if you want to force him into making a mistake," Angel whispered and he drifted around Carter.

Carter's upper lip curled in amusement. "Tell me, did you have to fuck that elf to get him to be your sponsor?"

Angel snorted. "Or not."

She laughed aloud. "Are you a twelve year old bully, or are you a grown man? Accusing me of sleeping my way into the Trials is pathetic."

A growl rumbled in his chest and he took two quick steps forward, raising his fist like he was going to back-hand her.

She braced herself for a fight, but the red suddenly fled from Carter's eyes and he stopped mid-step.

Dominance had a physical weight to it. Carter's dominance didn't affect her at all. No one that she had met could so far...until now. She turned slowly, eyes going to a man in his mid-thirties with hair so black it almost looked blue in the dim lighting.

Alpha Dominus -- an old term that simply referred to the alpha who ruled over all other packs, keeping the peace -- Ito was from an old werewolf family that had immigrated to America two centuries ago. They'd organized werewolves in the western hemisphere and laid down rules that eventually became the laws they all followed today.

His pack boasted over three hundred adults, a veritable army by normal pack standards. Ito had an almost unthinkable amount of strength to draw on, but it was his personal strength and dominance that allowed him to do so.

He glided forward, not a wrinkle in his suit or a hair out of place and stood before the two of them. Just by walking up this guy had accomplished what Carter hadn't. Amber felt like an imposter standing next to him

"Alpha Jason Carter, do you intend to challenge Alpha Hale?" Ito asked with a stony expression.

She'd never felt power like this before. His presence made her want to avert her eyes, tuck tail, and run away. She hated that feeling and forced herself to stand tall despite her shaking knees.

Carter looked away. "I will not stoop to challenging a *bitten* wolf."

"Then your continued discourtesy reflects poorly on all of us, Alpha Carter. I find your underhanded attempts to goad another alpha into a loss of control during our most important gathering personally insulting. If you are going to attempt such a thing, it should at least be done well," Ito said, his voice carrying through the hall. "You are dismissed for the evening. Tomorrow, you will either conduct yourself as is fitting an alpha of your stature, or you will be removed from The Gathering."

Silence fell over the crowd. Carter's face paled but he didn't say a word. He simply turned around and walked away.

Ito glanced at her briefly, a glimpse of distaste crossing his face before he walked away as well.

Whispered conversations filled the banquet hall once again, rolling over her like a wave. He had helped her, but not because he supported bitten wolves. Based on the look on his face, she was pretty sure he hated them just as much as Carter, if not more.

"That was interesting," Angel said, appearing right next to her.

"That was embarrassing."

"It could have gone worse," Genevieve replied as she appeared on her other side, not realizing she had been talking to the demon.

"I think drawing the attention of Ito is about as bad as it gets." She dabbed at the wet spot on the front of her dress with a sigh. "And now I stink."

Something tickled along the back of her neck, as though she were being watched. She turned around, eyes scanning the room but didn't see anyone.

That was odd.

"What?" Genevieve asked.

"Nothing." She shook her head. "I'm just paranoid. And definitely need that drink I was going for. Want anything?"

"I'll come with you," Genevieve said, glancing around the room suspiciously. "No one should be stupid enough to try something after that, but I'm not risking it."

Angel followed them and Amber felt that same, frustrating sense of thankfulness. He'd saved her ass back there and he wasn't even gloating. Yet, at least.

"Thank you," she whispered, the words quiet enough even she could barely hear them.

He caught her eye and winked at her. "My pleasure."

Shane caught up to them as they arrived at the bar, walking right through Angel unaware. "Hey, are you okay?"

"I'm fine," she said with a smile, catching Angel's scowl in her peripheral vision. "I had backup."

"I'm sorry I couldn't get involved––"

"Don't worry about it, Shane. You can't fight those battles for me. I know that."

Shane nodded, but he still looked extremely uncomfortable.

"He'll always have to put Jameson and his pack first," Angel whispered.

"What would you like?" the bartender asked, looking a little harried.

"Scotch, neat."

Angel grinned at her, the smile looking genuine for once. "Good choice."

CHAPTER 16

KADRITHAN (ANGEL)

Spending such long periods of time with Amber was beginning to take its toll.

Kadrithan downed an energy potion and waited for the sweep of magic to clear the exhaustion from his limbs. Nothing could remove the headache or slick of sweat that covered his body but a long, hot shower. However, he was not free to indulge in that yet.

There was one last person he needed to visit now that Amber was done dodging werewolves for the evening.

A brief knock on his door startled him. He wasn't expecting a visitor this time of night.

He opened the door and found Zerestria waiting outside. "What are you doing here?" he asked without thinking, shocked to find *her* visiting *him*. Despite his royal heritage, Zerestria outranked him as long as the war continued. "I'm sorry, my surprise has made me rude. Come in."

She raised an eyebrow but walked in without a snarky retort.

"No chastisement? It must be serious then," he commented as he shut the door, briefly checking the hall to see if there were any eavesdroppers.

She walked slowly toward the window, looking out over the dark landscape that was illuminated only by a red moon. "You should have come to me as soon as you suspected Raziel's involvement."

He stiffened. "I can handle Raziel."

Her pale green eyes bore into him. "This is not the time to let your pride get in the way of your decisions. I have not heard such foolish words from you in nearly two decades."

"We're not even sure it's him." He turned away, flexing his fingers uncomfortably as the energy potion made his skin prickle.

"Sure enough that you are preparing to *handle* him."

"How did you even find out?" he asked sullenly, feeling like a kid caught with his hand in the cookie jar. He was far too old for this, but Zerestria had a way of making him feel like an idiot.

"Venali complains loudly and often. Finding out wasn't difficult," Zerestria said, gaze turning back to the window. "Rafael Vida is a poor cover name, which is part of what worries me."

"He's moving more openly than he ever has," he said, putting their shared concern into words.

She nodded. "What is your plan?"

"I want to know why now. Something must have triggered this. I don't like that we've been blindsided by this." It had been gnawing at him since the conversation with Venali. Taking out Raziel could change everything for them but it was risky to attempt.

"We are indeed missing something." She shook her head, her shoulders hunching in farther. She looked tired...and old.

"This is an opportunity, and I'm going to find a way to take advantage of it."

She turned back to him. "Make sure you do, and that you don't get distracted."

"Distracted? I work toward our goals without rest."

"Your reports show a trend that you seem willfully blind to, and you have never given a *gift* to someone you have marked before. At the very least, it should have been in exchange for something."

Anger -- at himself and at Zerestria -- pulsed in his gut. "I have never had a mark that could be so easily manipulated. Having Amber's trust means I can ask her to do something without fulfilling the mark. That is valuable."

She waved away his argument. "I've known you long enough to see through your bravado. We are in the midst of a war. Sentiment has no place in your decisions."

A vision of Amber in that dress, red leaking into her eyes as she faced off against an alpha twice her size flashed through his mind. She appealed to him after so long dealing with the groveling, fearful scum that usually ended up with a demon mark. It was pointless though, and admiration for someone he needed to control was dangerous.

"I still have work to do tonight," he said finally, unwilling to discuss that further right now.

Zerestria nodded and headed for the door, clearly satisfied that she had made her point. "I'll be drawing on my sources to see what I can learn about Raziel's movements as well. We will meet again tomorrow."

He let her out, then shut and locked his door. His headache had grown worse and his mood had gone from tired, to angry and tired.

Plopping down on the chaise lounge, he took a deep breath, trying to center himself before his next visit. Red hair and hazel eyes flashed through his mind, pulling his focus from the task at hand.

"Damn you, Zerestria," he muttered. This hadn't been a problem before, but now that she'd put it in his mind, he was questioning everything. Amber had potential as a mark but he was *not* going to let anyone or anything distract him.

He shut his eyes and focused on the transition into the spirit realm. Evangeline still struggled with this, but he had done it so many times it was as easy as exhaling.

Passing through darkness, fire, and chilling cold, he found himself behind the mark he needed to speak to today. As always, he waited a moment to reveal himself. There was often more to be learned from silent observation than from actually speaking to the mark.

Laurel —— a human woman whose beauty rivaled that of the half angels thanks to their deal —— pinned her hair in place on top of her head, practicing her smile in the mirror. She did that when she thought no one was watching. It was an odd habit, but it did take practice to make a fake smile appear genuine.

.

CHAPTER 17

TOMMY

Tommy stood next to Ceri in the crowd. Objectively, he knew the tribe was pretty big, but seeing them all together was mind blowing. Hundreds of trolls were gathered in the field. The energy in the air thudded against his chest.

This event was held out in the middle of nowhere in the woods. He'd almost been convinced they had the wrong address after ten minutes driving down a long dirt road, but then they'd seen the other cars.

He'd looked around for Deward for fifteen minutes after they arrived before he'd stumbled across Deward's father, who assured him that Deward would come find him when he was ready. The man had seemed excited and proud and had slapped him on the shoulder hard enough to leave a bruise, which wasn't like him. Normally he was fairly calm and intellectual.

His tusks were also painted white, which was definitely not normal troll fashion. All of the adults had their tusks painted some color. Whatever was going to happen today was going to be different from the days spent training with the trolls.

He texted Amber real quick to see if the Trials had started yet. It would have been nice to be there to support Paul, but since it was at The Gathering the rest of the pack couldn't attend. They limited pack members for safety apparently.

Amber replied quickly.

No. He's going last, of course. It will be a couple of hours. Deward challenged you to a duel yet or whatever?

He snorted at his phone.

Nah, not yet. Don't sound so excited by the prospect.

Amber simply replied with:

:P

"This is quite the gathering," Ceri said, looking around curiously. She stood out among the trolls with her blonde hair and white, flowing dress. It was good to see her out of her robe, and even better to find she was freshly showered. She was starting to smell so strongly of sage it was hard to breath around her.

He put his phone away. "It definitely is. Everyone seems pretty hyped up for whatever is going to be happening."

Derek's scent drifted past Tommy and he looked back to find him jogging up. "Sorry I'm late. Did I miss anything?"

"Nope, hasn't started yet," Tommy said, watching Derek and Ceri do that weird smile-and-look-away thing. It was getting kind of hard to watch. "How was the shop today?"

"A little busy but I got everything done before I headed back to the house to shower. Income will cover rent on the building this month, which I didn't expect to happen so soon," Derek said with a proud smile.

"That's amazing!" Ceri exclaimed, her face lighting up like Tommy hadn't seen since before the sorcerer's attack. "You have a knack for business apparently."

A horn cut through the noise, starting out low and growing louder until Tommy was tempted to cover his ears. The crowd moved as one, flowing around the three of them toward a small platform set on the far side of the clearing.

"Must be starting," Tommy said, practically bouncing on his toes now that something was finally happening. The anticipation for this had been building for days, and Deward had been painfully cryptic about the whole thing. With the full moon tonight as well, there was a constant buzz under his skin.

"Did you ever figure out why we were invited?" Derek asked.

"Nope."

They found a spot with a view of the wooden platform. A lone troll stood on it. Despite the deep wrinkles on her dark green face, she stood straight. The old woman was actually kind of ripped.

She wore a deep, black jumpsuit with a thick, crimson rope tied around her torso in an intricate knot. A crest was pinned to the center, showing a large eye with a hammer in the iris. He'd seen that same image at the training center but hadn't ever paid much attention to it. It must mean something to this tribe.

The woman scanned the crowd, waiting for them to settle.

"Greetings, fellow tribesman," she said, the beginning of her speech casting a hush over the trolls. "We are honored to gather in our holy place. Honored to watch our children transform into adults."

The trolls clapped once in unison as if on cue. Tommy jerked at the same time as Ceri and they bumped into each other. He pressed his lips together to keep from laughing.

"We will celebrate this transformation by challenging them to be better than their parents and their elders. After all, progress demands the next generation be better than the last." She put her hand behind her back and walked the length of the stage, smiling out at the crowd. "Are we ready to begin?"

The trolls let out a bellowing cheer that *did* make Tommy clap his hand over his ears. Derek whooped and hollered right along with them.

A line of a dozen trolls, all Deward's age, filed onto the stage. They were all tusk-less. It took him a moment to pick his friend out of the line, but he spotted him on the far left. Deward's hands were clasped behind his back like the others. He stood tall and proud.

Each of the trolls had a handprint on their chest in varying colors. Deward's was white like his father's tusks.

The woman walked in front of them, as if inspecting the younger trolls. Abruptly, she paused in front of one of them.

"Pallia Bonebiter, who do you name?"

The female troll straightened her shoulders. Her thick, red hair was braided and tightly bound out of the way to the back of her head. "I name my sister, Yanni Bonebiter."

A cheer rose up from among the trolls as Yanni jogged toward the stage, joining Pallia with a grin.

"Any clue why they're naming people?" Ceri whispered.

He shook his head. "Nope, Deward didn't explain anything."

The crowed cheered as each troll stepped forward and named their companion. Tommy clapped along with them.

Finally, Deward stepped forward. He was the last to be chosen by the elder and looked tense.

"Deward Tuskbreaker, who do you name?"

The crowed went silent, awaiting his reply.

"I name my brother, Thomas Anderson," Deward said without hesitation, his voice booming across the space.

Tommy froze. That was his name. He didn't even know how Deward had found his last name, he'd never told him.

Ceri jabbed him in the ribs. "Go or you're going to embarrass him."

His feet started moving but he was in a complete daze. The trolls seemed just as stunned. The crowd parted as he walked but they were all whispering among themselves, looking back and forth between him and Deward in shock.

He hopped up onto the stage and walked over to stand beside Deward like the others that had been called up. Deward stared straight ahead without looking at him.

"Are you sure of your choice, youngling?" the woman asked, causing another murmur in the crowd. She hadn't asked that of anyone else.

Deward looked at him and nodded. "I am."

Great. Whatever Deward was doing was not only a surprise to him, it likely also broke with troll tradition.

Tommy clasped his hands behind his back with the others and stared out at the crowd defiantly. If Deward wanted him up here, then screw anyone that thought otherwise. He was good at breaking tradition. Inside his mind, the wolf howled in challenge.

CHAPTER 18

AMBER

Amber was pretty sure she was more nervous than Paul, and she wasn't even the one about to go out in front of hundreds of people to complete the Trials.

His entire pack was huddled in the waiting room. Two other alphas were completing the Trials before him and they weren't allowed to watch. They could hear the cheers and boos through the thin walls of the building though.

"I wanted to thank you again for agreeing to sponsor me. It was a risk to trust anyone that had been involved with Lockhart, but I appreciate that you took a chance on me," Paul said, extending his hand toward her.

She shook it firmly. "Hopefully you don't regret choosing me."

A mischievous grin spread across his face. "I like stirring things up on occasion. No regrets here."

Genevieve snorted. "I should hope not. I worked hard on those negotiations."

Paul's smile shifted toward genuine amusement. "You certainly did."

Amber looked between the two of them, understanding dawning on her. That flutter of annoyance and panic from the night before was starting to make sense. She'd wondered for a while if Paul was *interested* in Genevieve, and the more she watched them, the more it seemed like he was.

She narrowed her eyes at Paul. If he was making Genevieve uncomfortable, she'd gut him.

Paul caught her expression and cocked his head at her in confusion.

There was a brief knock -- which was good timing for Amber-- and Ito's beta opened the door. "It is time."

Paul nodded. "Let's get this done."

Amber walked with him toward the arena. The alpha that had just passed the Trials was rejoining his pack. Their excitement only made her more nervous. People were cheering for him, but she doubted they'd cheer for Paul.

This arena lacked the air of formality and tradition that the clearing in the woods where she had been tested had possessed. It was all new —— a temporary thing they'd set up for The Gathering. The shiny metal and pine seemed all wrong. Even her wolf agreed, growling unhappily in her mind.

The crowd quieted as Alpha Ito stepped forward. His cold eyes found her, and he seemed just as uninterested in speaking to her as he had the night before.

"Amber Hale, as the sponsor for Paul Greer, do you swear that he has maintained conduct becoming an alpha through the waning and the waxing of the moon?" Ito asked, his expression cold. His hatred of her was more terrifying because it wasn't reckless. She didn't understand it and she wished they'd never met.

"I swear it."

"Paul Greer, come forward."

Paul approached the stone —— the only thing here that wasn't new —— and stood before Ito.

A knife appeared in Ito's hand, seemingly out of thin air. It was nothing like the one Jameson had used in the ritual she had gone through. It was made of pure silver, even the handle which Ito was holding without flinching despite the smoke rising from his skin.

"By the Moon, who gives us strength. By the Night, who gives us sight. By the Wolf, who gives us life. Let the candidate's worthiness be measured." He held his hand over the stone and drew the blade across his palm, then squeezed a few drops of blood down onto it.

She felt the magic much stronger this time. It drifted around her like a cool breeze, refreshing her and the wolf.

Ito handed the blade to Paul who repeated the action. The two of them were illuminated by the moonlight for a moment as the urge to shift rolled through the crowd.

"Do you need an explanation of the first course?" Ito asked, cutting the moment short.

Paul shook his head. "I do not."

"Then begin when you are ready," Ito said as he stepped aside and pointed toward the starting mark, which was a red line painted on the grass.

Ito then gestured sharply at the crowd and they filed up onto the overlook. Amber and Genevieve led Paul's pack up to the right side after Ito while most of the crowd went to the other side.

Paul stripped down —— tossing his clothes to his unofficial beta—— without a hint of concern. She forced herself not to look away like a blushing virgin. This was normal. Totally normal. Not sexual in the least.

A blush crept up Genevieve's neck. At least she wasn't the only one affected.

It was odd looking down at the course from up here. It looked smaller than it had when she'd been the one facing it. Sometimes it was hard to believe it had only been a few months since she had been changed. It felt like years had passed with how much everything had changed.

Paul stood at the line, looking perfectly relaxed other than the subtle shifting of his muscles under his skin. There was a moment of complete silence, then he took off at a run.

CHAPTER 19

DEWARD

That had been reckless, but Deward couldn't find it in himself to regret it. The other trolls talked about bravery and inclusivity but he felt the tribe had become borderline xenophobic as of late.

In centuries past, it was just as common to choose someone outside the tribe to assist with your feat as it was to choose your sibling or cousin.

To be fair, other supernaturals seemed to care less and less about their customs. It was hard to find someone willing to assist you with something so challenging with no other reward than a sense of accomplishment.

He barely listened to the elder complete the ceremony, waiting only for the cue that meant they could leave the stage and he could finally give Tommy the explanation he deserved.

A cheer rose up from the crowd and the elder waved them off the stage. He grabbed Tommy's arm and dragged him away from the stage where they'd have a moment before his parents found him. Tommy was worryingly silent.

They paused just inside the tree line and he turned to his friend who faced him with crossed arms. "So, what did I just agree to? And why didn't you warn me, dude?"

Deward inclined his head in apology. "It's forbidden. Part of this ceremony is understanding who will come to your aid when called. Tradition dictates that you do not tell that person ahead of time." He took a deep breath. "Anyhow, part of entering adulthood is the opportunity to complete what we call a feat. It can be a feat of intellect, bravery, strength –– whatever we choose. We must discuss it with one of the elders and get their approval. My mother, for example, translated the Voynich manuscript, which was long thought to be impossible."

Tommy narrowed his eyes at him. "I got the impression it's not exactly normal to choose someone outside the tribe."

"Ah, no, it isn't," Deward admitted, straightening his shoulders in defiance. "It didn't used to be so uncommon a couple of centuries ago but things change. It's mostly just riskier. The people of the tribe know it is an honor while an outsider is more likely to refuse to help, which would make what I have to do much harder. Also, someone in the tribe has had to complete a feat of their own, so they may be able to offer more help." He paused, unsure if he should add this last part, but he wanted to be honest. "But you have risen to the challenge of adapting to a monumental change. I consider that a feat all on its own."

Tommy looked down, scuffing his foot against the dirt before responding. "You aren't going to get in trouble, are you?"

"I'm...actually not sure how my parents will react. My choice is supported by the values they taught me from the time I was a child, but this was not what most would consider the wisest choice."

"An unexpected choice is not inherently wrong," Deward's father said, appearing from behind a tree. He hadn't noticed his approach, likely due to nerves. Still, it was an embarrassing oversight.

His mother stepped out as well, her expression blank. "We heard your explanation to Thomas, however, it was superficial at best. You gave all the reasons why choosing him shouldn't be an issue, but I would like to hear *why* you have chosen Thomas to help you for this particular feat."

Tommy looked at him, apparently curious as well.

He clasped his hands in front of himself. This was one question, at least, that he was well-prepared to answer. "My reasons are as follows: first, his senses are keener than mine. Since I am searching for something this was a high priority. Second, we have shown excellent teamwork both in training and during our study sessions. A sense of camaraderie and ability to work together is paramount. Third, I trust Thomas, and I believe I have his trust as well. Choosing him without warning, was a final test of this, which was obviously a success. The challenging nature of the feat I've chosen requires that I have absolute trust in the person that will be helping me, and that they put the same trust in me."

Saying that much at once had left him out of breath, so he clamped his mouth shut and waited.

His mother searched his face for a moment before nodding. "You have thought this through carefully. I expected nothing less."

Relief flooded through him. "Thank you, mother."

His father walked over and pulled him into a hug, slapping him on the back. "I look forward to seeing you take on this challenge." He released him and turned to Tommy, wrapping him in the same hug. His friend looked a little stunned and returned the hug tentatively. "And I am glad that my son will have someone so highly qualified at his side."

"I'm, uh, glad he picked me," Tommy said with a shaky grin. He looked surprisingly emotional, which Deward hadn't expected.

His mother shook Tommy's hand, then turned back to him. "We must go help with preparations."

He nodded. "Thank you for your support."

They hurried off, leaving him and Tommy alone for a moment.

"What exactly have I agreed to help you with?" Tommy asked.

"The feat I have chosen is difficult, but I am sure we can do it quickly. There is a Book of Prophecies I believe was hidden near Portland by a powerful coven of witches a few centuries ago. I intend to find it and share it with the tribe," Deward said proudly, his pulse quickening at the thought. The future was difficult -- some would say impossible -- to foretell. Possessing something that could give them insight into the future would be fascinating. They could learn so much. "I've been preparing for this for six months, and we are given one month to complete it after today."

"Where is this book? Do we need to go look for it right now?" Tommy asked.

"No," Deward said, a grin spreading across his face. "Today is all about the Games."

"The Games?" Both of Tommy's eyebrows shot up. "Why does that sound so ominous?"

Deward laughed, excitement growing in his gut. "No need to be worried...unless you can't hold your liquor."

"Wait, what?"

CHAPTER 20

GENEVIEVE

Watching the Trials was different this time. There was a sense of anticipation in the crowd, but not because anyone really doubted any of the alphas would pass. This was just entertainment for them.

She'd been tense throughout the whole thing, but no one had tried to trip Paul during the obstacle course, or hurt his sense of smell in the maze. The fight with the bear had been miserable to watch even though Paul was never really in danger. It made the whole thing so much less stressful.

There were also only half the people here compared to the number that had attended Amber's Trials. Since The Gathering was limited to alphas and their betas, the audience wasn't filled with their packs.

Paul had just drunk the potion that would force him to shift eventually. He sat on the ground, head bowed from the strain of holding back the shift.

Amber leaned against the banister and shook her head. "It seems like such a long time ago, but it's only been two months."

"Yeah, it's weird to think about," Genevieve agreed with a sigh. Her hand went to the scar on her thigh. She could feel the ridges of it through her slacks. It had bothered her a lot at first, but now it was something of an anchor. She'd been through something that should have broken her and made it through to the other side stronger than ever.

The minutes ticked by as Paul battled the change. Fur crept up his forearms as claws sprouted from the tips of his fingers. Every time it gained an inch, he would force it back, but it was a losing battle. Still, as the timer ticked on, she realized his control was well above average.

Five minutes was the minimum and he was nearing ten. Only one other alpha had made it that far. It looked like he was going for top time.

With a deep breath, Paul rose to his feet and shifted smoothly, as if he was simply done waiting. He lifted his head and howled. His pack joined in, their enthusiasm bringing a smile to her face. Hopefully this meant they would fully accept him as alpha. Gaining the position had been a bloody, savage affair.

Ito stepped into the arena. "Alpha Paul Greer, we welcome you."

Paul dipped his shaggy, black head in acknowledgement, then trotted out of the ring, rejoining his pack.

"I'm going to go congratulate him," Genevieve whispered to Amber.

Her alpha nodded. "I'll join you in a few minutes, Jameson is waving me over."

She slipped through the press of bodies behind her and hurried down the stairs. The alphas that had passed the Trials were all sent to wait just outside the arena, so Paul should be somewhere down there.

As she rounded a corner, someone grabbed her arm roughly. She whirled on the assailant, finding a man who looked like he should be a wereferret rather than a werewolf. He pressed a finger to his lips and nodded toward a small, dark space under the stairs.

She was torn between telling him to take a walk and following him. He was practically shaking with nerves though, so whatever he had to tell her might be important. Or it could be a trap.

Gritting her teeth, she followed him, senses on high alert for an ambush. The sounds above them were muted by the thump of feet as people began walking around and loudly discussing the Trials.

Beads of sweat glistened on the guy's upper lip as his eyes darted around. "Don't tell anyone I told you this."

"Ok," Genevieve said as calmly as she could. "I won't tell anyone."

"The MIB is looking into your pack. And I don't mean casually. Carter is trying to get them evidence that you know more about all that no magic zone stuff. I don't want to be involved in this. The guy is fabricating evidence, you know? Someone is paying him to do it. But I can't just step down as beta and then end up an omega. So I'm staying out of it after this."

Anger surged through her, but she tamped down on it. Now was not the time to rage. "Thanks for telling me. That was really brave of you."

The man snorted. "Don't patronize me. I'm just doing this out of guilt. Remember, *I didn't tell you shit.* I'll deny it if you try to claim I did."

"Got it," she said with her best lawyer smile. "Anything else you want to pass along before you run away like a scared rabbit?"

He scowled at her. "Stay off Ito's radar. You think Carter hates bitten wolves? He hasn't got anything on that wily bastard."

"Noted." It wasn't anything she hadn't already suspected, but having it confirmed filled her with unease. There was nothing publicly available on his views which had led her to believe he didn't support bitten wolves. Knowing that he was actively working against them could be a problem in the future.

The man scurried off. She waited in the dark corner for a moment longer, not wanting it to be too obvious they'd been talking.

Her hands shook a little as she pulled her phone out. She thought about texting Amber but didn't want to dump this on her in the midst of all this. She could probably feel her anger and fear though, so she'd have to explain it somehow.

The MIB's involvement was serious though. The FBI handled most investigations, while the MIB –– Magical Investigations Bureau –– was only brought in for the most dangerous cases involving supernaturals. Honestly, it made sense considering a sorcerer was involved, but it scared her.

She texted Amber a brief explanation with reassurances it could be dealt with after the conference was over then shoved her phone back in her pocket.

"Genevieve?" Paul asked, sounding amused to find her hiding under the stairs. "What are you doing?"

"I was looking for you, but had to make a work call real quick," she said, burying the worry at the back of her mind until it could be dealt with. "You did amazing!"

"Thank you," he said, returning her smile. "I appreciate the support from you and Amber. Especially you."

A blush began creeping up her neck. "I…it's just been good to help someone succeed. Finding a sponsor is hard."

He shoved his hands in his pockets, some of the warmth leaving his face. He didn't seem angry, but he was pulling back. She let him.

"I'll see you around at the after party. My pack needs to run, and so do I."

"Congratulations again," she said with a soft smile.

He nodded and jogged back toward his pack. She retreated further back into the dark recess and put her head in her hands, wishing Amber was down here with her and that Mr. Ferret had never dumped that news on her.

CHAPTER 21

DEREK

Derek squinted at Tommy. The kid was drunk. Then again, so was he. Troll liquor packed a punch. He wasn't sure how he was still standing.

"You're not winning this one," Derek said, trying to force his eyes to focus down the length of the potato gun. There was no sight, after all, it *was* a potato gun, but he could still line it up pretty well.

Tommy scoffed at him. "Just because you're from Texas doesn't mean you can outshoot everyone."

He pulled the trigger, sending the potato thunking straight into the center of the target. "Nah, but ten years in competitive shooting in 4H does."

Tommy lined up his own shot, arm wavering unsteadily. It went wide, missing the target entirely. Tommy turned on him with a glare. "You...you cheated."

Derek ruffled Tommy's hair. "I'm just better, teen wolf."

"Don't call me that, *old man*," Tommy retorted, shoving his hand away. "Ceri, do something with him. His ego is getting out of hand."

Ceri snorted. "Don't think I can fix that."

"You totally could, Cece. We all know you're bangin'. Sound proofing can't hide your scent all over each other." Tommy immediately burst into giggles, making a gagging noise.

"Call me Cece again and I'll switch your head with your butt," Ceri said with a glare, her fingers twitching threateningly. "I know exactly the spell to do it."

Deward jogged over, half-tackling Tommy. "It's time for chess, come on!"

The troll dragged Tommy away amid a flurry of questions, pausing to grab another drink for both of them.

"He's going to end up barfing all over everything," Derek said, squinting so he could see better.

Ceri snorted and held a bottle of water up in front of his face. "I don't think he'll be the only one at this rate."

He grabbed the water and glared at her unsteadily. "Why aren't you drunk?"

"Maybe I can hold my liquor, unlike *some* people."

"Pshhhhh. You're way smaller than me." He put his hand on top of her head to demonstrate how short she was. "I could drink you under the table."

She brushed his hand away and stepped in closer. "I'm Irish. I have a clear genetic advantage."

He was pretty sure she was flirting with him. "Is that so?"

"It is so."

"I bet our kids will be able to hold their liquor *and* be tall. Then they'll be invincible."

She froze and her eyes went wide. "Our what?"

Whoops. What was in this troll liquor? "Ummm..."

"Derek, we're not..." she sighed, looking around for some kind of escape. "Drink lots of water. I'm going to, uh, go find food."

"Derek! Come play chess with us!" Tommy shouted, running back over and grabbing him by the arm.

He let Tommy drag him away without protest. Maybe Ceri would forget what he said. "I suck at chess, just so you know."

"This is better than normal chess. Look!" Tommy pointed at a raised, bamboo platform surrounded by a pit of sand.

"What is that?"

"Living chess. We get to be the pieces. Deward is running our team."

"How do we get to be the pieces?" Derek asked, the alcohol making his head spin.

"If someone moves to take another piece, they have to fight whoever is there. It's kind of like sumo, you have to force them out of their spot."

"Fighting while drunk? No way that could go wrong."

Tommy grinned at him. "Trolls are awesome."

Deward was directing the trolls he'd chosen around his board and handing out sashes. He gave Tommy two, nodding in greeting at Derek.

"We're white." Tommy draped a sash around his neck that had the symbol of a bishop on it, then pulled on his own that showed a piece Derek didn't recognize. "Alright, I'm on d1. You're on c1."

Derek squinted at the board. "Where?"

"Over here." Tommy dragged him to the spot third square from the left, then took the position next to him. Each square was about five feet by five feet, which made for a massive chess board. It made sense if they had to fight in the squares though.

Derek looked at Tommy, not sure what the symbol on his sash represented. "What are you?"

"The queen."

"That's an important piece, right?"

"They're *all* important but I have the most flexible movement. Oh, speaking of important, do *not* move unless Deward tells you too or it'll count as his turn."

Derek mock saluted him. "As you command, my queen."

Tommy rolled his eyes.

A whistle was blown and everyone quieted down as the last players scrambled to their spots. Deward stood to the right of Tommy, arms crossed and a serious expression on his face. Across the board, mirroring his position, was Deward's father, Olwen.

"E2 to e4," Deward shouted, his voice cutting through the silence. A hushed whisper rolled through the crowd as one of the trolls with a pawn sash moved forward two places.

"E7 to e5," Olwen countered. The black pawn moved forward, stopping right in front of his adversary. They glared at each other, both of them tense.

Derek expected them to brawl right then and there but they held their positions. Through the drunken haze, he remembered that pawns could only attack at an angle. Or something like that.

"F2 to f4," Deward said confidently. A second pawn moved forward without hesitation, taking up position next to the first.

Olwen chuckled. "Pawn takes f4. King's gambit accepted, though I did expect something more imaginative."

Deward grinned at the taunt. "We'll see."

The black pawn moved quickly, lunging at the white pawn diagonal from him. They struggled for a few moments, but the black pawn roared and shoved the white pawn. He lost his footing and fell out of his square. A cheer rose from the crowd. The black pawn helped the white pawn back up and patted him on his back, then the white pawn walked to the side of the board as the victor took his place.

"F1 to c4," Deward called out, not phased by the loss of his pawn. He and Olwen continued calling out their moves. Deward's other bishop took a pawn, then a few moves later, was defeated by one of Olwen's pawns.

Derek tried to follow along but he was iffy on the rules of chess on a good day. Tommy was called away and joined a few other pieces in surrounding a black pawn, but Olwen's queen was there too –– who Derek belatedly realized was Deward's mother.

"Bishop takes f4," Deward called out. No one moved.

The knight to his left jabbed him in the ribs. "That's you."

The black pawn that was surrounded waved at him . "Let's go, little human. Unless you're scared?"

He narrowed his eyes at the troll. So what if the guy had fifty pounds and five inches on him? He could take the green bully. "You wish, pawn."

Derek had been watching when this big oaf had tossed the last person off the board. The troll was relying on his size to push people around.

As he approached, the troll lowered his head like a bull. Derek stepped into the square with him and crouched slightly so it looked like he was going to make a stand. He'd been the runt of the family until he turned seventeen and filled out. He knew how to fight people bigger than him.

The troll charged, barreling toward him with three-hundred pounds of pure muscle and determination. Derek dropped and lunged forward, catching the troll at the knees with both arms, then lifted. He pushed off hard with his left foot, angling them just enough so that when the troll's feet left the ground, he tumbled right out of the square into Deward's mother.

Ceri was cheering in the crowd, a smile on her face. Seeing that felt even better than winning the spot.

Derek straightened and saluted the fallen pawn. "The bigger they are the harder they fall."

The troll laughed and stood back up, holding out his hand to Derek. "Well fought."

The moves continued around him. More and more white pieces fell as Deward directed his pieces across the board. He was moved once more, ending up all the way on the other side in enemy territory.

Tommy ended up a couple of spaces to his right. The crowd seemed very excited about this, shouting encouragement at Deward and Olwen, who directed his knight to challenge Tommy. The kid fought bravely but ended up getting stomped, his reflexes slow from the alcohol.

"Sorry, Deward!" Tommy called as he limped off to the side.

Deward simply smiled and said, "Bishop to e7."

He managed to recognize that meant him this time and hurried to the empty spot, waving at Olwen, who was diagonal to him.

Olwen sighed heavily.

"Checkmate," Deward said proudly.

Whistles and cheers erupted from the crowd as Olwen nodded, accepting his defeat. He met Deward in the center of the board, shaking his hand.

Derek followed the others as they returned to the crowd, clearing so the next game could get set up. He looked for Ceri for a few minutes but she was nowhere to be found.

"Hey, there you are!" Tommy said, running up behind him.

"Have you seen Ceri?" he asked.

"Yeah, she said she'd be back to pick us up but she had something to do." Tommy holding a drink for him. "Sorry, man. I heard the whole kid thing."

Derek took the drink and chugged it. "What game are we playing next?"

Tommy slung his arm around him. "I think a brutal game of Scrabble is just what you need."

He lowered his glass. "Scrabble?"

Tommy nodded solemnly. "Scrabble."

Shaking his head with a laugh, he followed Tommy through the crowd to the next distraction.

CHAPTER 22

AMBER

Just two more hours until she was free. All Amber wanted was to get home to her pack before the full moon was over. Shane had promised to drive her and Genevieve back tonight no matter how late.

The celebrations were getting...enthusiastic now that the Trials were over. Paul was maintaining his usual air of coolness, but the other new alphas were enjoying the open bar to its fullest extent.

She was surprised Angel hadn't showed up for the Trials or the dinner. It was disconcerting to find she felt vulnerable without him.

Someone tapped Amber's shoulder politely. She turned and saw a striking woman that she hadn't noticed at the conference.

Her black hair was twisted up in a fancy french knot. The blouse she wore wasn't anything crazy but it somehow managed to look more expensive than Amber's entire wardrobe. She suddenly felt severely underdressed.

"I hate to tear you away from the festivities, but I heard you'd been looking for me," the woman said with a warm smile that lit up her already strikingly beautiful face.

"I have?" Amber asked before she could think of a better response. "Sorry, I'm Amber Hale, what was your name?"

"Tatiana Vernier, a fellow alpha," the woman said, shaking her hand firmly.

"Oh," Amber said, smiling broadly in an attempt to make up for the awkward greeting. "I was starting to think you weren't actually here."

Tatiana laughed. Even that was elegant. "You've been...busy. It's not surprising you hadn't spotted me yet."

She snorted. "Yeah, busy is one word for it."

"If you have time now, I would love to chat. It seems like a good time to slip away without drawing too much attention."

"Sure, they don't need me for this," Amber agreed with a nod. She glanced back at Genevieve but her beta was distracted with Paul.

Tatiana led her away from the crowds to a small alcove hidden away in a corner. It was quiet here, almost as if the sound was magically cut off.

"I snuck away some snacks for us," Tatiana said, gesturing to two plates on a low table between plush chairs. She picked up one and settled in the chair near the wall. "Have a seat, relax. This is a just a chat between girls. No need to be formal."

Amber nodded and sat in the other chair. It was a little too soft so she had to scoot to the edge to keep from sinking into it.

"So, how long have you had a shaman in your pack?" Tatiana asked without preamble, as if it was a perfectly natural thing to ask.

Amber tensed immediately, her wolf rising up in her mind on alert for a threat. This was exactly what they'd wanted to avoid during this conference. How did this woman know? Had Jameson told her?

"You didn't think you were the only one, did you?" the woman said with a sly smile, seemingly amused at Amber's shock. "There aren't many of us, and none of us talk about it. It's a nice trump card, after all."

Amber cleared her throat uncomfortably. "Yeah, I guess I did think I was the only one. Or at least one of very few." Not even Angel could throw her off like this. Tatiana wasn't just a pretty face, she was calculating. "How long has the shaman been in your pack?"

"Oh, for years."

She picked up the plate Tatiana had offered her just to have something to do with her hands. "How does no one know you have a shaman in your pack?"

The other alpha leaned back and crossed her legs. She exuded all the confidence Amber wished she possessed. "Mostly because I make sure I'm easily overlooked. I also knew what it meant when I invited the witch into my pack, so it was simpler to keep it under wraps. I'm getting the impression you stumbled into this somehow, which frankly, is baffling. And interesting."

Amber couldn't help but glance nervously over her shoulder before nodding. "Yeah, we did stumble into it. Who told you...?"

"They can't hear us," Tatiana said with a wink. "And no one told me. I just did a little digging after that sorcerer attacked your pack. It was easy to put two and two together if you know what you're looking for, and I do."

"Ah, I guess it would be," she admitted.

"This witch, have you given her your pack bite?"

She frowned and resisted the urge to fidget. "No, is that necessary?"

Tatiana shrugged. "Not really. It can cement the pack bond and ensure a higher level of loyalty but that doesn't seem to be an issue for you. But that's enough of that, what did you want to talk to me about?"

"I just wanted to meet you. You were recommended by an acquaintance as an influential alpha. As a new pack, I thought this was an important opportunity to meet whoever I could."

"An acquaintance said I was influential?"

"Yep," Amber said, not volunteering anything else. She'd already given away too much in this conversation.

The demon mark flared on Amber's chest and she heard a strange thunk behind them, followed by a muffled cursing. Glancing over her shoulder, she saw Angel pounding against some kind of invisible barrier.

When she turned back to Tatiana, the alpha was staring right at the demon. Like she could see him.

"Every time I think I have you figured out, you surprise me again, Alpha Hale," Tatiana said, her dark eyes boring into Amber's. She didn't look upset. She looked very, very interested.

"Sorry?" Amber replied with an uneasy smile.

"Oh, don't be. Most werewolves are tedious." Tatiana turned and dug in her small, black purse for a moment, then pulled out a card and a pen. She scribbled on the back of the card then handed it to Amber. "My personal cell number is on the back. Let's talk again after the conference is over."

Amber took it, slightly dazed by the whole conversation. "Alright, I'll call you."

"I'll be very offended if you don't," Tatiana said as she stood, slinging the purse over her shoulder. "Looks like our absence is about to be noticed. It's best not to be seen together too much during this thing. Until next time, Amber."

"Yeah, until then." Amber watched her walk away. A few seconds after she disappeared from sight there was a low pop and Angel tumbled forward, finally released from whatever had held him.

He strode forward angrily, shifting into a human-like form as he moved.

"Before you yell at me, Vernier did...whatever that was. And she could see you."

He stopped abruptly in front of her. "Are you sure?"

"She was looking right at you and declared me a surprise, so yeah, pretty sure." Amber took a bite of the sandwich, chewing absently while Angel fumed and paced. "If she can see you, is that because she has a demon mark too?"

Angel shook his head. "No, that wouldn't allow such a thing."

"What about having a shaman in her pack?"

He paused. "Perhaps, but it wouldn't be an inherent skill. It would be something the shaman would have needed to cast in advance. That's honestly more worrying."

"Tatiana Vernier seems like the kind of person to be prepared for absolutely every scenario," she said, shaking her head in disbelief. "It's kind of inspiring."

"Now you just sound like you have a crush on her too," Angel muttered darkly.

Amber laughed. "And you sound jealous."

"Maybe I am."

She looked up and batted her eyes at the demon. "How could anyone resist swooning over me?"

If he thought she was going to take his teasing seriously, then he was going to be disappointed.

Angel glared at her for a moment before shaking his head and resuming his pacing.

"On a positive note, she gave me her number and wants me to contact her after this. Whatever it is you wanted me to get on her good side for might be possible."

"I have to figure out how and why she could see me before you do anything."

She shrugged. "I'm calling her within a week of the conference. She wanted me to, and I'm not about to offend someone who knows more about shamans than I do. We might need her help."

"I'm sure that's exactly what she wants."

"Maybe she's actually a demon." Amber shoved the last bite of sandwich in her mouth and set the plate aside as she stood.

"Where are you going?"

"Back to celebrate and make sure Genevieve is fine. Carter is still here, I don't want to leave her alone for too long."

"There is a lot to discuss. I need to know everything that woman said, word for word."

"Well, you know where to find me. But it's going to wait until later."

"Fine. Tonight." Angel disappeared in a puff of smoke.

Amber stood in the alcove for a few moments longer, replaying the conversation in her head. She wanted to trust Tatiana, but she was probably being manipulated. On the off chance the other alpha really did want to help, she had to take the chance.

CHAPTER 23

GENEVIEVE

Genevieve plopped down in the chair next to Amber and faced the rest of the pack on the couch. Tommy still looked groggy after a night of drinking but his werewolf metabolism saved him from suffering from a hangover. Derek and Ceri, however, both looked like they might be sick. She wrinkled her nose at the foul smelling tea they were drinking. It had stunk up the kitchen and was now infecting the living room.

Captain Jack rubbed against her leg. She picked him up so he could curl up in her lap. His claws pricked her legs through her jeans as he found a comfortable position. He didn't quite fit anymore. His back legs dangled over her knees.

"Why are we up this early?" Derek grumbled, his deep voice still rough with sleep.

"Because Gen and I spent the weekend getting threatened and y'all need to know about it," Amber said, leaning back and propping her feet up on the coffee table.

"Threatened?" Tommy asked in alarm.

Genevieve nodded. "Well, mine was more of a warning. My 'informant'," she used finger-quotes sarcastically, "aka...one of Alpha Carter's betas, pulled me aside after Paul's Trials. He didn't tell me what, exactly, Carter was up to but––"

"If you want to butt into our pack meeting, then make it where the others can see and hear you," Amber said testily, looking off to her left.

Kadrithan slowly appeared in a chair next to Amber, apparently deciding he *did* want to keep butting in. He didn't look at all apologetic for being a nuisance but that wasn't anything new.

Genevieve cleared her throat, making a point to glare at Kadrithan before continuing. "*But*, we do know it involves trying to manufacture evidence to give to the MIB to implicate us in working with the sorcerer." She dragged her fingers through Captain Jack's fluffy hair nervously. He started to purr. "In addition to all this, the organization Zachariah worked for released a statement yesterday evening claiming they intend to investigate his death, suspecting foul play by the werewolves due to the nature of his injuries. It's total crap but it makes us and Jameson's pack look bad."

"Appearance is all that matters in these sorts of situations. Your judge, jury, and executioner will be public opinion," Kadrithan said with a nod.

"What are we supposed to do? Hire a PR Manager?" Amber asked, looking completely at a loss.

"No, but I think we might need to speak directly to someone with the MIB."

Amber stared silently at the floor for a moment. "Or I might just need to deal with Carter. Personally."

"And what? Challenge him to a fight?" Tommy asked, exasperated.

Genevieve sat back and let them argue it out for a moment, going over all the options in her mind. They'd lose an outright battle even if Amber could take him, which she might be able to do. But that was a big if. They needed something more.

"Maybe all we need to do is discredit him," she said, interrupting Amber and Tommy's back and forth.

Amber pursed her lips thoughtfully. "That could work. I'm sure he's not exactly an upstanding citizen."

"My concern is that the MIB, and the general public, need someone to blame. If we don't hand them that, then it's going to be us," Genevieve said, crossing her arms. Captain Jack reached up and batted at her hand, dissatisfied that the petting had stopped.

"We've already told everyone about the sorcerer and that Zachariah was helping him. They didn't believe us," Amber objected.

"Because it wasn't believable. Demons are the bad guys," she said, gesturing toward Kadrithan who winked at her. "And angels are pure, wonderful creatures no one ever believes do any wrong."

"To be honest, I was there, and it still doesn't make sense to me," Ceri admitted. "Maybe Zachariah did go rogue."

Kadrithan laughed, the sound sending a warning chill down her spine. "Angels are pure. Bitten werewolves can't control themselves. Witches will stab you in the back." He shook his head dismissively. "I would have thought your pack wouldn't buy into stereotypes."

"I think I liked it better when he was invisible," Derek muttered.

"Demons are the ones forcing people into taking marks, not angels," Ceri said, staring Kadrithan down in challenge.

"It's quite impossible to force anyone into a taking a mark. Believe me, I've tried," he said with a mischievous smile.

"You're not exactly helping your point," Amber said, shaking her head. "And you could try being less vague. Do you know what the angels are up to?"

"Looking out for themselves, as always." Kadrithan glanced at Tommy. "Your troll friend might actually know more about that than most people."

"Deward? Why?" Tommy's brow creased with confusion.

"The trolls have always been the most neutral historians." Kadrithan stood. "This has been delightful, but I have an appointment to make. Do consider taking a closer look at what *actions* your pure angels take."

He disappeared in a puff of smoke, leaving behind nothing but the faint scent of sulfur.

"I don't know how you stand him." Ceri chugged the last of her tea with a grimace.

"I draw on the strength of the pack bond for patience daily," Amber said, letting her head fall back against the chair.

Genevieve snorted. "We're going to need a bigger pack in that case."

"Unfortunately, dealing with the MIB isn't going to be simple, but we can start with figuring out what Carter is giving them, I guess," Amber said, eyes searching the ceiling for answers.

"I'm going to talk to Deward about the history of the angels too, just in case there's something to that," Tommy said.

"Kadrithan is manipulating us," Ceri objected.

Tommy shook his head. "It didn't feel like he was lying. He's been dropping hints about something being off with the angels for ages. They tried to kill Evangeline just for being half demon. That's not exactly something a good person would do."

"We can look into it without throwing our allegiance on the side of the demons," Amber interjected. "It's a good idea, Tommy."

"Thanks," he said, casting a triumphant look at Ceri.

"Now, the next issue is something Ceri will have to decide," Amber continued. "Alpha Tatiana Vernier pulled me aside on the last day of the conference and asked me how long I'd had a shaman in my pack."

Ceri's face paled. "How did she find out?"

"She has a shaman in her pack and said that it's apparent if you know what to look for." Amber said with a shrug. "I don't think Jameson betrayed us by spreading that around. I'm actually not sure he understands that you are truly part of the pack."

"Did she threaten you?"

"No, she offered to help us. Answer any questions we might have."

"Talking to someone that has experience as a shaman would be very helpful, but..." Ceri crossed her arms and leaned back into the couch. "This other shaman was a witch first. Witches don't share spells unless they're in a coven, and even then there's always a trade. I really don't think Vernier or her shaman intend on giving us anything out of the goodness of their hearts."

"I agree. It's become apparent pretty much no one is that generous," Amber said with an unhappy twist of her lips. "However, we may need to try to get what we can from them until we figure out what Vernier is after. We'll be cautious, if you're up for it. I'm not going to push you into it."

Ceri nodded. "As long as we go in knowing there will be strings attached." She then hesitated for a moment before adding, "There is something else that's been bothering me. My spirit guide, the owl, asked me to find something in the spirit realm. When I got close, something pushed me back into my body." Ceri's jaw got tight like it always did when she got mad. "I've never experienced anything like that but I'm working on figuring it out."

Genevieve glanced at the spot the demon had sat. Amber's wolf had done that to him once before —— with unfortunate consequences —— but it would be good to know how it was done. Just in case.

Captain Jack jumped off her lap and headed toward the kitchen, meowing loudly.

"Yeah, yeah. I'm hungry too," she said, following him. There was so much to do to protect the pack and it felt like a timer was counting down over their heads.

She had today off, but tomorrow she had to be back at work at seven am. The thought made her tired but there was no way around it.

CHAPTER 24

CERI

Ceri hadn't missed her coven for even a moment since she joined the pack. Until now.

The experience in the spirit realm had shaken her confidence. It had been a long time since she had failed so utterly and it left her feeling like she was six years old losing to Siobhan in a stupid competition.

The thought of Siobhan made her want to throw up. A vision of her stupid, selfish cousin with her eyes gouged out, heart cut from her chest, and long auburn hair hacked off without care flashed through her mind. Seeing her like that had been the moment Ceri had almost given up.

It had been her fault Siobhan had even been involved. She'd gotten her killed. And yet, the pack was still relying on her. She had to try one last time to go to the spirit realm alone. If it was dangerous, it would be better for only her to be hurt instead of the entire pack.

However, she wasn't going to just try the same thing again. She needed to be better prepared for this attempt.

Carefully clearing away the pine needles and other debris, she drew a symbol in the dirt. A diamond within a circle large enough for her to lay in comfortably. She placed labradorite at the north point to shield against psychic attacks. Black obsidian was placed on the eastern point to protect against black magic, curses, and evil spirits.

On the southern point she placed staurolite to assist her as she moved into the spirit realm. The final crystal was placed on the western point. She'd thought about this one for a while before settling on Apache tear, a crystal often used in healing.

It was her just-in-case choice. The darkness hadn't hurt her last time, but it might if she managed to fight harder. She also wanted the energies of the crystal with her as she created this totem.

She'd studied this sort of casting a few years back. It was something that had gone out of style about a century ago, but witches used to claim a familiar -- or animal totem --

quite often. What she intended to create would strengthen the link between her and her spirit guide.

The spirit had taken to leaving feathers when it visited her as an owl. She'd been collecting them, unsure what to use them for until she'd found this spell.

She set the bowl of sage below the labradorite and lit it. The smoke curled around her knees, filling the circle. It's sharp, almost minty scent cleared her mind.

A breeze ruffled her hair as she picked up the three feathers she had selected for the totem and a length of cord. Deciding to consider that the spirit's blessing, she began.

"*Ligatus fuero.*" She wrapped the cord around the base of the feathers once. "*Aeris ligare.*" She wound it around again. "*Et volens liberum.*" Magic flowed from her fingers into the cord. The knot tightened and the remaining cord separated cleanly as though it had been cut.

The tawny feathers hardened, petrifying in the space of a single breath. Wind picked up around her. The trees came alive, creaking and swaying. Her awareness of the earth around her deepened.

She could *feel* bugs crawling across the dirt. A bird sitting on a branch. The leaves drinking up sunlight. Warmth filled her senses and she was tempted to disappear in it. To just float out of her body and enjoy this blissful escape from the hustle of her life. But she had work to do.

With considerable effort, she drew her attention back to her own body. Her heartbeat was slow and steady. She took a breath and focused on the movement of her chest.

Blinking to clear her blurred vision, she opened her eyes and looked down at the totem. The feathers were bone white. She traced the spine of the feather. Magic tingled up her finger in response.

A smile spread across her face. She had done it. Now she could go back to the spirit realm and face the darkness again.

"What are you doing out here alone?" Derek asked, startling her.

She looked back at him, unable to hide her guilty expression, feeling like she'd been caught doing something she shouldn't. They hadn't talked about the children comment he'd made while he was drunk, and it didn't seem like either of them wanted to, but it had made everything awkward. "I just wanted to try one more time to do it myself."

"They say the definition of insanity is trying the same thing over and over again while expecting different results," he said, raising an eyebrow.

She rolled her eyes and began tying her remaining cord to the totem so she could hang it around her neck. "I just missed something the first time. I'm going to be more cautious, not just walk in like I did before."

"Are you sure you don't need help?"

"I probably will, but I'd rather not put the pack at risk. If I can do it alone, it's better."

"That sounds logical on the surface, but something tells me it isn't."

She sighed and turned to face him. Apparently this couldn't be a short conversation. "I want to do this alone. Bringing in the pack has to be a last resort."

"Because you're worried you'll be putting them all at risk?"

She nodded firmly. "Yes."

"Then let me help instead."

"What? You can't."

"If the pack can do it, why can't I?" Derek crossed his arms as if daring her to say it was because he was human. That was one of her reasons. The other being an entirely irrational feeling of protectiveness toward him.

"It's still a risk…" she said weakly.

"I'm not part of the pack, so me going with you doesn't risk the pack, but it is safer than you going alone."

"What if I can't protect you in there?"

He laughed at her. Actually *laughed*. "It sounds like you couldn't even protect yourself. I'm going to watch *your* back, not the other way around."

She stared at him, trying to think up another excuse, but they were all weaker than the last. Accepting his help for now was probably her best bet.

"Fine, but if we run into something dangerous, you have to promise to bail, immediately," she said, narrowing her eyes at him.

"I'm not making a promise I have no intention of keeping. Let's just do this and be as smart as we can about it."

Ceri pressed her lips into a thin line and nodded. "You're difficult."

Derek just grinned at her.

Muttering to herself, Ceri grabbed the sage and lit it again. "Get over here and sit in the circle with me."

Derek hurried to join her. The circle was barely big enough for the two of them, mostly because he was over six feet tall and made purely of muscle.

She scooted around to face him with her legs crossed. "Have you ever done this before?"

He shook his head. "Nope."

"Alright. The important thing is not panicking. The spirit realm is…well, it's different. You don't move the same and you won't have your physical body." The owl landed just outside the circle. She couldn't deny being a little relieved it had come when she needed it. Normally it was the one to appear when it wanted to take her to the spirit realm. She hadn't been completely sure she'd be able to call it.

Derek glanced at the owl. "Do you talk to the owl?"

"Sometimes. In the spirit realm." She took a deep breath, already regretting all of this. "You ready?"

"Yep."

"Close your eyes and breathe slowly. We'll be there before you know it," Ceri said, looking up into the owl's eyes.

As easy as breathing, she drifted into the spirit realm

~

Snow drifted down in heavy flakes around them. Derek looked green as he peered over the edge of the cliff.

She wrapped her hand in his. "What's wrong?"

"I'm afraid of heights." His voice cracked slightly on the last word.

A laugh bubbled out of her lips before she could stop it.

He glared at her. "It's not funny."

"It's a little funny," she said, unable to suppress her smile.

"Are you sure we have to jump down there?"

"I have to but you can stay up here if you want. Or I can send you back to your body?" she suggested, raising a hand ready to do just that.

He batted her hand away. "I better not die."

With that, he launched himself over the edge of the cliff.

"Crap." She jumped after him, holding her limbs close to her body to fall faster so she could catch up. The wind caught them as she grabbed his arm. "We shouldn't separate you idiot!"

His eyes were squeezed shut. "I did...what...I had to."

"We're about to land," she said, pulling him in close so he didn't freak out when their feet touched the ground.

He tensed, hands gripping her arms hard enough to bruise. She smiled into his chest, doing her absolute best not to laugh at him. It was pretty amusing to see such a burly guy freaking out over a little cliff.

Their feet landed silently on the ground and she stepped back, making sure Derek wasn't going to pass out on her. He put his hands on his knees and took deep breaths.

The strange jungle was just as she remembered. Alien, green plants towered over them.

"Did we shrink or are these things just really tall?" Derek whispered, looking around warily.

"We're in the spirit realm, size is...relative here." The same creeping sense of unease she'd felt before was already making her feel watched. "Let's go farther in."

Derek nodded and started walking. She followed, feeling like she was moving through molasses. Frowning, she watched him walking unimpeded.

He stopped and looked back. "Are you coming?"

"How are you walking without effort?"

"Can you not?"

She shook her head. "It's like trying to wade through molasses."

He strode back to her. "Let me carry you then."

"What? No--"

"Ceri, it's the most efficient way to move. Give me one good reason why not."

She sighed. "Fine."

He scooped her up like she weighed nothing and walked confidently into the forest. It grew warmer the farther they went. The strange plants stood closer together, blocking out the sky.

Even though she wasn't walking, she felt herself growing more and more tired, as if existing in this place took effort.

"Are you still okay?" she asked.

He nodded. "I feel like we're being watched but I can still move just fine."

She glanced back over his shoulder and her heart almost jumped out of her chest.

"Stop and put me down," she said urgently.

He complied. "What's wrong?"

"Look," she whispered, pointing at inky-black darkness creeping up behind them. It spread over the ground like water, crawling up the trunks of plants as it flowed around them. The entire forest behind them was encased in the darkness. They couldn't go back.

"What the hell is that stuff?"

"I don't know."

"What do we do?"

"I don't know! Just-- shut up and give me a minute to think." Her hand went to the totem around her neck. It was time to test it out.

She lifted her other hand and cast a simple light spell. A brilliant flash of white light exploded from her palm. However, instead of pushing the darkness back it surged forward and swallowed the light, snuffing it out.

"Get behind me." She grabbed Derek's arm and dragged him away from the darkness.

"It's behind us too. Maybe we should have kept moving."

She turned and saw that he was right. It had them surrounded. Gritting her teeth, she decided the only thing she could do was face it head on.

"Stay here, and trust me." She waited for his nod before marching forward and wading into the darkness. Just like last time, she immediately began to fade.

Derek grabbed her arm and yanked her toward him, shielding her from the darkness with his body. "Fight it."

"I can't!"

"Yes, you can."

Her hand was slowly reforming but Derek was dissolving instead. She only had as long as he could shield her before she'd be pushed out of the spirit realm once again.

She shut her eyes and buried her face in his chest. The darkness slithered up her legs.

"*Illuceo.*" Her magic flared out, beating back the darkness.

"It's working, do it again!"

She chanted the spell over and over but using magic here was sapping her strength much quicker than she expected. They had minutes at best. This wouldn't work.

With one last, forceful push, she grabbed Derek's hands and yanked them both out of the spirit realm.

She fell back, her head hitting the ground painfully. The two of them lay inside her circle, panting.

"I'm sorry," she whispered.

"Don't apologize. You did your best." He reached over and grabbed her hand, holding it tightly. "We'll figure it out."

She stared up through the tree branches and hoped he was right.

CHAPTER 25

AMBER

Amber paced the length of the living room as she chatted with Tatiana Vernier. It was a nervous habit; she hated being on the phone.

"Yeah, I can make this weekend work."

"Great! You can bring the whole pack if you want but I'll just be bringing Jean, my shaman. Text me the address of whatever restaurant you'd like to meet at," Tatiana replied happily.

"Will do. See you then."

"Stay safe."

She hung up and continued pacing the length of the room.

"Well?" Angel demanded.

"We're meeting this weekend to talk and share information. She's being very helpful."

He crossed his arms. "You forget I can sense your strong emotions. You're unsettled."

She stopped abruptly and sighed. "It's too easy. She said I could bring my whole pack. Maybe it's a trap."

A slow smile spread across his face. "This is the Amber I know and admire. You probably should be suspicious."

She threw her arms up in exasperation. "I thought you wanted me to become friends with her. She never would have introduced herself to me if I hadn't been asking around about her."

He snorted. "I don't appreciate it when people flip my plans around on me. She's up to something, so instead of being *friends* with her, you need to find out what she's after."

"I intend on doing that. We know she's not being completely up front with us."

"Maybe Genevieve can dig up something on her. She seems to have a knack for research. Anyhow, I must cut this meeting short."

"Tragic," she said drily.

"It is. For you." He winked and popped out of existence.

Her shoulders drooped in relief. All she wanted this morning was to have some time to herself, clean the kitchen, and maybe take a nap before heading into the mechanic shop to catch up on things before the weekend was over.

The sound of tires on gravel startled her. No one was supposed to be home for a while, and Ceri and Derek were out for a walk -- or whatever they were actually doing out in the woods alone.

She walked over to a window and peeked outside. A plain, black suburban that screamed federal agents was driving down their driveway.

"How the hell did they get through the wards?" she muttered, pulling out her phone to text Genevieve and Ceri.

Unlike last time the police showed up at their door, there was nothing to hide. She doubted they were coming to arrest her. There would have been more of them -- they tended to send in large forces for werewolf arrests.

She paced the living room, waiting for the knock on the door. Whatever questions they had, she would answer the same way she'd answered questions from the police. None of it was a lie unless you counted omitting how much they knew about Evangeline.

Finally, there was a brisk knock on the door. The cabinets fluttered at the knock. Great. Illya didn't like them. She took a deep breath, then walked over and opened it.

An elvish woman -- which would explain blowing through the wards -- and a human man stood in front of her. They wore expressions as severe as their black suits.

"How can I help you?" Amber asked, leaning against the door frame and crossing her arms.

"Agents Icewind and Horan," the woman said in lieu of a greeting, flashing her badge. The man was staring at her intently, but remained silent. "Are you Amber Hale?"

She nodded. "I am."

"Do you have a few minutes to talk?" Icewind asked.

"Sure." Amber remained in place. It was pure stubbornness, but she didn't want them inside her home. Her den. The wolf prowled in her mind, anxious to have intruders gone. Coming through the wards without permission was rude, and she didn't like that was how this had started.

A muscle in Icewind's jaw twitched. "May we come inside?"

"Oh, you're asking now?" Amber asked with a fake smile.

The elf's eyes narrowed at her. "The MIB has the authority to enter--"

"I'm really not interested in how you're throwing your authority around. You're not coming inside. I don't believe in encouraging poor manners."

The man's lips twitched as if he were fighting down a smile.

"Considering your pack is under investigation, I'd think you'd be more willing to cooperate with the MIB," Icewind bit out.

"I'm perfectly willing to answer any questions you have. Right here, in the doorway. Not sure what difference the location makes to you." Amber cocked her head to the side, staring Icewind down.

"During your confrontation with the sorcerer," Horan began, subtly flicking Icewind in the arm as if to tell her to back off. Maybe they were doing good cop, bad cop, "you stated that he was working with the half angel, Zachariah Hudson. Do you have any proof of this?"

"Other than seeing them together, no. I didn't have time to whip out my phone and take a picture," Amber said drily, pulling away from the staring contest with Icewind to look at Horan. He looked like your typical, clean cut jock but she sensed something more dangerous lurking behind the crew cut. He was actually paying attention.

"Understandable," he said with a pleasant grin. "We've come today as a courtesy to deliver these summons in person." He handed her a legal document. "In order to fully investigate the events of the attack, we need to speak with you and every member of your pack, and your brother. These interviews will be conducted at our office in Portland at the times listed in the summons. If any of you need to reschedule," he paused and pulled out a business card, "feel free to call me personally."

She took the card and folded it up inside the summons. "Sounds great. Looks like I'll be seeing you both again soon."

"Have a good day, Ms. Hale," he said with a polite nod.

Icewind turned around and headed back to their suburban without comment.

Amber stood in the doorway until they had driven off the property, her fingers gripping the summons so hard she tore a hole in it.

CHAPTER 26

DEWARD

A chill wind rustled through the branches as Deward crouched in front of a moss covered boulder. He brushed a chunk of the moss away. It was two hours after dawn Monday morning but the waning gibbous moon was still visible in the sky. Its light caused the ancient rune carved into the base of the boulder to glow slightly, making it much easier to find.

The lines had faded but he was sure this was what he had been searching for. Six months spending every free moment with his nose in books. Sleepless nights translating obscure texts, some meant to mislead you to hide this secret.

The entrance wasn't in the city like many who had looked for it thought. It was miles away, deep in the woods, most easily spotted the night after the full moon.

Trolls couldn't wield magic like a witch or elf, or shift into a different form like a werewolf, but they could mold magic that had already been created. It was part of why casting magic at a troll was less effective than it would be against any other race.

This rune was a built in key, of sorts. A witch could unlock the entrance with ease. It would take him a little more effort. He placed his palm against it, dew sending a chill through his palm, and drew on the magic that filled the boulder. It was old and tremulous, but enough was still there.

The boulder split in half with a low pop. He jerked his hand away and took a step back as it began to move. The two halves pulled apart, tendrils of light clinging between them like taffy. They slid through the dirt as though they didn't weigh half a ton each.

The light dripped onto the ground and the earth below then melted away revealing an opening. It led straight down.

Carefully, Deward approached the edge and peered down into the dark hole, anticipation flooding through him. He couldn't see the bottom.

He hadn't expected to find the entrance to the old tunnels this quickly. It was possible, if everything tonight went well, that he could be the first to complete his feat. To do so would be an honor, and if he was honest with himself, immensely satisfying.

Pulling out a flashlight, he aimed it downward. The light reflected off a damp, stone floor. It was hard to judge the distance but it certainly wasn't far enough to injure him if he hopped in.

Deward's phone buzzed. Tommy was only five minutes away.

As he looked down into the beckoning void, he made a snap decision to enter the tunnels now. Tommy was almost here. It was only a minimal risk.

Cold air rushed up from his toes as he dropped down. Fear bloomed in his gut when the ground was slightly farther than he expected, but he managed to tuck and roll with the impact.

The cavern he had dropped into wasn't large. A single tunnel lead further down into the earth, and into darkness. The stench of the place made him want to climb right back out but he wasn't going to turn back now.

There was something rotten down here. Perhaps the tunnels themselves were decaying. They'd been hollowed out by witches before Portland was even founded and were supported with magic, but magic could not endure forever. It, too, would rot and crumble over time.

He had a love for history, which is what had led him to choosing this feat. Whether or not the Book of Prophesies could really help someone tell the future was beside the point. Finding the hidden room which contained texts that might have come from the Library of Alexandria would be an achievement in itself.

Based on his research, it was likely the room would contain quite a bit of magical history. Enchanted books, cursed robes, and even a seeing glass –– something used to spy on your enemies that had been outlawed two-hundred years ago.

He hesitated again, but Tommy really would be here any moment. Quickly texting him that he had dropped down into the tunnels, he hurried toward the opening that led down. Tommy could follow his scent easily enough, and it's not like there were turns one could get lost among. The tunnels simply went...down.

Witches had practiced their magic underground –– quite literally –– for a long time. There were many reasons for this, chief among them a need for secrecy. Before the world became more civilized, their greatest enemies had been other witches. Not to mention anyone willing to steal their spells and sell them to the highest bidder.

Much like the place where Tommy's pack had faced off against the sorcerer, this used to be a haven for the witches. The coven had simply vanished one day, as far as he could tell. It was another mystery he was very interested in finding the answer to.

Unease crept through him. It felt unnatural, as though there were something here trying to persuade him to leave. He slowed and glanced behind himself but he was still alone.

The light of his flashlight gleamed dully on the damp walls. They had been perfectly smooth when the tunnels were made but over the years, they had roughened. Water slipped out of a thin crack in the ceiling, dripping down onto the stone floor with a steady patter. It echoed through the tunnels like a panicked heartbeat.

He pushed through the feeling and walked farther down. It began to fade and he spotted the rune that had cast the spell just around the turn. Glowing blue moss had grown over half of it, sucking at the magic like a parasite. Even a year ago, the feeling of unease may have been unbearable to push through.

Glancing at the time on his phone, he was torn between heading farther down, or waiting here for Tommy. The magic was unpleasant to pass through and it would be a little rude to ask Tommy to do it alone.

Perhaps he could go a little farther, then come back...

Deward froze. There was a scuffling, as if a rodent was scurrying through the tunnel ahead of him. He lifted his flashlight, expecting to see the flash of yellow, beady eyes, but there was nothing.

With a frown, he looked at the ground and the walls. There was dust and moss but there were no droppings. No bugs. But there were tracks in the grime. Human footprints.

How had he missed it? It should have been the first thing he looked for -- a sign that he wasn't the first to find this place.

The scuffling noise was louder this time but it was obvious it was footsteps, not some small animal like he'd first thought.

"The fool..." a girlish whisper floated past him.

Slowly, he turned, using his flashlight to illuminate the tunnel behind him. There was no one there.

Pushing down the fear with the logic he was raised to use, he went through the possibilities quickly. Cloaking magic that hid them from view. An old protection meant to scare away intruders through hallucinations. Or...they were above him.

He took a quick step back and looked up. The beam of light lit up an elvish woman that looked more ghoul than human. Her hair was filthy and her pale skin was streaked with dirt and grime. She was held against the ceiling in a cradle of vines like some kind of spider.

"Who are you?" he asked as calmly as he could. Her eyes were covered in a white film as though she were blind.

"Cursed among men," she hissed as she lowered down toward him.

He began moving backward at a slow but steady pace. Tommy was almost here. He would have backup soon, not that he wanted Tommy to walk into this unaware. Slipping his hand into his pocket, he maneuvered his phone and hit speed dial for Tommy's number.

"What do you want?"

"The truth!" the elf screeched as she twisted and dropped to the floor. "You...you will be able to see. You have come with the same folly. You are mine."

"What do you--"

She lunged at him. He turned to sprint away but vines shot out at him from every direction. They wrapped around his legs, his throat, and his arms. Sharp thorns dug into his flesh until blood dripped onto the stone floor.

He struggled against it all, reaching into the magic binding him to fight back, but this elf was strong. So much stronger than him.

She appeared in front of him and leaned in close, her pale eyes boring into his own. "A gift for a fool," she whispered as her cold hands pressed into his cheeks.

He saw nothing....

Nothing....

But...

Blood and flame that fell from the sky.

Light and darkness.

Death.

CHAPTER 27

KADRITHAN (ANGEL)

Kadrithan wasn't looking forward to his next visit. It was necessary though. He'd given the woman a task when he'd last seen her -- the first step in fulfilling her mark. She'd been less than pleased and he needed to know that she had completed it as instructed. It wouldn't be a surprise to discover that she might be avoiding it. It appeared she was staying at her house outside the city -- something she only did when she was trying to run away from something.

With a final exhale, his spirit formed and sight, sound, and smell returned to him. All at once, he wished they hadn't.

Blood. He almost gagged as the scent of it overwhelmed his senses. It was fresh. Bright red was spread over the white, marble floors of the bathroom. In every direction the walls were painted in a fine spray. Whoever had donated it was no longer alive. There was too much for even a werewolf to have survived. If it had been her...

He stood frozen for a half second before forcing himself to move forward. There was no threat to him while he was still invisible to everyone in this realm.

His logical mind had already accepted that his marked was dead but his heart still pounded in anticipation, hoping against all reason that he would find some other unlucky bastard dead in the next room.

There should have been some sense of danger from her when she was attacked, but he had felt nothing. Perhaps she had died too quickly to feel fear.

He followed the smeared trail of blood. The initial attack had taken place in the bathroom but the body had been moved. There were no footprints in the blood, which was odd, to say the least.

The trail led into the bedroom. Her body hung directly in front of a picturesque window, dangling from ceiling like a fly caught in a spiders' web. A web made of some strange, black material glinted in the sunlight streaming into the room.

Walking closer, he inspected the webbing before he looked at her. He needed a clear mind for this part. Every detail was important.

The material was strange. Up close, he realized it had thorns as if it were some kind of plant, but it was clearly made of something else entirely. It was less than an inch thick. Everywhere it had pierced her body it had gone through cleanly without ripping or tearing.

Glancing around the room to ensure he was still alone, he materialized in the realm and tried to break a piece of the webbing off. His fingers burned as soon as he touched it causing him to jerk away and almost slip in a puddle of blood.

A door opened downstairs, someone shouting a greeting. They were in for an unfortunate surprise. He faded from sight so he could watch their reaction without being seen.

Leaving footprints in the blood was an unfortunate mistake, and likely to confuse the police, but there was no way it could be traced back to him at least.

"Laurel, what are you doing? We're going to be late!" the woman shouted, clearly impatient.

Kadrithan glanced at the dead woman. Her face was blank and her eyes glazed over in white. She'd been wearing her bathrobe and a thin white slip when she'd been attacked. It was speckled with blood on the front from the arterial spray.

It was possible some sort of spell was used to keep her from fighting back. It wouldn't have been difficult to sneak up on her. She wasn't a fighter, and as a human, had no magic to defend herself.

The woman's footsteps grew closer, an angry clack of high heels against the floor. "Laurel. Seriously. I came all the--"

The door slammed open and the woman choked on the next word. Her eyes went wide, the blood drained from her face, and...she passed out.

Kadrithan sighed. At least that gave him a little more time to examine the scene of the murder before police swarmed it and got in his way.

He wanted a piece of the webbing to examine. Of course, he couldn't take it back with him but he *could* carry it with him in this realm long enough to get it to another of his marked. If he could manage to break off a piece.

It would take a nearly impossible amount of effort but finding this murderer was of the utmost importance. Laurel had been integral to his plans.

With a sigh, he braced himself for the strain this would create on his physical body, then poured magic into his spirit until he became solid.

Yanking a pillow case off one of her pillows, he wrapped it securely around his hand, then punched a slender thread of the webbing. It snapped free, tinkling to the ground and shattering like glass. Apparently, it was fragile.

Careful to keep from touching it again, he adjusted the pillow case and carefully broke off a piece.

"Ungh..."

The woman was stirring behind him. It was time to go.

He ran toward the stairs, jumping over the woman who still hadn't managed to open her eyes. The strain was already tiring him, but all that mattered was getting this as far away as he could before he was forced back into his body.

His marks acted like tethers to this realm. He couldn't simply arrive and go wherever he wanted. It was impossible to go too far from them. At some point, he would simply hit a wall.

The only reason he'd been able to go to Laurel was because she'd been recently murdered. By sunrise the day following her death, her mark would be void. They'd never been able to figure out why it didn't vanish immediately, but it was useful. Perhaps the soul lingered after death.

If he could make it to the woods, he could hide this until he could send someone else to retrieve it.

As he ran, he noticed that −− for some odd reason −− Amber was very close and she was moving straight toward him.

Taking a chance, he changed directions and moved as fast as he could toward his other mark, shifting the power that tethered him to this realm to her.

The effort it took to do that nearly brought him to his knees but he pushed through. It would be safer if he could get it to her.

CHAPTER 28

AMBER

Amber sprinted through the house. Tommy was panicking, and not in a small way. He was *afraid*. She growled as she grabbed her truck keys then yanked the front door open. She'd been getting ready to join Derek at the mechanic shop but that wasn't happening.

The truck roared to life as she cranked the key in the ignition. She peeled out of the driveway. It was a good thing she'd just given the truck a tune-up or this might have killed it.

The highway flew by as she drove as fast as she could. Tommy wasn't that far. She should be able to get to him in less than ten minutes as long as she didn't have to slow down.

When he'd rushed out of the house this morning to help Deward she hadn't even been worried. Tommy was always safe with the troll. Deward was sensible and cautious, or so she had thought.

The miles flew by, her worry only increasing with every passing moment. Three more minutes. Just three more until she'd be close enough to shift and run to him. This was faster for now.

A man dressed in an old-fashioned black suit leapt out in front of her truck. She almost ran over him but managed to slam on the brakes and swerve in time to avoid hitting him.

"I don't have time for this," she snarled, ready to drive off immediately before his face registered. The angle of the jaw and the nose…it was Angel. "What in the hell…"

He ran up to her door and yanked it open. "Take this. Keep it safe."

"I don't––"

He shoved a shiny, black piece of something in her hands and disappeared in a puff of smoke. With no explanation.

Grinding her teeth together, she quickly wrapped it in a dirty napkin laying in the seat then shoved it in the glovebox.

"Annoying, stupid, needy demon," she muttered as she steered back into her lane and took off as fast as the old truck would allow. She was starting to think a sports car might be more practical.

Tommy's fear was mixed with anger now. That could be either a good sign or a bad sign but it meant he was alive. She pushed strength toward him through the bond as quickly as she could.

Her phone rang.

"What?"

"What's wrong?" Genevieve demanded.

"Tommy. He went to meet Deward for that feat thing, but now all I'm getting is fear and anger."

Genevieve was silent for a moment. "Could that be part of the feat?"

"He's too scared. Something is wrong, I can feel it. Tommy said it wasn't dangerous when he rushed out to meet him." Amber's fingers tightened on the phone. She should have gone with him. Should have helped instead of letting him run off by himself. She should have – –

"Amber, whatever insane thoughts are running through your head right now, stop it. I can feel it and that means Tommy can too. Don't make this harder for him when he's already scared."

She forced herself to take a deep breath and push her own fear down, walling it off from the pack. It was a stupid loss of control.

"Thank you."

"Where is he? Do you have an address?"

"No, but I'll text you and Ceri with my location when I get closer . Can you call her and explain? Derek too?"

"Yeah, drive faster."

Genevieve hung up and Amber dropped her phone in her lap, mashing the accelerator down even harder. The truck's engine roared as she sped down the narrow highway.

They must have met somewhere in the woods. She was heading away from the city.

There were sirens in the distance and her eyes snapped to the rearview mirror. She was speeding but she hadn't passed any police. She really hoped they weren't after her. The last thing she needed was to get picked up by the police right now.

She was so close to Tommy. Making a snap decision, she drove the truck down the next small road she saw, parking it on the side of the road in the grass. She stripped down quickly then shifted, grabbing her clothes in her mouth, just in case.

The wolf howled in her mind as she raced through the trees. She strained her senses, listening for shouting or sounds of fighting but there was nothing. Tommy was close enough that she should be able to hear him by now.

She slid to a halt, kicking up the pine needles that coated the forest floor. It felt like she was close enough to touch Tommy, almost like…he was below her.

Nose to the ground, she searched for his trail. She found Deward's first and followed it. It mixed with Tommy's and led to a boulder that had been cracked in half. There was a hole between the two pieces of stone leading down into darkness.

She plunged down through the opening without hesitation. Her paws hit wet stone and she slipped a little. This place smelled wrong. It was full of old magic and...blood.

Dropping her clothes, she sprinted down the only path she could take. Her howl echoed off the walls of the tunnel. If there was anyone else down here, they'd know she was coming, but she didn't care. She would tear them apart if they'd hurt Tommy.

As she rounded a turn, unnatural fear tugged at her mind but she shrugged it off. She was too angry to care about being scared.

She almost ran into Tommy when she found him. He was standing –– thankfully unhurt –– in the middle of the tunnel staring at blood spattered on the floors and walls.

He looked at her, anger and fear in his eyes. "Something bad has happened to Deward."

CHAPTER 29

TOMMY

Tommy paced from one side of the tunnel to the other. He wanted to charge ahead and find someone to fight but he couldn't be stupid right now.

"There's a single set of footprints after this point," Amber said, pointing past the place where Deward's blood sat in puddles on the grimy floor. "But two, including Deward's up to the point. They had to have carried him away somehow."

"He weighs two hundred pounds. It would have taken a werewolf or some kind of spell to carry someone that heavy without letting them touch the ground at all. There aren't drag marks," Tommy said, forcing himself to look at this clinically like Deward would have. The anger would help later when they killed whoever had hurt him, but right now, it was only a distraction.

The moment he felt the pull on his mark, Tommy remembered he was supposed to meet with Evangeline this morning. He'd forgotten in the midst of the chaos.

She materialized into a golden blob but didn't speak as she floated toward him, obviously realizing something must be wrong.

As her light touched him, he was filled with warmth and felt some of the panicky fear ease. Amber glanced at him in confusion but didn't question it.

"The rest of the pack just arrived, they'll be down here in a minute," she said instead, squatting down next to the largest pool of blood.

"You're getting better at sensing us through the pack bond, aren't you?"

She nodded. "It's becoming more clear. I used to suppress it to give y'all privacy but now I can filter out most of your emotions while still sensing where y'all are."

"I felt it...when you were sending me strength earlier. It was weird. It was like you were right behind me."

"That is weird. Glad it worked though."

Amber rose from her crouch. "I'm going to get the others while you update Evangeline on what's going on."

"Can you see her or something?" he asked, curious how she could always tell instantly.

She shrugged. "No, but I think I can sense her maybe? It's subtle. You always look at her when she appears too. I think I do the same thing with Kadrithan."

"Yeah, I guess you do."

Amber took off toward the entrance at a jog, leaving him and Evangeline alone for a moment.

"What's happened? Who's hurt?" she asked urgently. "It wasn't you, was it?"

"No, it was Deward." Tommy dragged his hands through his hair. "I was meeting him here to help him with his feat –– some troll rite of passage he asked me to complete with him –– but he went in without me. I got a call from him and heard a woman speaking in the background but I couldn't understand her, then he screamed and the call cut off. By the time I got here, this was all that was left." He gestured at the blood. "No footprints. No sign of him."

"Shit."

"Yeah."

Evangeline was quiet for a moment, hovering low to the ground over the blood like she was searching for clues. "Have you gone further into the tunnels to look for him?"

"No, Amber wanted to wait for the pack. Deward wasn't a pushover. Anyone that could take him out like that is a big threat to any of us."

He could hear Amber filling the others in as they approached. They were getting close.

"Is it okay if the others know you're visiting me? They already know about the mark."

She hesitated, the light shifting jerkily as she bobbed in place. "Yeah, no reason to hide it really. And I want to help. I can scout things out ahead. Nothing can see me or hurt me."

"That would be really helpful. Better to know what we're getting ourselves into."

"I'm going now. Don't go too far before I come back."

He nodded and she zipped away, light trailing behind her like a shooting star just as the others rounded the corner.

"Evangeline is scouting ahead for us," he said, nodding at the rest of the pack in greeting.

Ceri ran to him, wrapping him in a tight hug. He melted into her, burying his face in her hair to block out the scent of Deward's blood for a moment.

"We're going to find him, okay?" she whispered as the others started discussing what had happened again, giving them a little privacy.

"I know. We have to." Deward had trusted him. He should have been here. Deward should have waited.

She pulled back and squeezed his shoulders. "Amber said he called you. What did you hear?"

He took a deep breath, forcing himself to remember the strange conversation. "It was mostly incoherent. There was a woman rambling about fools and lies I think. He tried to ask her what she wanted but that's when he started screaming. It happened really fast."

"Alright, knowing it was a woman is important. That will help narrow things down. Has Evangeline found anything yet?"

He shook his head. "I don't know but she's heading back toward us I think. She can only go so far from me."

Evangeline appeared around the curve. "Went as far as I could. Nothing yet."

"Amber, Evangeline said she went as far as she could but didn't find anything yet. I've got to move farther down so she can keep scouting."

Amber nodded. "Let's go. Tommy, with me in front. Genevieve, take up the rear and keep your ear out for *any* sounds of movement. Ceri and Derek in the middle. Ceri, do you have anything that could detect traps or any magic that might be waiting for us?"

"A few things," Ceri replied as they all got into position. "I'll see what I can do while we're moving."

Any other time, Tommy would have laughed at how organized they were now. They'd come such a long way as a pack and Amber had really stepped into her role as alpha. But...he couldn't bring himself to smile when Deward was in danger. Or dead.

This was like losing Ceri all over again but they had no way of telling how he was doing.

Evangeline pushed ahead of them as they walked. He felt a constant tug on the mark as she stretched their connection to its limits to scout for them.

He glanced at Amber, wondering how much Kadrithan could help them if he wanted to. It was possible things like that were a little different for Evangeline since she was only half demon. Still, it made him wonder. It would be good to know the limits of Amber's demon.

They walked silently down the narrow tunnels. He strained to hear everything he could but it was weirdly quiet. There was nothing alive down here, not even rats. He wasn't sure if the magic kept them out or they just didn't like the feel of it. He certainly didn't.

There was an abrupt tug on the mark and Tommy's hand flew to his chest. "I think she found something, let's hurry."

Amber nodded and they broke into a run, moving as fast as they could without leaving Derek behind. The light from his flashlight bounced unsteadily making it hard to see but they had other senses that could warn them of danger.

The tunnels sloped steeply downward before a sharp curve. As they rounded the bend, Evangeline came into view, bobbing in front of a room.

"I can't open the door but I went inside. There's no one in there, but someone did burn everything inside," she said in a rush.

"There's no one in the room. She said someone burned everything in it though," Tommy said, running ahead toward the door.

"Wait!" Ceri shouted, jogging after him. "Let me check the door first. There could still be a trap or curse Evangeline can't sense."

Tommy paused just in front of the door and nodded impatiently. "Fine."

Magic flowed from Ceri's fingertips and the handle glowed brightly, then the whole door. She stepped back and nodded.

He yanked the door open. Smoke hung heavy in the air, unable to dissipate. Some magic must have contained it to the room.

As soon as he crossed the threshold the stench of burnt paper filled his nose. The room was filled with ash. Whatever was in here had been burned a few days ago at least. The ashes were no longer smoldering and the room felt cold.

"Stand back, out of the way of the door, I can clear this out," Ceri said, walking in as well.

He stepped back out of the room and rejoined the others as Ceri began chanting in Latin. Her words echoed off the stone, reverberating in his chest.

The smoke swirled around her like a slow-motion whirlpool. She drew it in tighter and tighter until it was condensed into a black cloud, then thrust her hands at it with one final word.

It blew out of the room and around the bend before expanding again with a pop.

"Best I can do right now, sorry," Ceri said with a shrug.

"It'll help us look for his scent..." Amber trailed off, staring at the floor in confusion. "Ceri, don't move. Are those Deward's footprints?"

Tommy looked down near Ceri's feet, and sure enough, bloody footprints big enough to be Deward's were scattered all around the room. If it weren't for the blood, clearing out the smoke would have blown them away.

"Then he started walking here? That doesn't make sense. These aren't...there's no sign of a fight. How could they get him to comply like that?" Tommy asked, hurrying back into the room.

"Mind control of some kind perhaps, though that sort of magic is particularly hard to pull off, especially for only one person. Was anyone talking or even breathing in the background when Deward called you?" Ceri asked.

He shook his head. "No, I don't think so."

"There are dozens of possibilities, but the simplest may just be that whoever this was had already overpowered him once and threatened him into compliance. Or..." she hesitated for a moment. "Or gotten him to comply by threatening you, if they knew you were coming. How long did it take you to get into the tunnels after Deward called?"

"A minute, maybe." What Ceri was implying sunk in slowly and he felt his heart drop. "He could have been down here while I was back there."

"Hey," Amber interrupted, grabbing his shoulder. "Don't start with that. Even if he was, this person could have just taken both of you if you'd tried to rush after him. Then we wouldn't know anything about what had happened. You made the right choice."

Tommy nodded absently, as he stared at the bloody footprints, tracing their route. They stopped in front of the wall. "These don't lead to anywhere."

"Could be a hidden back door out of here," Derek said, shining his flashlight parallel to the wall. The uneven texture of the wall was highlighted, along with a subtle crack that would have been hard to see without the light. "Ceri, you got anything for this?"

"Maybe――"

Amber walked up and stomp-kicked right next to the crack. The stone groaned as it slid in, dust falling to the floor. "Looks like you were right."

"Well, that's one way to open it," Derek said with a shrug.

Amber stepped back, then kicked it again, harder this time. He felt her draw on the pack bond, using their strength. The stone door slid back a foot. He couldn't see anything but darkness beyond it.

Ceri walked toward it with a frown. "I don't like what I'm feeling from in there. Don't kick it again."

Amber cringed and stepped back slowly. "Did I trigger something?"

"No, its..." Ceri leaned toward the crack, eyes slipping shut as she focused on something the rest of them couldn't sense. Her fingers twitched, magic lifting from them and seeping into the opening. "Black magic. There is some sort of curse on this tunnel."

"Can you break it?" Tommy demanded. They had to be able to go after his friend. "Would this have cursed Deward?"

Ceri shook her head. "No to both. I've heard about these curses before. They're used as a sort of ward. I would need a coven to break something like this. It was made with at least thirteen witches over the course of thirty days. Even after all these years, this is still more powerful than any curse I've ever encountered. The witches used it to protect their escape route, so whoever took Deward through here would have had some kind of amulet that allows them to pass through unharmed, bound to them by blood. If they hadn't given him the same, then Deward's entrails would be...well...it would be obvious."

"I have to tell his parents he's been taken," Tommy said, his lips settling into a grim line.

"I'll go with you," Amber said, putting a hand on his shoulder.

He nodded, dread filling him. If he had just shown up a few minutes earlier...

Evangeline drifted up behind him, filling him with her light again. "I have to go. I'm sorry. I'll come back as soon as I can."

He nodded absently, dreading the news he was about to have to deliver.

CHAPTER 30

AMBER

Amber kept a hand on Tommy's shoulder as they waited for the elder to join them. Deward's parents had taken the news stoically, looking at the pictures they'd snapped of the blood, the tunnels, and the room without a hint of emotion.

They'd asked questions -- smart questions -- then Deward's father had left to fetch the elder.

Deward's mother, Ithra, walked back into the room carrying a tray of refreshments. "Please, eat and drink. You have had a trying day."

Amber accepted a tall, ice cold glass of tea and a plate stacked with sandwiches. Tommy just shook his head, his eyes never leaving the ground.

Ithra sat down across from them, the only sign of her distress the tight grip on her own glass.

"I'm sorry I didn't have his back. I was supposed to," Tommy said quietly.

Ithra's lips pressed into a thin line and she shook her head. "It is not you who should apologize, but my son. He foolishly walked into a dangerous situation alone. It is his poor decision that has caused this, not any action or failure on your part." Ithra's eyes flicked to Amber. "Your pack is not under any obligation to involve yourselves in this."

"Deward is Tommy's friend, we want to help. We will do everything we can to find him and bring him back," Amber said firmly. She was fond of the troll and even if she hadn't been, she would never just turn her back on someone in need.

Ithra inclined her head. "Thank you."

Deward's father, Olwen, opened the door, letting the elder in ahead of him. Tommy had mentioned her, and she was just as he described. Fierce. Her age showed in the lines on her face but not in her posture.

"Alpha Hale, Thomas Anderson." The elder nodded at each of them. "I understand Deward has been kidnapped and possibly murdered during pursuit of his feat?"

Tommy nodded. "Yeah."

"Before we continue, I must mention that if we intervene to rescue him, his feat will be forfeit--"

"Are you kidding me?" Tommy interrupted angrily. "How is that even a concern right now?"

Amber grabbed Tommy and jerked him back when he tried to stand. "Enough, Tommy."

She got his anger, but this felt like part of a ritual, not just misguided priorities.

The elder, not reacting to his anger, looked to Deward's parents for their answer.

"His life comes before any other pursuit," Ithra said calmly. "The feat is hereby, forfeit."

"As elder, this is heard and accepted." The elder clasped her hands together and bowed her head formally. "Now, we may continue. What assistance can the tribe offer?"

Olwen pulled up a chair for the elder, then sat down next to his wife. "What information did Deward share with you concerning his feat? As per tradition, we knew only the goal, and nothing else."

The elder nodded. "During his preparation, Deward discovered a diary and parts of a map that had belonged to a witch who was cast out of the coven that built the tunnels Deward was taken in. This coven was known for their wealth of knowledge. It is believed the founding witch had escaped from the Library of Alexandria with some of their most important texts before it was destroyed. His goal, as you know, was to find a book of prophecies. He believed he knew where this book had last been stored and that he could find the entrance to this hidden place very soon."

"And it was in those tunnels?" Tommy asked quietly, looking regretful for his outburst. The elder nodded. "Yes."

"Is it possible someone else was after the same thing? Was Deward the only one with this knowledge?" Ithra asked.

The elder shrugged. "He had the original copy of the diary and a torn map. Perhaps someone else had the other half, or found their way to the same place through a different route. Deward was not aware of any outside threats when we last spoke. Did he mention any to you, Thomas?"

Tommy shook his head. "No, he made it sound easy, to be honest. He was..." he paused and took a deep breath. "He was pretty sure he could finish his feat first."

"Do we need to call the police and file a missing person's report?" Amber asked. She really didn't want to but if they needed the police's help, then she'd accept it no matter the risk.

Olwen shook his head immediately. "We will handle this as a tribe unless it becomes absolutely necessary to involve outside help. We take care of our own."

"I understand." Werewolves often did the same thing. Anything that could be dealt with internally was. No one wanted to bring the intrusive attention of the authorities into their midst. Laws and traditions often...clashed.

"Olwen said that Deward's trail lead to another passage that you could not pass through. Why is that?" the elder asked.

"There is some sort of curse on it that the witch in our pack, Ceri, says she cannot break without a large coven helping her," Amber said.

Ithra frowned. "That is, perhaps, a problem I can work on with her if she would be willing. Trolls do not use magic like witches or elves, but we can manipulate it in our own way. Perhaps joining with the power of the tribe, we can give her the strength to break it."

Amber eyebrows shot up. "That is a very interesting idea. I'll talk to her about it as soon as we get back. I think she would be willing to try but she'll know better than me what's possible."

"I will search through the notes Deward left here concerning his feat and see if I can find any other clues that may lead us to wherever this woman may have taken him. Perhaps there is another place this coven hid their valuable items," Olwen said.

"I'm going to search the forest for their scent in the direction the tunnel went," Tommy said, fingers wound tightly together. "The part we went through curved a little but headed basically in one direction. Maybe the rest is the same."

Ithra nodded and rose from her seat. "I believe this is all we can do tonight. If anyone discovers anything, please share it at once."

"We will," Amber said before draining her glass of sweet tea.

Tommy silently followed her back to the truck. Pain emanated from him like a dark cloud. She silently sent strength to him through the pack bond. There were no assurances she could give him to make this easier.

CHAPTER 31

TOMMY

Tommy leaned back into the couch. He couldn't sleep. He flipped the TV on just to have some noise. The silence left too much room to think.

He was about to change the channel when a news helicopter circling over a familiar length of highway caught his eye. Tommy frowned. He'd driven that way when he was going to meet Deward. He turned the volume up a notch and leaned in, listening intently.

"Laurel Teller, a TV actress and model, was found by her best friend yesterday morning violently murdered in her own home. We have Thomas Arnold reporting from the scene of the crime. What can you tell us, Thomas?"

The second reporter stood in front of a two story, modern home. Police cars blocked a view of the lawn. The place was swarming with officers.

"Good evening Karen. Unfortunately, we don't know much at this point. Our contacts with the police have been unable to comment, however, we were able to find out that there was no forced entry. It's almost certain that whoever murdered Ms. Teller used magic to get in and out. In fact, it appears the MIB is actually joining us on the scene right now. We'll see if we can get a comment straight from the authority."

The reporter and his cameraman rushed after the MIB agents that stepped out of their sleek, black suburban but were ignored.

He pulled out his phone and searched the internet for Laurel Teller. A ton of articles popped up, the top ones linking her to a couple of pop stars and...an angel.

He skimmed the article, skipping past the pointless fluff until he found the information on the angel. Apparently, they didn't know his name, but whoever he was, he owned the houses she lived in. The cars she drove. The credit cards she shopped with. Everything.

There was a certain status that came with being picked by an angel. They called them Blessed, which he'd always thought was a bunch of crap. They were *blessed* alright. The angels showered the men and women they chose with money and gifts, the Blessed women popped out a couple of kids, then it all tended to disappear.

What bothered him though was the connection to the angel. It felt like too much of a coincidence after everything that had happened. A half angel had been involved with the sorcerer, now an angel's mistress shows up dead less than a mile from where Deward is taken by a powerful magic user.

Could the murderer be the same person as the kidnapper? Could it be an angel somehow?

Amber padded into the living room. "What's wrong? Your racing heartbeat woke me up."

He shoved his phone at her. "This human, someone attached to an angel, was murdered a mile from the tunnels the same morning Deward disappeared."

"That must have been why I heard sirens on the way to meet you," Amber said with a frown. She grabbed his phone, reading about Laurel's attachment to the angel. "Is it related somehow?"

"I think so. The news is saying whoever killed her did it with magic. The MIB showed up to the scene while they were reporting."

She took a deep breath, her lips pressed into a thin line. "This isn't good."

"No, but it's a clue. Do we go to them? Tell them what happened?"

"I don't know. I'm not sure they'd trust us considering our pack is under investigation. It also doesn't look good to be linked, in any way, to another death."

Tommy slumped back onto the couch. "We have to do something."

Amber opened her mouth to say something but stopped, eyes darting to the side. Kadrithan must have appeared.

"It's in my glove box, why--" She rolled her eyes. "It's perfectly safe there. Do you need it back?"

Tommy watched the one-sided exchange silently. He wished he could hear what Kadrithan was saying.

"We've had more important--shut up and listen," she said, crossing her arms. "Tommy's friend Deward went missing in some tunnels less than a mile from where you ran out in front of my truck, which just so happens to also be the location of a murder. You know anything about that?"

Amber stared the demon down, anger flashing through the pack bond at whatever his response was. "Keep bullshitting me and I'll put that black thing down the garbage disposal."

He raised his eyebrows. Kadrithan must be really pissing her off.

"Fine, then you're explaining *everything*."

Amber stomped toward the door. "I'll be right back."

Genevieve appeared at the top of the stairs. "What the hell is going on?"

"I may have figured something out but apparently Kadrithan is involved. Amber is making him explain something."

Ceri and Derek walked into the living room from the hallway. He was wearing her fluffy, purple robe.

"Everything okay?" he asked tiredly.

"Just wait for Amber to get back." Tommy pushed off the couch and headed to the kitchen. He hadn't been able to eat dinner earlier and his stomach was protesting the lack of food.

Woggy's head popped up from the silverware drawer as he approached, his cheeks stuffed full.

"What have you gotten into this time?" he asked while signing along with it.

Ears dropping sheepishly, Woggy held up a half-eaten spoon. He signed *sorry* and *hungry* with his free hand.

"Aw hell, we forgot to give you lunch and dinner, didn't we?" Tommy signed the question, but he didn't know quite enough words to form the whole thought. Woggy seemed to understand though and nodded forlornly.

You sad. You angry. Woggy signed back. *Waited. Hungry.*

Sorry. Tommy signed with a sigh. He opened the fridge and pulled out the leftover pizza and some canned chicken. "Here you go."

Captain Jack meowed as he ran into the kitchen looking for a treat as well.

"We probably forgot to feed you too--" Tommy stopped abruptly, taking in the cat's size. He was bigger than he had been yesterday, he was sure of it.

"He's still growing," Genevieve said with a sigh from the entryway to the kitchen, confirming his suspicions. "I'm starting to wonder if someone cast a spell on him or something. It's weird."

Shaking her head, she went into the pantry and got his cat food, filling his bowl to the top. "Growing boys need lots of food," she murmured, stroking his back as he started chowing down on the dry food.

Woggy tugged on Tommy' sleeve, long fingers straining to reach the chicken. He took the paper off then handed the pixie the can -- they'd learned they really didn't need to open it for him.

The front door opened and Amber stomped back in, still arguing with Kadrithan about something.

He met Genevieve's eyes and they both sighed before heading back to the living room.

"Visible. Now," Amber demanded.

Kadrithan came into view, though he was more of a wonky, shadowy blob than a person. Tommy frowned. That was odd. The demon was all about appearances and being intimidating. It was almost like he *couldn't* do anything more right now.

"Give it to the witch," Kadrithan demanded.

"Not until you tell me where you found it and what it is," Amber said, clutching a dirty napkin in her hand.

Kadrithan's shadow darkened. For a moment, Tommy thought he may not answer. "I found it at the murder scene."

"At Laurel Teller's?" Tommy asked in alarm.

"Yes. It is a piece of what killed her. *However*, I don't know what it is, which is why I brought it to you in the first place. I can't touch it or properly analyze it. Give it to her and have her do it."

Ceri glared at the demon. "You don't get to order us around."

"Ceri, please do it. I think whoever killed Laurel Teller may have taken Deward. We need to know everything we can. Do it for me, not him," Tommy pleaded. He wasn't above getting down on his knees and begging if it came to it.

Her shoulders slumped. "Fine, give it here."

Amber handed over the dirty napkin. Inside it was a slender, black piece of something that looked almost like obsidian. It was shiny and perfectly smooth other than what looked like a thorn jutting from it.

"This is strange." Ceri examined it carefully, tapping it quickly with her finger. She frowned, then picked it up from the napkin. "It doesn't burn me."

"What kind of magic created it?" Kadrithan asked, drifting toward her.

Ceri frowned and glared at the thing. She never had liked not knowing things. "It's hard to say. My first instinct is elvish but I've never seen anything like this from an elf. Their magic is very elemental, and this is neither wood, nor stone. It's not a plant either despite the thorn."

"If it's elvish, maybe Thallan could say for sure what kind?" Tommy suggested.

Ceri visibly shuddered. "Even if he did know, he'd never tell us. Illya, however, might." She shut her eyes and took on a strange glow. A shudder went through the house, then Illya's specter appeared in the living room.

She smiled serenely at them, her pale green hair drifting around her shoulders in a breeze only she felt. "Ceridwen."

"Illya, we need your help," Ceri said, holding the piece out to her. "Do you know what this is?"

Illya drifted toward her, eyes alight at the chance to be useful. She stopped abruptly when she got close. The cabinets in the kitchen all flew open. The doors began rattling and the floorboards swayed under their feet. "Corruption. Get it out."

Ceri quickly wrapped it back in the napkin. Derek grabbed it from her and ran for the back door, which flew open to let him out, then slammed shut behind him.

"Who could create that?" Ceri asked quickly, glancing around nervously.

"Someone who has turned their back on all that is good. A murderer and corrupter," Illya snarled, her delicate features twisting into a hateful mask.

"An elf though? Or a witch?" Tommy asked. They had to get answers before Illya tore the house down around them.

"An elf."

"Thank you," Ceri said, lifting her hand and releasing whatever magic she had used to summon Illya. The elf's specter disappeared with a pop and the house went quiet.

"Well, that was terrifying," Genevieve muttered, plopping down on the couch.

"Those tunnels were built by witches, but is it possible an elf could access that... amulet, or whatever you called it, to get through that curse on the back exit?" Amber asked.

Ceri nodded. "Anyone with magic could manage it."

"This troll that disappeared, what happened?" Kadrithan asked.

Tommy quickly re-explained it, including the phone call and the woman's voice on the other end.

"Maybe this elf killed Laurel, then went back to the tunnels and Deward was just in the wrong place at the wrong time," Genevieve suggested.

"Maybe, but why did she take him with her and not just kill him? Taking him is harder and riskier," Tommy said, joining her on the couch. He was bone tired but sleep just wasn't going to happen tonight.

"She must need him for something; perhaps to frame for the murder," Kadrithan said, drifting back and forth in front of the couch like he was pacing. It was weird to see him doing such human things.

"You can only show up places where someone you have marked is," Tommy said, something dawning on him.

Kadrithan stilled. "And?"

"Laurel had one of your marks."

"Had, being the operative word, since she is now dead."

Amber frowned at him. "Was she killed because of something you asked her to do?"

"I highly doubt--"

Amber's glare cut off his response.

He sighed dramatically, the shadows twisting in irritation. "I don't know. I was visiting her to check on her progress on the task I had given her, but she was already dead when I arrived. She had to have been killed after sundown the previous day, or her mark would have already faded, but I believe she was killed perhaps an hour before I arrived. Maybe less."

"What task?" Tommy asked.

"That is not something I will be sharing no matter how much Amber glares at me. I have told you enough tonight. You have the information you need to find this elf that took your friend." Kadrithan disappeared with a low pop.

Amber growled, baring her teeth like she was in wolf form. "I'm going to strangle him."

"He was more useful than he usually is," Tommy said, leaning his head back against the cushions and staring at the ceiling. "We have way more information than we did two hours ago."

Genevieve picked Captain Jack up and set the massive cat on both their laps. "True, the only question is, what do we do now?"

.

CHAPTER 32

TOMMY

Tommy had no intention of running into Thallan while he was here. Since it was before dawn, the old drunkard should be passed out somewhere.

He jumped, catching the lower edge of the second story balcony and hauling himself up over the banister. Once safely on the balcony, he stopped and listened intently for footsteps. There was nothing.

The board covering this window had come loose. He pushed it inward, cringing at the loud crack when it broke near the nails on the other side.

He stepped through the opening and replaced the board. The hallway was dark and musty. Rain had been leaking through the gap in the board for a while and the carpet under the window was still soggy with it, unable to fully dry without sunlight or airflow.

Thallan was crazy but he had also been obsessed with killing Kadrithan. Right now, Tommy needed information. He knew the elf wouldn't be forthcoming but there had to be something around here that could explain more about demons and angels. Maybe even something about how an elf could take over someone's mind. All he knew was that he couldn't sit still.

With no idea where he should go, Tommy simply picked a direction, heading left down the dark hallway. The hall was lined with empty bedrooms, their doors open since there was nothing left inside to protect.

However, at the end of the hall there was something different. One room was sealed off like a tomb. Boards had been haphazardly nailed over it. He pried them off one at a time. If Thallan sealed it off, then it was probably the best place to look.

With one last cautious glance over his shoulder, he pulled off the last board and opened the door. A wave of fresh air rolled out of the room, catching him by surprise.

Stepping inside was like stepping into an oasis. Despite the dim light of the moon filtering through the windows, it felt bright and fresh inside. The curtains were thrown open, revealing what would have been a beautiful view of the garden once upon a time.

The tall windows were lined with plants, all of them still in bloom. Whatever sickness was sucking the life away from the mansion hadn't touched this place yet.

A shawl hung from the back of a brightly colored plush chair that looked out of place with the rest of the subtle decor. He wandered farther in, noting a book with a slightly crumpled receipt tucked in its pages had been left on the seat.

As he looked around, he realized this must have been Illya's study. Thallan probably boarded it up right after she died, leaving it exactly as it had been when she died.

He pulled the door shut then began searching the room more thoroughly. The book on the chair was something on magic in botany, which made sense considering all the plants that were scattered throughout the room. It smelled nice in here.

He spent a few minutes searching the shelves, but it quickly became clear there was nothing that would help him here. Illya had been into growing things, not demons or angels. It really was too bad she'd died. She seemed like a wonderful person.

It was hard to do quietly, but he managed to get a couple of boards back in place. The rest were a lost cause. Hopefully if Thallan found them, he'd think he tore them off in a drunken rage or something.

Unwilling to give up the search so quickly, Tommy wandered the second floor. A dried vomit stain at the bottom of a stairwell caught his attention. The stairs must lead up to the highest floor of the house. If Thallan was still going up there it was worth searching.

He stepped over the dried vomit and hurried up the stairs. It had been much more pleasant in Illya's room, to say the least.

The stairs wound upward, the walls closing in the higher he got. Thallan's scent was heavy here but not fresh. He figured the old bat must lurk up here often. If it was possible for an elf to turn into a vampire, Thallan would probably volunteer.

At the top of the tower, an open door beckoned him into a small, circular room. Stained glass windows colored the pre-dawn light that filtered into the room, giving everything a reddish cast. He stood in the doorway for a moment taking it all in.

If the rest of the house was decaying, this must be the rotten heart. Some of the floorboards were warped as if the roof had a leak. Trash, including broken bottles of cheap liquor, littered the floor. It was a mess.

He wrinkled his nose as he stepped inside. Thallan had *definitely* spent a lot of time in here. The stench of cigarettes overpowered any other smells. For once, he was thankful.

Walking around, he poked piles of trash with his foot to see if anything helpful was buried underneath. A half-broken bookshelf to the left of the door held a few dust-covered tomes. Poetry. Elvish history. Philosophy.

He sighed, about ready to give up when something caught his eye. In the corner was something...dark. The already dim lighting seemed to be unable to reach it but there was nothing casting a shadow on it. The scent of sulfur cut through the smell of the cigarettes as he slowly approached it. Kicking aside a pile of crumpled paper, he found a book.

It was bound in old leather, cracked and worn, with a strange symbol stamped on the front. He picked it up and flipped through the bent and torn pages. There were various summoning spells inside, none of them legal. At the very back was one simply titled: Demon.

This must be what Thallan had used to summon Kadrithan and make that deal with him. He read the summoning spell intently. It didn't require much. Most of the instructions were simply notes on how to bargain along with examples of various common mistakes.

There was one note, however, that caught his eye. It didn't make any sense.

While one should use caution around demons, it is the Great Deceivers around whom one must exercise the greatest caution. Do not be blinded by false promises from those that cannot be bound to a promise unlike the Demon.

"Who are the Great Deceivers?" he muttered, flipping back to the beginning of the book in search of clues.

A crash downstairs interrupted him. It was time to go. He tucked the book under his arm and sprinted back down the stairs, leaving out of the same window he entered through. There was no way he was risking getting caught by Thallan in there.

Hopefully he wouldn't notice the book was missing anytime soon.

CHAPTER 33

CERI

The tarot card was sitting on her pillow. Again. Ceri grabbed it and stomped into the kitchen, ready to put it down the garbage disposal this time. Looking at it was supposed to get the little weasel to *stop* showing up everywhere.

When she yanked her door open, she almost walked into Amber. She had a book tucked under her arm.

"What are you reading? You never read." As soon as the words came out of her mouth, she realized how rude that sounded.

Amber scowled at her. "I read. I'm just busy…"

"I was just surprised."

"You still meeting with Ithra today to talk about that curse?"

"Yeah, just as soon as I have some coffee." She narrowed her eyes. Amber was avoiding her question.

"Great." Amber nodded uncomfortably and tried to scurry away to her room without answering what the book was.

Ceri grabbed it before she could get away.

"Wait––" Amber cut herself off with a sigh, then crossed her arms, waiting for Ceri's reaction.

The book was old and the pages were protected with magic. She opened it and saw the book was on tarot.

"Still determined to figure out this stupid card, I see." Ceri muttered, flipping through the pages.

"Well, a tarot card appeared for me too when I ran into that guy. I'd rather know as much as I could about it than nothing, even if it might be total crap," Amber said firmly, as if she'd rehearsed this argument in her head before.

She rolled her eyes. "It *is* crap."

"How do you know? You do magic. Why is this any different?"

"Fortune tellers are all about illusion and conning you."

"Dr. Stone isn't trying to con us. He didn't ask for money, just offered help if I wanted it, then told me to research it myself."

Notes in a strange text were scribbled in the top corner of one of the pages. "Where did you get this book?"

Amber scratched her head and shifted on her feet. "Kadrithan."

She slammed the book shut. "Are you serious? What did he get you to agree to in exchange for this?"

"Nothing," Amber snapped, truly irritated now. "He said it was a gift, no strings attached. I'm guessing he just wants me to trust him or something. The book helps. I still don't trust him. It was a win-win."

"I don't like it," she muttered, staring at the book like it might bite her.

Amber sighed. "You've really got to let go of your prejudices."

"I don't--"

"Yeah, you do. Maybe these tarot cards can tell us something. Is yours still following you around?"

Ceri glared at the card in her hand. "Yes."

"Mine isn't. It seems content that I'm trying to figure it out. Keep the book. Read about your card. Maybe it will help. If it doesn't, I'll slap Dr. Stone around until he gets them to go away." Amber crossed her arms, daring Ceri to argue with her.

"Look, it's experience not some kind of preju--"

"I'm taking Tommy back to the woods to look for Deward. Good luck." Amber walked back into her room, shutting the door behind her and cutting the argument off.

Ceri was half-annoyed, half-impressed. Amber knew she'd look at the stupid book now because she'd challenged her. Sighing, she glared at the hideous card again. If she was being honest, she was somewhat curious what it meant. She was also worried it would be something bad.

There was nothing to do but find out unless she wanted to spend the rest of her life haunted by a sassy tarot card.

Resigning herself to her fate, she slipped back into her room, shutting her door firmly behind herself. She'd never live it down if the pack caught her reading this.

Woggy poked his head up from the nest he'd made in her bedroom window, squeaking imperiously for his breakfast. She felt guilty after forgetting to feed him the other night and had been conned into delivering him breakfast in bed.

Grabbing a can of tuna from her drawer, she handed it to the greedy little pixie, then settled back in her bed. This book was very old, possibly the oldest thing she'd ever held. Maybe tarot and fortune telling was crap but she couldn't deny how cool it was to get to examine a piece of history like this.

She flipped through long-winded introduction expounding on the *venerable and arcane arts involved in channeling magicks through the hallowed vessels of the tarot cards*. She rolled her eyes. At most they were a psychological trick favored by con artists.

Impatient, she flipped through until she saw a full page drawing that matched the tarot card Dr. Stone had given her. The fat devil leered at her making her skin crawl. She flicked him on the nose, feeling dumb for letting a drawing get to her like this.

With a sigh, she began reading the description.

Rather than signifying doom, as one might expect from a card whose appearance is moste evil, The Devil, which is the fifteenth card in the Major Arcana, may instead represent the shadow self. It calls attention to the darkest desires which hide within our souls.

Let it call you forth to action. Root out this darkness and take control of it. This darkness may be fear of something within or a threat from another, and fear will always limit any of us blessed with the gift of magick. One must always deal with the shadows within lest they consume us or weaken us.

The Devil may also warn us of a situation from which there is no hope of escape. Let traps and betrayal not catch you by surprise if this card appears for you. Root out the darkness lurking around you.

"Well, isn't that positive," she muttered, her eyes drawn back to the demon and the two people chained at his feet. As she stared at him, she felt a tug. Her vision darkened and she felt the same oppressive warmth that had pushed her out of the spirit realm. It pressed in all around her, suffocating her.

She grabbed the totem hanging from her neck and its power flared around her, shoving the darkness away. Tossing the book to the side on the bed she gasped for breath, heart still racing from the moment of panic.

Woggy grunted as he munched on some tuna. She was jealous of him. His biggest struggle tended to be trying to convince them to feed him an hour earlier than normal. The pixie life was a simple one. He didn't have unwanted visions of darkness that seemed to be haunting him after an ill-advised trip to the spirit realm.

The tarot card drifted into her view. She sighed, staring at the pushy thing.

"What do you want me to do? I read the book. It's not helping."

The card shimmied, floating closer to her.

"You want me to look at you again?"

It bounced mid-air excitedly.

"Fine." She held out her hand and let it flip into her palm. It didn't look any more appealing upside down but at least this time she wasn't overwhelmed with another vision. "Are you warning me about some darkness within, or a terrible, unavoidable situation?"

The first thought that came to her was that it was both. She frowned, feeling a slight tingle of magic in her fingers.

"Was that...you?"

The card twitched.

"Can't you just pick one? Does it have to be both?"

The insight bloomed in her mind as clear as if the card had spoken to her. The answer remained the same: both.

Just what she needed to hear before she met with some trolls to try to break an ancient curse.

CHAPTER 34

CERI

She'd never had much to do with trolls. Not for any particular reason, the circles she ran in had simply never overlapped with the intellectual trolls. Her family and coven hadn't been big on sharing or on mingling with races that couldn't wield magic like they could.

Knocking on the door, she waited nervously for someone to answer. After two failures to make any progress in the spirit realm her confidence was at an all time low. Her talents lay in breaking spells other witches had cast though. Theoretically, she was the best possible person to help with this.

Ithra opened the door. She wasn't quite what Ceri had expected. A finely-made, white silk blouse flattered Ithra's dark green skin. Her hair was bright blue, just like Deward's, however it was pulled back into a braid instead of a mohawk.

"You must be Ceridwen," Ithra said, extending her hand. "I am Ithra Tuskbreaker, pleased to meet you."

"Yes, pleased to meet you as well," Ceri said with a smile.

"Come inside and make yourself comfortable. The elder and my brother –– who is most familiar with curses –– will be joining us today."

Ceri followed her inside, admiring the inside of the troll's home. It was spotless, not a speck of dirt on the ground or a single thing out of place. The decorations were minimal. Instead of pictures of family, they had hung framed math equations and essays. She couldn't help but smile at that.

Ithra led her to a room on the second floor. The elder –– who she recognized from the day spent with the trolls –– and another troll whose muscles looked likely to bust out of his shirt nodded in greeting.

"This is my brother, Velgo, and Elder Xenya," Ithra said in introduction. They all shook hands, getting the formalities out of the way. "Please, tell us what you know of this curse."

"How familiar are you with spells cast by witches?" Ceri asked.

"I have spent my life studying your magic. I am as familiar with it as one can be without being a witch," he said with a humble nod of his head.

"Excellent, that will make this easier." She reflected for a moment on what she'd felt at that doorway. "The curse has faded in power, which is good for us. The problem lies with the sheer number of witches involved in creating it. I believe this course of retreat was a last resort for them, so the power they poured into the curse was amplified by their determination."

"How large was the circle that cast it?" Velgo asked.

"Thirteen witches large, at least. Similar to the runes that hid the main entrance to the tunnels, I believe they cast it alongside the cycle of the moon."

Velgo nodded as he walked over to a large whiteboard that took up one of the walls. He began writing down notes with handwriting that was unfairly perfect. "How many witches do you estimate you'd need to break it?"

"Three."

He stopped, looking back at her in surprise. "That's not many. Amber said you thought you'd need a large coven to break it."

She shook her head. "Not a large one, simply a skilled one. However, there is not a single witch in Portland I would trust to help with this."

"I believe the tribe can help you by standing in as a coven," Elder Xenya said.

"I am certainly willing to try, though I have no idea how many more trolls I would need in place of a skilled witch." She paused, noting a frown tugging at the elder's mouth. "I am completely uneducated in how a troll can manipulate magic."

"That will take some experimentation," Velgo said, unconcerned. "I believe the best test of that will be casting a spell with you first. We certainly can't have our first attempt at channeling your magic be done with a dangerous curse."

"That's logical. Perhaps..." she'd dismissed the idea initially because she didn't have a coven to help her, but if the trolls could, that would change everything. "We might be able to scry Deward, see where he is and what he's doing."

Ithra's head popped up at that. "If it is at all possible, I want to try."

Velgo tapped his marker against the whiteboard. "Theoretically, if we can act as your coven, then scrying would be as good a test as anything else. It is fairly complex."

Ceri nodded in agreement. "I brought as much as I could with me today, however we would need a gallon of fresh water, not distilled."

"There is a creek two blocks from here, will that work?" Xenya asked.

"Yes."

"I'll fetch it." The elder hurried out of the room, leaving them to the rest of the planning.

Ceri threw herself into the joy that came with planning a spell like this. It had been a long time since she'd been able to share this with someone and she'd forgotten how thrilling it was.

If Deward's life hadn't been at risk, she could have even called it fun.

CHAPTER 35

AMBER

There was no trail in the woods. No one had passed this way in ages. Amber shifted back and yanked her shirt on in annoyance.

Tommy was justifiably frustrated as well. His emotions were pounding through the pack bond like a headache.

"They can't have just disappeared completely."

"We might have to wait for Ceri to break that curse to pick the trail up."

Tommy sighed, dragging his hand down his face. "He could be dead by then. If he isn't already."

She shoved her feet back in her shoes. There was nothing she could say to that. He was right.

"Maybe we should go to Laurel's house and try to catch the scent of the murderer. It's only been a day, there's a chance we can trace her back to wherever she was before the murder."

Her head snapped up. "A crime scene is the last place we should be wandering around."

"If someone is there we'll hear them and we can leave."

She hesitated, but knew she would have done it for Ceri in a heartbeat. Deward needed their help. "Alright, let's try. But if anyone is there, we turn right back around."

"Yeah, I don't want to get arrested any more than you do."

Instead of driving closer to Laurel's house, which would be suspicious, they walked through the woods. Amber listened intently for any sign they weren't alone but other than a few birds, the forest remained silent.

Laurel's home was part of some kind of estate that butted up to a state park –– which is where they'd been searching. The trees and underbrush were dense so she wasn't able to see the house until they were almost on top of it.

STEPHANIE FOXE

Wordlessly, both she and Tommy stopped, taking cover behind a large tree as they scoped the area out. The yard and driveway were empty, guarded only by yellow police tape strung around the property. Based on the varying scents, dozens of people had passed through here recently.

"I don't hear anyone, do you?" Tommy whispered.

She shook her head. "Nope, but we're still going in *carefully*. Just in case."

Tommy nodded curtly and ran toward the house, staying low. She followed him with all her senses on high alert.

They stopped and pressed their backs against the outside of the house, checking one last time to ensure it was vacant.

"It's weird they left it empty, isn't it?" Tommy asked in a hushed whisper.

She shrugged. "Maybe they can't afford to have someone sit here. Not really sure how it works."

"You think they have the place warded?"

"We'd be able to smell the magic if they did. Just keep moving slow."

Tommy nodded, stepping back to look up at a second story balcony. "Let's go in up there. Less likely to be warded if any of it is."

Amber shrugged. "Alright, stand back. I'm going first."

"Sure thing, alpha," Tommy said with a hint of amusement in his tone.

She threw him a mock glare before launching herself up to the balcony, catching the top of the banister easily. It was too bad she couldn't do all this when she and Dylan had been sneaking out of the house as teenagers. It had always been getting back in unnoticed that had been difficult.

Throwing her legs over the side she dropped onto the balcony and paused. The house remained silent and no magic tingled over her skin. She waited three breaths, just in case, but it was clear.

"Are you meditating up there or what?" Tommy hissed from the ground.

"I'm being *careful*," she said, leaning over the banister to glare at him. "But it's safe. Get up here."

"Finally." He jumped up and pulled himself over with a practiced ease that made her think he'd done it before.

Amber tugged on the window but it was locked. "Well, should have thought about it being locked. Any other ideas?"

"Scoot over."

She raised an eyebrow at him, but did as requested.

He peered through the window then nodded his head. "I can open this."

"I'm not even going to ask how you know how to do that."

"Probably for the best." He pushed both hands firmly against the window and began moving it up and down in incremental motions. Slowly but surely, the window lock began to raise.

"Is it seriously that easy?"

The lock came free and the window slid up. "Yep."

"Wish I'd known about that last time I locked myself out of my apartment," Amber muttered as she followed him into the the house.

634

Tommy smirked at her, then gestured down the hallway. "After you."

The house was newly built and the interior had all the trendy decorations she saw on TV. Light gray walls, tall windows with gauzy curtains, and abstract prints hung without a frame. It all felt impersonal, like a stage instead of a home.

"She must not have lived here very long, her scent hasn't...settled into the place, you know?" Tommy said quietly.

"Yeah, I know what you mean. It's like she barely ever walked through here." Amber frowned, poking her head into what appeared to be a guest bedroom. It smelled like bleach and fabric softener. No one had slept in here in months, if ever.

"Some news articles did say she mostly stayed in the city. This was her 'country house,'" he said with finger quotes, "that she stayed at when she was fighting with her boyfriend –– the mysterious angel."

The hallway opened up with a wide staircase leading down to their right and a balcony that overlooked the entryway. Little evidence markers were laid out in various places, including a single bloody footprint that trailed down the stairs like someone had hopped on one foot all the way down.

"That looks a little big to be a woman's footprint," Tommy said in confusion.

"Maybe it's Kadrithan's. He grabbed that piece of evidence, I guess he stepped in her blood somehow."

Tommy grimaced. "Must have been a lot of blood."

Amber stepped around the evidence markers, following them into a large bedroom. The center of the room was empty except for dried blood that had spread across the floor. Straight above the blood, the ceiling had strange holes in it.

She walked around it, stepping into the bathroom, and immediately regretted it. The scent of blood still hung in the air like a fog. Seeing it splattered against the walls like red paint reminded her of that crazy, old vampire Bram and his little basement of horrors. A shudder ran down her spine and she turned away. Even if there was a scent hidden under all that blood, she'd never be able to find it.

"Who would do something like this?" Tommy asked quietly from the doorway of the bedroom.

"I don't know. Let's search the rest of the house. There's nothing that can help us in here."

Tommy didn't argue, gladly retreating back into the hall ahead of her. She took a deep breath of clean air as soon as she was a few feet away from the scene of the murder. The lingering smell of blood was still there, at the back of her throat, but it was better out here.

"We should check downstairs," Amber said, wanting to put more distance between herself and the carnage in that bathroom.

"Sure, maybe the murderer came in through the front door. The police didn't find any sign of forced entry. According to the news at least." Tommy jogged ahead of her, skipping over the bloody footprints.

They spent a few minutes sniffing around downstairs, coming up with absolutely nothing new.

"She's got to be erasing her scent somehow. Elves always smell like flowers and dirt, it'd be obvious if someone besides police had been in here," Amber said, sighing in frustration.

They heard the car turning into the driveway at the same time.

Tommy froze, looking at her with wide eyes. "We can't go out the front door."

"Back upstairs, now." They'd gotten too cocky and let their guard down. She pushed Tommy ahead of her and sprinted up the stairs after him.

They made it just around the corner when the front door swung open. It was too late to get out of the house. If they opened the window now it'd make noise. They were stuck.

Frantically searching for a hiding spot, she decided on a guest bedroom and shoved Tommy inside, scrambling in after him. She held her breath as she strained her ears for another sound. The voice grew louder, their footsteps drawing closer to her and Tommy.

After a moment, the voice became clear. It was Agent Horan. She was surprised he was here considering he was supposed to be meeting with Genevieve in about an hour –– she was the first of the pack that would have to be interrogated.

"You're going to have to move faster. I can only drag this out for so much longer. It was hard enough to clear this crime scene out today." Horan paused for a long moment. "No, that's not good enough. Have it by this weekend or I'm out."

Tommy's hand tightened on her arm.

"This conversation is pointless. Do what you were hired to do or neither of us will be getting paid. I'm dealing with my problem. You need to deal with yours."

Amber frowned. If he was talking to Carter, did that mean both of them were being paid by someone to make them look guilty?

"Yeah, I've got it. The forensics team is going over the place again tomorrow. They'll find it then. Now, stop worrying about what I'm doing, and take care of your end of the deal." Horan ended the call, muttering insults to himself as he moved something heavy in the bedroom Laurel was killed in. After a brief moment of silence, he grunted, moving the heavy thing back. "I better get that bonus."

With an annoyed sigh, he tromped out of the room and back toward the stairs. Amber slumped in relief against the wall. That had been way too close for comfort.

She and Tommy waited in the empty room until they heard him driving away, then cautiously slipped back into the hallway. Once again, the house was empty.

"I'm starting to feel like I'm in a corny filler episode of *Werespy*," Tommy muttered as they walked back to the murder scene.

"Did you actually watch that show?" Amber asked with a laugh, the adrenaline giving her energy she had no outlet for. "It was so bad."

"Hey, it's a classic," Tommy objected, his nose twitching as he tried to sniff out where Horan had been in the room.

She snorted. "I don't think a soapy spy drama that was cancelled after one and a half seasons can be called a classic."

Tommy glared at her but didn't bother trying to argue. "He left it behind the dresser."

They moved it with little effort. Sometimes she forgot how much extra strength being a werewolf gave her. It was just normal now.

She crouched down by the dresser. Half of a flower preserved in resin was laying on the floor as if it had been broken and knocked under the dresser during a struggle.

"What is it?" Tommy asked.

"I have no clue, but he planted it here, so it can't be good. I'm taking it." She picked it up carefully, turning it over in her hand. It had broken near the top, ripping the bloom in half. Horan was clearly trying to frame someone for this…but who?

CHAPTER 36

CERI

Ceri stood just inside the circle, her hands held out over the silver bowl of water. Velgo and Ithra stood in two connected circles, chanting quietly in Latin. Spells were most powerful when cast by witches in groups that were prime numbers. Three, five, seven, etc. Adding Xenya as the fourth would have weakened them.

The world fell away as she sank into the spell. Her heartbeat synced up with the steady rhythm of the chants. With each inhale, she let her magic fill her body a little more.

When she had cast spells with her coven, each of them had controlled the flow of their own magic. This was vastly different. Witches all had a deep well of magic, the trolls, however, seemed to be a conduit. She drew the magic through them from the earth itself. It allowed her greater individual control but would never give her the power a real coven would provide.

She pushed away the doubt. It would be enough for this. She had enough magic within herself and the pack to break the curse if she could complete this spell.

"Saturo."

Their magic seeped into the water. It darkened. The surface rippled in agitation. Her lips continued forming the words of the chant but all her attention was on the scrying bowl. Slowly, the water lifted from the bowl, spreading out above it in a thin disc.

Tendrils rose from the surface, winding together to form legs, then a torso. As Deward took shape, the echo of him began to move. Sharp, jerky movements as though he was fighting someone. Red seeped into the figure's outstretched hands, dripping back down into the scrying water.

Her vision stuttered and shifted, drawing closer and closer to Deward until he was all she could see. With one final push, she was within him, seeing out of his eyes. It was blurry and everything seemed too slow.

He looked down at his hands covered in blood.

Hurry, a harsh whisper came from behind him.

The hands moved. The feet moved. She saw an elf, darkness folded around her like a shroud, beckoning him to follow.

Lies and tricks. It is hidden, the harsh voice said again, frustration clear in their tone.

We must find it. The words rumbled out of Deward's chest this time.

The figure ahead of him stopped and turned on Deward. *Someone watches.*

The other person drew nearer, pale eyes shining from within the shroud of darkness. They looked into Deward. Into her.

Get out.

Ceri dug in, pouring more power into the spell. She wasn't leaving until she was ready.

It is not time yet.

Pure, furious magic hit her. She fell to her knees, fingers clawing the floor as she gasped for air.

"No!" she screamed, clinging to the spell with all the magic and stubbornness she could bring to bear. She wouldn't lose like this. Not again. "Show yourself!"

She wanted to see her enemy. She was sick of fighting the unseen. Sick of battling against darkness she didn't understand.

It is not time yet.

A wave of magic even stronger than the last hit her and the spell shattered. The scrying water exploded, raining down on everyone in the room.

Ceri lay on the floor, tears mixed with the cold water running into her eyes.

"Ceri!" Ithra cried, dropping to her knees beside her. "Are you hurt?"

She shook her head but found herself unable to move. Her body ached as though she'd been physically hit.

"What happened?" Velgo demanded as he rolled her over and helped her sit up.

Her teeth chattered as she tried to recover from the shock of that much magic battering her mind. "The elf. She--she forced me out. But I saw him."

"Deward is alive?" Ithra asked, emotion showing in her voice for the first time.

She nodded. "But he's helping the elf. I don't understand why. Must be--must be mind control or something else."

"Do you know where he is?" Ithra asked.

"No," she shook her head. "But they killed someone. There was blood...on his hands."

Ithra stood abruptly and walked to the other side of the room, her back to the others. "We have to stop him. He would not want to be a part of this."

Ceri let Velgo help her to her feet. "This is still a rescue mission, Ithra. If this elf is controlling him somehow, then we can save him. We can break her power over him."

Ithra nodded but still looked upset. Ceri could hardly blame her. Even if they did rescue Deward, it was likely he had just killed someone. There may not be a happy ending to this and everyone in the room was smart enough to understand that.

She couldn't justify using blood magic to track down Selena, but in this moment she was sorely tempted to use it to find Deward. He didn't deserve any of this.

CHAPTER 37

GENEVIEVE

Dressed in her best suit, with her hair arranged in a neat french twist, Genevieve felt as ready as she could for this interrogation. They called it an interview but she knew better.

She was glad she was the first to go though. After this, she'd be able to coach the others on what to expect and how to handle the questions. She'd also be attending as their lawyer, which the agents legally had to allow. Luckily, she was also going to have some help today.

"You really didn't have to do this," she said.

Her boss waved a hand at her. "One of the perks of working for a law firm is an excellent defense team at your beck and call. Besides, it counts toward my pro bono."

Genevieve laughed and pulled open the door to the MIB office. It was a big building but not a pretty one. They'd built it to be functional, so it was boxy and gray.

The inside wasn't any better. Dull, burnt orange carpet muffled their steps as they walked to the receptionist desk. The walls were beige –– an unfortunate shade that looked dirty rather than neutral, though that could have been the glare of the fluorescent lighting reflecting off the carpet.

She smiled at the woman sitting behind the desk and got a blank look in return. "Genevieve Bisset, here for my appointment with Agents Icewind and Horan along with my lawyer, Ms. Susan Lau."

"IDs," the woman replied, holding out her hand. Once they'd both dug them out of their purses, she scanned them, then printed out temporary visitor passes they had to pin to their chests. "That way, third floor." She pointed toward some elevators to their left.

"Thank you," Genevieve said politely, not bothering to smile this time.

"Friendly bunch, aren't they?" Susan said as they walked away.

"Apparently."

Her boss had intimidated her when she'd first met her. She was gorgeous in a stop-and-stare kind of way, with sleek black hair and a slender frame. The more they'd worked together, the more she'd come to appreciate her intelligence and sharp wit. Susan didn't care who you were within the law firm, the only thing that mattered to her was the effort you put into your work.

The elevator let them off on the third floor, which looked exactly the same as the first except for the windows. The natural light did nothing to improve the look of things.

They arrived at the office designated in the summons and found the door already open. Agent Horan rose as soon as he spotted them in the hallway.

"You're early," he said with a smile as he rose from his desk, his eyes flicking from her to Susan. "And you brought company."

"Didn't want to keep you waiting," Genevieve said as she shook his hand. "This is my lawyer, Susan Lau."

"Ah, a lawyer wasn't necessary, this is a casual chat, but of course she's welcome to stay," he said with an easy smile. "Have a seat, my partner will be back in just a moment."

Genevieve glanced at Susan, who had put on a neutral expression as soon as they'd walked in. Something about Horan made her skin crawl. She didn't like his attitude or his subtle digs. No one in their right mind went to talk to someone investigating them without a lawyer.

They sat down in the two chairs across from Horan's desk. The budget must be thin these days based on the peeling leather on the armrests.

"I'll get the formalities out of the way while we wait on my partner," Horan said, that same, easy smile still plastered on his face. The longer he held it, the more disingenuous it appeared. "The MIB is investigating these no-magic zones. Since your pack was involved––"

"My client's pack was not involved, they were the victims of an attack," Lau interrupted with a fake smile of her own.

Horan cleared his throat and nodded. "Of course. Anyhow, with the appearance of the largest no-magic zone yet, we have a responsibility to the public to fully investigate the incident. And your pack's *alleged* involvement."

"Who is alleging the Hale pack had any involvement in the incident? It was clear from their statements and the police reports that they were victims in the attack. Is that in dispute?" Lau asked.

Horan waved her questions away. "This is a routine part of a thorough investigation. We have to rule out certain possibilities so that we can move forward with other leads. If it's not done now, it could be brought up in a future trial and raise reasonable doubt with a jury."

"Of course," Lau said, using that particular tone she saved for when she absolutely didn't believe what someone was telling her.

"I'm sorry, it appears I'm late," a woman said from behind them.

Genevieve glanced back at the other agent. Unlike Horan her expression was flat, bordering on irritated.

"This is my partner, Agent Icewind," Horan said, nodding at her as she walked around to stand behind his desk. "Icewind, this is Genevieve Bisset and her lawyer, Susan Lau."

Icewind shook their hands briefly then leaned against the wall behind his desk, sipping on a cup of coffee. "Please, continue."

She had pale blonde hair with a subtle blue tint to it. The severe expression on her face made it look like it might crack if she ever attempted to smile.

"Now that we're all here, let's get started," Horan said with a grin, like they were all hanging out for fun. She didn't like how dismissive he was. He either thought they were stupid or that pretending everything was fine would get more information out her.

He was going to be disappointed.

Horan pulled out a file folder and flipped it open, scanning through a list of information. "Your pack met with the sorcerer at this location, is that correct?" He pulled out a picture showing the ruins of the old, stone house, as well as the scene of the fight, and pushed it across the desk.

"I wouldn't say met with, but yes, that's where we fought the sorcerer in order to rescue our pack member, Ceridwen Gallagher," Genevieve said.

"And, before the incident, did you have any prior contact with this woman?" He pulled out another picture and slid it across the desk as well. It was of Siobhan. Dead.

Genevieve looked away immediately, not wanting to linger on the grotesque image. "No, I did not."

Susan flipped the picture over and slid it back toward Horan. "Is your intention to traumatize my client? This is uncalled for."

"Apologies," Horan said, spreading his hands magnanimously. "I'm simply trying to establish a timeline."

"I never met Siobhan while she was alive," Genevieve said firmly, feeling bile rise in the back of her throat despite her determination to not let this idiot get under her skin.

"Of course, I'm sorry to bring up these bad memories." Horan shuffled through the file, blessedly silent for a moment. "Let's move on to the days leading up to the incident. Was Ceri's kidnapping a surprise to you?"

"Of course. If we'd had any clue it was coming she never would have been taken like that."

Horan nodded and pulled out something she didn't expect to see at all. A picture of her and Paul. She wasn't even sure where it had been taken. "You have a close relationship with Paul Greer."

"My alpha sponsored Paul for his recent Trials, so yes, I do," Genevieve said, not liking what Horan was insinuating at all.

"How long have you known Paul?" Horan continued.

"Since before the attack. He helped me with a case after he successfully challenged the previous interim alpha. What does this have to do with anything?"

"Just establishing your connections." Horan pulled out a picture of what looked like a fiery comet shooting through the sky over Portland. "This is the only picture we have of the *alleged* demon involved in the attack. Did you have any contact with this demon?"

"No. We went over this a dozen times with the police."

"What did you see that night when your pack fought the sorcerer?" Horan pressed.

She bit down on a sigh. "We fought the sorcerer and Selena Blackwood –– whose whereabouts we've gotten no updates on, by the way –– and rescued Ceri. There was no demon around the no-magic zone. Only a sorcerer and a half-angel who ran away at the beginning of the fight, attacking Tommy on his way out."

A frown creased Icewind's forehead at Genevieve's answer, but she didn't comment. Horan continued his line of questioning but Genevieve did her best to pay attention to his partner's reactions. There was something off between them, almost like Icewind was surprised by what he was asking. That was...interesting. And possibly useful.

"I don't appreciate the implication that my client lied in her original statement, Agent Horan. Anyone who has gone through a traumatic event will struggle to remember details, which is why eye witnesses often disagree on things as simple as the color of a van at a crime scene. If you brought my client here just to throw out wild accusations, then we're going to have to end this interview now," Susan said, staring Horan down.

"I'm not making accusations, I'm just asking questions––"

"With all due respect, Agent, I've been in this business for a long time and I know an accusation when I see one. You're asking leading questions and attempting to trap my client needlessly. If this was, as you stated at the beginning, a casual chat, then your tone is out of line."

Icewind pushed off the wall and walked around to the side of the desk. "One last question, then we can call it a day."

A wave of anger passed over Horan's face at her interruption, but he leaned back in his chair and said nothing.

Susan nodded. "Go ahead."

"Do you have any knowledge concerning the whereabouts of the demon that was spotted in the area during these attacks?"

Genevieve looked her straight in the eye and told the truth. "No."

"Thank you, you're free to go. Have a good day."

She didn't hesitate to get up and follow Susan out of the office, though she motioned for her to walk a little slower once they got a few feet away.

"Have you seen my keychain? The one with the flower in it?" Icewind asked, a tension to her voice that seemed like it was leftover from the interrogation.

"No, did it fall off somewhere or something?" Horan asked dismissively.

"I don't know. Must have."

The conversation continued with nothing of importance mentioned. They must know how good werewolf hearing was and were expecting her to try to listen in.

She climbed onto the elevator after Susan but felt no relief when the doors slid shut. This wasn't over, not by a long shot. They were just getting started.

CHAPTER 38

TOMMY

Tommy stared at Woggy and the new pixie. Woggy wouldn't meet his eyes, just kept signing for dinner, then pointing at his 'friend'. He was pretty sure this meant Woggy had a girlfriend -- who was probably getting in through the cat door they'd installed for Captain Jack and Woggy, which, in hindsight, was inevitably going to end up with the whole pixie swarm in the house.

With a sigh, Tommy grabbed two cans of tuna. There was no way he'd be the one to break up this romance.

"Are you sure you're okay?" Amber asked, following Ceri into the kitchen.

"I'm annoyed but otherwise fine," Ceri said, adjusting her bun on the top of her head. "I'm more worried about Deward."

Tommy had an irrational urge to shift and run into the city and just tear it apart until he found his friend. He sighed. That wouldn't help anything though.

"You're sure he killed someone?" he asked as he threw away the tuna can wrapper.

Ceri's expression softened. "No. I saw blood on his hands, but there could be another explanation. Scrying isn't an exact magic, it shows impressions and emotions more than exactly what is happening in the moment."

Genevieve's car turned into the driveway.

"Finally, she worked so late today," Tommy said, hurrying to meet her at the front door. They'd been waiting for her to compare notes for the day. Even Derek was already back.

"Wait, why are there two pixies?" Amber asked.

Ceri laughed at her.

Tommy pulled the door open just before Genevieve reached for the handle. "Come on, dinner is on the table. We've been waiting on you."

"Sorry," she said tiredly. "I have to catch up on all the work I missed while I was at that stupid interrogation."

"I take it that went well?" he asked, raising an eyebrow.

"Be glad I went first."

He wrapped an arm around her shoulder and steered her toward the dining room. "Pizza will make it all better. We got one with all meat, just for you."

"You know the way to a girl's heart," Genevieve said, dumping her bags on the floor and rushing ahead of him.

Derek jogged downstairs, his hair wet from his shower. "Did I miss anything?"

"Nope, Gen just got back."

Once the pack was finally corralled into the same room, stuffing their faces with pizza, Amber took her place at the head of the table.

"Ceri, can you catch Gen up on what you found out with the trolls today?"

Ceri swallowed her bite of food and nodded. "In order to see if I could work with the trolls to break that curse on the tunnels, we decided to practice casting a spell together. We scryed Deward. What I saw wasn't very clear, but I believe Deward was fighting someone alongside that elf. It looked like there was blood on his hands. The elf said something about lies and tricks, and that something was hidden. I think they may be looking for this thing together."

"Any clue what that thing is?" Gen asked.

"Nope." Ceri sighed. "The other bit of bad news was that the elf noticed me scrying and managed to overpower me. Doing that alone, while I was channeling the spell with the trolls, means she's way more powerful than any elf I've ever met. Kind of like a sorcerer is more powerful than a solitary witch."

"Illya did say the magic she used to kill Laurel was corrupt. Maybe she's some kind of elf sorcerer," Tommy suggested.

"It's looking like that might be accurate," Ceri agreed.

Amber picked a black olive off her piece of pizza with a scowl. "How'd the meeting with the MIB agents go, Gen?"

Genevieve grabbed a third piece of pizza. "Horan is bad news. He spent the whole time trying to unsettle me. He even shoved a picture of Siobhan in my face with..." she waved her hand in front of her eyes, "just to upset me I think."

Ceri shoved her plate away, looking like she'd lost her appetite. Derek put his hand on her thigh under the table and she leaned against his arm.

"However, his partner doesn't seem to be on the same page with him. They might be playing us but I think the tension I sensed there is real. And I think we can use it."

Amber nodded. "Horan is definitely up to no good. Tommy and I searched the murder scene today––"

"You did *what?*" Genevieve demanded, her voice cracking in outrage.

"We were careful. And I'm glad we did, because while we were there Horan showed up and planted some evidence. You still have it Tommy?"

He nodded and pulled out the flower. "It's broken off something else. No clue what. I thought he'd be planting something to frame Amber. This has got to be for someone else though."

Genevieve got up and walked over, taking it from his hand. "A keychain. With a flower."

"What?" he asked, completely confused.

"As we were walking away I heard Agent Icewind asking Horan if he'd seen her keychain. One with a flower in it. She'd apparently lost it."

"Wait, he's framing his partner for the murder?" This was completely unexpected.

"That's what he meant by 'his problem' when he was talking on the phone," Amber said, dropping her pizza on her plate. "Remember? When he was on the phone he said 'I'm dealing with my problem, you deal with yours'. Maybe Icewind is getting in the way of whatever agreement he has with Carter."

"We have to warn her somehow," Ceri said quietly, still looking pale.

"I agree, but since we've thwarted Horan's plan to frame her, I think we need to wait and see how he reacts before we tell her," Genevieve said, looking over at Amber. "We need a way to get Icewind on our side and get her help. I think we'll need a way to prove Horan is out to get her before she'll fully trust us."

Tommy sighed. "If Deward is connected to the person that murdered Laurel like we think, we also need to find him before the MIB solves the murder. If they ever do with the way Kadrithan tracked blood everywhere."

"I need to confirm that with him, just in case there is someone else involved we don't know about," Amber said, picking at the crust of her pizza absently.

They'd learned a lot today but were left with more questions than answers. As usual.

His mind went to the book he'd found in Thallan's tower. Part of him didn't want to admit he'd been in there snooping around, but he knew he had to tell the others. Too much was at stake to be keeping secrets.

"There's something else I need to show you guys. I'll be right back." He hurried up to his room and grabbed the book. It still stunk of sulfur and black magic.

Ceri stiffened immediately when he walked back into the dining room. "Where did you get that?"

"You're not allowed to get bent out of shape about where I got it," Tommy said firmly. "We need to know more about the history between angels and demons so we can figure out what's going on."

Ceri sighed. "You stole it from Thallan's house, didn't you?"

No one had seen him. He was sure of it. Ceri would have dragged him away from Thallan's house by her ear if she'd suspected anything. "How'd you know?"

"You don't have a car. It had to be from somewhere pretty close."

He shrugged and nodded. "It was up in that tower thrown in a corner, so he probably won't even notice it's missing."

"What's in it?" Amber asked.

"Tons of old black magic spells." He flipped it open to the back and handed it to Ceri. "And instructions on how to summon a demon. I'm guessing this is how he summoned Kadrithan and got the mark."

Ceri frowned at the old book as she read the spell. "I'll copy down this spell, but then I'm burning this."

"That bad?" Derek asked with a chuckle.

"It's disgusting and dangerous in the wrong hands. So yes, that bad."

"The important part is one of the warnings with the summoning spell." He walked around to Ceri's side and pointed out the paragraph. "It basically says anyone with a demon mark should be more worried about the 'Great Deceivers' than the demons."

"There's someone worse than the demons out there?" Amber asked skeptically.

He shrugged. "Bad enough some black magic witches left a warning about them."

Ceri drummed her fingers against the page. "This is *really* old. They could have been referring to any number of things, even another coven. Witches can be a little...dramatic sometimes."

"Or they could be talking about the angels," he suggested quietly.

"That's a stretch, Tommy," Ceri said tiredly. "I know you think the angels are up to no good, and honestly I'm starting to agree, but this doesn't prove anything."

"I'll keep looking. Maybe Deward's family will know something. Kadrithan did suggest the trolls were more reliable historians."

Ceri nodded. "I'm visiting them again tomorrow. I can ask."

"I want to come with you."

"It'll have to be after your meeting with the MIB agents," Genevieve interrupted.

He covered his face with a groan. He'd forgotten about that. "Are you sure I can't skip it?"

Genevieve snorted. "That wouldn't look suspicious at all."

He stared at the leftover pizza sullenly, his skin crawling with irritation. "I'm going to go for a run."

"I'll go with you," Genevieve volunteered, surprising him. She hesitated at his expression. "If that's okay?"

"Yeah, company would be nice." Normally, he'd want to just be alone, but the wolf craved the comfort of pack. Genevieve was also the least likely to pry. She understood the need to just run and forget about the real world for a little bit.

CHAPTER 39

AMBER

They needed dirt on Carter, and Amber had an idea how they might be able to find some on short notice. However, this was one trip she was making alone. There was no way she ever letting any of the pack near Bram if she could help it.

Visiting the old bat wasn't exactly her idea of a good time, but sacrifices had to be made. In this case, her blood. And her mental well-being.

She'd let Genevieve know where she was going and why she needed to see Bram alone. Her beta hadn't been happy about it but had agreed it was the best way to approach the vampire.

Turning down the narrow road, she spotted the old, brick building the vampire lived in. The same guard was standing near the chain link fence. Hopefully he remembered her, or this might be a very short visit.

She rolled down her window as she came to a stop and leaned her head out with a smile. "Hello again."

The vampire pushed back his hood as he approached, returning her smile. His yellow eyes reflected back the light of her headlights for a moment until he passed the hood of her truck. "Shane's friend, welcome back. What brings you here today?"

"I'd like to talk to Bram, if he's available."

The vampire looked over his shoulder and she heard someone say something, but couldn't make out what over the rumble of the diesel engine.

"You're in luck, he is. Go ahead."

The gate slid open and she drove through, parking in the same open spot as last time. There was a different guard at the door this time but they let her through without comment, seeming completely uninterested in who she was or what she was doing here.

As she walked in, the sickening smell of blood hit her just as hard as it had the last time. She ground her teeth together and forced herself to keep walking. Shane wasn't here to distract her, something she was already beginning to regret. He would have come if she had asked. This whole going-it-alone thing might backfire horribly.

The only light inside the old building came from the TV. A couple of people were sprawled out on one of the couches scattered throughout the room watching it or snoring.

She paused at the top of the stairs that led to the basement. Bram was willing to see her but that didn't mean he'd actually help her. Taking a deep breath, she walked down the stairs.

The door at the bottom opened immediately and Bram smiled up at her, shirtless, just like last time. His pale eyes glowed faintly in the darkness. "Welcome back, Amber."

"Thank you for seeing me," she said politely.

He grinned at her, his sharp incisors making it look more menacing than friendly. "Of course, any friend of Shane's is always welcome here. Please, come in." He stepped back and waved her inside.

She nodded and jogged down the last couple of steps. The room was just as she remembered. Those creepy paintings covered the walls. The ones that wouldn't fit were stacked in corners or still propped up on blood-spattered easels.

"What brings you here today? Or are you here simply to have your portrait done again?" he asked hopefully.

"I figured a portrait was part of the deal," she said carefully.

"It does foster a sense of…generosity in me," he said, waving his hands with a dramatic flourish.

"Before we start, I did have one question. Just something I've been curious about, if you don't mind answering."

He nodded as he grabbed a fresh canvas, setting it on an easel. "Go ahead, you've peaked my interest."

"Did you know Selena Blackwood was helping the sorcerer?"

"I suspected many things and had proof of none."

"Why didn't you warn me?"

He paused, meeting her eyes. "I gave you what you came to me for. Nothing more, nothing less."

She shoved her hands in her pockets with a sigh. "Right."

"Would you like to draw the blood yourself again?" he asked, gesturing to the draw kit already laid out on the table.

"Definitely." She sat down and opened up the supplies she needed. She wasn't nearly as nervous last time. The shock of what Bram did had worn off. It was definitely weird, but so was turning into a wolf. She could handle weird.

Amber slid the needle in, relieved she got it on the first try. It had been a while since she'd drawn blood. Other than her last visit, it was longer than she wanted to think about.

"What brings you to my lair today?" Bram asked, pupils dilating at the first squirt of blood into the tube.

"Alpha Jason Carter." She readied the next tube. It was filling quickly because of her rapid heartbeat. Maybe she wasn't as calm as she thought. "Someone is paying him to give false evidence to the MIB in an attempt to prove my pack was involved with the sorcerer that created the no-magic zones around here."

"That isn't very nice," Bram said, sounding amused.

She switched the tubes out. He picked up the first one and held it up to the light, rolling it back and forth to watch the blood cling to the sides.

"No, it isn't. Anyhow, I need to discredit him. Or find something on him that I can use to get him to stop." She resisted to urge to snatch the tube back before he started making out with it or something equally disturbing. "I know he's done something he shouldn't have. A guy with an ego that big will have screwed up, probably in a big way. I don't have a lot of time to find out how. Can you help me?"

Bram swayed in rhythm with her heartbeat. "I could."

She ground her teeth together, willing herself to stay calm, but her increased heartbeat gave away her irritation. "Why do I feel a but coming?"

"I doubt I could find what you need in time to help you." He collected the tubes and rose from the chair opposite her. "And to be frank, which I do think you prefer, you can't afford me. The blood gets you a meeting but it does not pay for what you're asking. The risk is too great."

She stuck the bandaid on her arm. Crooked. And wrinkled. She tried pointlessly to smooth it down, wishing once again that she'd brought Shane. "Why don't you think you could find it in time?"

"You are currently three moves behind, darling. Whoever is plotting against you has been doing so for weeks, if not longer. It's too late to cut off the ambush. You are already surrounded. Metaphorically, of course." Bram emptied the vials of her blood into a bowl, careful to get every last drop, then moved to his canvas.

"So, what? I just have to walk into this metaphorical ambush?"

He shrugged, dipping his brush in the palette. "You have to beat them outright."

She sighed. "You make it sound easy."

"It is simple, not easy. There is a difference."

His paintbrush moved in quick strokes across the canvas. The smell of her own blood drifted through the room, sending a shudder through her. There was something horribly intimate about letting him use something that had been inside her like this.

"You said I couldn't afford you but...what if I could come up with the money some-how? What kind of price tag are we talking about?" She didn't want to walk out of here empty-handed. Maybe she could scrape the money together, or get a loan. There had to be a way.

Bram added a few more strokes before answering. "You are close to seeing what is happening. The big picture. But you do not understand what you are asking of me."

The angels. The MIB. Carter. Ito. It was all politics and grudges that ran deep. "You'd have to pick a side, wouldn't you? If you helped me with this."

Bram inclined his head with a smile. "Bravo, you *are* learning."

She put her head in her hands. "I hate politics. I didn't want any of this crap."

Bram laughed. "This is why I like you. You're straightforward. What you see is what you get. That is also why they hate you. You've upset the natural order."

"If they had just left me alone, their precious natural order could have stayed how it was," she grumbled, rising from her chair. "Thanks for the advice. It was helpful even if it wasn't what I was hoping for."

His pale eyes met hers. "It was my pleasure."

"I'll see myself out. You can keep the painting this time too." She headed toward the exit, mentally patting herself on the back for not sprinting away.

"Won't you look at it this time?" Bram asked.

She paused on the stairs. She didn't want to look at the painting but she also didn't want to piss Bram off. He seemed to like her. Enough to indulge her questions at least. It's not like it would hurt anything to look at the painting even if she did hate it.

"Fine." She turned around but didn't find what she was expecting. Last time, she'd looked dangerous. All fire and anger. This was...different. "That's not me, that's..."

"It is you, very much so," he crooned, fingers caressing the edges of the canvas.

A pair of deep red eyes stared out of the face of a wolf, teeth bared in a warning snarl. There was still anger and a sense of threat, but the eyes were *powerful*. They were *alive*.

She tore her gaze from the painting and saw that Bram was staring at her.

"Yes, I captured you very well." He smiled, his long, white fangs pressing into his lower lip.

CHAPTER 40

KADRITHAN (ANGEL)

"Everything has changed. This pack has been pulled into this and there is nothing we can do to change that now." Kadrithan filled his glass. This wasn't an evening for temperance.

"Pour me one as well," Zerestria said tiredly. She accepted the glass and settled herself on the opposite end of his chaise lounge. "What did you tell them."

"The bare minimum. They know Laurel was my mark but nothing of the task I gave her." He took a drink, letting the elven whisky burn its way down his throat. "However, if this continues, they will find out more soon. Whatever this troll has gotten mixed up in will bring them into direct opposition of the angels. Of Raziel himself."

"You must delay the explanation until the right moment. As long as your mark is on their alpha, you control the pack, but having their trust would be even more powerful."

Kadrithan stared blankly into his glass, contemplating everything that had happened. "I can handle the pack and Amber. What troubles me is this elf."

"Me as well," Zerestria admitted. "This murder has hurt our plans but I do not think that was the reason for it."

"Neither do I." He thought back to the crime scene. Laurel's body had been put on display. There was a message there, though he had no idea who it was meant for. Raziel? Himself? Someone else entirely? "There's something that's bothering me."

"And what is that?"

"Killing Laurel is pointless. She was the third-favorite mistress of Raziel, not the first. Torture and kidnap make more sense. There were things she knew that might help someone move against Raziel but he won't care that she is dead, he will simply replace her."

"Perhaps they had a personal grudge. Laurel had a life and enemies outside of Raziel."

"Perhaps."

"The only way to know for sure is to find Laurel's murderer. Venali finally managed to get that mark he's been after the last month. Use him however you need for this."

Kadrithan gave her a blank stare. "You are so generous."

"The angels moved against the western front after a decade of peace. Our resources are drawn thin."

The reminder that he was being kept away from the fighting set a mixture of guilt and anger boiling in his gut. "Some days I think we should just fight them and end this."

"That is a battle we would lose and you know it. I am just as frustrated at being stuck in this empty castle as you but we have a job to do. The fate of this war depends on us, Kadrithan. We will never defeat the angels so long as we are bound by this curse."

There was a brief knock, then the door to his study swung open. A messenger scurried in, carrying a sealed envelope. "Venali sends an urgent message."

Zerestria grabbed the envelope and tore it open, reading the note quickly. "Leave us."

The messenger shut the door behind himself.

She turned to him with a frown. "Someone broke into Raziel's estate. Two guards were killed."

"That escalates things."

"It certainly does. If they took it——"

"We weren't sure Raziel kept it there. That's why I needed Laurel to find out." Still, the idea that the very thing they'd been hunting had been snatched out from underneath their noses at the last moment was enough to make him want to punch a hole in the wall.

Zerestria was silent for a beat. "We have to know."

"Send Venali to deal with those MIB agents. I have to search for this elf personally."

She nodded. "Time is of the essence."

CHAPTER 41

EVANGELINE

Light flooded her room, waking Evangeline out of a dead sleep.

"We've gotta go. Get up now," Katarina said, tossing her always packed backpack at her. She caught it right before it hit her face.

"What's wrong? Are they here?" she asked, scrambling out of bed to shove her feet in her shoes. She slept with her clothes on now. They never knew when they'd have to move again. She hoped it was somewhere warmer this time.

Tommy thought she was still in Mexico relaxing on a beach. Unfortunately, that had only lasted a few days before she'd been woken up at a dawn and told to run.

"How do they keep finding us?" she asked as she ran after Katarina into the main room.

"We don't know, which irritates me," Katarina said with a scowl.

Charlie burst through the front door. "Let's put a little hustle on it, ladies."

"Where is––"

"Waiting in the Jeep."

She'd begged her uncle to send her mother somewhere safe but apparently the safest place was with them. He couldn't spare the resources to assign anyone else to protect Eloise, and her end of the deal required her to stay with Evangeline as long as she was alive regardless.

Despite the darkness, she saw clearly as they ran to the Jeep. She hopped in the back, sliding over to sit next to her mother, who grabbed her hand to reassure her.

Katarina sat in the back with her rifle, eyes scanning the snow covered trees around them. The woods were eerily silent.

Charlie slammed on the accelerator, throwing her back into the seat. They bounced over the uneven terrain, tires slipping in the snow that had built up on the narrow road overnight.

She squeezed her mother's hand, wishing she wasn't trapped in this hell. She should be with Tommy, helping him search for his friend.

It wasn't dying that scared her. It was how vulnerable everyone around her was. Charlie was human. Breakable and vulnerable like her mother. Katarina, for all her skill with a gun and magic, was only one woman.

"Heads down," Katarina whispered.

Evangeline pulled her mother down, then draped over her shoulders, shielding her as much as possible. They'd argued about it the first time they'd had to do this, but her mother eventually accepted it since *she* could heal from a bullet wound fairly quickly but her mother couldn't.

They stayed perfectly silent as the Jeep rumbled down the road. She hated how much noise it made. It always felt like a giant neon sign pointing at them: HERE THEY ARE, COME KILL THEM.

"Three behind," Katarina whispered, before firing off a shot.

Evangeline covered her ears with her hands, trying to preserve some of her hearing. A second shot rang out, then a third.

"Two remaining, coming up left side."

"We got company on the front side too," Charlie said, slamming on the accelerator. "Eva, go."

She opened the door and burst out into the open, kicking it shut behind her. The momentum of the Jeep gave her the speed she needed to charge at the attackers ahead of them. It was wolves, two of them. Their eyes glowed yellow in the headlights.

In the time since she'd killed that half angel Zachariah, she'd learned a few things. She thrust both hands out ahead of her and fire bloomed from her palms in a wave. It swept toward the wolves who separated, running in opposite directions to avoid the attack.

Steady gunfire continued behind her as Katarina laid down cover fire. She'd hold them off as long as she could.

Evangeline lifted her hands, lighting a ring of fire around the now stopped Jeep. If they wanted them, they were going to have to pass through it to get to them.

A howl rose up from the forest. Another joined it, then another and another. She couldn't tell where they were coming from, just that they were surrounded. The haunting sound made her skin crawl.

She lifted off the ground with a hard push from her wings and searched the darkness for the mercenary pack. If she could find the alpha, it would de-stabilize them.

There was a yelp and a clump of trees shook. Katarina must be in the woods now. She spotted a flash of eyes amongst the trees and dove at them, sending flames before her. At first, she'd been hesitant to do this sort of thing, but she'd burn down the entire forest if that's what it took to survive and protect her mother.

She landed in a small clearing, smoke thickening the air as the trees burned around her. They were close. She could feel them watching her.

Paws thudded into the ground behind her and she shot up, flipping backwards as the wolf passed beneath her. They always went for the legs first to slow you down, just like real wolves. She'd learned that the hard way.

A bullet hit the side of the wolf and he stumbled, sliding to a stop against the tree. She heard the next one coming and met it head on with a blast of fire that rolled over it. It rolled in the dirt trying frantically to put out the flames but didn't have a chance before another bullet drove through its head.

She and Katarina were a good team.

"Kat!" Charlie's shout cut through the woods.

Evangeline ran back toward the Jeep, heart pounding in her chest. They'd gone too far, gotten too aggressive. This pack was smarter than the others. They weren't just chasing her.

The alpha was charging toward Charlie, unconcerned about the shotgun pointed at his face. Before Charlie could get a shot off, the massive wolf slammed him into the side of the Jeep. It raised its head, ready to strike, when the back of its skull exploded. The wolf slumped to the side, revealing her mother with the rifle still held to her shoulder.

"Charlie, you okay?" Eloise shouted.

"Peachy keen," he hollered back. "But stuck under this throw rug. He's heavy as hell."

A mournful howl went up, echoed by only one other wolf. She waited, standing between Charlie and the tree line until Katarina ran out, slinging her rifle over her shoulder.

"They're retreating. Let's go."

She pulled the dead alpha off Charlie and helped him up to his feet. There was a nasty gash on the back of his head from where he'd hit the Jeep and he wasn't standing up straight.

"They sure aren't screwing around anymore," Charlie said, spitting out a gob of blood.

"I don't understand," Evangeline said, tucking her hand in her sleeve and brushing glass off his shoulders.

"Something must have changed to give them a sense of urgency," Katarina said with a shrug. No matter what happened, it never seemed to phase her. She spilled blood with the same ease that she made a cup of tea in the morning.

Evangeline stared at the carnage around them feeling numb. They'd survived this attack but the next might be worse. The angels could send more people. They might send a sorcerer next time.

She curled her hand into a fist. When her uncle finally bothered to show up, he better be prepared to give her some answers.

CHAPTER 42

TOMMY

"You have quite the juvenile record," Horan said, pulling out a thick file. "Breaking and entering, theft, more theft, vandalism. The list goes on for a while. I'm surprised you managed to avoid jail time."

Tommy just stared at him. Was his record supposed to be a surprise? It's not like he'd forgotten. Everything he'd done had been in order to survive though and he refused to let some MIB stiff make him feel bad about it.

"You seem to be fond of bringing up things that have no relevance to the current investigation," Genevieve said, sounding bored.

The other agent stood behind Horan like some kind of silent guard. He couldn't get a feel for Icewind at all. She *looked* angry but her heartbeat was slow and even.

Horan gave Genevieve a sharp smile. "In my experience, the context of a person's life has great relevance to my investigations."

Icewind's eyes flicked to Horan and her frown deepened.

He shuffled through a thick file, unaware of his partner's disapproval. "In the weeks leading up to the incident with the sorcerer, you had contact with a woman named Selena Blackwood."

Tommy nodded. "Sure. She got me fired."

"Was this a chance meeting?"

"Pretty much. She had a grudge against Ceri and tried to hurt this pixie that's kind of our pet. I just got in the way."

"Interesting." Horan scribbled down a few notes.

"A grudge over a pixie?" Icewind asked, raising a skeptical eyebrow.

He nodded. "It sounds dumb but that's what started it."

"A pixie is an odd choice in pet. Most people consider them pests," Icewind said.

"They shouldn't be either –– they can understand us and talk with us. We're teaching Woggy sign language."

Both of Icewind's eyebrows shot up. "Sign language?"

"The pixie is a quick learner," Genevieve said with a sharp smile.

Horan cleared his throat. "Have you had any contact with Selena Blackwood since the incident with the sorcerer?"

"Unfortunately, no."

"Unfortunately?" Horan asked, looking up at him.

"I'd rather she wasn't out in the world doing who knows what. I'm surprised the police haven't been able to find her after all this time."

"It is interesting how completely she has disappeared." The way he phrased it sounded like an accusation. Tommy resisted the urge to roll his eyes.

"I spoke with your father yesterday and was surprised to learn you'd had no contact with him for a very long time. He was concerned to hear you had joined a werewolf pack."

"Why the hell are you contacting my father? He has literally nothing to do with this," Tommy objected, unable to stop some anger from leaking into his voice. Even Icewind looked shocked, her heartbeat picking up in pace for the first time.

Horan looked up, mock surprise on his face. "I was simply doing my job, of course. I didn't realize it would upset you. Your father did express an interest in reconnecting, by the way. He has been looking for you for a while."

"I highly doubt that," Tommy said drily.

"Since you do seem to have a contentious relationship, I should warn you that he might try to contest your current, uh, living situation," Horan said, waving dismissively at Genevieve. "Perhaps that's something you can work out before he contacts the local police."

"Amber became his legal guardian the moment he submitted to her as his alpha. Regardless of the legality of the bite, his father lost custody of him in that moment. The only person that could dispute that is Tommy himself." Genevieve stood, motioning for him to join her. "This meeting is over and you can expect a call from your superior after this. Threatening my client is out of line."

Icewind remained silent, looking at Tommy rather than Genevieve. He held her gaze, challenging her, and he could have sworn that for a moment she looked apologetic.

Horan leaned back and spread his arms. "I have not threatened Tommy in any way."

"We both know that's not true." She turned on her heel and Tommy quickly followed her as she marched out of the room.

They were silent until they got on the elevator.

His hands shook as he shoved them in his pockets. "You weren't bluffing about my dad not being able to do anything, right?"

"No, I wasn't." She reached over and squeezed his shoulder. "The case that established that was kind of a crap show, but you're safe. Your dad has no legal authority over you."

They hurried back to the parking lot. He sure as hell didn't want to stay here any long than necessary, and it seemed Genevieve didn't either.

"I don't trust that dude and I don't think the other agent does either," Tommy said as he buckled his seatbelt.

Genevieve frowned. "What gives you that impression?"

"She was uncomfortable the whole time. Didn't you see that look on her face?"

"I thought it was RBF or something. She's not the most pleasant of individuals," she said with a shrug.

He shook his head. "When Horan was being an asshole, *her* heartbeat sped up. She's not happy with what he's doing. We know Carter is feeding Horan information, and we suspect Horan is trying to frame her for Laurel's murder. I think if we talk to her she'll listen."

Genevieve tapped her fingers against the wheel, staring thoughtfully out the window. "You up for a little espionage?"

The memory of running through The Market trying to avoid Lockhart's men made him cringe. Everything he'd learned from *Werespy* had turned out to not work in real life. Who knew TV shows were so misleading.

"Uhhh, sure? Who are we spying on."

"RBF."

He followed her gaze and saw Icewind climbing in a beat up elf-spelled hybrid. Those things had been popular when they first came out until everyone realized how hard it was to get them fixed.

"Let's do it."

CHAPTER 43

GENEVIEVE

Genevieve kept her distance, making sure not to drive in the same lane as Icewind to reduce the chance of being spotted. Tommy thought they could trust her, and he was probably right. He had a knack for figuring people out, but she needed to be sure. She also wanted to go into a conversation like that with as much information as possible.

Tommy slumped down in his seat and sighed. "I think she knows we're following her."

She slowed down and let a car cut in between them. "Why?"

"Seriously? She took four right turns. We're literally going in a circle."

"Oh…" She'd been so focused on keeping track of her she hadn't noticed. "Look, I'm a lawyer not a spy. I guess I suck at this."

"We should just talk to her like normal people. Instead of creepy stalkers."

"I feel like walking up and saying 'hey, your partner is framing you for murder' is just a little sudden."

Tommy sat up suddenly. "She's pulling into that parking lot."

"Crap."

"We have to talk to her now or we'll look even guiltier."

Genevieve sighed and pulled in after Icewind. She parked a couple of spots away so as not to look threatening. Icewind didn't look all that concerned when she climbed out of her car though. In fact, she looked amused, which wasn't an expression she'd expected to see on the woman's normally stoic face.

"Come on," Tommy said, hopping out of the car.

She turned the car off and climbed out as well. This was embarrassing but there was no running away now.

"Fancy meeting you two here. Randomly," Icewind said drily as they approached.

"Yeah, huge coincidence," Genevieve agreed, crossing her arms.

Tommy took a deep breath. "We were following you."

"No kidding," Icewind said sarcastically. "Care to explain why, or should I just arrest you?"

"You can't arrest us—"

Tommy cut her off with a jab from his elbow. "Your partner is trying to frame you for the murder of Laurel Teller."

Genevieve wanted to sink into the ground. She couldn't believe he'd just blurted that out.

"Which we found out because he is also working with a werewolf named Jason Carter who is giving him false information to try to prove our pack was working with this sorcerer."

"So you're following me, and not him?" Icewind asked, looking at the two of them like they were insane. At this point, that was justified.

"I wasn't a hundred percent sure we could trust you," Genevieve said, trying to reclaim some of her dignity. "It's clear you and Horan don't exactly see eye to eye, but we didn't know how much you suspected, if anything."

Icewind shoved her hands in her pockets. "I see. Do you have any proof Horan is trying to frame me for a murder that -- as far as I know -- has absolutely nothing to do with you or your pack?"

Tommy looked at her and she sighed. He wanted to show her the keychain.

"I know I can't get anything legally binding, but I want your word that if my client shares this information with you, you will not use that information to press charges."

Both of Icewind's eyebrows shot up. "That's a pretty big ask."

She had no intention of budging on this. "Believe me, he did you a favor. You owe him."

They stared at each other for a moment, neither of them breaking eye contact.

"Fine," Icewind said, finally dragging her eyes to Tommy. "I give my word not to arrest you for whatever illegal thing you did that has supposedly helped me."

Tommy pulled the keychain out of his pocket. "Does this look familiar?"

Icewind snatched it out of his hand. "Where the hell did you get this?"

"So, hypothetically, I went to Laurel Teller's crime scene for a....really good reason. And, hypothetically, Horan showed up and hid it under a dresser in the room she was murdered in while telling someone on the phone that he was 'dealing with his problem' and that the forensics team would find it today when they did another sweep."

Icewind stared at the broken piece of her keychain. "That explains his foul mood this morning." She pocketed it and looked up at them. "You do nothing with this information. I'll handle it."

"You've got to be kidding me," Tommy said, completely exasperated. "He's working with someone that's trying to frame our pack for conspiring with a sorcerer. We have to take them both down!"

"This may come as a surprise, but breaking into a crime scene during an active investigation is *illegal*. No one at the MIB is going to take your word over his that he planted this at the crime scene." She crossed her arms, staring them both down. "I will file a report with Internal Investigations as soon as I have something concrete to give them. They'll handle it, and until they do, I'll be watching Horan."

"And Carter?" Genevieve asked.

Icewind sighed and pursed her lips. "He won't be a threat once Horan is under investigation. If you can find some kind of evidence that he's been talking to Horan, it could help. Just try to be a little more subtle than you were with me."

"We can be subtle," Genevieve said with more confidence than she felt.

Icewind snorted. "I'm sure."

"We'll be in touch soon. Hopefully." She grabbed Tommy by the elbow and nodded goodbye at Icewind, dragging her packmate back toward the car.

"If I catch you following me again, I will arrest you," Icewind shouted after them.

"Noted!"

Once they were safely back in the car, she turned to Tommy. "You're telling Amber when she gets done meeting with Vernier."

"Why me?"

"I'm your beta. I get to order you around."

Tommy rolled his eyes. "Just keep telling yourself that."

CHAPTER 44

AMBER

Amber shouldn't have answered the call but she'd been worried something bad had happened. She really did worry too much, and it had gotten her in trouble this time.

"Why didn't you tell me about Deward? I can help," Shane said, clearly frustrated.

"I just didn't think about it. We're handling it. I can't drag you into every bad thing my pack gets tangled up with." She pinched the bridge of her nose between her thumb and forefinger, not understanding why this was even an argument.

"You can drag me into all of it. I'm your friend, Amber. Hopefully more than that if you ever get a chance to be normal."

Silence hung between them for a long moment. "If you want to help us find Deward, then you can, but right now Ceri and another alpha are waiting on me to join them. I have to go."

"Alright. Just call me after, okay?"

"I will."

She hung up and hurried inside. It was a nice restaurant. Vernier seemed like the kind of person that preferred upscale establishments so she'd chosen based on that. Part of her felt stupid for wanting to impress Vernier, but she'd tried to remind herself it was reasonable. She needed to be on good terms with the alpha if Vernier was going to help them.

Taking a deep breath, she slowed her pace and her breathing before rounding the corner. She could feel where Ceri was through the pack bond. It led her toward the back of the restaurant to a booth tucked in the corner. Ceri was laughing about something. A full on belly laugh. That had to be a good sign.

Vernier spotted her first and waved. "I was starting to think you'd bailed."

"Sorry about that. Just had to take that phone call. Council business," Amber said as she slid in next to Ceri, who scooted over to give her a little more room.

The woman next to Vernier wasn't as strikingly beautiful as she was. In fact, Amber would describe her as plain. She had thin brown hair and a nervous expression, like she'd rather fade into the flowery wallpaper than make small talk.

"Amber Hale," she said, extending her hand across the table.

"Jean Yawler," the woman replied, shaking briefly with a clammy palm. "Nice to meet you."

"She's been Tatiana's shaman for almost four years," Ceri said with a smile. "They've learned so much together."

"That's awesome to hear. Did the two of you have a mentor? Or was it something you've learned on your own?" Amber asked, looking between the two of them. Tatiana seemed so untouchable compared to Jean. They were an odd pair.

Jean's eyes flicked to Tatiana, waiting for her to answer.

"When my great-grandmother was a child, her pack had one of the last shamans." Tatiana leaned in and crossed her arms on the table, smiling wistfully as if lost in nostalgia. "She passed that knowledge down to me. She didn't know everything of course, but it was enough to guide Jean and I after we found each other."

A waitress approached with a tray full of desserts. Amber leaned back as she set the plates on the table.

"We ordered one of each dessert since we've all already had lunch," Ceri said, dragging a big slice of raspberry cheesecake over to herself.

"We should meet more often," she said with a laugh.

"Want to split this disturbingly large piece of chocolate cake?" Tatiana asked, putting the plate in between them. It *was* worryingly large.

"Sure." She picked up her fork with a smile and carved out a bite. It was rich. The ganache filling between the layers was *almost* too much, but it had a thin mascarpone layer right above it that evened it out.

"Now," Tatiana said, patting her lips with a napkin and turned to Ceri. "You've been a shaman since you joined the pack and seem to be coping fine. Is there anything in particular you're struggling with?"

Ceri shrugged, picking at her cheesecake. "It hasn't really been a struggle. Not that part. We are learning as we go."

'That's great. You're a natural," Tatiana said with a grin.

Amber couldn't help but notice Jean's eyes darting away at that comment like she was embarrassed. "How's the brownie sundae?"

Jean nodded. "It's good."

"The Gallagher Coven was a rising star for a long time," Tatiana commented, licking her fork clean. "I'm surprised you left."

"Yeah, uh, sometimes family is…difficult. Amber and I found each other at the right time." Ceri stabbed her cheesecake with a little more force than was necessary. "Did you leave your coven to join the pack too, Jean?"

Jean's eyes finally moved to Ceri and she nodded. "I didn't have a coven. My family coven was already full. I would have made it eight witches."

"Ah. Lucky finding a pack then." Ceri smiled but Jean didn't reciprocate. "There's so much more potential as a shaman I think. Some things are harder but having the power of the pack behind me feels better than being in a coven ever did."

"I bet," Jean said with a nervous chuckle.

"Since Jean was never officially a part of her family's coven, she's never had access to a spell book. I've shared with her everything my grandmother left me." Tatiana patted Jean on the arm. "But it is more limited than the spells you would have access to. So, I'd like to propose a trade."

"A trade?" Ceri repeated.

Tatiana nodded. "Share spells with us and we will teach you more about what it means to be a shaman. What you can do. What you *shouldn't* do. The four of us can learn together."

"That's an interesting idea. We'll have to think about it and talk it over with the whole pack, but I really appreciate the offer. You're more helpful than I would have ever expected," Amber said, glancing at Ceri who was nodding along.

"Oh, Ceri, could I get your number real quick? I have Amber's but not yours." Tatiana pulled out her cellphone, looking at Ceri expectantly.

"Sure." Ceri took the proffered phone and put in her contact information.

Amber nudged the last bite of cake toward Tatiana but she waved it off as she took back her phone.

"All yours, Amber. I'm stuffed."

She finished it off gladly, glancing at Jean once again. There was just something about the way she sat there so quiet that bothered her. Maybe Jean was shy but...that's not what her gut was telling her. It reminded her of how Tommy acted at first. Scared and beaten down.

The waitress came by with the check, which Tatiana snatched up before Amber could grab it.

"My treat," Tatiana said with a grin as she handed it back to the waitress with her card. "We'll give your pack some time to think all this through. I don't want to pressure, even though I am excited about the potential here. I really think it'll benefit both our packs."

Ceri nodded. "It is an exciting opportunity. Let's keep in touch while we think it over."

"Absolutely." Tatiana glanced at Jean. "You done eating?"

Jean nodded.

"I have another appointment, so unfortunately we'll have to rush out, but I'm looking forward to chatting again." Tatiana stood, pulling on a tailored, knee-length jacket. "It really has been a pleasure."

Amber and Ceri slid out of the booth as well.

"Likewise," Amber said, shaking her hand.

They walked out of the restaurant as a group, parting ways in the parking lot. Tatiana had a limo there to pick her up, which was honestly not all that surprising.

"Who gets a limo to drive them around downtown Portland?" Ceri asked, shaking her head in disbelief.

"Something tells me Tatiana was born in a limo." She hesitated for a moment. "Did Jean seem off to you?"

Ceri wavered her hand. "I couldn't decide if she was shy or...scared of me. It's like I intimidated her."

"You can be kind of scary." She smirked at Ceri just in time to see her indignant response.

"I am *friendly*."

She snorted. "You are surprisingly competitive and a little bossy. Normally. However, today you were the most relaxed I've seen you in weeks. So if Jean was intimidated, I don't think it was by you."

"I guess we need to try to find out before we agree to do anything with Tatiana's pack. She's charming but that doesn't mean she's trustworthy."

"Yeah." Amber shook her head. "Nobody is that nice, are they?"

"I would say you're that nice but you're actually pretty grumpy."

"Ha. Ha," she said drily. "You needed to run some errands while we were out right?"

"Yeah, is that still okay?"

"I was going to see if Shane will meet me at that coffee shop that's a couple of blocks away while you run them." She shoved her hands in her pockets, feeling awkward. "Unless you want company?"

Ceri shook her head with a knowing smile. "No, it's fine. *Excellent*, even."

She rolled her eyes. "Don't you start too. Gen is bad enough."

Laughing, Ceri waved and headed toward the car. She pulled out her phone and texted Shane. Hopefully he could join her and she wouldn't end up sitting alone in a coffee shop for a couple of hours.

Can you meet me at that coffee shop on the corner of 24th and Thurman? I'll catch you up and get some much needed caffeine.

He responded immediately.

Sure. It's a date ;)

She felt herself smiling like an idiot as she put her phone away. Thankfully there was no one there to see her. Enjoying the cool weather, she took her time walking along the crowded sidewalk. The sunshine had drawn everyone out this weekend and downtown Portland was even busier than usual.

The crosswalk flashed the walk sign just as she reached the intersection, so she hurried across the road. It was quicker to cut through the alley up ahead than to follow the road around the whole block.

The alley was even cooler than the street. A breeze picked up, ruffling her hair around her face and carrying with it a strange scent. It smelled like magic but...different. Off somehow.

"Where is your demon?"

Amber almost tripped over her feet at the sudden question. She hadn't heard anyone coming. A hand closed around her arm as she turned to face whoever had asked. She jerked back with a snarl. "Let go––"

"Where?" the woman asked again, tapping her finger directly against the place on Amber's chest where the mark lay.

She looked at the woman in shock. What was the deal with everyone being able to see Angel or her demon mark all of a sudden?

CHAPTER 45

AMBER

"What are you talking about?" Amber asked, deciding to play dumb. There was something wrong with the woman that had stopped her.

"Lying and searching and...and..." The woman would have been beautiful if she'd been clean. As it was, it looked like she'd been rolling around in a dumpster.

Amber held her breath for a moment. The smell was hard to bear this close. "I'm sorry, I don't understand what you're saying."

"The...the...curses and eyes and lies," the woman insisted, her fingers digging into her arm hard enough to leave bruises.

"Do you need help?"

"So many." The woman shook her once, hard.

Amber reached over and gently pried her fingers off, unwilling to hurt someone that was suffering like this. As a nurse she'd had to treat people with mental illnesses before. Staying calm and not overreacting was important. She needed to get her phone out and call for an ambulance though. Someone in this state shouldn't be walking around the streets alone. If she grabbed someone else, she might get hurt.

"Can you come with me? I can get you lunch. Something to drink?" she asked asked gently.

Bright green light blinded her and she flew backward, hitting something hard. She tried to roll away but sharp points dug into her skin, holding her down.

It took all her control, but she forced herself to go still. The wolf strained against her hold. She wanted to shift badly.

A moment later her vision cleared and she blinked rapidly. The spell had trapped her in a tangle of thorny vines. Every time she moved they tightened, so she continued to hold still. The woman was gone.

Taking a deep breath, Amber found the pack bond in her mind and took stock of who was closest. Ceri was still nearby, but Genevieve and Tommy were closer. They'd probably all felt her momentary panic and the shock of pain through the bond. Alarm and worry was coming at her from all of them.

Genevieve was moving fast to her location. She must have shifted.

Amber sank into the pack bond. It was stronger than the last time she went this deep. Ceri's magic had woven into it, along with something else. The only thing she could relate it to was the power she felt on the nights of the full moon.

I'm okay, they left, she thought at the pack as hard as she could. They hadn't tested the whole communication through the pack bond thing that they were supposed to be able to do now that they had a shaman in the pack, but it was worth a try. Hopefully her intention had been clear. Some of Tommy's panic eased, but Ceri didn't relax and Genevieve didn't slow down at all.

She'd been pinned in an odd place. It was out of sight of passersby down the narrow alley. The vines covered her completely, though she could see through the cracks.

A door opened to her left from the back of some restaurant and a woman walked out carrying a trash bag.

"What the hell?" The woman stared at the mass of vines in annoyance. "Freaking elves. Why are they always trying to grow crap in weird places."

A vicious growl echoed off the concrete as Genevieve skidded around the corner, racing toward her. The woman with the trash screamed, threw the bag at Genevieve, and ran back inside.

Her beta slid to a halt about a foot from the vines, breathing heavily. Genevieve sniffed it carefully and circled around trying to see her more clearly.

"I'm okay, Gen," she said with as little movement as possible. "I just can't move or they tighten. Ceri is on her way too, I can feel her getting closer."

Genevieve sat on her haunches and growled unhappily at the vines. A piece of lettuce was stuck to her head from the trash she hadn't completely dodged.

"Yeah, I feel the same way." Her arms were in an awkward position. The temptation to just shift and try to tear her way out was getting greater by the moment.

With an angry huff, Genevieve shifted back. It was mesmerizing to watch the fur roll back. During the full moons she was always too caught up with the urge to run to notice things like that.

"How the hell did you manage to get caught like this?" Genevieve asked, crossing her arms.

"Crazy homeless woman. Guess I startled her. Where's Tommy?"

"I left him with the car. He's driving to us."

The back door to the restaurant opened again and two guys burst out, sliding to a halt when they saw Genevieve standing there butt-naked.

"What the––" the first one stammered, eyes wide.

"My alpha was attacked in the alley. Sorry to startle that other employee," Genevieve said with a big smile as she put her hands on her hips.

"Hello!" Amber said from where she was trapped, making both of them jump.

One of the men finally snapped his eyes back up to Genevieve's face. "Yeah, uh, no worries."

"Bye-bye now," Genevieve said, shooing them back inside. "We'll handle this, but the elf mafia could return at any moment and you do *not* want them thinking you're involved."

Both the men paled and scrambled back inside, slamming the door shut behind them. Amber was pretty sure she heard a deadbolt sliding into place as well.

"Elf mafia?" she asked with a laugh.

"They've actually been creating a serious issue around here lately. Don't you keep up with the news?"

"Not at all. I avoid it."

"Ceri is almost here," Amber said with relief. The areas where the vines touched were starting to itch.

"What have you gotten yourself into now?" a snarky voice asked. Angel was barely visible through the vines.

Amber shut her eyes and sighed. "Don't start."

"Who are you––oh. Hi, Kadrithan. You know it's rude to appear to just Amber, right?"

The pull on the demon mark increased and Angel stepped out of the shadows looking more or less solid. His face wouldn't quite come into focus though. "You're the only one who ever *wants* to see me, Genevieve."

She snorted. "I'd just rather see you than know you're floating around invisible, insulting my alpha."

"Such loyalty," he mused, his tone suggesting he didn't think that was a good thing at all.

"Alternatively, you could just go away," Amber suggested. Her humiliation didn't need to be seen by anyone else.

"I second that," Ceri said, appearing at the end of the alley, her purse slung over her shoulder. "We were barely apart for five minutes and you're already in trouble. You're lucky I was already in town with you or you'd have been waiting for a half hour while I drove here."

"Next time I'll plan better," Amber said drily.

Ceri stopped next to Genevieve and looked at the vines curiously. "So, what happened?"

"The unfortunate combination of magic and a mental illness. I should have just called the police right away."

"Ah. This looks like elf magic. Are you sure it wasn't…could whoever took Deward be targeting you?"

Amber shrugged, and immediately regretted the movement when the vines tightened. "I doubt it. The lady was completely out of it."

She dug around in her purse for a moment, then pulled out a small, glass bottle. "This will only hurt a little bit."

"What––"

A flash of light and heat burst over her. She bit down on a scream. The vines retreated immediately and she shoved free of their grasp, and whatever the hell Ceri had thrown on her.

Someone grabbed her arm and jerked her farther away, lifting her off her feet. She stumbled on the landing and had to cling to Genevieve to stay upright.

Panting and still shaking from the shock of the pain, she whirled on Ceri. "Only a little bit?"

The witch laughed at her. "Telling you it's going to hurt a lot doesn't help. It's like ripping off a bandaid, I just had to do it."

"The way you yelped *was* amusing," Angel agreed.

Ceri smiled at him before catching herself and crossing her arms with a frown. "Are you sure this wasn't related somehow? Could someone have paid the elf to attack you?"

She shrugged. "If they did then the attacker was a great actor and a terrible assassin. She seemed legitimately mentally ill. It was just bad luck."

"I don't like the timing," Angel said, walking around the burnt remnants of the vines.

"I dislike agreeing with the demon, but...I don't like the timing either," Ceri admitted. "It's way too much of a coincidence for you to be randomly attacked by an elf...while we're hunting down an elf."

"Well..." Amber itched at a dry spot on her arm that was still healing from the light burn she'd received. "She did grab me and ask where my demon was. So it is a little suspicious."

Angel's head snapped up. "What?"

"I was heading to the coffee shop to meet with Shane. The elf asked as I was walking by, then grabbed me. I thought it was just a random question..." she trailed off, feeling a little stupid based on the way everyone was staring at her. Something about the woman had just made her not think twice about what she said.

"You're normally just as suspicious as I am," Angel said, drifting around her.

Her head began to ache as she tried to recall exactly what the woman had said. "Eyes... and lies..." Her vision swam and she had the urge to run. They shouldn't be asking these questions. The woman was crazy, it didn't matter. "It was nothing. Y'all are overreacting. I should go before I'm late."

"Amber, look at me," Angel demanded sharply.

She put her hands over her ears and shook her head. The wolf howled wildly in her mind, thrashing against her control.

Warm hands closed around her arms and jerked them away. Her head snapped up, gaze locking with Angel's. His eyes burned with power.

"What is happening to her?" Genevieve yelled in the background.

"A curse is affecting her," Ceri said tensely.

Amber couldn't see any of them. The demon's gaze held her in place. It felt like he was looking *into* her.

Fight it, his voice echoed in her mind. *You're stronger than this. Draw on the pack bond.*

The wolf crashed to the forefront and pulled on the bond with all her might. Amber felt her consciousness wavering and let the wolf take control as much as she could without shifting. Something was wrong but the wolf knew what to do. She knew how to fight it.

Power rushed into her from the pack, laced with a hot, violent magic she'd never felt before. It had to be Angel's. She didn't think he could really act without a demon's mark in return, but it seemed he could.

His grip on her arms tightened and he ground his teeth together. She felt his hands begin to tremble as she fought through the tangle of the curse that had latched onto her mind.

A screech lanced through her mind and the curse snapped. At the same moment, Angel shouted in pain and disappeared.

Amber blinked and found herself staring up at the sky. Ceri poured a cool, sweet liquid over her face that washed away that last of the confusion.

"What happened?"

"I don't know, but we need to find that elf. Now," Amber said pushing Ceri away so she could stand. "She knew Kadrithan by name and I think she has Deward. Or the curse does."

"What?" Ceri asked in confusion.

"The curse garbled her words. She was asking me where Kadrithan is because she knows he is looking for Raziel's key, whatever that is. She said she's seen many futures and that we have to find it soon." She stood and looked around. "Where is Kadrithan?"

"He vanished," Ceri said as she packed up her bag. "Worry about him later. Let's try to catch up with the elf."

Amber pressed a hand to her demon mark. It felt *strained*. What had he done?

CHAPTER 46

CERI

"Can you smell her?" Ceri asked, following Amber as she paced back and forth along the sidewalk. This should be going faster.

"Her scent is everywhere, then it completely disappears. Sorry, I'm not actually a bloodhound," Amber grumped at her. There were dark circles under her eyes.

"I can't track it either," Genevieve said, clearly annoyed. "Tommy, what about you? Anything?"

He shook his head. "It's just like in the tunnels. She's got to be hiding her scent somehow. Has Kadrithan come back yet?"

Amber shook her head. "No and the mark feels...strained and weird. Kind of like it did when my wolf banished him."

Ceri looked around them, taking in this area of the city. Tall trees grew up between the tightly packed buildings which mostly housed coffee shops, pizza, and a couple of elf cafes that offered meals enhanced with magic. It was after lunch now, so the area was quieting down.

Tiring of the wait, she dug through her bag, hoping she had something to make this easier. Chalk for a circle of protection. A necklace with a crystal pendant that *might* work. She also had the totem she had created which would give her spells a little extra oomph. "I could try a tracking spell."

Amber deflated a little. "I think we're going to have to. It's like she walked in circles then vanished."

"She's crazy, but she's also powerful, as evidenced by her rooting you like she did. And noticing me during the scrying attempt. Come on, I need to go back to the place she attacked you."

Amber followed her. "Why do we need to go back there?"

"White magic tracking spells are finicky. The best focus I can use for it is a place where the target recently cast magic."

Tommy and Genevieve jogged over, trailing after them. They hadn't gone far from the alley. She could still feel the magic tingling over her skin when she turned between the two buildings. The vines, once green, were already black and decaying.

"I don't have much time," she said, hurrying to standing in the place Amber had lain.

She grabbed the chalk and drew a quick circle of protection. It would be stronger if it were carved into dirt, but she needed to do this where the elf and Amber had their confrontation, and the area was all concrete.

Grabbing the pendant next, she held the crystal between her palms and slowly filled it with magic. It would act both as a battery and a magnet, drawn inexorably toward its target.

Once it was filled, she stepped into the center of the circle and focused intently on their target. The elf's magic lingered in the air like a bad smell.

"*Quaere invenique.*" The pendant zoomed out from between her palms like a dart, catching on the necklace that she had wrapped around her fingers.

"This way," she said, leading them to the left in the direction the pendant was pointing.

"That would have been useful while you were...." Amber trailed off.

Ceri forced herself to smile. "It probably would have saved you some time. It's too bad they can't be made ahead of time. The magic would run out by the time you needed it."

"Ah, figures."

Amber's phone rang and she cursed when she saw the caller ID. "I forgot about Shane."

"Talk to him. You can catch up in a minute, we won't confront her without you if we find her," Ceri said, waving her away.

Tommy jogged up to walk next to her. "Can you tell how far away this elf is?"

"No, only the direction. It's a pretty limited magic. Though, it does have a range of a hundred miles, so she's still in the state."

"Great," Tommy muttered.

"How are you holding up?"

"Fine other than feeling utterly useless."

"I--" The pendant slipped out of her fingers as it was drawn abruptly downward. Ceri stopped and stared at the sidewalk. "She's below us."

Tommy looked down at the ground as well. "Think anyone would notice if we dug a big hole in the street?"

"That *might* be a little obvious."

"Maybe we can go down a storm drain or something," he suggested, eyeing a nearby manhole.

Genevieve jogged over. "What's going on?"

She gestured at the pendant. "Somehow, the elf is below us. I assume more tunnels. I really don't understand why the witches burrowed under everything in the area, but apparently they did."

"Then it has to be connected to the tunnels Deward disappeared in. You and the trolls can break the curse right?" Tommy looked both hopeful and desperate.

She released the tracking spell and tucked the pendant in her pocket. "We can try."

CHAPTER 47

KADRITHAN (ANGEL)

Kadrithan rarely made mistakes and he never did anything reckless. Until today, apparently.

He rolled off the chaise lounge and immediately vomited as the room spun around him. The strain of fighting that curse had pushed him so far beyond his limits he was surprised he was still conscious. If Amber didn't have two souls, it would have been impossible.

His muscles began cramping as he crawled toward the bathroom. It would be unbearably undignified if he had to call for help, so he pushed through the discomfort. He needed to start keeping his medicinal potions near the chaise instead of so far out of reach.

As painful as his condition was, the realization of what they were dealing with consumed all his thoughts. A prophetess. He hadn't seen one of those in a century. Of course, she was cursed as well. It looked like the standard one that kept anyone from believing her by making her seem crazy. It twisted the words as they left her mouth.

The woman would be just as insane as she appeared by now though. The twisted magic of a curse warped whoever was afflicted by it. That was part of why he had risked so much to push the curse out of Amber before it could take hold. She was too valuable to lose at a time like this.

This better earn him massive amounts of trust, and perhaps a favor. He would have to push for that after the time this setback was going to cost him. It might be a full day before he could travel again. With everything going on, that was less than ideal.

He managed to pull himself up to the cabinet without vomiting again and grabbed the potion he needed. It tasted almost as bad as the vomit but as soon as it slipped down his throat the muscle cramps eased and the nausea was washed away.

Slowly, his breathing eased and his heart rate slowed to normal. He stared at one of the potions in the cabinet. He was tempted to take it now but it was only a temptation.

Distilling magic was a lost art. Another thing the curse had taken from them. He held the glass vial up to the light, admiring the vibrant substance inside it for a moment. It was translucent but gleamed with colors that he wasn't sure actually existed. Looking at it made his eyes ache.

With a sigh, he put it back in its spot and shut the cabinet door. He'd have to pay the price for what he did today.

He would get back to Amber as soon as he could but while he recovered there was something he could do here. This cursed prophetess was after something. That's how the curses always worked. It drove them to fulfill some prophecy, even if it killed them. It also explained Deward's kidnapping.

In order to fulfill whatever prophesy this elf had fixated on she needed help. And she had found it in the tunnels when she had spread the curse to the troll. Deward was helping her now.

Kadrithan stripped off his soiled clothes. If the elf was after Raziel, that could mean only one thing. The prophecy had something to do with Raziel's key. Which meant it had something to do with *him*.

CHAPTER 48

TOMMY

Tommy stared at the note. It was Deward's handwriting. It was in his *room*. On his *pillow*. Deward's scent filled the space. He had been here while they had been running around downtown Portland looking for him.

He dragged his hands through his hair then turned around and kicked his chair into the wall. Fur crept up his shaking hands as he tried to hold back the shift. His anger hadn't gotten the best of him in a long time but he wasn't sure he could hold this back.

His door flew open and Amber ran into the room, already half-shifted herself. "What is it?"

He sat down heavily on his bed and picked up the note and held it out to Amber. He hadn't read it yet. "Deward was here."

Amber straightened, the red glow in her eyes fading. "His scent is pretty fresh in here."

"The window was open when I got up here. I haven't been keeping it locked since we have the wards and everything."

She took the note finally. "Tommy, we must find Raziel's key before many futures are lost. Tell the demon time is running out. You must trust me." Amber lowered the note and looked at him with a worrying amount of pity in her eyes. "The curse has him too, then. This is almost exactly what that elf said when she grabbed me."

He put his head in his hands, staring at the floor to avoid the look Amber was giving him. "Has Kadrithan shown back up yet to explain what the hell Raziel's key is?"

"No. I think he might have been hurt when he helped me with the effects of the curse."

"Great."

Amber sat down next to him. "Any chance Evangeline might recognize the name? Or know what Deward is talking about?"

"I don't know and I don't have any way to contact her. She always comes to me." He frowned. "Actually, I should have heard from her last night."

Amber tapped the note against her fingers nervously. "Then we have to do what we can on our own. Kadrithan said the other day the trolls are historians. Ceri is planning on trying to break that curse tomorrow. While she's doing that, we can talk to Xenya, the elder, and see if she knows anything about Raziel or this key. We can ask about the curse too."

"Yeah."

Amber patted him on the shoulder. "You want me to leave you alone for a while?"

He glanced up at her. "You're getting better at not hovering."

She stood and did a little bow. "Yes, I am. You should be proud." Pausing in the doorway, she hesitated.

"Just say it."

"If you need *anything*, I'll be downstairs."

"Feel better?"

"Loads." She shut the door firmly behind her, leaving him alone in the dark.

He stared out the window and just felt sorry for himself for a moment. This was supposed to have been fun. Him and Deward, searching for a missing book. Maybe he was cursed to ruin every good thing he got.

A hard tug on the demon mark snapped him out of his pity party.

"Why does it feel like you've gone full emo?" Evangeline asked as she appeared, flooding his room with light.

"Has anyone ever told you that you're great at being comforting?"

"Nope."

"Shocking."

She sighed loudly and floated over toward the bed. "What happened?"

"Deward is cursed. We don't know why or how, but he's working with the person that kidnapped him, and I think it's all tied up with the angels. And Kadrithan."

Evangeline's form shifted, condensing into a human shape. She held out her hand and he twined his fingers in hers. "Is he being helpful? I can yell at him if not."

"Amber was affected by the curse and he did something to help her, but I think it might have backfired somehow. He disappeared and Amber says the mark feels strained."

"Well, shit. That explains why he didn't show up when…" She let the thought trail off.

"When what?" he asked, looking at her suspiciously.

She cleared her throat awkwardly. "You're not allowed to be pissed at me. You were safer ignorant."

"Eva, what aren't you telling me?"

"I'm not in Mexico. We were only there for a few days."

"Why?"

"Because we're being hunted. We're moving a lot to try to stay ahead of them."

He pulled his hand away and stood up. "By the angels?"

She nodded. "They send mercenaries to do their dirty work, but yeah."

He started pacing, feeling like he was stuck in a cage. "I don't understand why they want you dead that badly."

"Me neither. Kadrithan still won't explain." Her human form dissolved and she snapped back into the floating ball of light. "But, look, this isn't important right now. I have people protecting me. Deward needs all your focus."

"I just...I feel like it's all connected somehow. We're missing something. Kadrithan keeps warning us about the angels. We're being targeted by freaking everyone right now. Other werewolves -- who are being paid off by someone -- and the MIB." He stopped and shook his head. "Why us? Why now?"

"I don't know, but--crap. I have to go. I'm sorry."

"What--"

"I'll be back. I promise." She disappeared.

Tommy stood in his room, staring at the spot she had been in. She could be fighting for her life right now and he had no idea where she was. There was absolutely nothing he could do.

CHAPTER 49

AMBER

"He hasn't come back," Amber said, pressing her hand to her chest. The demon mark still felt wrong. Faded and stretched.

Ceri sighed. "I wish I could see that as a good sign."

"Me too." Her brush caught on a tangle and she set it down, coaxing the knot out of her wet hair with her fingers instead. "Never would have guessed I'd end up worrying about a demon."

"I still don't trust him." Ceri picked up the brush. "Sit. I'll brush it out."

She scooted down from the couch and sat in front of Ceri. Captain Jack took that as an invitation to crawl into her lap. His claws pricked through her pajama pants as he settled into place. The monster had to weigh at least forty pounds now. He was closer to the size of a dog than a cat now.

"I don't trust him either. He's lying, or at the very least, withholding information still. It's just...he put himself on the line to help me with the effects of that curse. Either I'm important enough to keep alive or he has a heart after all."

Ceri was silent for a while, just brushing her hair. She let her eyes slip shut. This was soothing. She'd never had a friend she could relax with like this before. When her mother had brushed her hair it had always been rushed. The woman hadn't exactly been...tender.

Captain Jack batted at her hand until she started petting him. He'd gotten awfully comfortable around her. It was probably because she'd stopped trying to kick him out of her bed. Genevieve liked him best, but she was pretty sure *she* was the cat's favorite.

"There are very few people in this world that are cackling, evil villains," Ceri said quietly. "Sure, some of them are about as evil as you get. Cold hearted, power hungry, and mean. The reason I don't trust Kadrithan is because he's after something. As long as you are helpful to him in achieving that, he's going to try to keep you alive. The second you aren't, he'll turn on you. In some ways that's more dangerous because you won't see it coming."

STEPHANIE FOXE

She knew it was true. It was what she'd been telling herself from the beginning. It had been easy to hate him for a while after he'd called in the mark. He'd been so angry and honestly, just plain rude.

"What are you guys doing?" Genevieve asked, padding tiredly into the living room.

"Contemplating the moral code of demons," Amber said drily.

"Fascinating." Genevieve plopped down next to Ceri and leaned her head on her shoulder. Captain Jack grabbed her foot and tried to gnaw on her toes. "What's the conclusion?"

"Not to be trusted," Ceri replied for her.

"Despite the lack of trust, it does worry me that he hasn't come back yet." She cringed when Ceri hit a knot.

"Sorry," Ceri said, setting the brush down to get the knot out more gently.

"All of this seems to be tied up with whatever it is he's after. I don't like that it's also somehow connected to whoever took Deward."

"I can agree with that. And..." Ceri sighed as if it pained her to say the rest. "I'm glad he was there to help you fight off the effects of that curse. I don't think I would have been able to stop it."

Amber snorted. "Don't worry, I won't tell him you said that."

"I'd deny it if you did."

Genevieve glanced up at the stairs. "How's Tommy?"

She sat forward, wrapping her arms around her knees. "Upset he can't do more. Just like we all are."

"Tomorrow morning we'll break the curse and get some answers," Ceri said decisively.

Amber smiled into her knees. This was the Ceri she knew. Confident. A force to be reckoned with.

688

CHAPTER 50

CERI

Ceri parked behind what she assumed was Ithra's car. The trolls had beat them here.

Tommy ruffled his fingers through his hair. There were dark circles under his eyes that matched her own. Apparently no one was sleeping well anymore. "You sure you can do this?"

She turned the car off and dropped her hands in her lap. He deserved an honest answer but she didn't want him to lose hope. "I'm not going to lie and say I can do it for sure but I'm going to try. I am *pretty* good at this magic stuff, so the odds are in your favor."

He took a deep breath and nodded, forcing a smile onto his face. "I guess that's all anyone can ever do."

"Let's go get this over with," she said, patting him on the shoulder.

They climbed out of the car and joined the rest of the pack on the walk to the tunnel entrance. Everyone was silent and a little tense. She couldn't blame them. It felt like everything hinged on this.

Olwen and Ithra nodded in greeting as they approach. Velgo was examining the runes that had guarded the entrance, recreating them carefully in a notebook.

"Xenya," Amber said with a nod in greeting, which Xenya returned.

Ceri hadn't noticed the elder leaning against a tree. She'd blended into the forest completely.

"Are you ready to begin, Ceridwen?" Ithra asked.

"I am if you and Velgo are."

A round of nods from the group confirmed they were, so she began the descent into the tunnels.

The air down here was just as stale and wrong as it had been last time. If anything, the stench of decay was even more prominent, as if leaving the entrance open had accelerated it. Ithra and Olwen maintained their stoic focus even as they walked past the area stained with Deward's blood now. It had dried, leaving dark smudges. She was glad she didn't have the wolves' sense of smell.

Relief lightened her steps when they reached the room. Soon, this would all be over with. As she stepped across the threshold, it seemed as if the curse sensed her. Sensed her intent.

"Alright, Velgo and Ithra can stay in here with me. Everyone else has to wait outside the room. There will be backlash as we break the curse. It's going to fight back."

Olwen pressed his forehead against Ithra's, whispering a quick word of encouragement before following the others back into the hall.

Ceri took a deep breath. This was for Deward, but until it was done, she had to forget he existed and focus on the magic.

She righted a charred bench and set her bag on it. It was still solid enough to work. She laid out her supplies one by one. This circle couldn't be drawn in chalk or even carved into the stone. For it to protect them from the backlash of magic it had to be something more.

Normally, this would be when she'd drain some poor goat of their blood and paint it on the floor. It was borderline blood magic, something witches liked to ignore. She was sorely tempted to do that now but her instincts told her it would be a mistake.

As a shaman, she was drawn to nature. Defiling nature for a brief taste of power went against everything she had come to believe was right and good. There had to be a way around it. She'd spent all night thinking about it and going through the options. She wasn't sure if the solution she'd settled on would work but she had to try.

Taking a deep breath, she pulled out her jar of dirt. She'd taken it from the garden near the guest house last night. It was from the pack's den, blessed by an elf, and it -- theoretically -- would help to ground and protect her.

"Is that dirt?" Velgo asked, clearly confused.

She cleared her throat. "Yep."

"What is it for?"

"The circle. I use white magic, especially now that I've joined the pack. I had to find an alternative to animal blood."

Understanding dawned on Velgo's face, as well as excitement. "Dirt is an interesting choice. What made you choose that medium?"

"A combination of things. The earth is solid and for this aspect of the spell, that's what I need. There are rules we can fall back on for spell-casting but I've found the greatest power comes from somewhere else. Intuition or...imagination." She couldn't help the smile that tugged at her lips. Magic was her passion. "My family excelled at using that skill to invent new spells or bend existing ones. It also allowed us to be really, really good at cracking wards. Hopefully those skills will help me today too."

"Have you never broken a curse before?"

She shook her head, smile fading. "I've cast them but never broken one. Never had a reason to."

"Are we ready?" Ithra asked as she walked up to them.

"Almost," Ceri said, unscrewing the lid to the jar. "I need to make the circle and cleanse the room."

The two trolls stepped back. Ceri lit the sage, letting the sharp scent of it clear out the lingering stench of smoke. Hesitating only for a moment, she picked up the totem she'd made and hung it from her necklace. Perhaps it would come in handy today.

With that done, she carefully poured out the dirt in a large circle. Next, she set out the three candles that would be part of the ritual and a single bloom she'd also taken from the garden.

Breaking a curse required speed, power, and an understanding of the curse. She was sure she could act fast enough but she wasn't sure working with the trolls would give her enough power. Understanding the curse was another thing entirely. In order to analyze it, she needed to see it.

Stepping into the circle, she cast the first spell of the evening. Magic crawled up her neck, over her cheeks, and melted into her eyes. This never failed to unsettle her. She'd only had to cast this twice before and she hadn't liked it then either.

She opened her eyes and looked at the curse. It was woven into the stone, the edges frayed from years of decay. Whoever had designed this hadn't wasted time making it elegant. The spell was utilitarian. All blunt force power and no intricacies. That made her job simpler, if not easier.

"Step into the circle then light the candles," she said, her voice barely above a whisper.

The trolls joined her in the circle, the three of them standing in a triangle. Velgo and Ithra leaned down, lighting their candles in unison with her. The flames flickered wildly as if wind was blowing through the room.

She picked up the sage in one hand and a flower in the other and held them out in front of her. It was time to begin.

"*In terra. Ad lucem. Et sacrificium.*" She crushed the flower in her hand, letting the petals fall to the ground by her feet. "*Sumo imperium.*"

Green tendrils of magic rose up from the ground within the circle like flowers sprouting from the ground. They extended toward the curse as Velgo and Ithra continued the chant.

The magic became an extension of her body. Another hand or foot to direct as she willed it. The pack bond grew in her chest, fueling the spell.

She turned her gaze to the curse, then slammed the magic into it. Sparks flew as green crashed into black. A loud screech filled the room and echoed through the tunnels as the competing magics strained against one another. Her hair lifted around her head as the cursed door began to shake.

Moving quickly, she struck at the weak points, driving the black magic back. It was frayed and weakened by time but it still held the power of a full coven.

She drew sharply on her connection to Velgo and Ithra. Her temporary coven was non-traditional but together, they were enough. The trolls possessed more magic than she had expected. Ithra felt different today. More determined. Perhaps her love for her son gave her more power than usual.

Ceri gritted her teeth and continued battering the curse with all her strength and skill. Thread by thread, the curse unraveled. But instead of fading away, it creeped up the magic she had cast at it. She shifted the spell, moving to block the encroaching curse, but it was too late. All at once, inky black magic surged toward her. She grabbed the totem hanging around her neck with her free hand.

"*Contego!*"

Wind swept up around them and pushed back against the curse. It wouldn't be able to hold it off forever though. She had to end this.

Holding on tightly to the air totem, she waded into the midst of the swirling magic. There was one last piece of the curse clinging to the stone. One last weak point.

It was hard to spot it through the haze of green and black, but as soon as she saw it, she directed the full force of the spell to attack that single point. Everything froze, silence hanging in the air for a long second, then, it imploded.

She was dragged forward, her feet slipping along the stone before the backlash of the magic exploded outward in a shockwave.

She slammed her hand down on the center of the circle and a protective shield flared up around her and the trolls. Dust sprinkled down from the ceiling as the tunnels shook.

Tommy appeared in the doorway behind them. "Did you do it? Is it over?"

Standing slowly, she nodded at Tommy. All traces of magic were gone. "It is. We did it."

She looked back at the doorway. The stone was twisted as if it had melted. It wasn't really stone anymore. The curse had changed it. Warped it.

The longer a curse was attached to something, the worse the damage it left behind. She squeezed her eyes shut. They needed to find Deward. Soon.

CHAPTER 51

TOMMY

Tommy shifted back to human form and pulled on his clothes, keeping his back to the rest of the pack until they confirmed they were dressed as well. He had to stay stooped over because the ceiling here wasn't quite high enough for him to stand up straight without bumping his head.

They had walked for miles. After close to an hour, he'd insisted they shift and run ahead to see how far it went. The coven that had built this tunnel had been insanely dedicated. They must have been smuggling something because he couldn't fathom any other reason to build tunnels this extensive.

But now they were finally at the end.

"My GPS isn't working down here," Genevieve said, shaking her phone like that might help it get better signal.

"We were going east the whole time. We've got to be under Portland somewhere," he said, looking up at the escape hatch. It *had* been rusted over but it was obvious someone had opened it recently.

There were footprints all over this area. As well as something even better. A scent. Deward had been here with that elf.

Amber put her hands on her hips and looked up at the hatch suspiciously. "Alright, I'm going up first."

Anticipation mixed with dread made his heart pound in his chest. They could find Deward up there.

Amber twisted the handle. It turned silently and the hatch popped open. She moved it to the side and jumped up to grab the edge of the opening, pulling herself up just high enough to see.

She dropped back down and looked at him, confused. "They aren't there right now but this is not what I was expecting."

"Is it safe to go up?" he asked.

She nodded and waved him ahead. He pulled himself up quickly and saw what she meant.

"Is this...a museum?"

There were shelves neatly lined with paintings and boxes. Old statues stood in rows, some missing arms, other heads. He scooted out of the way and dusted himself off.

The section of the floor they'd come up through would fit neatly into the tile, making it invisible when closed. Amber and Genevieve crawled out after him.

"Aha! My GPS is working now." Genevieve tapped at her phone for a moment, then frowned and looked up. "It says we're in the Portland Art Museum."

Amber's nose twitched and she wandered off through the shelves. "They've been this way recently."

"How are they getting in and out of the museum's storage room without being noticed?" Genevieve wondered aloud.

"Probably the same way they've been hiding their scent." He wiggled his fingers at her. "Magic."

"Gen, can you call Ceri real quick and update her?" Amber asked.

"Sure."

"Tommy, come with me. Let's see if we can find where they're getting out."

He nodded and jogged over to Amber, picking up the scent she was following. It didn't smell like they spent that much time here.

The path led them through the shelves toward a door that required some kind of code to go through. He paused a few feet away, nose twitching as he noticed that while this path had the strongest scent, it split off.

"Wait. I think the elf has been this way too." He followed the lighter scent.

As he moved away from the well-traveled path, it became easier to follow. It was the elf's scent but...it was different. Lacking something. It was also older.

It led to an office door with a sign on it-- Dr. Cassandra Lightvine. He tested the handle and found the door unlocked. Tentatively, he pushed it open.

Light spilled into a messy office. Tacked to a corkboard on the far wall were pictures he recognized. This Dr. Lightvine had been to the tunnels. She'd inspected the runes. There had been curses in that tunnel that she had broken in order to get to the room that had been burned.

She'd found the Book of Prophecies.

CHAPTER 52

GENEVIEVE

Genevieve was hunched over her laptop, scribbling down notes of Cassandra Lightvine. She should have been working but right now, this was more important.

Cassandra wasn't just a museum employee, she owned it along with some kind of community garden center, an old house in downtown Portland, and a historical society.

From what she and Tommy were able to put together, the elvish family had been collecting quite a bit of the old covens holdings. They must have known about the tunnel for ages and maintained the back door entrance when they built the museum. After her parents had died about twenty years ago, it had all been left to her.

What she wasn't sure about was whether Cassandra was working alone or not.

There was a knock on her office door and she quickly minimized her search. "Come in!"

To her surprise, Agent Icewind walked in. She looked around the tiny space, which was just big enough to fit her desk and a chair. "Nice office."

She snorted. "It's literally a converted closet. How can I help you?"

"I warned you not to follow Horan."

Genevieve's brows shot up. "We haven't been. Why do you think we are?"

Icewind frowned at her, fingers tapping restlessly against her crossed arm. "How do I know you aren't lying?"

She sighed and threw her hands up. "I don't know. I'm just not. We've had more important things to do."

"Where were you yesterday?"

She pulled out the pictures and notes they'd taken from Cassandra's office. "Running through tunnels built by witches a couple of centuries ago."

Icewind picked up one of the pictures. "Okay…"

"Actually, this is something you should probably know. Consider it an anonymous tip, but the woman that took these photos is the same person that killed Laurel Teller. At least that's our working theory. Her name is Cassandra Lightvine."

"Is that so?"

She nodded. "She's an elf. We think she found something and ended up cursed. I have no idea why she killed Teller but..." Sighing, she thought through her options quickly, but decided it was time to give Icewind a little more information. "She kidnapped a friend of our pack. We think he's cursed now too."

"Let me guess, this *friend* hasn't been reported as missing to the police."

Genevieve shook her head.

"Did he help this woman kill Teller?"

"No. He was taken right after her murder though."

"You people have a knack for getting mixed up in some unfortunate situations," Icewind said drily.

She shrugged. "Unlucky I guess. You never did say why you thought we were following Horan, by the way."

"He was acting weird this morning. Nervous." Icewind set the picture back on her desk. "I'll look into Lightvine. If you find anything else, do us both a favor and call me instead of investigating it yourself."

"Of course," Genevieve lied.

Icewind sighed heavily and turned to leave, shaking her head. "Don't be stupid, Bisset."

The agent shut the door behind herself and Genevieve slumped down in her chair. This was getting complicated.

They might have the name of the person that had taken Deward but they didn't know where to find her. Amber was on her right now to check out the other places Cassandra owned but she doubted the crazy elf would be there.

She shuffled through the pictures, hoping something would jump out at her. A clue. An explanation. They hadn't found a single reference to Raziel's key in any of the books or photographs despite Deward and the elf talking about it.

Raziel sounded like an angel's name but that was just a guess. Of all the times for Kadrithan to go MIA, this was possibly the worst.

Her phone rang. She glanced at the caller ID and almost dismissed the call when she saw it was Steven, but she'd been too absent lately. He deserved better.

"Hey--"

"Gen, I think someone is following me," Steven whispered.

She froze. "Where are you?"

"In the school library. I noticed them when I left my dorm room. They aren't students. I think...I think they might be werewolves." His voice shook with fear.

"Describe them to me."

"One guy looks kind of...weaselly."

Jumping out of her chair, she sprinted for the door. "Listen. They are from a pack that are targeting us. Do not let them find you or take you. Do you have the emergency kit?"

"Okay. Okay." There was a rustling noise. "I, uh, I do have it. But suddenly I don't feel super confident about using it."

"Steven, you have to. I'm coming for you but I'm fifteen minutes away at least. I won't get there in time."

CHAPTER 53

AMBER

Amber pulled into the tiny parking lot -- there was room for exactly two cars -- in front of the Lightvine Historical Society's headquarters. The name sounded impressive, however the building was anything but. It was hidden in an old subdivision among cookie-cutter houses. This one stood out for the simple fact that it was old. Unfortunately, it was also falling apart.

The grass hadn't been mowed in what looked like months. Plywood had been tacked up inside a broken window no one had bothered to repair. Beer bottles scattered all over the uneven porch.

She stepped onto the porch, a board creaking under her foot, and knocked loudly of the front door. There was no reason to think anyone would be in there but she had come here to find out.

It was deathly silent inside. No heartbeats, no footsteps. She sniffed the door, checking for any signs of magic but it seemed whoever owned this place hadn't bothered to protect it magically either.

Her phone rang, cutting through the silence. "Hey Shane, what's up?"

"I'm sorry."

She stopped, her senses going on alert at the tone in his voice. He was upset. "For what?"

"Due to recent allegations, my alpha has determined that it would put our pack in a dangerous position if I were to continue helping you. Our packs are not allies and I have overstepped."

Rejection curled in her gut. It was an ugly but familiar feeling for her. "You sound like you're reading a prepared speech. You could at least tell me yourself and not just parrot whatever bullshit reason you were given." She realized belatedly that she was almost shouting by the end.

"I can't help with Deward and I can't see you until your pack is cleared by the MIB," he

S T E P H A N I E   F O X E

continued in a quiet, even tone. "I'm sorry, Amber. I argued against it but there are bigger things at stake here and I can't…I have to put my pack first."

Hearing what Angel had said to her at that party echoed back from Shane's own mouth was too much to take.

"Fine." She hung up. There was nothing more to say. He couldn't tell her what she wanted to hear. The worst part was that he was making the right decision. They weren't dating. She wasn't his girlfriend. He owed her nothing and his pack everything.

There had been potential there but it had never gotten off the ground. There was always something getting in the way.

A car stopped on the street behind her and she looked over her shoulder to see Agent Horan stepping out of a black suburban. If she had been in wolf form, her fur would have been standing on end. He looked way too smug for this to turn out in her favor.

"Agent Horan, I didn't expect to run into you all the way out here," she said pleasantly as she walked back down off the porch. If her day hadn't already been bad enough, this was the moldy cherry on a poop sundae.

He looked at the house. "What are you doing here?"

She shrugged and glanced back at the house as well. "I was thinking about buying a place in town. Not sure this is the right house though. Can I help you?"

Horan's expression shifted to mock pity. "Unfortunately, I'm going to insist you come back to the MIB with me. I have a warrant for your arrest."

"What?" A thousand thoughts were racing through her mind. She hadn't done anything she could be arrested for and she really hadn't thought Carter would be capable of drumming up something that could put her in this position. Another question niggling at the back of her mind was, how the hell had Horan found her? Only pack knew she was going to this address. It wasn't exactly on her normal route.

Then, the worst thought. Had Shane known this was coming and not warned her?

Horan pulled out an official looking document. "It's a warrant for your arrest. I assured my superiors you would surrender yourself peacefully so we didn't have to send a team with guns out to your house."

This was crap. He knew it. She knew it. And he knew that she knew. The problem was, if she resisted or ran, he really would have something to arrest her for. And it would make her look bad.

"I'll call my beta to come pick up my truck then," Amber said pulling out her phone.

Horan nodded congenially. "With me, please." He stepped back and pulled open the door to the backseat of the suburban. It had a partition cage separating the front seat from the back made of thick steel with what she assumed was bullet proof glass on top.

She was torn between fleeing what could be a trap and facing it head on. Running now would put the whole pack at risk though and she couldn't justify it.

She called Genevieve as she climbed into the back of the suburban. Her phone rang once then went to voicemail.

"Genevieve, Agent Horan has just picked me up with a warrant for my arrest. Please come to the MIB when you get this message." She hung up, proud of herself for relaying all of that information calmly despite the building rage. This was an abuse of power. She

700

should be able to trust someone in his position but he was a worthless, greedy, cowardly, piece of crap instead.

"We have to make a quick stop on the way, but it'll be just a moment," Horan said, smiling at her in the rearview mirror as he turned left, taking them farther into the subdivision.

"A quick stop?"

He nodded as he pulled over to the side of the road behind another car. A muscle car with a gaudy paint job, to be specific. When Carter stepped out and walked toward them, she tried to open her door. It was locked.

"Horan, let me out or I'm going to break your door."

"You can't break it. It was made with werewolves in mind." He turned back to look at her through the bulletproof glass. "Do yourself a favor and sit quietly and listen. I don't want to have to gas you, but I will if I think you pose a threat." He pointed to a small vent in the ceiling that would fill the backseat with gas that she knew would sedate and weaken her. The addition to police cars had been all over the news for a while. Civil rights groups hadn't liked it one bit. Right now, she didn't like it either.

The other passenger door opened and Carter climbed in, settling into the seat next to her. He adjusted his suit jacket and crossed his legs, looking completely at ease. "Give us a minute, Horan."

The agent climbed out and shut the door, leaving her and Carter alone. Her instincts –– wolf and human –– told her this was a very, very bad situation to be in. She doubted this was about killing her. There were easier ways. This was about intimidating her.

"You know, one of the problems with smaller packs is that you can't be everywhere at once. It's why we encourage large packs to stay together," Carter said, stretching his legs out as far as the space would allow. He seemed perfectly at ease, if not a little eager. "Right now, someone who a normal, well-run pack would be able to protect is being attacked. However, you left them vulnerable."

She opened her mouth to object when a flood of fear rushed down the pack bond. Genevieve. She was in trouble. Gritting her teeth, Amber gave her strength. The only thing she could do to help right now.

"What have you done?"

"Me? Nothing at all. I'd never do anything to hurt another pack." He smiled, all teeth, like a wild animal growling.

Amber's hands curled into fists. It would be so simple to jump across this car and rip his throat out but she knew Agent Horan would claim it was murder. "You didn't just bring me here to gloat. What do you want?"

"Disband your pack. Join a different one. As a peace offering, I'll even let you choose. I bet Jameson would take you in. He seems to have a soft spot for you."

Genevieve's panic fluttered in her chest next to her heart. Carter must have threatened Jameson somehow. Enough that he'd force Shane to call things off.

She leaned in, holding Carter's gaze. "No."

He grinned. "That's what I was hoping you'd say."

"Why? Are you planning on finally fighting me yourself instead of sending minions to do your dirty work."

He opened the door and stepped out of the suburban, the smug expression never leaving his face. "I'll see you again, Hale."

Carter walked away. She curled her hands into a fist. Bram had been right. She was out of her depth with all this plotting and scheming.

The driver's door opened again and Horan peeked his head in. "Looks like there was a mix up and there *isn't* a warrant out for your arrest after all." He hit a button and her door unlocked. "Apologies, you're free to go."

She stepped out slowly, moving into Horan's personal space. He took an involuntary step back. She could smell the instinctual fear wafting off of him from having a predator so close. Red bled into her eyes as she pulled on the dominance that made her an alpha.

"Keep in mind that to them, you are expendable."

"To who?" he asked, playing dumb.

She brushed passed him, doing her best to maintain an even gait. She wanted to sprint back to her truck but she knew she was still being watched.

CHAPTER 54

∝∽

GENEVIEVE

Genevieve raced through the library parking lot on two legs. She wanted to shift but if Steven was hurt she'd need her hands.

As she rounded the building, the burn of silver dust was the first thing to hit her nose. The second was the smell of Steven's blood.

His back was against the brick wall and a stream of powdered silver was shooting out of his repurposed mace canister. Two wolves were advancing on him, their lips curled back in a snarl.

Genevieve howled, shifting as she raced forward. The larger, black wolf broke off and ran toward her. She darted to the side, leaping onto the wall then pushing off to land on his back.

His teeth sunk into her back leg but she had him by the scruff of the neck. She bore down, shaking his neck hard enough that he lost his footing and his grip on her leg.

The pack bond swelled in her chest and strength flowed through her. Steven's shouts cut through the snarls but she couldn't understand him.

She bit down on the wolf's vulnerable belly and ripped a chunk of flesh away. He howled in pain and scrambled backwards. Pressing her advantage, she struck again, opening a deep gash on his neck.

He didn't just retreat this time; he turned and ran. The other wolf followed.

She was tempted to give chase but Steven was sliding down the wall clutching his arm. His textbooks were strewn all over the pavement along with his shredded backpack.

Shifting back to human form, she raced to his side.

"Oh god. That was terrifying," Steven said shakily.

"Where are you hurt?" she demanded, hands hovering above his arm awkwardly. She didn't know what to do. She didn't even have a first aid kit.

"Just...just my arm." He moved his blood-coated fingers away from the wound. It would need stitches. His eyes drifted down her body. "You're naked."

"That doesn't matter, we have to go. They might come back. I don't know why they ran like that. Two against one they could have taken me." She helped him to his feet, holding him upright when his legs nearly gave way.

"My books. I can't just leave them here. I need my notes for...for my thesis."

"Are you serious?"

"It's important!"

"Fine, lean against the wall." She made sure he was going to stay upright this time, then hastily gathered the books and the notepad. The silver dust coating them burned her skin immediately but she didn't care. She barely felt it.

"Crap, it's burning you, I didn't think––"

"It's fine. Come on." She gritted her teeth against the sting of the silver. Her muscles were weakening every place that it touched, only offset by the strength that Amber was sending her.

Steven leaned on her as they hurried back to her car. She threw the books in the backseat. Her phone, which was sitting in the center console was ringing off the hook.

"Answer that," she instructed Steven as she peeled out of the parking lot.

"Hello?"

"Steven? What the hell is going on?" Amber demanded, half-shouting.

"I'm with Gen. I got attacked by two werewolves but I'm okay. Mostly"

"Is Gen hurt?"

"No, she's fine. Well, she touched silver powder."

"Get back to the house as fast as y'all can."

"He needs stitches!" Genevieve shouted, knowing Amber would be able to hear.

"I don't think it's safe to go to a hospital. Carter just had me temporarily arrested. I can stitch it up," Amber said.

Genevieve mashed down on the accelerator. "He *what?*"

"I'll explain at the house."

"She hung up," Steven said, lowering the phone.

She nodded. Tears stung at her eyes as the adrenaline began to fade. "I'm sorry. I'm so sorry."

Steven put his good hand on her shoulder. "It's not your fault."

"It's literally my fault. You were attacked because I'm dating you. And I left you vulnerable. I'm a terrible girlfriend."

"You came to my rescue. If anything, I'm a terrible boyfriend for needing to be rescued." He was silent for a moment. "Thank you. For coming."

Her grip on the steering wheel tightened. "I think you should stay at the pack house until this is all over."

"Not even going to argue with you," he said with a short laugh that ended with a hiss of pain. "Ow. Moved too much."

CHAPTER 55

AMBER

"I didn't realize nurses could give stitches," Steven said as Amber adjusted the angle of his arm.

"They can't most places. I got an advanced certification to up my chances of getting a job." She tied off the last stitch, glad her skills weren't any rustier. "It didn't help with the job search but I guess it's a good thing I learned."

He lifted his arm, inspecting her work. "Is it going to scar?"

"Yes, but it won't be too large once it's fully healed. Ceri's potions will help and, if you really hate it, the elvish stuff can make it good as new."

"No way, I want to keep it," he said with an unexpected grin. "I can tell everyone I was attacked by a werewolf. This will give me cool points. And this experience is going to be really helpful with my studies. There's just something...different about facing off against a giant werewolf that wants to kill you. I could see the bloodlust in their eyes."

"Yay?" she said hesitantly. Steven was odd but she figured this reaction was better than him freaking out.

Ceri hurried back into the dining room with another salve and a basket full of potions. "Genevieve was *covered* in silver dust. Did she roll in it or something?"

Steven cringed. "No...that was my fault. I asked her to get my textbooks and it got all over them when I was spraying it at the other werewolves."

"Ah. Are they still in her car?"

He nodded. "I'll get them out and clean it. I don't want it getting all over her again."

"I can help. We'll have to clean it carefully," Ceri said, pulling out her salve.

"So, umm, Gen didn't get a chance to really explain what's going on," Steven said hesitantly, looking back and forth between the two of them.

"Well, it's complicated." Amber tossed the last of the bloody bandages into the trash next to her foot. "The reason you were attacked was to try to scare me into compliance. Or just scare me."

"Attacking the squishy humans is smart," Steven said, nodding along like this was some kind of science experiment and he was fine with being the guinea pig.

Ceri gave him a baffled look, shaking her head. "Generally the squishy humans aren't happy to be targeted."

"Oh, I'm not *happy* about it, it's just that it makes sense." He gave Ceri his arm so she could apply another potion. "What are they trying to get you to do? Or not do?"

She hadn't even had a chance to explain that to the pack. "Let's wait for the others. I won't leave you out of the loop though, promise."

"Hey Ceri, I'm out of the soap stuff. Do you have any more?" Genevieve shouted from the bathroom.

Ceri hurried out of the dining room to help her.

"Steven, I had a question. This is a total long shot, but you've studied history and magic. Have you ever heard of Raziel's key?"

He frowned. "That name Raziel sounds angelic. I haven't really studied their history."

"Ah okay."

"But I'll look into it. Is it related to what's going on?"

She sat back and shrugged. "We think so, we're just not sure how."

"Yeah, I'll be right over," Ceri said as she walked back into the room. She hung up her phone with a deep sigh. "Bad news. Thallan has gone missing."

CHAPTER 56

CERI

Ceri hurried across the lawn. In the midst of all the chaos, she'd forgotten about Thallan. And apparently that had been a mistake. She was tempted to just let the crazy elf stay missing –– he was probably locked up in a drunk tank somewhere –– but she felt weirdly responsible for him.

The doctor's motorcycle was parked near the porch and the front door was standing open when she jogged up.

Dr. Stone was waiting for her just inside the entryway. "Any idea where he might be?"

"There's a bar that has an early happy hour I think he's been going to. I'll have to find the address." She pulled out her phone and searched the name of the bar. "How has his therapy been going? I know you can't share the details but could you tell me if he's...improving?"

"I thought it was going well when he stopped raging so much but I was mistaken." Stone scratched his stubbled jaw. "He's a crafty old bastard."

"What did he do?"

"I'm not sure yet, which is what worries me. He's up to something though."

"Great," Ceri muttered. "Can I text the address to the number you called me from?"

Stone nodded. "That'll work."

Something tapped against her shoulder and she looked back to see the tarot card that still haunted her was waving at Stone.

"Ah, I see our little friend is still with you."

Ceri sighed. "I looked at it and listened to what it had to say. Why won't it go away?"

Stone approached, coaxing the card out from behind her back. It hovered above his hand, basking in the attention. "That's a good question. Typically, it means the lesson the card is trying to teach you is still being missed. With this little guy, it could also mean you don't understand what you're being warned about still. Or...you haven't found what you need yet."

"That's all very vague." Ceri glared at the card. This was why she hated tarot. Every piece of advice was just vague enough that everyone could relate to it, without actually meaning anything. It was nothing more than a mind trick.

"It's vague until it's not," Stone said cryptically.

She could feel the enamel grinding off her teeth as she held back what she wanted to shout at him.

The serious expression on his weathered face cracked after a moment and he laughed, hand to belly. "You should see your face."

Even the tarot card seemed to be laughing.

"Seriously? This is how you entertain yourself?" she demanded, hands on hips.

"Sorry, I couldn't resist," Stone said, wiping tears of amusement from his eyes. "Anyhow, to be *less* vague, try asking the card to show you what you're missing. I guarantee it's trying. Whatever this is, it's something you've been avoiding dealing with for a while. I suspect you already know what it is and just don't want to admit it."

"That's ridiculous," Ceri said, unable to look at it him as the memory of her spirit fading from the spirit realm as the darkness pressed around her flashed through her mind.

He shrugged. "Whatever you're afraid of, it's better to face it than keep running."

"I'll let the others know Thallan is missing. Call me if you find him, please."

"Will do." He nodded in farewell, then headed to his motorcycle. She stood there, lost in thought, until it rumbled to life and Dr. Stone left.

CHAPTER 57

EVANGELINE

Snow floated past her window. She'd been staring outside absently for what felt like hours.

She kept expecting to see a shadow pass by. They'd been attacked so often lately she could barely get her muscles to unclench. Sleep was impossible. Especially with the nightmares.

If it wasn't memories of blood and bullets when she closed her eyes, it was fire. Her demon side was growing stronger. Her uncle wanted her to find someone else to give her mark to in order to increase her power further.

She suspected the real reason was that it would balance out the growth of her angel side. With a wave of her hand, she changed the view out her window to a beach. Palm trees, aqua-blue water, white sand. Even though she knew it was just an illusion, it still looked real.

The view stuttered and wavered before shattering, revealing the cold once again. She sighed. There was no escaping reality for long.

"Evangeline," Kadrithan whispered from the shadows. "I don't have long."

She shot upright. "Where the hell have you been?"

"We don't have much time so I cannot explain everything as in depth as I would like." He stayed in the corner of her room, nothing more than a blob of darkness in an already dark corner.

"We were attacked twice in a week," she said angrily. "You should have been here."

The shadow grew darker, a flash of angry red streaking through the center. "I was injured."

"So was Charlie."

"You'll have to yell at me later, Eva. I need to tell you about your parents, and the reason you are being hunted so intently."

Evangeline went still, her heart pounding in her chest. "About time."

‐

CHAPTER 58

GENEVIEVE

Genevieve tossed her keys on the kitchen counter with a sigh. She'd been hoping to come home and see Steven but Derek had *stolen* her boyfriend.

Instead of sitting at the house alone all day, Steven had opted to go with Derek to the mechanic shop. He knew nothing about truck engines. Or motor oil. Or...wrenches. Derek had claimed they were going to bond as humans.

She opened the fridge and glared at the emptiness that greeted her. The one day she got off early, and she didn't even get extra time with her own boyfriend.

A vaguely familiar sounding car came down the driveway. It was quiet. She tilted her head to the side and listened closely. Maybe even elf-spelled. There was only one person she knew that drove a car like that but she had no idea what Agent Icewind would be doing here.

As she headed toward the front door there was a polite knock. The front door unlocked on it's own.

"What the hell, house. You're supposed to keep strangers out not just let them in," she muttered, jogging to get to the door before the house decided to just open the front door all on its own.

She peeked out the window and saw Icewind standing outside, just as suspected. When she went to open the door, it flew back, almost hitting her.

"Excited to see me?" Icewind asked in confusion.

She cleared her throat. "Something like that. The door sometimes...malfunctions." Shaking her head, she put on a smile. "Anyhow, what's up?"

Icewind crossed her arms. "I've been suspended."

"What?"

"Horan, the dirty little rat, reported me for harassing and stalking a suspect. I don't know how much he paid that asshole to lie, or how he got photographs of him in my apartment without me noticing, but it worked." Icewind shook her head, a muscle in her jaw twitching as she ground her teeth together. "I'd kill him if I thought it'd help me get my job back."

"Great. Well, come on in. I assume you didn't just come here to deliver the news in person," Genevieve said, stepping back and waving the agent inside.

The cabinets fluttered as Icewind crossed the threshold and she could have *sworn* the house made a noise. She frowned. That was a weird response to a visitor but the house didn't seem upset at least. Maybe she really liked elves.

Ceri walked into the living room, flipping through a book distractedly. "Who was knocking––"

Icewind nodded in greeting. "I should have known it was you that somehow convinced him to let this pack move in. You did almost talk me into changing my mind about seeing him."

"Wait, you two know each other?" Genevieve asked, looking at the two of them suspiciously.

"Sort of. She's Thallan's daughter. He asked me to track her down–– that was the favor I did for him ages ago. I found her address and spoke with her in person. It was actually really easy since her friends were willing to talk to me but not Thallan. I had no idea she worked for the MIB." Ceri stopped rambling and turned back to Icewind, her brow pinched in confusion. "When did you change your name?"

Icewind chuckled. "After you found me. I didn't want my dad to be able to track me down again so easily. I moved too."

"Understandable," Ceri said with a smile.

Icewind looked around the living room. "It's weird being back here. I remember my..." She took a deep breath, sorrow passing over her features. "My mother and father building the place. My mother built the wards herself. She spent a lot of time out here."

That explained why the house was so excited to let Icewind in. She was welcoming her daughter home.

"Is Amber heading back yet?" Ceri asked.

Genevieve shook her head. "Nope, they're all still running around town."

"She was the one that talked Thallan into letting the pack move in here, by the way," Ceri said. "He turned me down flat when I tried to call in the favor."

"Can't say that shocks me." Icewind sighed deeply, clearly not fond of her father or any reminder of him.

"Oh, and you should know, your father went missing yesterday. I think he's probably just...in a drunk tank somewhere, but I haven't been able to find him."

Icewind nodded, pursing her lips in disapproval. "I suppose it shouldn't be a surprise that he drinks now."

"Well, um, I'm sure we'll find him. Do you want us to call you when we do?" Genevieve asked.

"No. Definitely not." Icewind shook her head firmly. "I just came here to let you know I was suspended and –– against my better judgment –– offer to help. Whoever framed me did so because I was getting in their way. I know I'm not the real target."

"Yeah, that's us apparently," Genevieve agreed with a sigh. "I'll have to talk to Amber but I think she'd gladly accept your help."

"What can you tell me about Jason Carter? I think he was involved with my suspension and you mentioned him the other day."

Genevieve nodded toward the dining room. "I'll show you my notes."

CHAPTER 59

AMBER

Amber parked on the street near the coffee shop. She'd gone to Cassandra Lightvine's house, and like the historical society, it was deserted. A house that big should have staff or guards but it had neither. What it *did* have were wards she couldn't get past. She'd have to come back with Ceri and see if they could get in.

Tommy and Deward's father, Olwen, had come up empty handed searching the garden center as well. They were already headed home but she had decided to make a quick stop before joining them.

The bell on the door tinkled as she walked into the coffee shop. It was fairly busy, with most of the tables being taken up. There was one free in the corner so she dropped her jacket off to save it then went up to the counter to order.

"How can I help you?" the barista –– a young girl wearing a sticker that said *I'm new* on her apron –– asked nervously.

She smiled, trying to put her at ease. "Just a London Fog."

The barista tapped at her screen, looking over her shoulder for help.

"Earl grey tea with milk, vanilla, and lavender, if that helps you find it," Amber whispered.

A blush spread across the girls' face. "It does, thanks." She moved through the choices a little more confidently, then looked up with a smile. "Four fifty."

Amber handed over cash. "Keep the change."

She watched people file in and out of the coffee shop while she waited for her drink. They were all so blissfully ignorant. She used to come to places like this all the time when she was in school, and she never thought about demons or angels or evil, cursed elves.

"Here's your drink," another barista said, handing her the warm cup.

"Thanks." She headed unhurriedly over to her table and sat down. Just for a few minutes, she wanted to enjoy her tea and not worry about anything.

"Amber Hale, may I join you for coffee?"

She looked up and froze when she saw the man who had asked to join her.

To say he was beautiful would be incorrect. The exacting symmetry of his features and the elegant way they were arranged was beyond that. Everything about him was perfection. Not a strand of his deep, black hair was out of place. She hardly noticed his clothes, only that they, too, were exactly as they should be.

She met his eyes -- deep gray orbs flecked with light that hinted at mysteries and hidden pleasures -- and felt a pull to walk up to him. Her fingers ached to trace the curve of his cheek.

The wolf dug its claws into her mind and power flooded her body as she resisted the siren call of the angel's gaze. She tore her eyes away, heart pounding with exertion.

He looked around the coffee shop, as if noticing for the first time that everyone in there was staring at him in shock.

"I'm sure no one would mind giving my friend and I some privacy?" the angel asked, his words taking on a strange, melodic lilt. The air shimmered around each person. One by one, they filed out of the coffee shop. Even the baristas.

He turned his inhumanly perfect face back to her and smiled. "That's better."

A red haze filtered over her vision as the wolf rose to the front of her mind. She let her take control. This creature standing in front of her was dangerous.

This perfection was alluring and intimidating...and it felt wrong. The pull to fall at his feet was wrong. The way her heart pounded in her chest at his smile was wrong.

She stared at his nose, refusing to meet his eyes again. "What do you want?"

He settled in the chair across from her, leaning toward her across the table. "I just wanted to speak with you."

"Why?" she asked, her hands trembling as power washed over her in waves. She was being rude but she was terrified that if she gave into the urge to please him, then he would be able to make her do anything.

"To thank you for your efforts to stop that terrible sorcerer. It was very dangerous to fight him. You were brave," he said, his words sinking into her skin like sunshine after days of rain. It made her want to lean in and soak up more of that feeling.

She pushed back in her chair, the dissonant growling of her wolf giving her just enough clarity to resist. "We did what we had to."

"Don't diminish your achievement," he said, placing his hand on hers before she had a chance to jerk it away. His fingers closed a little too tightly around her hand. "Not many would have risked so much, even for a friend."

His skin was smooth but strangely cold against her own. Trembling, she reached for his wrist with her free hand and yanked it free. Fear and a strange sense of shame washed over her as she set his hand back down on the table, away from her.

"Do not...touch me..." she gasped out, barely able to speak through the effort of not begging forgiveness. This was insanity but she never let someone touch her when she didn't want them to. The wolf writhed under her skin, moments away from forcing a shift.

"I'm sorry, I didn't intend to upset you," he said, leaning in a little closer but not moving to touch her again. "You look distressed, so I won't keep you long. My presence can be quite overwhelming. As thanks, I wanted to offer you a gift. I can erase your demon mark."

Her heart nearly stopped in her chest. "That's…impossible."

"For you, yes, but not for me," he replied easily.

For a moment, she was tempted to say yes, but strangely his offer distressed the wolf even more.

This was a gift with strings attached and she knew it, even if he didn't say it. Claws extended from her fingertips and it took all the strength she could pull from the pack bond to hold back a full shift.

"No." It was all she could manage to say. If she said another word, she was afraid it would be yes. She hated Kadrithan sometimes but this creature terrified her more. He was in her head, trying to influence her. Kadrithan, for all his faults, had never done that.

A frown marred the angel's perfect face. "I am surprised at your answer, Amber. Are you sure you won't reconsider?"

She shook her head. "A deal…is a deal."

"I'm sure you were manipulated into it. There is no shame in freeing yourself from someone who has lied to you." The pressure his power created intensified. She felt small and weak.

She curled her hands into fists and dug the claws into the palms of her hands. Warm blood trickled down her wrist and the pain cleared her mind, just a little. "No, thank you."

He nodded forlornly. "If that is your decision, then I can only hope you will change your mind soon." He pulled a box from his pocket. "I also wanted give you this, as a gesture of good will. Please do not reject both of my gifts."

He pushed the box across the table toward her then leaned back, lifting the pressure on her mind just a little.

She stared at the box like it might bite her. Part of her wanted to reject this too but she was worried what he might do. Even with the strength of the pack bond she wasn't sure she could fight the angel alone. Or at all.

Willing her fingers not to shake, she opened the box. A delicate necklace sat on a black silk lining. The gold chain was so thin it looked like it would snap at the slightest tug. Extending down from the chain were glittering diamonds, each bigger than the one above it. It was luxurious and beautiful. And completely unnecessary. She couldn't help but notice that it would have gone perfectly with the dress she wore the last day of the conference. The message was clear: *I've been watching you.*

She swallowed uncomfortably. "Thank you."

"It is my honor to reward your efforts." He rose from the table and smiled down at her. "Until we meet again, Amber. Remember, if you change your mind about the demon mark, the offer still stands."

The sound of her name on his lips sent a thrill down her spine. "Okay," she choked out.

The bell tinkled as he walked out, taking his strange influence with him. Her vision twisted and blurred as air rushed back into her lungs. She grabbed the edge of the table to stay upright, heart pounding and chest heaving.

The necklace sat there, sparkling innocently in the sunlight. She smacked the box shut.

The other customers began filing back in.

"Was that an angel?"

"She's so lucky she got to talk to him!"

"They're just as hot as everyone says."

Their stupidity made her want to scream. How had they not noticed he had forced them all to walk outside? How could they think that was fun and not terrifying?

She snatched up the box and sprinted outside, leaving her untouched tea behind. She had the irrational urge to cry.

Biting the inside of her cheek, she focused on putting one foot in front of the other until she made it back to her truck. It took three tries to get the key in the door. Another two to get the key in the ignition.

Her phone was ringing but she ignored it, driving home with a death grip on the steering wheel. The jewelry box taunted her from the passenger seat. It was tempting to toss it out the window and keep driving. She wondered if the angel would know if she threw it away.

She took a twisting route back home, checking for anyone following her, not that they didn't already have her address.

The pack bond was alight with worry and she did her best to let them know she was okay now. She couldn't talk to them yet. Whatever that angel had done to her had terrified her. If she hadn't had the wolf, he could have manipulated her so easily. She would have done anything for the chance to feel his hand against hers or the slightest acknowledgement.

She'd heard stories about how amazing and wonderful angels were, and that must be why. They didn't let people think anything else about them.

Kadrithan was right. They weren't pure or anything else. They were worse than the demons.

There was a tug on her demon mark and Kadrithan appeared as a little, red devil next to her in the truck.

She almost cried in relief, which was not normally how she felt when he showed up. "Where have you been?"

"Recovering. What the hell is wrong with you?" he asked, taking in her expression with alarm.

She stopped at the gate to the property and turned to face him. "An angel showed up and talked to me."

Kadrithan's face darkened. "What did he want? Did he threaten you?"

She laughed hysterically, unable to stop for a long moment. Resting her forehead on the steering wheel she attempted to catch her breath. "No, he offered to erase your mark."

There was a beat of silence. "You didn't accept his offer."

"No, I didn't."

Kadrithan shifted into his human form and leaned toward her. "Why not?"

She looked up at Kadrithan, unable to hide her fear behind her usual mask of bravado. "What the hell are they, Kadrithan? He was not...he was not good."

The demon sighed and looked out the window, thinking something over in his mind. "Perhaps it is time I tell you."

CHAPTER 60

KADRITHAN (ANGEL)

Kadrithan had never seen Amber quite this undone. Even when Ceri had been dying, she had remained fiercely determined through her desperation. The angel had completely terrified her, which, despite being worrying, he took as a good sign.

If the angel hadn't scared her, it would mean the angel had a hold on her and he wouldn't be able to trust her ever again.

"This angel, did he tell you his name?" he asked finally.

Amber briefly let her head fall against the steering wheel, shoulders drooping with exhaustion. "Can you just answer my question for once?"

"I will, but I need to know which of them approached you. It's important."

She sighed, rubbing her hands down her face. They were streaked with dried blood.

He grabbed them. "I thought you said he didn't hurt you."

She scowled at him but let him examine the wounds. "He didn't. I partially shifted and dug my claws into my palm to keep him from doing...whatever it was he was doing. He didn't say his name, by the way."

"Hmm, smart," he said, releasing her hands. She grabbed a napkin from the pile in the center console and started trying to rub off the blood. "What did he look like? Describe him."

She shrugged. "It was hard to focus on what he actually looked like, other than disturbingly perfect. He had black hair and gray eyes though. Do you want me to describe the effervescent twinkling of his eyes? Or his perfect, ivory skin?"

"No, that's quite enough," he said, rolling his eyes. She hadn't been visited by one of the archangels, thankfully, but it was nearly just as bad. "I believe it was Zelas that met with you. He is powerful but ultimately not our biggest concern." He paused, noticing Ceri running down the driveway. "It appears we have a visitor. I think it would easiest if I just explained this to the whole pack at once."

"Crap, she called three times while we've been sitting here." Amber put the truck in drive and rolled down her window. "Just get in, Ceri. I'll explain it all in a minute."

Ceri glanced at him suspiciously but nodded and climbed in the passenger seat, forcing him closer to Amber, not that he minded.

"What is this?" Ceri asked, picking up a velvety black jewelry box. Something you'd put a necklace in. That was an odd thing for Amber to have in her truck. She wasn't one for jewelry and trinkets. Apparently, Ceri agreed.

"The angel gave it to me as a gift. It matches my dress from the conference. They've been watching me," Amber said sourly.

He took the box from Ceri and opened it. She was right. He snapped the lid closed again. "Throw it away. Don't keep it in the house."

"I'll destroy it," Ceri said, taking it back from him and holding onto it with a white-knuckled grip.

Amber parked quickly and they all headed into the house. Everyone was there, their faces showing their distress at the ordeal their alpha had just gone through.

"Sorry I couldn't block all that," Amber said awkwardly as she locked the door behind them. "And for freaking out after."

"What happened? Was it his fault again?" her brother demanded, directing a glare at him. Derek's bushy beard was puffed out as if he'd been pulling on it.

Another human, this one wiry and nerdy, hovered behind Derek. He pushed his glasses up on his nose in a nervous gesture. Genevieve put a protective arm around him when she saw his eyes on the man. Interesting. That was not the sort of man he'd expect her to choose.

Amber shook her head. "No, for once it wasn't." She sighed deeply and shoved her hands in her pockets. "An angel approached me at the coffee shop. Using some kind of weird magic, he made everyone in the coffee shop get up and walk out. Including the baristas. It was like he entranced them all."

"What? That should be impossible. Controlling that many people at once..." Ceri looked horrified.

Amber nodded. "Yeah, it was terrifying. My wolf was the only reason he didn't entrance me too. It was a struggle. I *wanted* to please him. I was barely able to resist the pull."

The cat-that-wasn't-a-cat prowled into the room, purring as it approached him. He'd been avoiding the thing so as not to draw attention to it, but there wasn't much he could do this time.

"Get over here, Jack." Genevieve scrambled to scoop up the cat before it touched him, scowling at him as if it were his fault.

"Did the angel try to hurt you?" Tommy asked, speaking up for the first time. The boy was always quiet, but rarely idle. Tommy was very observant, something that could be troublesome for him eventually.

"Not physically. Now, hear me out on this before any of you get mad, because whatever this angel was offering me, it was going to come with serious strings attached." Amber waited for everyone to nod before continuing. "The angel offered to erase Kadrithan's mark."

She pressed her lips into a thin line, waiting for the pack's reaction.

Ceri was the first to speak, but she didn't look angry, only confused. "They can do that?"

"After a fashion," he answered for Amber. It was time to explain a few things to the pack, despite the risk. He couldn't share everything of course, but now that an angel had threatened their alpha, they were ready to hear some of the truth. "They can shift it to someone else, who will agree because the angel has manipulated them into it. That person would immediately be killed, of course. Unless he was offering simply to kill Amber, which is possible."

"That's horrible," Ceri said, confusion shifting to disapproval.

"Hardly the most horrible thing Zelas has ever done, I can assure you."

"Zelas? That was the angel's name?" Ceri asked.

He nodded. "Zelas is an envoy of one of the five archangels."

They didn't need to know that archangel was Raziel just yet. Names had power, and he needed to preserve as much of his own as he could.

"You said you would explain what the angels are," Amber prompted, impatient for him to get to the point.

He sighed and summoned a chair, sitting in front of the pack. His power filled the room, dimming the sunlight. It was a strain still but holding their attention was worth the effort.

"Angels and demons. Light and darkness. Everyone has accepted this for centuries. However, it was once the opposite. Demon is a name given to us by our mortal enemies, the parasites that now feed on the human race without repercussion."

With a wave of his hand, he summoned a weak illusion of an angel. Beautiful. Artificial. An angel could have made this look real. Feel real. This was the best he could do.

"Angels are incubi and succubi. Masters of illusion and manipulation. They feed on humans, and humans alone. Magic users can be manipulated or tricked, but the magic that flows through them protects them from being fed on."

Amber stared at the illusion silently, taking in everything he was saying. This reveal was important. If he struck the right note, then she would be on his side, once and for all. If he didn't...he could lose them.

"I'm sure you felt it, Amber. He would have been like the sun, warming you and drawing you in. He would have tried to touch you as much as possible, and you would have craved that touch."

She nodded, anger burning in her eyes. "He tried, I shoved his hand away."

"They're feeding off what, sexual energy?" Genevieve asked.

"They feed off your soul, your life force, whatever you prefer to call it, in order to extend their own lives," he said, tearing his eyes away from Amber for a moment. "Seduction is simply the easiest way to gain enough physical contact to do so efficiently. Lust also further clouds their victim's judgment, making the task even easier."

"What are demons then?" Ceri asked, a challenging tone to her voice still.

"We are the fae."

Tommy's head snapped up. "What? I've never heard of them."

He chuckled and spread his arms wide. "Now you have. Our name and true nature has been lost to history."

"But you act like a demon. The fire, the smoke, the deals in exchange for a chance at someone's soul," Amber objected. "Why?"

"A very, very long time ago, the incubi made the final move in a long war. With the help of some witches they had entranced, they cursed every living fae, and every fae born from that moment forward."

Ceri's face paled. "The size of the coven needed..."

"Three hundred seventy three witches combined their power with the five archangels."

The witch sat down heavily on the couch. "It's an insane thing to do, but it's possible."

"What was the curse?" Tommy asked, ever perceptive.

"You saw the effects of it in Evangeline," he said, meeting the boy's eyes. "We will die without someone wearing our mark. Painfully and slowly. They sought to make us parasites as well, and they succeeded."

His eyes flicked back to Amber, taking in her reaction. Her elbows were resting on her knees and her hands were clasped tightly together. Her lips were pressed into a thin, disapproving line. Good. She was angry –– and that meant she believed him.

"What does Evangeline have to do with the curse?" Tommy asked, his dark eyes boring into him. "That's why you're protecting her, isn't it?"

"Nothing," he lied easily. "She's my niece, and despite the unfortunate circumstances surrounding her birth, I will always protect my family."

Tommy sat back and crossed his arms, looking unconvinced. That could be a problem but as long as he could put off more questions about Evangeline until the right time, perhaps it could be avoided.

"The fae have been fighting with the angels since the time of the curse. They attack our lands just often enough to keep us from growing in power enough to challenge them. Recently, these attacks have increased. Most of us agree that we are running out of time. At some point, we have to fight back or the angels will utterly destroy us. These areas where magic is being destroyed are an even more worrying sign."

That caught the witch's attention. "Why?"

"The angels want to destroy magic in this world. Completely."

Color drained from Ceri's face. "Is that possible?"

"Apparently, it is. They've only been testing the spell so far. Since they haven't eradicated magic yet, I can only conclude that they cannot. They are missing something." He sat back in his chair, folding his hands in his lap. "Along with breaking this curse, I have been searching to discover an answer to *what* they are missing so I can make sure they never get it."

"Do they want to destroy magic because it keeps them from feeding on magic users?" Amber asked, glancing at her friend with worry.

He nodded. "Yes."

"We can't let them do that. Any of it," Amber declared, a familiar, stubborn look coming into her eye.

And just like that, he had them.

CHAPTER 61

CERI

Ceri sat on the front porch watching the sun go down. Kadrithan had left them with questions. Fear. Disbelief. Tommy had insisted he was still not telling them something, and she agreed, but what he had told them was enough. There was a war coming.

They would have to fight. Everyone would. It didn't matter if they were a witch, a werewolf, or an elf. The angels wanted to take magic away from all of them.

The front door opened and Amber walked outside. "Thought I'd find you out here."

She gave her alpha a wan smile. "It's our spot I guess."

Amber walked over and sat down on the swing next to her with a tired sigh. "I suppose so." She pushed them into a gentle rock before pulling her feet up underneath her. "Are we doing the right thing by helping him?"

Ceri pulled her cardigan a little tighter around her. "We can't sit by and do nothing. That's all I know for sure."

Amber snorted. "The last time I decided I couldn't stand by and do nothing I ended up getting bitten by a werewolf on a full moon. We all know how that turned out."

"I think it turned out pretty well, minus the various trials and tribulations," she said, nudging Amber with her shoulder.

"There will be more of those if we do this. Worse ones, probably." Amber looked back through the window. "We'll be risking everything."

"I think we're too far in to back out now, to be perfectly honest."

"That seems to be how it goes."

They lapsed into silence as the sun dipped below the horizon. Reds and oranges stretched across the sky like watercolors over the jagged, dark silhouette of the forest. Her mind strayed to the spirit realm and to the tarot card. To her own darkness.

"Amber," she said hesitantly, all the emotions she hadn't wanted to face bubbling up inside her chest. "I'm sorry."

Amber looked at her with genuine concern. "What for?"

"I should have known better. I left that night by myself, ignoring common sense, and the entire pack paid for it. It's my fault you ended up stuck with another demon mark. It's my fault you nearly killed Derek and Genevieve. It's all my..." Her breaths started coming in gasps as tears poured down her cheeks. "All my fault."

Amber leaned over without hesitation and pulled her into a tight hug. "I never blamed you for that, but if you need to hear it, then I forgive you."

"I almost used blood magic to track down Selena and Deward," she said, all the dark things tumbling out of her at once. "I think about it all the time. About killing the other pixies and cutting out their hearts. Sometimes, I can even justify it in my head."

"You didn't go through with it," Amber said, arms tightening around her.

"Because I'm weak," she whispered.

Amber pulled back and looked at her very seriously. "Because you *aren't.*"

"I have a way to find them and I haven't, I just--"

"No. There is a line, Ceri, and there has to be. There are some things we cannot do no matter how important the cause is."

She took a deep breath, trying to calm the panic that had her whole body shaking. "What if I step over it?"

"Then I'll pull you back, just like you would do for me. That's what the pack, what family, is for."

"I need your help. There is something in the spirit realm and I can't get it alone. I think I know why now, but....I'm not strong enough on my my own."

Amber pulled back slightly and brushed away her tears. "What do you need?"

"I need the pack to come to the spirit realm with me. There's this...darkness there. I think it's what the tarot card has been trying to warn me about." She hesitated, not wanting to think about it's meaning, much less say it aloud. "This is going to sound kooky, but I think the darkness is something within *me.* The spirit realm can manifest terrible things if you go into with evil intent."

"Is there anything you can do to clear your intent before we try again? Meditation? Stick sage in your hair?"

She smacked Amber on the arm. "Don't mock me."

"I'm not! I just don't know how it all works."

Sighing, she hopped off the swing. "Come on. If we're going to do this, I need to get everything ready and tell the rest of the pack."

〜

Ceri finished the circle and surveyed her work. Since the sun had already set, they'd parked Amber's truck in the yard and were using the headlights to illuminate everything.

Normally, she'd do this inside, but with the pack it felt right to be outdoors under the moon. Satisfied everything was in order, she turned around to find Tommy standing right behind her.

"Derek said you took him to the spirit realm the other day."

She nodded. "Yeah. Why?"

He lightly punched her shoulder. "You could have asked for help sooner! I would have gone with you too."

Crossing her arms, she stared him down. "Well I'm asking now."

Amber jogged up. "We ready to do this? It's getting late."

"Yep. Alright, everyone inside the circle." She'd made it way bigger than normal. Everyone needed to be able to lay down, toe to toe, and still be inside it.

Genevieve, who had been quietly arguing with Steven, seemed to come to some sort of agreement. They hugged and Steven took a seat on the steps to the back porch, ready to keep watch over them while they did this.

Woggy, along with the whole swarm of pixies, were also gathered on the back porch watching curiously. There was a pile of leaves in front of them that looked like their version of popcorn. They signed to each other, sporadically, mixing squeaks in with the signed words. The pixies really were making it their own.

Amber was the last to step inside, and when she did, Ceri felt something change. Clarity filled her, giving her a sense of purpose. Red bled into Amber's eyes and her sense of the pack bond heightened.

"Whoa, are you guys feeling that?" Genevieve asked in a hushed whisper, as if afraid to break the spell.

She nodded. "Yes."

"Is that a good sign?" Amber asked.

"I hope so. Everyone lay down." She settled herself on the grass, her toes bumping together with everyone else's. "Remember, don't panic and stay *together*. No matter what happens."

There were murmurs of agreement from around the circle. She stared up at the crescent moon and let its soft light give her warmth.

A flap of wings startled her slightly as the owl settled at her head. It hooted in greeting.

"Can you take all of us?" she asked quietly.

Its head appeared in her line of vision, the luminous orange eyes drawing her in like gravity had been reversed. She took that as a yes.

A breath later, and she was standing on the cliff above the clouds. Snow was drifting down from the heavy clouds overhead. Lightning cracked, followed by the distant rumble of thunder.

She turned around to check on the others but stopped in shock. Derek was there, appearing human just like last time, but the others...were wolves. And they were way bigger than normal.

Amber's stooped her head to meet her eyes, cocking her head to the side as if to ask, *what's next?*

"Can you guys still understand me?" she asked, looking curiously at her pack.

Genevieve yipped happily, while Amber and Tommy nodded. Tommy's attention was mostly on the storm brewing overhead, his tail twitching nervously.

Derek joined her at the edge of the cliff. "We have to jump again, don't we?"

"Yep. Want me to hold your hand?" she asked with a smirk.

He glared at her. "Maybe I'll just push you instead and stay up here enjoying the view."

"Push me and I'll turn your pillow into a spider nest."

He lifted his hands in surrender. "Geez, you didn't have to take it there."

Rolling her eyes, she turned to the others. "We have to jump. You'll float to the bottom, so just try not to think about it too hard."

The wolves approached. Amber looked at her once for confirmation, then huffed and leapt off the edge. Before she could hesitate, Ceri jumped after her.

They floated down slowly. Cold turned to warmth, and the strange jungle came into view. Perhaps it was her imagination, but it looked more menacing than she remembered.

Derek let out a sigh of relief as they landed, finally opening his eyes. "I can't understate how much I hate that."

"Hopefully after today, we never have to come back. It's not really my favorite either."

Fur brushed against her arm as Tommy pressed himself lightly to her side. His ears were drawn as he looked warily around them.

"Yeah, it doesn't feel very welcoming here, does it?" Ceri said, patting his side. "Let's go."

Amber took point, leading them deeper into the dense jungle. Their footsteps were muffled by the heavy air.

The slightest breeze stirred her hair, carrying a hint of a whisper. She paused, looking around for the encroaching darkness, but it hadn't shown itself yet.

Genevieve stopped abruptly, stepping out of the line they had formed. Her ears swiveled as if she were searching for a noise.

"What is it?" Ceri asked, unconsciously stepping back into Derek.

Genevieve ignored her, glancing at Amber who must have given her some kind of approval because she moved away from them.

"What is she doing? We need to stay together!" Ceri objected, torn between running after Genevieve and staying with the others.

Genevieve, however, didn't go far. She stopped a few feet away and lifted her head, growling at something above her. Ceri followed her gaze. The darkness that she had been looking for on the ground flowed above them, sliding from tree to tree.

"Get back!" Ceri shouted, grabbing the totem hanging around her neck with one hand as she began chanting.

Still weak. Still afraid, the darkness whispered in her mind. *Still alone.*

Before she could finish her spell, the darkness fell over them like a net.

CHAPTER 62

CERI

"Keep chopping like that and you'll fail before we even get started."

Ceri looked down. Her eye of newt was half-squished and the edges where she had cut were jagged.

Her grandmother placed a fresh eye in front of her. "Start over but don't fall too far behind."

"She might as well quit now. She's never been able to keep up with me," Siobhan quipped from the other side of the room, smirking at her over her grandmother's shoulder. She flipped her long, red hair over her shoulder. "Ceridwen is weak."

Ceri narrowed her eyes at her cousin. "Shut up, Siobhan."

She could make this potion in her sleep. Her stupid, stuck-up cousin would be sorry once she had control of this coven. It was her birth right. Grandmother had chosen *her*.

No one could stop her. Especially not Siobhan. This was everything she'd ever...

Her vision blurred for a moment and she blinked in confusion. Why was she here? It felt like there was something she was supposed to be doing...something important.

"Back to work!" her grandmother barked.

Shaking off the unease, she gently held the eye of newt in place, careful not to crush it this time. The razor sharp knife cut through it like butter. Thin, even slices, just like she'd been taught.

She pushed her board forward for examination at the same time as Siobhan. Grandmother walked over to *her* board first and inspected it without expression, then moved to Siobhan's work table to do the same thing.

"Pass. Gather the final ingredient."

Siobhan flounced over to a cage Ceri hadn't noticed. Bony, gray pixies huddled in the back corner, squeaking shrilly as her cousin opened the small door to the cage. They tried to stay away from Siobhan's hand but she was fast, striking like a snake and grabbing one.

Two pixies clung to its arms but she shook them off and pulled out her prize, closing the door as she pulled out her arm.

"Ceridwen. Don't just stand there gawking, get one," her grandmother snapped.

"What?"

"A pixie, child. Or have you gone daft?" A warning glint shone in grandmother's eye as she glared at her. If she didn't act now, the punishment would be swift and unpleasant.

She didn't know why she was hesitating. They were just pixies. She didn't care about pixies. They were pests.

Swallowing down her discomfort, she marched over to the cage. Her traitorous fingers shook as she opened the little door.

When she stuck her hand inside, one of the pixies marched forward toward her hand instead of cowering like the others. Another tried to drag him back, but it shook off their hand with an imperious squeak. The pixie stared up at her defiantly, there for the taking.

"Ceridwen, don't waste my time!"

Her grandmother's voice startled her into action. She grabbed the pixie that had walked up to her. It must be an especially dumb one.

The pixie didn't struggle on the way back to her work bench but it was trembling. Stupid little pest. She glanced back over her shoulder and saw the other pixies watching. They wouldn't like what they were about to see.

"The cut on the wings must be clean. Don't waste any of it. Make sure you get the hearts too, those don't need to be fresh," her grandmother said, crossing her arms and glaring at each of them in turn.

Siobhan held her wriggling pixie down and grabbed her knife with the other. It was an awkward affair to cut off the wings while they were moving, but they had to be taken while the pixie was alive or it just wasn't the same. The potion would be weaker.

Using a finger to stretch the wings out, Siobhan placed her knife as close to the pixie's back as she could get it. Then, with a smooth press, severed them cleanly. The pixie shrieked in pain, a piercing noise that made Ceri's head hurt.

"You going to do it too, or just watch, loser?" Siobhan taunted, holding up the delicate little wings and wiggling them at her.

Ceri looked down at her pixie and it looked back up at her. "Stop looking at me like that," she muttered, slamming it down on her table harder than was necessary. Still, it stared up at her. Almost...defiantly.

She stretched out the wings with her finger and picked up the knife. The pixie wasn't struggling. Why wasn't he struggling?

Her hand shook as she held the knife over the wings. This was for the coven. For power. For everything she'd ever wanted. She had to do this. This was just the price of doing magic. Something had to pay it.

The pixie's heartbeat fluttered under her palm.

"Enough hesitation, Ceridwen! Do it now or I will remove you from this coven," her grandmother snarled, anger contorting her features.

Ceri's hand wouldn't stop shaking. The pixie patted her hand, then made a strange symbol with its fingers. Somehow she knew it meant *I love you*. That didn't make sense. Pixies didn't love. They didn't speak.

A flash of memory cut through her confusion. *Woggy.*

She dropped the knife and grabbed the pixie, holding the pixie protectively against her chest. "I won't do it."

Her grandmother advanced on her, shoving everything off her workbench in a fit of rage. "I trained you! I taught you everything! How could you be so weak after all that?"

"I'm not weak!" Ceri shouted back, her shaking hands betraying the very thing she wanted to deny.

"You're scared to hurt a pixie!"

"It doesn't deserve this!"

"No one gets what they deserve, only what they take!" her grandmother shouted, spittle flying from her lips. "And if you won't take it, then I will!"

"No!" Ceri took another step back. "You won't take anything! You're--" Confusion swept over her once again. "You're dead. You're both dead."

Siobhan rolled her eyes. "Do I look dead?"

"You did when..." Ceri shook her head, feeling something strange tugging at her. There was a voice, someone yelling for her in the distance. "This isn't real."

Siobhan groaned in irritation. "Don't be stupid, Ceridwen. Of course this is real."

"You're dead. The sorcerer killed you."

A cold wind swept through her. She curled in on herself, collapsing to the floor and burying her head in her knees. The scene shifted, the work room and her grandmother disappearing.

"Only because you let him kill me," Siobhan snarled.

She looked up and saw Siobhan's lifeless face staring back at her. Eyes gone. Beautiful hair hacked off. "You were too weak. You failed me."

"I'm sorry. I didn't know they'd hurt you."

"Sorry isn't enough!" Siobhan screamed, her pale hand reaching for Ceri.

A vicious growl startled Siobhan and she whirled around to face the intruder. A large, ruddy wolf walked toward them, her eyes glowing blood-red.

"Amber." Remembering the name gave Ceri strength. This was an illusion. This wasn't real.

Siobhan lunged at Amber, but the wolf walked through her like she didn't exist. Ceri rose and met Amber halfway, pressing her head to Amber's.

Points of light broke through the darkness around them, like stars appearing in a dark sky. They grew larger and larger and the darkness began to crumble. As the light touched her legs, the numbing cold fled from her limbs.

The jungle was gone along with the strange, oppressive warmth. She curled her fingers into Amber's fur to stay standing and looked around.

"Where the hell are we?" she whispered, afraid to speak too loudly in the cavern. It was maybe twenty feet across but the ceiling must have been fifty feet high. Wind and snow howled outside, whistling past the narrow entrance.

"I don't know," Derek replied.

She turned around and saw the rest of the pack was with them.

"The darkness swallowed you up," Derek explained as he pulled her into a hug.

"Amber decided to go in after you. When the two of you reappeared, the jungle was gone and we were here."

The wolves gathered around them. Tommy licked her elbow and sniffed her carefully, as if to make sure she was real.

"Are you okay?"

She nodded into Derek's chest. "Yeah, I'm okay. That darkness wasn't what I thought it was though. It wasn't anything I created. It was a trap."

"What kind of trap?"

"An illusion spell. One that drew on my worst fears to make them real. If I hadn't been able to break out of the dream I was trapped in, I would have stayed here until my body wasted away and I died." She took a deep breath, the gravity of the situation finally hitting her. "That's not the kind of thing I could have broken on my own."

"Then I'm glad you weren't alone."

Amber barked sharply, then nodded toward a raised dais a few feet away. Laying on the surface was half of a broken, clay tablet.

Curious, Ceri walked up to the dais. "This must be what the spirit wanted me to find."

"Should we take it?"

"I think so." She reached for the tablet but just before she could touch it, electricity exploded through her, throwing her backwards like a rag doll.

"Ceri!" Derek shouted, running after her.

"It didn't hurt," she reassured them, rolling back up to her knees. "But I think it reacted to my magic somehow. It was...odd."

Derek looked back at the tablet thoughtfully. "I don't have any magic."

"I could be wrong," she said, rising to her feet. Her spirit felt a little wobbly but she'd been through worse.

Derek brushed past Amber and jogged back up to the tablet.

"Derek, don't--"

He picked it up. Nothing happened.

"Huh. Guess it just doesn't like witches."

She looked at him incredulously. "Are you kidding me? You could have been hurt!"

"It didn't hurt you!" he shot back.

"That's not the point! That was insanely risky!"

Amber cut their argument off with a whiny howl and motioned for them to look up. The ceiling of the cavern was crumbling.

"Oops."

Ceri glared at Derek. "Everyone, stand together, just like we laid down."

The pack quickly arranged themselves around her and she pulled them back toward their bodies. The ceiling of the cavern caved in with a loud crack as a strong wind hit them, pushing them out of the spirit realm just before the rock rained down on their heads.

As the spirit realm was fading from view, she caught a glimpse of the tarot card that had been haunting her. It gave a little goodbye wave, then disappeared in a shower of golden sparks.

CHAPTER 63

AMBER

Amber jerked upright and blinked water out of her eyes as she patted her body. Rain was pouring down and she was soaked through, but she didn't care.

She was back in her body. No more spirit wolf. "Let's never do that again."

"I second that," Genevieve said with a groan, her limp, pink hair plastered to her face. "Not a fan of jumping off cliffs or not being able to speak or watching Ceri writhe in a mass of darkness."

"Jumping off cliffs?" Steven asked in alarm, leaving the shelter of the porch to see if Genevieve was okay.

"What do I do with this?" Derek asked, holding up the broken half of the tablet they'd seen in the cavern.

With his always impeccable timing, Kadrithan appeared in front of Amber. The rain hissed as it touched his skin, turning into steam instantly.

"This is not the time," she groaned, rubbing at her demon mark with a grimace.

The demon ignored her, focusing on the broken tablet in Derek's hand instead. "Where did you get that?"

Derek hid it behind his back. "None of your business, demon."

"You have no idea what you're holding––"

"Then explain what it is," Amber interrupted, crossing her arms.

"Why is the human holding it?" he asked instead of explaining. He always had a billion questions and never any answers.

"Kadrithan––

"I have to be sure," he said, relenting slightly. "Can the rest of you touch it?"

"I'll try again. It wouldn't let me in the spirit realm," Ceri said, smoothing her wet curls back out of her face. Her cardigan was falling off her shoulders it was so heavy with water.

"Are you sure that's a good idea?" Derek asked, hesitating to let her near it.

"I'll be careful," she reassured him.

Derek nodded reluctantly and held the broken tablet out within her reach.

Taking a deep breath, Ceri moved her hand slowly toward it, stopping about an inch away, then shook her head. "I still can't touch it, and if I do, it will actually hurt me in this realm."

Kadrithan nodded and turned away, facing Amber. "You have to hide this and keep it safe."

"Why?"

"It is half of Raziel's key."

They all went silent at that. Cassandra, the crazy elf had talked about it, as had Deward in the note he'd left in Tommy's room.

"What, exactly, is Raziel's key?"

Kadrithan clenched his jaw tightly, looking away as if searching for a way to get out of explaining it.

"You're going to explain and you're going to do it now," Amber demanded, thrusting her finger at him.

"Take it in the house," Kadrithan said, crossing his arms behind his back. "I need to speak with Amber alone."

No one moved. They all looked to her for direction, ignoring his orders entirely. Part of her wanted to refuse and make him explain now, in front of everyone, but based on the stiff set of his jaw, she had a feeling he wouldn't.

Turning to Derek, she nodded. "Go ahead and get out of the rain. I'll explain everything to y'all once I get some answers. Even if I have to beat them out of him."

Derek, holding the tablet close to his chest, cast a glare at the demon as he headed inside. The others trailed after him. Genevieve closed the door behind them but reappeared at the window and stood guard there.

"Walk with me," Kadrithan said, turning and floating toward the tree line.

She obliged but she wasn't happy about it. After he'd explained the true nature of the angels to them, she'd expected he would just be honest with them. Apparently that was expecting too much.

They reached the edge of the forest and she stopped, finding shelter under a tall tree to keep most of the rain off. "This is far enough."

He turned to face her slowly, his features sharpening as he drew on the mark. His feet touched the ground and he looked more solid than she'd ever seen him.

He smoothed his hands back through his wavy, black hair. She suppressed the urge to mock him when she noticed that he needed to shave. The rough stubble looked out of place above the old-fashioned suit he wore but now wasn't the time for banter.

Tapping his fingers restlessly against his crossed arms, he caught her gaze. "I need you to understand how important this is. What I am about to share with you is information that I have killed to protect, and would kill again to do so."

That was ominous. Taking a deep breath, she nodded. "We have the thing, I need to know what *exactly* it is and why it's important."

Angel rubbed a hand across the back of his neck. "It's part of the curse, as well as the key to breaking it. Or, at least half the key." He spoke as if she were dragging every word out of him.

She looked back toward the house and her pack. Right now, sitting in their living room, was the source of a curse that had cast an entire race into ruin. Everyone would want it. "Will the angels know it's gone?"

"I don't know."

"If they do, will they know we took it?"

He exhaled sharply. "I don't know."

She pressed her hands into her eyes and told herself to stay calm and not rage at Kadrithan just because he was here. This wasn't his fault, for once. They'd gone into the spirit world and retrieved this without knowing what it was. This was on them. "What do you know?"

"This will change everything. If I could take it back to the demon realm with me, I would," Kadrithan said, his arms held stiffly behind his back. Even when Evangeline had been in danger he hadn't been this desperate. He leaned forward and took her hand, holding it between his own. "Please protect it."

She stared at him in shock. "I'm surprised you aren't calling in your demon mark."

"If you aren't doing this willingly, it won't be enough. And..." He released her hand and sat back, jaw clenching. "I don't intend to ever call in that mark. I need you to help me until this is over."

"And when is it over?"

"When we win the war."

She leaned back against the tree and fiddled with the hem of her shirt. "How long has this war been going on?"

He was silent. The only sounds were the rain beating the forest canopy and her heart thumping painfully in her chest. She'd never thought about it, but he had no heartbeat at all since he wasn't really here.

"Kadrithan, how long?"

He sighed. "Centuries."

She squeezed her eyes shut. This was insane. Demons. Angels. Centuries long wars. She didn't want any of this.

"Amber, I'm begging you. We can win this. You don't understand how close we are. We have half of the tablet, we are close to finding the rest. We have Evangeline--"

"She is a child." Amber pushed off the tree and advanced on him, anger at this whole mess rushing through her. "And you said she wasn't involved in this."

He took a step forward, invading her space. "I never would have told you if it had been an option. My niece's role in this is pivotal. If I could free my people without her and let her be a child, then I would. But the incubus took that option away from us."

"Is she even really your niece?"

He smoothed his hair back with an angry swipe. "Yes. She is."

"I don't know which of the things you've told me are truth and which are lies. How am I supposed to believe any of this?" she demanded, throwing her hands in the air. "For all I know, it's *all* a lie."

"It's not!" he shouted, all pretense of control now gone. "You must understand the position you have put me in! We are fighting for survival. For our freedom. I owe you nothing. Not explanations, not the truth. *Nothing.*" He grabbed her by the shoulders and pushed her back into the tree. "But I have given you both because I need your help."

She yanked his hands off her shoulders and shoved him back. "That's not how this works, Kadrithan. You're asking me to put my life and the lives of everyone in my pack on the line for this. So yes, you do owe me explanations and the truth. If you want us to fight this war with you then *we are part of it.*"

His lip curled in derision. "You are not fae––"

"I don't give a shit." Her hands shook with anger and the wolf moved restlessly in her mind. A red haze filtered across her vision as she drew on the power of the pack. On her strength as alpha. "You do not own me."

He pressed his thumb into the mark above her heart. "You sure about that?"

She grabbed him by his fancy collar and dragged him down to her face. "I am. You need that mark just like you need me. Don't forget that."

Gently, he unwound her fingers from his collar, but didn't move away. "Whatever you need to tell yourself to sleep at night."

"What are you planning on doing with Evangeline?"

He rolled his eyes and finally moved back. "Why are you so hung up on that? I'm not planning on sacrificing her life if that's what you're worried about."

"It was a thought that crossed my mind."

Sighing, he leaned his shoulder against the tree next to her and crossed his arms. "She has to live to help us, not die."

"To break the curse?"

"Yes. The only person that can break the curse is someone with both fae and incubus blood." He shook his head. "They must have thought no one from either race would be stupid enough to screw the other, much less have a child with their enemy."

Amber frowned. "Who are her parents?"

"My sister and an incubus I never met."

"Did he rape her, or…?" she asked tentatively.

"No. It was *love*, of course. Nothing makes people stupider."

"Does Evangeline know all this?"

He nodded with a sigh. "Yes, I told her everything. It was time. She raged at me, cursed both angels and demons, and then agreed to do whatever was necessary because she wants to be free of this curse just as much as the rest of us."

Amber sat down and put her head in her hands. "What else do you need to break the curse?"

Surprising her, Kadrithan slid to the ground next to her, staring blankly up through the trees. "The halves of the key, joined once more. The blood of enemies in their veins, wielding light and fire. The twilight hour, when day meets night. In the space between realms where spirits dwell. Only then shall what has been wrought be undone."

"That was poetic. Is it some kind of prophecy?"

He shook his head. "Prophecies are guaranteed to come true, this wasn't that reassuring. It was accompanied by a warning that if this was not accomplished before, and I quote, 'the gift of the fae is become corrupt', then it will never be done."

Tilting her head to the side, she pinched her brows together. "What is the gift of the fae?"

He was quite for a moment before turning his face toward her. "Magic."

She swallowed around the sudden lump in her throat and tried to process what he was saying. "The fae...gave everyone magic?"

"That's what the legends tell us. It was a very long time ago. My ancestors were powerful and immortal. They took a liking to the humans and the ruling kings and queens shared a portion of their magic with those they favored. Giving away this magic weakened them but they did not care, they thought they were still too powerful to be touched." His tone became wistful, almost nostalgic for a time long past. "Over time, they realized that their magic had been leaking away and they had lost more than they realized. They stopped it, but by that point, the fae were greatly weakened. It was that gift that allowed the incubus to strike us down, using the very gift we had given to the humans."

"Were you alive back then?" Amber asked quietly, afraid to break the spell. He was rarely this open.

"Yes, but I was very young when the curse struck us down."

She turned her gaze back to the sky. The rain was slowing down. "The war has been going on your entire life."

"Yes."

"This thing the angels are doing to the magic, that's what the warning is about, isn't it?"

He nodded. "That is what I fear."

"I need you to promise me something." She looked at him, his coal black eyes meeting her own.

"What?"

"Promise me that you will not lie to me again, not even by omission. If we are going to help you win this war, I have to be able to trust you. And you have to trust me."

He held her gaze, frustration and indecision warring in his eyes. "You are asking more than you realize."

"I think honesty is a fair trade for my life."

"You are going to be the death of me."

She snorted. "I think I should be saying that to you."

His hand brushed against her cheek, startling her. She tried to jerk away, but he slipped his hand around the back of her neck, holding her in place, then pressed his other hand to the mark. "I swear on this mark that I will be honest with you, and I expect the same in return."

Her heart pounded in her chest as the heat of his hand sank into her skin. She licked her lips nervously feeling suddenly parched. "Then it's settled."

His thumb brushed against the pulse point on her neck before he pulled his hand away and sat back. "Good. Can you hide the tablet wherever it was your witch stowed Evangeline when the police were searching the house?"

She cleared her throat and pushed up to her feet, brushing the dirt and pine needles off her butt. "I'll ask Ceri."

"I'll be back in an hour. I have to inform the others what your pack has found."

"Alright."

Kadrithan disappeared in a puff of smoke but she didn't move. Still shaking, she lifted her hand to her neck where he'd held her. It was still warm.

CHAPTER 64

TOMMY

"But he lied," Tommy objected, pacing behind the couch. Pissed off didn't even start to cover it. He wanted to strangle someone. Preferably the demon.

"Yes, he lied," Amber said stiffly, glaring at the tablet sitting on the coffee table. Captain Jack was winding through her legs, rubbing his face against her with a loud purr. That cat was getting weirder by the day. "I think he's told us everything now but I can't be sure."

"Why did you agree to help him if you can't be sure?"

"Because I *am* sure that the angels are our enemies. They've been trying to kill Evangeline, which we saw with our own eyes. And when that angel approached me in the coffee shop, he tried to get into my head. If you had felt it..." Amber shook her head, lips pressed into a thin line. "It wasn't right."

"That is unusual." Steven pushed his glasses back up on his nose, continuing to mutter to himself, and leaned a little closer to the broken tablet. He was busy recreating all the symbols on the tablet in his notebook. Tommy was glad someone had thought to do it before they hid it away.

He stopped pacing and scuffed at the carpet with his bare foot. "Kadrithan said Eva knows? About the curse and how she has to break it?"

"Yes, he said he told her."

"Well, no matter how we move forward, I think we all agree that we should hide the tablet if we can," Ceri said, standing and walking over to it.

He certainly didn't want anyone to be able to walk in here and take it after all the trouble they'd gone through to retrieve it. Amber was right, the angels were their enemy. As far as trusting the demons, he was still unsure, but they were the least of evils for now.

Everyone nodded in agreement, except Steven.

"I'm almost done, just one moment." He drew a little faster.

"Steven, just take a picture with your phone," Genevieve said, exasperated.

He froze, pencil hovering over his paper. "Oh. Why didn't you suggest that sooner? That would be much easier." He pulled out his phone and quickly snapped a picture, then motioned to Ceri that it was all hers.

Ceri shut her eyes and swayed lightly in place, getting that spaced out look she always had when she was connecting with Illya. The floor shifted slightly and the cabinets in the kitchen banged around, then, Illya's specter appeared.

"Is everything alright?" Illya asked, her hands clasped tightly in front of her chest.

"Wow," Steven said breathlessly, making notes without even looking at the paper.

Tommy shook his head with a smile. Watching Steven be awed by magic was the only bright spot in this crap heap of a week.

"Illya, can you hide this? Like you hid Evangeline and Eloise when the police came?" Ceri asked, pointing at the tablet.

The elf approached it, inspecting it carefully. "It's very powerful."

"Yes," Ceri agreed. "That's why we need to hide it and keep it safe."

Illya stuck her hand in the tablet and her face screwed up in concentration. For a tense few seconds, everyone was silent, then Illya let out an annoyed huff.

"I can hide it for a while, but not forever. It's very powerful."

"How long do you think?"

"Perhaps a few months."

Ceri let out a sigh of relief. "That will have to be long enough."

"As you wish," Illya said, dissolving into a green mist. She enveloped the tablet and then it just...disappeared. Along with the coffee table.

Ceri released whatever hold she had on the house and shook her head to clear it.

"So much for the coffee table," Genevieve muttered.

Amber rolled her eyes. "We'll get a new one."

Captain Jack meowed and trotted over to the newly empty space, sniffing it suspiciously. His tail swished as he pawed at the carpet.

"Well, we've officially confused the cat," Tommy said, leaning against the back of the couch. "When is Kadrithan supposed to come back?"

Amber looked at the clock on the wall. "In a few minutes."

Tommy dragged his hands through his hair. Everyone was still on edge. He could feel it vibrating through the pack bond. Normally he couldn't sense anyone but Amber. Something had changed. It had been slowly growing for a while. Going to the spirit realm must have accelerated it.

Needing space to think, Tommy retreated into the kitchen. He grabbed a cold soda out of the refrigerator then shut the door, leaning against it. The can hissed as he popped open the tab. Captain Jack came in to investigate, but when he saw it wasn't wet food, turned and left again.

Sipping on his drink, he thought through the recent revelations. Knowing for sure that Deward's disappearance was connected to the angels did nothing to reassure him, but it might help them find him.

The silverware drawer rattled and inched open, then a head popped out. It wasn't Woggy though. It was his girlfriend –– who they really needed to give a name. She set her prize on the counter then shimmied her way out of the drawer.

"Hey there," he said, signing along with his words.

The pixie squeaked in surprise and toppled over.

"Sorry to scare you." He smiled and nudged the spoon toward her, which she grabbed and held to her chest protectively. They'd really had a thing for the silverware lately. Maybe spoons were a delicacy. "Where's Woggy?"

He knew that if she was here, Woggy wouldn't be far away. They'd been inseparable lately. Sure enough, at the sound of his name, Woggy's head popped up from behind dishes drying on the counter.

A thought struck Tommy. It was so simple. They couldn't track down Cassandra and Deward, but they knew what the two of them were after. Raziel's key. They'd already found one half of it. Maybe they could find the other half too. Then, Deward would come to them.

"You look like you've just thought of something," Amber said, joining him in the kitchen. "Also I need in the fridge."

He moved away, leaning against the counter instead. "I did think of something. We've been putting out all this effort trying to find Deward, but we're going about it all wrong. We just need to find the rest of Raziel's key like Deward said in his note, then I think he and Cassandra will come to us. I'm not sure exactly how this curse or prophecy works but it's driving them to find it."

Amber nodded along as she grabbed a soda from the refrigerator as well. "That makes a lot of sense. And based on what I talked to Kadrithan about, finding the rest of the tablet needs to be done soon."

Smoke drifted around a corner, accompanied by the smell of sulfur. Kadrithan grew up from the smoke, appearing in his more human form. He looked around, not at any of them, but searching for the tablet. "Where is it?"

"We hid it just like you asked," Amber said.

He nodded, some of the tension leaving his shoulders. "Good."

"Is Evangeline okay? Amber said you told her she's part of all of this." Tommy crossed his arms and scowled at the demon.

Kadrithan lifted an eyebrow as if surprised he cared. "She is well, and remains safe."

"For now," Tommy muttered. He followed them back into the living room and sat down next to Genevieve. She slung an arm around his shoulder in solidarity.

Amber rubbed her forehead tiredly. "What did your..." she waved her hand in the air, searching for the word, "people have to say?"

"Zerestria had much to say, none of it very comforting. The elders are gathering quietly to prepare to escalate the war." As he spoke, his hands clenched tighter and tighter. He *really* didn't like sharing information.

"Who is Zerestria?" Tommy asked, happy to continue the torture. He told himself it was revenge for all the lies Kadrithan had told Evangeline, but he knew it was just for himself.

The demon looked back at him, brows drawn together in annoyance. "The elder I work most closely with."

Amber shifted from foot to foot restlessly. "Is there any sign that the angels –– this Raziel –– know that we took the tablet?"

"No. Fortunately, he seems unaware so far. Zerestria does not believe he would be able to discover who took it even if he did become aware, but there is still a risk."

Ceri pulled her cardigan tighter around her and began fiddling with the hem of her sleeve. "In the note Deward left for Tommy, he mentioned Raziel's key. They've been looking for it. Where is the rest of the tablet?"

"Tommy and I were just talking and he thinks that if we find the rest of the tablet, the curse will make Deward and Cassandra come to us. We need to find it for them," Amber said.

"That's the problem. I don't know where it is." Kadrithan stood there stiffly, as if telling the truth made him physically uncomfortable. Served the demon right as far as he was concerned.

"You know, I'd forgotten this, but the day Cassandra approached me she was asking for *you*," Amber said, narrowing her eyes at Kadrithan. "She specifically wanted to talk to you to find Raziel's key. She thought you knew where it was."

Kadrithan's frown deepened and he looked away thoughtfully. "If I knew where it was, I would have stolen it long ago. It's odd she assumed I knew where it is."

"The message Deward left said to tell Kadrithan time was running out. They both seem to think you know something or need to do something," Tommy said, pulling the note out of his pocket. He'd kept it with him since he found it. "Here."

"I can't hold it. Appearing like this requires almost too much effort as it is. I'm still recovering from helping Amber with the curse," Kadrithan said.

Amber frowned. "You were hurt?"

"Exhausted. Using great amounts of magic outside of a deal in exchange for a mark is very taxing. I did more than I should have, and have been paying for it ever since."

"Ah..." Amber turned away, resuming her pacing.

Tommy unfolded the note and held it out for the demon to read.

He nodded when he was done. "I've never encountered a curse of prophecy quite like this one. This elf has no reason to know who I am and we have done *everything* possible to keep the angels from suspecting we are searching for the tablet."

"But they know now," Amber said quietly.

Kadrithan nodded sharply. "Most likely."

"Could the rest of the tablet be in the spirit realm where we got the first half?" Tommy asked.

"No, it's here, in the human realm. Based on what we *do* know of this elf and the Book of Prophecy, I suspect it is nearby. Raziel has always preferred this area, visiting it often. I think he does so to keep an eye on the tablet."

Genevieve propped her feet up on the coffee table. "Did Cassandra kill Laurel Teller because she thought she might know where it was?"

Kadrithan nodded. "I suspect so. She also recently attempted to rob another of Raziel's other properties –– a place we had been watching as well. Based on Raziel's reaction, she did not find it there."

"I think I was scrying Deward when they tried to rob Raziel," Ceri said, staring at her hands as if caught in the memory. "They'd killed someone, and talked about lies and tricks. Saying 'it is hidden'. She must have been talking about the tablet."

Steven sat forward, his notebook balanced on his knee. "Perhaps we need to make a list of all the places it *could* be. I can research it, dig through the history books. My school's library--"

"History," Tommy exclaimed. "You told me to talk to the trolls to find out the truth about the angels. You said they were the best historians. Is there a chance they might be able to piece together where Raziel has hidden it?"

"It's...possible."

"Perhaps having someone that can provide context will make it even more likely," Amber said, crossing her arms and looking pointedly at Kadrithan.

"You want me to reveal myself to the trolls?" Kadrithan asked incredulously.

She nodded. "Yes. They're searching for their son. They'll do anything to help him, even work with a demon I suspect."

"Deward knew about Evangeline and didn't care I had a demon mark. His parents will understand."

"Then it's settled." Amber grabbed her jacket off the hook by the door. "Steven, with us. If the rest of you could stay here, that'd be great. I don't feel comfortable leaving the house empty since she's holding the tablet for us."

Ceri nodded. "Of course, I don't mind staying."

Tommy was as anxious as he was excited. They were finally getting somewhere. They had a plan.

CHAPTER 65

AMBER

It was dawn. No one had slept a wink. Amber propped her feet up on the side of the truck, folding her hands under the back of her head, and watched the sun lifting over the horizon.

Everyone else was consumed with research. They had lists, maps, charts, and stacks of books. Once Kadrithan had needed to leave to rest, she'd escaped out here. She couldn't help with this part. History and research wasn't her thing.

She could stitch someone up, replace a transmission, or punch a werewolf in the face but she could *not* read dry history books for hours on end. Being cooped up in the midst of all that was starting to grate on her nerves so she'd come out here for some fresh air.

This used to be her and Dylan's thing. Laying in the back of this truck, talking about their dreams. His big plan had been getting the bite, then becoming a big rock star. He couldn't sing or play an instrument but that didn't matter when they were laying under the stars. Anything felt possible.

"You wouldn't believe what I've gotten mixed up with, Dylan," she whispered, watching the last of the stars fade away as the sky brightened. "Werewolves were just the beginning. I'm literally fighting angels now. Is that cooler than a rock star? I think it is."

For the first time since he'd died, remembering him didn't feel like a knife in her chest. The grief was still there but so was the happy, hopeful feeling he'd always inspired in her.

Her phone buzzed with a text from Tommy saying they'd found something. She sat up with a groan and hopped over the side of her truck. A faint hint of leather and cheap cologne made her pause. She knelt down, sniffing carefully to find the source of the scent.

It was coming from above the tire in the wheel well. She shone her phone's flashlight into the space and saw a small black thing stuck to the metal. It was flat and square and almost unnoticeable. If she hadn't been looking for something she never would have seen it.

She pulled it off, careful not to break it and brought it to her nose. The scent was faint but she was sure she recognized the scent as belonging to Horan. That asshole had been tracking her. It must be how he found her when she was at Lightvine's house the other day.

She shoved it in her pocket and headed back toward the house. This pissed her off but it would have to wait. Finding the rest of Raziel's key and getting Deward back were way more important than an MIB agent on a power trip. She'd deal with Horan when it was all over.

CHAPTER 66

CERI

Ceri accepted the tea Derek had made her with a grateful smile. She'd felt lighter since they'd returned from the spirit realm. The doubt and guilt that had been plaguing her since the fight with the sorcerer had lifted.

"So, have you changed your mind about tarot cards?" Derek asked as he stirred a heaping spoonful of sugar into his mug of tea.

She scoffed at his suggestion. "No. Most people using tarot are full of crap."

"But not all of them?" Derek sipped his tea smugly.

She narrowed her eyes at him. "I'm not letting Dr. Stone get anywhere near me with those cards ever again."

Genevieve stuck her head in the kitchen. "Someone just pulled in the driveway."

Ceri's heart jumped into her throat. The angels couldn't be here already, could they? "Who is it?"

"I think it's Alpha Vernier."

Setting her tea down on the counter, Ceri followed Genevieve to the window that looked out at the driveway. Sure enough, it was Tatiana that climbed out of a black suburban.

"It's weird of her to show up unannounced. I'll go talk to her. Call Amber."

Genevieve nodded and pulled out her phone.

"Stay inside, Derek. I mean it," Ceri said, waiting for him to agree before pulling open the front door and walking out to greet Tatiana. She put on a pleasant smile. "What a nice surprise."

Tatiana returned her smile. "I certainly hope so."

"If you're looking for Amber she won't be back for about a half an hour." Ceri stopped a safe distance from Tatiana and leaned against the porch banister.

"I'm here to talk to you, actually," Tatiana said with a wink. "Can we walk?"

Ceri hesitated. Alarm bells were going off in her mind. There was something wrong here. However, she didn't think Tatiana was here to hurt her.

"Sure," she said finally, walking down the steps to join Tatiana.

The alpha slipped her arm into Ceri's then started toward the gate, walking at a slow pace. "It's been quite the week, hasn't it?"

"I suppose," Ceri hedged, not sure what Tatiana knew and what she was guessing at.

Tatiana stopped and turned to her. "We should be honest with each other."

She raised an eyebrow. "That would be good. Why are you here?"

"Because you need me as much as I need you."

"Really?" She didn't like where this was going. She didn't like that Tatiana had come when Amber wasn't here. And she didn't like that Jean wasn't with them.

"Your pack is being investigated by the MIB and Carter has all but openly declared war on your pack." Tatiana sighed, as if it pained her to say all this. "You need knowledge and protection Amber can't give to you. She's sweet and very well-intentioned, but she's managed to get herself a leech that will never let go," Tatiana said plainly. "You can see that, can't you? Out of all of them, I thought you'd be the most clear-headed about the situation."

Ceri's mind was spinning. "Are you suggesting I leave my pack?"

Tatiana leaned in and wrapped her hands around Ceri's. "I'm inviting you to join mine."

"I can't--"

"You *can*. Amber never gave you the pack bite. Walking away from them is as simple as choosing it." Tatiana gave her hands a quick squeeze and leaned back. "This *is* a choice, though. I won't try to intimidate you into joining my pack. The facts are plain to both of us, and the threats you will be facing if you stay are out of my control."

"I'm not leaving my pack," Ceri said, incredulous Tatiana would even suggest it. All this had been a ploy to try and lure her away from Amber. "The fact that you'd even want someone who would turn their back on their pack as soon as things got dangerous makes me question not only your judgment, but your character."

Tatiana's face darkened at the insult. Red flowed into her irises and she seemed to grow bigger, the air humming with her anger. "I have been civil throughout this conversation, how dare you--"

"It doesn't matter how sweetly you say it." Magic rippled over Ceri's skin. Tatiana had claimed she wouldn't try to force things, but she could no longer take her at her word. "You're leaving, and if you try to hurt my pack, in any way, I will make you regret it unto your dying breath."

Genevieve walked out onto the front porch and crossed her arms. "You heard her. Get off our property."

Tatiana never took her eyes off Ceri. "You will regret this, and when you do, you will come crawling to me to beg for your salvation."

"I don't beg," Ceri snapped. She drew on her magic and the power of her pack, letting it flow around her. Wind lifted her hair and electricity crackled through the air. "Now leave while you can still walk."

Tatiana turned on her heel and stomped back to her suburban, slamming the door after she got in. Gravel spun under her tires as she gunned it down the driveway, leaving a cloud of dust behind her.

Ceri, her anger growing by the minute, marched back into the house.

"Amber will be back in about five minutes. They were already on their way when I called," Genevieve said, still staring at the gate. "I'm going to shift and watch the perimeter, just in case she tries to come back."

"Good idea," Ceri said, pacing the length of the living room.

Derek stepped in her path and caught her by the shoulders. "Take a deep breath before you set something on fire. There are literally sparks shooting off your fingertips."

She looked down and saw her fingertips were crackling a bit. With a frustrated sigh, she began releasing the magic she'd drawn on when telling Tatiana to go the hell away. "I'm not going to set anything on fire."

"Uh huh. Sure."

"I can't believe she was playing us this whole time. Amber really liked her."

"It was a dick move," Derek agreed, pulling her into a hug.

She wasn't sure when he'd become the person who knew how to calm her down, or when burying her face in his chest made her feel like she was home. It was just so easy with him.

A thought occurred to her and she jerked away, her mind racing.

"What's wrong?"

"Nothing. I just realized something is all."

The front door flew open and Amber ran inside, looking around frantically like she expected her to be gone. "Where is Tatiana? I'm going to eviscerate her."

"She left, but that doesn't matter right now," Ceri said, walking over to her alpha. "Give me the pack bite."

Amber looked at her in alarm. "Can witches even become a werewolf?"

"No, but that's not what I'm asking. Don't change me, just give me the pack bite. Cement my bond with the pack. There is a difference between the two. A bite from an alpha on any day other than the full moon won't change you. It's how alphas accept new werewolves into their packs." She pulled up her sleeve, extending her bare arm toward Amber. "Vernier was lying when she said it was unimportant. I didn't realize that until I was talking to her today. I will never fully become a shaman until you do it. We'll be stuck in this state of transition forever."

Amber's expression hardened, her anger at Vernier for her lies and manipulation echoing through the pack bond. "I understand."

"Are you sure this is a good idea?" Derek asked warily.

"I'm positive." Her heart pounded in her chest as Amber gently lifted her arm toward her mouth. This was going to hurt. Amber met her eyes, waiting to get final confirmation that she was sure about this.

Ceri nodded firmly. "Do it now."

Amber's teeth lengthened and her eyes glowed red as she bit down on Ceri's forearm. There was pain, sharp and hot, as her blood filled her alpha's mouth. But she barely noticed it as magic surged between them.

For a moment, it felt like Amber was draining her, sucking all the life and magic from her body…but then the flow of power shifted. The power of the pack crashed into her, filling her back up. It flowed back and forth between them until she could no longer feel where her magic ended and the strange, feral power of the wolf began.

She could feel them. Amber. Tommy. Genevieve. An awareness of the pack sat in her chest like a second heartbeat.

Amber slowly lowered her arm, blood staining her lips. "That was different."

"No kidding."

"Your eyes are glowing."

She turned to the mirror hanging by the front door and saw she was right. An intense, blue light burned in her eyes. Not yellow like a regular werewolf, or red like an alpha. Something different.

CHAPTER 67

GENEVIEVE

Genevieve had run the full perimeter of the property after Tatiana had left. Her muscles burned in a good way and the hot shower she'd taken after she'd gotten back had left her feeling like she'd had a massage.

She decided the pack didn't shift and run often enough. They still went about things like they were human so often, only shifting on the full moon or when they absolutely had to.

Steven wrapped his arms around her waist and planted a kiss on her neck. "You smell better."

She whacked him on the arm -- gently, unlike last time when she'd accidentally left a huge bruise. "Rude."

"Just being honest." He turned her around and held her tight. "I'm glad I've gotten to see more of you."

"Me too. This is going to sound bad but...I didn't think I would like it this much. It's nice having you here."

"Is that so?" Steven said, a teasing tone in his voice. "You don't want me to move in, dooo yoooou?"

She laughed nervously. "What if I did?"

"Wait, seriously?"

Genevieve.

The impression of her name drifted through her mind. She knew it was Amber that had said it, but she also knew Amber hadn't said it out loud.

"What's wrong?"

"I think I heard...that can't be possible."

She grabbed her clothes and quickly pulled them on.

"Wait! You can't run off now!" Steven complained.

"I'll be right back!"

She raced downstairs. She had to know what Amber had just done. This was in no way related to fleeing the conversation with Steven.

Amber was sitting cross legged on the floor with Ceri in the middle of the living room, her eyes shut in concentration.

"How did you do that?"

Amber's eyes shot open and she twisted around in place with a huge grin. "It worked?"

"I heard my name, but it was in my head?"

"Yes!" Amber threw her hands in the air in celebration. "It's actually working!"

"That book you found that talked about all the changes the pack would go through with a shaman was right!" Ceri said, grinning like a lunatic. "The pack bite made all the difference!"

"Does this mean we can actually talk through the pack bond now?" she asked, excitement growing in her chest. This was so *cool*.

"With practice, yes. That took way too much effort and concentration to be practical in the middle of a fight or anything like that," Amber said, still beaming with pride. "I can't believe it actually worked."

"I want to try next," Tommy said, dropping to the floor next to Amber.

Genevieve's phone started ringing in her room. She groaned, but ran back upstairs to answer it. If it was her boss and she missed the call, there'd be hell to pay.

Steven held it out for her, looking resigned that they wouldn't get to talk about what she'd said for a while.

"Hello?"

"I need...help..." Icewind grunted, pain clear in her voice.

"Where are you?"

"Sending you...location..." There was the ping of a message, then a thunk.

"Icewind?"

There was no reply.

"Crap. Amber! We have a problem!" Genevieve shouted as she shoved her feet in her shoes.

CHAPTER 68

TOMMY

Tommy helped Amber lift Icewind onto the dining room table.

"Who attacked you?" Genevieve asked, cradling her blood-streaked face in her hands.

"Wolves," Icewind slurred out, her eyes rolling back in her head.

"Tommy, get gauze from the bathroom," Amber said as she ripped Icewind's shirt off to find the source of the bleeding.

"Horan...following him and they...they caught me--" Icewind hissed in pain as Amber pressed down on a gash across her stomach.

Tommy shook himself out of the daze he was in and ran to the bathroom, grabbing the first aid kit from under the sink. He wished he could plug his nose somehow to escape the smell of blood. He was really starting to hate it.

"Here," he said, handing Amber a bundle of gauze.

"Ceri, do you have anything to stop this bleeding? We have to do it fast," Amber asked as she pressed the gauze to the wound. "Tommy, come hold pressure on this."

He hurried around to the side of the table and put his hand where Amber's had been. The blood soaking through the bandages was hot and sticky. He could feel Icewind's sluggish heartbeat under his palm.

"Yes, I'll get it."

"Shouldn't we take her to a hospital?" Tommy asked, watching her face grow paler by the moment.

"There's no time now." Amber worked intently, wrapping the worst of the wounds first. The elf was covered in bite marks, chinks of flesh missing in some places.

Bile rose in his throat and he had to look away. They'd torn her apart. It was a miracle she was still alive. He had no idea how she'd managed to run away like this. They'd found her crawling through the woods.

Icewind grabbed his arm, startling him. "My father..."

"We'll find him, I promise," Tommy said, hoping he sounded reassuring. He was pretty sure Thallan was still missing.

"No, he––" Icewind's face lost all its color and she fell back, unconscious.

"Uhhh, Amber, she passed out," Tommy said frantically.

"I know. Ceri! We really need some potions now!" Amber shouted over her shoulder.

Ceri came running back into the room and dumped an armful of supplies on the table. "Tommy, give her the blue ones."

"Can I let the pressure off on this?"

"Yes, I'll hold it," Amber said, reaching one hand over and taking his place.

He grabbed the blue potion and opened it with shaking fingers. Grabbing her jaw, he pulled her mouth open and poured the potion between her lips. Some dribbled down the side of her face but the effect was immediate.

She surged back to consciousness, her whole body jerking as she coughed.

"Hold still!" Amber shouted, practically throwing herself across Icewind to keep her from coming off the table. "You have to stay as still as possible or you'll tear everything back open."

Icewind grimaced, her teeth grinding together. "Everything hurts."

"Green one, Tommy," Ceri said, opening a jar of salve to treat the bad wound on Icewind's stomach.

He grabbed the next potion. Icewind opened her mouth this time, making it easier to feed it to her. As the bright green potion hit her tongue, she relaxed with a sigh.

"Need that schtuff all da time," she muttered, smacking her lips happily.

"What is in this?" Tommy asked, carefully setting it down before any got on his fingers.

"It's a strong painkiller. Also creates euphoria," Ceri said as she held the gash closed as Icewind's skin began knitting back together. It wasn't perfect, but it closed enough for the bleeding to stop.

"Icewind––"

"Call meeee Neia. Dat's my name," Icewind said with a giggle. "Neeeeeeeiaaaaa. Like a horse!"

Tommy met Amber's eyes. She looked like she was having just as much trouble not losing it as he was.

"Neia," Amber said, sounding like she was being strangled. "Who attacked you?"

"Wolfie boys and wolfie girls." She lifted her head off the table and frowned exaggeratedly. "My daddy was there."

"Thallan was there when you were attacked?" Tommy asked. Surely she had to be misremembering.

"Yup. Yup yup. He saw it all. Set them on fiyah! But he was helping them. I heard him. Heard him telling them allllll about you guys."

There was a loud banging on the front door and the house shuddered. Everything groaned and moved, sounding like a roar.

Genevieve ran into the room. "Thallan is at the door."

"Did anyone follow him?" Amber asked, wiping her bloody hands off on a rag.

"No, doesn't look like it."

Derek jogged up behind Genevieve with his shotgun. "Want me to make him leave?"

"No," Amber said, her expression going hard. "He's going to tell us what the hell he's been doing. Ceri, do you have anything that can make Neia less..." She waved her hand at the loopy elf.

"Yeah, but it will bring back the pain," Ceri said.

"Give it to her. I think she'll want to be coherent for this. If not, we can dose her with the good stuff again."

Ceri nodded and opened a small jar with a murky brown liquid, holding it under Neia's nose. Tommy grimaced, even from here it burned his nose.

Neia jerked, the glassiness leaving her eyes as she came back to full coherence. Her jaw tightened as the pain returned with it.

"Where is he?" she demanded.

"Outside. He can't get in the house. Your mom...banished him," Ceri said uncomfortably.

"My mom is dead," Neia said in confusion.

Amber shook her head when Ceri looked to her. "We'll explain later. Do you want to talk to him? We need to know what he's been doing."

"Yes. I want him to look me in the eye when he tries to explain why he's been working with those assholes," Neia said through gritted teeth.

"Alright. I can carry you outside," Amber offered.

Neia tried to move her legs, but stopped, panting from the pain. "Yeah, can't walk."

Amber very gently scooped her up, but that still caused the elf pain. With all her injuries, it was unavoidable.

The pack moved to the door as one. Genevieve waited until they were all there, then opened the door.

Thallan was pacing angrily in front of the porch, his hair disheveled and his shirt scorched. "Where is she?"

Amber moved to the front. "You've got a lot of nerve coming here making demands."

"I made a mistake," Thallan whispered hoarsely, hunching in on himself as he took in his daughter's injuries.

"What did you do?" Neia demanded.

"I didn't know you'd get hurt," he pleaded, reaching for her despite the distance between them.

"What did you do?" she demanded, biting off each word as she said it.

His eyes skittered to the ground. "A woman came to me. An angel. I told her they knew where the half breed demon was. That they'd protected her." He pulled out a cigarette, lighting it with shaking hands. "I didn't know they'd hurt you."

"You *idiot*," Neia snarled. "How could you betray these people?"

"I just wanted that demon to get what was coming to him," Thallan said, sounding unconvinced by his own words.

"That demon saved my mother from a slow, painful death. I wish she was still alive too, but he had nothing to do with that car accident. He helped us." The anger had faded from her voice, replaced with sorrow, which Tommy understood. Thallan was a great man brought low by grief and bitterness. It was hard to hate someone so pathetic.

Thallan took a long drag on the cigarette, not looking at anyone. There was no defense to what he'd done and he knew it. It was just another mistake. Another betrayal.

"What's done is done," Tommy said, crossing his arms and turning his attention to Icewind. "The angels were going to target us eventually regardless. The only thing that matters is getting to Deward."

Amber nodded. "Ceri, can you make it to where Thallan can't leave his house?"

The elf didn't react to the request, just kept sucking on the cigarette like it was his lifeline.

"I can," Ceri said without hesitation.

"Genevieve, take Thallan to his house with Ceri and make sure he doesn't get away."

"No problem," Genevieve said, walking toward Thallan and cracking her knuckles.

"With me." Amber led the rest of the pack back inside. She laid Icewind down on the couch. "Tommy, get the good painkillers again."

He hurried into the dining room and grabbed the last green potion. Icewind took it, drinking down the contents greedily. It hit her fast and she collapsed back into the cushions with a giggle, her eyes drooping shut.

Amber crossed her arms, shoulders tight with frustration. "We don't know what move the angels will make next so we have to be ready for anything. No one is going anywhere on their own until this is all over."

"Is she going to be okay?" Tommy asked, looking at the now sleeping elf.

"Yeah, I think so."

Tommy's phone rang. He pulled it out and saw Ithra's name on the caller ID.

"Hello?"

"Tommy, we've found it."

His heart jumped into overdrive. "The rest of Raziel's key?"

"Yes. We're on our way to your pack's house. We'll need a plan if the tablet is where we think it is."

Tommy met Amber's eyes and she nodded. "We'll figure something out. We're going to get Deward back, no matter what."

CHAPTER 69

KADRITHAN (ANGEL)

Kadrithan sat across from Zerestria, lost in thought. She held her glass out for a refill. He poured her the rest of the elven wine.

She tilted the glass in a slow circle, watching the plum-colored wine cling to the sides of the glass. "Despite my misgivings, I agree that the time for caution is past."

"This will start a war." He'd been arguing for this for the last thirty minutes. It was ridiculous of him to hesitate now, but he was. This would change everything. There would be no going back to their semi-peaceful enslavement.

"Yes, it will." Zerestria drained her glass. "The elders are in agreement. They gave their approval last night."

He looked up sharply. "Then why did I have to waste a half an hour convincing you it was the right thing to do?"

She snorted. "You were convincing yourself, not me."

"That was my favorite wine," he muttered, grabbing their empty glasses and tossing the bottle into the trash.

"Mine as well," she said with a laugh. "Go to your wolves and get the rest of the key." She paused at the door and looked back. "Be careful."

He inclined his head toward her. "Always."

Kadrithan stood at the window for a few minutes after she'd left. Red dust kicked up by a wind storm pelted against the glass like rain.

He pulled the worn picture of his younger sister from his breast pocket, smoothing his thumb over the wrinkles. Her smile was bright and carefree. She should have been able to stay that way.

"We're almost there, Faylen. Just like I promised." He tucked the picture away and pulled his mind back to the task at hand. It was time to fight back, just like he'd wanted for so many years. He hadn't expected to be so hesitant to finally take action.

He laid down on his chaise lounge and shifted around until he found a comfortable position. This was going to take a while.

Focusing on the warmth of Amber's mark, he let it guide him through the darkness, fire, and cold. Sounds and sights slowly flowed toward him as he stabilized, choosing to remain unseen until he knew what was going on.

There were more people here than he expected.

"Xenya says the other elders are still uncertain. She is talking to them now," Olwen said, shaking his head unhappily.

"The temple Raziel built is only twenty minutes away. We should go tonight even if the tribe won't help. We should just go now," Tommy said with more heat than he realized the boy even had. His normally placid features were screwed up with anger. Anger directed at his alpha.

"And then what? Kill everyone inside and hope the tablet is actually there?" Amber replied calmly. Inside, she was anything but calm. She was frustrated, angry, and terrified. It always amazed him how tightly locked down she could keep her emotions when she wanted to.

"So you won't let us do anything?"

"That's *not what I said*," Amber snapped, some of that frustration leaking into her voice. "I just want to try to scout the temple out first. We're going to get Deward back, Tommy. I promise."

They must have found the tablet, or at least found something worth checking out.

Ithra -- the missing troll's mother that he had met recently -- laid a hand on Tommy's shoulder. "She's right, Thomas. Rushing in blindly could result in our failure and death, then there would be no one to save my son. Take a deep breath and think it through."

All the bluster went out of the boy and he turned away, pacing restlessly.

Kadrithan drifted through the group, trying to better gauge the tempers of everyone involved. Surprisingly, Ceri, the witch, wasn't in the room. Normally she had a voice in these decisions.

Genevieve was standing near the front door with her arms crossed and her lips pressed into a disapproving line. She seemed unhappy with all the options being discussed.

Deward's parents were calm despite the tension they clearly felt. They were ruled by reason which could make them easier to deal with. More predictable than the others if nothing else.

"We need help," Amber said, rubbing her hands down her face. "I don't want to leave the house or Icewind unprotected but we'll need everyone if we're going to attack a place that big."

This was why he liked Amber. She made things easy on him.

He flowed into a visibility, taking on his human form. "I may be able to help."

Every eye turned to him. The trolls looked startled but the pack, who knew him better at this point, simply looked annoyed.

He smiled pleasantly.

Amber narrowed her eyes at him and put her hands on her hips. "Help, how?"

He ignored her and looked at Ithra. The mother. She was the one he needed to sway to his way of thinking. "The curse that affects all fae limits my ability to use magic. Without those limits, I could help the pack find and reclaim the rest of Raziel's key. I could find your son."

Ithra cocked her head to the side curiously, suspicion growing in her eyes. "What is your point?"

"The only way I can temporarily lift the limits of the curse is through the so-called demon marks. These deals allow me to act in the interest of whoever bears my mark in order to accomplish whatever they have requested."

Tommy's head jerked up. "You want her to take your mark."

Kadrithan nodded, unconcerned. "I want to help."

"Like hell you do––"

"Enough," Amber cut Tommy off.

She didn't look convinced that his motives were pure but she *was* defending him. That was good enough.

"Kadrithan, why are you offering to 'help'?" she asked, putting a rather derogatory emphasis on the last word.

Once again, he looked to Ithra when he answered. It was *her* that he needed to convince. "I've been fighting the angels for centuries. They have killed my sister and others I cared for. I am offering to help you because I need the rest of the tablet. My motives are entirely selfish."

"You have got to be kidding me," Tommy muttered in the background.

He ignored the kid, holding Ithra's gaze. She did not appear to be upset by what he had said.

Ithra looked back to her husband. He nodded slowly, a sad expression on his face. She returned her attention to him. "You are not offering to find Deward, specifically, are you?"

"No." He clasped his hands in front of him, as close to begging as he was willing to get. "Like Tommy has stated previously, if we find the tablet, Deward and this elf will come to us. The curse that binds them to the prophecy will drive them to seek us out. Take my mark and ask me to help the pack retrieve the tablet so that I can put all my power behind this task."

He made the mistake of glancing at Amber after he said that. She looked...disappointed. As if he'd betrayed her trust somehow. He'd been honest, just like he promised her –– something else that was likely to turn out to be a mistake.

"I will accept this deal," Ithra said, surprising him with her quick decision.

"If you're not sure, we can figure something else out," Amber said hesitantly.

Ithra looked back at her with a calm smile. "You have said the demons are not our enemies. Do you think he will try to harm me later?"

"Not intentionally, but he will use you. He will call in the debt the mark represents."

"Just as I am using him now to help my son? That is something I can accept."

Amber nodded in acceptance. "As long as you're aware of the risk."

Ithra looked back at him. "I'm ready."

"When we go to the temple I will give you my mark. I only have so long to act after making a deal." He held his hand out to her. "Until then, let us shake on it."

Ithra put her green hand in his and shook it without even the slightest tremor of uncertainty.

CHAPTER 70

AMBER

It felt like everything was moving at light speed and slow as molasses all at the same time. They were hurtling toward something they couldn't take back. Toward a fight with an enemy bigger than any they'd ever faced.

Ever since she'd given Ceri the pack bite, those changes had been flowing through the pack as well. She felt out of control.

A warm hand squeezed her shoulder. "Hiding in your room is very thirteen-year-old girl, not what I expect of an alpha."

"Shut up, Angel." She stared out her bedroom window, refusing to look at him. "This could get my entire pack killed."

"I'll be there. Your pack has a good chance of success."

She turned to face him. "Will you do everything you can to keep them all safe?"

"I made a deal––"

"I'm not talking about the deal with Ithra. I'm asking you if you will do everything you can to keep them safe."

The demon stilled, accepting the gravity of her question. "Yes, Amber. I will."

She nodded, swallowing down the fear that had left a lump in her throat. "Good."

With a decisive nod, she marched out of her room to rejoin the rest of the pack. Kadrithan was right, hiding in her room right now was inexcusable. The pack needed her there and they needed her to be strong.

Before she reached the living room, her phone rang. She pulled it out of her pocket with a groan. It was an unknown number. She contemplated dismissing the call but she didn't like the timing.

"Hello?"

"I've been looking at your most recent portrait and I think it may be one of my favorites," the vampire said, practically purring.

"Bram?"

STEPHANIE FOXE

He chuckled. "The one and only."

"Oh. I'm surprised you're calling." She slipped back into her room, shooing Kadrithan away when he tried to listen in. "How can I help you?"

"When you visited last you chastised me for not warning you about Selena Black-wood's involvement."

She waited but he didn't continue. "I guess I did. It wasn't intended to be disrespectful--"

"Oh hush," he said, cutting her off. "Don't get all hesitant on me now. I'm calling to make up for it."

"Make up for it how?"

"A rather surprising delegation comprised of Alpha Dominus Ito, Alpha Carter, and a few other important packs are headed to your house."

She ran through the house, jerking the blinds aside, half-expecting them to be rolling up the driveway right then. "Why?"

"I think you already know. I would not recommend running, by the way."

"This is the ambush you were talking about, isn't it? The one where I just have to beat them."

"Indeed it is. You have half an hour. Good luck, Amber." He hung up without further pleasantries.

"What's going on?" Genevieve demanded, jogging up behind her.

She lowered the phone, a million thoughts running through her mind. This was the worst possible timing. They were too close to getting the tablet and rescuing Deward.

The tarot card appeared in front of her. The figure on it seeming at peace despite the discomfort of his situation. She knew what she had to do.

Grabbing the card out of the air, she turned to the others. "The rest of you have to go find Deward and the tablet. You need to leave now."

"What are you talking about?" Kadrithan asked.

"Carter is headed here with Ito. I don't know what they have planned but I know it's meant to stop us. Y'all can still do this without me. You have to, and you have to go now."

"No, I'm staying with you," Genevieve objected, throwing her hands down.

"You aren't. You're going to protect the others since I can't go. That's an order, as your alpha." She drew herself up, letting her authority flow into her words. "This is not up for debate. This fight is mine and I have to do it alone so the rest of you can save Deward."

Ceri, who was standing at the end of the hallway nodded. "With the pack bond, we're never truly apart. Don't forget that."

Genevieve, who still looked pissed, turned away. "Let's go. Ithra, you have the address?"

Amber met Kadrithan's eyes. He nodded, and mouthed *I promise*. He would protect them.

CHAPTER 71

AMBER

Quiet had settled over the house. The pack was long gone but she could still feel them, like always. The wolf prowled inside her mind, waiting patiently for the challengers to arrive. She was not afraid anymore.

She heard them coming before she saw them. The rumble of engines drifted past her, carried on the steady breeze. There were dozens of vehicles headed toward her. It wasn't just Carter coming. It was all of them.

The first car -- which was actually a limousine -- turned down her driveway. It had little flags sticking up on either side of the hood with some sort of coat of arms on them. She rolled her eyes at the self-importance it must have required to attach flags to an already showy car.

Following the limousine, a line of cars and trucks filed in through the gate. She'd had Ceri drop the wards and open it before she left to make it easy for them. They spread out and parked, not caring about tearing up the lawn. Not that it mattered considering how the estate was looking these days.

The limousine driver climbed out and hurried to open the door for his boss. Ito stepped out, adjusting his suit jacket with a sharp tug. Following him was someone she had expected to see here. Still, the sight of Zelas, the angel that had approached her at the coffee shop, pissed her off.

Ito might hate her for his own, misguided reasons, but he was still letting the angels use him. He was nothing more than their puppet.

Amber sat and waited as the wolves gathered, forming a half circle around the front of the house. Her fellow council members were here along with their packs. Even Jameson was here, with Shane right next to him. She ignored them -- and the thumping ache in her chest. They hadn't called. Hadn't warned her. They no longer mattered.

Once the group seemed settled, Amber rose from her seat and walked down the front steps of the porch. The rocks of the driveway were cool under her bare feet.

"Welcome to my home," she said pleasantly as she nodded in greeting at Ito.

Ito lifted his cold eyes to her own. She waited for the weight of his dominance to make her legs shake again, but it washed over her like a weak puff of air instead. Here, at her home, protected by the power of a shaman and her pack combined, he couldn't reach her.

"Amber Hale, you have been accused of colluding with demons -- an enemy of all humanity -- and of threatening the peace werewolves have maintained with the angels and human governments." He paused, stepping aside. "Let the accuser step forward."

The crowd parted and Jason Carter strolled to the front, looking very pleased with himself. "For these crimes, I formally challenge Amber Hale, in front of these witnesses. Let truth favor the victor."

Ito stood by Carter. "Amber Hale, how do you respond?"

They intended for this to be a spectacle. To make an example of her: this is what happens when a bitten wolf oversteps.

Bram had told her she'd have to beat them outright. It was almost like he knew what they had planned all along.

"So is this like drowning a witch? If she floats, she's guilty, and if she drowns, she's innocent?" Amber asked, tucking her hands in her pockets.

Red leaked into Ito's eyes. "Accept the challenge, or kneel and choose death. You will not mock our traditions."

She resisted the urge to roll her eyes. It was difficult. Meeting Carter's gaze, she took the only choice she had. "I accept the challenge."

Ito turned to the crowd, hands behind his back. "Will anyone protest this challenge?"

Jameson stepped forward, and as quickly as hope bloomed in her chest, it was snuffed out. "The local council will not protest this decision."

Carter snorted at that, then winked at her. He'd done this. Turned the council against her, taken Shane from her, and blocked off every avenue of escape. He thought he'd already won, as if she had no chance in a fight against him. The wolf peered out of her eyes as she smiled at him. He was wrong.

"Who will stand as witness for Alpha Jason Carter?" Ito asked, his voice carrying across the space.

"I will." Tatiana stepped out of the crowd and stood behind Carter, a self-satisfied grin on her face. She met Amber's eyes and the grin widened. "I stand as witness for Jason Carter in the formal challenge laid out against Amber Hale."

Ito nodded his head in acceptance. "Your witness is recognized." He turned back to the crowd. "Who will stand as witness for Amber Hale?"

"I don't need one," she interrupted. Her pack wasn't here and it was unnecessary anyhow. There were almost a hundred people gathered here. They weren't exactly short on witnesses.

"That is not your decision to make," Ito said sharply. "There must be someone to stand as your witness if you are to accept this challenge."

Her eyes strayed to Shane but he was staring at the ground.

"I will!" A shout came from behind her.

Amber turned and saw Icewind staggering out the front door in obvious pain.

"I stand as witness for Amber Hale in the formal challenge laid out by Jason Carter." Icewind straightened slightly, holding herself up on the porch banister.

Ito's teeth ground together in irritation. He must have thought it would be that easy. "Your witness is recognized."

Carter stepped forward, pulling his shirt off over his head. "Let's do this."

Always with the nudity. Pushing away her human concerns about modesty, Amber unbuttoned her shirt, holding Carter's gaze the whole time. He would get his fight, but he wouldn't like how it ended.

Once they were naked, Ito stepped between them. "You will shift, then when I say begin, you will fight to the death. Only one of you will be permitted to leave this ring."

Carter shifted immediately, exploding into his wolf form with a howl. He was bigger than average with fur as black as his heart.

She leaned into her shift, letting it flow without effort. When her paws hit the ground, she realized something was different.

"Why is she so big?" someone in the crowd whispered.

She shook out her fur and kept her focus on Carter. Nothing else mattered until he was dead.

Ito moved back and stood with the others. A breathless anticipation fell over the gathered wolves. No one spoke. No one moved.

"Begin."

CHAPTER 72

GENEVIEVE

They all felt Amber shift. That meant she was going to fight. Genevieve dropped the last of her clothes to the ground. She wouldn't be fighting alone.

She stared at the temple standing on the hill. It looked like it had come straight from Rome with tall columns all around the outside. There was some kind of inner chamber she couldn't get a good view of.

Of course a rich angel would not only build himself a temple, but use it to hide a powerful magical artifact.

"Xenya is still talking to the tribe," Ithra said, worry lacing her voice.

"She'll be able to convince them. Have faith, my love," Olwen replied, pressing his forehead to hers.

Genevieve felt a little bad for overhearing. It was hard to give people privacy when you could hear everything they said, but she always did her best.

They'd all been hoping the tribe would come help. If they weren't here yet, she doubted they would come at all. It was up to them. Three werewolves, a human, two trolls…and a demon.

Kadrithan had disappeared, promising to return quickly. He had two minutes to get back here before they were going to just do this without him.

Tommy jogged up to her, pulling leaves out of his hair. He didn't even flinch at her nudity and she barely gave it a thought –– it was hard to care about at a time like this. "I counted ten guards. They smelled like magic but I'm not sure if they're angels or something else. It was hard to tell from so far away."

She turned to Ceri, who was creating some kind of spell next to them. "How are things coming?"

"Good. Almost done," Ceri said distractedly.

Derek was standing a few feet away, his shotgun slung over his shoulder. He looked relaxed and she envied him. She was all wound up with nerves and worry. Amber had always been with them for stuff like this. This time, she'd been left in charge and she got why Amber always worried so much.

It was harder when the decisions were yours to make. She hated it. She didn't want to let the pack down.

Kadrithan stepped out of the darkness in front of them. He looked more solid than normal. "Ithra, are you ready?"

The troll stepped forward and nodded. "I am."

Olwen put a hand on his wife's shoulder, squeezing it gently.

"Do you agree to accept my mark in exchange for my help retrieving the second half of Raziel's key and protecting everyone here tonight?" Kadrithan asked.

Ithra inclined her head. "I do."

He placed his hand on her chest over her heart. "A debt for a debt."

Ithra repeated the phrase, not flinching as the demon's magic burned into her skin.

Genevieve's nose twitched at the unsettling scent -- a mix of sulfur and fire.

"I'm done," Ceri said quietly, looking out at the temple and ignoring what was happening behind her.

"It's definitely going to get their attention?" she asked nervously. A lot was riding on this. If they couldn't draw most of the guards away it would be a hard fight for everyone going to the temple.

Ceri nodded. "Oh yeah. No chance they'll miss it."

Genevieve looked at Olwen. "You still good with being bait with me?"

He nodded. "I'm faster while Ithra will be more able to help Ceridwen. It is the best task for me."

Cracking her knuckles, she nodded decisively. "Then let's do this. No point in wasting any more time."

"Alright, no turning back once I do this," Ceri said.

"Sounds goods. Keep them safe, Tommy, alright?" Genevieve said, clapping him on the shoulder.

"Keep yourself safe. I still don't like you doing this. There are a lot of guards."

"That's exactly why we need to." She squeezed his shoulder one last time. "Go ahead, Ceri."

She crouched down, pressing her hand to the edge of the circle, and said something in Latin.

A fire started in the circle. It grew higher and higher, rising up above the trees. Once it was at least thirty feet tall, it sprouted legs, then a torso and arms. Horns rose from the head, wreathed in smoke.

A booming voice echoed through the forest. "I will enjoy watching this temple burn." Then, the fiery demon cackled maniacally.

Kadrithan looked at Ceri and raised an eyebrow. "Really?"

She snorted. "I think my impression is pretty spot on."

Genevieve rolled her eyes. "Hurry up and get to the temple or this will all be wasted."

She dropped to all fours and shifted, not waiting on them to stop gawking at Ceri's distraction. Olwen nodded that he was ready and ran in the opposite direction as her.

Their job was to keep the guards that came to investigate busy. They'd take them out if they could but making sure the guards chased them and not the rest of the group was the most important part of the plan. If the others could get in and out quickly, they might be able to avoid a fight altogether.

In this form, the pack bond was even more apparent. She could feel Amber drawing on it for strength. If she focused, she knew she'd be able to see through Amber's eyes but she resisted the urge. Amber was fighting so that they could do this. She couldn't waste the opportunity by being distracted.

Her feet padded silently against the forest floor as she raced toward the temple. A branch cracked ahead and she slowed, listening for footsteps.

To her left. A small group, maybe three or four people.

She changed directions, getting ahead of them, then ran straight toward them. They had to see her for this to work.

They were getting close now. She'd miscalculated before. There were at least five of them and they smelled like magic. This was going to be risky.

Picking up speed, she wove through the trees. She needed to strike first with this many of them. She'd only have the element of surprise once.

Instead of heading straight toward them, she changed angles, coming at them from the side. It was dark but she could see perfectly.

A woman walked at the edge of the group, magic crackling at her fingertips. Genevieve picked up speed, muscles straining at their limits, then launched herself at the woman's neck.

Her jaws snapped closed on air, but her back paws dug into the woman's gut, tearing through her flimsy shirt. She leapt away immediately as gunfire cracked through the air. Dirt splattered against her flank as bullets hit the ground.

The woman was screaming, hands pressing uselessly against her wounds.

"Kill the wolf!" One of the men shouted.

She launched herself behind a tree just in time to avoid a bolt of lightning. It hit the trunk of the tree instead and burst into flame with a loud crack.

It looked like they had more than one witch. That was unlucky for her.

Keeping as low as she could, she kept running. She'd wanted to stay close to the group but since they had guns, she could only keep so close without risking getting shot.

With a frustrated growl, she switched directions, running perpendicular to them to get on their other side. She'd just have to take on a little risk if it meant keeping their attention.

The underbrush was thicker up ahead. She crouched down behind it and waited. It was hard to hear over her own pounding heart. She swiveled her ears, letting the wolf come to the forefront.

It wanted to hunt. Corral their prey into a vulnerable position and take them down one at a time. It didn't give a crap what kinds of weapons they had. Fear slowly faded into the background of her mind, replaced by cold determination.

She moved silently through the trees to flank them. They had guns and magic but they were intruders here. The wolf understood how to blend into the shadows of the forest, where to step, how their prey would move. She could smell their fear on the wind.

Two men with guns walked slowly in the rear about twenty feet apart. They had spread out too far, a mistake they would not realize until it was too late.

She stalked forward, low to the ground, until she was within range of the man on the left. Muscles bunching under fur, she waited until he was mid-step to launch herself at him.

Her jaw closed around the back of his neck and she bit down hard, shaking her head viciously as her claws dug into his back. His neck snapped before he even got a chance to scream.

The body fell to the ground with a heavy thump.

"Eric? You okay, man? " the other guard called.

Genevieve faded back into the woods, circling around behind him as he walked slowly toward them, his gun held at his shoulder.

She waited until he was just a few feet away before charging at him. He yelled when he saw the body, swinging around and shooting wildly, all his bullets hitting trees.

She leapt, coming at him from the side. Electricity blasted through the air and struck them both. It knocked her off target and she hit a tree, stunning her. Her muscles twitched and jerked painfully. Gunfire followed and a bullet ripped through her front leg. It missed the bone but she couldn't move it.

She forced herself to stand and stumbled away on three legs, taking cover behind a clump of trees.

"Where did she go?" the other witch demanded, fear making his voice quake.

"I don't know! Why didn't you hit her again?"

"Shut the hell up! This was supposed to be an easy job! Now Eric is dead and--"

Gunfire interrupted the complaining as one of the men sprayed bullets into the trees. Luckily for her, in completely the wrong direction.

She'd have to move soon though. She nosed at her leg and the pain nearly overwhelmed her. It was healing but with a wound this bad, it would take time. Too much time.

Forcing herself back up onto her three good feet, she looked around for an escape route. She had to make a run for it or instead of being a distraction, she'd just be dead.

Before she could take a step, she heard footsteps. Someone new was coming and she was blocked in.

Her ears flattened against her head and she bared her teeth. If it came down to it, she wasn't going down without a fight. They'd pay in blood if they wanted to kill her.

The footsteps drew closer, then stopped abruptly. She froze as well. What the hell were they doing?

A whisper in a strange language cut through the silence, then the guards behind her screamed.

She creeped around a tree and peeked out, freezing at the sight that met her eyes. All three of the remaining guards were dead. Black vines that glinted in the moonlight held them suspended above the forest floor, piercing their bodie in dozens of places.

"Angry fools and...liars."

Genevieve turned around slowly. A woman with stringy blonde hair streaked with dried blood swayed unsteadily in front of her. Her eyes were solid white.

Behind her stood Deward.

"Where?" the elf demanded.

Genevieve shifted. She didn't try to run, there was no point. "The temple."

Deward stood behind the elf silently. Just staring at her. Like the woman, his eyes were solid white. They both smelled like old blood and sweat.

Genevieve's head began to ache as she looked at them. She knew them, right? The troll...he looked familiar.

The wolf pressed its claws into her mind and clarity filtered back into her thoughts. She scooted away, unable to stand as she fought off the effects of the curse.

She didn't fight the shift. She needed the wolf. Lifting her head, she howled.

The pack bond grew inside of her and she pushed the image of Cassandra and Deward toward Tommy with all her might. Her vision blurred, mixing with his as she saw through his eyes and he saw through her eyes. She broke the connection immediately. It was too disorienting and he'd seen enough.

She half-expected the elf to kill her but the woman turned and walked away instead. Deward stood there for a moment longer before he followed.

Genevieve collapsed back into the dirt in the midst of the bodies. She had to get back to the others and help, but first, her leg had to heal enough to walk.

Light exploded over the temple, blasting through the trees like a wave. The sudden brightness blinded her.

An enraged howl followed. They were in trouble, but she couldn't move. Something was wrong. The healing on her leg had stopped. A slow, deep burn spread up into her flank.

"Shit." Those were silver bullets.

CHAPTER 73

AMBER

Carter didn't hesitate to attack. Perhaps he thought he could take her out right away. He was certainly arrogant enough to be that stupid.

She hopped out of the way of his charge and snapped at his hind leg, teeth missing by less than an inch. They circled each other, lips curled back in a snarl as the crowd looked on. Their anticipation pounded in the air. All these people had come here to watch her die. It was sick but it wasn't because they were werewolves. It was because they were horribly human.

Her wolf wanted to win this fight but she had never taken pleasure from watching others fight. She measured herself against the other wolves, wanting to assert her dominance, but that was very different from watching this for entertainment.

Carter attacked again, jaws snapping at her legs. She moved quickly but he seemed to be able to anticipate which direction she'd dodge. He moved diagonally, cutting off her retreats, forcing her toward the edge of the circle. If she let herself be cornered, this would be over quickly, and not in the way she hoped.

She dropped low to the ground, growling as he circled around her. He charged in as expected, but this attack was faster than the others. Too fast. He hit her, knocking her off balance. Teeth grazed her side, tearing open a gash. She whipped around, ignoring the pain, and snapped at his leg, forcing him back just enough to give her breathing room.

Let me take control, the wolf whispered in her mind.

She rarely heard the wolf speak but something had changed. Her connection to the wolf was stronger. Giving Ceri the pack bite had accelerated everything.

Taking a deep breath, she sank further into the wolf. Their desires and instincts flowed together until instead of two souls in one body, there was only one. Something greater together than they were separate.

Her teeth lengthened and her body grew in size. Magic –– pulled from the earth –– filled her with strength. Awareness. She was more than just a wolf.

Carter took a step back, a growl rumbling from his chest. Whispers of confusion spread through the gathered crowd like wildfire.

Amber lowered her head and began closing the space between them. She knew Carter's patience would only last so long. He would attack first again and she would make him pay.

In the blink of an eye, Carter shifted his hind foot and leapt at her. She didn't dodge his attack this time. Crouching low, she lunged forward then shot up. Her teeth sunk into his vulnerable belly as he landed on her but he was heavier than she'd expected.

They hit the ground and his bulk drove the air out of her lungs. She ripped at his gut, her hind legs scrambling against his as they fought for footing and dominance.

She twisted, getting her flank out from under him, but he managed to catch her foreleg in his jaws. Pain shocked through her system but she didn't hesitate. With an enraged growl, she bit down on his shoulder and shook her head sharply.

He yelped in pain and released her leg. She tried to push back up to her feet but he used his weight to keep her from standing back up. Carter was just as oversized in wolf form as he was in real life. She had grown in size but he was still stronger and he had fought like this before.

She pushed the doubts away. There was no time to be afraid. She had to win. They moved in a blur. Red and black twisting together with punches of white teeth, blood-streaked.

This couldn't go on forever. Already her muscles were beginning to protest the exertion. Adrenaline sucked at her limbs, both giving her energy and taking it.

They broke apart for a moment, both panting and dripping blood from their wounds. Their eyes met, neither one of them willing to look away.

In this moment, the rest of the world didn't exist. Not politics. Not laws. Nothing but two alphas, each unwilling to submit to the other.

With the wolf at the forefront of her mind, she saw the strike coming before he moved and darted to the side. He was only slightly faster, but it was enough. His claws dug into the side of her face. It was deeper than any of her other wounds. It felt wrong, as if he'd used magic to create the wound somehow.

He got his shoulder under her legs and tossed her back, landing on top of her as she slid in the dirt. She howled in anger and something snapped inside of her. The pack bond exploded inside of her and, all at once, everything became clear.

CHAPTER 74

✌

KADRITHAN (ANGEL)

The attack had come out of nowhere. Their distraction had worked. The temple had been empty...until Derek had picked up the tablet.

"Don't let them get it. I'll be right back," Kadrithan said, shoving Amber's vulnerable human brother down behind the marble dais.

"What are you doing--"

Derek's protests were cut off as Kadrithan returned to his body with jarring speed. The room spun and he thought he might vomit.

He hadn't expected Raziel himself to show up at the temple. Not so soon.

Fighting against the spin of the room, Kadrithan ran for this bathroom. He threw open the cabinet and grabbed the the vial of distilled magic.

Without hesitating, he unstoppered it and poured the gleaming liquid down his throat. He had to use this now. They had no chance of fending off Raziel and getting out alive if he didn't. The deal required it, as did good, common sense.

The vial fell from his fingers as the magic burned through him. He dropped to the ground and laid down on the bathroom floor, not worrying about cleanliness or how sore he'd be when he returned again.

With magic pounding in his veins, he searched his mind for the link to Ithra and fought his way back to her with reckless speed.

It was so easy this time to step into the human realm. His feet -- more solid than he had ever managed on his own -- touched the ground. Horns grew from his head and fiery wings exploded from his back, tearing straight through his shirt and jacket.

A shotgun blast echoed through the marble temple but it wasn't enough to drown out the sounds of fighting. Raziel hadn't come alone. A dozen lesser incubi and half breeds blocked the exit. Magic hung in the air like a fog.

One of the half breeds screamed in pain as a wolf's teeth sunk into the meat of his calf. He stumbled and swung around to take aim at Tommy, but was stopped short when a spear drove through his chest, coming out clean on the other side. Ithra ripped the spear free and twirled it around, knocking aside a blast of light from one of the lesser incubus with a battle-cry.

Ceri was fending off Raziel but slowly losing ground. Wind swirled around the witch as she fought the angels with bright bursts of flame and sharp gusts of air. Her hands were in constant motion as she kept up a steady chant. Magic pulsed through the air. More magic than he thought was even possible for one witch. It still wouldn't be enough.

Raziel, crowned in a halo of light, waved his hand through the air and she was tossed back without effort.

Kadrithan flew toward her, catching her just before she hit a wall. The force of her impact sent him stumbling backward but he could take the blow. It would have broken her. He set her on her feet and moved between her and Raziel.

"Get away from the temple with the others. As far as you can go," he said urgently. This fight was his and when they clashed, no one nearby would be safe.

A black wolf raced toward the angel, howling in rage, but Raziel simply waved his hand again. Light struck out like a whip and tossed the wolf aside.

"Tommy!" Ceri shrieked.

"Get him and run!" Kadrithan said, shouting over the noise. He couldn't waste any more time babying them. Raziel wasn't going to wait.

The angel's gaze landed on him and a smile split his inhumanly perfect face. "Kadrithan, my old friend."

He walked toward the incubus scum, drawing his sword smoothly. "Friend? We were acquaintances at best."

The incubus laughed, the sound like chimes in the wind. He'd heard Raziel's real laugh though and it wasn't so kind.

"Do you intend to model for me or are we going to fight, *friend*?" Kadrithan taunted. He was eager to plunge his sword into Raziel's gut. He wanted to hear him squeal in pain like the pig he was.

The incubus smiled and the false beauty dripped from his face like melting candle wax. Cold, pale skin replaced the effervescent warmth of the illusion. The halo vanished. The brilliant white, feathered wings faded away.

What was left was the truth. A man with cruelty in his eyes and a whip burning with cold light clutched in a bony hand.

"Let's dance, demon," Raziel said with a sharp smile.

They raced toward one another, moving inhumanly fast. Neither of them were human. They were stronger, faster, more powerful.

The whip cracked through the air. He smacked it aside with the flat of his sword and launched himself straight up into the air, his wings moving as he needed instinctually. It had been so long since he'd been able to do this, especially in the human realm, but his body remembered how to move. Evangeline had no idea how lucky she was to be able to do this at will, or how powerful it made her.

He dove at Raziel, sword held close to his body, ready for a quick strike. The incubus didn't wait for him. He darted out of the way, spinning in a tight circle and striking out with the whip once again.

A sudden blast of wind knocked the whip off kilter and him nearly out of the sky.

Ceri, walking backwards toward the dais continued chanting. Her hair floated all around her head and her eyes glowed blue. That was new.

The incubus shrieked in rage and lashed out at the witch. Kadrithan took the opening and swung his sword, letting magic flow down the blade. Fire billowed from its edge and flew at Raziel in a white-hot crescent wave.

Raziel was forced to step back, missing his strike at Ceri, to shield himself against the attack with a shield of light.

"Leave, Ceridwen!" Kadrithan shouted. He didn't have time to make sure she didn't get hurt. Raziel wasn't just any incubus. This fight would push him to his limits. Perhaps beyond them.

"No! They'll just follow us." The witch pulled a strange, feathered necklace out from her shirt. "Deal with Raziel, we'll take care of the rest."

"Fine. Stay out of my way." She was just as stubborn as Amber. No one in the pack was ever willing to just cooperate with his plans. It was infuriating.

He launched himself at Raziel again, going on the offensive. With the distilled magic buzzing through him, he felt reckless. This was as close to free as he'd felt in a century.

"You cannot hope to beat me!" Raziel shouted as he spun in place, whip snapping out with a crack like thunder.

"That's something a man afraid of losing would say!" He drove his sword into the floor, cracking the marble as flames raced along the ground toward the incubus. Once close to Raziel, they exploded upward in a shower of super-heated rock.

A shield of light surrounded Raziel. It grew in brightness, then exploded with a flash, blinding him. He shot upward. Raziel would use the light to hide his next attack. He had to keep moving until he could see again.

The whip wrapped around his foot, dragging him back down with a vicious yank. His wings bent awkwardly and he swung in a wide arc, smashing into one of the gaudy statues near the wall. He rolled away immediately, narrowly avoiding the bolt of lightning that crashed into the statue, finishing it off.

"No!" Derek's shout was followed by three quick shotgun blasts. A group of four half breeds were converging on him and Ithra. Ceri was a short distance away, casting frantically, but separated from them by an angel.

With a growl of frustration, Kadrithan launched himself at the group, slicing through two of them in one swing. He sent a bolt of flame into the back of the angel, getting its attention just long enough for Ceri to regain the upper hand.

Raziel's whip wrapped around his wrist and he was yanked backward. He tossed the sword to his left hand and swiped it over his head, the enchanted metal cutting through the whip with an awful, keening sound.

He jerked his wrist free but realized he couldn't close his hand. The burns from the light had gone too deep. He'd have to continue the fight with his off hand. This was not a fight he could handle at a disadvantage.

Raziel had brought too many men. His attention was split between the pack and Raziel. He'd promised Amber he would keep them safe and he couldn't break that promise.

Casting away the doubt and fear, he charged at Raziel, sending fire ahead of him like a stampede. The incubus was forced upward, propelling himself toward the ceiling in a blaze of crackling lightning.

Raziel's whip struck down, nearly landing a blow on his cheek. He dodged it, counter-attacking with another wave of fire. They danced around each other. Light and fire. Angel and demon.

Kadrithan began to feel the drain of the fight. If he'd not had the distilled magic, he would have already been forced to return to his physical body. He could not keep this up forever.

With a series of quick attacks, Raziel forced him backward toward the pack. He managed to deflect each strike but the incubus was moving too fast for him to counter. It was as if the incubus had simply been toying with him before.

"Your relationship with this pack is quite fascinating," Raziel said with a growing smile, thin lips stretched over sharp teeth. He lifted a hand toward Derek. "Would your little alpha forgive you if they didn't all come home?"

He raced to put himself between Raziel and the pack but he was too slow. Lightning exploded from Raziel's palm, racing toward Derek. It seemed as if everything was moving in slow motion. A black blur passed in front of Derek, taking the brunt of the attack. But not all of it. Tommy let out a yelp but it was drowned out by Derek's shout of pain.

Tommy crashed into Derek and they both hit the ground in a tangle of limbs, the tablet flying from Derek's hand and sliding across the floor.

Raziel raced for it immediately, shouting orders for his minions to help.

"*Tempestas!*" Ceri shouted, enraged. Wind blew from the back of the temple, sending them all flying back. Kadrithan flared out his wings and let the air currents propel him upward.

The angel Ceri had been fighting charged her and the spell faltered, giving Raziel an opening. Even as Kadrithan flung an arc of fire at Raziel, the incubus struck out at her. Raziel's whip connected first, barely deflected by a sharp gust of wind.

A group of three half breeds got in between him and Raziel, casting a wall of light that blocked his advance. He was separated from the pack. They wouldn't be able to hold against Raziel. Tommy and Derek weren't moving. Only Ceri and Ithra, who had been injured at some point, now stood between Raziel and the rest of the pack. And more importantly, the tablet.

"Raziel, Keeper of Secrets," a hoarse whisper floated through the room. "Your lies will be undone."

Kadrithan raised his sword and took a step back, searching for the source of the words. An elf walked into the temple behind him, her eyes milky white, and the black aura of a curse hovering around her.

She lifted her hand toward Raziel. "The halves of the key, joined once more. The blood of enemies in their veins, wielding light and fire. The twilight hour, when day meets night. In the space between realms where spirits dwell. Only then shall what has been be wrought be undone."

Raziel flung a bolt of lightning at her. She didn't move, simply lifted her other hand.

Black vines shot up from the ground, running Raziel's leg clean through. He screamed in pain and the lightning fizzled out.

Kadrithan rushed him, ready to strike the incubus down, but the vines did not hold him. Raziel shot up, parrying the slash of his sword with a spear of light he summoned out of nothingness. He forced the incubus back, bearing down on him with quick, aggressive strikes. If he let Raziel get his footing back now, he'd lose this fight. He had to end this.

With a bellow, he knocked Raziel back several feet, putting space between them. He lifted his sword to the sky and let the fire within him roll up onto the blade.

The fae were not mere witches, nor anything else born of this world. His people had given magic to the humans. They *were* magic. Even now, crippled by this curse, he was more than any of them.

Raziel pressed his hands together, light pulsing between them as his arms shook. This would be their final attacks. It was do or die.

"I'll see you in hell, Raziel," he said, his voice shaking with the strain.

The incubus smirked. "Not likely."

The two attacks slammed into one another; fire so hot it burned white and the blisteringly bright crackle of lightning. He could not see where one ended and the other began.

Sweat dripped down his brow as he strained to control the spell. Raziel was struggling as well. Blood flowed freely from the wound Cassandra had given him. She had weakened him.

Ceri's chants echoed throughout the temple. She had joined hands with Ithra and Olwen in a hastily drawn circle. Her magic joined the attack, battering Raziel from every direction. Wind whipped the incubus's hair into a frenzy.

He bared his teeth at Kadrithan, fury blazing in his eyes. "You will pay for this."

Then, his spell collapsed, overwhelmed by fire and wind. A cry of pain was drawn from Raziel's throat as he was thrown back, landing on the broken floor in an undignified heap. His hands burned almost to ash.

Kadrithan walked toward him slowly, relishing the moment and his victory. He would take Raziel's head and plant it on a stake in front of the temple.

He stopped near Raziel's head and looked down at him. "You could not hold us down forever."

"That's where you're wrong," Raziel whispered, a smile spreading across his face.

Kadrithan tried to step back but it was too late, Raziel was already casting his attack. The illusion fell from the incubus's hands. They weren't burned at all.

A spear of light drove toward him. The attack was too close to dodge.

CHAPTER 75

AMBER

Strength. Power. Magic. It was all around them. She was nothing but a conduit.

Carter struck down, intending to get his jaws around her throat. She twisted under him and he hit dirt instead.

He might be wearing the skin of a wolf, but at his core, Carter was nothing more than a man. She drove her back paw into his balls, claws digging into him ruthlessly.

He yelped and threw himself backward in a frantic bid to protect himself. That was all the opening she needed.

She charged after him and slammed him into the ground. He could not kill her. He could not take her pack from her. He could not scare her into submission.

Her jaws closed around his throat. He thrashed under her. Frantic. Desperate. Afraid.

She bit down harder, cutting off his oxygen. The more he fought the worse he made it. His muscles spasmed as he struggled for oxygen he couldn't get. The blood vessels in his eyes popped from the pressure. She *felt* him begin to die.

It was slow. Horribly, painfully slow. Every second felt like minutes as his thrashing weakened…then stopped. She knew if she let go now, he'd come back to consciousness.

Lifting her gaze to Ito's, she bit down harder. Bones cracked under her powerful jaws. She waited until his heart stopped. Until the buzz of life in him flowed back into the earth.

When she was sure, she dropped Carter's lifeless body into the dirt at her feet, then lifted her head and howled. The crowd joined her, acknowledging her victory. Honoring her in their own way. Ito, however, remained silent.

She had won this fight but they had taken her choice from her. Ito had forced her to kill in order to live.

Tired and angry, she shifted back to human. Her face ached. The other wounds were healing but she could tell something was wrong with that one. It would be a problem for later though.

"Are you happy?" she asked, holding Ito's gaze. "Or would you like me to rip out his heart and lay it at your feet?" She walked toward him, magic and power still pounding through her limbs with every heartbeat. She nodded her head toward Zelas, hovering on the fringes of the group. "Or, should I lay it on an altar before the angels. This was their doing after all, wasn't it?"

Ito scoffed. "The angels? What do they have to do with this?"

"They paid Carter to orchestrate all this. I'm sure he was happy to do it, but I was surprised to find out *you* were involved."

"I have done nothing but support a pack who sought to protect our kind from foul influences," Ito said with a sneer. "Perhaps I should have challenged you myself."

Amber was done being frightened by anyone. She met Ito's eyes, facing all the cold hate she found there without backing down. "Are you really so scared of me?"

His expression hardened as a murmur went through the crowd. "What reason would I have to be frightened of you?"

"I think you're terrified to admit you're wrong. I'm sure you don't experience that often, but every time I manage to succeed it tips the scale a little further in favor of bitten wolves being equal to born wolves. Why you need to feel superior to me, I do not know." She shrugged, holding his gaze steadily as he brought all his strength to bear. His power electrified the air, but it couldn't touch her. Not anymore. "Even now you need to see me cower, but I won't."

A low growl rose from his chest. "You have no idea what you are talking about. I have watched you toy with power you do not understand, wearing the mark of demon. Any power you have is stolen and underserved. Your successes prove nothing except that a bitten wolf is a desperate, pathetic creature grasping after things never intended for them."

"Desperate?" Amber asked, cocking her head to the side. "Desperate was paying someone to change a human against their will. Threatening me, getting me fired, getting me evicted. Hiring a witch to sabotage my Trials. A grown man throwing whisky on me to see if he could get me mad enough to make a scene. Desperate is approving a formal challenge based on lies just because you needed me to fail. I have fought back to survive, nothing more and nothing less. The only desperate people I see here are the born wolves that have attacked me, over and over again, for nothing more than pride."

"That is enough!" Ito snarled, stepping forward as if he would strike her.

"I agree. That is enough," Jameson said, walking out of the crowd toward her. "I did not protest this challenge, as you requested, but enough is enough. Amber has broken no laws, human or werewolf. She defeated Carter in a formal challenge. Is our Alpha Dominus going to violate his word and strike her down?"

Ito's eyes bled red. "I should."

Jameson stepped in front of her, his pack spreading out behind them protectively. "I expected you to be more honorable. If I have been mistaken, then you will have to go through me to fight her."

Ito looked at each of them and straightened. "So be it, Jameson. You have chosen your side."

The Alpha Dominus turned and walked away. The crowd dispersed, everyone returning to their vehicles except for Jameson and his pack.

She watched them leave silently, every instinct screaming at her to get to her pack as quickly as possible. They were fighting for their lives.

CHAPTER 76

TOMMY

Cassandra and Deward were both running toward Raziel. If Deward got in the way of that spell, he'd die. Time slowed as Tommy launched himself through the air. He didn't care if this meant they lost, or if Raziel got away. He couldn't let Deward die. He had to save him.

He hit Deward in the side and they tumbled to the ground less than a foot from Kadrithan and Raziel. Deward bellowed in rage.

Cassandra made it though, throwing herself in front of Kadrithan just in time. The light drove into her chest, running her clean through and stabbing into the demon. She fell back into Kadrithan's arms, her body convulsing as hot blood poured over his hands.

Deward tried to get out from under him, but he held his friend down.

"Attack!"

A great shout rose up, echoing throughout the temple as at least thirty trolls charged into the temple. Xenya, the elder, ran straight at Raziel, wielding a wickedly spiked metal flail. The incubus took a step back, watching as all his men were overrun by the trolls.

"This isn't over," Raziel hissed, limping backward.

Light split the air, rising up through the roof of the temple and rending the ceiling in two. Raziel shot upward, fleeing like the coward he was.

Deward's struggles stopped abruptly and he went limp, laying on the broken marble as if he were dead. Tommy wanted to shift and help him but while Raziel had fled, the others hadn't.

A spear burst through the chest of the angel standing over Tommy. His eyes bulged in shock as blood bubbled from his lips. Ithra yanked the spear free, twirling it around her in an elegant display of violence, thrusting and slicing every time one of them made the mistake of getting too close to her son.

Tommy forced himself to move, charging at the next attacker. His muscles ached with exhaustion and the burn from Raziel's lightning on his back made it hard to breathe but he couldn't stop now.

With trolls here to help, the rest of the fight went quickly. In what felt like an eternity compressed into the blink of an eye, it was over. He limped back to Deward, paws slipping in the blood-slick covering the floor.

Kadrithan was cradling Cassandra. She lifted her hands to his face and whispered something that made him stiffen. Tommy couldn't hear it and he didn't care anyhow, not right now.

With a whimper, he shifted back to human form. His body was fighting to heal but he had more wounds than he realized. Cuts, both large and small, covered his limbs.

Ithra dropped her spear and knelt next to Deward, shaking him slightly. "He's still breathing."

"He...collapsed when Raziel...left," Tommy gasped out between pained breaths. He looked around for Ceri. She could help. "Where's Ceri?"

"With Derek. He's injured as well," Ithra said, smoothing her hand over Deward's forehead.

"Where's Genevieve?"

Ithra looked around. "I don't see her."

"I have to find her." He forced himself upright, waited for the room to stop spinning, then rose to his feet.

"Are you sure you can?" Ithra asked, looking at him with worry.

He nodded firmly. "Yeah. No other choice. I'll get Ceri to come help Deward."

Walking away from his friend so soon after finding him was hard, but he wasn't the one who could help him right now. Only Ceri could if it was the curse that was still affecting him. And Genevieve needed him, he could feel it. She was in pain.

He limped over to Ceri, who was with Derek behind the dais. There were burns on his hands and feet from where the lightning had exited his body. The tablet they'd fought for sat innocently on the ground right next to him -- untouched by the fighting.

"Is he going to be okay?" Tommy asked tiredly.

Ceri nodded shakily. "Yeah, just need to get him back to the house."

"Deward collapsed when Raziel left and isn't moving. Can you help him?"

She dragged her hands through her hair. "Yeah." Leaning down close to Derek, she smoothed his hair back. "Will you be okay?"

He nodded, his face white as a sheet from the pain. "Yes. Go."

"I have to go find Gen," Tommy said as they walked back toward Deward. "She's hurt somewhere out in the woods still."

"Alright, take this," Ceri said, pulling out two vials. "One for you and one for her. It'll give you a boost of energy and heal you, just a little."

He downed it immediately and relief spread through his limbs. The pain was muted and the worst of the exhaustion faded into the background. He took off at a run -- which was more of a jog, but it was as much as he could manage right now. Part of him wanted to shift, but he knew it would use up what little energy he had regained.

He left the temple, and let the pack bond guide him. Being able to feel it like this was new but the wolf knew how to use it. It was as easy as breathing –– well, easier than breathing right now. Breathing hurt.

He smelled the magic and metal of their guns as he drew near. It almost drowned out the scent of Genevieve's blood. Picking up his pace, he moved as quickly as he could until he felt himself drawing close to Genevieve.

"Gen?" he shouted.

There was a weak yip in response and he turned around, spotting her tail near a bush. He raced to her side, dropping to his knees next to her. Her leg was a mess of blood and bone.

"What's wrong? Why isn't it healing?" he asked, unstoppering the potion Ceri had given him.

She whined, unable to speak, but he felt her answer as sure as if she'd spoken it. Silver.

"Crap, Gen. Take this." He poured the potion into her mouth and she lapped it up greedily, letting out a sigh of relief as it began its work. "I'm going to have to pick you up."

She huffed but didn't argue. He got one arm under her shoulder, then quickly shoved his other under her flank. She yelped, fighting him as he picked her up.

"Hold still or I'll drop you!" he shouted, holding on for dear life. He didn't want to hurt her anymore, but he was too weak to carry her if she struggled too much.

A sudden warmth filled him, like the sun breaking through the clouds. Strength that wasn't his own filled his arms and legs. Amber was getting close and she was helping.

Genevieve stilled in his arms, her head lolling to the side. He broke into a run. They had to get the silver out of her, fast.

CHAPTER 77

❧

CERI

Ceri was beyond bone tired. She was pretty sure she was sleepwalking. Every time she turned around she expected to see another angel hurtling magic through the air but it really was over. She smoothed a hand over Deward's hair. The fighting was over at least.

"We have to do it now, but I'll need more than just the two of you with how exhausted I am," she said, looking up at Deward's parents. "Would the tribe be willing to help? I'd need twelve of them to make a circle of thirteen. A lucky number."

"I'll ask," Olwen said, rising and hurrying over to Xenya.

"How hopeful should I be?" Ithra asked quietly, her hand wrapped tightly around Deward's wrist, as if she was the only thing holding him here.

Ceri took a deep breath. "I am almost certain he will live. But––" she added, cutting off Ithra's sigh of relief. "He will not escape this without consequences. The curse has been on him too long."

"What will happen to him?"

"We can't know until the curse is lifted."

Ithra nodded firmly. "Then I will worry about it later."

Tommy burst in through the temple door carrying Genevieve, who was passed out in wolf form. "Ceri, she has silver poisoning."

"I can help with that," Xenya said, walking back with Olwen. A group of trolls she assumed were the volunteers followed them. "You deal with the curse, I will take care of your wolf until you are done."

"Thank you," Ceri said, suppressing her worry for Genevieve as best as she could. Everyone was hurt. Everything had gone wrong. She could only fix one thing at a time and this required her full attention.

Kadrithan laid Cassandra's body out of the way and approached her. He was hurt too, blood trailing down his chest and burns on his wrist. "I have to leave."

"Alright."

"I made sure Derek has Raziel's key. Hide it as soon as you can and tell Amber to keep her guard up. I don't know when they'll retaliate."

She nodded, part of her not caring about the tablet or the demon's stupid war right now. "I'll tell her."

He hesitated, then lifted his hand to her forehead. As soon as his skin touched hers, she was filled with magic that burned through her like a wildfire.

She gasped, jerking away in shock. "What the hell was that?"

"I promised to help." Before she could demand an actual explanation, he disappeared.

She lifted her hand. It was shaking, but not from exhaustion this time. He'd given her some of his magic somehow. Curling her fingers into a fist, she turned to the others. It was time to break this curse. She wouldn't waste the demon's gift.

"Form a circle around him. We don't have time for elegance. I'll have to break it with brute force." She walked over and stood at Deward's head. The volunteers gathered around her; Ithra at her right and Olwen next to his wife.

"Wait!" Amber shouted, running into the room. "Let me help too."

She wanted to cry with relief at seeing Amber here. Her alpha took the place of the troll to her left and grabbed her hand.

Up close, she realized Amber was hurt. Angry red claw marks, half-healed, covered her right cheek. "Your face, what happened?"

"I'll explain later," Amber said, squeezing her hand gently.

"Okay." Ceri turned back to Deward and shut her eyes. "*Nos ligare.*"

Her magic rushed through the circle, binding them all together. As it settled into the group of thirteen, everything came into focus. The power of the pack, of the trolls, of the earth.

She opened her eyes and looked down at Deward. The curse covered his head like a veil. Impenetrable darkness. She let go of Amber's hand and knelt on the hard marble. "*Et non est tibi. Eum dimittere.*"

The curse rose up, screeching in protest, but she reached through it -- into it -- and ripped it away. It fought back, trying to overwhelm her, but Kadrithan's magic reached out of her and burned it away like it was nothing. Whatever fae magic was, it was more powerful than anything she had seen before.

Deward twitched, taking a gasping breath as his eyes snapped open. They were still milky white.

"Did it work?" Ithra asked.

"Yes," Ceri said sadly.

Ithra dropped to her knees, gathering Deward up in her arms.

"Mother?" Deward asked, touching her shoulders in confusion.

"Yes, Deward, it's me," she said, pulling back and touching his cheek.

He flinched back in surprise. "Why can't I see you? Where am I?"

Ceri turned away. She didn't want to watch this.

Tommy was standing just behind her, watching the scene unfold in confusion. "What's wrong with him?"

"He's blind."

CHAPTER 78

AMBER

Amber ran her fingers through Genevieve's fur even though she was still asleep. It was more to reassure herself that she was still breathing, still alive, than it was to soothe Genevieve. The silver had gone deep. Even with the strength she was sending her from the pack bond, it would be hours before she could shift back. The injury was taking so much of Genevieve's energy to heal that it was slowing everything down.

Ceri walked in and collapsed in the chair next to her.

"How's Derek?"

"Getting better fast with the salves." Ceri put her head in her hands. "It's a good thing I couldn't sleep for weeks or I wouldn't have all these extra potions laying around."

She snorted. "Silver lining."

"The stuff I gave you should have faded those scars by now," Ceri said, pushing her hair out of the way to get a better look.

Amber tugged her hand away. "It won't. It can't."

"Why?"

"An injury inflicted by another alpha doesn't always heal right. Jameson explained it before I left. I'm stuck like this, but it's okay." She forced a smile. "Scars are kinda badass, right? Like Steven said. I can tell everyone I got in a fight with a werewolf."

Ceri laughed but it didn't reach her eyes. "An alpha werewolf no less." She cleared her throat. "Are they, uh, going to come get Carter's body?"

"I have to give permission to his beta to retrieve it for cremation. I didn't have time. Just had to kick everyone off the property so I could get to y'all." She snorted, dropping her head to Genevieve's side. "They think I'm making a statement but I'm really not. I want it gone."

"Not so bad to make everyone a little scared of you, I think," Ceri said, leaning back in her chair.

"Is Tommy still with Deward?"

"Yeah, he won't leave his side. Can't blame him. Deward isn't...taking it well."

"Is there no way to heal the blindness?"

Ceri shook her head. "Not since it was caused by a curse."

She resumed running her hands through Genevieve's fur, a nervous habit at this point. "This didn't turn out well."

"We all made it through alive."

"Barely. If I hadn't given you the pack bite..." She shook her head, pushing the thoughts away. "Vernier ended up helping us, even if it wasn't on purpose."

"I'm sure that pisses her off," Ceri said with a scowl. "I still can't believe Jameson didn't do anything to stop them. I really thought he was on our side."

"I think he is, just not enough to be willing to sacrifice his pack for us. I can't really blame him. He doesn't owe us anything."

"It's not about owing us something, it's about doing the right thing. He shouldn't have caved to Ito." Ceri's face darkened. "Shane shouldn't have just dumped you on his alpha's orders either."

She shrugged. "At the end, Jameson stood up for me when it looked like Ito wouldn't honor the results of the challenge. I managed to kill Carter but I wouldn't have been so lucky with Ito. And as for Shane –– he picked his pack over me. I would do the same thing."

"I'm still going to be pissed at him. Genevieve might try to kill him when she finds out."

Amber snorted. "I might let her."

Tommy walked in, looking somber. "How is she?"

"Still asleep but not in pain," Amber said, waving him over. "She can feel that we're with her."

He walked over to her head and dug his hands into her fur. It calmed him too. She'd given up on suppressing the pack bond for today. It seemed they all needed it, the reassurance of being able to feel each other through it.

Derek hobbled in too and dragged a chair over to sit next to Ceri. She frowned, wondering if she could give the pack bite to a human too.

CHAPTER 79

GENEVIEVE

"My father is willing to make a statement. That should help with the investigation," Icewind said, leaning against her elbow tiredly.

Genevieve took another sip of the awful tea Ceri was making her drink and grimaced. "That's good."

"It means I have to talk to him for at least another few weeks. I'm tempted to just tell him no and figure something else out," the elf muttered.

"Suck it up, buttercup. Horan is still a threat to the pack. If Thallan can help, he's going to have to."

Icewind groaned. "You owe me for this."

"I saved your life! *You* owe *me*."

Steven bustled back into the room. "You haven't finished your tea yet!"

She glared at him. "Quit hovering. I'll finish it eventually."

"But Ceri said you need to drink it before it gets cold or it won't be as effective," he protested, advancing on her like he might try to force it down her throat.

Icewind busted out laughing and rose from her seat. "All I'm going to say is: karma."

The elf continued cackling as she left the room. Abandoning her to Steven's mother-henning. To *torment*.

"Steven, I swear I will kick you out of the house if you don't stop," she said, taking another drink to pacify him. It was still awful.

He huffed in annoyance and crossed his arms. "How is your leg feeling?"

"Better," she said honestly. She wiggled her toes for him. "Now that the silver is out of my system, it's actually healing."

He nodded, still standing there tensely.

"Steven, I'm going to be okay. I promise."

"I know."

"Then what's wrong?"

He looked away, hands curling into a fist. "I just feel a little useless. I was sitting in this house, hiding, while everyone else was out fighting. I didn't even have the guts to walk outside when Amber needed help."

She grabbed him and pulled him down onto the couch beside her, leaning her head against his shoulder. "It's selfish, but I'm glad you didn't go outside."

"You can't mean that--"

"Shut up." She planted her hand across his mouth to keep him from interrupting her again. "You've been dragged into this and it sucks. Honestly, they probably wouldn't have even accepted you as a witness for Amber. Werewolves don't tend to count humans for much. Icewind being an elf made a difference. Also, you were just attacked by werewolves. Anyone would have doubts about walking out in front of the same people that attacked them the day before." She lowered her hand. "So, just...just let it go. I don't need you to be some kind of knight in shining armor beheading monsters for me. I just need you to survive, okay?"

He nodded mutely.

"And I want you to move in. With me. Now."

"Are you--"

She slapped her hand back over his mouth again. "Don't say anything, just nod yes or no."

With wide eyes, he nodded yes.

"Okay, good." She settled her head back on his shoulder and glared at the murky brown liquid in her mug. "I hate this tea."

CHAPTER 80

EVANGELINE

"Where to this time?" she asked, settling into her seat in the Jeep.

"Portland."

"Seriously?"

Charlie nodded, chewing on his toothpick. "Your uncle said we're done hiding out. Apparently, the pack is going to need ya."

"Do they know we're coming back?"

"Not yet." He took out the toothpick and pointed it at her in the rearview mirror. "And they won't hear about it ahead of time. They're being watched. If you tell Tommy, the angels might figure it out."

"Oh come on, they're not psychic––"

"No arguments," Katarina said, reaching back to smack the side of her head with a quick strike she was too slow to avoid. She rubbed it, scowling at the elf, who didn't look the least bit apologetic. "Safety first. Always."

She slunk down in her seat with a sigh. "I hate you both."

Her mother laughed at her. "We all know that's a lie."

"Then I hate Kadrithan."

Charlie snorted. "Who doesn't?"

Even Katarina smiled at that.

She looked out the window, watching the trees fly by. Going back made her nervous because it meant things were about to get messy. Hiding was easier than fighting. Hiding was safer. She wasn't ready for this. Kadrithan kept claiming she was strong and that she had a destiny to fulfill. A literal prophecy was depending on her.

"Here we come, ready or not," she whispered, her breath fogging up the window. She drew a frowny face in it.

CHAPTER 81

TOMMY

"Just get out."

"I'm not leaving." Tommy crossed his arms and glared at Deward, even though he couldn't see it.

Deward rolled over in bed, facing the wall. He hadn't been angry. Or scared. He hadn't been anything. Once they'd gotten him home, Deward had just laid in bed staring at nothing.

Tommy sat down on the edge of the bed, not touching him, just staying close. "You can't just give up, Deward. They're looking for a way to fix your sight. Maybe they'll find something, but even if they don't, you're still alive. We'll find ways to cope."

Deward remained silent.

"What do you need, dude? Come on, just talk to me."

Startling him, Deward rolled over abruptly. "Kill me."

"What? No. Why would I do that?"

"Because I remember everything. Everything we did." Deward sat up, grasping wildly until he caught Tommy's arm. "I killed innocent people and I can see their faces. It's like I can't open my eyes and they're always there. I need it to stop."

"Maybe Ceri has something to help you sleep––"

"You don't get it," Deward said, shoving him away. "I can't live like this."

"You know it wasn't you that killed them. It was just the curse."

Deward collapsed back onto the bed, hiding his face with his hands. "You don't understand. You can't."

Tommy tucked a foot up underneath him. "I guess I can't, but I'm still not leaving. You said we were brothers. Brothers don't abandon each other just because things have gotten hard."

They were silent for a moment, both of them lost in their thoughts.

He shifted uncomfortably. "I'm sorry I didn't get there in time to stop her from taking you. When you texted me, I took a minute to feed Captain Jack before I left even though I knew Ceri would feed him again when she got up. If I hadn't done that..."

Deward dropped his hands, sighing heavily. "She would have just taken you too."

"Maybe, maybe not."

"Are you trying to prove to me that regret is pointless?"

"No, but if it's working, then yes."

Deward snorted, a ghost of a smile tugging at his lips. "Your logic is flawed."

"Pretty sure I'm not the only one with flawed logic right now."

Deward turned his head away, plucking at the bedding nervously. "I'm mad that I can't see."

"Me too. It sucks."

"Eloquently put."

"I'm a high school drop out, what do you expect?"

"I spent months tutoring you! I expect a more varied vocabulary, at the very least," Deward said, crossing his arms.

"Guess you'll just have to keep working on me."

The troll shook his head, smoothing down his blue hair. It was frizzy after being washed for the first time in a week. "I don't know how to deal with this. Every time I try to think about the future, all I can think about is everything I've lost. I can't read, Tommy. Do you understand how much that changes? No college. No learning. No books. It's everything––" He stopped, unable to say anything else.

Tommy grabbed his arm. "We'll find a way to cope. You won't be doing this alone, even if that means I spend ten hours a day reading to you."

Deward reached over, wrapping his hand around Tommy's arm. "Okay."

CHAPTER 82

AMBER

Amber stared through her window into the backyard, watching and listening. She knew sleep wasn't going to come any time soon. Not after everything that had happened today.

She was surprised the angels hadn't come for their precious 'key' already. Kadrithan had warned her not to let her guard down and she had no intention of doing so. She grabbed her jacket, intending to go out and patrol the property but a familiar tug on her demon mark stopped her.

For the first time, it was followed by utter relief. She whirled around as Kadrithan stepped out of a pillar of smoke looking very human. "About time."

"I had to update Zerestria and help them prepare for retaliation. Don't worry, I was keeping an eye on you. If I'd sensed any danger I would have come."

She scuffed her bare foot against the carpet. "You kept them all alive."

"Not on my own. They fought well."

"Just let me thank you, jerk," she muttered.

He raised an eyebrow. "That looked painful."

"Well, I'm not repeating it, so I hope it sounded sincere too." She crossed her arms and stared him down, feeling off-kilter. They'd been flipping back and forth between enemy and ally so quickly lately that she wasn't sure how to act around him anymore. His promise not to lie to her had left her even more confused. "So, how long do we have? Do you know what they'll do?"

"Not long, a week at most. You're going to have to leave."

"What?" Her head snapped up and she frantically suppressed her connection to the pack bond. She didn't want the others feeling this until she knew for sure what they were going to have to do.

"They know where you live. Staying here, waiting for an attack, is insanity. I want you to leave and meet up with Evangeline in a couple of days, as soon as everyone is healed. She's already on her way to Portland."

STEPHANIE FOXE

"We can't leave. This is our home." She hadn't realized how much it had come to mean to her. This house. The security of having a *home* again.

"Surviving is more important than any place," Kadrithan argued, irritation clear on his face. "I'm trying to keep you alive."

"And keep Raziel's key away from them."

"Yes, but believe it or not, it matters to me whether or not you survive this," he said, closing the distance between them.

She walked backwards until her knees hit her bed, sitting down hard. "Oh."

He groaned in frustration, dragging his hands down his face. "You have been a great help to me. I don't intend to sacrifice your life needlessly. I can't force you to leave, and I won't, but the angels *will* come for you and your pack. They will come for the key. You can't be here when they do."

"Will they hurt Illya if we're not here?"

"I don't know." He summoned a chair and sat down across from her.

Captain Jack slipped in, pushing the door open a little wider. He wound through Kadrithan's legs, meowing pitifully when he realized the demon –– or fae, though it was hard to think of him as anything other than a demon –– wasn't solid.

Dejected, he made his way over to her instead. She patted his head absentmindedly, barely even having to lean down to reach it. He just *kept* growing.

"Where could we even go? It's not like we can run forever."

"I have allies, marks I can call in."

She pulled her hair over her shoulder and began braiding it, needing to do something with her hands. "I can't decide this without the pack."

"Of course," he said, clasping his hands in his lap. His eyes strayed to her cheek, something unhappy flickering in his dark eyes. "I didn't expect a decision tonight. You've barely recovered."

"Carter managed to make sure I'd never forget him," she said, waving at the scar, not wanting it to be the elephant in the room. The others had all shied away from looking at it.

A muscle in Kadrithan's jaw twitched. "You defeated him. That's all that matters."

"Yeah." She looked away, remembering the way he'd twitched underneath her as he'd died. Even without the scar, she never would have forgotten him. He wasn't even the first person she'd killed, which felt odd to realize, but his death had been the most intimate, not something she'd done in the haze of a fight. It had been horribly deliberate. "Anyhow, is there anything else I should know?"

"No, I think I've told you everything." He stared silently at the cat for a long moment, then his head popped up. "Oh, there is one thing that I have not told you. Something I'm sure you'd consider in violation of my vow to not lie to you ever again, even by omission."

She crossed her arms and took a deep breath, steeling herself for more bad news. "What is it?"

He pointed at her feet. "That is not a cat."

She looked down. Captain Jack was winding between her feet, purring. "I know, he's a savage beastie with an unnatural love for human food. What's your point?"

"No, you're not listening. It is not a cat at all."

Amber eyed the not-cat warily. She'd never trusted that mangy creature. Apparently, that was one hundred percent justified. She was going to kill Genevieve for bringing it home. "Then what the hell is it?"

"A fae creature called the chimera. They're attracted to trouble," he said with a smirk. "And fae. He must have smelled my scent on Genevieve when she was at the shelter and lured her in. They're very persuasive."

"They can use mind control?" She continued backing away slowly, but Captain Jack just followed, rubbing and purring like he was an innocent little kitty and not a savage chimera.

"Not quite. They simply look for caretakers. They're very lazy."

"Oh, so it's not like dangerous or anything?" she asked hopefully.

"No, they're quite deadly. Even I'd be hard-pressed to kill one if it decided it wanted me dead."

"And you are *just now mentioning this*," she whisper-shouted at him, afraid of startling the chimera. "I've been sleeping with it, Kadrithan. It sits on my head at night. Claws at my legs. Are you saying it could have *eaten me?*"

He shrugged. "Yeah, but you keep it well fed, so it probably won't. Anyhow..." He stood and smiled, as if the conversation was over. "I need to go, but I'll see you early tomorrow."

"What?! You can't just leave—"

He disappeared in a puff of smoke.

Amber lifted her leg out of reach of Captain Jack and began slowly creeping toward the door. He followed her, meowing curiously. She made it to the door and slipped out, slamming it shut behind her.

"What's wrong?" Ceri asked, coming out of her room right across the hall.

"We need more cat food."

MAKE A DIFFERENCE

Reviews are very important, and sometimes hard for an independently published author to get. A big publisher has a massive advertising budget and can send out hundreds of review copies.

Leaving an honest review helps me tremendously. It shows other readers why they should give me a try. It also shows Amazon that readers are enjoying the book.

If you've enjoyed reading this book, I would appreciate, very much, if you took the time to leave a review. Whether you write one sentence, or three paragraphs, it's equally helpful.

Thank you :)

P.S. Who's your favorite character? Let me know in the Facebook group.

https://www.facebook.com/groups/TheFoxehole/

Follow Me

Thank you so much for buying my book. I really hope you have enjoyed the story as much as I did writing it. Being an author is not an easy task, so your support means a lot to me. I do my best to make sure books come out error free. However, if you found any errors, please feel free to reach out to me so I can correct them!

If you loved this book, the best way to find out about new releases and updates is to join my Facebook group, The Foxehole. Amazon does a very poor job about notifying readers of new book releases. Joining the group can be an alternative to newsletters if you feel your inbox is getting a little crowded.

Facebook Group:
https://www.facebook.com/groups/TheFoxehole
Newsletter:
https://stephaniefoxe.com/#Follow-Me
Goodreads:
http://goodreads.com/Stephanie_Foxe
BookBub:
https://www.bookbub.com/authors/stephanie-foxe

MORE BY STEPHANIE FOXE

The Witch's Bite Series is a complete series that follows Olivia Carter –

I'm the only healer in a hundred miles, yet I'm probably the poorest in over a thousand.

Opening my very own apothecary is the only thing I really want in life, well that and a steady relationship. Lofty goals when you have a felony record for selling illegal potions. Healing neckers for the local vamps, while not all that glorious, has helped me build a good reputation. Then the cops show up at my door asking questions about a dead girl and trying to pin the murder on my employer. Next thing I know, I'm dodging fireballs in parking lots, and my favorite vampire is missing.

If you crave fast-paced, potion-slinging, snarky witch's, with a side of slow-burn romance, then you'll love Olivia Carter. This witch bites back, literally.

~

Stephanie Foxe also writes with her husband Alex Steele. In The Chaos Mages Series you will meet Logan Blackwell and Lexi Swift as they solve crimes in a world full of magic and myths, much like in Misfit Pack.

What else could go wrong?

I'm a detective with the IMIB - International Magical Investigations Bureau. I eat good food, drive fast cars, and I work alone.

Because no one can keep up with me.

When my boss dumps an unwanted partner in my lap, I'm told to figure out how to play nice, or I can kiss my job goodbye. My job is my life. Losing it is not an option.

There's no time to complain before a vampire explodes, a werewolf beats the mayor's nephew to death with his own arm, and some very determined assassins start popping up everywhere where we go.

One misstep and it's not my job I'll have to worry about losing. It's my head.

I may not be a big fan of rules, but I sure as hell believe in doing the right thing. Whoever is hurting innocents will pay. One way or another.

What else could go wrong, you ask? Losing a bet and ending up with pink hair. Apparently.

www.StephanieFoxe.com
www.AlexSteele.net

facebook.com/StephanieFoxeAuthor
goodreads.com/Stephanie_Foxe
bookbub.com/authors/stephanie-foxe